THE CALL OF FIFE AND DRUM

Books by Howard Fast

THE DINNER PARTY
THE IMMIGRANT'S DAUGHTER
THE OUTSIDER
MAX
TIME AND THE RIDDLE: THIRTY-ONE ZEN STORIES
THE LEGACY
THE ESTABLISHMENT
THE MAGIC DOOR
SECOND GENERATION
THE IMMIGRANTS
THE ART OF ZEN MEDITATION
A TOUCH OF INFINITY
THE HESSIAN
THE CROSSING
THE GENERAL ZAPPED AN ANGEL
THE JEWS: STORY OF A PEOPLE
THE HUNTER AND THE TRAP
TORQUEMADA
THE HILL
AGRIPPA'S DAUGHTER
POWER
THE EDGE OF TOMORROW
APRIL MORNING
THE GOLDEN RIVER
THE WINSTON AFFAIR
MOSES, PRINCE OF EGYPT
THE LAST SUPPER
SILAS TIMBERMAN
THE PASSION OF SACCO AND VANZETTI
SPARTACUS
THE PROUD AND THE FREE
DEPARTURE
MY GLORIOUS BROTHERS
CLARKTON
THE AMERICAN
FREEDOM ROAD
CITIZEN TOM PAINE
THE UNVANQUISHED
THE LAST FRONTIER
CONCEIVED IN LIBERTY
PLACE IN THE CITY
THE CHILDREN
STRANGE YESTERDAY
TWO VALLEYS

THE CALL
OF FIFE
AND DRUM

Three Novels of the Revolution

The Unvanquished

Conceived in Liberty

The Proud and the Free

by
HOWARD FAST

Citadel Press   *Secaucus, New Jersey*

Published in 1987 by Citadel Press
A division of Lyle Stuart Inc.
120 Enterprise Avenue, Secaucus, NJ 07094
In Canada: Musson Book Company
A division of General Publishing Co. Limited
Don Mills, Ontario

Queries regarding rights and permissions should be
addressed to: Lyle Stuart, 120 Enterprise Avenue,
Secaucus, N.J. 07094

Manufactured in the United States of America

Library of Congress Cataloging-in-Publication Data

Fast, Howard, 1914–
    The call of fife and drum.

    Contents: The Unvanquished — Conceived in liberty —
The proud and the free.
    1. United States — History — Revolution, 1775-1783 —
Fiction. I. Title.
PS3511.A784A6 1987   813′.52   86-31714
ISBN 0-8065-1027-7

INTRODUCTION

$\mathbf{B}$ACK IN 1938, soon after my wife and I were married, we bought a two-seater 1931 Ford, and set off to see America. In the course of this trip, we spent a day at Valley Forge, where a national park had been established and where General Washington's winter encampment had been reconstructed. I don't know what Valley Forge looks like today, almost half a century later, but at that time, the replicated encampment was crude enough to give one a sensation of how it might have been when the Continental Army wintered there.

I was deeply touched. We bought all the historical literature available at the spot, and when we came home, I immersed myself in whatever I could find on Valley Forge. Since that time, there has been an enormous amount of serious scholarship and publication on the American Revolution. At that time, there was surprisingly little. As it appeared to me then, the Revolution was a dimly remembered incident of minor importance and major confusion. Being as poorly educated in American history as most of the population then—and now—I found myself putting together a long list of questions and very few answers.

I think I felt that writing a story of what had happened might clarify it for me, whereupon I sat down to produce a book which eventually became *Conceived in Liberty*. I was twenty-three at the time, and I already had behind me three novels, none particularly distinguished and none of which struck a spark to the literary world, much less setting it on fire. With *Conceived in Liberty*, reviewers took serious notice for the first time that here was a young writer called Howard Fast, and that his work might eventually have possibilities. "At least it explodes with life," a reviewer said. The novel was reviewed in *The New York Times* literary section and in the *Herald-Tribune* literary section, and if the reviews were not raves, they were at least generous.

On my part, I had found a subject that was to intrigue me for years to come, in the course of which I would publish five more books on the period, each of them examining another aspect of the American Revolution. I must say that to my delight, two of these books have been used as school texts, so that several generations of Americans have been able to participate, at least in their imagination, in that extraordinary event that brought this country into being. Of the six books I wrote on the subject of the Revolution, five were novels and the sixth a history of the Battle of Trenton and the events leading up to it, the first detailed examination of that event in the past hundred years.

Here, in this volume, are three novels out of the five. The first, in order of publication, was, as I say above, *Conceived in Liberty.* Even as it was published, the events that led to the United States' involvement in World War II were taking place, and shortly after Pearl Harbor, my second book on the subject, a study of George Washington and his conduct of the retreat from New York City in 1776, was published. That was titled *The Unvanquished,* and it was published in 1942. *Time* Magazine said it was indirectly the most important book yet published on World War II, since it went to the roots of what was to be America's supreme effort.

Eight years passed before the third volume in this collection saw print—eight years during which the country, having destroyed Hitlerism in conjunction with the Soviet Union, turned from the hot war to a cold war that would go on interminably. The passionate patriotism expressed in *The Unvanquished,* the will of a small band of rebels to make a decent world for themselves, preached a song of hope and survival at the time of Pearl Harbor. Twelve years later, when I wrote *The Proud and the Free,* the situation had changed. McCarthyism was the rule of the time, and a kind of fear never known in the past now stalked America. So much of what we believed in twelve years before had been turned on its head; yet at this moment of terror and despair in America, the seeds of the great civil rights movement were being sown. Thus, I turned my attention to another part of the American Revolution, the months before the final victory at Yorktown. By this date, the small, ragged band of volunteers who were the subject of my first two novels had swelled into a large, war-hardened army, the backbone of which was the Pennsylvania Line, as it was called. Victory was in the air, and the unity that had cemented the various regions and classes of America no longer prevailed. *The Proud and the Free* was written during what is remembered as the lowest moment of American democracy in the twentieth century. While I feel that the book is a valid picture of the incident it portrays, it is history seen from a specific moment of the future. But this, indeed, is the case of all history.

I think that the three books will give the reader some new insights as to the origin of America. They will certainly not bore you.

— HOWARD FAST

THE
UNVANQUISHED

To Sam and Peggy

CONTENTS

PART ONE

BROOKLYN

1

THE FOXHUNTER

WITH the heat running like warm water from the sides of the room, backed by three closed windows and a closed door, he slept badly and restlessly, waking up, closing his eyes firmly, dozing, prodded into consciousness, fighting consciousness because he was a man who slept well most of the time, rolling over from a wet spot on the pillow, dreaming, recalling, forgetting, finding a painful ache in all the packed, broad, slab-like pictures that went to make up his memory.

While the night candle next to his bed burned, dim under its sooty cover, he could look at his watch and mark the hours, one o'clock, half past one, two o'clock, surely five o'clock, ten minutes after two, until the candle burned down.

Sometime during that night, awakening, he became afraid, and his sweat turned cold. He shivered and trembled and sought reassurance in the deep pockmarks that covered his face. His eyes searched the unending dark, but there was no object, no end, no faint trickle of light through the tightly sealed windows. His fingers traced out the pockmarks, nose and chin and mouth and forehead and thinning hair and back to the pockmarks; and in the dark his sense of objects drifted away, the pocks deep holes, the nose a monstrous thing, the chin an ungainly wedge.

He rolled over, threw off the single blanket that covered him, and groaned, "Patsy, Patsy." Then he buried his face in the wet pillow.

The grey dawn crept into the room and revealed him. He was awake and sitting up in the tangled disarray of his bed. His linen nightshirt had wrinkled and twisted itself up above his knees, and his long bony legs stuck out like the props of a scarecrow. He looked haggard from lack of sleep, older than he was, and incredibly thin.

1

He rolled over to the edge of the bed and shuffled his almost grotesquely large feet across the floor, seeking his slippers. When his toes found the soft caves of felt, he stood up, crouching for a moment with the instinctive gesture of a very tall man. He stretched and yawned before he went to a window and threw it open. The air outside was a little cooler, and he breathed deeply of it. It was still only half morning, still too early to know whether the day would be fair or foul, roofed with a blue sky or with angry clouds; but hot it would be with the sickening wet heat that was the prize of New York City and no other place in all the land.

After a few moments at the window, he told himself, "It will rain," for out of the east came the faintest rumbling and grumbling of angry storm clouds; and he was sleepy enough to think no more of it than that, storm clouds, rain, mud, rubbing his eyes with his enormous hands, shuffling around the bed and sitting down in a spindle-legged chair.

As he sat, the thunder came again, but different, in staccato bursts that forecast ruin instead of rain; and the big man leaped out of his chair and lurched toward the window, losing his felt slippers, leaned out of the window and called, "Billy! Billy! Billy!"

He hadn't a big voice, but he could make it snap like a lash. Pulling his nightshirt over his head, he stamped around naked, calling, "Billy! Billy!"

He was skin wound on bones, with broad shoulders and broader hips; clothes would cover his lankness and give his huge frame an impression of strength. When a colored man came running into the room, the first words were for clothes.

He was calm suddenly, dressing himself with the aid of the colored man. He sat on the edge of the bed, pulling on his stockings, his buff breeches, his high black boots; and as he wore the clothes, he became a different man, stronger, wiser, vaster. His long, skinny body assumed more human proportions as the huge knobs of bone disappeared under the broadcloth and linen. His thin red hair was combed from its disarray flat back against his head. Only his tired grey eyes remained to tell of the sleepless night.

He washed in a white china bowl and then got into his blue jacket. If he heard the rumbling thunder now, the fears and apprehensions it evoked were tight-locked under his uniform.

"Shave you, sir?" the colored man asked

"Later."

"Two gentlemen waiting," the colored man said.

2

"How long? Why didn't you wake me, Billy? Haven't you more sense than that?"

"Just a few minutes."

"How long is a few minutes Billy? You have less sense every day."

"Maybe five minutes, sir."

The big, bony, stooping man, fully dressed now in a buff and blue uniform, left the bedroom. As he entered another room which he called his office, he straightened up and threw back his shoulders with a visible effort.

That same buff and blue uniform had made a stir in Philadelphia something over a year ago. A tall, tall man, long-faced, shy, but very well dressed, had sat down with the Second Continental Congress, wrapped in his buff and blue and in the deepest mantle of silence, and had sat and sat and sat without ever saying a word. His silence became something physical and alive; everyone else wanted to talk, and everyone else did talk. Things were moving; it was revolution, and the world was dropping into pieces, and the pieces had to be sorted out, and when someone suggested a humble and dutiful petition to the King of England, John Adams roared, "Oh, the imbeciles! The fools! The damned, damned fools, with their talk of petitions!"

And in all the crazy riot of talk, the tall man in buff and blue said nothing, heard everything, and kept his quizzical grey eyes fastened more or less intently upon the meeting.

"Who is he?" a member from Massachusetts asked.

"Nobody important."

"In that uniform?"

"Well, he's nobody important; he's a farmer from Virginia. His name's Washington."

"Washington?"

"Wash-ing-ton."

"Who ever heard of a name like that?"

"That's *his* name. He's rich."

The member from Massachusetts nodded, a merchant himself, putting the uniform at forty pounds, the lace at three, the shoes at four. "He never speaks?" he inquired.

"No."

"Just sits there?"

"Yes."

"Washington—" the member from Massachusetts said thoughtfully.

And John Adams told his cousin Sam, "I like him."

3

"Why?"

"He knows how to keep a still tongue."

"Maybe he's got nothing to say," Sam suggested.

"No — people who have nothing to say spend all their time talking about it," John said. "That man Washington, he's said nothing and he's chairman of four military committees. Nobody ever heard of George Washington of Virginia, but they look at the uniform and they look at the way he holds his head and they hear how much money he's worth, and then they vote for him without thinking any more about it."

"How much is he worth?" Sam asked.

"As much as any man in America."

Sam grinned and said, "Commander in chief?"

"Why not? Look at the way he wears his uniform, the way he sits on his horse."

"Some won't like it," Sam Adams said slowly, thinking of a people's revolution, but also of what it meant to be as rich as any man in America.

"The North won't like it, but the South will. We already have the North, and now we need the South, to be more precise, Virginia."

"I wasn't thinking of that," Sam said. "I was thinking of Hancock. He wants like all the devils in hell to lead this business."

"You want it too, don't you?" John Adams asked, squinting at his cousin.

"I can't wear a uniform," he replied sourly. "Still there'll be hell to pay for Hancock."

"Let it then. I'm going to nominate this Washington."

And now, nominated, appointed more than a year, this tall, forty-four-year-old planter, foxhunter, farmer, still found it difficult to think of himself as a general.

With a curt nod he greeted the two men who were waiting for him, and nodded for them to speak. They hadn't slept either; their eyes were red and their faces were dirty and their clothes were limp with sweat. They were from General Putnam, they told him.

"Billy," he said, "get these gentlemen something to drink." And he told them, "Sit down, gentlemen. You've come a long way and its hot. Sit down."

His judgment was quick and certain and damning, because they were afraid, one of them a boy of eighteen or nineteen and the other a sallow man in his thirties, but both of them afraid and dirty and tired, dressed in old homespun and linen shirts that had once been white but were now muddy brown. The big man thought: "What am I looking at? A lieutenant and a captain, or a major and a colonel?" His army! They were Yankees with clumsy movements and nasal New England accents, and he had to cover his contempt by staring at the grained wood of the table where he sat. He had a physical abhorrence of physical fear; it was something twined in and out of the whole fabric and pattern of his life. He had always been a sickly man, and he had the sickly man's intimate knowledge of death; fear to him was real and black and terrible, and for that reason, being almost without the habit of introspection, he despised fear in others.

In these two, the messengers from General Putnam, fear was as hot and wet as the day itself. It slid from their lips as they poured out their story. They had come over from Brooklyn.

How had they come?

They stared at him amazed, not comprehending how his mind needed details, hundreds of little details for him to piece together, meaningless details when the world was falling apart.

They had rowed across in a skiff. They couldn't get a boatman. The younger one began to blubber; you would think with a message from General Putnam, they could get someone to row the boat.

"When was that?" the big man cried. "When did it start, you fools? Answer me!" He pulled out his watch; it was six o'clock.

That was what the younger one was trying to tell him, blubbering that they couldn't get a boatman, that they had to row themselves. The sallow man thrust out his palms in proof and showed the blisters. He had never rowed a boat before. He hadn't enlisted to row a boat; he wasn't a sailor. They had run all the way from the landing; well, he hadn't enlisted for that, to row boats and to run his fool head off.

"Get out of here!" the foxhunter roared. "Both of you—get out of here!"

He sat at the table while Billy brought in some breakfast, while through the open window came the distant rumble of cannon.

He shouldn't have lost his temper at those two, he told himself. His temper was a hot iron on hairsprings, an outpouring of all the inhibitions bound up so tightly inside of him. It was something he had wheedled and flailed and coaxed and beaten all of his life; and until he had come up here to the North to take command of the army, he had believed it under control, flung back, hammered down and tight in chains.

Before that taking of command, he could clearly remember the last

5

time he had lost himself. It had been during a clear, glorious afternoon at Mount Vernon, when he sat in his saddle with the pack sprayed out in front of him, looking for game, a fox or a deer or a hare, with his horse's hoofs drumming sweet music and the smell of green things on the cool breeze. The pack raised a scent, but he reined in, his eyes on a flight of dark birds silhouetted in the sky over the Potomac. The picture was fixed and lovely until a shot from the river bank sent two of the birds twisting down in their death.

In that moment, like a taut thong snapping, he went insane with rage against the poacher who crouched in a canoe by the bank, a steep hill-slope away. The foxhunter put his horse over the suicidal slope of the hill, plunged down to the river, flung off his horse and rushed at the poacher, who was trying to get his canoe clear of the bank. The poacher, seeing this fantastically tall man charging at him, fired his gun in desperation; but the foxhunter crashed past, ripped the fowling piece out of the man's hands, and then deliberately beat the poacher to within an inch of his life. He dragged the poacher out of the canoe, through the water, up on the bank, punishing him all the way as a dog punishes a terrified rat.

The memory wasn't good. He hated poachers, but he hated no man enough to justify losing himself in rage. After that incident, for a long time, his temper had been carefully under control—until he came to the army, until he made up his mind that there was nothing else to do but fight. When that time came, he put on his buff and blue uniform of a colonel in the Virginia militia.

The pride of getting the command had lasted until he saw his army. The command was everything and all, and he remembered telling his wife, "Patsy, they've given it to me, all of it. I don't know why, but they've given it to me. To me, do you understand?"

Then he added, "I'm not the man for it, Patsy—why should they have given it to me?"

"Why?" he kept asking himself afterwards. "Why?'

But he was proud, no longer a foxhunter, but something else, so mighty in his pride, so big and strong and splendid that nobody, looking at him, could doubt that he was the right man, the only man, standing like a god, six feet two and a half inches with a broad impassive face, cool grey eyes, and because he said so little and had an air of knowing how things should be done. But like a boy, rewarded beyond belief or estimation, he told himself again and again, "They've given it to me," thinking of how it was that afternoon in the Congress when John Adams rose and talked about qualifications needed for a com-

6

mander in chief, everyone taking for granted the fact of his speaking for Hancock, and Hancock himself flushing, moving with nervous little jerks, biting his lips, smiling sheepishly when Adams said something particularly lush, and then cocking his big head as Adams said:

"Gentlemen, I know these qualifications are high, but we all know they are needful in this crisis in this chief. Does anyone say they are not to be obtained in this country? In reply, I say they are; they reside in one of our own body, and he is the man whom I now nominate — George Washington of Virginia."

It fell like a bombshell, and Hancock's face suddenly became a lump of flesh, without expression and without features. The Virginian reacted more slowly; he had been staring at Hancock, and it was only moments later, as a memory, vague and poorly defined, that he heard his own name spoken. He got to his feet somehow, still staring at the suffering Hancock, and then turned and shuffled from the hall, as if he had done something unspeakably wretched.

Only afterward, bit by bit, the exultation came.

That was until he saw his army, New England men sprawled outside of Boston, besieging the British, picking their noses, bickering and complaining in their metallic, offensive Yankee twang.

After that his temper wore as thin as a piece of old and frayed cloth.

He read Putnam's message as he ate his breakfast. Sometime early this morning, the battle had begun, and things were going badly. Putnam didn't say how bad things were, but they were bad enough. He couldn't see much more than his own corner and everything was confused, but it was bad enough.

Putnam wanted more men.

The Virginian shook his head. How had it come to this? He sat here at the breakfast table, his body as inert and helpless as a bundle of wet rags, staring at cakes and honey, and over there in Brooklyn his army was fighting a battle, its first battle, the first battle of the Continental armies of the thirteen colonies. And he sat with nothing to do, no thoughts, no solutions, only the dreadful horror of a person caught in a trap of his own making.

He was not brilliant; even his dreams were formal things, and when he had made himself a picture of an army, before he had ever seen the army that was to be his and was to fight for the independence of the colonies, his picture had been a neat conception of many thousands of orderly men in orderly uniforms. They would wheel and march and attack and retreat and charge and fire just as an army should, and he in his buff and blue uniform would ride at their front.

And the Yankees outside of Boston hadn't a uniform to a regiment, and aside from eating and sleeping they were superlative at lying on their backsides and complaining.

Still, Putnam wanted more of them, more Yankees, for what they were worth. This was the real thing; this was a battle. Over, across the river, in Brooklyn, men were hacking at each other, cursing at each other, shooting their unwieldy, rusty firelocks, and dying and running away. For him, at his breakfast table, there was the booming of cannon, clearer and nearer now.

From Boston, after the British fleet had given up the city and sailed away, the big Virginian marched his army down to New York. At the time that had seemed like an obvious thing to do. It was almost like a victory, the way the English had been forced out of Boston. There was no fighting to speak of after he had taken command; but the British didn't know whether the thousands of New England farmers, sprawled around the town, were an army or not. Anyway, they didn't give two damns for Boston, and they sailed away and left it.

New York was something else. Placed like a gate at the mouth of the Hudson, it was the key to the whole colonial situation, and who controlled New York might control America. Or, at least, so the foxhunter had thought. Others thought differently; others thought that New York City might be a death trap, and they pointed to the maps and said, "See how it lies; what will you defend? Manhattan? It lies like a finger stretched out, with a broad river on either side of it. Hold the bay end, and the English sail their navy up the rivers and cut you off, neat as they please. Long Island? Another finger with water for the British to sail on. Staten Island? Even worse in the same way."

The big man shook his head. He had on his side the Congress, who wanted the city held. He considered himself their servant, for all his pride, and he liked to think of them as an august senate, such as had sat in ancient Rome. If they wanted the city held, it should be held, some way, somehow. And he had twenty thousand men. They were Yankees, for the most part; they were a slovenly, shambling rabble of militia, and on the march to New York they had sprawled aimlessly over miles of road. But still there were twenty thousand of them and they were an army.

And now Putnam had sent him a message for more men, all of it working out in the worst way, the worst possible way, half of his army in Brooklyn, trapped by the British who had sailed around Long Island, another part here in New York, waiting to be trapped; nothing was lacking but that the British should sail the rest of their fleet up the East River and put an end to a comic-opera revolution that had appointed a foolish, prideful Virginia gentleman as its commander in chief.

2

THE BATTLE

HIS TROUBLE was to know where they would strike or how they would strike or when they would strike. He wasn't a general, he wasn't even a soldier, he was a foxhunting plantation owner; if he tried to think out the whole complicated matter of military strategy in the defense of New York, the endless ramifications puzzled and bewildered him. His instinct was for a thousand small and concrete details which he could construct into one single fact, all of it shot through with the even thread of orderliness. Here there was no orderliness and no single fact.

The British might seize Long Island, so he put a part of his men on Brooklyn Heights, directly across the river from Manhattan. Or they might, on the contrary, seize New York itself; that meant a part of his army must remain in Manhattan. Another part to defend upper Manhattan, another for the Jerseys, another for the Highlands—and so on. And how many were sick? And how many deserted each day?

He no longer said, as before, that he had twenty thousand men.

He was all a bundle of hurts and pains as he left the room, his breakfast untouched. But he walked stiffly and certainly, and they said, "Look at him, he knows how things are going."

He stood in the street outside, and aides and officers crowded around him.

"Listen to the guns, sir!"

"Shall we be going across?"

"My regiment, sir. I have my regiment ready."

"No, mine, sir!"

Boys of eighteen and nineteen talking about regiments. He managed what was so hard for him, to smile.

He was not a revolutionist, so he would say to himself, over and over again, "My country, my country, my country." He would think of the river, flowing softly and gently by his acres, and he would think of the cold dirt in his hand, being crumpled farmer-wise, until grain by grain it slipped through his fingers; he would think of the house and the barn and the grass and the trees, and there would be many solid things for him to place his feet on. He needed solid things.

There was nothing solid about revolution. It was a shimmering unreality, and the only concrete form it took in his eyes was to produce thousands and thousand of slovenly, dirty, tobacco-chewing, nasal-voiced Yankee farmers.

So he said to himself, "My country, my country," shaking his head slowly like a bulldog who has put his teeth into something and will hold on vise-like until death severs the head from the body.

He knew now, this morning, August 27, 1776, that he had made a terrible, tragic mistake in trying to defend Brooklyn. His huge, grotesque body held a nature as soft as it was eager; and childlike was the trust he put in persons who knew more than he did. Their number was legion.

One of them was a General Charles Lee, a soldier and a darling of all the people who knew the Virginian was no soldier at all. Lee, a disgruntled, bitter soldier of fortune, hating a life that had given him nothing, leaped on the bandwagon of revolution; and logically he was the man to lead the army. But he was objectionable and ugly, whereas the foxhunter was a pleasant gentleman and magnificent in his bearing; Lee was penniless, and the foxhunter was, perhaps, the wealthiest man in all the colonies. For all that the war would be fought by a dirty rabble, money remained the crux of the situation, and people wept when they heard that the Virginia farmer had refused to take a penny for his services.

The foxhunter wrote to Lee, humble with a man so much wiser, and asked what the soldier would do about New York. Lee's answer was that he would build fortifications on Brooklyn Heights.

It was five days now since the British had ferried most of their German troops from Staten Island to Gravesend on Long Island. The Virginian had watched the action impotently, having no ship in his navy bigger than a rowboat; and then he made his answer, desperately, by sending six more of the dirty, tobacco-chewing regiments into the death's trap of Brooklyn.

Then, for five days, nothing happened, and the dull, sinking fear that he was to know for many days and weeks and months to come, lumped up in his breast. If he had been a real general, he would have taken advantage of some dark night and pulled all his troops back into Manhattan; if he had been a self-confident fool, he would have sent more and more regiments across the river and into the trap which the British had so neatly created. Being neither, he left his army divided, part in one place and part in another, hoping against hope for a miracle to save him from the looming disaster.

There was no miracle.

About three o'clock in the morning, on August 27, 1776, the British began their advance.

They had twenty thousand men on Long Island, a good part of them German mercenaries, altogether the best-officered, best-trained fighting force in the world at the time. There were less than ten thousand American colonials facing them on Brooklyn Heights. The ten thousand were a rabble of militia that had only one thought in common, the desire to go home as soon as possible.

General Nathanael Greene, whom the Virginian had placed in command, lay in bed with a raging fever. Greene was only thirty-four years old, a Quaker, a good man, solid and dependable, with brains in his head. He was young, but the whole army was young—boys who wanted to show the world what dreams they had. But Greene was sick, and in desperation the Virginian gave the command to Sullivan. Then his faith in Sullivan went out like a dying candle, and desperately—more desperately than ever now—he gave the command to Putnam. The generals bickered and fought, and their troops took up the quarrel.

The Virginian sent troops over, more and more of the slovenly, high-voiced Yankees, with their huge muzzle-loading firelocks and their baby-faced commanders. And all the while he was in a frenzy of apprehension that the British left on Staten Island might attack his depleted Manhattan garrison.

He still prayed to God that he might win the battle, the very first battle, the initial test of George Washington, commander in chief. He knew something of how the battle was going, of what was happening, but not a great deal.

He knew that a fatal mistake had been made; not his; his mistakes were plenty, but this was not one of his. From their redoubts on Brooklyn Heights, the Americans had fanned out to take places in a range of low hills that extended from the Narrows inland almost to the East River. There were three passes through these low hills, and two of the passes were fairly well defended, while the third was almost completely ignored. This neglect of the third pass was the fatal mistake.

It was two hours before daybreak on the twenty-seventh when the advance guard of the British army reach the inland pass, the Jamaica pass. The British expected a stiff battle, and come forward cautiously, but to their amazement they found the pass guarded only by five sleeping officers. Like school children playing at war and all wanting to be generals, this rebel army was laden with officers, sometimes as many in a regiment as there were private soldiers to do the fighting, their attitude being, "Dammit all to hell—if you reckon yourself high and mighty enough for an officer, I do too, as good a man as you are."

They wore feathers in their caps, since having no uniforms there was nothing to distinguish one from another, and out of that love for cockades came the mocking tune of the British:

Yankee Doodle went to town, riding on a pony,
Stuck a feather in his cap and called it macaroni —

The five sleeping officers were awakened by bayonet pricks in their buttocks, and warned that if they made any outcry the steel points would be driven at their throats.

"I do allow," one said sleepily, and the others said nothing at all, only rubbing the sore spots on their buttocks and regretting that they had not followed an earlier impulse to put away their guns and go home.

"Rebels," a British officer said scornfully, the way he would say pigs or goats or cows.

"What command?" another asked.

"Huh?"

"Bless your sleepy souls, what command?"

"Milishy, mister," a seventeen-year-old grinned.

"Milishy," the others chimed in.

"But the regiment? The regiment?"

"Just milishy," they insisted.

"Oh, merciful God," the officer said softly, and then the five captives were taken away and the British column went on. Word was sent back that the left flank of the American army had been turned and was now wide open, and though the British command could hardly believe its senses, it didn't hesitate to take advantage of the gap. A frontal attack was launched at the right flank for diversion, during which time hundreds and hundreds of redcoat troops poured through the wonderful gap to take the Americans in the rear.

"And after that?" the big foxhunter asked grimly. He was not a man for regrets; when a thing was done, it was done.

"After that it was hell, just hell, just bloody, bloody hell."

He stood so calmly, so still, the Virginian, that those around him thought: "He's not human — or maybe he doesn't understand what happened."

He didn't know the full story of the disaster until he had crossed the river and got to Brooklyn himself. Afraid to leave Manhattan open for an even greater debacle, torn because his men were fighting a battle in Brooklyn and he was here, at last he crossed, and then the battle was almost over. His face remained as placid as a death mask when they told him what had happened to his two generals, Stirling and Sullivan.

They held the front where the German mercenaries advanced in frontal attack. That was after the cannonading which in its distant echoes had penetrated the Virginian's airless bedroom. The cannonading did little enough harm, but it frayed the nerve of the Yankee farmers, who had dozed uneasily over their guns all night.

Then came the German Jagers, marching knee-deep through the drifting mists of the morning, their green uniforms blending in with the trees and bushes, their drums playing, their bright bayonets dipping and sparkling.

"Hessians," the Yankees told each other. The farm-bred boys, eighteen and nineteen and twenty years old, stared with wide eyes and gripped their guns with wet palms. Along with their unreasoning hatred for the Germans was an aching fear. The big, ox-eyed, green-clad, guttural-voiced mercenaries were beyond their comprehension.

"Hessians," they told each other.

Still they would have made a stand, tried to make one, blowing off some of their unwieldy guns, holding for just a little while the ragged front of their line, except that suddenly, from behind them, sounded the drums of the redcoats. They looked around and saw that they were attacked from two directions. They tried to stand up before the Germans, and volleys from the redcoats slashed into their backs. They whimpered and moaned, and screamed that they were betrayed. They tried to retreat, and the columns in red drove them back into the arms of the Germans. They tried to swing their great, rusty twenty-five-pound firelocks in defense, and the razor-sharp bayonets of the Hessians slashed out their guts. They fell on the ground and wept for their mothers, and the ox-eyed German peasants rammed slivers of steel into their backs.

They had never fought in any battle before, except the few of them who made the stand at Bunker Hill. They had never killed or been killed. The leisurely wash of their lives had rolled gently around many box-like, white village churches in many New England towns; and for all the times they had sat in taverns and talked of freedom, they were paying now.

They ran every which way, and the Germans yelled and laughed and ran after them. They cowered back against trees, and their breath sighed and died as the bayonets cut through them and bent on the wood.

They hid in fields, and the Germans hunted them out and pulled them up and dragged them along, shouting, "Yonkee! Yonkee! Yonkee!"

The hell went on for hours. between the wooded line they tried to hold and the American base fortifications was a slow creek running through a treacherous bog. The panic-stricken colonials floundered into this trap, threw away their guns, and sank deeper and deeper into the mud. And behind them, ever, came that guttural, mocking cry, "Yonkee! Yonkee! Yonkee!"

General Sullivan was in a cornfield, trying to hide. He crept between the tall stalks, and watched the Hessian boots trample past him. He lay very still, but not still enough. Three straw-haired Germans dragged him to his feet, and grinning, bore him off as their own, personal prize.

General Stirling ran, alone, not through fear, but alone with the enemy all around him, his men gone, his brigades scattered like chaff, the redcoats pot-shooting at him like men after ducks, never knowing their prize was a general, not a tobacco-chewing cockade brevet, but a real enough general who himself had once worn the red coat of Britain. He ran and ran until his feet were heavy as lead, until he blundered into a German patrol which grinningly made its second capture of an American general.

When the Virginian had crossed the river and come into the rear lines of the battle, his officers, colonels and majors and a general, came trailing to tell him how bad it was, how it couldn't be worse.

"We're done," they tried to make him understand. "All done, all finished, all done—"

He went up to the top of a hill, where he could watch the battle complete itself, and he knew that they were right, that everything was done, that nothing was left, that the impossible scheme had played itself out.

He stood there with the whole horrible picture spread before him.

14

the bog lay at his feet. He could almost see the faces of the Hessians as they cut up and herded out of the fight the pleading Yankees. He saw a Maryland brigade drive into the redcoat flank in a vain effort to hold open an avenue of retreat. Grapeshot raked them and tore them to pieces. In the bog, the Yankees crawled like insects. The Hessians were making a holiday of it, and the wind carried to him, faintly, the guttural refrain of joy, "Yonkee! Yonkee!"

And someone was saying to him, "General, what shall we do now?"

"Now?"

He was thinking of how it was to be made commander in chief of a whole army.

"Now?" he repeated. "What is there to do?"

He walked along slowly, nodding his head, muttering, wondering, trying to recall all the long line of mistakes that had gone into the making of this. He tried to remember what he knew of war, of battles, of defeats, and his head ached, and his whole lank body was wet with sweat.

A Colonel Hart, mud-stained, asked him, "If they come on to attack us here—?"

"Then wait until they are close by," the foxhunter said slowly, as if repeating a lesson he had learned in school. "Then just wait until they are close by before you fire."

But it was all over and all done, and he knew it; and nothing in the world could help him now, not advice to his frightened men, not waiting until the enemy was close by—but nothing at all now.

3

THE MARBLEHEAD FISHERMEN

THEY all admired him a great deal, as he walked up and down behind the lines, his steps measured, his long body severely erect, and his brow only slightly furrowed, like nothing ever seen in the way of a commander whose army had been sliced to pieces and whose hopes had been shattered. With his great height, he bulked high out of the confusion of dispatch runners, anguished colonels who had lost their regiments, heartbroken captains of nineteen and twenty, generals who had served their first and last command.

Morning had worn into midday, and midday into a hot, sulky afternoon, and now the murky sun was sinking behind the Palisades. The battle was not yet over, but only because the British had paused to rest from the wonderful sport of chasing and killing and capturing New Englanders. They had driven them into a cul-de-sac, ringed by strong masses of troops on three sides and water on the fourth; and feeling that the motley army was securely in his grasp, the British commander was in no hurry to close the issue and lose men who could not easily be replaced.

The retreat, which had become almost a rout, ran into the American entrenchments like slow flood waters over bottom lands; and all that long afternoon terrified and beaten men staggered out of the bog and woods. They were bewildered and frightened, each of them immersed in his own personal catastrophe, each of them certain that the whole thin dream of revolution was done with, that nothing remained except to save his own skin.

They streamed past the big farmer and clustered into huddles of panic-stricken humanity. They avoided his eyes, but some of them glanced back at him after they had passed, fixing their gaze on his muddy boots.

Almost two thousand of them never came out of the bog and the woods.

It was not the first time the Virginian had lost. The whole warp and woof of his life was woven with losses and disappointments and unfulfilled dreams. Inside he suffered minutely over minute things; his humility was real because it evidenced itself not in a complex of inferiority, but in an understanding of inferiority. He, who placed courage above almost all virtues, knew his own cowardice; he, to whom love was as necessary as the air he breathed, had lost the only woman he ever loved; he, who wanted the affection of all men, had never had a real friend; his heart went out to every child he had ever seen, yet he never had children of his own; he worshipped learning because he knew his own ignorance and how painful and involved were the workings of his mind. His love and lust for life were matched only by the thin thread which connected him with life, and his long, frail body lingered constantly at the edge of darkness.

As night fell, he continued his tireless pacing, asking only one question of the broken men who came to him:

"How many have we lost?"

They didn't know; the forlorn battlefield of Brooklyn was still a scrambled jigsaw puzzle that would not be put together entirely for years and generations to come. Whole regiments had vanished. Generals and colonels and majors and dozens of lower ranks of officers had disappeared as completely as if the earth had swallowed them. Some said a thousand were lost; others said fifteen hundred; others said three thousand.

General Putnam came over to where Washington paced and said, "Whatever it is, we're hurt sore."

The commander in chief nodded his agreement, and Putnam marveled that a man could be composed of so little blood and so much rock and steel. Putnam thought it would be better if he would curse just a little at the wreckage strewn about them.

"It will be dark soon, and suppose they attack again, after it's dark—"

"They may," the foxhunter agreed.

"But my God almighty, sir!" Putnam said shrilly, "we're in no condition to resist another attack."

The foxhunter turned his cold grey eyes on the general, and Putnam wilted and swallowed and mumbled something or other.

"If they attack, we will fight again," the foxhunter said.

"Yes."

"It's important for them to understand that we will fight again. The battle isn't over, general."

The Virginian resumed his walk, telling himself again and again that the battle was not over, but knowing, after he had fumbled sufficiently in his memory, that somehow for him, for George Washington, things were always the same, that dignity was not competence, that the ability to make foolish youngsters love a gangling farmer was not the virtue of a commander in chief. Now his army was cut to pieces, strewn about with their backs to the water; and in some ways it was much as if they had taken the theme from his life. From the horrible nightmare of Braddock's defeat up to now, everything that he had a hand in, that mattered, had been torn into shreds and strewn about. His big, clumsy hands laid waste wherever they fumbled, and like the bad music he made on his flute, it was always the same tune, played over and over without variation.

Still there must be something now; even when things came to an end, men struggled before they died. There must be something, but no one else would think. He had to walk back and forth, calmly for all the horror inside of him, and force his heavy wits to function, since there was no one else who had any wits about him at all.

They were all watching him. Through the gathering dusk he could see the hundreds of white faces turned toward him, and out of the intermittent drumming of cannon he could hear their whispering. He was General George Washington of Virginia, and you could tell by his walk that he had something up his sleeve.

To Knox and Putnam, standing over to one side, with their backs against a wickerwork bastion, the commander in chief loomed like a giant against the golden twilight sky. Knox, chief of American artillery—what there was of it—was a boy of twenty-six, bright-eyed, very fat, red-cheeked, loving four things passionately, books, his guns, his wife, and his commander in chief. The tall, skinny foxhunter was like a god in his eyes, calm, beyond fears and uncertainties, beyond all the lusts and hurts of human flesh. Before the war, Knox had been a bookseller, an ambitious bookseller who dreamed of some day becoming another Ben Franklin, a publisher who nurtured talented young writers and brought out endless editions of wonderful books. Now, as chief of artillery, he loved his black, stub-nosed guns as tenderly as he had regarded his first editions, and now his dreams were of a thousand pieces all belching in even volleys.

He lusted after guns, hoarded them, treasured them, counted them morning and night. His men made crude jokes about his sleeping with his guns, yet if he could be with them, he would sleep nowhere else. Now his pain was personal and singular; regardless of what happened his guns would be forfeited to the enemy, the few precious cannon that had been trundled and dragged from every corner of the land. He felt bereft and naked, and as he stood next to Putnam, his whole attitude was hopeless dejection. For all that, the figure of the foxhunter, out-lined against the sky, had power to elevate him, to take him out of himself for a moment.

"Look," he told the general. "Look at him."

Morosely, Putnam said words to the effect of his looking, since there was nothing else to do.

"How quiet he is," Knox marveled.

"He'd be that way if the skies fell upon him."

Putnam resented Knox's turn of phrase, his endless bad quotations from bad books. "They did," Putnam growled.

When the began to pester him to lie down and sleep for a while, the big man realized that his inhuman mask of calm had accomplished something; it had taken them, at least for the moment, out of them-selves, out of the individual pools of misery and defeat that each man had crawled into.

That it was for the moment, he realized full well. It needed only the light of morning to bring the renewed assault of the well-rested, victory-flushed British and Germans, and this time there would be no retreat for the defeated American rabble. They would be pushed back to the river and slaughtered like ducks in a game pond.

No one would ever know what it had cost him to maintain that mask of calm all afternoon and evening, while he wrestled with his problem. Forcing his mind to function, forcing himself to reason calmly and slowly, he had placed before himself a choice of three courses of action. Three there were, and no more than three, and hour after hour he searched each one for every last possibility it held.

The first, the most obvious, the easiest, was surrender; and something inside of him longed to give up the crazy, futile struggle, to get rid of the cowardly rabble he called his army, to lay down his sword in stately dignity and go back to his quiet home on the Potomac. Some would despise him and hate him; others would praise him; and some, like Patsy, would understand. But this, the obvious way, never fully reached his consciousness; it existed in the deep pit of doubts that tormented him; but he could not fully consider it because he could not fully admit to himself that he would even consider such a prospect. Death would be the same sort of surrender and bring the same sort of peace, but he was not yet at a point where he would admit to himself that nothing remained but to die.

The second alternative was to fight. If he were to assemble the brigades and tell them that he had decided to hold his ground and fight the British to the last man, they would not cheer or smile or mutter proud words about dying for their country; they would only look at him blankly with their already-dead eyes, and then those among them who were boys — as most of them were — would begin to weep quietly as they remembered the folks at home in the neat little villages. The half-foreign element, those who had crept out of the ghettos and slums of Europe and were revolutionists body and soul, might cheer his decision, but they were only a fraction of the whole, as bad fighters as the rest, many of them speaking no English, most of them weak and sickly and undisciplined.

Some of the officers, men like Knox and Putnam and Carter and Dee, big, healthy young men who loved danger for its own sake, and feared nothing on earth, would follow him into hell. But a handful of officers cannot win a battle. He thought wistfully of those men as he numbered them off, envying their brute-like physical courage which

19

was never troubled by doubts or fears or sickly pain.

To fight would not even be glorious, for the already-defeated Americans would break at the first British charge and run screaming from the merciless bayonets of the straw-haired Germans. To fight would achieve the same results as a surrender, except that a few hundred more Yankee boys would die, and another thousand would suffer with festering, gangrenous wounds. And if they fought, there would be none of the genteel terms of surrender; death he could bear, but not the gallows.

"And the revolution?" he asked himself. It was difficult to think of the revolution now, of anything abstract as opposed to the fact of the army that was his to save or see destroyed. If they stayed and fought, the revolution would not matter a great deal.

One alternative remained — retreat. Retreat would save his army, at least until the British had reorganized to attack the island of Manhattan. Retreat might give him a chance to rally his frightened men, and retreat would unite him with still-untouched brigades which he had left to defend the city. Of all the three courses, retreat was the only one which he could consider reasonably, and retreat was the only one which was utterly impossible.

For one thing, there was certainly not time to make preparations to evacuate an army which still numbered thousands of men. It was dark now, and the confusion of the stricken battlefield had been replaced by the confusion of the hopeless camp. The only thing that kept them at their barricades at all was the knowledge that the cold waters of the river lay at their backs, that there was no place to go. Whisper the word retreat, and the brigades would claw and fight to be the first at the water's edge.

For another thing, there were no boats. And if there were boats, who could row them and keep calm and steady under fire?

He saw the officers of his staff standing around him, and realized that he had been pacing back and forth in that way for hours.

"Sir, have something to eat," Knox pleaded.

"Yes, of course. Have you eaten, Harry?"

"Sir? Yes, I ate, sir."

"Stew?"

"But good, sir, very good, sir," the fat bookseller nodded. "And wine — I saved a bottle."

He managed to smile and nod; and given that signal of his inner peace, they crowded close to him and led him away. He saw how eager they were to be next to him, to brush his hand with one of theirs, to

20

take comfort from his big, handsome figure. They were only boys, and they were frightened and heartsick, and he was so calm and assured that they were sure he held the solution for all their woes in his tightly clenched fist.

The foxhunter was thankful for the darkness of his tent; his throat had choked up and his eyes were foolish with tears. He had never had children of his own, but now they were like his own children, the young officers who had crowded in, one of them kneeling and gently removing his boots, another helping him out of his coat, another unbuckling his sword, and all of them so gentle and understanding. It was almost a caress when their hands touched him. He realized now that he had not deceived them, that they knew as well as he that this was the end of their fantastic adventure.

A captain of eighteen piped, "Easy, sir, lie down here, and I'll puff out this pillow."

Carter folded his coat with loving care.

Knox said, with love and importance, "See, sir, the boots are right here by the bed. Just drop your feet into them."

Putnam, older than the commander in chief, prescribed a good night's sleep. "And then we all see matters differently," he said huskily.

"Sir, shall I drop the tent flaps?" the captain squeaked.

They tiptoed out, leaving him alone in the darkness. He lay there for almost an hour, but he couldn't sleep. Instead, his thoughts slid back through the weeks and months to the time when he was riding north from Philadelphia to Boston to take command of his army. The whole long, slow ride was blurred by his fears and anticipations; from town to town they had gone, reviewing company after company of militia, the big farmer making so many speeches that he acquired a formula: "— my sincere pleasure in being here before you this day, this being a most glorious occasion." All of which did not take away his wonder as to how they would greet him, the Yankee New Englanders who had fought at Bunker Hill, and who were waiting for him now outside of Boston.

And finally he came before them, sitting on his horse in buff and blue, such a long, handsome, aristocratic figure as they had never seen before; and he saw what his army was, the mass of Yankee rustics in homespun, thousands of them slouching on their big firelocks, staring at him curiously, flinging remarks at each other, spitting crudely, and somberly chewing fat cuds of tobacco. And out in front were the officers, boys mostly, some young men, and one or two old men, but as

Yankee as the rank and file, and much more somberly cold and hostile in their judgment of him. He was Virginia, and they were Massachusetts, Vermont, New Hampshire, Maine, Rhode Island, and Connecticut, and between the two worlds was an infinite limbo; he might go into that limbo, they might too, but how could either get across? He remembered thinking to himself at that time that during his life he had met some hard men; cut-throats, robbers, Indian fighters of the backwoods who for years did not eat from a plate nor lay their heads on a feathered pillow, privateer sailors who were no better than pirates, kilted Scots clansmen of the Fincastle highlands; yet altogether none so hard as these New Englanders who were hard in their own Yankee way, hard and cold, with icy blue eyes, or eyes black as bits of charcoal.

"They hate me," he had written to Martha after that first review. "They all hate me and, I am sure, regard me as the meanest sort of outlander; they, who hypocritically scorning slaves, make of themselves worse slaves than tenant farmers, pecking and scratching at their bit of rocky, unhospitable soil. . . ."

When he met with his officers in the first of what he liked to call his councils of war, they stared coldly and significantly at his lace cuffs, his silk stockings, and his black pumps. And they disagreed with him wherever they could unobtrusively, in their own sly Yankee fashion. He felt their satisfaction when one of their cuts went home and it seared him — to whom it meant so much to be loved and admired by others.

Then how was it, he asked himself now, lying in his tent after they had left him, that the change had come about? He didn't know with any certainty, and almost fearful of introspection, he could not look inside of himself for an answer. He himself had not changed, but only gone on in the line of his duty, doing the things he hoped and believed a commander in chief should do. He could not realize that in going on alone, he had drawn them after him, gaining in stature as he fell back on his belief in himself and the path he followed.

Every bone in his body ached as he pulled on his boots, got into his coat, and buckled on his sword. He went outside and walked over to one of the fires, so that he could look at his watch. It was just half past three in the morning.

Walking slowly down the line of entrenchments he pretended to inspect them. As he passed, the men on duty snapped to what they considered military alertness. Some of them grinned anxiously; others sulked. A few saluted.

He realized that the British lines could not be very far away. The cannonading had stopped, and in the morning stillness, he could hear the voices of the Hessians. He wondered what they were talking about. He had seen a good many of the Germans, prisoners and deserters, and their ox-like stolidity disturbed him more than it puzzled him. For all his disgust at the arrogant independence of the New Englanders, it was better than the abject willingness of the Hessians to obey orders, anyone's orders. There was something terrifying about the big, shuffling, straw-haired peasants.

The Virginian reached the end of the lines and turned back. Already, a dirty-grey hint of morning had crept into the sky, and now he walked more slowly, like a condemned man who has used up the few hours of grace remaining to him and holds back because his destination is implicit. Somewhere a cock crowed, and somewhere else a dog began to bark.

A boy came running, round-cheeked and cockaded as a lieutenant, panting for breath as he saluted and stared at the big man.

"Yes?"

"Yes, sir, General Washington. I was to tell you reinforcements are coming over from the city."

"General Mifflin?" the foxhunter asked calmly.

"Yes, sir, yes, sir." The big man's calm was like cold water poured on the boy's excitement. "Yes, sir—sha'n't we give those bloody lobsters the devil now?" The boy could hardly keep from hopping up and down. "They'll attack at dawn, won't they, sir, don't you think so, sir, begging your pardon—" His voice sighed out as he realized his temerity. "General Putnam said you might come down to the water—if you weren't sleeping, if you wish to, sir."

"We'll go in a little while," the Virginian said calmly.

"In a little while, sir?"

He nodded, noting the effect on the boy. It wouldn't hurt for word to go around that Washington wasn't worried, so little worried that he was hardly interested in the number of men coming over from the city. It was better, at any rate, than to let them know that the reinforcements were coming to their death because the commander in chief hadn't the strength of mind to give up what he had already lost, but must drag more and more of his men into the hopeless trap.

For five minutes more he struggled between a desire to appear a hero in the boy's eyes and a longing to know what was happening on the river bank. Finally, he looked at his watch and said, "We'll go now, lieutenant."

The boy led the way proudly, shoulders thrown back, hoping that many of his friends would see him strolling with the commander in chief. As they walked, a faint, mist-like rain began to fall, and with the rain, a furious and buoyant hope sprang into the foxhunter's heart. In the rain, flints wouldn't spark and gunpowder would become a sodden, unexplosive mess. In the rush of hope, he felt his whole body trembling with excitement, yet he forced himself to walk calmly by the boy's side and to speak in even, unworried tones.

"What is your name, sir?" he asked.

"Tom Lackway, sir, begging your pardon."

"There's no need to beg my pardon. How old are you?"

"Seventeen, sir."

The big man raised his brows.

"Seventeen this April past," the boy explained hastily.

"I see. When did you receive your commission?"

"It's only a brevet cockade," the boy said anxiously, forgetting his "sir" for the first time. His hand roved to the feather he wore in his cap. "Yesterday," he said softly.

"Was your officer killed?"

"No—he run away," the boy said.

It was raining in earnest when the Virginian reached the riverfront, and the church spires and gabled roofs of New York were already dim in the mist. His cocked hat was drooping, and his uniform was entirely shapeless by now. he kept his face impassive, but his hand was trembling as he shook hands with Mifflin.

"Three regiments, sir," Mifflin said proudly. Mifflin was an ambitious man; at thirty he had been sent to the Congress. Now, at thirty-two, he was a general. Given a fair share of years, he was often dazzled when he thought of the heights to which he might rise. He was impatient, and a little jealous of a man he considered so very dull.

"I heard there was rough going yesterday."

The Virginian nodded. He felt Mifflin's contempt, saw in it one tiny piece of the contempt of all quick, intelligent men for a blunderer. He knew he hadn't the courage to tell Mifflin to turn around and send his men back to New York. So he stood there silently, watching the troops disembark.

There was a sense of order evident, the first bit of actual order he had seen since he came over to Brooklyn. The boats were sliding back and forth smoothly and expertly, and the men at the oars rowed as if they had done nothing but row all their lives. So fascinated was he by this expert performance that he allowed the imperturbable mask of his face to drop for a moment, long enough for Mifflin to note the expression and nod proudly.

"They know about boats," Mifflin said, nodding at the boatmen.

"They do know about boats," the foxhunter agreed mentally. He himself lost all sense of security where water was concerned; he could not think in the terms of a navy or even water barriers, that being one of the reasons why he had allowed himself to be drawn into the terrible cul-de-sac of Brooklyn. But even to him it was plainly evident that these men knew and enjoyed their work. They were leathery-skinned, long-faced Yankees, but they wore an air of confidence that the New England farmers did not possess. And there was uniformity in the blue jackets and stained oilskins most of them wore. Uniformity was one of the many things his army lacked; at least these men at the oars were of a kind.

"Who are they?" he asked.

"Glover's regiment, Marblehead fishermen. I didn't want my men blundering in the river all day—and these men know how to row. Maybe they can't fight, but they know about boats—they should; they've been fishermen all along."

"Fishermen," the foxhunter said softly. "How many are there?" The rain had increased, and now he laid his big palms against the drops, eagerly, almost with sensuous relief. The morning was growing on, and still there was no sign of a British attack.

"Six or seven hundred."

His mind fought with an idea. He didn't hear Mifflin ask whether or not they would be better off taking shelter out of the rain; his mind was plodding down a maze that might lead out of ruin. But he told himself, doggedly: "I must do it alone, alone."

For the first time in his life, he attempted the task of crawling into the minds of little, frightened men. He must plan a retreat, a retreat which the rain had given one single, slim chance of success, yet he alone out of the whole army must know that retreat was contemplated. If anyone else knew, the terror of the defeated army would turn into panic. He had wanted to lead an army, a proud, disciplined army; instead he was leading a frightened rabble of children and fools. But he understood something of them now; he no longer deluded himself.

"Sir?" Mifflin demanded.

For ten minutes the big man had stood motionless and silent in the pouring rain. Putnam, old and tired, came plodding down the slope to join them. Mifflin glanced at him, past the big man, and shrugged his shoulder helplessly, as if to indicate that the Virginian had gone off the loose end entirely.

"Sir?" Mifflin asked again.

Wherever the commander in chief stood, in his gaunt height, a knot of officers gathered. Now they crouched in an impatient circle, waiting for him to come out of the rain.

"I don't think they'll attack today," Putnam observed, not sagacious, but sourly aware of sciatica and rheumatism. "Why should they fight in the rain when they can sit in their tents and wait for the weather to clear?"

Nobody wanted to suggest retreat, yet it was the prime thought in the minds of each of them, a certainty that had to come from the Virginian. They stared at him expectantly, and he braced himself.

"We won't retreat, gentlemen," he told them.

Now their faces said that he had gone insane.

"Gentlemen," he informed them quietly, "we are going to bring over reinforcements and we are going to take our sick and wounded back to New York. Today I want you to gather every boat on this river, every barge or skiff or scow. I want boats brought down from the North River and I want every fishing craft out of the Sound you can lay hands on—and I want them all brought here, to the Brooklyn shore. I want you to get those boats. I want you, Colonel Glover, to keep your fishermen here, on the riverfront—do you understand, on the riverfront?"

Then, weak, tired, but in a subtle way he had never known before, triumphant, he shouldered through them and walked back to the entrenchments. He was not a good hand at deceit; it was the least of his virtues; but the mere fact that he could cloak his intentions at all amazed him curiously.

4

THE RETREAT

HOURS passed while he sat in his tent, looked at his watch now and then, and listened to the drizzle of rain on the canvas. There was nothing to do but think; at least twenty-four hours would have to pass before the boats began to arrive in any sort of quantity.

He realized that sooner or later he would have to divulge his plan to his officers. No one man, alone, could put into effect the retreat of any army of thousands. The duplicity would be too strained, too thinly drawn; and if one single factor went wrong, the whole structure would crash down like a house of cards.

Still, at this moment, there was nothing to do, and the very fact of his sitting quietly in his tent would reassure the army. The boys who were his officers could not match his patience; they hopped and squeaked, and every five minutes one of them would thrust his head into the tent. The commander sat at a little camp table, writing calmly, and the boy would whistle and go back to tell the others what he had seen.

"He looked up at me."

"Yes?"

"And didn't say a word, just looked at me."

"Annoyed?"

"No—I wouldn't say that he was annoyed."

"Smiling?"

"Maybe a wee bit amused."

"Christ, he's a cool one!"

And as the night wore on, the Virginian lay down on his bed, and rolled feverishly from side to side, pleading with himself for sleep. Doubts and fears paraded mockingly; all the British had to do was to sail their fleet up the East River and cut off the American retreat once and forever. Knox's six- and nine-pounder popguns could make no impression on their mighty ships of the line, while a single broadside from their carronades would blow the Marblehead men out of the water.

Then why didn't they? What held them back? What were they waiting for?

Why, why, why? he asked himself, drifting into an uneasy doze that brought memories walking like ghosts. He woke and looked at his watch, and saw that only a few minutes had passed.

In the wet, dismal dawn, he sat in his tent with Knox and Putnam and Mifflin. The tent drooped and leaked; there was an uneven rhythm between the drops inside and the drops outside, and the floor of the tent was a pancake of sucking mud. Putnam and Mifflin sat together on the sway-backed bed; the foxhunter sat at his rickety camp table, and Knox on a low ammunition box with a huge pewter pitcher of stale beer between his legs.

"What are you waiting for?" Mifflin demanded.

"Loggerhead," Knox said, drawing in his huge stomach and regarding the beer intently.

"Put in the rum and molasses."

"When the loggerhead comes," Knox said patiently.

"What the devil's the difference?"

"He's right, when the logger comes," Putnam nodded.

"It's the only way," Knox said. "Otherwise you spoil it."

"He's right," Putnam agreed. "You have to wait until the iron's hot."

"Damfool superstition," Mifflin muttered.

The Virginian shook his head wearily and tapped his long fingers on the table. "Gentlemen," he said quietly, "the flip can wait."

"Sorry, sir," Knox said. He poked a finger into the stale beer and licked absently.

"We're going to retreat," the Virginian said. His voice was humble, almost pleading. There seemed to be no future and no end to the word retreat.

They stared at him bewilderedly. Knox was the first to look away; his round boyish face was puckered and frightened. He picked up a tin pan of molasses from the floor and let molasses run into the beer. It ran slowly and obstinately, and while Knox poured, a skinny, pock-marked runt of a boy poked into the tent, carrying a red-hot iron.

"Loggerhead, sir," the boy squeaked.

"Give it to me," Knox said.

"The rum!" Putnam reminded him gruffly.

Mifflin took up a bottle of rum and poured it into the pitcher of beer, and then Knox plunged in the red-hot poker. The whole mess sizzled and steamed, giving off a foul, leathery smell. The pock-marked boy watched, fascinated, until a glance from Putnam sent him scurrying away. Knox, meanwhile, had set the poker aside and was pouring the concoction into earthenware cups.

The commander drank from his mug slowly. No one had proposed a toast, no one wanted a toast. Mifflin, Knox and Putnam filled and refilled from the pewter pitcher with grim earnestness.

And Mifflin muttered, "I can't understand that, sir, about retreat. I can't understand it, sir. I brought over my men and now you tell me retreat. I can't understand it, sir. Why shouldn't we fight them?"

"There's nothing else," the Virginian said. "The men won't fight— God knows if they ever will. And if the British sail up the river, that's the end of it. It's better to have an army that won't fight than no army at all."

"Sir, if you tell them to retreat," Knox said, "It'll be worse."

The big man nodded. How many times in the past twenty-four hours had he pictured thousands of panic-stricken men fighting madly to be the first into the boats! "You won't tell them," he said. "After dark, tonight, order certain regiments to be relieved, one by one. Each to think all the rest are holding the line. Maybe that way—"

"—sick and tired," Putnam was muttering. "Can't hardly move my hip."

"—most can be taken out of this. General Mifflin, I want you to man the redoubts with your men and hold them until I give word that you are to go."

"And get rid of me as he got rid of Stirling and Sullivan," Mifflin thought.

Almost tearfully, Knox asked, "But what about my guns, sir—what about my guns?"

"Spike them."

"All of them? Can't we take a few over, sir?"

The big man shook his head.

"All my beautiful guns," Knox whispered. He had downed too much flip, and he was almost maudlin now. "My beautiful guns," he sighed.

The rain went on. The commander threw a cloak over his shoulders and walked back and forth through the camp. The men were frightened and wet and miserable; they had no tents over here in Brooklyn, most of them, and they lay around in a sick sort of despair. They gave the commander in chief hardly a glance as he passed; they had made no effort to keep their muskets out of the rain, and there was hardly a piece in the camp in condition to fire.

Any sort of attack would have swept them away like over-ripe wheat; they had lost all semblance of any army; they lay where they were only because each and every one of them realized the hopelessness of retreat. Some of them, the sixteen- and seventeen-year-old boys for the most part, were still whimpering like hurt puppies over the shock of the rout. The Maryland and Virginia troops held themselves apart, still in some semblance of order; it was their private grudge that they had taken too great a share of the battering, and it needed only a tiny incident to send them at the throats of the New Englanders. The New Englanders, for their part, had discussed the miserable showing and defeat of the revolutionary army with Yankee thoroughness, and they were convinced now that the officers who led them had deliberately betrayed them. Given the chance, a good many of them would desert; and many were now planning how they would manage it, once they were out of this devilish Brooklyn trap. But others would go on, betrayed or not, because this was something they had started at Concord and Lexington and would finish because their need for freedom was more organic than logical. They had to be free; it was part of their blood and flesh, and any sort of servitude, real or imagined, was like a raw cancer inside of them.

Every movement of the foxhunter's tall, straight body was an affront to them. They cursed him for what they knew him to be, a stupid, heartless Virginia foxhunter.

Their common sense told them that he, the wealthiest man in America, could have no real interest in the war. His hardness and bitter temper were constant subjects of discussion among them. Even that outlandish name of his was an affront to them. Washington—who in all hell had ever heard of such a name?

His feet hurt. Through all the pains of a sickly body that had been denied sleep for sixty hours, the pain of his feet was most persistent. And as the dreary afternoon closed, with the British still patiently waiting in their tents for the rain to stop, he decided that he could not walk another step. He called for his horse, mounted, and rode down to the riverfront; as he rode he dozed constantly, and he had to pull himself awake again and again with a definite effort of will.

Now that all preparations had been completed, he was certain that the retreat would not come off successfully. It was inconceivable that the British, who were only a few hundred yards away, should allow this beaten wreck of an army to withdraw in safety. He saw ruin and disgrace and the gallow's noose, and tired as he was his thoughts took on the drift of a fantastic nightmare. He wondered vaguely what force made him do one thing after another; he had never thought a great deal about forces.

At the riverfront, he was amazed by the number of boats the Marblehead men had gathered. They were only now beginning to approach the Brooklyn shore, but the river up toward Hell's Gate was alive with bobbing craft of every description. They came out of the murk of fog and rain in an endless stream, driven by the wind and the laughing, rain-soaked fishermen, and the same fog and rain hid their approach from the British fleet, stationed out on the bay. And the Marblehead men were enjoying their task; sick to death of endless marching and drilling, they had turned at last to a job that suited them, and they alone of all the army worked well and quickly and efficiently. Their colonel, Glover, was a Salem man himself; he had

30

raised the regiment of fishermen; he knew his men, what they were capable of, and how to get the last ounce of work out of them.

As the boats came in, Glover was having them moored and beached, stripping them of all gear except that absolutely necessary to a ferry, and assigning a crew of men to each boat. The larger boats, sailing gigs and a few cutters, were kept separate, so that they could have room for a circular tack. As dusk fell, the massed boats made a solid rank on the riverfront.

Knox came crunching down to where the commander sat on his horse. The boy's pudgy face was twisted with despair.

"About those guns, sir," he said.

"Yes?"

"Where are we going to find more guns when we spike those?"

The big man shrugged.

"An army fights with guns," Knox insisted doggedly.

"And with men — and we have neither."

They looked at one another, the bookseller who had once dreamed of being a successful publisher and the foxhunter who had once dreamed of having many peaceful years — with the woman he loved and children of his own.

"I'll start to spike as soon as it's dark," Knox said.

"Quietly as you can."

"You can't spike a gun quietly, sir," Knox said morosely. "I'll do my best."

"And when it's done, send your men down here to be taken across the river."

At about seven o'clock, Glover came over to report that his boats were almost all in, as many as could be expected, and that he was ready to start ferrying when the word was given. A dozen officers had come down and clustered around the commander in chief, making him realize again that the only force capable of stirring the broken army lay in his thin, weary body. He looked at the officers with bloodshot eyes, staring at face after face, wondering vaguely that these children should be colonels and majors and generals, and then, singling out one, said, "Bring down your regiment and put them in the boats."

"Retreat, sir?"

"No, you fool — I'm relieving your regiment, sending them over to the city for rest and dry clothes. The rest of you go back to your posts."

He almost laughed aloud, it was such a silly, childish deception. He

31

walked his horse down to the boats, that he might be on hand to supervise the embarkation, and there in the flickering light of a lantern held by one of the fishermen, he began to doze again.

"Sir?"

He looked up sleepily.

"You looked somehow sickly," the fisherman grinned.

"Get to your post!"

"Yes, sir—"

"Get to your post! By God, Glover, keep your men in hand!" They were the only ones left he could discipline; the rest were beyond discipline.

He sat there, trembling with fatigue, biting his lips to drive away sleep until the blood ran down inside his mouth.

He was astonished to discover how well the scheme worked. Its very simplicity was the factor that made it successful. Each regiment, believing that it alone was the lucky one, believing that it alone was to be relieved, crept down to the riverfront in the deepest silence. Their fear was not that the British should hear them; as an enemy and a factor to be considered, the British had vanished entirely from their minds: their fear was that their less fortunate comrades should hear them and destroy this, their last chance for life and liberty.

After the first regiment had left the Brooklyn shore for the dim lights of Manhattan, the Virginian's weariness vanished. There was still a chance, and it appeared to be a good chance. His thought-process was meticulous, but all his grown life he had sat at card tables, and the heady lust for a stake placed on a good deal was deep in his blood. He drove his horse back and forth, being everywhere at once, shepherding the men into the boats as he would a herd of sheep. As with many sickly men, he had an almost inexhaustible store of nervous energy; later he would pay the price, but now he was a furious, challenging man on a horse.

He spared no one. The boys who called themselves generals wilted under the lash of his tongue. The Marblehead fishermen, who were already laboring super-humanly, were not laboring well enough. He dragged the patient Glover over hot coals, and when the Salem man dared meekly to protest, he roared, "I'll have no back talk, sir! God damn you, do your duty!"

He had been born in a saddle and weaned like a colt, the foxhunter; as he rode now, the horse was of his flesh and slave to his flesh.

The night wore on and still the regiments came and still he herded them into the boats. He had lost count, and when he asked his aides they knew no more than he about how many were left holding the lines. But they were exuberant, heady with the success of the maneuver.

"Let me go see, sir," one of them, Scammel by name, begged.

"Yes. But leave Mifflin."

"What?" Scammel had reared his horse.

"I said leave Mifflin and bring the others. Mifflin goes last."

"Yes, sir." Scammel dashed away.

"I don't think he understood you, sir," Glover observed.

But another regiment was creeping down from the heights, and the Virginian rode off to direct them to the boats. Nothing would go wrong now.

The orders he had given Scammel, which Scammel did not understand, yet hastened to carry out, fearing to face the commander with his confusion, set off a chain that threatened to blow all his plans sky-high. Scammel dashed up to Mifflin and told him that the commander in chief desired him, Mifflin, to march all his troops down to the boat landing to be embarked for New York.

"My troops or them?" Mifflin demanded, pointing to the thinned, nervous ranks of New Englanders, as contrasted with his own fairly well-disciplined regiments.

"Your own troops, I think," Scammel said.

"You're sure?"

"That's what he told me."

"And them?" pointing to the New Englanders.

Scammel shook his head, and Mifflin shrugged, giving orders for his men to abandon their places in the entrenchments and fall into line. The New Englanders watched open-mouthed, trying to comprehend the fact that while Mifflin's fresh troops marched away, they were to be left for a sacrifice, they who had fought so well and shed so much of their blood in the battle of Brooklyn. For just so long as it took them to comprehend the fact, they stood there and watched, and then the spell broke and they bolted. And every brigade within sight or hearing joined in the flight.

The wave of men was like a flood rolling down to the boat landing. They gave themselves to panic and fought and clawed. They climbed over each other's heads; they crawled between feet; they punched and ripped and tore; they wept in terror and pushed their comrades into the black waters of the river. They cursed the Marblehead fishermen hysterically, and the fishermen fought back with clubbed oars.

And in the center of it, roaring like an enraged beast, was the commander in chief. He was everywhere at once, furious and terrible — and quelling them; it was like cold water poured on hot flames, and out of the wretched sizzle came a single moment of deep silence.

"Get to your ranks!"

They gave way before him and cowered; many of them sank to the ground and wept into their trembling hands. And the big man rode through them, looking neither to the left nor to right.

When he found Mifflin, he had himself almost under control once more, enough to keep from flinging himself on the general with all the terrible fury he was capable of, enough to sit rigid and demand, "Why did you withdraw, Mifflin?"

"I had your orders."

"God damn you, no! You had no orders!"

"By God, I did!" Mifflin raged. "Didn't you send Scammel to me? Didn't you order me to fall back?" His eyes ran with tears of rage and he slapped his hands helplessly against his thighs. "Didn't you send Scammel to me, didn't you?"

The foxhunter climbed down from his horse, walked over to Mifflin, and took the man by the shoulders.

"Didn't you send Scammel to me?" Mifflin sobbed.

The Virginian was restored to sanity now; he was able to recall the question in Scammel's eyes that the boy had not dared to ask.

"What did Scammel tell you?" he asked Mifflin.

"To come down here!"

The Virginian shook his head. "Forgive me."

"Sir?"

"I'm sorry, General Mifflin, believe me. It wasn't Scammel's fault nor yours. I don't know what I'm saying sometimes."

"What are your orders, sir?" Mifflin asked hoarsely, feeling then, at that moment, that he would have died for the tall foxhunter, and gladly.

"Go back to your post and hold it until I send for you."

"I'll hold it until hell breaks loose," Mifflin whispered.

It was close on morning, and the fog had lifted. The Virginian sat in a boat with Knox and a schoolboy captain of artillery whose name was Alexander Hamilton.

"Push off, sir?" the Marblehead man at the tiller asked.

"Just a moment."

34

The oars wavered and dropped to the water. The captain of artillery pointed to the slope where Hessians were already scrambling through the mud.

"Better go now, sir," Knox said morosely, still mourning the loss of his guns.

"We'll go," the big man nodded.

The tillerman fended off and the oars scooped at the water. As the boat glided out into the river, the Hessians formed up and let loose a volley.

The commander in chief hardly moved; he was dozing already, and in moment more he would be asleep. He didn't want to think now; he still had his army, for what it was worth, and there would be time for thought later.

PART TWO

MANHATTAN ISLAND

5

THE ARMY OF LIBERTY

ON AUGUST 29, the good burghers of New York City had gone to sleep with the comforting knowledge that the patriot army was somewhere else. And these good men, solid men who knew the price of things and minded their own business, asked only one thing of the patriot army—that it be somewhere else.

When they woke up, on August 30th, they discovered to their horror and dismay that the army of liberty had returned. Not in the best order, it is true; there was no beating of drums and playing of fifes; there were no Yankee farmers in close rank, trying to march as if they were soldiers; there were no gay cockades and arrogant boasts; instead there was a bedraggled, crawling thing that occupied the city in silence and misery.

When the burghers came out in the morning to open their shops and swing back their shutters, they saw the soldiers of liberty moving through the streets, wet, glassy-eyed, and beaten.

The commander in chief slept in a deep cavern of darkness that was only faintly punctuated by pinprick musket flashes; he slept not restlessly, but log-like, chained down by weariness; and afterwards everything from the moment he stepped into the boat to leave Brooklyn was masked by that same fog of weariness. He hardly remembered how he dozed on the seat with the muskets roaring behind him, nor did he recall his stammering insistence that he had left something behind him. He had no memory of taking off his clothes, of sipping at a glass of wine someone held out to him—and of falling asleep while he sipped, of giving orders in a faint, dream-like whisper.

In his sleep, the battle became more vivid and more terrible, and once he woke with the grating cry of "Yonkee, Yonkee" ringing in his

37

HOWARD FAST

ears. But after that he slipped back into a deep and restful slumber.

He slept through the morning and afternoon, and as evening came on, he still slept. His officers, for all their desire to know his plans, did not have the heart to wake him. Younger men than he, their stretch of wakefulness had been neither so long nor so painful, and now they were up and gathering in little knots around the house where he slept.

Their talk was all of the battle and the incredible escape from Brooklyn, none of them seemed to realize the full import of the loss they had sustained — a full fifth of their effectives on the Brooklyn shore. Their youth gave them a heady, insane confidence; out of their farms and their shops, they had come to this magnificent adventure, and when the adventure threatened to end abruptly, they had escaped, and therefore one thing followed absolutely:

They would always escape.

The army of liberty slept too. They had crawled into whatever dark corners they could find. Above Canal Street, there were dozens of old Dutch barns, and each of these barns was crammed full of patriots, snoring and complaining, shaking with fever and trembling with fear. Some of the Yankees lay in the gutters, and others slept curled against doors of houses that were closed to them. Two lieutenants and four privates lay on a wet tent fly, spread in the mud of Bowery Lane. A church was filled with moaning wounded, but there were neither doctors nor nurses to attend to them. A boy lay dead on Pearl Street with his face in the mud, but the worthy burghers regarded him as they might a dead cat or a dead dog. The Jewish Synagogue on Mill Street was packed so full of sick and wounded that there was no room left for the old men to pray; they stood outside and listened to the cries of the tortured creatures that had once been their sons and grandsons. In Fraunces Tavern a half company of Delaware Swedes had finished all the rum on hand, broken most of the furniture, and gone to sleep on the floor. On Bowling Green, fourteen Poles, all that was left of a brigade, had built a fire of driftwood and sat around it, not for the warming of their bodies but of their poor, lonely souls. They knew not one single word of English; they sang their mournful Slavic songs and remembered the days when they had fled like beasts through the desolate Pripet Marshes; and they told each other that it was always the same when men looked around for a way to make themselves free. Two men, a Virginian and a Rhode Island Yankee, had fought like devils in the bushes north of Old Slip, and the Virginian left the Yankee with his throat cut and his blood running out.

38

They slept through the morning and most of the afternoon, but toward evening they began to awake and their courage returned to some degree. They came out of their dark holes and sought for something to quench their thirst. They stormed the taverns, and with a mug or two of flip under their belts they became heroes. There was not a man among them who had not killed his share and more than his share of the cowardly British, and what they had done to the Hessians was something for their grandchildren to hear. They cursed the Virginia squire who had mismanaged everything, and they said what a damned fortunate thing it was he had men he could depend on. As more and more red-hot loggers came out of the fire, as more and more flip flowed into their bellies, their boasting turned into a desire for action, and bands of Yankees set out to find some of the God-damned Virginians, and bands of Maryland men set out to revenge the deaths of their comrades by breaking some Rhode Island heads. Arm in arm, Pennsylvanians roamed the streets,filled with sullen hatred for everyone, and Down Easters swore they would make New York a hell spot for any filthy tidewater aristocrats they could find.

Pitched battles raged, and cobblestones and clubbed muskets left broken heads behind. A jeweler who had the reputation of being a Tory, but who had stayed on in New York protesting his love for the patriots, had his shop broken into, and a whole brigade of Connecticut men strutted with watches and pins.

Two boys came out of the jeweler's house and went after the Connecticut men. Their names were Aaron Burr and Alexander Hamilton; Hamilton, a wraith of a lad with violet, girl-like eyes, lit into the Connecticut brigade like a fury out of hell. There were other splashes in the whirlpool; Knox beat in the heads of two drunken Virginians who had torn the clothes off a Dutch girl, and old Israel Putnam went through street after street, driving Yankees out of the mud with his bare sword, while he tongue-lashed them in a way that could be heard blocks off. Other officers followed his example, and as night fell on New York, the town became a bedlam of cursing, pleading officers, drunken soldiers, weeping boys, and bitterly complaining citizens.

The bickering was endless and childish—over muskets, knapsacks, handkerchiefs, loaves of bread. In the mad scramble out of Brooklyn, everyone had grabbed what he could, and everyone claimed everyone else's possessions. Now, with brigades scattered through the narrow streets, with drunkards lost, forgetful even of the name of their regiments, weeping for comrades they had seen killed when they ran away, with hundreds of deserters racing like mad for tne wooded hills of Harlem Heights, the situation was well-nigh hopeless.

Yet the baby-faced officers persevered, and presently as the night wore on, some sort of order came into being. And later, once more, the army of liberty slept.

Billy brought in six bottles of Madeira. "Instead of flip," the fox-hunter said diffidently, smiling a little in the first feeble attempt at a joke that his young men had heard in many days. He was very fond of Madeira, and now that he had slept and rested and changed his clothes and combed his hair, nothing else would do.

The dozen or so officers who sat crowded close to the round table made up a sort of council of war. The Virginian had summoned them to talk about the retreat, the future, and the revolution: Knox and Putnam and Mercer and Mifflin and Spencer and Clinton — and others, generals, major generals, colonels, and the boy Hamilton who could write so well, sitting to one side with his open notebook on his knee, his own nineteen years slightly in awe of these men in their late twenties and early thirties.

When they first gathered at the table, the commander in chief had not yet appeared. He sat over a little table in his bedroom, painfully composing a message to the army which had been so miraculously restored to him. When he wrote it was with difficulty and even with shame, for he spelled badly, and in a time of magnificent penmen, his penmanship was not of the best. He had a love of words that verged upon humble supplication, yet all his life words had eluded him. He could not transpose emotion into letters; if the world fell on him, he could only report that there was a disturbance, and if his heart was breaking, it made him ashamed and self-conscious to say that he was somewhat uneasy.

It was difficult enough to compose what he believed, but now for an hour he had written and scratched out a mockery of the truth, finishing with something he hardly dared to read through.

"They'll laugh," he told himself. He made up his mind that if they laughed, he would not trust himself to words, but just stare at them with great composure and an even glance.

Before he left his bedroom, he examined himself carefully in the mirror. He set his face in a very calm and knowing expression, thinking with some satisfaction that they would say to each other afterward:

"He's got ice in his veins, not a bit disturbed. It may be bluff, but more likely he knows about things. That whole mess of Brooklyn doesn't disturb him."

He straightened his coat and smoothed out the wrinkles in his fawn-colored breeches. Billy had sewn two bits of lace under his cuffs, and now he let the lace droop onto his wrists in the lazy manner he managed so well. Instead of boots, he wore white silk stockings and black pumps—with a calculated purpose: so they might say that he was more prepared to dance than to fight, and certainly not disturbed. He looked at his watch, saw that he had kept them waiting for more than a half hour, and then he made his deliberate entrance, his six feet two and a half inches stiff as a ramrod.

When the wine had been poured, he proposed the first toast. "To the Continental Congress," he said calmly, wondering grimly how long it would be so, how many days or weeks at the most before the toast would again be to "His Gracious Majesty, the King." And the boys around the table reflected his thoughts, drinking soberly, thoughtfully.

The second toast he made to "America." His men looked at him curiously and uncertainly. It was facetious of him, or clever, or foolish; he was a Virginian. They were Yankees, most of them, and they could never forget that he was a Virginian. And the word America had a strange foreign sound in their ears.

"To America, gentlemen," he had said.

The third toast was for the gallant men who had died, shot through or pinned in the back by a sliver of steel or trampled underfoot. Looking at their faces he realized that they were thinking more of the men who had run away than of those who had died. "Let it be that way"—he said to himself—"only judge not."

The fourth toast was for the future, for the success of their arms, and now he saw them looking at him as if he had mentioned something foul, not to be spoken of.

The fifth toast was for them, his officers, and as he proposed it he saw the red flushes mantle their faces, and he felt choked and lonely in their esteem.

Bill brought more of the Madeira.

The sixth toast was for him, for "His Excellency, George Washington, Commander in Chief of the Continental Forces."

"Thank you, gentlemen," he said quietly, almost miserably, hating himself for the manner in which he had prepared and developed this whole scene, calculating every reaction in the headstrong boys who followed him.

He sat for the most part in silence, letting them talk as they wished.

41

In his own mind, he knew what he desired to do and knew how impossible it was. What he wanted was retreat, constant retreat, long, hard marches that would never allow his men to stay for a moment in one place, never allow them to think, never allow them to desert. The business in Brooklyn had given him some insight on one terribly important fact: that it was his army that counted. By the grace of God, he still had his army, and nothing else mattered. He would take his army and go away — burn New York to the ground and give the British only a heap of ashes for winter quarters when they took New York — go on for months if necessary, go on across the great green bulk of the Alleghenies, but keep his army intact and together.

Yet he knew it was impossible. Congress had made him commander in chief to fight battles, and to fight battles they had given him an army of Yankee children.

"We're safe enough," Knox was saying. "We're on an island. An island's like a good fort; you can hold it forever."

"And we're like to be there forever."

"I say to hell with all that and burn the town, and get out and leave them the ashes."

"Burn it?"

"Burn it! That's what I say. Burn it!"

"I live here, sir!"

Scorn and hate and bickering destroyed the radiant warmth of the toasts, and chairs were pushed back; and then military tactics thrust into a well of personalities.

"Gentlemen," the big man said.

Then they sat in silence for a while, their commander telling them that he had wanted to burn New York, but that Congress forbade it and that he would hear no further talk on the merit or lack of merit in any Congressional policy.

"Retreat, sir?"

He shook his head. "We'll try to hold some of the city," he said.

They looked at him perplexedly. Was this another of his tricks? He had been damned clever at Brooklyn.

"We must make sure of Kingsbridge," he said, allowing just a faint note of hopelessness to creep into his voice. Kingsbridge was a way off the island at its northernmost tip, a wooden bridge crossing Spuyten Duyvil.

Old Putnam was afraid and he shook his head; he felt ancient and foolish in that circle of hotheaded boys.

Mifflin, a little drunk, regarding the foxhunter more highly than ever after the incident at Brooklyn and the Virginian's selfless apology, said, "Whatever comes, we can hold Fort Washington—we can hold it until hell freezes over!" And then there was a moment of silence, for the fort was his own, the first place named after him, to give him dignity and dignity to the Congress that had elected him, the first place in all the broad miles of America called Washington. Yet it was almost never called that in his presence; instead they spoke of "the fort" or "that hill north of the Heights."

"We can hold Fort Washington," Knox said shyly, stressing the name. And the others nodded.

He felt that he could not bear much more of this; his life had been with his kind, Virginians and aristocrats, not Yankee boys; he had never been loved. Respected, admired, but not loved. Still there was a heady sort of joy in knowing that they would follow him anywhere, to hell if necessary, but anywhere he chose to lead. It was something he had not done deliberately; they had hated him at first, but for their hatred he returned a measure of justice. The rest, that he might appear fearless, honorable, wonderful to look at, something to regard with admiration, did not occur to him; their love of him left him puzzled and deeply moved, the more so since he had no complete understanding of their reasons.

"We will do what we can," he said helplessly.

"We must not fight them here," old Israel pleaded.

"What we can do and must do—"

"We should abandon the town!"

"No!"

Spencer, drunk on six glasses of Madeira, cried, "By God, hold the city and blow the filthy swine to hell!"

"You're drunk, sir," old Israel said evenly.

"Sober enough to see you in hell, you damned old lady!"

"Spencer, hold your tongue!" the Virginian said icily.

After that, the long silence was a dumb admission by each and every one of them.

"You will form your brigades," said the commander in chief. "You will get them out of the streets and take away whatever they have stolen. Common thieves will receive thirty lashes, and for desertion a hundred, and for rape five hundred. I want that understood. I want them paraded. For those of your men who threw away their muskets, find something, if not muskets at least a pike or a pitchfork or a knife. I have written out an order for the men—to encourage their spirits and to give them some feeling of devotion. I will read it to you now, and then I will have my secretary make copies for you to read to your brigades tomorrow. Here is the order as I have written it:

"Now, our whole Army is collected together, without water intervening, while the Enemy can receive little assistance from their ships; their Army is and must be divided into many bodies, and fatigued with keeping up a communication with their ships; whereas ours is connected and can act together; they must effect a landing, under so many disadvantages, that if officers and soldiers are vigilant, and alert, to prevent surprise, and add spirit when they approach, there is no doubt of our success.

"The General hopes the several officers, both superior and inferior, will now exert themselves, and gloriously determine to conquer, or die—From the justice of our cause—the situation of the harbor, and the bravery of her sons, America can only expect success. Now is the time for every man to exert himself, and to make our country glorious, or it will become contemptible."

He had finished speaking, and it was out, and he stared straight ahead, waiting for them to laugh. No one laughed. He looked slowly at Knox, whose eyes were filled with tears.

Meanwhile, one of a thousand deserters had been caught by the patrol at Kingsbridge. The man, a Vermonter, fought and struggled, and finally collapsed in impotent rage when he saw escape was hopeless. Curiosity impelled the soldiers of the patrol to open the huge bag he was carrying. It contained a ham, a lady's silk dress, and assorted products of six or seven other New York shops. All that they understood, and even admired his very capable looting. But the presence of an eight-pound cannonball stumped them.

"What's this?" they demanded.

"A ball, ye damn fools."

"What for? Why are you stealing ammunition?"

"Lor', ye damn fools, I'm bringing a bumper for my maw to ground out mustard with "

6

ONE TERRIBLE SUNDAY MORNING

R IDING from the little cluster of houses that was called New York, a country village on the southern tip of Manhattan Island, up to his headquarters in Harlem, in the cool Saturday afternoon of September 14th, the Virginia squire reviewed the events of the past two weeks.

All in all, he had not done badly; and he reflected with some satisfaction that the defeated rabble which had fled so miserably from Brooklyn Heights had once again some semblance of an army. Two weeks ago, immediately after their return to New York, he had almost lost hope; men were deserting, not singly, nor even in groups of ten and twenty, but in whole brigades. All discipline had been forgotten, and the army had terrified New York, rioting through the streets, brawling, looting, raping and killing. Pitched battles had occurred between the Virginia and North Carolina brigades and the New Englanders, and the whole army appeared to be in a state of rapid dissolution.

Only by the grace of God had the British refrained from some attempt to make a bridgehead on Manhattan, and now he dared to hope that they had held back too long. He had regrouped his forces into three divisions, one under the command of old Putnam, assigned to hold the city itself, another under Heath to hold the northern bottleneck of Kingsbridge, and the third under Spencer to hold the body of Manhattan in-between. He was uncertain of Spencer, whom he did not completely trust and whom he considered a fool; but the only other major general available, Nathanael Greene—whom he trusted and liked—was just recovering from the fever which had laid him low before the Brooklyn affair. Spencer would do until Greene returned, and now, in the bright coolness of the autumn afternoon, the Virginian felt wonderfully exhilarated and not at all disposed toward worry.

There had been times during the past two weeks when he had been so sick with despair that all the strength had gone out of his body, when he had lain on his bed, in hopelessness, for hours on end. As when, for instance, the Congress had lost courage entirely, flinching from the thousand and more men lost on Brooklyn Heights, and had sent Dr. Franklin and Mr. John Adams to talk with General Howe about surrender. He, their servant, could not protest; he was a soldier taking orders; but heartbroken, he had pleaded with those around

45

him, those he knew and had come to love as he had never loved men — Knox, Putnam, Mifflin: "Why, why, why? Why surrender?"

"No," they told him. "It won't turn out that way; there won't be any talk of surrender."

"They let me fight the battles," he said miserably, "and then they send Adams and Franklin to talk about surrender. It doesn't matter that men have died for liberty."

"It matters, sir," they tried to convince him.

"Franklin's an old man; he's got no guts."

"He won't give up."

"And Adams put me here. Is he afraid now?" And then he said, "They're all afraid, that's the long and short of it. They're afraid and they want to give up. God help us, that's all, they want to give up."

Afterwards, when the discussions had produced nothing more than a flow of keen wit from Dr. Franklin, the Virginian tried to understand why he had been so shaken by the thought that the revolution might peter out after the disgraceful rout of Brooklyn. He was slow and awkward at introspection, which he regarded as something slightly sordid, yet he probed himself enough to realize that there were other reasons that the desire to prove himself a leader of some quality instead of a fool. What those other reasons were, he didn't quite know; certainly there was no real bond between himself and the rabble of Yankees, backwoods Southerners, and foreign revolutionaries he led; yet there was a drive and a force, and an ache in his heart for something unseen yet tremendously powerful and forthright.

But today, he had dismissed the painful and rather nasty business of introspection; he had dismissed fears and worries and doubts and had given himself to the good feeling of a wind in his face and a hard dirt road under his horse's hoofs. Riding through the lovely woods of mid-Manhattan, with meandering brooks, silver-faced ponds, and stone-hedged fields on either side of him, he thought that never in his life, even on the shores of his beloved Potomac, had he seen country so placidly beautiful. He was a farmer and countryman, out of many generations of farmers and countrymen, and he reacted to things instinctively and gratefully, to a flight of birds dark against the rosy sky that rimmed the black Palisades, to the waving surface of bright and golden wheat in the neat Dutch fields, to the exquisite scarlet of the early turning red maples, to a windmill looping against the cold green sky of the east, to little pink lizards swarming over the dust of the road, to the baying of hounds in the spirit of an evening chase, to a tiny red-cheeked boy teetering on top of a split rail fence — to fading sun, and wind and scudding clouds.

It was a moment when life was inordinately good, good beyond measure to this thin man whose love of life was sensuous and grateful.

Along with him, there rode a troop of about a dozen light horse, one of the few cavalry units in his army, fat Colonel Knox, grinning and happy to be near the man he worshipped, young Burr, sent along by Putnam to accompany the commander in chief back to his headquarters on Harlem Heights, and a Lieutenant Grayson and a Captain Hardy. The light horse had not been light horse for very long, and they found it difficult to keep in order, two abreast and two abreast; instead they bunched up and strung out as the procession wound along, and the officers were in such good spirits that they hadn't the heart to criticize.

The men began to sing, chanting their everlasting ditty about Yankee Doodle and the pony he rode to London Town. The verses were endless, most of them smutty, but the Virginia squire screwed up his face not at the content but at what he considered a wretched melody. His own taste was for Mozart and Bach, and now he had a nostalgic memory of the hours he had spent with his flute, painfully picking out the difficult counterpoint. He was like a child about his music, living it, quick with eagerness when a new piece came over from London, sitting alone behind a locked door and making the air sigh with wordless outpourings, yet ashamed of the fact that in this as in everything else, he was mediocre.

They rode on northward, turning east from the Bloomingdale Road which wound along the river bank, cutting across the fragrant meadows, threading through the wall of trees that humped like a backbone north and south over the whole island, stopping at a farm to drink from a mossy wooden bucket, and then turning north again under the high ridge of Morningside Heights into the gathering twilight. From there it was only a few miles to the house which he had selected for his new headquarters.

This house, a graceful, white Georgian structure, which was almost painfully reminiscent of Mount Vernon, had belonged to Captain Roger Morris, and was one of many magnificent homes scattered among the Dutch farmlands of the island. Captain Morris had prudently gone to England to await the ignoble end of the miserable rebellion, and his wife was with some Tory friends in Yonkers, spending long evenings discussing the Yankee scum. In their absence, the Virginian had taken over their house, ostensibly because it was more or less centrally located, about three miles south of Kingsbridge and nine miles

47

north of the city; actually, because sitting as it did, on a grassy lawn over the Harlem River, it was another Mount Vernon.

He arrived there late that night, past midnight, and remarked cheerfully to his secretary, Robert Harrison, who had waited up for him, that he was glad the next day was Sunday and that he could look forward to a day of rest.

There was little enough rest. He had hardly started to undress before a panting messenger burst into the Morris house and demanded to see the commander in chief.

"He's gone to bed," the Virginian heard Harrison say.

"Well, I reckon he'd better git up."

"Mind your tongue, damn you!"

The Virginian came onto the stairs and said, "That will be enough, Harrison. I'll talk to the man."

The messenger could hardly help from grinning at the skinny naked torso sticking up out of the tight breeches.

"Well, what is it?"

"About four, five thousand British air crossing over onto that island from the Long Island way."

"What island?"

"Montresor's," the messenger drawled.

"Who sent you?"

"Spencer."

"General, damn you!"

"General," the messenger grinned.

Stifling his rage, telling himself that he would remember that face and teach the fellow a thing or two when there was time, the big man dashed upstairs and flung on his coat. Without any explanation, he ran out of the house, leaped on his horse, and galloped through the darkness, giving the beast its head. In less than an hour, he saw the fires of Spencer's camp.

"It's all right," Spencer drawled lazily, raising his brows at the naked flesh that showed under the commander's coat. "I'm digging a trench alongside the river. They're on the island, but they won't come over here tonight or tomorrow with what I've got waiting for them. It's all right."

The big man rode back to the Morris house slowly. His elation had passed away; his bones and muscles ached, as they did in the Virginia lowlands when a storm was brewing.

*   *   *

They were Connecticut troops selected to hold the bank, he was told afterwards, and that same Saturday evening Spencer had sent them marching down the bank of the East River to make breastworks against a British landing. It was a poor choice, not because the Connecticut men were in any way inferior to the New York or Pennsylvania men, but because the Connecticut brigades had been less carefully watched, and thus out of six thousand, some four thousand had succeeded in deserting. The two thousand left were disgruntled and bitter, and their feelings were not elevated any by their being forced to march mile after mile through the blackest of nights on a twisting little path that followed the bank of the East River.

The leader of the Connecticut troops, a Major Gray, was disgruntled too; he was close on to forty, and he was thoroughly disgusted with being a major in an army where there were generals in their twenties and thirties.

When the troops reached the portion of the bank they were supposed to defend, a section about four miles north of the lower tip of Manhattan, the order was given to halt, remove knapsacks, and man the entrenchments. The entrenchments, as they were, consisted of a hastily dug ditch, about a foot deep; and word was passed to deepen the trench and construct an actual breastwork of the excavated dirt and of logs and branches lying about in the woods behind them.

No one made any real effort to follow these orders. The troops were tired and angry, and confident enough that nothing would happen to be content with a ditch a foot deep. They sprawled out, some of them in the ditch, some of them on the ground in front of it and behind it. Most of them slept, but there was enough responsibility among the officers to cause them to post sentinels and make some effort to keep a watch.

Not that they could see anything; the night was as black as ink, and even the still waters on the East River, a few feet in front of them, were hidden in the darkness. But it was reassuring to hear the voices sounding back and forth:

"All is well!"

"All is well!"

For about an hour the silence was unbroken, except by the lonely calling of the sentries, and then there began many strange, muffled noises, creakings, strainings, splashings. The noises started, stopped, and started again, and the sleeping Yankees began to stir restlessly.

Presently, to the mournfull call of the sentries, there sounded what was almost an echo out of the black river:

"Not so well!"

The sentries stopped dead still in their slow pacing.

"Hello?"

"Hello," came back the ironic echo.

"There be someone out in that river," a sentry said prosaically.

There was giggling and gurgling among the straining and creaking.

"All is well," the sentry said uncertainly.

"Not well—not at all!" came back from the black river.

The captains and lieutenants held a council, and then some of them crept silently to the water's edge; but there was nothing to see, absolutely nothing.

"A boatload of British," a captain reported to the major.

"Yes, I guess so."

"Shall we give them a volley, sir?"

"What for? You can't see them."

"That's so," the lieutenant nodded slowly, and then added, almost triumphantly, "They can't see us."

"Oh, damn it, go to sleep," the major said

The captain went back to sleep, but the sentries, once they discovered that there was nothing ghostly about the voices coming from the river, managed to make the night more interesting by injecting a little Yankee humor. The repartee went on through the long, slow hours.

The grey of dawn unfolded the darkness without haste and through the lifting mists the Connecticut men saw what they had thought to be a boatload of British—four mighty ships of the line, anchored prow to stern with broadsides facing them, guns rolled out, and gunners standing by. And beneath the guns, along the whole line of the ships, were boats full of British marines.

The Yankees stared, rubbed their eyes, and stared again. They began to talk in anxious excitement, and the officers ran up and down the lines, waking up those men who still slept.

But no one fired. Minutes passed; the sun broke through the mist and cast an enchanting halo about the tall spars of the battleships, and still no one fired. It was all too unbelievable, too unreal, too fantastic; it was a strange, terrifying, colorful picture, the tall ships with their hundreds of open gun ports, the gun crews standing by with ramrods and powder sacks, the ship's officers, poised on poop and quarterdeck, coolly watching the American lines, the marines crowded into the boats, but metallic and disciplined none the less, their red coats bright as fire and their bayonets nicking at the sky.

And still the Americans stared in horror and astonishment.

Then, on the British decks, pipes began to twitter, sounding like foolish sparrows in the clean, still morning. The oars in the longboats and barges dipped down, and the wide flotilla of marines began to move toward the shore.

Major Gray gave a hoarse command, and there was the snickering sound of hammers scraping on firelocks; but no one heard an American musket fire. For at that moment, one of the British officers let his hand drop, and an inferno of fire and hell and roundshot and grapeshot was let loose on the world. The four ships became roaring furnaces of destruction as the combined broadsides, enough to blow any vessel in the world out of the water, were discharged into the American lines.

The Connecticut men never saw the ships of the line again. A solid wall of smoke had formed in the river, a rolling, ghastly pall broken only by ribbons of light as the gunners reloaded and discharged fresh broadsides. They tried to aim their muskets, and found the weapons ripped from their hands by an almost solid blast of grape. They tried to rise up, and the grape struck them down and tore them to pieces. They tried to call to their friends and saw that their friends were lying headless and dead.

Yet they stood it and died, not breaking until they realized that the boats of the marines were nosing out of the smoke, saw the redcoats leap into the water, form, and march for the shore with machine-like precision, wet bayonets like lace in the smoke. Then they broke; then the boys and young men of Connecticut leaped from their trenches and fled inland. And even now the grape pursued them, lashing over the heads of the redcoated marines.

They ran inland for perhaps a hundred yards, throwing away their guns as they fled, before they found some relief from the dread panic that had overtaken them. They felt the smoke and grape behind them and saw green fields slashed with the morning sunlight. And over the fields they saw a column of men marching in closer order, men they knew were their own—for who else would be on the mainland of New York?—men they ran to with sobbing cries of welcome.

And then the Yankees stopped; the marching men were in green. And someone shouted, "Hessians!"

They tried to flee; they cast about desperately; behind them were the marines, in front the Germans.

The big guns of the battleships had ceased fire. There was a new

51

stillness, broken by a derisive shout:

"Yonkee! Yonkee! Yonkee!"

They plunged away wildly, but not wildly enough; and in their ears, punctuating their own screams and mocking their pain, came that horrible roar:

"Yonkee! Yonkee! Yonkee!"

New York, the town itself, clustered tightly on the southernmost tip of Manhattan Island. It was still more a village than a city, though it had spread above the old wall that the Dutch settlers had built as a stockade against the Indians. Already, at that time, people had begun to call that lane Wall Street. The town itself was full of crooked little avenues, fronted mostly by red-brick, step-roofed Dutch houses, although of late the building style was almost entirely Georgian, as in most of the mid-Atlantic colonies. It was a bright, cheerful little town, and it had as its prosperous hinterland the wooded hills and green meadows of Manhattan Island.

In accordance with Washington's plan, Old Israel Putnam had taken command of the city itself, garrisoning it with five thousand men. These were, for the most part, New Jersey and Pennsylvania militia, men who had stood up to battle just a little better than the New England Yankees and were therefore very contemptuous of the Massachusetts and Connecticut and Rhode Island troops. Aside from that it was good policy to keep the mid-country men apart from the Yankees, for they could hardly meet each other without a pitched battle occurring.

The five thousand militia were camped on the outskirts of the city, the greatest part of them on its northern edge and on both lower riverfronts. Putnam had noticed the movement of British vessels in the bay on Saturday afternoon, and during that black night, certain sounds coming from both rivers made him suspect that at least one or two of the big ships of the line were being kedged up the rivers. But young Burr, riding back from Harlem, assured the old man that Spencer had dug entrenchments all along the East River front, and that patrols were covering the whole Manhattan shore of the Hudson. So Putnam went to sleep, more or less uneasily, and slept until he was awakened by the thundering British broadsides.

He struggled into his clothes, ran outside, and found that his Pennsylvania and New Jersey militia were already in a turmoil. The guns had turned them out of their camps like rabbits out of a bramble patch, and they were crowding nervously through the narrow streets and grassy lanes of the town.

52

The Unvanquished

Aaron Burr, haggard after an almost sleepless night, had already heard the worst. He hung over his lathered horse in front of Putnam's headquarters and told the old man what he knew.

"They've landed!"

"British?"

"Hessians, too—on both sides of the island."

"How many?"

"I don't know," Burr cried hoarsely. "How can I know how many! Thousands, I guess."

Old Putnam shook his head; one hand he held on his tinny sword trembled violently. "They couldn't have landed," he insisted.

"Thousands, I tell you."

"If they landed, we're caught like rats in a trap—"

The boy nodded, his slim body arched with excitement.

"Retreat—"

"Right away, there's no time to lose—don't you see, on both sides of the island."

"Yes, yes," Putnam faltered.

"Right away, I tell you."

"If we could join the general," Putnam said vaguely.

"But they're between us," Burr pleaded. "On both sides of the island, don't you understand! And then if they come together, where will we go—into the river?"

The old man kept nodding.

Afterwards, for long years, Burr had a silent, bitter scorn of those who said glibly, "Retreat is easy." He knew that it was easy to advance, but a man is dying when he retreats, and it's not easy to die.

It was not easy that day. The hot morning sun baked all movement out of the autumn winds, and the tall golden wheat in the Manhattan fields stood stiff and motionless. In the city, the burghers opened their windows and doors and saw the Continental militia streaming north through the narrow lanes. Word of what had happened spread like fire, and only for a few minutes was there anything orderly or self-possessed about the Pennsylvania and New Jersey men. Then they pressed forward, and soon they were running, and soon they broke out of the city, and then almost all of the five thousand men were swarming north in a wild panic.

They ran and outdistanced their officers. They crowded the little lanes and they spread like quail across the fields. They broke through bushes and blundered in woods. The whole breadth of the island was filled with frightened men racing frantically for freedom before the British closed their trap.

Some, as they ran, held their muskets with blind instinct; others threw their muskets away; others fired insanely at their own comrades. Some fell and died, stabbed by their own bayonets, and officers died, shot through by men they tried to command.

Most of them, as they ran, verged to the west, where the Bloomingdale Road made a dusty path to Kingsbridge; others swerved eastward and presently, half dead of weariness, stumbling, crawling, falling, came in with the hacked remnants of Spencer's New Englanders. There, on the eastern shore, it became a horrible, tragic, melee, Yankees, Pennsylvanians and Jersey men staggering along blindly, croaking with parched tongues, and trying like terrified children to shield themselves from the glittering bayonets of the Hessians. And the Hessians stabbed ponderously and intently, dry themselves as they croaked, "Yonkee, Yonkee," driving the boys and children onto the metallic, redcoated ranks of the Royal Marines.

Henry Knox, in the city with Putnam, had arranged what few cannon remained to him, with gentle and loving care. Some he set with their noses sniffing at the bay, others flanking them, others back a bit on an elevated platform with their snouts down, ready to spit grape and cannister, and others barking gallantly at the mouths of the East River and the Hudson. For all that, it was a futile gesture; he had no guns capable of more than stinging the great ships of the line; his little popguns, six- and eight-pounders, would make a noise and a flash, but would hardly be heard above the killing roar of a British broadside. His other guns, his wonderful, precious monsters that could hurl a forty-pound mass of metal, had been spiked in the mud of Brooklyn.

The result of that loss was an almost insane desire on his part to hoard what guns remained. The boy, whom others boys called colonel, was a born collector; once he had collected minerals, then leaves, then insects, then books, and now guns. He knew every gun in his batteries. He had walked hundreds of miles through frozen forests to bring some of the guns from the Canadian border. He had fished guns out of the water and lowered others from mountains. He had polished them with his own hands and designed his own carriages for them. He had no desire to kill; he had long ago decided that he was on the right side; then he stopped thinking about it and thought only of how many cannon he could gather. His deadly earnestness, his devotion to the Virginia foxhunter, who was the opposite of him in almost every particular, and his utter unselfishness, made him seem a good deal older than his twenty-six years. And his massive, slightly ridiculous body and almost pathetic lack of cleverness made his men love him.

On this Sunday morning, when the British broadsides rocked the island into wakefulness, when the headlong flight to the north began, Knox turned the other way and went to his guns. He went without haste stolidly and gloomily, without giving orders for anyone to follow. He had no plan, no thought except that he wanted to be with his guns, that he didn't want to run any more.

His gunners, who were stationed near the batteries, made no secret of their desire to run away. They started to go, and only stopped when they saw their colonel standing moodily beside one of his cannon, for all the world like a boy suddenly made an orphan and waiting with the terrible knowledge that there is nothing to wait for. They paused and stared at him, and then some of them went back and then the others. And then a Captain Miller said simply, "The army is running away, colonel."

"Yes—" Knox came out of his trance slowly.

"There's nothing we can do here."

"The guns are here," Knox said, and his thought was that when he left these guns, there would be nothing else, absolutely nothing else.

"Sir, it's no use staying here," the captain argued.

"You don't have to stay here," Knox shrugged.

"But my God, colonel," the captain said vehemently, "what good will it do to stay here and let the British have us along with the guns?"

"You don't have to stay here," Knox repeated.

"But my God, colonel, just because those other bastards ran away—"

"Yes, they ran away." Knox spoke the last two words slowly, savagely.

The artillerymen shifted around, but no one made any move to go, the men scuffing their feet and staring at the ground, and one boy of fifteen sobbing unashamed. From the north came the shrill sound of the fleeing army and over and above it the dull boom of the British broadsides.

For a few minutes no one said anything, and then a Plymouth boy, seventeen years old, a lieutenant in rank, piped cheerfully, "Lor', colonel, if we're all a-going to die, this is a mighty poor place. There's a pretty little hill some miles to north of here where we could ring the guns and make a fight. Shade trees, too," he added eagerly.

"It's almighty hot here," someone else offered.

The men began to chuckle, half in fright, half in excitement at the wonderful venture they were proposing when all the rest of the army had run away.

"What hill?" Knox demanded.

"Bunker's, they call it."

Knox saw the smiles on the faces. It was a good sign; the one half-victory that raggle-taggle army had won had been on another Bunker Hill. He came alive, gave directions for loading the ammunition carts, and sent some of the men away to see whether they could find a horse or two. Three ancient nags resulted from the search, and they were harnessed to three of the eight-pounders. The men themselves dragged what others of the guns they could manage and the ammunition carts. In a little while, the motley procession was under way, creaking slowly through the littered streets of the town, where countless knapsacks, rusty bayonets and ancient muskets marked the trail of the American army.

The townspeople, who were already making ready to welcome the British, whose attitude toward the Continentals was good riddance to bad rubbish, lined the streets to grin at the slow-moving batteries. Children ran along, screaming, "Get a horse! Get a horse!" And dozens of brightly painted ladies, whose living had gone with the army, screamed and cursed and spat at the gunners and pelted them with all the filth that lay in the gutters. Looking neither to the left nor to right, Knox labored at the wheels of one of the guns, the sweat pouring from his forehead.

When the sweat-soaked procession finally got to Bunker's Hill, they found it already occupied. General Silliman, a heavy, plodding, sullen man, had kept most of his regiment together and steered them off onto the hill. There they lay over their muskets, half afraid, half defiant, and almost murderously bitter now that their first panic had left them.

"What are you going to do?" Knox asked, unable to believe his eyes.

"Let those bastards come. We'll know what to do," Silliman growled.

Knox nodded. He didn't know Silliman very well and had never felt drawn toward the man, but now they were together, two of them with one thought. Knox was coming out of his black mood and passing into a state of mingled fear and exultation. Putnam's army had melted away, and from their little sun-drenched hill they could see nothing but a tiny brook and a placid white farmhouse. Knox knew it was the end; the revolution had melted in a scummy pool of panic and rout; the harlots of New York would laugh and blaspheme for months perhaps, but in time even they would forget. He, at least, would not

hang from a gibbet nor rot in jail nor spend his years in some lonely
backwoods town, lying about glories that had never been. He would
die here, giving his life for a cause he had believed in and had the
courage to fight for.

"Batteries two and five up on the hill!" he cried. "Ring and load
with solid shot! Batteries one, three and four, flank action with cannister and grape!"

A ragged, tremulous cheer floated up from Silliman's men, and they
came running to help drag the guns up the slope. Silliman nodded and
nodded wordlessly, grasping Knox's hand. Then, in the next few
minutes, all was action and excitement in which even fear and hopelessness were forgotten—so much so that almost no one noticed the
rider who was spurring his lathered horse down the road toward them.

It was Burr, more haggard, more tired than ever, so dry he could
only croak until one of the artillerymen held up a canteen for him to
drink from. Then, after he had spat out a mouthful of sand and
swallowed twice, he demanded angrily of Silliman, "My God, general,
what's all this?"

"You can see that. We haven't run away."

"Oh, Jesus Christ, I know! But do you know that in one hour from
now, the British will have cut you off—completely?"

Silliman tightened his mouth and shook his head.

"Oh, Christ, oh, Jesus Christ," Burr cried, "is that it, is it suicide, is
it all you can think of to kill a regiment that had guts enough not to
run away? Will that give us our liberty? Will that make the revolution?"

"We've run enough."

"You've run enough! You've run enough! You sit there on your ass
and tell me you've run enough!"

"God damn it, major, I'll not have you talk like that!"

"I'll talk as I damn please!"

"God damn it, no! I won't take that from any twenty-year-old fool!"

"You'll take it!" Burr almost screamed. "You'll take it because twenty
or not, I'm man enough to—"

"Burr!" Knox roared.

The boy subsided and lay on his horse's neck trembling and pouring
sweat. "All right, Harry," he said in a hoarse whisper. "I'm sorry. I'm
right, too. I'm sorry."

"Colonel Knox," the artilleryman said evenly.

"All right, Colonel Knox—only for the love of God, Harry, come with me and don't stand up for these crazy heroics."

"Is it heroics to want to stand instead of running away—instead of running away always? Did you see what happened in the city today?"

"I saw it."

"And now you want us to run away."

"I want you to live, that's all—to live."

"For what?" Knox demanded. "What's left?"

"The revolution, and that's more than death! Death's no good! That doesn't help! I swear to God, Harry, believe me!"

"I won't leave my guns."

Burr turned to the men, his white face a mask of desperation, his voice shrill and penetrating, "Do you hear me? Do you want to die? Is that all you want, you dirty Pennsylvania bastards? There's an army at Kingsbridge that's going to fight, maybe for twenty years, maybe forever, but all you dirty Pennsylvania bastards want is to die!"

A roar of anger answered him, and the boy, tired as he was, judged their temper perfectly. "Follow me!" he screamed, and spurred his horse to the north, not even looking back to see how they spilled down the hill and ran after him. Even Silliman went, at the tail end, cursing Burr at the top of his lungs.

The artillerymen were left. They had stayed with Knox, and now they stood without moving, looking at him, serving him and placing in his hands the decision of life or death. He couldn't speak. Sobbing, he started north, and with their heads and arms hanging limply, they followed him.

They didn't look back to where all the bright guns stood more lonely than any living men.

Only the dead did not hear that crashing broadside from the four British ships of the line.

On that Sunday morning, the commander in chief had awakened before dawn, after a night of deep slumber. Billy, who slept outside the room, who could hear in his sleep when his master rolled from side to side, helped him to dress in the candlelight, wagging his black head and chuckling happily.

"A good night," Billy said.

"Yes, better than most."

"Getting better than it was after you left Missis Patsy."

"A little better," the Virginian smiled. He was in high spirits this morning.

"Going to set the skillet on," Billy said, running down the stairs.

58

"Going to set the skillet on," he sang, "and get the water boiling."

The Virginian's breakfast, as always, was cakes and honey and tea. He ate with a good appetite, noticed that Harrison had not yet awakened, and decided that he would go out for an early inspection of the troops holding the line in Harlem. Billy had anticipated his thought, and when the big man came out of the Morris house, the Negro was standing there with the horse saddled and ready. Washington mounted, waved, and set off down the road at a smart canter.

The first grey of dawn had dispersed the inky blackness when he rode past the tired sentries into Mifflin's camp. Mifflin, with a few regiments, formed the most northerly outpost of Spencer's division, holding a thinly manned line across the waist of Manhattan. Now, early as it was, the general stood dressed, grinning happily as he recognized the tall form of his commander in chief. He waved an arm and opened his mouth to speak when the four broadsides rumbled in the distance.

The Virginian stiffened, bent, and then spurred his horse through the awakening camp. Mifflin ran for a horse, but before he could mount the Virginian was out of sight.

Washington rode four miles, lashing his beast heartlessly, before he saw the first and fleetest of the panic-stricken army. By then the mists had lifted and the sun had put a golden glaze on the meadows and wheatfields and orchards. He had driven his horse recklessly, leaving the road, clearing a wall with a bound, a brook, a fence; he rode full into them, saw them as far as he was able to see, hundreds and hundreds of men, men crawling, running, hiding, staggering.

He pulled in his horse and tried to talk to them; he rode slowly across their front, but there was no recognition in their blank eyes. They ran on. One fired at him.

He yelled at them, "Halt!"

They swarmed past him.

"Do you hear me?" he called.

He pleaded, "Halt!"

"You know who I am! I'm your commander! I'm your general!"

"Halt!" he shrieked.

"Get behind the stone walls!"

"Use your guns!"

They swarmed on, like rabbits driven by long-eared dogs.

"By God, halt!"

He spurred his horse again. He rode among them, lashing until the quirt was torn from his hand. He drew his pistols, but the guns missed fire, soaked as they were with sweat. He flung the pistols at them. He drew his sword. He rode among them, cutting, slashing, screaming at the top of his lungs, pleading, begging, slashing again—but they ran on.

He rushed across the fields like a demon. His voice screamed and raged until it cracked.

And then he no longer urged his horse, but sat there without moving while they fled past him. The sword dropped from his loose fingers and fell into the wet, jewel-like grass, lying all a-sparkle in the bright dewdrops. His spine, braced like a ramrod, had lost its support; he sagged in his saddle like a long bag of disjointed bones.

He saw the column of British coming, marching smartly, only a few hundred yards away, the marines like red ribbons fluttering where there was no wind. Yet he didn't move; it seemed to him that he was suspended in a void; he felt that he was dead, and wondered vaguely why he could still see and hear and feel.

The British were only a hundred yards away now.

He saw Mifflin next to him and heard Mifflin's voice as from a great distance.

"Come away, sir, please, please," Mifflin was begging.

There were others around him. Why did they want him to come away when he was already dead?

"Please, sir, please."

He saw how Mifflin's face was contorted.

"Please, sir."

Then he gave Mifflin the reins and allowed his horse to be led away. It didn't matter that the British were firing at him. Nothing mattered.

7

THE GRACIOUS MRS. MURRAY

THE BRITISH army had been trained to fight; it had been drilled and drilled and drilled until it had emerged as the finest fighting machine in the world; it would march into hell and high water with impassive calm. The British general who boasted that he could lead his army onto the sands of the channel beaches and order it to march across to France, and have it march until the last man's head had disappeared under the water, was not exaggerating; he was stating a fact; in the same way he could lead his army to the edge of a cliff and have it march over rank by rank, and there would have been neither hesitation nor annoyance among the redcoated soldiers.

But there was nothing in the training of British troops that told them what to do when the army they were supposed to fight ran away. A retreating army was one thing; then they were supposed to pursue in close order with the purpose of breaking morale and sowing disorder. But this was not even a retreating army.

By the time General Howe had landed a substantial amount of his troops in New York City, there was not a hale Continental to be seen, only the sick and wounded, packed into the churches and synagogues. The weather was very hot, and the portly Howe was very uncomfortable; among the many things American which he disliked intensely, the weather stood well in front. One could never be sure of the seasons; summer became winter and autumn became summer, and a mild spring day could occur in January as well as any other time of the year. The weather was as beastly, as stupid, as inconsistent as the Americans themselves.

With the thermometer at ninety-two in the shade, with the redcoat columns standing packed in the narrow streets, General Howe had to sit in his damp saddle and receive the congratulations of a committee of earnest, grateful, and well-to-do citizens. Phineas Thatcher, the grain merchant, voiced their gratitude.

"I have no desire, Your Excellency," he said, "to dwell upon our miseries, upon what we have suffered from this rascally band of thieves and cutthroats.

"Ha — quite true," Howe nodded impatiently.

"Nor to put forward our patience as loyal subjects of His Most Gracious Majesty —"

"Quite true."

"But to welcome you as our liberator —"

"Of course, of course," Howe agreed, wondering whether this would go on forever.

"Our protector —"

They were finally under way and out of the town, the long column crawling over the road like a gorgeous scarlet snake, the drums and fifes playing, the regimental banners held proudly, the artillery rumbling and grunting like a counterpoint to the steady thud, thud, thud of marching feet. At the head of the column rode General Howe and his aides, all on white horses, making as pretty a sight as the peaceful

61

country lanes of Manhattan had ever seen. And all around them, in the meadows, on the road, were evidences of the Americans' headlong flight—knapsacks, muskets, belts, hats, powder horns, bags of shot, old bayonets.

"They must have been in a frightful hurry," one of the aides observed.

"Beastly hot to hurry," Howe sighed. "Provincial energy, even in retreat, is most amazing."

"They won't go far."

"Why," Howe complained, "do provincials talk so much? We could have been on our way an hour ago if not for all that talk, talk, talk."

They rode on; the heat increased; their beautifully pressed, colorful uniforms became limp and wet. Presently, they met the first of the Hessians, who had landed further up the island, from the East River. Laughing and shouting, the Hessians herded along groups of American prisoners, clusters of dirty, frightened boys who could hardly walk for weariness. They were very proud of their achievement, the Hessians, but the redcoats marched by looking straight ahead, not even deigning to notice them.

"War is dine commander?" Howe demanded of some of them.

They shook their heads and went on with their prisoners.

"Stubborn beasts!"

"Dine commander?" Howe insisted, wondering why they could not understand their own tongue.

"Bad business, breaking order like that," one of his aides observed.

"The devil take them," Howe said. He was hot and tired and bored, and he had nothing more to look forward to than a wearisome day of collecting American prisoners. He had expected a battle, certainly stubborn resistance in attempting the most difficult operation in military practice, the establishing of a bridgehead against an entrenched enemy, and instead there was nothing less than a complete melting away of Washington's army. He had a good deal of respect, almost admiration for the tall, stubborn foxhunter, and as a Whig, many of his sympathies were with the revolutionists, at least abstractly.

He felt no hate, only an impatient desire to meet the Yankees in battle and administer a sound and sportsmanlike drubbing, something that would end the war as, he considered, all wars should be ended, in a mood for the gentlemen on both sides to sit down at a table and exchange toasts. But this—this utter panic, this foul cowardice—turned his stomach; the revolution was over; the ideals were blasted and had gone the way of all other ideals; and it was so very hot.

He was glad that he would be sailing back to England soon.

An officer of the light infantry, who had been landed from boats a few miles north of here, came riding to meet the column, saluted, and gave Howe more details of the flight.

"We can have them all before night," the officer said eagerly.

"How many would you say?" Howe asked, not with too much interest.

"Ten thousand, perhaps, here on the island."

"A good catch," Howe sighed, taking off his hat and wiping his brow.

"If you'll only hurry, sir!"

"There's time enough."

"Yes, sir, of course, sir—but it's my opinion that a few thousand of them are directly across the island, west of here. We could cut them off, you know, like snaring rabbits."

"Yes, certainly—you know, I'd give my soul for a drink. I don't like the idea of these Jagers breaking ranks; find someone who can talk their beastly doggerel."

"Yes, sir. They've been taking prisoners, got almost five hundred."

"They shouldn't break ranks. Whose house is that, over there?" He pointed to a pleasant Georgian house, set back about two hundred yards from the road, with a shady veranda and a rolling green lawn. Two colored servants were occupied in taking down wooden shutters that had evidently been put in place when the dawn bombardment began; and on the veranda three ladies sat and fanned themselves.

"I don't know, sir. I suppose they broke ranks to pursue the enemy."

"It's bad for discipline. Do you suppose they'd offer us a drink?"

He didn't wait for an answer, but started his horse off for the house, waving for his staff to follow him and calling back for the files to stand fast. Still arguing his case, the light-infantry officer followed, the whole colorful party moving at a smart trot to where the ladies sat.

The ladies rose, more excited than alarmed; General Howe swept off his hat and smiled so gallantly that in a moment they were smiling too. They were all three of them younger than thirty, and they all had that innocuous charm that Howe considered the most wonderful thing about the American colonies. One was blonde and blue-eyed, with hair like combed flax; the other two were dark; they were all quite pretty.

"I most earnestly command your pardon," Howe said, "but I and my men are dying of thirst, and seeing this haven of shade and restfulness, like an oasis in a desert—"

They were laughing as Howe dismounted, bowed, and presented

63

himself. "William Howe, humbly at your service."

"Your Excellency!" they cried, and dropped in very graceful curtsies.

"Please, the honor belongs to your humble servant," Howe insisted, and went on to present Colonel Bently, Colonel Jameson, Major Lass, Captain Loring, Captain Atterbee, Lieutenant Greystone, and Lieutenant Bart. They were all most honored.

The ladies, who had certainly never seen such a magnificent display of uniform and color and polite bearing before, introduced each other as Mrs. Murray, Mrs. Van Cleehut, and Miss Penrose. Miss Penrose was the blonde, and she stilled even the captain of light infantry's desire to be somewhere else. They chattered and curtsied until General Howe gently reminded them of his thirst.

"Oh, what savages you must think us!" Mrs. Murray cried. She clapped her hands, called one of the servants, and told him to bring some iced punch and some claret. "You must forgive us," she explained to General Howe. "I know you would prefer port, but unfortunately port is so hard to come by here in the provinces."

"And claret will be ambrosia," Howe said.

"It's so cool inside," Mrs. Murray smiled. "If my humble house could —"

"Your humble house is a haven of refuge," Howe interrupted gallantly.

It was after lunch had been served and the whist tables were being set up, that Miss Penrose remarked how perfectly miserable the poor men out in the road must be. The endless column of British troops seemed from this distance like a raw red ribbon flung on the sun-soaked meadows. None of the men had moved from their places, and it seemed that they would stand there in their ruddy glory for all eternity.

Colonel Jameson rubbed his mustache, peered out of the window, and declared, "Not at all, not at all, my dear. Soldiering, you know, not a picnic, not at all a picnic." The colonel had been so attentive that the young subalterns could hardly do more than gaze at Miss Penrose from a distance.

"Why must war be?" Miss Penrose demanded passionately. "I couldn't sleep a wink after dawn with those horrible guns firing all the time, and then all morning those wretched men came running past, until Mrs. Murray put up the shutters and said there was nothing else to do but sit quietly and hope the house would not be burned over our heads."

"War, you know," the colonel shrugged. "Nasty business for ladies."

"James wanted to fight," Miss Penrose told them incredulously, not explaining who James was. "But mother packed him off to England. James always had a temper."

"Nasty business for ladies," the colonel said again, wagging his head and including all the others in his apology.

Mrs. Murray was calling Colonel Jameson to make up another four at whist. Miss Penrose didn't play whist, and immediately all the subalterns decided that they were very poor hands at cards.

By tea time, Howe had finished his third bottle of claret, and was ready to swear to God that never in his life had he spent an afternoon with more devilishly charming company.

"But we are rebels, you know," Mrs. Murray protested.

"Oh, come now, my dear Mrs. Murray!"

"Rebels, bosh! There are no more rebels," Colonel Bently said comfortably.

On the subject of rebels, Mrs. Van Cleehut said that her husband was in Philadelphia and would stay there until the last of these wretched persons had left New York. "Really, they're quite horrible," she smiled. "You should have seen two of them this morning, all over dirt and filth, trying to hide in the carriage house."

"Jackson made short work of them," Mrs. Murray explained.

Miss Penrose said, "It would be different if they had uniforms. You would think, wouldn't you, that those persons and their Congress would have uniforms, if they're going to have an army, I mean, anyway some sort of uniform," glancing admiringly out of the window to where the redcoat files still stood in the sun.

"They're so miserably poor," Mrs. Murray smiled. "None of the better people will have any part of them."

"I hear the Schuylers and Pintards and Beekmans are with the rebels."

"Some—oh, yes, the best blood has dark spots. The Roosevelts and Bensons and Hoffmans have gone off with that rabble, too. But they'll learn. They'll come back dragging their fine feathers in the dust."

"To the end of the war," Howe said, raising his glass and starting on his fourth bottle of claret.

"You do think so?"

"By all means. Nothing left but to take prisoners."

"It's been so disturbing."

"Nasty business for ladies," Colonel Jameson agreed.

"And prices have gone up impossibly," Mrs. Murray added.

At dinner time, General Howe protested, "No, no—you've been too charming and too gracious, Mrs. Murray, but we are uninvited guests."

"But you can't know how secure we've felt since you're here," Miss Penrose insisted.

"One is fighting a war," General Howe said. "Not a very pleasant business, but a man's duty."

"But you said yourself that the war was over this morning," Mrs. Murray pointed out.

Jackson brought the general his fifth bottle of claret.

The afternoon passed and evening came, and a breeze rustled through the fields and trees of Manhattan. Candles were lit in the Murray house, and a tinkle of dishes and the sound of laughter came through the open door.

Meanwhile the last fleeing American had passed on north and found refuge behind the lines at Harlem.

8

VIEW HALLOO

OLD PUTNAM, nudging Mifflin, said, "Speak to him."

"What?"

"Speak to him."

"What? What should I say to him?"

"I don't know, speak to him. My God, don't you see, somebody has to speak to him?"

"What?"

"Anything. Tell him to come out of the rain."

"Just that?" Mifflin said stupidly, and added, "Would you tell him to come out of the rain?"

"I can't speak to him," Putnam said, thinking of how he had run away with an army running after him.

The rain had come with darkness after that terribly hot and sultry September day. It came strong and keen and cold and lashing, but it meant respite; for British guns could not fire at Americans who had thrown away their guns. It gave the beaten Yankees a chance to crawl through the American lines at Harlem and to lie shivering, without tents, even without clothes in the drenching downpour.

This American line, manned by Mifflin's brigades, by Massachusetts men, Marblehead fishermen, Boston militia, Middlesex farmers, still held firm; perhaps only by virtue of the fact that the British and Hessians had not yet pushed that far north of Manhattan Island.

The entrenchments had been built on the northern slope of a deep and narrow valley that cuts the island two-thirds of the way from its southern tip. Deep and narrow at Claremont on the Hudson, broadening out as it approached the East River, it was called at that time the Hollow Way. It was a good position, even for a shattered army, for to make an attack, the British would have to come pouring down one slope, cross the bottom of the valley, and climb the other slope. All the afternoon and evening of September 15th, frightened Connecticut, New Jersey and Pennsylvania militiamen had staggered into the Hollow Way and found security behind the Massachusetts entrenchments. Beaten and spiritless, they sprawled on the ground and listened to the mocking jeers of the New Englanders, who, not having been attacked nor encircled, could boast of their courage, forgetting what their courage was two weeks ago on Brooklyn Heights.

The midlanders had no heart to reply. They lay almost without movement, watching dumbly the officers' efforts to collect a brigade here and a brigade there, hardly moving when the cold rain began.

Walking through the shattered troops, the Virginian looked neither to left nor to right. But after he had passed, the men nodded at him and asked each other whether they had seen his eyes. Connecticut men gained importance by detailing his actions of the morning and describing how he had gone completely insane, lashing at them with his sword.

"Took Jones' pinky off," one of them said.

Another displayed a welt behind his ear. "Got me there with his stock."

"He's addled," another decided. "Gone and walked away and addled. Lookee at his eyes."

In a muted voice, a Hartford boy told how the commander in chief had sat on his horse and waited for the British to kill him.

Knox and Putnam and Mifflin and Knowlton and Burr stood together under a tree and watched the Virginian pace back and forth in the pouring rain. It was past midnight already, and he had been walking like that, back and forth and back and forth, for almost four hours. His pace never changed and he walked always in the same line, and under his boots the ground was mashed into spongy mud. His blue coat was limp and shapeless and one of the cocks of his hat had come loose and hung over his ear, pouring a steady stream of water down onto his shoulder. His long arms hung limply by his sides and sometimes the grotesquely huge hands clenched and unclenched.

Knox, who could not stand much more of it, added his voice to Putnam's begging Mifflin to go over and speak to him. And Putnam reiterated, almost pitifully, "Tell him to come out of the rain."

"All right," Mifflin nodded, and walked over to his commander in chief and said, "Please, sir—"

The tall man stopped in his walk, peered at Mifflin inquiringly, and then began to walk once more.

"Please, sir, come out of the rain."

"What?"

"I said, come out of the rain, please, sir. Please. You're soaking wet."

"Wet? What are you trying to tell me, Mifflin?"

"You're wet, sir—you're soaking wet. You'll catch a death of cold."

"I'll thank you to mind your own damned affairs, Mifflin," the Virginian said quietly.

"Please, sir, say what you want to, it's no good in the world to stay here and catch a death of cold."

"I'll thank you, Mifflin, to go to hell and be damned."

"Please, General Washington—"

Now Knox had joined Mifflin, Putnam just a little distance behind him. Washington stopped pacing and demanded, "What is this, gentlemen? Have you no duties, no brigades—?"

"Please, General Washington, come out of the rain," Knox said, and then his voice broke and he turned away, and they all stood there helplessly around the tall man.

And then the foxhunter said softly, "We'll go to my headquarters, gentlemen. We're none of us dry, are we?"

Knox and Mifflin took him up to his room. While Billy was out, heating a loggerhead for a mug of flip, they undressed him. He was meek and sleepy, and he made no protest when they helped him into bed and covered him with blankets. Knox supported his head and shoulders while he drank the flip, and a moment later he was sleeping as soundly and peacefully as a child.

When the came out of his room and Billy looked at them inquiringly, they nodded and said, "He's sleeping," gently and considerately, as if the colored man were a father and entitled to know.

"He ain't sick?" Billy asked.

"No—" Mifflin shook his head. "Not sick, I don't think." Mifflin didn't know what more to say; there were no words for what had happened in the tall, weary body. And Knox, not trusting himself to speak, sat down in front of the fire and stared at the curling flames. And in the licking, curling tongues of fire, Knox found neither peace nor hope; waked out of a dream, his dogged, unimaginative self could not find another to replace it. So many things were gone: for the tall foxhunter, honor, since he was a Virginia aristocrat; but for Knox, a great deal more than honor, a round, comfortable wife, a warm home, many books, many hopes, a nation, a republic, a screaming vision that had banged on his eardrums until he was ready to lay down his life and fortune for his country, his miserable, dirty little backwoods country.

"Flip, gentlemen," Billy said, taking another loggerhead out of the fire and filling the kitchen where they sat with the good, homey smell of burnt sugar.

"Will you drink?" Mifflin asked Knox.

Then the two of them, sitting on either side of the hearth, drank mug after mug of the boiling hot rum with deadly and silent earnestness.

They were good and drunk when they went out on the porch, a while later, hard drunk, mad and bitter and black, lost from joy and all the good things of drinking, lost even from lust and savagery, from dirty ditties and bad humor, holding onto each other and walking slowly across the broad veranda of the Morris house. The rain had stopped; there was the ghost of a moon, and in the misty night a sentry paced back and forth over the sloping lawn. And Knox, glancing over his shoulder at the magnificent portico, thinking of the Tory owner, mouthed a foul imprecation.

Mifflin nodded in savage agreement.

The commander in chief was up a little before dawn, as was his custom, and he appeared rested and composed after the few hours' sleep he had had. He had dressed quietly and quickly, and now he sat at the breakfast table eating pancakes and honey and listening to Adjutant-General Reed, who was full to the neck with information gathered by a patrol sent to investigate the British movement. About Reed, a delicate, almost languorous young man of thirty-five, there was a certain feminine timidity—accented by his cameo-like features and his large, violet eyes. He was possessed of a sensitivity that kept him in the background when other men suffered, as if he were afraid to test his own capacity for being hurt, and sometimes the Virginian felt that Reed feared him.

Thus, the day before, knowing that there was nothing he could do, Reed had done nothing, only watch the gathering ruin through half-closed eyes and cringe inside of himself and bite his full, round lips. Then, very early in the morning, when men stunned into absolute impotence the day before could think of nothing and therefore did nothing, he selected the most reliable body of men he could find and sent them out to discover just where the British were and what they intended to do.

This patrol was led by a man called Thomas Knowlton, a Yankee who had not been convinced at Brooklyn Heights that all Yankees were cowards. There he had been with a regiment of Connecticut troops, and not running away himself, he was amazed to find that a number of other men had stayed by him and duplicated his feat of not running away. One in particular, a Coventry schoolteacher called Nathan Hale, when questioned by Knowlton as to why he had stood absolutely motionless and uncovered in a rain of British grape, had answered, "Because there was no place to go—" and then added thoughtfully, "They don't know about a revolution. It's not a diversion. It's either the beginning or the end."

Knowlton was not certain that that made sense. He was a professional soldier more than a revolutionist; he had picked this side of the fight because he was a Yankee, because his one pride, after being clean-shaven, was to be his own master, and because the only time during his adult life he had been moved to tears was on seeing an old farmer, who had lost everything, go to work for someone else, losing his soul as his old feet moved him toward a means of existence. Knowlton's inclination toward freedom was not logical; he reacted like a vixen in a trap, who bites off her own leg to go back to her pups and her death. The only thing he thought of particularly was that if he got together a group of men who would not run away every time a gun was fired, they would be worth something. Spencer reluctantly gave him permission, and Knowlton formed a little patrol of sharpshooters with the twenty-one-year-old Hale and seventeen-year-old Morton and nineteen-year-old Lake as his captains. Nobody in the patrol was over thirty and most were under twenty, but even the children shared in one trait, that at Brooklyn, for some obscure reason, they had not run away.

This was the patrol which Reed had sent out to look around and see where the British were. And now, sitting across the breakfast table from his commander, he pleaded his cause earnestly.

"Don't you see, sir," he said, "the redcoats know we are beaten, if you'll forgive me, but they know it, they know it!"

The big man looked at his handsome adjutant stonily. "I don't have to be reminded of that, Mr. Reed," he said.

"But that's the point, sir, that they know it! If we hit at them now, they go reeling back."

The big man shook his head listlessly, and in answer to his unspoken words, Reed cried, "But that was yesterday, sir! What good is yesterday?"

"It serves to remind us," the Virginian muttered.

"But we can fight!"

"No, Mr. Reed, we can't fight. We can't even run away—decently."

The adjutant spread his hands and admitted his defeat. "I'm sorry, sir. I was wrong; I concede it," he said. "But what about the patrol?"

"They will come back," the big man said dully. "They have legs to run with, so they will come back."

They rode down from the Morris house to the lines at the Hollow Way, where they met Mifflin, who glanced at Reed significantly. A little behind the Virginian, Reed spread his hands and shook his head helplessly.

For the tall farmer, today had ceased to exist. There were only memories and a compulsion that kept his body moving and performing certain necessary things. He was living in all that had come before this nightmare of senseless defeat; the years of his life had buckled together, and twenty years ago seemed like yesterday; the present was a long, heartbreaking pause, and there was no tomorrow. And out of his memories, jumbled and formless, came all sorts of things, good and bad, a time when a pointer puppy, loving with the infinite, unselfish love of a beast, had looked into his eyes as it became sick and died, leaving him with a grief so strangely full that it was not too different from what he had felt when his wife's daughter, Patsy, his own, beloved, darling Patsy, had died, setting her poor, sick mind at rest. Grief was not all bad; it could have a kinship with love. And he could remember now going to a neighbor's house where there were sixteen children, sixteen laughing, handsome healthy brats, frolicking around him and mixing grief with a love he could not bear, he who had never had a child of his own, forcing him to lock himself into one of the out-

71

buildings and sit with his face in his hands, grieving not for sixteen children that could never be his, but for a nameless pointer puppy and a half-insane stepchild.

But this, all of this that had been yesterday and for three weeks before that, was not grief and not fear, but despair so numbing that it broke his pride.

Because it was better to move than to stay still, he had walked his horse through the front line of his entrenchments, through the spread of dirty New Englanders and midlanders and over the bottom of the Hollow Way. Reed and Mifflin followed him, afraid in their hearts of what he might do left alone and riding in the direction of the British. It was a bright, clean morning, cool and comfortable after the heavy rain of the night before, with the song of birds in the air, the crowing of cocks and the baying of hounds. A sharp wind blew across the Hudson from the Palisades and wound down the valley, tossing dry leaves and causing trees to sway gleefully.

They had started up the slope that led to Morningside Heights, when they heard the splutter of musket fire, sounding from what might have been a mile's distance. The big man stopped his horse and listened without any show of interest, but Reed spurred up and cried, "That's Knowlton's patrol, sir. They've made some contact, and now they can draw them on."

The big man didn't move. The sound, which once would have vitalized him with energy, left him undisturbed and uninterested, listening without hearing to Reed's proposals to draw the British into a trap, to reinforce the patrol Knowlton led. Reed talked and talked, while the musket fire continued, and then his voice died away and he looked at Mifflin's grim face for some sort of sympathy. Then the two of them sat on their horses in silence.

It was after the firing stopped that Reed said, "They'll be coming back now. But they made a fight of it, sir. You'll not deny that they made a fight of it. You could tell their shots from the volley fire."

Still the Virginian didn't move.

The first of Knowlton's men appeared through the brush and woods. They were not running, but walking backwards with measured steps, their pieces in their hands, without panic or haste or disorder. Some were wounded, limping along with their arms over comrades' shoulders, and others were carried. Knowlton himself appeared, huge, bear-like, grinning and waving at Reed until he noticed the commander in chief. The little patrol gathered itself together and began to move at a run to where the three generals sat.

And at that moment, a view-halloo came winging down from the heights.

It was the last, bitterest thrust. It cut into the Virginia foxhunter, because he knew it was meant for him; it sang merrily over the bright air, canting from a half-dozen trumpets:

> *A hunting we will go,*
> *A hunting we will go,*
> *We'll catch a fox and put him in a box,*
> *And then we'll let him go.*

For him, for the foxhunter, there was no need to see what was transpiring behind the screen of woods in the fields and meadows of Morningside Heights. The gentlemen, the bloods and snobs and macaronies, were having a game, a game inspired by their own delicate, rapier-like British sense of humor, a game measured to hit precisely what it was aimed at, a foxhunting backwoodsman, a provincial who in his own way had dared to consider himself something of a gentlemen.

He would understand it, if no one else in the army did; he would know how precisely a snob can destroy a human being by refusing to admit the simple fact of his existence; he would know how they had destroyed his wretched mockery of revolution by turning it into a foxhunt, by gaily finishing it in a sporting fashion. He could picture them so clearly, riding along in the fine morning with their dragoons behind them, sniggering and prodding the winded trumpeters to keep sounding the view-halloo, knowing that he would hear it somewhere, somehow, calling to each other:

"Yoicks! Yoicks!"

He had leaped off his horse and had his big hand tangled in the jacket of the startled Knowlton. "Tell me, you Yankee bastard," he roared, "are you afraid?"

"By God, no sir!"

"Not of me, not of them?"

"I'm not afraid of anything on God's green earth," Knowlton said coolly.

"Then tell me, could you lead a party down that valley to the left of here and scale the eastern side of the heights—and come in behind those—foxhunters?"

"I could try it," Knowlton grinned.

"Then try it, God damn you! Reed, go with him! Take a regiment, no, not Yankees—take Weedon's Virginia men and Major Leitch! And remember, behind them, not a foxhunt, a beartrap!"

Reed waited to hear no more; he was off, spurring his horse back to the lines to pick up the Virginians, while Knowlton mustered out his wounded. Meanwhile, the view-halloo had twisted down toward the Hudson.

The foxhunter turned on Mifflin and pointed toward where the gorge opened on the river. "I want a frontal attack in that direction," he said curtly.

"A frontal attack?" Mifflin asked stupidly.

"General, do I have to repeat a thing twenty times to get it into your head? I want a diversion; I want a few hundred of your filthy Yankees, if you can find that many to hold their guns and shoot them off, to advance on the southern slope. For at least a half hour; after that they can run away!"

Mifflin nodded and swung away; his emotions were a tangle of rage and joy.

Knowlton led his Connecticut men and Leitch his Virginians up the glacial outcroppings that frosted the eastern edge of Morningside Heights. They climbed silently and quickly, their heavy muskets slung over their shoulders where they had slings, or else thrust through holes torn in their shirts. So intent were they upon breasting the cliff that for the moment the Virginians and Yankees forgot their deep and mutual hatred. Knowlton was completely happy, understanding only vaguely the change that the taunting bugles had wrought in the foxhunter, but realizing nevertheless that the Virginian had passed through a moment of hell, realizing too that in their brief verbal exchange they had come as close to each other as men may who approach as strangers, exchange blows, and come off blood brothers.

Knowlton's was not a deep nor an intricate nature. He was neither an intellectual nor a revolutionary, but a man who loved action and excitement and the comradeship that went with a camp. He had wanted to get into the fight that had been brewing for so many years, and as a result he was here; and it satisfied him somewhat to believe that he was on the right side. He hadn't thought it out in detail, and he was content to take the word of men who could spin a feeling into a reasoned argument. He was fighting on the side of freedom because to him freedom was bald and simple; it was the opposite of being put in jail, chained down and bound around.

He and Reed had not begun their climb far enough south of the Hollow Way; instead of coming in behind the British, they topped the cliff and blundered square into the flank of a column of green-clad Hessians, cautiously feeling their way toward the American lines.

A German officer happened to be looking at the cliff-edge when Major Leitch placed both palms on a rock and cautiously drew himself up to ground level.

"What ist das?" the German cried

Leitch roared like a trapped bull. Knowlton vaulted up beside him, and the Virginia and Connecticut men followed, cutting hands and faces on the rocks in their mad haste to reach the top.

The cry, "Yonkee, Yonkee?" was running down the line of Jagers. An officer spurred up on his horse and yelled:

"An die Gewehre!"

Precise as dolls hung on strings, the Germans halted, presented arms, and revolved into a wide formation. Still roaring, Leitch raised his pistol, aimed at the officer who had first seen him, and shot the Hessian through the heart.

"Legt an!" the man on horseback cried.

The line of muskets dropped, like wet wheat in a strong wind.

"Feuer!"

The blaze of musketry crashed into the faces of the Americans. Three bullets, two in the belly and one in the hip, stilled Major Leitch's roaring; he rolled on his face and groaned and bled out his life. Knowlton, waving at his men, shouting, trying by the motions of the long arms to pull them over the cliff, received a round musket ball full in the temple. Reed caught him as he fell.

"Legt an!" the order came again.

Still the Americans fought at the rocky ledge.

"Feuer!"

There was no breasting that storm of shot. With insane stubbornness, the Americans clung to the ledge, but they could not climb over onto the heights. They laid their muskets on the rock and discharged them, and then, clinging to the cliff surface like goats, tried to reload. It was entirely hopeless.

Reed backed down, supporting the great weight of the dying Knowlton, and with the aid of two of his Connecticut Rangers laid him down on a sheltered ledge of rock. In all the noise of the skirmish, Reed had to bend very low to hear what Knowlton was trying to say. It was something about the foxhunter, and pointing to the ledge, Knowlton said, "Tell him—because I was wounded, I had to stop here. Tell him I wasn't afraid —"

Mifflin ordered Lieutenant-Colonel Crary to take about two hundred Massachusetts Yankees and create a diversion. When the men were told off, Mifflin strode across their loose line and said to them, "You don't have to fight, there's no guts in you for that. But for one hour you're going to stand up on that hill across the valley, and so help me God, I'll kill the first man who runs away."

They stared at him sullenly and made no answer; their homespun shirts blew loosely in the wind.

"March!" Mifflin said.

They started off across the valley bottom, walking first, then beginning to run. The foxhunter, spurring down on Mifflin, demanded to know why they were running.

"I don't know, sir," Mifflin said uneasily.

They pressed into the woods, and until they reached the top, Mifflin could see their shirts, spots of white in the green. They passed over the top, and a moment later a crackle of musket fire broke out.

"There is your diversion, sir," Mifflin said.

The big man waited for them to come back; he waited for them to come pouring down the slope as fast as their legs would carry them. He looked over his shoulder, and saw that all along the line of entrenchments thousands of the dirty, beaten Yankees were standing up and listening to the musketry.

The firing went on, and Mifflin said softly and incredulously, "Oh, my God, they're holding."

The Virginian stared at the slope that should have been full of fleeing men, but was strangely empty.

"They're holding, sir," Mifflin repeated.

"Damn you, Mifflin, don't you think I have ears and eyes! Get out of here! Take a regiment and reinforce them!"

Himself, he drove up the slope. Mifflin was calling after him to return, not to go into it alone, but he plunged his horse on through the trees, onto the heights until he came to where a thin, stubborn line of New Englanders crouched behind a stone wall. They had already beaten off a charge of dragoons, and now they mutely faced a smart column of light infantry that was marching down on them, still about four hundred yards away.

He pulled in his horse just behind them and stared at the Yankees as though they were men from another world. In the meadow beyond the wall, two dragoons lay in the deep grass, and the rancid smell of gunpowder still lingered on the air. The Yankees turned to look at him, but only a few officers saluted; they didn't cheer at the sight of the commander. And he, on his part, gave no orders and said nothing.

The light infantry came nearer, their regimental battle flags waving, their drums playing briskly. They were only a hundred yards away and still no shot had been fired, when Mifflin came hurrying up with the regiment. With him was Greene, still deathly pale from his long sickness, but with burning eyes.

"Putnam's coming up with another five hundred, sir," he called.

There was a crashing sound further back, and glancing over his shoulder the big man saw Knox and young Hamilton, straddling a two-horse team that dragged one of their light field pieces. And in front of him, the Yankees, seeing the reinforcements come running toward them, scrambled over the stone wall and charged the British infantry. There was no order, no formation, no method, only hundreds of yelling, screaming New Englanders swarming down on the British, firing, clubbing their muskets, clawing at the bayonets with their bare hands, laughing, sobbing and dying — and forcing the British back.

The Virginian followed them into it; he yelled the way they yelled; he sobbed and laughed; he knew this was no fight according to military standards and he didn't care; he cared only that he led men willing to fight. He roared at Mifflin to hurry Putnam and the five hundred. He sent an aide flying to Knox to see if he could wheel his cannon out to their flank and rake the British. And a moment later he sent another aide racing after Mifflin with orders to bring up not only Putnam's five hundred, but five hundred more deployed in a wide skirmish line to protect his raving mad Massachusetts men from encirclement.

Meanwhile, the single column of British light infantry, who had expected no opposition whatever, whose intention had been only to feel out the Continental line, found itself vastly outnumbered and reeling back before what seemed to be a screaming mob of lunatics. It gave back and back, and the Yankees, seeing for the first time British regulars giving them ground in the open field, went completely berserk. They forgot that guns were made to be fired, using them instead as clubs, using their hands and feet and rocks, rushing, smashing with their heads and shoulders, kicking, clawing. Yet the British held their close order, unable to reload yet presenting always the glittering points of their bayonets.

They had retreated almost a mile before the Yankees, when the Hessians, having put a finish to Reed's disastrous attempt to flank them and attack in the rear, swung westward and struck the American flank. At

HOWARD FAST

the same moment, a battery of artillery opened on the other flank with grape; and two columns of redcoats, drawn by the firing, came up at double-quick to support the light infantry.

The Yankees gave back, their whole front torn and mangled, but they didn't run away. They walked backwards, clubbing, striking, cursing, carrying their wounded, clinging to each inch of ground until they were again at the lip of the Hollow Way; and then screamed in derision as the British refused to follow them down into the valley and chance a frontal attack on the American lines.

They had been beaten, but they hadn't run; they had held onto their guns and kept their faces to the enemy; and they were as proud as the foxhunter who sat on his horse again as straight as a ramrod, his heart choking so that he couldn't say a word to the grinning boys pressed around him.

PART THREE

WESTCHESTER

9

LET FREEDOM RING

WITHIN a few hours after the British occupied the city, New York had cast off whatever faint affection it had at one time held for the revolutionists. A stranger might have remarked that there was something like a contest raging among the good citizens as to who had despised the rebels most. Certainly the wealthier citizens vied desperately in the sending out of dinner invitations to the officers of the various British regiments. It was a great and desired honor to net a general, a good deal to net a colonel or a major, and young captains and subalterns were by no means to be sneezed at. And in their feelings, the good families of New York were quite sincere; from the beginning they had known precisely on what side their bread was buttered.

That went for the aristocracy and the wealthy; the middle classes breathed a sigh of relief and felt that now they could unlock their shops and take down their shutters. For them, the occupation meant stability; it meant that they could resume business as usual, not on promises to pay and worthless paper money, but for good, solid, shining gold. It meant that in the thousands of British troops and sailors, they would have valuable customers, and it meant that perhaps, in the Port of New York at least, overseas trade would be resumed under the protection of British guns.

In fact, hardly anyone at all felt anything but joy or relief in the fact of the British occupation. New York was overflowing with a worthless scum that had trickled into the city from all the surrounding countryside, men who had never done an honest day's work in their lives, who had attached themselves to the revolutionists until it appeared that the Yankees might have to fight, and women who plied the oldest trade. Of these last, there was truly an amazing number in the city, literally thousands, ranging in age from girls in their teens to toothless old crones, and ranging in appearance from beauty to ghastliness. Where they had come from, no one knew; it seemed incredible that the thin fringe of settlement could have supplied so many ladies of shady repute. When the Yankees had occupied the city, these ladies were an unabashed raggle-taggle worthy of the New England rabble; but now that the British were here, they blossomed out in an amazing display of finery. They strutted all over the narrow, twisting streets, displaying their feathers and silks and whispering their prices into the ears of any and every redcoat, German, or Highlander they met. And the good burghers tolerated them and were even glad of their presence, for they were a sort of a certification against rape of decent women, the citizens saying, "Who will pick the forbidden fruit when apples grow everywhere?"

In the weeks following the British landing, the city took on a holiday appearance; there were dinners and balls and more dinners and parties and dances and receptions. Not only among the ladies who sold their charms, but among the so-called honest citizens the female outnumbered the male. Men of substance had taken themselves to Canada and England, many of them leaving their families behind and the younger bloods, hating the revolutionary upstarts as only one American could hate another, had hied themselves to Westchester to join the forces of a certain Robert Rogers. This Robert Rogers was a cold, calculating, and strangely cruel soldier of fortune, who had already, some years before, made a name of blood and brutality with his Rogers' Rangers.

Robert Rogers had made a reputation out of his complete contempt for the human species. For him no cause had any more to recommend than its strength, and his belief that might makes right was not intellectual but purely physical. Loving nobody, not even himself, he despised the rabble who had taken it upon themselves to remake their small part of the world. His life had been like the path of a burning ball, leaving a wake of death and misery, but after many years of defeats and misfortunes he was at last coming into his own as the leader of the young Tories of New York and Westchester. As yet, he had no more than a nuisance value, hanging on the fringe of the American army, cutting out sentries, catching deserters and facetiously lynching them, developing and refining the delicate arts he had learned from the Indians and from the Corsairs of North Africa with whom he had had a good deal of experience.

New York City had given both ways. Young men, the sons of tradesmen and workers, had alienated their fathers and broken their mothers' hearts by dealing with a flimsy, foolish underground organization called The Sons of Liberty. When it came to action instead of words, many of them had joined an artillery company led by a West Indian boy named Alexander Hamilton. Now they too were gone, and they and the bloods had been replaced by the British and an infiltration of worthless, illiterate tramps.

Among the few in New York who did not welcome the British were the Jews—who saw their hopes and dreams flee with the tattered Yankees. Instinctively, they had cast their whole fortune with the revolution. Every Jew able to bear arms had joined the insurgent army; their emotional impulse had caused them to speak out violently, and once they had crossed the bridge, they had destroyed it behind them. They had left no way back; they had filled their synagogues with wounded and their parlors with plots, and they had given their cash with the impulse of a gambler who plays one card to win or lose all. Now their youth had gone away with the Yankees, except for those who lay in their cellars moaning with gangrenous wounds.

This was not a new situation for them; it echoed and re-echoed back through all the long, dusty hall of history. The women sat in their houses, behind locked doors and barred shutters, weeping quietly, shedding the only tears that were shed in New York for the defeated and the dishonored, and the old men gathered in the synagogue to pray that this, the last retreat of the exiled, might still retain some hope for a promised land. Only one, a consumptive Polish-Jewish immigrant called Haym Salomon, a frail, thin man, too weak to bear arms and therefore left behind, bared his teeth as he addressed a group of desperate plotters in the cellar of his house, coughed blood, and swore to God that this was only the beginning.

In this New York, in the early evening of September 20, 1776, a young man wandered from street to street, his progress quite aimless. His suit of plain brown homespun was patched at elbow, knee, and seat, and his old round hat had the flat brim that was then much in favor with upcountry folk. He was very young, only twenty-one, and his clear blue eyes and red cheeks made him appear even younger. He had the ambling, slightly hesitant gait that country people so often assume when they are in an unfamiliar city, and his whole attitude was that of an innocuous sightseer.

When he saw a redcoat, he gawked and grinned, and once he picked up a rusty Yankee bayonet and tested its blunt edge with a curious finger. His steps took him everywhere and nowhere, from the East River slips to the old fishing shacks along the Hudson, and from the uptown Dutch windmills to the smooth sward of Bowling Green. On Bowling Green, the British had ranged a battery of sixteen-pound carronades, and in these the young man took an almost childish interest. He edged closer and closer, until he was able to touch their cold surface with his hand.

" 'Ere, now," the sentry said. "None of that."

"They're wonderful big guns," the young man remarked.

"Well, I seen plenty bigger. Now, get along, get along!"

He was found loitering next to a rambling warehouse that the British had converted into a military storeroom, and he was soundly cursed and sent on his way.

Uptown, a few blocks north of Wall Street, he was stopped by a patrol and questioned as to who he was and what business he had in the streets of New York after dark.

"I came down out of the Jerseys," he told the sergeant blandly. "I was looking to join up with Major Rogers."

"And what dirty ragback in New York ain't looking to join up with Major Rogers?"

The boy shrugged.

"Now get off the streets and mind your business, or you'll do your joining in gaol," the sergeant warned him.

After that, he stayed in the darker alleys and bolted like a rabbit when he saw the lantern of a patrol coming. He was very tired, having slept only a few hours in the past three days, but he didn't care to go to any of the inns or public houses; there was just a faint chance that someone might recognize him. As the evening wore on and his weariness increased, he thought of going to a Jew's house, throwing himself on the mercy of the owner, and begging a bed and shelter. But the first house he chose was empty and desolate, with a redcoat sentry in front of the door, and then he felt that approaching another would be like thrusting his hand into a hornets' nest.

Again and again during that evening he had been stopped by ladies of the street, to all of whom he gave the same answer, "I have no money." But now, halted by one and mumbling the same words, he found his arm caught and held.

"Don't go away," she said.

Just that slight presure on his arm made him feel like an animal in a trap and showed him on what thin threads his nerves were strung. He wrenched away, turning to look at her as he did, seeing a dark-eyed, slim girl, heavily and vulgarly painted, wearing a torn lacy gown and a green hat with a bedraggled feather dropping over her shoulder.

"What are you afraid of?" she grinned.

"Nothing. I haven't any money."

"I didn't ask you for money." She was looking at his handsome boyish face with frank admiration. She faced him and the world with cocky defiance, her arms akimbo, her little chin tilted up. "You're a Yankee, ain't you?" she demanded.

"No—"

"Well, what are you afraid of? I ain't a bloody lobster." He started to walk away, but she skipped after him and took his arm again. "What are you afraid of? I know you're a Yankee. I seen you before when the army was here."

He turned slowly and looked at her with such dumb desperation that she recoiled in fright. He took hold of her wrist and held it so tightly that she gave quick little animal gasps of pain. And then he saw her eyes go wider as she looked past his shoulder.

"Oh, let go! There's a patrol."

He glanced quickly, saw the bubble of light, and bolted. He heard her running after him, and when he came to the end of the street found his way blocked again by another swaying lantern. Caught between the two, his senses battered at the blank walls of the dark little alley, his body fought for knowledge, and his feet munched the ground hopelessly, until wakening to her grasp on his hand he followed her into a crevice, a hole solid with darkness, through a door and into darkness beyond, standing close to her after the door had closed and listening to her panting breath.

"There, now," she whispered. "You're strong—my whole hand hurts."

He giggled nervously in the darkness. The pressure of her warm body against his thigh and chest upset him, and now that he couldn't see her, only smell the strong perfumes she had poured onto her hair and clothes, he could feel gratitude for her refuge and offer his thanks to something other than the painted tart who had accosted him on the street.

"I got flints. You want a light?" she asked him.

"No."

The reply was too quick and too definite; he felt her body stiffen, and for the first time in his young manhood he sensed the unseen, indefinable effusion of hurt. He faltered, found his pride and background, and remembered what she was; he remembered sermons in a white clapboard church where sinful women were described simply and certainly, the devil behind them and hell in front of them; and he repeated, "I haven't any money." And then he was glad he couldn't see her face.

She took his hand and led him across the room and told him to sit down. The hard, straw-filled bolster whispered under her weight, but she was not near him now. He sat awkwardly and stiffly, his back straight and his hands clasped, but weariness was returning and the mere fact of a bed made him long for sleep.

"What's your name?" she asked him.

"Nathan Hale."

"Are you a rebel?"

"Yes." There was no more need for concealment; somewhere, his Yankee shell had been broken.

"You run away from the army?" she asked him.

"No."

"I could have let them lobsters get you," she complained plaintively, for the moment her voice emerging from the darkness a little girl's voice. "All you Yankees care about is money—all you tell me is that you got no money. I don't care."

"I want to thank you for taking me in here," he said carefully and precisely. He felt large and strong and important, and more a man than he ever had before in his twenty-one years. But she didn't answer him, and after a moment or two, he realized that she was crying, the noise in the dark like the purring of a lonely cat. He sat uneasily for a while and then fumbled clumsily for her, touching a warm arm and then a soft breast, drawing back, excited and tired, fighting his own silent struggle with sin. He had to force himself to speak, and his lips were dry as he asked her name.

"Helen," she said.

"Well, don't cry," he told her.

"I'm not crying. You can stay here until they go away, if you want to."

He nodded, forgetting that in the darkness his every action was hidden from her, and then sat still, half-dozing until he felt her hand touch his sleeve.

"How old are you?" he asked.

"Twenty-one."

"I'm eighteen," she said. "Are you married?"

"No."

"You got a girl you bundle with?" she inquired simply.

Again the darkness prevented her from seeing the reaction on his face. The straw rustled as she moved closer to him, and her fingers tightened on the homespun, feeling for the flesh of his arm.

"Where you from?" she wanted to know.

"Coventry, Connecticut." He was half asleep, his hardly overcome passion making his weariness lascivious and as sweetly heady as wine, and as he spoke his lips barely moved, his voice a whisper.

"Lie down," she said, pushing him back, and he allowed himself to yield, drawing his feet up on the rustling straw. She sat beside him and stroked his round cheeks, while he lay in delicious comfort, mechanically answering her questions as he drifted into sleep, once protesting that he would dirty her bed with his mud-stained clothes.

"That's nothing," she laughed, and he let her take off his shoes. "I never been to Connecticut," she said. "Is it pretty?"

"I hardly remember," he whispered.

"You a farmer?" she wanted to know.

"Schoolteacher."

"Never! No!" A note of deep and sincere reverence crept into her voice. "Real? For sure?"

"For sure. I went to Yale College," he added, not wondering, in his drowsiness, why he should want to impress this little harlot with that.

"Never!" And then she confessed, "I can't read."

He giggled sleepily.

"I can't even read," she repeated, in a tone that one would confess to God an inability to create worlds and fling them out into space.

In the celler of his house, in candlelight that gave him the appearance of a shrunken-limbed imp, the consumptive little Jew, Haym Salomon, plotted and pleaded and coughed into a cambric handkerchief. With him were a Scotch riverman, a fat Dutch shopkeeper, a wounded Pole who spoke almost no English, and the aging but fiery-eyed beadle of the synagogue. It was a terrible and desperate thing that Salomon was nerving himself and the others to do, and they had been arguing about it since early in the afternoon; now, only a few hours before midnight, they were worn out but still had arrived at no conclusion.

They sat in silence and stared at each other out of red-rimmed eyes. They knew that soon, very soon, they would have to come to a decision, one way or another; but in this pause they were able to form the first vivid and complete picture of what their plans meant. Here was a city, New York, the key to America, the finest harbor, the best anchorage; here was food and shelter and comfort, and here was the enemy. Here was the snug nest, unapproachable by land, but capable of being defended almost forever by Britain's powerful navy; here was a poisoned thorn stuck into the side of America that would make the land twist with agony whatever else happened.

There was one way out, a way that Washington had foreseen long since, but which Congress had forbidden, a way that every practical military observer in the colonies had known was the only way. An ulcerous sore which cannot be healed must be gouged out; New York must be destroyed, burned, left a heap of smoking cinders that would give comfort neither to the Tory partisans nor to the British and German invaders. If innocent people must suffer, then that was simply the price one had to pay for revolution. Revolution was not a game; it was a one-way road with inferno raging behind the men who traveled it.

"And you can't look back," Salomon broke the silence.

The Dutch shopkeeper shook his head stubbornly. "Destruction does not make a solution," he said with his thick accent.

"You can't look back," Salomon insisted.

It was a little after midnight that Nathan Hale awoke, groped through his first sensation of blindness in the pitch-black room, rolled over on the straw, and remembered how he had come to the place. His recollection of the girl, immersed as it was in darkness, was fuzzy. He could not re-create through the pitch. Fumbling, moving his stocking feet across the floor, he found his shoes, put them on, and stumbled toward where he thought the door to be, possessed by an urgent need to be out of the place and into the fresh air.

Not until he had opened the door and allowed the silvery starlight to stream in, was he able to make out anything of the place where he had slept, the windowless cube of the room, the bed, a chair, and a blob in one corner which let him know in a rush of shame and misery that the girl had not shared his bed, but had given him in his god-like elevation the place of comfort and honor. He did not have the courage to go back and wake her; instead he stumbled down the street, his Yankee shell of sufficiency and right shattered in many places. He walked on and on, the short sleep serving only to accentuate the aches in his tired body, and he had come at least six or seven blocks from the harlot's house before he realized that New York City was beginning to burn.

At first the licking tendrils of flame were so unreal that their impact was meaningless, and not until the streets were full of hurrying, shouting citizens did he realize the full significance of the fire. Then he too ran along with the others, propelled by the instinctive knowledge that where the press was thickest and where the excitement was greatest his most certain safety lay. Not alone that; he was boy enough to love the fury of a fire and be caught up in all the futile, senseless gestures of the volunteer firemen; and this, with the colorful army uniforms, the screeching harlots, the booming alarm cannons and the wildly yelling citizens, was more colorful than any of the tiny blazes that had brought rare moments of action to Coventry. In common with all Americans in that time of small towns and primitive fire-fighting methods, he was convinced of the omnipotence of any fair-sized blaze, and only opposed it because that was the one emotional outlet of a person attending the catastrophe.

By now the old Dutch houses were going up like the tinderboxes they were, and the crackle of flames and the sound of falling rafters and walls was like the noise from a battlefield. Night was turned into day, and to Hale the brightly illuminated streets, packed with night-shirted citizens and British redcoats trying desperately to clear a path for the hand-pumps, were wonderfully reminiscent of those vague pictures he had garnered from his study of ancient history; and he thought to himself, in a sudden thrill of elation, that this was as surely the end of an era as the burning of Rome while Nero fiddled. In that moment of incendiary glory and crazy excitement, he forgot the punishing and bitter defeats of his comrades and thought only of how puny and helpless the British were while their conquered city burned.

At that moment, some miles to the north, Robert Harrison had dragged the Virginian from a sound slumber to a window that faced the glowing southern sky. For a while, the two men stood there, still not fully awake, speculating upon what might have caused that wonderful, unearthly glow. Harrison decided, as calmly as he could, "I would say, sir, from all indications, that New York is on fire. Certainly nothing within our own lines could make a glow of such proportions." And then he cast a quick, keen, sidewise glance at the Virginian, to see whether the expression on the long face might denote joy or elation or disappointment. But the commander's features were incredibly placid, and all he said was, "Please see that my horse is saddled, Mr. Harrison."

As he rode south, the big man noticed that the glow was increasing, until by the time he approached Harlem the southern sky was filled with a sunburst of glory and fire. At first he had considered that perhaps a single large house was on fire or that one of the enemy ships in the river had been set alight, but now he realized that nothing less than a whole city in flames could brighten the sky in such a fashion.

Thrilled and elated as he was by this almost miraculous accomplishment of all he had dreamed of doing and — held helpless by a timid Congress — been unable to do, he nevertheless determined to make no gesture nor action until he had accurate information about what had happened.

In a clearing on a hill to the north of the Hollow Way, he dismounted, and there one by one the members of his staff joined him. Knox, Putnam, Mifflin, Spencer, Silliman, Greene, Reed, Smallwood, and perhaps a dozen others. They stood in a close, silent group, the most verbose of them speechless in the presence of this awful and wonderful destruction. A few of them were religious men, most were freethinkers, and some were atheists, but the least believing of them felt the awe and solemnness of the occasion.

For hours they stood and watched, until the star-speckled sky haloing the fire, turned into grey mist, and the bright morning sun transformed strange terror into mere actuality.

When Nathan Hale remembered the painted little tart who had given him shelter in a hard-pressed moment, it was too late; and when he tried desperately to find the miserable alley where she possessed a windowless cubbyhole, a bed and chair that made a home, he found himself confronted everywhere by a wall of raging fire. He ran and stumbled and bruised himself and thrust through crowds and shouldered redcoats aside; but always the laughing flames were ahead of him.

He came away, finally, hating the city and all it contained, telling himself, "I'll go back now. I've been here long enough, and I know all that I'll ever know. They wouldn't want me to stay here any longer."

He walked north, away from the fire and the crowds, but he was very tired, and when he saw a shed with some hay in it, he burrowed into the hay and fell asleep; he fell asleep easily and quickly, out of pure exhaustion.

In the morning, when he awoke, the fire still burned, closer to him than before, not so impressive in daylight, but more ominous in its crackling insistence. He cleared the hay from his hair and clothes, endured some scathing remarks from the owner of the shed, who saw him emerge, drank some water from a trough where he doused his head and face, rubbing off the soot, and continued his progress north.

Now he no longer saw the excited, half-crazy crowds of the night before; people were calmer and more deadly; the damage had been done, and they were searching for some sort of vengeance. The flames could not be stopped, but there were still rebels and rebels could be made to suffer. Once he saw a screaming wretch dragged by at the end of a noose, and again he saw a bearded old Jew lying dead in the street.

As he came to the outskirts of the city, he went more cautiously, but it took him only a little while to realize that redcoat patrols were on every road and path. Again and again, he attempted to make his way north out of New York, and again and again he had to double back on his own tracks; he was beginning to feel like a trapped beast, nervous, sweating, his eyes red and tearful from the smoke. Once he had to run for it, leaping stone walls and finding refuge for the moment in a chicken house among the cackling hens. He left there and crawled along a fence, burrowed through a briar patch and found a moment's peace in a bit of woods. He found a little brook, lay down on his stomach, and drank until he could hold no more. He went cautiously through an apple orchard, edging from tree to tree, until he came to the fringe of a broad meadow. The highroad ran about a quarter mile to his left, and on it he could see the crimson blob of a patrol. To the north were woods and shelter, shelter that might continue all the distance to the Hollow Way. Stooping low, he began to run across the meadow.

He was almost across it when the patrol sighted him and let go with their clumsy muskets. He twisted away and saw redcoats at the edge of the woods; he ran to the right and then saw the green of Hessians cutting off escape in that direction.

He doubled back and saw four dragoons driving their horses straight at him.

His coat torn, a long gash across one pink cheek, his full lips trembling just a little, he stood in General Howe's headquarters and faced Major Rudly Clare and stared at Major Clare's blinking, somewhat bored lashes. Major Clare sat behind a table on which were spread pieces of paper scribbled over with notes and bits of rude map-making. In a tone as bored as his glance, Major Clare said, "You don't deny having written these?"

"No, sir. They were found on me."

"You write an excellent hand."

There was a shade of wistful pride in the boy's voice as he said, "I'm a graduate of Yale College, bachelor of arts, sir."

"Really? I'm an admirer of your provincial centers of learning. What's your name?"

"Captain Nathan Hale."

"Never mind the title. What regiment?"

"Colonel Knowlton's Connecticut Rangers, sir."

"Rangers — oh, my aunt, what a bloody variety of services you beggars have! And where is your regiment now?"

"I couldn't say, sir."

"You couldn't say!" The major's voice betrayed a shade of impatience. "Damn it all, boy, you're a spy — don't you understand?"

The boy nodded, his bright blue eyes creasing with sudden realization.

"Damn it all," the major said, "these papers — civilian clothes, at the fire — "

"We have no uniforms," the boy said helplessly. "We none of us have uniforms."

The major fingered the papers for a moment or so, and then said to the sergeant standing beside him, "Take him out to Cunningham and have him hanged in the morning."

The sky was so blue the next morning, and the wind was blowing and the birds singing, and the grass green and crunchy, and the maple leaves turning their wonderful nutty crimson. And in the crowd that had gathered to watch the hanging, there was hardly anyone who didn't remark on the perfect weather, for in the fall the weather in New York can be like the weather nowhere else in the world, with the strong wind traveling from over the Palisades, making little whitecaps on the Hudson, with all the scent and smell of a million miles westward sighing down on the queen of cities.

When he came out, to the rumble of muffled drums, he had only one prayer, one single prayer to God to give him the strength not to be afraid, not to be a part of all the fear he remembered, the fear that had sent them running from Brooklyn, running from New York, the fear that had robbed them of dignity and glory and beauty, the fear that let little girls sell themselves and become tarts, the fear that made free men speaking his own tongue sail across three thousand miles of sea to take away his and his comrades' dreams, the fear that built stony shells of retreat for all his kind. So he clenched his hands, bottled his heartsickness inside of him, and walked across the greensward.

He looked like a child, with his red cheeks, his blue eyes, and his sandy hair, and he was woefully, pathetically brave, trying to smile, trying not to think of the little bit he had lived, the one woman who had offered herself to him and been refused, his mother and his father and all the gawking faces of the Coventry rustics when he had walked away to war, trying not to realize that this was the last part of fresh air, blue sky, green grass.

And then, in the end, the whole thing broke down, and he knew only that he wanted to live, to go back to the warm embrace of the others, the poor, ragged devils who were making a terrible and wonderful and mysterious thing called revolution.

But they didn't know, the good citizens of New York who stood and watched a red-cheeked boy with a tremulous smile on his face, standing and waiting to be hanged.

10

HOW THE FISHERMEN WERE NOT AFRAID

LIKE a flaming meteor out of the south, General Charles Lee descended upon the beaten army that crouched on the lip of the Hollow Way. For days and weeks, his coming had been anticipated; the New Englanders nodded wisely and agreed with the Southerners upon this point, that as a soldier and a leader, Mr. Lee had everything the Virginia foxhunter lacked. They pointed to the manner in which he had repulsed a British attack on Charlestown; they read aloud his military prognostications; they wrote his strategy in the sand; they exalted his courage; they praised his cunning. The most miserable, loutish, craven Yankee in the revolutionary rabble protested stoutly that he would have been the best soldier in the world if only General Lee had been there to lead him. Already they had pushed every bit of blame, every single mistake onto the bony shoulders of the foxhunter; now they speculated upon how differently everything would have gone had only General Lee been in the saddle.

And in great measure, the foxhunter agreed with them, for deep in his own heart he knew only too well that as a military man Charles Lee was everything that he, George Washington, was not. His reverence for Lee was deep and sincere and unselfish, the same reverence he had held, a long time ago, for his wonderful brother, Lawrence Washington—for Lawrence had been all that he was not and all that he held so dear—graceful, charming, courtly, a leader of men and a fantastic adventurer; and that was the reverence the Virginia squire had for all the world's great and brilliant men, who moved ahead without doubts and fears. Constantly, in those trying days, he had written to Lee, telling him of this and that, hanging on to his replies as pearls of wisdom. And every letter from Lee only served to convince him of his own unworthiness and Lee's superiority.

And now, at last, Lee was coming here to Harlem.

It didn't matter that some of those who would follow the Virginian into hell did not share his opinion of Charles Lee, that Knox fairly bubbled with dislike of Lee, that Putnam sneered openly, that Green said he would trust Lee with anything that was nailed down but with nothing that was not, that Reed mentioned certain other factors at Charlestown as having more to do with the repulse of the British than General Lee. They could not shake Washington's faith, the more so since he realized that their own regard for him was shaped by anything but military factors.

When Charles Lee strode into the encampment on Harlem Heights, those of the army of liberty who had never before seen him were more than a little astonished at his appearance and at the dozen dogs that yapped at his heels. They were all of them dog masters, owners of one dog, even two dogs, and some few the possessors of hunt packs; but for a general on campaign to be followed by a howling dozen—that was too much. You could hardly hear the man speak for the uproar which his dogs made when anyone approached him.

His appearance, too, was very unusual; he was tall and fantastically skinny, not in the way of Washington, with big, fleshless bones that could hide themselves under a uniform coat, but thin as a reed, narrow and long, narrow sloping shoulders, no hips, tendril hands, a long nose, a small mouth, and almost no chin at all. He spoke in a high-pitched voice, blinking his eyes rapidly and affecting the English "Beau Nash" drawl. Another British affectation was his habit of seeing only what he wanted to see, whether the object was a hundred yards away or right under his nose.

For all his unusual, almost out-of-the-world appearance, Lee was a good soldier, a far more experienced soldier than anyone else in the American army. He was that strange thing, a man born into battle; and in all his forty-five years he had never known any other life than that of the army. He was a soldier in the same fashion that one man is a painter and another a butcher. He did not and never had fought for a cause or a reason or an impulse, nor to inflict wrong, nor to right a wrong. He fought because soldiering was his trade, and while he didn't always sell himself to the highest bidder, having an eye to glory and advancement, he certainly never let ideological purposes influence him.

He liked to boast that he held a commission in the British army at the age of eleven, and possibly it was true. He was the English-born son of an officer, and he had no memories that were not of army life. He had fought in almost every corner of the globe, in America during the French War, in Portugal, in Poland, anywhere and everywhere there was a market for a sword or a gun. When he turned to America once more and was offered a position second only to the commander in chief, he demanded a thirty-thousand-dollar guarantee before he would accept. His price was high, but trained soldiers who were also English gentlemen did not grow on every tree; and therefore his bid was accepted—with the feeling among most people that at thirty thousand dollars here was a better bargain than the foxhunter, who came without price and even with the understanding that there would be no payment.

Admire him they did, in the way the midland bumpkins and the nasal-voiced New England rustics admired anyone who came from the old country, not as an immigrant, but as a free soldier of fortune; but like him even they could not. God knew, they boasted enough. They had to cry out loud to reassure themselves, spread thin as they were on the edge of nowhere; but their boasting was nothing compared to the drawling value Charles Lee put on himself. His price was thirty thousand dollars, and he made sure that no one would undervalue him.

He approved of the Morris house, where the foxhunter had had his headquarters these past weeks; he filled his pocket with black cigars from the humidor and lashed the placid Billy with contempt, his attitude toward Negroes learned and overlearned during his Southern stay. He kicked the turf of the lawn—which the Virginian treasured and preserved in its soft green beauty—and let his howling dogs into the lovely Chipendale parlor. At the table, in the cool, chaste dining room, he fed his dogs along with himself, and told jokes so filthy that they offended even the ears of his fellow officers, men bred and raised on very strong meat, as stories and songs went. And the Virginian bore it all tolerantly, even gladly.

Lee had not been at headquarters more than two hours before he demanded a council of war, telling Washington exactly which men, in his opinion, should attend. The officers came without eagerness, filing into the shadowy dining room of the Morris house, taken aback by Lee's sprawling presence in the commander's seat at the head of the table. When the Madeira was poured, Lee proposed the toasts; when the discussion was opened, Lee took it and held it.

Sitting almost motionless during the discussion, which waxed high and then waned, heated and then slowed, calmer, bitter in the memories it evoked, Washington retreated deeper and deeper into the shadows thrown by the candles, not moving, but effacing himself none the less.

Lee's first words were a comment on the insanity of their position. He put into corrosive expression what most of them had been thinking for months, that without a powerful navy the defense of New York was utterly hopeless. Viciously and barely, he drew a picture of what would have happened to the miserable little army had the British only followed a course that any sane commander would plot. He was certain on that score; for him, war was a science; and his contempt for the British and their methods was as obvious as his confidence in his own. But that very fact turned the officers present against him.

"Damn it all!" he cried. "We must get out! There's no other way to it. It's a filthy, bloody trap, and if those marvelously stupid lobsters only had the sense to put a ship up the river and turn its guns into Kingsbridge, we'd be here until hell froze over."

They knew he was right, and for that reason they snarled at him.

"We held them for weeks," Putnam growled.

"Why don't they take the Hollow Way if it's that simple?" Reed wanted to know.

And Greene pointed out, "There's no way in the world to take Fort Washington. Ten men and a battery could hold it until your hell freezes over."

"Oh, you bloody fools!" Lee drawled. "Ten soldiers could drive your New England stench out of it in an hour."

They wrangled; they almost came to blows, shaking the frail table; they spoke of duels and challenges; they called each other names: and through it all the big man sat without speaking, without voicing any opinion. Lee didn't know them; they were not like any soldiers he had ever seen, not even like the gentry of the South; they were bumpkins, rustics, shopkeepers; they were boys, and he had not seen them, unafraid, lead other boys who were terribly, woefully afraid. To it all, he had one answer: "You bloody damned fools."

In the end they leaned back exhausted, and the Virginian's decision, gentle after the row, came out of the shadows. "General Lee is right," he said quietly. "We can't fight—here of all places. Perhaps we can't fight anywhere. We are going to leave New York and retreat. Perhaps we will try to hold the fort that bears my name and perhaps we will not; I don't know yet. But our way, our only way, I tell you, gentle-

94

men, is to retreat until we have made ourselves into an army. We have one advantage—that we don't overestimate ourselves. Do you know, gentlemen, that when I went away from my home I thought it would be for a little while? It will not be a little while, gentlemen, but a long time. We will retreat, if we have to, over the mountains where there is a forest twice as large as Europe. But someday, gentlemen, we will become an army, the sort of an army General Lee has had experience with, and then we will turn around—and then we will not run away."

For a long time the Virginian repeated those words to himself. "We will not run away, we will not run away, we will become an army, we will become an army."

He tried to make an army. Awkwardly, he plodded through what measures he could conceive of, trying to mend this and fix that, lecturing, advising, scolding, pleading. At some of his efforts, Lee nodded benevolently, but for the most part the thin Englishman drifted through the camp like a guest of honor, telling endless tales of his experiences on the battlefields of Europe, the moral of all being that no cleverness was like the cleverness of General Charles Lee.

And the Yankees loved it; they loved his cleverness; they loved his obvious hints about who would be the commander in chief in time to come; they loved his many small findings, as contrasted with the virtues of the Virginian.

When men deserted by the tens and twenties and fifties, Lee could afford to shrug his shoulders at this strange army, but when some of them were brought back and the commander in chief grimly ordered them to be whipped until the blood ran from their backs, the Yankees told each other that the Virginian was a stonehearted tyrant. The day, every day, was one steady plague of mutiny, desertion, thievery, and complaint.

•Yet hard on the council of war, the commander's veneration for Lee found confirmation; for the British at last did precisely what Lee had predicted they would do sooner or later. They sent a force through the East River into the Sound, in a flanking attack on Westchester, an attack planned to cut off the American army and end its existence.

The flanking movement should have worked. Under cover of night and fog, British boats crept up the East River searching for an outjutting bit of land called Pell's Point. But the fog further confused their none too accurate geography, and they landed instead at Throgg's Neck, also an outjutting of the Westchester coast, but almost an island, since it was connected with the mainland by a wooden causeway.

A fourteen-year-old Dutch boy, Peter Rauch, was digging clams on the beach when he heard the British voices. His wits were keen, keen enough to send him running barefooted for a whole mile through the night to the camp of a red-faced Irish colonel by the name of Hand, who disliked the British but had a deep and generous hatred of Tories, and who had dragged his regiment into Westchester in the hope of meeting the dashing Rogers and some of his green-clad rangers.

Peter Rauch burst through the sprawling men and descended upon Hand with a torrent of Dutch, waving his arms wildly, nor did he calm down until the Irishman had picked him up by his belt and shaken him, puppy-like, in the air.

"Now what is it in English?" Hand demanded.

"Der lobsters!"

"Where?"

"In der wasser, in der boats, I tink maybe dey come up from der town, like how you say, dis," and he made violent rowing motions with his hands.

"Rowing?"

"Ya."

"How many?"

"I chust hear dem, I don see dem."

"Where will they be landing, boy, do you know?"

"I tink, der way dey go, dey go in der neck."

"Can you lead us there, boy?"

"Ya, ya, ya," gleefully avenging his ancestors, who had lost New Amsterdam.

And an hour later Hand's men were ripping up the causeway and yelling their peculiar Pennsylvania derision at the British.

The big man studied his map, one long finger laid on Throgg's Neck, and tried to understand and anticipate what the British would do next. He was caught, yet in a way the British were also caught, though only a torn-up causeway and a few muskets kept them back; it was a question of whether he could get his army out of New York before the British returned to their boats and landed somewhere else on the Westchester shore.

He thought not. He was under no delusions concerning his army, and he had learnt by now that there was a most definite difference between retreating and running away. He had seen his army run away once, and the memory was bitter; all that had saved them then from dissolving like a cloud of gas was the fact that they were on an island and that most of them could not swim. Now the very thought of what might happen, if he were to pick up his army and race from Manhattan with part of the British behind him and another part threatening to cut off his front, made his blood run cold. No, his army must move slowly, deliberately, gently; it must move in a close mass, so that the men could crowd together and feel each other's warmth, and it must have the knowledge of a solid rear guard behind it.

The rear guard was less of a problem than the British force on Throgg's Neck; the Delaware and Maryland troops had held once before, and they might hold again, but there were so few of them. And Throgg's Neck—

He put his finger back on the map and forced himself to plan and contrive; he said to himself, hopelessly, "If there were only five hundred more who would stand and fight."

Riding through Westchester, along the Sound shore, he and most of his staff had agreed that Pell's Point would be the most likely place for a British landing attempt, and to that consensus of opinion, Lee had added his own. For the moment, the British were frustrated on Throgg's Neck, but what would happen when they slipped away and found the next spur of land, without a torn-up causeway to hold them back?

As he sat there, thinking, planning, contriving, there came to his mind's eye the picture of several hundred men in blue peajackets and stocking fishermen's hats; he was back in the desolate cul-de-sac of Brooklyn, watching the rolling, unhurried gait of the Marblehead men. They were Yankees, nasal-voiced, shell-encrusted, boastful, yet in a way different, lashed by a thousand days of wind and salt sleet, quietly aware of death and not seeing too much difference between lead bullets and an icy-cold sea. He had seen them with oars in their hands, and now he wondered how they would be with muskets.

He sent for Colonel Glover. The man was his own age, tightly knit, light-eyed, with the very slight, grudging smile that his kind would permit themselves for a Southern outlander.

"Can your men fight?" the Virginian asked.

"Maybe they can."

The Virginian indicated Pell's Point on the map. "I think the British will land there," he said. "I don't want them ashore until the army is out of the island."

"Uh-huh."

"Can you do it?"

"We can try," Glover said.

"It may be twenty-four hours, it may be forty-eight, but I want them held until all danger of encirclement is past."

"Uh-huh," Glover nodded.

And then they shook hands, Washington's smile as thin and grudging as Glover's own.

The fishermen took up their position that night, grumbling, swearing, dragging by main strength — for they had no horses — the three tiny field pieces allotted to them, stumbling through brush and fields and briars, and finding finally a stone wall which suited them. Near as they were to the Sound, they were nevertheless sullen over the fact that they had had to abandon the fleet of small boats which they gathered for the retreat from Brooklyn. Vaguely, they felt that this was a war which should be fought as much on the sea as on the land, and they had the small boatman's contempt for the mighty British ships of the line. They knew that their light Salem fishing smacks could dance merrily around the lumbering giants, and they asked no more than a chance to set the invading fleet ablaze with fire boats and then go home. Instead, here they were crawling through the poison-ivy patches of Westchester, tearing their faces, hands, and clothes in the endless briar tangles, and going God alone knew where.

When they had settled down behind the stone wall and primed their muskets, Glover lit his pipe and called up his officers for instructions. Of the sixteen men who gathered around him, nine had been captains of their own boats, three had been country schoolteachers who went out for cod when classes were off, one had been a parson, one had been a shoemaker, one had been a carpenter, and the last was Hiram Threemercy Ploughman, one of the most skillful and famous figure-head carvers on all the Gloucester coast. They were hard, sharp men with long faces and long noses and salt in their blood, and they were in the war because freedom for them was not an ideal but an obsession.

"Them" — Glover said, puffing at his pipe and nodding at the grey haze of dawn that was showing over the sound — "will be coming from yonder."

They waited.

"We'll be a-setting here," Glover continued.

They nodded sagely.

"We'll keep a-setting here," Glover said.

The parson said, booming in the darkness, "Lord God of Hosts, Mighty Jehovah, kindle thy wrath against the iniquitous, strike down them that would profane Thy Holy Name and give might to the virtuous and the God-fearing, and damn the Church of England!"

"Amen," said the others.

They loaded the cannon heavily in their own peculiar way, not with shot, but with the sweepings of a blacksmith's shop, rusty nails, bits of wire, old iron bolts, broken horseshoes, pieces of glass, and finely minced pewter pots and pans. They had no ideals nor illusion about the war, and there was in them a cold streak of Puritan ruthlessness. They were not riflemen, and their huge, wide-bore muskets, some of the bell-mouthed ancient matchlocks, came in for the same treatment of rusty nails and old wire. Not being riflemen, but being Yankees and efficient, they turned their muskets into shotguns and then sat and waited.

With the dawn, the British came marching down to sweep them away.

The fishermen waited calmly. The sun poked up out of the Sound, and dawn was a pink burst of glory, blood-spotted by the red coats of the British. They had tried Throgg's Neck and found the causeway torn up, but here there was land for their feet and nothing had ever stopped the redcoat columns where there was land for their feet. They marched in with their fifes playing and their drums beating, with their shakoes swaying and their glittering bayonets slicing the morning air. And when they were thirty yards away, the fishermen let go with the sweepings of a blacksmith shop.

They were fishermen; they had seen cod squirming and bleeding when the hooks were pulled out, but they had never seen a whole field of men like a slippery deck of cod; they were hard, as their fathers and grandfathers had been hard, but they were not hard enough for this, not hard enough to keep the blood in their faces and not hard enough to keep from retching.

Still, they reloaded.

The British came again, straight and precise, as if the whole field had not already been harrowed with death, and again the sweepings of a blacksmith shop tore out their life.

They came again and again.

They came hard on the run, pressing through the field of death to the stone wall, and the fishermen dropped their muskets, seizing the long, hooked poles that were tools of their trade, and using them as pikes.

All morning the British attacked in a senseless spectacle of bravery that was as stupid as it was glorious, and all morning the rusty nails of the coldly efficient Marblehead fishermen hurled them back.

At noon, Howe withdrew what was left of the redcoat light infantry and threw the green-clad Hessians into the battle; and they came on with their harsh battle cry of "Yonkee!" They had none of the cool precision that took the cockney boys of London into that blazing hell; they came on dogged and furious, and they died the same way. They raged up to the stone wall and they were thrown back. They spotted the field with their green coats and their bulky knapsacks and their unwieldy shakoes.

All through the afternoon the attacks went on, and all afternoon the fishermen beat back the sweating, gasping Germans. Three or four of the fishermen had died and a dozen more were wounded, but in the field in front of them lay more than five hundred British and Hessians. Even the faltering mentality of General Howe, never penetrated by fear of anything on God's earth, could not stand any more of this. He drew off his men, and gentle evening hid the horror of Pell's Point.

While the Marblehead fishermen lay behind the stone wall at Pell's Point, the commander laboriously began to evacuate his army from Harlem, to begin what he felt would be a retreat of many long years. Up to now, he had been the commander in chief of an army that proposed to fight the enemy and destroy it; but only by the grace of God, by the virtue of falling rain, by the calm stamina of six or seven hundred Yankee fishermen, had this enemy been kept from completely destroying his own army. Defeat had become so constant a fact that victory was not even to be thought of; only ways and means of retreating in good order were to be considered. And out of all this there was coming to the tall Virginia farmer a strange and curious knowledge: that wars and freedom of men are not won on a battlefield.

He did not have complete understanding of this new awareness yet; but the change in him was indicated by the acquisition of an almost godly patience. Mount Vernon, in its sunny glory, seemed very far away, indistinct, part of a dream; and though he still looked forward to his return there, it was something neither immediate nor calculable. Mount Vernon was no longer the solid, eternal fact of house, barns, smokehouse, storehouse, winehouse, orchards, fields, lawns, shadetrees: all that — and it was his life, for he was no man to exist inwardly, but only in the radiant warmth of good, solid fact — had been laid on the table, and Mount Vernon, which had been his, was no longer his, only a promise.

His patience was incredible; he had made for himself a simple credo, "My friends I will trust and my enemies I will endeavor to destroy." He no longer blamed and scolded and raged, and when things were done wrong, as most things were, he gave the impression in a most matter-of-fact way that on such a basis even the best armies in the world operated. Over the whole comic-opera war he presided in such simple dignity that even Charles Lee was moved to a certain respect.

"If only he wasn't such a fool," Lee thought.

But when the young hotheads, Knox, Mifflin, Mercer, McDougall and the others, came raging to the Virginian with news that Lee had said this and Lee has said that, he closed his ears and sent them on their way with the plain statement, "General Lee is a good and loyal soldier, gentlemen. That is all I ask of any of my staff."

A month ago, a year ago, the things Lee and certain others said about him would have turned him mad with anger; but he was not the same man that he had been a month ago and a year ago.

The Yankees trailed north. Brigade after brigade, some with arms, more who had thrown away their arms, they trudged north, through the narrow bottleneck of Manhattan, over Kingsbridge and into Westchester, escaping from the trap while Howe hurled his wonderful troops at the Marblehead fishermen. From the Hollow Way, which had been the Continental defense line, to White Plains, where the Virginian had been accumulating supplies for the expected retreat, was a distance of eighteen miles, less than a day's march for a trained corps, but more than a day's march for this broken, defeated army.

The Virginian had hoped and planned to establish another camp and make a stand at White Plains, but now he realized that such a policy would serve to play directly into the hands of the British. They only needed to surround his army to end the war, and sooner or later they would realize that and act accordingly. Therefore he changed his plans; already he had word that Glover and his fishermen were momentarily holding the British in check. With the main army out of Manhattan, he would place a rear guard at White Plains, while the stores were removed. After that, he would retreat —

But Greene, hating Lee as bitterly as he did, persuaded the commander not to give up New York entirely, but to leave a garrison of three thousand men at Fort Washington, which Green and Knox believed could be held forever.

Lee's opinion was: "That, sir, is the final piece of insanity."

101

Licking itself like a great wounded lion, the British army moved inland and north. In the darkness, the Yankee fishermen had slipped away, having shot out all the rusty horror they used to load their guns, yet not before they had inflicted, considering time, and the number of men involved, one of the most awful defeats the British army ever suffered in all its military history. Yet what they had done was in the way of a sideshow, a brief effort to delay a landing attempt, an action that passed almost unnoticed in the dark pall of defeat.

11

HOW OTHERS WERE AFRAID

ONCE the army of liberty was out of Manhattan, across Kingsbridge and sprawling through the low hills of southern Westchester, the Virginian felt a great relief. He had accomplished one thing that again and again in his dreams had promised to be the worst of debacles, the removal of his army from Manhattan Island. But the relief was short-lived, for the water-barrier that had kept his men from wholesale desertion was now removed, and in the promise of sudden dissolution, he began to lose the sense of reality. On his horse, he felt himself a big, awkward farmer, holding aloft two huge hands that were filled with powdery sand, sand which he could not hold, which sifted away, which dissolved, which puffed away on savage bursts of wind, which resolved into laconic and merciless communications:

"Sir, I'm sorry to say fourteen of my men deserted."

"It was no fault of mine, Your Excellency, the Vermont rifle regiment has gone home."

"We caught six deserters, but over a hundred escaped."

"The Carolina Republic's own Loyal and Devoted Artillery Company has slipped away with two six pounders."

"The Gadby Rangers are gone, sir. I don't know when they left camp."

"Captain Atterson walked off with all his men."

"Lieutenant Jones and six of his men."

"Colonel Arlen—"

"Eleven of the Pennsylvania Rifles."

"Captain Bixbe—"

"Seven of my regiment, sir, with two ho'heds, all our powder, and what am I to do for munitions?"

"Twelve of the Third New York."

It filled his ears and hammered into his head, a dreadful, relentless repetition, a dogged reiteration. Ten men, six men, nine men, a hundred men, two hundred men—and if it continued, very soon his hands would be empty. He pleaded with his staff, "Keep the men close and post sentries at night."

But one of the boys said, "Sir, even the sentries run away."

So he rushed north, hoping that mere impetus would keep his army together.

The densely wooded hills of Westchester were in many ways a no man's land. Major Robert Rogers and his rangers had instituted a sort of guerrilla warfare, which heretofore had been devoted mainly to burning the homes of revolutionist sympathizers and inflicting other minor deviltries upon them—desultory rape and banditry, some lynching, and a good deal of riding on a rail, the second being viler and more terrible than the first, since it consisted of seating a man on the sharp edge of a plank, with a fifty-pound weight hanging from either foot, and keeping him there until he fainted away or died, or screamed and wept and pleaded for mercy. The revolutionist party, though greatly outnumbered in Westchester, had come to a position which in any case makes very good revolutionary material—they had no more to lose. They retreated into the tangled forests of the Pocantico Hills and the dense marshes and lonely lakes of the Mahopac region, and from there they sallied forth in raids and counter-deviltries. They burned and raped and stole on their own, until the whole pretty woodland country had earned itself a nation-wide reputation for lawlessness and disorder.

To travel alone through Westchester, whether to White Plains, Tarrytown, or Dobbs Ferry—or to any of the lovely old Dutch villages that clustered along the Hudson bank and in the valleys and on the shore of the Sound, was a worth a man's life, whether he was Tory or revolutionist. Already the fields had gone to seed, fruit trees were untended, and lonely houses were either black ruins or armed and barred like fortresses. Perhaps no other section in all the colonies had felt so intensely the bitter and unrelenting hatred of civil war.

And into this region, now, came a new diversion, two armies of about thirteen thousand men each, one a mass of beaten, frightened Continentals, pouring up out of Manhattan Island, the other an orderly and wonderfully trained fighting machine of British and Germans, come up by boat to the region near New Rochelle and driving north and west on a sharp angle, calculated to cut off and trap the Americans. It was a slow race, in which the British were held back by their fear of pitfalls and ambushes and by their ignorance of Westchester geography, an ignorance which had induced the Admiralty in London to issue an order for the English fleet of mighty three-deck ships of the line to sail up the Bronx River and harry the Americans along its length. Thus Howe made all sorts of elaborate preparations to force a crossing of the Bronx River, only to shake his head in bewilderment when he discovered it was the tiniest and prettiest of woodland brooks, never deeper than a few feet and never wider than a few yards. The Americans were restrained by their very inability to march as an army.

And around both armies like a pack of famished wolves lurked the irregulars. They shot down deserters, cut off stragglers, and knifed sentries. They fought their own horrible war while the two masses of men jockeyed for position.

Position, to the Virginian, was an eternal hope. Dreaming at night, or dreaming awake in the daytime, he won battles, simply because his tactics were correct, even inspired, and his men were not afraid. And that made him say to himself, "Next time, if I do it right, if I plan everything the way a soldier would, it will be different. I will win."

To him, it was so plausible and obvious. He himself was not afraid; all the fear that had been his was gone in the knowledge that there was no way back, that from here on he could travel only in one direction; and he could not see why with his men it should be otherwise. Even experience was blotted out by that pleading hope. Thus when he found himself at White Plains, in a position that might be held even against the forces of hell, he said to Charles Lee, "If we could stop them here, general, we might change everything." Yet it was more a hope than a statement. His army was building entrenchments on a line from the meandering little Bronx River to a swampy lake. There were hillocks and there was a general rise of ground in their direction, and Lee recognized the entire thing as a tactical picture out of some old and formal military manual. For a moment he was caught with sympathy for this blundering, foolish farmer, who could never be either a leader or a soldier, and who, bound as he was by his slow mind, could only see the part and never the whole of anything.

But Lee still burned over the affront that had been placed upon him by disregarding his advice and leaving a garrison at Fort Washington. He was brutally noncommittal.

"We might drive them back to the Sound," the foxhunter dreamed.

"Or they might go around us and have us in a bloody trap," Lee said.

"No, they won't do that," the foxhunter murmured, and of this he was quite certain. He knew the contempt the British felt for him and his army—a contempt which would make the English scornful of surrounding what they could defeat in battle.

Afterwards, what came to be known as the Battle of White Plains, remained as a confused, bad memory in his mind, of no great importance in itself, but as the beginning of his greatest debacle—of that black horror that stayed with him as an uneasy ghost and rose to torture him in dreams.

In itself, the battle was not so different from his others; some of his men fought, but most of them ran away, the difference being that this time it was not Yankees who ran as if the devil himself was behind them, but Delaware and Maryland brigades, men of his own southland and men he had put some trust in. Yet they ran just as hard as Yankees, just as fast, and they threw away their guns in the same fashion.

He had put these regiments on a strong point called Chatterton's Hill. He had seen them bedded down behind stone walls, with cannon protecting their flanks, the artillery consisting of two field pieces in charge of the boy, Hamilton. It pained the Virginian to be prodigal with his cannon, so few pieces were left after the losses at Brooklyn and New York, considering the pieces that had been set aside in the beginning to defend Fort Washington and Fort Lee. It seemed to him that every time his army was driven from a place, it left behind such a vast store of munitions and arms as could never be replaced; and then it was root and search and lay hands on some iron balls here, a few kegs of powder there, some old muskets, matchlocks, pikes, rusty bayonets. Each time, it was like putting together an army once more, out of nothing.

At any rate, Hamilton fought, whipping his gunners into standing by, loading the cannon, and firing them; but it took only a single man wounded in the thigh to make the Maryland men break and run. Then it was the old heartbreaking story, officers pleading and yelling for the men to make a stand and the militia running wildly, without purpose and direction from the close, precise ranks of attacking British. Once again, by the hundreds, the Continentals fled like rabbits, crawling into whatever shelter they could find, hiding themselves in the brush, in the tall grass, burrowing into piles of dead autumn leaves, climbing trees, crawling into the caves of animals.

General McDougall, a New Yorker, leading a regiment of New Yorkers, mostly placid blue-eyed Dutch boys, did manage for a while to stem his end of the retreat. He got his men to stand at a stone wall, but when the British sent a company of light dragoons to dislodge them, they broke and fled much the same as the others.

And again, there was darkness with its saving grace.

The Virginia squire was becoming hard. He didn't slump in his saddle, nor did all the world fall away in a broken ruin. The change in him had been slow and painful; nevertheless it had happened. He had watched his men run away, yet all the emotion those around him could see was a more definite set in his jaw. Lines were forming, around his eyes, around his mouth, and something vastly more eruptive was happening within him. He had no sympathy for the tears of anger young Hamilton shed, nor for the rolling, resounding curses of the slow-witted and earnest Putnam.

"We're still here," he said of his army, as if in accomplishing that they had achieved more than the British.

"Except five hundred or so who have run away today," Lee reminded him.

"They'll come back," he said grimly. "When it's dark enough and quiet enough, they will come back."

And McDougall could only groan, "Those bastards, those dirty, cowardly bastards—"

"I don't blame them about the horse," the Virginian said evenly and judiciously. "They're not used to horses charging. They'll learn about cavalry. They'll learn that a man on a horse can die as quickly as a man on foot. They'll learn other things."

His faith was no longer exuberant; it was grim, it was becoming slightly terrible, and even old Putnam was afraid of the gathering ice in his grey eyes. From day to day, they, his aides, his friends, his enemies, could not perceive what was happening to the big, shy farmer from the Potomac, who had once thought of himself primarily as a fox-hunter and who had desired nothing more than the love of those around him; but they felt and saw the results, and sometimes they were afraid—and sometimes they were made happy with a desperate, lonely sort of pride. As for instance the time two days after the rout on Chatterton's Hill, when two of Rogers' Rangers were dragged into the Continental camp.

They were Westchester gentlemen brought face to face with one of their own kind, the foremost gentleman of Virginia, the aristocrat of the Potomac, the foxhunter; they, too, were foxhunters. A pink coat bound the three with chains that had been forged centuries ago, setting them up and over the world of little, frightened men; and therefore they swaggered a little until they began to realize what the stony set of his face meant. He asked them, "What are you?"

One was a handsome, tall, ruddy-faced blond man of thirty-five or so; he answered for the other, a thin-faced boy in a perfectly tailored suit of green buckskin.

"Captain Lacey of Major Rogers' Rangers, sir, and this is Lieutenant Albert."

"I don't know of a Major Rogers," the foxhunter said coldly.

They stared at him blankly.

"I know of a certain Rogers," the foxhunter said.

They waited, the older one cautiously feeling for an opening.

"And I hear he is an Englishman of sorts," the foxhunter went on. "But what are you?"

The older one blundered into this opening. "We hope and trust, sir, that you as a gentleman will give us the consideration that is our due. We are fortunate in addressing you instead of those —" he saw his blunder and stopped.

"What were you going to say?"

"Nothing."

"What were you going to say? What were you going to call my men?"

"Continentals, sir."

"We call ourselves Americans," the foxhunter said evenly. "You are not an Englishman, and I don't know what to call you, and that buckskin you wear, gentlemen, is less than dirt. I don't consider it a uniform and you were within our lines, so properly I have the right to hang you. But you called upon my consideration as a gentleman. Sergeant, take them away and give them two hundred lashes apiece."

In this time, directly after the Battle of White Plains, the Continentals stood upon the brink of an abyss, their backs against the Hudson, their front crumbling and awaiting the final stroke by General Howe. Why General Howe never delivered that blow, the Virginian was not to know for many years to come, and even then he was not certain he had the true answer. Perhaps Howe could not believe that an army of thirteen thousand men would simply fall to pieces if he prodded at its front.

The Virginian knew that it would, light as the prodding might be; in his heart and soul, he knew that he had come to the end of his rope, the final end and the single end, not as at Brooklyn and Harlem, where there was the alternative of retreat, not even as on that terrible Sunday morning when a whole division of his army, numbering thousands, had fled headlong through New York; but the end where there was no retreat.

There was no retreat, and this was the end, and if he dared to move his cowed Yankees the British would leap on them and destroy them. He had alternatives, but they were all the choices of a condemned man before the trap is sprung. His army had been split into three parts, one at Fort Washington in New York, one across the Hudson at Fort Lee, and the third part here in Westchester; and each of the parts was attempting with all the ability of the individual members, to desert him.

And what he did was the whole key to the change that had occurred inside of him: he went about his task as though he were a victor among victors; he inspected regiments; he punished deserters; he wrote letters to Congress; and in the evening with his men around him, he drank Madeira and toasted, "The Congress, gentlemen, and a quick and happy victory."

There was a certain peace of mind in knowing so surely the road he had to travel, not the length of it, but the single direction it took.

PART FOUR

JERSEY

12

THE FORT CALLED "WASHINGTON"

On THE bright, cold morning of November 12, 1776, the Virginia foxhunter stood on the shore of the Hudson and watched the brown-skinned Marblehead fishermen expertly ferry a brigade of his troops across to Jersey. Life was good and the wind was in his face and two mugs of hot flip were under his belt, along with cakes and honey and a pot of tea, enough to bulge comfortably and give him the good, morning content of a man who has eaten well. He had read a letter from his wife and written one to her, and the night before with three bottles of Madeira inside of him, he had danced for three hours straight. It added up—with the sun and the wind and the crisp leaves and the cold, glistening belly of the river.

If he had love, admiration, respect for any body of his men, it was for these same Marblehead fishermen, for all their dispassionate New England efficiency and for all their very apparent contempt of him and his kind. He was as foreign to them as they were to him; he could imagine them gawking at the gracious Georgian beauty of Mount Vernon and going into their cold Yankee rage at the sight of his Negro slaves in the fields. They had their ways, and their ideas were set; his own ideas had never been set, and he envied men who could go straight about their work with such certainty of purpose. Again, in a way, he was afraid of them, knowing that with five thousand like them he could sweep the British back into the sea—but not knowing, not even able to imagine what five thousand of them would do after they had finished with the British.

This morning he was in no mood to examine the future. His troops were on their way to Hackensack, in Jersey, where he had established his new encampment, and he looked forward to a brisk ride down the Palisades to Fort Lee. Behind him, dispositions had been nicely made, and it seemed that his position was better than it had ever been before. Two thousand men under General Heath were holding the upriver Hudson highlands, and another five thousand were in Westchester under the command of General Charles Lee. It was true that there had been a good many desertions, but in all he was wonderfully fortunate; for having had Washington completely at his mercy after the Battle of White Plains, Howe had hesitated to attack. The Virginian found no explanation of this course; it was so obvious to him that Howe had only to launch a frontal attack to have the whole American army fall to pieces. Like a doomed man, the Virginian had waited and waited, composing himself for an end that did not come. A few reports came to him from the British camp while Howe frittered away his opportunity; some said that Howe had not yet recovered from the terrible, bloody memory of Pell's Point; others speculated that he did not dare to end the revolt summarily, since feeling in England for the rebels grew higher and higher, and there was a possibility that the spark might leap across the Atlantic and set fire to the British Isles. But all of this was speculation; and when finally Howe turned around and marched his army back to New York, the Virginia squire knew that he was saved. But he had not and never would have any clear notion of why destruction had avoided him.

By now, he already had more than four thousand men in Jersey. When he had established himself at Fort Lee and given the fishermen the job of drawing off the garrison of Fort Washington, in Manhattan, he would have almost eight thousand men on either side of the river — and be in a position to execute a pincer movement against the British, who had been pinching him rather tightly.

All in all, it seemed that the tide had turned.

When they had crossed the river, the commander in chief received a salute from his troops and watched them march smartly away. They too were more cheerful, relieved at having the Hudson River between them and the English. He, himself, with only two of his staff, cantered down the cliff road toward Fort Lee.

All that day and that evening, the holiday spirit remained with him. At the house where they stopped to spend the night, a rambling Dutch farmhouse, there were two little girls, one six, the other eight. It was almost their bedtime when their shyness and the big Virginian's dignity had worn off, but an hour was left for him to sit in front of the dining-room oven and tell them stories while the loggerheads baked. He was not a good story-teller; for all that he lived outside of himself,

110

his lips wet with the wind of the whole world, he was not able to make a description alive nor an action exciting, merely stating sedulously:

"Six Indians were hiding in the woods and we had to shoot them to go through the woods, and then there were ten more Indians hiding up on a hill, whereupon we shot them—"

The little girls shivered, and the small one in his arms crawled closer, and what he said didn't matter at all, he was such a magnificent man, higher than a giant, with his wonderful blue jacket and his buff trousers, and shadows from the fire on the fascinating little pockmarks on his face. When the story was over, the eight-year-old said simply. "That was good. Papa says you're a good fighter, but you drink too much"—all with her curious Dutch accent.

"What?"

"Why do you drink so much?" the girl insisted sadly.

"Not too much. Not any more than anyone else."

"Papa said," the girl persisted, still very sadly, "that when you came here tonight, you would drink him out of house and home."

He reached Fort Lee about noon of the next day, and discovered to his amazement that instead of beginning to withdraw the troops from Manhattan Island, Greene had reinforced them. The Virginian said nothing until he had the handsome young Quaker alone in his tent.

"By God, Nathanael, what sort of damned insanity is this?"

"Insanity, sir?"

"Yes, insanity. Why didn't you make preparations to evacuate the fort? Why did you send more men into New York?"

"To hold the fort, sir."

"Hold it? It can't be held!"

"Good heavens, sir, why can't it be held? Because that damned renegade Englishman, Lee, told—"

"Greene!"

"I'm sorry, sir."

"It's not enough to apologize to me, General Greene," the big man said evenly. "I want you to understand now and for the future that General Lee is second in command to me in this army, and that his orders are deserving of all the respect—that a Yankee can muster."

Greene stared at him, and then shook his head dumbly. "My God, sir," he whispered, "What more can I say? Do you want me to kneel down at your feet? I will if you want me to." There was no mockery in his voice.

After that, after a minute or two of silence, the Virginian asked gently, "Do you think, Nathanael, that the fort can be held?"

"Forever!"

"Not forever. For a week, a month?"

"A month! Sir, please give us a chance! They've had New York, all of it their way; now only give us a chance."

"I'll give you a chance," he agreed.

Greene nodded, not trusting himself to speak.

That same evening, the big man rode west to where his troops were encamped at Hackensack, some five miles from Fort Lee at the top of the Palisades. At Hackensack, still crowing over the fine weather and the fact that the British army was some distance from them, the men were in good spirits, the more so since so many of them were Jersey men, and would no longer have to cross a mile-wide river if they decided to desert and go home. The mass of the Yankees had been left with Lee, and the slightly less-tattered Jersey men, eating better than they had for weeks and with no prospect of battle in the near future, had in some way come to the conclusion that they were a victorious army, a belief bolstered by the number of Passaic and Patterson girls who had already attached themselves to the new encampment. The troops clustered around the big man when he arrived, and cheered him more heartily than they had in weeks. Standing close to a cheerful, blazing fire, he told Knox about it.

"I like the looks of it, things were so much worse. They're better now. I was worried before because Nathanael pleaded to hold Fort Washington." He always said that name haltingly, feeling an almost childish pride in the fact that a place, a fortress of the republic, had been named for him, for an obscure Virginia farmer.

"You'll let him?" Knox demanded eagerly.

"Yes—but Lee—"

"Oh, damn Lee, sir! I'm sorry, forgive me, but you must let us fight, sir, you must!"

"Yes, if he can hold it, it may turn out to be a thorn in the side of Howe. Congress wants it held."

"Until hell freezes over, sir, believe me. We weren't beaten—we retreated, but we weren't beaten. Look at me, sir. I'm an officer of artillery, but where are my guns? In Brooklyn, in New York, at Fort Washington and at Fort Lee; but I swear to God, sir, that if I lose them all, it will be the same, we won't be beaten. We had no guns when we started—" The young bookseller was fairly dancing.

"Knox!"

"Yes, sir?"

"Go to bed," the big man said, somewhat morosely.

"Sir?"

"I said, go to bed," the big man repeated.

Puzzled, Knox stared at him, and then turned silently away; while the commander in chief began to walk through the sprawling, noisy camp. He walked slowly, with long, measured steps, his head bent forward slightly, his pale grey eyes barely open, barely reflecting the many lights of the fires. His long arms hung by his side, and though he looked straight ahead of himself as he walked, he was conscious of the thousand and one movements all around him, the buzz of talk that died into sibilant whispers at his approach, the laughing groups of men and those who were not laughing, the mumbling and grumbling, the songs, mournful, lonely, haunting Dutch and Scotch and Welsh airs that had lingered in the Jersey hinterland for a century, preserved as they had been in the old country where they had been sung for five centuries. He saw the disorder, the ragged tents, the unkempt, fat, back-country wenches who giggled and tried to hide from him, the pigs that rooted in the piles of waste, dumped anywhere and everywhere by the soldiers, who made no attempt to dispose of it, the stacked muskets and bayonets rusted so that they could only be melted off the barrels, the few skinny horses that pulled the creaking provision wagons, and the unprotected mounds of food and ammunition.

And as he walked, the gay elation of the past few days vanished, and he was filled with a sense of foreboding. It was only through constant contact that he could forget what manner of an army he led; let him go away for a day or two days, and he would see it with new eyes, as he was seeing it now, and he would fall victim to the old and terrible hopelessness. It was no use blaming Knox and the others, he told himself; they did the best they could. They were brave and gallant—yes, gallant—men, even if it was not the gallantry of a Virginia gentleman but the buffoonish clowning of shopkeepers and artisans.

He turned back to his tent, and there, by the light of two frolicking candles, sat down to write a letter to his wife. But when he had spread out the paper and dipped his pen in the ink, he found himself suddenly attacked by a fever-like wave of homesickness. It was so sudden, so absolute, so imperious that he let go of the quill and sank forward over the table, his face in his hands, his breath sighing between his fingers, his whole inward mind concentrated lushly and pitifully upon Mount Vernon. At that moment, as he had never before desired anything, he wanted to be back in his home, living the life he was made for, the life of a farmer and foxhunter, rising in the morning and eating his first breakfast alone in the kitchen, having two or three cups of good strong tea, riding out over the fields when they were still wet with the night's dew, cursing his spotted dogs good-naturedly and contemptuously, out of sight and hearing of anyone, raising a fox perhaps and chasing it for a mile or two until it escaped and left his dogs with their tongues hanging and their small minds puzzled, returning to his house full and brimming with life, having a second breakfast with Martha, who was pettish in the morning, not gloriously alive as he was, going over his accounts, a meticulous business he secretly loved, gloating over his past two weeks' winnings at cards, momentarily angry with a neighbor who got the best of him in a deal with pigs, welcoming guests for lunch, listening to good talk, eating good food, drinking good Madeira, sipping good brandy, lounging on the veranda for an hour of politics, out over the fields and then two hours of cards before the change for dinner—the way a man lived, not too easily, yet not hard, bored a great deal with his own content and wanting an adventure, a single, great, glorious adventure.

He sat for a long time with his face in his hands.

Late in the afternoon of the third day after he had arrived at Hackensack, a messenger from Fort Lee drove into the encampment on a lathered and winded horse. The messenger brought news that the British had attacked Fort Washington and that General Greene thought General Washington should know the state of affairs.

"And what is the state of affairs?" the big man demanded.

"I should say very good, sir. I should say the garrison is most enthusiastic. There is no doubt that they have already taken a heavy toll of the British."

For just a moment, the big man stared at the sweating, grinning messenger, and then he strode abruptly to his horse, mounted, and cantered off along the road to the Palisades. When he reached the edge of the high cliff overlooking the Hudson River and Manhattan Island, it was already dark. From the direction of Fort Washington came the occasional dull boom of a cannon, and now and again little fingers of light reached out of the darkness. Certainly, it did not look like a general attack, and he could hear no sound of musketry.

"Where is General Greene?" he asked Major Galloway, who had been left in charge of Fort Lee.

"Across the river, sir."

"And General Putnam?"

"Also at Fort Washington, sir."

For about fifteen minutes the big man paced back and forth, nervously and anxiously, peering at his watch again and again, straining his ears to hear some sound from across the Hudson, and his eyes to make out what might or might not be a battle. At last he could stand the suspense of waiting no longer, and he demanded of the major, "Is there a boat down at the landing?"

"I believe so, sir."

"Then get me someone with a torch to light the way down. I'm going across."

"Yes, sir — if you think it advisable."

"Damn it, major, I don't require your doubts concerning the advisability of my actions."

Meekly, the major crept away, returning with a militiaman, who carried a blazing pine torch. In its ruddy, dancing glare, the big man climbed and stumbled down the twisting path to the boat landing. He woke a sleeping boatman, climbed into the sternsheets, and pushed off from the shore himself. He sat in the stern, and when the oars poked at the water, roared at the boatman, "Damn you, row!"

They were halfway across the river, when the Virginian heard the creak of oarlocks and the lap of water. "Who's there?" he called.

"American!"

"American!" his own boatman shouted back.

"Hello, who's there?"

"Nathanael, is that you?" the Virginian asked.

The two boats drifted together, the boatmen hooking the gunnels, and the big man was able to make out General Greene and General Putnam. Putnam's lined and rather sour face nodded in greeting, while Greene grinned happily and reached across the boat to take the hand of his commander.

"I'm glad to see you, sir," he said. "I'm terribly glad to see you."

"What happened over there?" the Virginian demanded impatiently. "Have the British attacked?"

"Not yet, sir, not yet — just shooting a cannon or two to keep us on edge, and we had a poke or two back at them to keep them on the same edge. No, they haven't attacked, sir, and just listen to this — it's glorious, I tell you, sir, it's glorious. Howe sent in a man to ask Magaw for surrender; you know, sir, the way they drawl and look down their noses, some matter like this: 'Sir, Colonel Magaw, General Howe offers you gentle and generous terms of surrender; but if he should be forced to carry the place by assault' — assault, sir, *Your fort* by assault —"

"Go on, Nathanael."

" 'If he should be forced to carry the place by assault, then he cannot promise to hold back his men from extremities.' 'Assault?' Magaw answered, talking down his nose the same way. 'Really, sir,' Magaw said, 'I can't believe that His Excellency would carry out a threat so unworthy of himself and the British nation ' And then, sir, Magaw said, 'But give me leave to assure His Excellency that, impelled by the most glorious cause that mankind ever fought in, I am determined to defend this post to the last man, sir—to the last man. Tell His Excellency that.' "

"I never suspected Magaw of such a turn for rhetoric," the Virginian murmured.

"But isn't it glorious, sir? I must write it down and send it to Knox for a time when the history we are making is already made."

Putnam coughed, and the foxhunter said, "Tell me about the fort and leave go of the rhetoric for a while, Nathanael. I'm worried—"

"No, please, sir, don't worry; it's all right. We have them this time, and they'll batter their heads against us until they've broken them. I tell you, this is the turning point we've been waiting for."

The Virginian shook his head wearily, but Putnam said, "I think Nathanael's right, sir."

"We've had to retreat before," the foxhunter murmured. "There's no retreat out of there. How many men are in the garrison?"

"Almost three thousand by now. They'll do the retreating, not us. I give you my word, sir."

"We'll see, Nathanael. I wanted to go across tonight, but I suppose—" He shrugged. "Boatman, row back to Jersey." He sat in the boat, silent, humped over, until they reached the landing under the Palisades.

The geography of the tiny finger of land that comprises northern Manhattan Island is neither complex nor difficult to understand, the finger itself being less than a mile in width and no more than four miles from its northern tip to where it broadens into the fat belly of the island. In peculiar American terminology, it is called a panhandle.

The defense of this panhandle had been obvious to the foxhunter, to Greene, to Knox, to Magaw—to any one of the amateur soldiers who had wanted so desperately to hold on to some little bit of Manhattan; not only obvious but enticing. The place seemed made for defense; it appeared destined for a last-ditch stand; it spoke aloud to the reeling, beaten revolutionists:

"Come to my bosom and fly your colors; and so long as man remains alive, I will stand by you."

Deep in their hearts was plain knowledge of the futility of their struggle. The officers and the men under them wanted to stop running; they wanted a place where they could stand and fight for a cause, which if hopeless, was nevertheless all they possessed. They wanted to take a toll; they wanted to hit back; their thoughts said:

"God damn you, come and get me! Here I am! I can't run away, even if I want to. But every step you take, you'll pay for! Every rock you climb, you'll make slippery with your blood. This won't be easy; this won't be Brooklyn and New York and White Plains all over again! If you want the wolf, come and dig him out of his lair! And it won't take you a day nor a week nor a month."

That was the way their thoughts went, and their resolutions. They had had enough of running away. Some three thousand of them primed their guns and set about holding the panhandle until hell froze over.

From the Hollow Way, which had been the line of the American army in Manhattan, and which was some five miles from the northern tip of the island, the ground sloped up steadily for about three miles, and then divided into two ridges, one extending along the Hudson River and the other along the Harlem River. These two ridges were about the same height, each a few hundred feet above sea level, each with rocky, steeply sloping sides, and between them the land sloped down sharply to Spuyten Duyvil Creek, the trickle of water which connected the Harlem River with the Hudson. The two ridges did not extend to the end of the panhandle, but stopped abruptly just a mile south of the creek. A deep gash furrowed the panhandle at this point, and north of it was a third hill, just about the same height as the other two.

Each of these three hills was magnificent from the point of view of defense, yet each suffered from the same deadly drawback—that if one went, the other two would become untenable. The fort named after the foxhunter, the single and splendid tribute of an obscure provincial confederation to an obscure farmer, sat on the Hudson River ridge, a small stone structure which at its best could hold two or three hundred men comfortably. As with Fort Lee, across the river, a steep and rocky path led from the fort to the boat landing below.

Colonel Magaw, who was in charge of the fort's defense, had realized how difficult it would be to hold Fort Washington and no more than the fort. Two or three hundred determined men behind the stone bastions might hold the place for a week or two; but cut off and surrounded, they would sooner or later be starved out, and all the while they would be hammered by cannon placed on the other two hills. Knowing that and knowing the fort's drawbacks, Magaw had evolved the grandiose scheme of holding the whole panhandle until such a time as the Virginian might feel strong enough to attack New York and drive the British back into the sea. He had talked Greene and Putnam into his way of thinking, and had got them to pour more and more men into northern Manhattan.

On the night that Greene and Putnam rowed across the Hudson River, Magaw had three thousand men under his command, and these men had already been placed in their various defensive positions. Spreading a map in front of the two generals, he triumphantly pricked off position after position, challenging them to find a loophole in his scheme.

"Here" — he explained, drawing his finger across the panhandle, some two miles to the south — "are the Pennsylvanians, eight hundred of them. Let the lobsters come up from the south, and we'll have a merry welcome for them." Magaw was a little man, with bulging eyes and round cheeks — and a great awareness of his destiny. "And here" — he went on, pointing to the hill that overlooked Spuyten Duyvil — "are the Marylanders. Riflemen," he explained, as if they had not know that. "Baxter is over the Harlem, with his militia, but they won't come that way. Anyway, I think I've covered everything."

"No one covers everything," Putnam said sourly.

And Greene remarked, "It will be all right, if we don't run away."

He was getting old, thought the foxhunter. He had awakened in the cold morning full of little aches and pains and discomforts, and when he tried to raise his left arm, the joint groaned and stabbled like fire. If he had been at home, Martha would have sent him to bed and kneaded the shoulder herself with smelly bear grease; but here he had to pretend to ignore it. If Billy were here, then perhaps he could confide his woe to the Negro; but Billy was at Hackensack, and the Virginian could have no more called in an orderly and asked him to massage his shoulder than he could have walked naked in front of his assembled men.

He dressed alone, awkwardly, standing barefoot on the ground in his long woolsey underwear, pulling on his clothes, struggling with his high black boots, groaning as he bent the arm to get into his shirt first and then his jacket. His toilet was messy and miserable, and no matter what he did, he felt unkempt; and when he left his tent, it hurt him to hold himself straight.

Though it was hardly light, Greene and Putnam and Mercer were already dressed and waiting for him; and he got some small satisfaction out of reflecting that they had slept no better than he had. It was a constant drain on his conscience to know that he was so troubled with countless fears when all the men on his staff were dashing and gallant, never troubled by the dark horror of death or mutilation. He sat down with them to have his breakfast, but throughout the meal he said nothing and hardly ever lifted his eyes from his plate. He knew that if he said anything, it would be in the way of worried supposition about the three thousand men on the other side of the Hudson. So he sat at the camp table with his back toward Manhattan, and all through the meal resisted the impulse to glance behind him — although he knew well enough that the Manhattan shore was shrouded in mist.

His silence tripped and presently halted the conversation of the others. Mercer, never loquacious, said practically nothing, and Putnam, whose puffy face was rather yellow, complained morosely about his liver. Greene kept quiet until the meal was almost done, and then he observed, "See, sir, the mist is lifting!"

"It usually does," the big man agreed, restraining himself from an impulse to glance over his shoulder.

"The flag is flying," Greene nodded with proud emphasis. The flag was a battered old rattlesnake banner that had been dyed a violent purple, but Magaw was inordinately proud of it, and swore he would keep it at mast until the cloth rotted.

Mercer agreed in respectful silence. He was one of the strangest characters in all that strange army, a withered Scotsman and old professional soldier, silent, gloomy most of the time, but with a fire of rebellion burning deep and quiet inside of him. He never spoke of liberty, of freedom, of any of the catchwords; his purpose was never verbal, and the only hint of his thoughts was a certain glitter in his grey eyes.

After breakfast, the commander in chief embarked on a tour of inspection, striding purposefully through the camp, finding fault with a dozen things, which was never difficult, giving two captains and a lieutenant a bitter tongue-lashing because they had not shaved for three days — in all killing an hour before he allowed himself to return to the cliff-edge and look at the farther shore of the Hudson. Greene, who had been waiting, handed him a spyglass, and the big man had to concentrate on the steadiness of his hands as he focused it. In the glass, a doll's world came to life, the little star of the fort, the flag rip-

119

pling in the sunlight, the tiny figures of men. It all seemed so secure and so orderly that for the first time in three days his mind was put at ease.

"It's a good fort, sir, believe me," Greene said.

The big man shrugged and continued to stare through the glass.

By eleven o'clock there was still no sign of a British attack. The Virginian felt he could no longer control himself if he did nothing but stand here on the wrong side of three-quarters of a mile of water, waiting and watching. He knew that his presence at the fort could serve no purpose, yet he had to indulge in some sort of action. He remarked casually to Greene, "I think, Nathanael, that we ought to go across and see how things are."

"Good, sir! You'll be pleased. Will you want General Putnam?"

"Let him come if he wishes to."

On their way to the boat landing, they were joined by Mercer, who gloomily asked whether he alone would have to watch a "leetle show" from the wrong side.

"You can come, general. There's nothing likely to happen over here."

They reached the foot of the Palisades and climbed into a boat. The two Marblehead men at the oars, quite overwhelmed to have four generals to ferry across, spat on their hands and rowed manfully, cocking their ears for juicy bits of gossip that might be repeated later. But all they got was a mumbled and tiresome complaint from Putnam about the state of his liver and an old Highland recipe from Mercer: a cup of barley, the jelly of a sheep's hoof, and four fingers of whiskey, divided in three parts for three meals—said to be very good for the liver. Greene said nothing, and the commander in chief kept his eyes on the Manhattan shore.

They were halfway across the river, when a furious roll of cannon split the air, the sound like a blanket of thunder all over the shore and the river.

"They're at it!" Greene yelled, and the big man snapped at the boatmen.

"Damn you, why don't you row?"

"We be rowing," they answered stolidly.

As the boat grounded, the Virginian leaped into the water and led the rush up the steep path to the fort. Halfway there, his heart was pounding, his breath coming in short gasps. He forced himself to go more slowly, knowing that he should present a calm and unworried

appearance when he entered the fort. As he neared the fort, Magaw
bounded out to meet him, saluting and grinning, raising his voice to
talk over the rumbling cannonade.

"Well, they're at it, sir!"

"I can see that, colonel. Are your men holding?"

"By God, sir—they'll hold until doomsday! Of course, the fort itself
isn't under fire yet—your fort, if I may say so, sir, in the manner of a
toast. They're butting against the outposts, and they'll butt a long
while before they knock them off those two hills. We're prepared to sell
our lives dearly, every one of us, to the last man."

"I don't want lives sold," Washington said wearily. "I want the fort
held."

"It will be, sir."

"I want that path down to the boat landing defended very actively,
both as a line of communication with Fort Lee and as a means of
retreat if that should be necessary."

"It won't be necessary, sir!"

"Nevertheless, Colonel Magaw, I want you to understand the importance of keeping that path open. If necessary, after darkness tonight, if
we find the tide of battle not sufficiently in our favor, you may call
upon me for reinforcements."

Magaw could not refrain from rhetoric. "Believe me, sir," he said,
"my only desire is to give them such a knock that they will go reeling
back out of New York and free our beloved soil of their presence."

"Holy God," Putnam said, "he's worse than Knox."

The Virginian shrugged and walked into the fort. The men cheered
him. They were Southerners, most of them, and they yelled that it was
time they were given a chance instead of the God damned Yankees.
They waved their muskets and their hats and they danced on the battlements, yelling:

"Come on, you bloody lobsters! Come and get it! Come on, you God
damned bloody lobsters!"

I was not the sort of thing the foxhunter approved of, not when
there might be cold and bitter work to be done in just a few hours.
There was no reason for them to feel certain that the fort was invinci-
ble, that it would be a lark to defend it. He reflected that these men
had been too long outside of his command, but he also realized that
this was not the time for discipline.

He climbed onto the battlement himself and looked through his spyglass at the two hills that were under attack. On the one directly across
from him and facing the Harlem River, he could make out men mov-

ing through the woods, but as yet there was no sight of the British scarlet or the Hessian green. The other hill, the one to the north, was too heavily wooded to reveal anything of action that might be progressing there. From south of the fort, where the eight hundred Pennsylvanians were attempting to hold the whole neck of the panhandle, there came the sound of intense musketry, but there too the battle was hidden by a screen of trees.

He had been on the battlements for about ten minutes when Greene climbed up beside him and said somewhat nervously, "Sir, I think we should be going now."

"Why?"

"No one believes more strongly than I that this place can be defended, but if they should cut that path to the river, you may have to be here for a week or a month."

"I was determined to see some of the action, Nathanael."

"Please, sir. I will remain here if you want me to."

The big man shrugged; there was good sense in what Greene proposed. "We'll all go off now," he agreed, "and have some dinner across the river. If we wish to, we can return tonight."

Before he went, he shooks hands with Magaw, who clasped his big hand fervently and promised again to hold the fort for six months, if that had to be.

As they got into the boat, the commander in chief twisted around to look at the fort again.

"What is it, sir?" Greene asked.

"Nothing."

And Putnam said, "They're too damned sure, too damned sure."

They all sat facing the Jersey shore, except for the two boatmen, who now that they had been given no orders to hurry pulled slowly, with long, powerful sweeps, a rhythm, now, now, now—until suddenly it was broken, and with his oar poised in the air, the boatman nearest the commander stared back at the shore they had left, popeyed. And so, slowly, the foxhunter, Greene, Putnam, and Mercer turned around, and the boat, loose on the tide, began to swing broadside. And they didn't speak because what they saw was the impossible and incredible, the place they had just left, the boat landing occupied by a guard of redcoats and a long file of redcoats climbing up the path to the fort, the path that would be kept open, that had to be kept open, come what might.

The boat rocked, a little less than halfway out on the Hudson, but far enough out for them to observe the whole sweep of the shore of the panhandle, the meadows that led up to Fort Washington from the south and the big wooded hill to the north. From the north, men were slipping and sprawling headlong down the hill, in a frantic effort to get back to the fort before they were cut off by a division of redcoats marching through the gorge with beating drums and flying banners, the Continentals unaware that they were already cut off by the British who had taken the path and the boat landing.

The big man reached out, and someone—afterwards, he never knew who—put the spyglass in his hand.

In the south, it was more horrible. The Hessians were there, attacking the eight hundred Pennsylvanians, and the Pennsylvanians were running, and the Germans were running too. The big green-clad Jagers were having a field day. Over all the other noises of battle floated their wild warcry.

"Yonkee! Yonkee!"

The Pennsylvanians ran as if all the devils of hell were behind them. Many were Germans themselves, simple peasant folk who had come to America many years ago to put the Prussian specter behind them; but here were the terrible green-shakoed Jagers, with their long broad-blade bayonets, come three thousand miles to inflict their vengeance, yelling as they cut into the backs of the Pennsylvanians, spitting them like pigs. For the four generals in the boat, it was near and real and tragic, lit by sunlight the way a theater stage is lit by footlights; and they could do nothing but sit and watch the slaughter.

And as if the Jagers knew that four generals of the Continental army were watching, the performance became more terrible. The Pennsylvanians were flanked; they were butchered; they were pinned against trees; they were driven screaming into the river, while the Hessians hung over the bank and pot-shotted them.

Putnam began to curse. He stood up in the boat, roaring, "You bastards! You dirty bastards! You filthy, murdering bastards! God damn you! God damn you! God damn you!"

Greene put his face in his hands and began to sob.

Mercer whispered, "The poor bonny, bonny lads."

And one of the Marblehead fishermen said, "The Lord is my light and my salvation; whom shall I fear? The Lord is the strength of my life; of whom shall I be afraid? When the wicked, even mine enemies and my foes, came upon me to eat up my flesh, they stumbled and fell—"

The foxhunter said nothing, his face so white that the pockmarks

123

stood out like scars of the damned.

The boat, swung broadside by the tide, swayed and tilted, while little whitecapped waves lapped at its hull. The Palisades, covered with autumn colors, stood like a wall of flaming glory, and all the broad beautiful Hudson was splashed with golden sunlight.

The second act now began. All the outposts, all the carefully planned defenses devised by Magaw, were crumpling; and the Continentals fled toward the tiny fort that could hold no more than two or three hundred persons. They scrambled up the rocky sides of the gorge to the north, they spilled out of the meadows to the south, and they fled from their lines on the hill over the Harlem River. Some of this the men in the boat could see, and some of it was hidden from them; but the whole tragic purpose of what was happening was evident enough. More and more men poured into the fort, five hundred, a thousand, fifteen hundred, two thousand. They were packed in like cattle, unable to move, unable to sight a gun, unable to fire a cannon for fear of killing a hundred of their comrades—and still more Continentals came, clawing over the stone walls.

At last a point was reached where the fort could hold no more, where the panic-stricken late arrivals could not reach the walls through the press of bodies, where they fell back and made a second wall of human flesh.

There was never a question of defense. Like a ripe plum, almost three thousand men of the American army fell into the lap of the British. The net tightened. The grinning, triumphant Hessians swarmed in from the south, the light infantry breasted the eastern cliffs, and close-ranked redcoat troops marched stolidly up from the river. And from the north, the dragoons pushed their panting horses over the wooded hillside.

In another hour, it was all over; the purple rattlesnake flag hauled down and the British Jack up in its place.

The big man lowered his spyglass, pressed it together, and in a harsh whisper told the boatmen, "Row across—"

Greene couldn't look at him. The handsome young Quaker sat hunched over, his arms hanging limply, his whole body racked with sobs.

Putnam had become an old, old man. When he lifted a hand, it shook violently; when he tried to speak, his voice cracked and broke;

when he turned to the foxhunter, his face bore the deeply grooved imprint of pain.

"My fault—" he was trying to say.

Greene looked up.

"My fault," Putnam repeated, with miserable insistence.

"No, no," Greene said brokenly. "I wanted it, I wanted the fort to be held—all the time I wanted that."

The Virginia foxhunter said, "You, General Greene, and you, General Putnam, and you, General Mercer—when you go ashore at Fort Lee, you will remember that you are officers in my army, you will remember that you have a duty both to yourselves and your men, and you will strive to present an appearance compatible with your position."

Knyphausen, the Hessian, with his grinning Jagers behind him and in front of him, clearing a path, pushed into the fort.

"Wo ist Euer Hauptmann?"

The Continentals, pressed back at bayonet point, stared sullenly.

"Euer Hauptmann!" the Hessian roared.

A trembling backwoods Pennsylvania German answered, "Dort," pointing to Magaw, who stood with the unseeing eyes of a man destroyed, body and soul.

"Er spricht Deutsch," Knyphausen smiled, adding, with all promise for the future, "Schurke!"

Magaw stepped forward, head nodding dully.

"Wie heisst Er?"

Magaw looked around him slowly, at the Jagers, at the bayonets, at his packed, beaten men.

"Wie heisst Er?" Knyphausen repeated.

Through his misery, Magaw comprehended the intent, if not the meaning of the words. "Colonel Magaw," he whispered.

"Sein Rank?"

Magaw nodded helplessly, and Knyphausen, pointing to Magaw's sword, barked, "Hundsfott, ged er den Degen!"

Magaw slowly shook his head, while the Jagers roared with laughter.

"Den Degen," Knyphausen repeated.

Now, at last, Magaw understood, and trying to keep himself straight, erect, as befitting an officer of the republic, unbuckled the sword that had been bought with the shillings of his friends and the pennies of their children, and presented to him in a little white church by a pastor who had enjoined him to go out and do his duty by God and his conscience. He handed it over, ashamed of the tears in his eyes, and Knyphausen, receiving it, nodded slightly and said, "So!"

Even the Jagers did not laugh now.

Greene, plunged in blackness, scraping the bottom of hell, had hidden himself in his tent where he would not have to present an appearance compatible with his position and lay on his bed, face down, trying to realize what a man does when he has ruined not only his own life but that of his best and dearest friend, and when he has almost single-handedly destroyed his country. For Greene could see no future; nor could he see the tattered, ragamuffin little army recovering from this devastating blow.

Whether others were to blame or not, he blamed himself, knowing that it was almost entirely on his insistence and pleading that the Virginian had overruled his own and Lee's decision to abandon the fort. And now all was gone: hope and future and the revolution itself. He thought to himself, if only he had died, if only he had remained at the fort, if only he had gone out with the Pennsylvanians and spitted himself on a Hessian bayonet, if only he could go into the darkness that had been the reward of so many better men—

He heard the sound of someone entering the tent, and rolling over, he saw the high, bent figure of the foxhunter silhouetted against the flap, but only a black shadow without expression or intent. He got off the bed and onto his feet.

"Sit down, Nathanael," the foxhunter said.

Greene sat down and waited, steeling himself for the inevitable blow.

"It's been hard, Nathanael, hasn't it?" the foxhunter said.

"Sir?"

"I think it will be harder."

Greene stared at the tall man, trying to make out his features, his expression, trying to glean some evidence of his feelings.

"This is only the beginning," the Virginian nodded gently. "God only knows where we are going or what we are making or what the end will be; but we go on."

"Sir?"

"Do you understand, Nathanael, we go on?"

Greene got to his feet, found the other man's hand, and held onto it as if it were the only real thing in a bizarre world of nightmares.

"Sir—" He was glad the foxhunter could not see the tears in his eyes.

"Always, Nathanael."

"Always, sir."

* * *

Down the dusty road to New York City marched 2818 men of the Continental army, strung out over a mile of the way, feet dragging, arms hanging, and faces miserably white under the dirt and blood. On crude stretchers they carried their wounded and dead, and inside of them were all the dead hopes of a nation. And as they marched the Hessian drums ruffled and the British fifes sang; the wind blew the brown autumn leaves from the trees and fluttered the rattlesnake flag, carried by a group of triumphant Jagers.

As they neared the city, more and more curious, laughing citizens packed the roadway and hundreds of trulls and sluts ran along the Continental line, shrieking their opinions of the defeated men, cursing and spitting at them, darting between the redcoats who tried to fend them off. Small boys showered the Continentals with clobs of dirt and rocks, and they began the cry that was presently taken up by all the citizens:

"Where is Washington? Where is Washington? Where is Washington? Show us Washington! Who is the great George Washington? Which one? Where is he? Show him to us! Show us the rich man! Show us the richest man in America!"

They chorused: "A hunting we will go, a hunting we will go, we'll catch a fox and put him in a box, and then we'll let him go."

"Washington!" they demanded.

"Show us Washington!"

"Who caught the fox?" they sang. "Who caught the fox? Who caught the fox?"

They swirled around every officer who wore the buff and blue of his commander, laughing and screaming.

"Washington! Washington!"

Again and again, the redcoats beat them off, and again and again they were back with "Give us Washington—we want to celebrate his great victory?"

The fifes and rums of the Jagers took up the tune of *Yankee Doodle*, and the trulls sang:

> *Yankee Doodle went to London,*
> *Riding on a pony,*
> *Stuck a feather in his cap,*
> *And called it macaroni. . . .*

Over the noise of all this, a British quartermaster sergeant was trying to report to his colonel on the spoils, reading monotonously:

"146 of cannon pieces.

12,000 of shot, shell and case.
2800 of muskets.
900 of pikes.
1400 of bayonets (bent and rusty, a shame to see, sir).
400,000 of cartridges.
270 of swords—" and adding:

"Sorry, sir, this blood uproar—"

Walking on the high cliff of the Palisades, that night, he held it all inside of himself, the bereaved, the lonely, the terrified; he who had failed and always would fail, a dull Virginia farmer, a man who held water and sand in his fingers, but never anything solid or substantial, a man who had loved the wife of his best friend and held the love inside of him, like a charge of explosive, and then had seen her go away to add hopelessness to pain, a man who had loved an idiot stepdaughter and then kneeled by her bedside, pleading and whimpering for her not to die, a clown without wit or laughter, a clown without grace or hope of salvation.

13

HOW THEY WENT INTO JERSEY

RIDING from Hackensack to Fort Lee, a few days after the British capture of Fort Washington, Henry Knox sought for words to say to the tall man beside him. Knox had been at Hackensack when the fiasco at Fort Washington occurred, and the first definitive news of it he had was a note from Greene, a confused, hopeless confession. Knox liked Greene, as a man and as a friend—aside from the fact that the two of them, along with Mifflin, Putnam and Mercer, constituted almost all the support the commander in chief had. Now Knox wanted to say something in defense of Greene.

"A man makes a mistake which any man could make," he began.

"Sir?" The Virginian glanced at him curiously.

"Any man, I mean, sir, any man. I had a note from Nathanael, and my God, sir, I wonder that he hasn't killed himself—"

"Harry, don't be a damned fool!"

The tall man rode on, looking straight ahead, and Knox, feeling he had said too much already, could find no more to better it. He was not an imaginative person; he had to look a fact in the face, and the fact now, to all intents and purposes, was that the revolution had finished itself. Even a well-trained, well-supplied army the size of this could not stand the shock of the loss of three thousand men with supplies, guns, ammunition; and they were not a well-trained, well-supplied army.

"I'll stay," the bookseller thought to himself, wondering just how long it would be, whether three weeks or three months.

Putnam wasn't a young man like the others, but a Yankee farmer fifty-eight years old and not in the best of health, wanting peace and security, but security especially more than anything else on earth. There were no fires in him; he was old and dry, and he wanted a roof over his head.

For him, the reasons toward rebellion had been neither tangible nor furious. With his hired man he had been building a stone wall on his farm, his back aching as he chipped the rocks and set them in, his mind concentrated, if on anything, on that old New England dictum that good walls make good neighbors—when a rider had pounded up with news of what had happened at Lexington and Concord.

"I don't like it," Putnam said, shaking his head.

"You remember old Shep Featherlee, he's dead, they shot him."

"They shouldn't have done that," Putnam said, knowing already that old as he was his peace and security were both gone, that he would have to drag his aching bones somewhere and do something, not a rebel and not a democrat, but standing by the dictum that good fences make good neighbors. And here, now, a year and a half later, it had washed out, the revolution, the crazy comic-opera war, the dirty, frightened Yankees—and he wondered whether there was anything else but to go back to his farm and grow old and rotten inside.

A long time ago, not in months nor years, but as time goes, in changes of many things, they were organizing the militia in Rhode Island, and young Nathanael Greene had been made a general—by virtue of the book he was always reading, *Military Tactics as Practiced in Continental Lands, with a summary of those virtues which go into the making of a competent officer.* He had drilled the militia with the book under his arm, to the complete admiration of a knot of giggling, fascinated girls. He was handsome as a devil, only thirty-three, and he was a self-made man.

There was an old friend of his father's, a Quaker, who had taken him aside one afternoon when the drill was over, and said, "I would have a word or two with thee, Nathanael."

"Yes?" Greene still smarted from the fact that without being permitted to say a word on his own behalf, he had been disowned by the Quakers. Now he stood stiff and impatient in his new uniform.

"Thee are going to war, Nathanael?"

"Yes."

"And thee will make thy peace with they conscience?"

"I know what I have to do."

"Thee knows, Nathanael; but have thee considered that never since this world began came good out of evil."

"I'm not concerned with good and evil," he said, thinking of other things he might, but somehow could not, say to the old man, not the rights of man, the freedoms, the liberties, but the glorious adventure that promised a future without limit.

Now, thinking back over the months to what that old Quaker had said, seeing no future without limit, but instead one sharply defined and tragically proscribed, he tried to make for himself some plans, some intentions; he tried to relate himself once more to the Virginian and to the army of liberty.

Reed, the adjutant, sitting in front of a fire at Hackensack after the foxhunter had ridden away with Knox, thought about the past and the present and found nothing to hope for in the tall, awkward, blundering Virginia farmer. It seemed to him that he was living through the more or less historic moment when a movement dissolves, and his delicate fingers crept anxiously around the veins and muscles of his neck. Hanging would not be pleasant; and in the flames every wisp and twist of fire took the shape of a gallows.

A little while before, he had seen five hundred Vermont farmers march calmly out of the encampment, not as deserters, but as clear-headed Yankees who knew that the jig was up and were going home while their heads were still on their shoulders. They were the last of the Yankees on the west shore of the Hudson, and behind them they left only sullen, discontended midlanders, Pennsylvania and Jersey men.

Reed sighed, rose, and went to his tent. He took out quill and ink and paper, and began to write, addressing himself to General Charles Lee:

". . . I do not mean to flatter or praise you, at the expense of any other; but I do think it is entirely owing to you that this army and the liberties of America, so far as they are dependent on it, are not entirely cut off. You have decision, a quality often wanting in minds otherwise valuable, and I ascribe to this our escape from York Island, King's Bridge and the Plains; and I have no doubt, had you been here, the garrison of Mount Washington would now have composed a part of this army; and from all these circumstances, I confess, I do ardently wish to see you removed from a place where there will be so little call for your judgment and experience, to the place where they are likely to be so necessary. Nor am I singular in my opinion; every gentleman of the family, the officers and soldiers generally, have a confidence in you. The enemy constantly inquire where you are, and seem to be less confident when you are present. . . ."

When Knox and the Virginian arrived at Fort Lee, Greene had alarming news for them. About six thousand British soldiers had crossed the Hudson five miles north of Fort Lee and were already advancing inland in a broad circle which was intended to cut off the fort and surround the encampment at Hackensack.

"They want to make a whole end of us," Greene said bitterly but hopelessly. "They know they can do it, and by God, I see no way to stop them."

"Have you started to evacuate the fort?" the Virginian demanded.

"How can we evacuate? We have no horses, no wagons. I thought if we could hold them off for a time—" He and Knox stared at each other, and then Greene said helplessly, "My God, where will the end be?"

"Evacuate the fort," the tall man said.

"My God, sir, the tents, the provisions, the cannon—what are we going to do—"

"Evacuate the fort, General Greene. Immediately."

"And leave everything?"

"Everything."

"By tomorrow perhaps we could have horses for the cannon," Knox pleaded.

"Now!"

The foxhunter sat on his horse and watched the men stream out of the fort. They left behind them the tents standing, the big iron camp kettles cooking on the fires, the cannon primed and loaded. He rode behind them as they fled toward Hackensack; he drove them as a cattle herder drives stock. When they showed signs of slackening, stumbled or fell, he roared at them and whipped out them with his quirt. It was a wild and grotesque race, hundreds of men running, panting, walking, running again down the road to Hackensack. The birth of a nation became a foot race with a tall, pockmarked farmer bringing up the rear, and the audience was four Dutch children—who stood along the road and watched with charmed detachment, munching curds and bread—and a light dragoon who watched from a hill and then rode back to Lord Cornwallis to report.

"Too late, sir."

"They left the fort?"

"They're running down the road to Hackensack as if the devil himself were behind them."

He wanted his men counted, he told Knox.

"Sir?"

"Counted! My God, Knox, do I have to repeat an order seven times?"

"No, sir, only the desertions—"

"I'm not blind. I know there are desertions."

"But, sir—whole regiments."

"I want them counted."

It only took Knox a few hours to make the count. He came back and reported, "Two thousand, nine hundred and eleven, sir."

The tall man stared at him, and Knox said, "I'm sorry."

"You're sure?"

"I'm sure, sir."

And then the tall man nodded.

It rained as they plodded from Hackensack to Newark, not gently, but a strong, steady, cold pouring. It turned the road to mud, and there was no sound except the constant slop, slop, slop of their steps. They walked hunched over to protect themselves, their heads bent, their arms crooked around their muskets. The front ranks mashed the mud, those behind dug deeper, and when it came to the end of that mile-long column, the road was a bog. The foxhunter was at the head of the column, with Reed on one side of him and Putnam on the other; they were all three of them soaking wet, but Putnam, the old man, shot through and through with rheumatic pains, suffered most. Farther down the line, Greene straddled a sorry nag. Knox walked with Captain Hamilton and the fragment of artillery left them, while Mercer brought up the rear. Mifflin had gone the same day to Philadelphia, to plead with the frightened Congress for more men.

As they rode along, Reed asked the Virginian, "Where will we camp?"

"Newark, perhaps."

"And then retreat?"

The tall man shrugged.

"For how long?"

"I don't know."

"We can't retreat forever," Reed said.

"We can, I think. Almost forever."

"Where?"

"Pennsylvania."

"And if they follow us there?" Reed insisted.

"Westward."

"Where?"

"Across the Alleghenies."

It ended in a blank, a vast, unexplored wilderness, a million square miles of wild, dark forest that was incomprehensible to Reed, that meant pain and more pain to Putnam—but which, to the foxhunter, was only a continuation of a road that went in one single direction.

Whenever a horse could be found and spared, reasonably strong, sound of wind, it was dispatched with a pleading letter to General Charles Lee, who was in Westchester with more than five thousand New England Yankees. The letters were all of the same tone, begging Lee to come across the Hudson and join the Virginian with his army. But Lee had plans of his own.

Even for a mercenary soldier, there was a difference between thirty thousand dollars and destiny; and day by day, destiny had been coming closer and closer to Charles Lee. Destiny sat on his shoulders when he looked at himself in his mirror and contemplated his long, unattractive face; destiny was with him when he crooned at and caressed his pack of dogs. Destiny was in the letters he received from Joseph Reed and so many others who were dissatisfied and impatient with the blundering Virginian.

Lee had cast his fortunes with this crazy revolt of farmers and mechanics and tradesmen, and now the whole insane structure was tumbling. To run out would be too simple and too unprofitable; there was nothing waiting for him at the hands of the British, only contempt and dishonor. But suppose he were to rescue the almost inert carcass? Not mutiny; for one thing, he had been born and bred a soldier, and to mutiny against a mutiny was not only against his nature, it did not make sense. But suppose he waited patiently until the ripe fruit fell into his lap? The pattern of the future was clear enough; the foxhunter's army was dissolving like wet sand. It might hold together for ten days, for twenty days, for thirty days; thirty days was the limit he put on the business. Thirty days would see the army on the west shore of the Hudson gone, and the foxhunter in front of a British court martial. For his part, he had only to wait and to put off the Virginian with excuses, and in a month or less he himself would be commander in chief of the Continental armies. Certainly, there was no one else suited for the place, and certainly his army would be the only rebel army of any size left in America.

The Virginian could not forget the simile of the sand. Again and again, he stared at his big hands, fumbled with them, opened them and closed them. His hands were too big to hold a quill comfortably, even if he had been a scholar, even if he could have handled words, spelled them, reared them into intelligent sentences. It was agonizing pain for him to write, yet he sat in his tent at Newark, his candle burning, writing and writing, to Lee, to the terrified Congress, to the governors of the colonies, pleading for men and supplies, for cannon, stopping very often to feel at his neck and wonder what it meant for a man to be hanged for high reason and how it felt when the trap dropped and the rope tightened. Once he would have been sick with humiliation at the thought, but now it was merely a way for a man to end, and he managed to smile grimly as he rubbed his long, creased, sunburnt neck.

His thoughts now turned very often to Mount Vernon, to a part of his life that was drenched with sunlight, to little, fat Martha, to the white buildings and the green fields, memories harder to regain now that winter was approaching. It was strange, but the fact—which he now accepted—that he would never again see Mount Vernon, did not disconcert him too greatly. No one knew better than he how incredible his present position would have been to the man he was five, or even two years ago, the beaten commander of a fast-vanishing army, a lank bewildered man in a shapeless, faded uniform—sitting in a leaky, torn tent with a broken-spirited, dirty rabble of New Jersey and Pennsylvania boys around him. But he was not that man; that man couldn't have had such lonely, terrible pride, now the only thing left to him— pride in something that had not existed for him then and which he could not well put into words even now, which he could think of only as certain rights of man.

The tattered army fled out of one end of Newark as the British entered the other end of the town. Knox and Hamilton and a few others loaded a twelve-pounder with grape and flailed the streets with metal in a frantic bid for a few moments more of grace; and then they ran, leaving the cannon behind him. The whole army was running, sprawled out over the road that led to New Brunswick. The advance guard of the British was too small to attack the Continentals, but the dragoons climbed up on the Newark rooftops and cheered the army of liberty on its way.

Marching down to New Brunswick, they had their first brief flurry of snow. It had been summer when they began the retreat from Brooklyn Heights, and now it was almost the end of November, and they still wore the same clothing. If anything, they had less, for here and there along the way they had dropped this and that—a knapsack, a blanket, a jacket. Their stockings had long ago worn through, and there was no hope of replacements. Dirty toes poked through their shoes, and the shredded soles, where they still existed, were paper-thin. Wool, the manufacture of which had been forbidden in America, was almost unknown among them; their shirts were linen, their breeches homespun, neither material very warm nor lasting.

Winter came slowly, but now at last is was here, the damp, bone-penetrating winter of the Jersey flats, cold and wet and nasty; and on the muddy or frozen Jersey roads they began to leave their trademark, their insignia and single sign that marked them from all others for years to come. It was an ooze of blood, a stain from a thousand dragging feet, a dark spotting on the road that advertised: "Here walked the army of liberty"—for all who wanted to see or cared to read.

It was not only the cold. They began to feel the dull ache of starvation in their bellies, for the fields were gleaned clean, the cattle were driven away, and the barns were locked against them. The good Jersey citizens had taken a lesson from the good citizens of New York; this was not their army, this rabble, this bastardly conglomeration of foreigners, children, and madmen. The Jersey houses were shuttered tight, and the Jersey farmers had their guns loaded. More men of the army of liberty during that time died at barn doors than before the guns of the British; and deserters, tens and hundreds of deserters, made crazy with hunger, had their brains blown out when they approached houses to beg for food. How it had happened, so suddenly, the poor devils themselves did not know; themselves, they were Jersey and Pennsylvania men, yet suddenly they were an alien army in an alien land, every hand turned against them, every door closed to them, every window barred to them, and death waiting if they should venture only a few hundred yards from the main army.

As much as they wanted food and clothing, they wanted answers, desperately. There was only one man who had any; he was a small, ugly Englishman, with a long pear-shaped head. His name was Tom Paine.

He had fire in his eyes. He walked with them, with a musket slung over his shoulder, and the musket was almost as big as he was. He shared their food, and he sat around the fire with them. He was sick with them and lousy with them and tired with them and dirty with them. And he had answers.

He preached; they would have hated him if he were clean and hand-some, but he was dirty and ugly. They were never quite sure what he was; they couldn't make out whether he was an officer or a private; sometimes he was one and sometimes the other; he was neither when he stood up at the fire in the evening and said, in his curious Thetford accent, "Patriots, listen to me! Come and take comfort, for I swear to you there is comfort to be taken!"

They would come out of the corners and press around the fire where he stood, nudging each other, grinning a little self-consciously. "Tom Paine," they would tell each other, and nod.

He would single one out of the crowd and demand, "Patriot, what is your name?"

"Burk Hopper."

"Burk Hopper, why are you fighting with this army?"

"Damned if I know!"

"Then let me tell you—then let me tell you for a sign and a banner to lead you in the fray. Let me tell you that there is nothing on this earth more glorious than a man's freedom and no aim more elevated than liberty. . . ."

If it had been anyone in the world but Tom Paine, they would have laughed or cursed or killed him. But the words came out of Tom Paine like a prayer and a benediction, and there was fire in his eyes. They were martyrs, and he let them know it, drawing an inner stuff of fierce wonder from beneath their rags and filth. So they crouched and listened to him, picking their noses, spitting, pulling the little knotted hairs from their beards, nudging each other.

"That makes sense."

When he asked them, "Am I superstitious?"

"No! No!"

"Am I a damned Salem Puritan?"

"No!"

"Have I ever condoned the persecution of Jew by Christian, of Catholic by Protestant?"

"No!"

"Then you can believe me when I say to you as a man, only a man, no more than a man, that there is a God!"

Then they waited expectantly, knowing what was coming; for they had been told it a dozen times before.

"I say there is a God Almighty who will not give up his people to destruction by tyrants!"

Then there came an intellectual discord. "Now wait a minute, Tom—looka here. I ain't making to doubt you, but looka here at the lot of us, dirty, lousy—do we look like God is with us? Are we winning or are we losing?"

"I say that we are winning!" he thundered. "I say that should the ground open up and swallow us to the last man, we would still have won, for the world will not forget! We are a peaceful people, a humble people who took up arms only for the sacred rights of man! Be damned with who wins the battles on the field, my triumph is here!"—striking at his thin chest.

There was one night when he sat with a long, battered drum between his bony knees, tilted so that the top of it would catch light from the fire, using it as a desk and writing furiously, one devoted soldier beside him to hold the ink and another to sharpen the quills he bent and ruined in his rush of thought. In the place where he worked, a dead silence reigned; for word had gone around that Tom Paine was at it, and there was only the resonant mutter of the drum as the quill scratched back and forth.

As he wrote, more and more men crowded around the fire, until finally looking up, he saw the reddened burning eyes of more than a hundred fixed on him. Then he began to read what he had written, bending over the drumhead, his low voice beating back like a roll call down the ages:

"These are the times that try men's souls. The summer soldier and the sunshine patriot will, in this crisis, shrink from the service of their country; but he that stands it now, deserves the love and thanks of man and woman. Tyranny, like hell, is not easily conquered; yet we have this consolation with us, that the harder the conflict, the more glorious the triumph. . . . Heaven knows how to put a proper price upon its goods; and it would be strange indeed if so celestial an article as FREEDOM should not be highly rated. . . ."

And the foxhunter sent letters to Lee, pleading for help, for a thousand, for even a few hundred of his Yankees, for—if nothing else—the regiment of fishermen. Only now, with the desertions increasing daily in spite of Tom Paine's roaring, with the British hounding him day and night, did he realize what a store he had placed on Glover's men, what it would mean to know that there were six or seven hundred long-faced fishermen who would not run away. His councils of war were now almost wordless, himself facing Knox and Greene and Putnam and Mercer, the order of the day always the same, retreat; all that coupled with his desperate insistence that they should make counts so he might know how many or how few men were left.

At New Brunswick, two whole brigades of Pennsylvania men had announced their intentions to return home. He told Greene to have them surrounded by what loyal men he could muster and Knox to load a cannon with grape. He himself didn't know what he would do if the Pennsylvania men refused to lay down their arms. The midlanders began to walk, their bayonets level, their faces set with a desperation they had never shown against the British, and Greene looked helplessly at the Virginian. In that moment, the whole torn fabric of revolution might have dissolved in bloody ruin, but the tall man shook his head and the two brigades marched out of the encampment with no opposition.

The tall man couldn't retreat inside of himself. He pleaded with old Putnam afterwards. "What should I have done?"

"I don't know."

"Would you have fired?"

"I don't know. A man goes the way he sees a thing."

"And if he doesn't see anything—?"

He trusted Reed and was able to say to him, "You know how near the end we are, Joseph."

Reed nodded.

"I've written to Lee again and again. God knows what he's doing—he's a wise man and a good soldier, I can't criticize him. But he won't help us. Perhaps he can't help us.

There was a curious, half-frightened expression on Reed's face.

"Go to Burlington," the foxhunter said hopelessly. "Tell them we need men. Tell them it's the end, the real end this time; let them feel their necks the way I've been feeling mine."

A frightened Jersey legislature sat at Burlington. "It won't do any good," Reed protested.

"Go anyway, Joseph. It's the only straw I can catch at."

Reed had not been gone long when the letter came from Lee, addressed to Adjutant-General Joseph Reed. The dispatch rider gave it to the commander in chief, whose first impulse was to send it on after the adjutant. Then it occurred to him that this letter might contain the ray of hope he had been seeking. There was no letter for himself from Lee, and since Reed had been taking care of a good deal of the correspondence, this might serve the same purpose. He opened it and read.

"*My Dear Reed*—I received your most obliging, flattering letter; lament with you that fatal indecision of mind, which in war is a much greater disqualification than stupidity or even want of personal courage. Accident may put a decisive blunderer in the right; but eternal defeat and miscarriage must attend the man of the best parts, if cursed with indecision. The general recommends in so pressing a manner as almost to amount to an order, to bring over the Continental troops under my command; which recommendations, or order, throws me into the greatest dilemma from several considerations. . . ."

He continued to read, his mind blundering down a narrow black passageway, endless and without light. He stared at the salutation, repeating it to himself over and over again, *My Dear Reed, My Dear Reed*. He put his finger upon the signature: Charles Lee.

"'Lament with you,'" he whispered to himself.

He stood up, an effort which required almost all his strength, and paced miserably back and forth between the dirty curtains of his tent. He groped for the shaking world and tried to place it upon an even keel. Reed was his friend, his adjutant, his companion; Lee was a servant of his Congress. The letter was a false and rotten lie, forged to create dissension, served to him just at that precise time when Reed was away on a mission to Burlington.

"A damned lie!" he cried, and his voice brought the sentry's head into the tent.

"What is it, sir?"

"Nothing—"

His hands were shaking as he read the letter over a second time, wearing his glasses now, peering at every word. No—that painful

139

scrawl of Lee's could not be forged; he knew the handwriting as well as he knew his own. Lee had written this letter in answer to another letter of Reed's, "obliging, flattering." As his army dissolved, his officers plotted against him, the men he had loved and trusted; and now whom could he trust? Greene? Greene would die for him, but he might have said the same of Reed. Mifflin?why had he gone off to Philadelphia so eagerly? Who knew what was behind Mercer's brown mask? Putnam? Knox?

"Oh, my God," he whispered.

Hour after hour he paced back and forth in the narrow space of his tent, staring dumbly at his colored servant when the man came in to say that dinner was ready, nodding without hearing to a message Knox sent him, walking and walking and prodding with his bony shoulders at the walls which confined him. There was no salvation, no solution, only a direction; and the direction was fixed, a thing without change, a focus for his life that would never be any different. He felt tired and frightened, because he knew now how completely alone he was; but once more his feet were on the ground and he knew they would remain on the ground until he came to the end of his road, whatever that end might be.

He sat down and wrote to Reed:

"The enclosed was put into my hands by an express from White Plains. Having no idea of its being a private letter, much less suspecting the tendency of the correspondence, I opened it, as I had done to all other letters to you from the same place and Peek's Hill, upon the business of your office, as I conceived and found them to be. This, as it is the truth, must be my excuse for seeing the contents of a letter which neither inclination or intention would have prompted me to. I thank you for the trouble and fatigue you have undergone in your journey to Burlington, and sincerely wish your labors may be crowned with the desired success. With best respects to Mrs. Reed, I am, dear sir, &c.

"GEORGE WASHINGTON."

14

HOW DESTINY SAT ON GENERAL LEE'S SHOULDER

MEN WHO knew and liked Charles Lee complained that he should
have been born a king, and indeed in his ugly features and consistent
melancholy there was something both kingly and devilish. He hadn't,
like the foxhunter, gone blundering into destiny; destiny had been
inside of him from as far back as he could remember, and as far back
as he could remember he had been conscious of that destiny. Yet in
one way or another, that destiny had eluded him; now, for the first
time, it perched on his shoulder.

And on his shoulder he was determined to keep it. He knew only too
well what a potential lay inert in the sprawling American settlements,
numbering as they did almost three million souls, and he had quite
come to the conclusion that he was the man to awaken that fire. He
was not worried about his ability to drive off the British; that would
come later. He already had his army, and all that remained was to
obtain supreme command.

On the fourth of December, deciding that he had waited long
enough, he had the Marblehead fishermen ferry his army across the
Hudson. The British, in Jersey, were between him and the foxhunter;
obviously, his army was the best-equipped and the strongest, and just
as obviously, the British would leave him alone and concentrate their
force upon destroying the foxhunter. All this he had carefully thought
out in advance, and he was so satisfied with his work that he could
afford a rare smile, lying back in his boatload of dogs and crooning to
them while they made the air hideous with their yapping.

If Charles Lee loved nothing else, he loved his dogs; he saw them
into the boat as carefully as a man would shepherd his children, and
on the Jersey shore the fishermen stared in amazement as he lifted the
dogs out one by one, standing in the water himself, and carried them
up onto land. The army had already started its slow march under the
second in command, General Sullivan, who had been exchanged
recently, after being made prisoner at Brooklyn, but Lee wouldn't
move a step until the dogs were fed. As meat was brought, he examined each piece carefully, threw some aside in disgust, and raged and
ranted until food to suit his choice was produced.

The army turned down the Jersey shore in the general direction the
Virginian had taken some two weeks before, but Lee's progress was so

141

sluggish that even the New Englanders complained about their marching. Ten miles a day was unusual; sometimes it was only five or six, and sometimes they sat around for days and did nothing but sleep and eat. Sullivan, who suspected that things might not be going too well with the forces of the commander in chief, began to grow uneasy, but since he was denied the privilege of reading Lee's dispatches and papers, he had nothing concrete to base his suspicions upon. The rank-and-file Yankees had no knowledge at all of what had happened to the New Jersey and Pennsylvania men; as far as they knew, the earth might have opened and swallowed them. For their own part, it was a peaceful and lazy march, and they were not moved to object too violently, the more so since the horror of Brooklyn and New York was still vivid in their memories.

Seemingly, the war had lost all plan and purpose, and as the weather turned colder, the New Englanders began to desert in increasing numbers. By the time a week had passed, Lee and his army were at Morristown, but in the march from White Plains, he had lost almost a thousand men through desertions. Now he was close onto the rear guard of the British, and therefore he slowed down his already snail-like pace. On the twelfth of December, Lee marched his troops out of Morristown, eight miles to Vealtown. His moment of destiny had almost arrived. Each successive pleading dispatch from the command put the tall Virginian in a slightly more desperate position. A week more, Lee estimated, and there would be both a new Continental army and a new commander in chief.

For one thing, Lee was sick of the stench of camp, of his doltish troops, of the boredom of a week's tedious marching, of the constant and uninspired questions asked by the members of his staff as to where they were going and what they intended. Glover, the leader of the fishermen, didn't like Lee, and he lost no chance to make it plain. If Lee threatened him, he threatened back, and when Lee cursed him, he cursed back. For the time being, Lee intended to do nothing; he wanted command first, and when he had that, he would give his troops a taste of discipline.

But now he was sick to death of the whole thing; after the troops had encamped at Vealtown, Captain Gunnerson told him about the tavern, and Lee was in a proper mood to respond.

"How far is it?" Lee asked.

"Three miles. But it's worth it."

Why not? Lee asked himself. A man can go crazy without a little relaxation.

"A blonde?" Lee asked.

"No, she's dark." Gunnerson made motions with his hands, and Lee felt his body tense with desire.

"Her name's Anna," Gunnerson said.

Lee said, "You know, I suppose, captain, that a man can go far with me, a man with discretion."

"I pride myself on my discretion, sir."

"Continue to!"

The captain nodded, staring at the thin, ugly, sorrowful man who in a day or a week would be the leader of a nation. He felt neither love nor repulsion and thought that he would have been better satisfied with a handful of shillings than with Lee's promises for the future.

Lee went in to his dogs, a tentful that stilled their yapping the moment he entered, rushed at him and climbed onto him to kiss and welcome him. He knelt down so that they could get at his face, and he became almost womanly with tenderness.

"Babies, babies," he crooned.

They crawled into his arms and licked his face and hands.

"Little babies," he crooned. "Be quiet. Be still. Lie down."

They lay down obediently, and he fished sweets out of his pockets. One by one, he gave them the favors, allowing them to lick his face in thanks.

"Tomorrow, I'll see you, babies," he said.

They knew he was going away, and they lay quiet and looked at him out of their big, melting eyes.

"Tomorrow—"

The tavern was at Baskingridge, three miles away, and Lee rode there with six men as a guard. He would have preferred to go alone, but he realized the unimpressiveness of a general arriving anywhere without a guard.

There were only a few wide-eyed Jersey countrymen in the tavern when Lee strode in and announced himself with a bow and a flourish of his cocked hat: "Major-General Charles Lee of the Continental army!"

The guards pushed into the inn behind him, grinning, clasping their big muskets clumsily and self-importantly. The Jersey farmers rose, bowed in return, but awkwardly, and retreated to one side of the room. A little innkeeper rushed out of the kitchen, bowing, rubbing his hands, licking his lips.

"A patriot, sir. You have entered the house of a true and loyal patriot."

Lee smiled as he noticed the girl behind the bar; she was all that Gunnerson had promised.

"And I welcome you to my humble house, Your Excellency."

"All right. I want dinner and a bed, a featherbed, do you understand?"

"Completely, Your Excellency."

"And a place for my men."

"In the carriage house, dry and snug and warm, too. May I say, Your Excellency, that never before in twenty-two years of keeping a decent and honest house, have I been so honored?"

"You may." Lee nodded magnanimously.

"Our food is simple, but tastily cooked. You will not be disappointed in our food."

Lee threw off his coat and slumped into a high wing-chair by the fire. "Bring me a bottle of wine, now."

"Claret, Burgundy, Madeira, Port?"

"Claret," Lee decided. He was warm; he was comfortable; he was being treated with dignity. The girl brought the wine, and as she stood between him and the fire, hidden from the rest of the room by the high wing-chair, Lee ran his hand lightly across her thigh. She almost dropped the tray, giggling and rolling her big black eyes.

"Oh, Your Excellency."

"Pour the wine," Lee said. "My dear, pour the wine."

As she bent and poured the wine, he caressed her again, and the feel of warm, smooth flesh under his hand made him shiver with desire.

After two bottles of wine, he was ready for dinner, and by then the inn was empty except for himself, the landlord and the girl. Whether she was the landlord's daughter or a servant, Lee didn't know; whichever the case, the landlord urged her on him. She served the dinner and stood by the table while Lee ate. And along with the dinner, which consisted of a fine roast duck, a meat pie, and a pudding, there went a bottle of Burgundy and then an earthenware jug of homemade peach brandy.

Not in many months had Lee felt so completely at ease, so mellow, so little put-out with the world. He had never been a very successful person with women, yet he had made enough advances already to know that the girl would be his without any fumbling courtship. When he asked her to sit at the table, she giggled and refused, but she arched toward him and rubbed her full breasts against his shoulder like a big, purring kitten.

He was full, bloated, his belly tight against his waistcoat, when he got up from the table and slipped into the wing-chair by the fire. The girl was preparing a rum flip for him, and he sighed with content as she plunged the red-hot loggerheads into the pitcher. And then, while Lee sipped daintily at his mug, she pulled off his boots and set his feet on a footstool. By now, in Lee's eyes, she had lost all her grossness; she was delicate and dainty and precisely what he had always dreamed of in the way of a woman, and even her giggle as he stoked her hair was like musical laughter.

"Ah, my dear," he said, "you're very good to me."

"It ain't like we have a general every day," she simpered.

"No, my dear, nor does a general always have a princess to ease his weariness."

"Go on," she giggled.

"A general's life is neither a bed of roses nor a path of glory."

She continued to giggle.

"He has the weight of an army and the destiny of a nation upon his poor shoulders."

"I seen a British colonel once," she remembered.

"Our enemies, we must treat them honorably, but harry them sharply."

"He had white britches and a red coat. He was pretty." She frowned and recalled: "He had a perook."

"My poor army fights in rags," Lee sighed.

"They stink," she said bluntly, thinking of how the six troopers had pawed her when she showed them their beds in the barn.

With his third mug of flip, his mood became melancholy, and all the miseries and wants of his life rose up to plague him. "The path of glory," he said, "is a lonely road. I am a miserable man, a lonely man, an ugly man. I have no friends but my dogs, and by God they're better than men. They're my babies, they love me, they trust me. You look at glory, my dear, because the buttons on my uniform glitter, glitter, but I'm a miserable man, a lonely man. No warm hearth for me and no roof over my head, and no sweet wife to say farewell to me, and no little children to call me papa, no, for me the camp kettle is all and I must dip into it like a brute along with the other brutes and lay my head on the ground. . . ." Maudlin tears rolled down his flat cheeks and his under lip drooped and his head swayed from side to side.

"Come to bed," she smiled.

145

"Bed with a whore," he mumbled. "That for the new commander in chief of the army of liberation."

She continued to smile as she helped him upstairs.

It was four o'clock in the morning when a pounding on the door of his room woke him. The room was black and his head ached violently and his mouth was huge and rank and leathery.

"Who's there?" he muttered.

The pounding continued.

"Who's there?"

"Major Wilkinson."

"Who in damnation is Major Wilkinson?"

"Messenger from General Gates, sir."

"Who?"

"General Gates."

"Go to hell and be damned. There's time for that in the morning."

"This is very urgent, sir."

Lee felt the soft, yielding presence of the girl, but the night before was shrouded in the mystery of countless glasses of wine and flip. He dragged her from under the covers and tried to make out her face in the dark, frightening her until she whimpered like a bewildered kitten.

"Who are you, you bitch?" he demanded.

"Anna."

"Who?"

She broke into a frightened explanation of the night before, but he exclaimed, "God damn you, you bitch, get out of here!"

She started for the door, sobbing, but he caught her in the dark and whispered, "Under the bed!"

"What?"

"Under the bed, God damn you!"

Still sobbing, she crawled under the bed, and Lee opened the door. The man called Wilkinson stood there with the little innkeeper, who was clad in a long nightshirt and held a candle in his trembling hand. Wilkinson was a boy of nineteen, smirking, his eyes full of nasty knowledge he had wheedled from the landlord.

"Well?"

"This letter, sir," Wilkinson explained, holding it out to Lee.

"Who sent you and what the devil does this mean?"

"General Gates. He's with four regiments up by Wallpeck."

"You're crazy! He isn't a hundred miles of here!" He plucked at the letter and held it under the candlelight. "This is addressed to

146

Washington!"

"My God, sir," Wilkinson said with mocking dismay. "I don't know where General Washington is. Neither does General Gates. Neither does anyone in this whole cursed country. Schuyler sent Gates down with four regiments because he heard Washington was bad. But the general couldn't find him, and I couldn't find him. I been riding around all night, sir. I'm so stiff I can't move."

"All right," Lee said, tearing the letter open. "All right. Get out of here. Put a blanket somewhere and go to sleep."

Not until after he had crawled back under the covers did a series of pitiful wails remind Lee of the girl.

"Come out," he said. He had taken the candle back into the room with him and now he was able to see something of her, her swollen face and red eyes and stringy hair down to her waist.

"Who are you?"

"Anna," she sobbed. "Anna."

He rubbed his eyes and pulled air down his tortured throat, and bit by bit something of the night before came back. He groaned and said, "Can you get rum?"

She nodded eagerly.

"Bring me a drink."

She came back with a can of the stuff and he gulped it, almost choking with the hot fire in his throat, but feeling better once it was down. The girl, dressed only in a thin shift, had seated herself composedly at the foot of the bed, from where she regarded him with curious wonder.

"General Lee," she said.

"What?"

She made a face and then giggled and rubbed her belly.

"Get out," he groaned.

She went to the door, giggling and glancing across her shoulder; Lee rolled over and buried his face in the pillow.

The candle burned out and dawn filtered through the dirty little windows. Lee sat up in the bed, staring ahead of him, hating himself, wretched, with a splitting headache and a sour stomach. He belched slowly and regularly, and his outstretched hands were yellow against the bolster. It was almost eight o'clock before he felt the strength or inclination to get out of bed, poke his feet into his slippers, and stumble across the room to where his coat hung. The very thought of the effort of dressing sickened him. He managed to get the coat on over his

147

nightshirt, and without washing he opened the door and went down-stairs.

Wilkinson was waiting, warming himself by the fire; when he saw Lee he grinned and stared as if his eyes were deceiving him.

"What are you looking at?" Lee demanded coldly.

"Nothing, sir," Wilkinson said, licking his lips.

"Me?"

"I'm sorry, sir." The apology was insultingly meek.

"Don't be sorry, damn you," Lee said, taking some small consolation out of the knowledge that Wilkinson was looking at the next com-mander in chief of the Continental army. He got over to the wing-chair and dropped into it, telling the boy more gently, "Get me a drink, major."

"Rum?"

"Rum," Lee nodded glumly. Pulling the chair closer to the fire, he drained the goblet and then toasted his hands and his bare feet. The innkeeper approached to ask about breakfast, but Lee growled and swallowed several times, shaking his head.

"About that letter, sir," Wilkinson began.

"Damn it, where do you think Washington is?"

"I don't know, sir—across the Delaware, perhaps."

"Well, I don't know either. I don't know whether he's alive or dead or whether he has an army. I don't think it matters. Damn you, don't look at me like that! I said I don't think it matters."

"Yes, sir. I'm inclined to agree with you." He grinned again, ingra-tiatingly.

"Get your breakfast if you want to."

"I'm not very hungry, sir."

"Well, damn it, don't stand there staring at me!"

Lee was still sitting apathetically by the fire when Colonel Scammel, his adjutant, arrived. It was after nine now, but the inn, being off the main road, had no customers, and Lee was the only guest who had spent the night there. The girl had hidden herself in the kitchen and all the squeaky threats of the landlord could not bring her into the parlor where Lee sat barefooted, his coat over his nightshirt.

Scammel was as surprised as Wilkinson at Lee's appearance, but he controlled himself somewhat better and remembered to salute.

"What is it?" Lee demanded, returning his gaze to the fire after a single glance at the adjutant.

"General Sullivan wants his marching orders, sir."

"Marching orders?"

148

"Yes, sir."

Lee frowned at the fire. "Why does he want marching orders?"

"I suppose, sir, that he didn't think you intended a permanent encampment at Vealtown."

"No? Well, damn it all, Scammel, where does he want to march to?"

"I don't know, sir. That's up to you."

"I won't have your damned insolence, Scammel!" Lee cried, turning fiercely on the adjutant, who met his glance evenly, but said softly, "I'm sorry, sir. I did not intend insolence."

"I'm sorry," Lee muttered. "My head is splitting."

"Is there anything I can do?"

"No—no. Have you a map?"

Scammel nodded and went outside to fetch the map from his saddlebag. When he came back, he spread it out on the table, and Lee dragged himself from the wing-chair to look at it. The letters, lines, rivers and towns blurred before his eyes. He tried to focus, supporting himself over the table with both his outstretched hands, until Wilkinson brought a chair and helped him into it. Gradually, the places on the map came into focus and outlined themselves; and with Scammel and Wilkinson standing over his shoulders, Lee traced a wavering line from Vealtown to Pluckamin. There his finger stopped, and Wilkinson and Scammel exchanged glances.

"Pluckamin," Lee said.

Wilkinson grinned knowingly.

"It's not more than seven miles, sir," Scammel pointed out.

"What!"

"I said it seems to be a very short march, sir."

"Why should it be a long one, Scammel?"

"No reason, sir. But General Sullivan is under the impression that we should be moving to join General Washington."

"Tell Sullivan we'll move at my own damned pleasure! Tell him that, Scammel!"

"Very well, sir." And Scammel swung on his heel and walked out of the house.

Lee stared after Scammel, and then he turned to Wilkinson and demanded querulously, "Did you see my army? Did you see their shoes? Did you see their clothes?"

Wilkinson nodded. Lee appeared full to the brim with self-pity, his red eyes becoming moist, his lower lip trembling. "Join Washington," he said, aggrieved and asking for pity. "Did you see their shoes? And how do I know where Washington is? Does anyone know?"

The major shrugged and sat down at the table, where the landlord was spreading the breakfast dishes. Lee, who had not been hungry before, now began to eat ravenously—eggs, pancakes, bacon, stuffing his mouth with chunks of bread as if he had been starving for a week. The girl came out of the kitchen and stood at the bar, giggling, her hands on her lips, her eyes reaching toward Wilkinson, who grinned at her and winked lewdly.

"Damned hussy," Lee muttered. He felt better now that he had eaten.

"Who is she?"

"Yours," Lee said, giving with lordly satisfaction. He pounded on the table, calling for the landlord to give him pen and ink and paper. "I'll burn the ears of your General Gates," Lee told Wilkinson. "By God, there's a new order coming, and I can make or break a man, Wilkinson, understand that!"

"Sir?" the boy smiled innocently, and then added, "I hope to be included. For me, sir, the old order's a filthy bitch."

"Make him or break him," Lee said pointedly. Wilkinson rose and walked to the window, and Lee grabbed the quill and began to write furiously:

"The ingenious maneuver of Fort Washington has completely unhinged the goodly fabric we had been building. There never was so damned a stroke; *Entre nous,* a certain great man is most damnably deficient. He has thrown me into a situation where I have my choice of difficulties: if I stay in this province I risk myself and army; and if I do not stay, the province is lost forever. . . ."

Wilkinson had been staring out of the window, from which point he could see something over a hundred yards of the road. When a party of British dragoons appeared from around the bend and dashed down on the inn with their pistols drawn, it was neither inconsistent nor impossible; it was the bad end of a bad little drama, all of which had given Wilkinson the impression of being inside a nightmare.

Lee had just finished writing his letter, and he was signing it when he heard the roll of hoofs. "What's that?" he asked Wilkinson, without turning around.

"British cavalry," came the strangely calm answer.

"Where? My God, how?" Lee stood there in disheveled impotence, one slipper off, his arms hanging tragically, his birdlike head thrust forward. "Where's the guard?" he moaned.

Wilkinson was already starting up the stairs.

"For God's sake, Wilkinson, where are you going?" Lee cried.

"To save my hide," the boy said cheerfully. "I'm quite fond of it."

The guards had stacked their muskets on the shady side of the house, and then, becoming chilled, had gone around to the sunny side to warm themselves, leaving the muskets stacked and on the other side of the inn. While they were basking in the sun, the girl came out with hot flip, and after they had finished the rum they caught her and almost came to a battle over which should keep his hands on the best parts of her. She was screaming with laughter and they were in the process of dragging her across to the barn when the British dragoons appeared. They let go of her and stared stupidly, while she stood poised in wide-eyed admiration of the gorgeous horsemen.

Then they broke and ran in every direction, the dragoons after them, riding them down and beating them with sword-flats.

Lee was standing by the fire, holding onto the wing-chair, when Colonel Harcourt of the Royal Dragoons entered the inn, and afterwards Harcourt said that he had never in his life seen anything all at once so funny, tragic, and pitiful. They were old acquaintances, and back in the years when Lee had been a British officer, the dragoons had been his own regiment. And now it seemed to Lee that some terrible, woeful irony had planned his whole stay at the inn, culminating it with this. Looking at Harcourt as he would at a ghost, Lee tried with a trembling hand to button his coat and hide the dirty, wrinkled nightshirt.

Harcourt smiled and nodded. "Pleased to see me, Lee?" he asked.

Lee sought for some sort of dignity, letting go of the wing-chair and drawing himself up, trying to hide the bare foot, swaying a little, feeling faint and nauseous. Captain Harris, whom he also remembered, pushed into the inn; Harris was young and handsome and immaculate. He regarded Lee with disgust.

"What are you going to do with me, sir?" Lee whispered.

"Hang you, I suppose," Harcourt replied callously.

"No—no. Oh, my God, no."

Harcourt took a perfumed handkerchief out of his pocket and sniffed at it delicately.

"You can't hang me," Lee whispered.

"What shall I do with him, sir?" Harris asked.

"Take him out and put him on a horse."

"You don't want him to dress, sir?"

Harcourt stepped back a pace, allowing the handkerchief to dangle and measuring Lee carefully from head to foot. "No — really, I don't think so," he drawled. "Really, I don't think so, he's so attractive as he is. Don't you think so, Captain Harris?"

"Sir," Lee pleaded, "for God's sake, let me put on my uniform."

"Aren't you wearing your uniform, Mr. Lee?"

"Give me the dignity of my rank."

"You have no rank," the colonel said harshly. "Take him out of here, Harris."

Wilkinson came out from under the bed and went to a window. The dragoons, with General Lee in their midst, were riding down the road in the direction of New Brunswick. Wilkinson brushed the dust from his uniform and went downstairs to the parlor, where the landlord was moaning that Lee had not paid his bill. "Two pounds," he told Wilkinson. "I'm a poor man. Seven dinners, eight breakfasts, feed for the horses, two pounds."

"Oh, go to hell," Wilkinson said to him.

He went outside. The girl was there, and she smiled at him and began to edge toward him. Some of the guards, wretched and bedraggled, were shuffling back toward the inn. The girl was very close to Wilkinson now, but she saw his face and stopped and pouted. The guards were sheepish and forlorn, one of them with a long, bleeding cut over his ear, and they kept eying Wilkinson, trying to gauge what his temper was. Now the girl came on again until she was close enough to put her hand on Wilkinson's arm. At that he whirled and slapped her brutally across the face.

"You slut! You dirty slut!" he shouted.

Sullivan, the general left in command of Lee's army, had only recently been a British prisoner. Taken at Brooklyn, he sat in a British jail until the Virginian got hold of a British officer who could be exchanged for him, and since then he had been serving with Lee in a not too cordial relationship. Suspecting Lee's intentions, he felt that the outcome would not only be the ruin of the commander in chief, but the end of everything that was left of the revolution. Nevertheless, for the time he could do nothing but obey orders, and when Scammel appeared with his weird tale of what had taken place at the inn, Sullivan shrugged and gave orders to break up the encampment and start off toward Pluckamin, thinking that a seven-mile march was better than no march at all.

It was about two hours after that, when the army was already on its way, that Wilkinson appeared. He had met Sullivan the night before, when he had come to camp looking for Lee and had been directed to the inn. Now Sullivan nodded brusquely, and Scammel said, grimacing at the memory, "You left our general in good health, I presume?"

Wilkinson smirked, licked his lips, and glanced with calm calculation at the two officers. A born plotter, completely egotistical, Wilkinson, superficially at least, was hard as rock; for all his nineteen years, he had plunged headlong into the wild scramble of ambitious men to make the revolution their own ladder to glory. The fact that Lee had been captured bothered him not one bit; he considered Lee a brute and a fool, stupid enough to be boiled in his own fleshpots, and therefore better out of the way. What troubled Wilkinson was a certain doubt as to how deeply Scammel and Sullivan were implicated in the widespread if loosely jointed conspiracy to ruin the Virginian, a conspiracy which until now had Gates and Lee as its chief supporters. Watching them keenly, Wilkinson let his news fall deliberately and baldly.

"In good enough health," he smiled, "but in the hands of the British."

They had been walking their horses slowly with the army, and now as if by spoken agreement, their horses came to a standstill, Scammel blinking, but Sullivan staring at the boy with hard, cold blue eyes. Sullivan dismounted, never taking his eyes off Wilkinson, and Scammel and the boy followed.

"That's not funny, you little brute," Sullivan said, unable to swallow his contempt of Wilkinson.

The three stood close together now, and beyond them the shuffling Yankees made an endless, drab panorama.

"You can go to hell, damn you, it's true!" Wilkinson said shrilly.

Sullivan turned to Scammel and asked, "What is this young bitch talking about?"

"I don't know, sir. I told you how I left Lee a little while ago and what he said. But he was all right then."

Wilkinson shouted, "You've go no right to talk to me like that, damn you, mister! I'm a major! I won't take that from you!"

"Shut up," Sullivan said, taking the lapels of the boy's coat in his hands, glancing sidewise at the marching men." "Shut up or I'll kill you, you dirty little son of a bitch."

The look in Sullivan's eyes cowed Wilkinson. "What happened to Lee?" Sullivan demanded, not letting go of the boy's jacket.

"Someone called the dragoons and they took him."

"Who?"

"I don't know."

"Who, Wilkinson? I'd as soon kill you as not!"

"Not me!" the boy protested. "My God, why should I want Lee out of the way? Why should I want the dragoons to take him?"

Sullivan let go of him. "Yes, why—" he said thoughtfully.

Wilkinson was almost in tears now. "I tried to help him," he improvised. "It was just me against all those dragoons—his damned guard ran away. I took a pistol in each hand and stood at the door and told them I'd shoot the first man who entered the house—"

Scammel laughed and Sullivan asked quietly. "Why didn't they take you, too, Wilkinson? Or didn't the dragoons have any use for you?"

"Lee gave himself up, and when I saw it was hopeless, I went upstairs."

"You're a dirty liar," Sullivan said.

Wilkinson managed to stay silent, but the look he gave Sullivan defined his feelings. His thin lips, white and pressed together, trembled slightly and Scammel thought, "Some day he'll put a bullet in Sullivan's back, unless he's killed first, which is not impossible."

"Go on with your story," Sullivan nodded.

Wilkinson told the rest and then gave Sullivan the letter, explaining, "Lee was writing this when they took him away. I saw it on the table afterwards." He studied Sullivan's face as the general read it, seeking some indication of his reactions and finding none. Sullivan glanced up.

"Do you know what's in it?"

"No," Wilkinson lied.

Sullivan handed it to Scammel, who read it and handed it back without a word. As Sullivan maintained a thoughtful and somewhat worried silence, Wilkinson gained confidence and began to bluster.

Sullivan gave him the letter. "Take it to General Gates," he said shortly.

Grinning once more, Wilkinson demanded, "And what shall I say General Sullivan intends to do?"

Scammel and Sullivan exchanged glances, and then Sullivan said softly and dangerously, "Give him the letter, and then tell him, Wilkinson, that I'm marching to join General Washington. Tell him that anyone who disagrees with my course of action can go to hell and be damned. Tell him that."

Somehow, the news that Lee had been captured got out and through the army, perhaps from Lee's guards who drifted back to their regiments, perhaps from the officers who had to be told the news and why the direction of the march was being changed. At any rate, only a few hours after Wilkinson brought the news, the whole line was alive with speculation, and the change of mood and intention was instantly apparent. Sullivan, still unable fully to comprehend the fact, asked Scammel almost pathetically, "But how would they know he was there at the inn? Unless that little bastard—yet he's in it up to his neck, with Gates and Lee, so why should he—?"

"Why shouldn't they know? Everyone knew. This country is filthy with Tories."

"I should have broken his dirty back!"

"I don't think he did it," Scammel said. "Why should he?"

"God knows."

The marching army seethed and boiled, and early in the afternoon came the first eruptive consequence of Lee's capture. Two hundred Massachusetts men marched stolidly out of the line. Sullivan spurred after them and reined his horse across their path, but they marched on around him and past him, their eyes fixed on the ground and straight ahead, their ears closed to his exhortations and cursing.

An hour later, one hundred men from Maine turned out of the line. Sullivan was a Maine man himself, and he begged them to wait only two or three days. He got off his horse and walked along with them, pleading, but it was no good.

The Jersey men went off by tens and twenties, by ones and twos and threes.

Sullivan knew what the Marblehead men had done at Brooklyn and Pell's Point, and now he asked Glover, "Will your men fire on deserters if I order them to?"

Glover shook his head sadly. "I don't reckon they will."

"Will they stand by me?"

"That's likely," Glover considered. "But they don't lean to slaying their own kind."

At six o'clock, a band of eighty Connecticut cavalry rode off into the night.

And during the night, almost two hundred Vermont and a hundred more Virginia men marched away. It took a regiment of Pennsylvanians a night's discussion for them to make up their minds, and in the morning they too marched away, three hundred strong. Sullivan didn't sleep that night; he went from regiment to regiment, pleading with all the tattered medley of captains, colonels, majors, lieutenants by the

155

score, even those who called themselves generals. He wrote orders; he threatened; he raved until he was hoarse. He went into his tent, drank almost a quart of rum, and wept tears of pity for himself, his country and his destiny. He woke Scammel.

"My God, what am I going to do?"

"I don't know."

"What can I do?"

"You can take what's left and order them to shoot deserters."

"That's no good—they won't. They're all thinking the same thing."

"How many have gone?"

"Close to a thousand, I reckon."

"I don't know what you can do," Scammel said, thankful that he was not in command. "I wish I did, but I don't know."

And the next day, a haggard, bleary-eyed Sullivan saw the same process continue. Massachusetts men, Rhode Island men, Connecticut men, Jersey men, New York men, Maryland men, Virginia men, they trickled off, they went off by regiments, by brigades, by ones and twos and threes.

15

HOW THE FOXHUNTER BECAME A DICTATOR

THE NURSERY rhyme, learned by the foxhunter so long ago when he was six or seven or eight, had lingered down the long passage of years, framed in its crusty hornbook with its steel engravings of little men with big feet and big noses, the way some small, unimportant things linger:

> *Run, run, run away,*
> *Run, run, run away,*
> *Because, because, you should know when,*
> *Again, again, again, again,*
> *You will run, run, run away.*

At Brunswick he had wanted to pause and rest and breathe a little and see if he could find some flour and warm clothes, and linger in the hope that perhaps here at last Lee and his five thousand would join him—and maybe give the militia a chance to come in. That hope, that phrase, "to come in," had become so forlorn and rusty. Congress like

156

to use it; Adams, Hancock, Franklin, Jefferson—they all liked to use it; it gave in a broad sense such a stirring picture, the farmers, the countrymen, the mechanics, the clerks, all dropping their ledgers and plows and tools and picking up their guns and marching proudly and forthrightly to drive the enemy from their land and establish liberty and freedom and justice for all time. But the empty, hollow actuality was barred doors, shuttered windows, a sullen musket warning: "Keep off, damn you beggars!"

New Brunswick, which meant at the least a rest for aching feet, a pause to look at themselves and count themselves, came to an end on December 1st, when Captain Peter Mendoz, nineteen, drove his starving, skinny nag up to the house where the commander in chief was quartered and yelled, "They're here, sir!"

He came out in his shirt, his long bony shoulders hunched inquiringly, a piece of bread in his hand. "Who?"

"The British, sir!"

He finished the bread in a mouthful, and then Billy was behind him helping him struggle into his jacket. He said, "Get off the horse, captain, and talk sense."

The boy explained frantically. "About a mile away."

"How do you know?"

"I saw them," the boy wailed. "My God, sir, I saw them."

"How many?"

"Oh, sir—the whole army."

The foxhunter began to run, with his long, loping, swaying strides, seeing Greene and calling, "We're marching, Nathanael!"

"When?"

"Now."

"Where?"

"Out of here."

"Where?"

"Tell Mercer and Stirling to start the Brigades!"

He saw Knox, a fat whirl of excitement and evidently aware of what had happened, and called to him, "Can you knock down a bridge, Harry?"

"Bridge?"

"Damn you, Harry, haven't you any sense? The bridge across the river."

"I never tried, sir."

"Well, knock it down, Harry. Put some guns there if they should try to cross—and knock down the bridge."

The bookseller had a pair of lungs like a foghorn; he rolled along bellowing, "Brigades on the march! Brigades on the march!" The whole encampment had become a maelstrom of men running for their equipment, officers shouting senselessly at them, and drivers trying to load up their wagons with whatever they could lay hands on. Through this Knox pushed his way, roaring for his artillerymen, wondering where he could find crowbars and hammers. He had never torn down a bridge, and the heavy wooden structure across the Raritan did not look as if it would collapse with just a little prodding, and all he could think of at this moment were hammers and crowbars. At any rate, it was small and short salvation, for most of the Raritan was no more than knee deep. He spied Hamilton and yelled.

"Alex, where are your guns?"

"On the river, sir. I was looking for horses."

"The hell with horses! Drag them over to the bridge and keep the British from crossing!"

"Yes, sir."

"Have you seen any crowbars?"

"Sir?"

"Crowbars! I have to knock down that damned bridge."

He shook his head helplessly and Knox went running on. A while later, when he had picked up a dozen men with axes and bars and hammers and gotten them to the bridge, Hamilton was already there, the cannon loaded and waiting. Knox led his men into the icy water, where they sneezed and shivered and attacked the piling and planks. Meanwhile, over their heads, the guns began to explode. It was about twenty minutes before the end of the bridge gave way.

On the bank again, shivering, dancing clumsily to warm himself, Knox saw the British drawn up on the other shore, just out of cannon shot, in precise and orderly rows of red and green. At the other end of the bridge lay the bodies of three light infantrymen, caught by grape as they tried to storm across. A British officer, whom Knox thought later to be Cornwallis, doffed his hat in a half-mocking, half-respectful salute, while the Highland pipers paraded back and forth, screeching an off-key version of *Yankee Doodle*.

"Damned, bloody, kilted savages," Knox muttered, and Hamilton ground his teeth in impotent rage.

"I suppose we'll have to spike the guns," Knox said.

"Unless we can drag them away after dark."

"Without horses?" Knox was thinking that by dark the British would have crossed the river and gotten in behind them, and wondering how

158

it would be to sit in jail, rid of all this nightmare. When he turned around to look, he could just make out the last of the Continentals, racing down the road toward Princeton.

Toward evening of the next day, the shambling remnant of the army of liberty reached Trenton. As a gesture, a pleading gesture that he should not be driven out of New Jersey without making some sort of a show, the Virginian left some twelve hundred men at Princeton, under Stirling, who had been exchanged, along with Sullivan, since the two of them were taken by the British at Brooklyn.

"But what will I do, sir?" Stirling asked, looking at the ragged, shivering, half-armed, half-starved brigades.

Almost wistfully, the tall man said, "Maybe some Jersey militia will come in if they know we are trying to defend their land."

"Defend them? Christ, sir, they hate us."

The tall man winced.

"Defend them," Stirling said. "The richest land in America, stuffed with food, and we starve in it."

"They don't understand," he whispered.

"They understand well enough how to keep their own bellies full."

"I know."

"And if the British come?"

The tall man shook his head.

"Twelve hundred men — look at them, sir! And the British have ten, fifteen thousand of the finest troops in the world."

"I know."

"But, sir —"

"Do the best you can," the Virginian said.

He sat in his tent at Trenton with Mifflin and Greene, and it seemed an eternity ago that he had flown into a rage at Mifflin at Brooklyn Heights and more than an eternity ago that he had once raced after hounds through the lush meadows of Mount Vernon. He could study that tall, handsome, aristocratic foxhunter of the Potomac with all the detachment that a man living has for one a long time dead, not with regret, but with the painful, certain knowledge that a whole world had died, as worlds died before, as they would again, leaving no future but only a dark and weary present to men who traveled a road between them.

He said to Greene, "I would like the men counted, Nathanael."

"There's no use doing that, sir," Mifflin said bitterly.

159

"Why?"

"The New York militia walked off today. We have less than a thousand left, between eight and nine hundred, I think."

"That can't be," the foxhunter said softly, unbelievingly.

"It is," Greene remarked stolidly. "Mifflin's right. The New York militia walked away. It was no use trying to stop them. We're too thin. If we had tried, the rest would have walked away with them."

"Eight or nine hundred," the foxhunter mused.

"I hate to think that it's the end, sir," Mifflin said miserably. "I hate to think that."

"There's Lee's army," Greene reminded them.

"If we ever see Lee's army again."

"We'll see them," the foxhunter said, but with no confidence, the way one speaks of all the goodness and forbearance of Providence.

"It seems only yesterday," Greene said, "that we were in New York with twenty thousand men."

"Yesterday's gone," the foxhunter said. "I want you to go to Philadelphia, Mifflin, and I want you to come back with men, all the men you can get. I want you to go in front of Congress, because they don't read my letters; or if they read them, they put them away where neither their memory nor their conscience will be troubled; but go in front of Congress, threaten them, bully them, plead with them if you have to—but come back with men."

"Come back with the moon," he might as well have said.

Knox, returning from holding the British at the Raritan River, little the worse except for a hacking cough, told the Virginian about the proclamation issued a day or two before by General Howe. "I commands all persons in arms against His Majesty's government to disband and return home," he explained. "If offers a free pardon to those who comply within fifty days."

"I expected something like that," the Virginian nodded.

"Will it hit us hard, sir?"

"Can we be hit much harder?"

"I don't know—word's running like fire through the countryside. They used to be afraid to admit they were Tories, but now they're damned proud of it. It's worth a man's life to travel alone in Jersey."

Almost at the end, the end was put off for a little while. Mifflin performed a miracle; he came back from Philadelphia with fifteen hundred militia, not soldiers, but at least men, white-faced Philadelphia

160

clerks and storekeepers, bookbinders and drapers' assistants, and carpenters and tailors. They were frightened, tired and aching from their march; the two-thirds who had muskets held them awkwardly and somewhat fearfully, and the rest were armed with pikes, swords which had but recently hung over mantelpieces, and ancient blunderbusses. They were raw, and their drilling and marching had been all a game until Mifflin threatened and bullied them into coming up to Trenton. Still they were men.

The Virginian shook Mifflin's hand, and something in his eyes disclosed how near he had been to the end. "How many are left?" Mifflin asked cautiously.

"Six hundred — "

Mifflin whistled.

"It was very close," the tall man admitted. He looked weak and tired, and his face had a yellow, sickly sheen. But a better evidence of his state was his loquaciousness; for explaining, he said more to Mifflin than he ever had before. "I tried not to let them know — they would have bolted, all of them. I broke them into small groups, and I kept them moving, anything at all in the world except to let them see that none of them were left. And general — I prayed — " He broke off, flushing, self-conscious; a little ashamed of himself, he turned brusque. "Have them enrolled with the adjutant, and then march them off to Princeton. Greene is there, and I'll be along later with what's left of mine." He turned and eyed the new militia:

"And, general, march them by twos — let these damned Jersey Tories see that we have an army, only — don't let them fight," he added.

He went back to his headquarters and called Billy, and when the Negro came, demanded, "Have you any Madeira left?"

Billy nodded.

"How much?"

"Six bottles."

"Bring them all," the foxhunter said.

He had never really been drunk, and this time the wine left him cold and miserable and tired. He drank mechanically and quickly and hopelessly, not to forget, but to remember, to unfasten the tight-packed, tight-locked patterns that had gone to make up his life.

It was no use, for he found it as impossible to remember as to make himself drunk. Mount Vernon was a faint dream, and no more than that, and the foxhunting Virginia squire that he had been at Mount Vernon was part of the dream. All that was gone, lost and unobtainable; and on the bleak road he now traveled a fortitude was required

161

that could draw no sustenance from the past.

All that mattered now was to exist, as an army and as a movement and as a cause; they ran, dodged, hid, and twisted; they stumbled, fell, crawled, but moved on somehow, and they no longer spoke of striking back. Not so long ago, the Virginian would not have run away; bursting with pride, he would have battered his handsome head into a bloody ruin; but now his pride had become something else, even as ends and values had changed.

On his way back to Princeton, to join his army, after he had sent the Philadelphia reinforcements on ahead, he met the vanguard of a fleeing mob. But the difference was that instead of becoming a raging madman, as once he had, he now observed his troops with cold and measured detachment, and when Greene appeared, asked him calmly, "What is it now, Nathanael?"

Greene was tired and pettish, having no sympathy even for his commander in chief. "The same thing," he groaned. "My God, what else would it be?"

"The British are in Princeton?" the tall man asked softly.

Greene nodded hopelessly.

"There was no chance to hold on for a little while, Nathanael?"

"No—no, don't you think I wanted to hold on? If we had been in army of regulars, we were still outnumbered three to one. But my word, sir, did you see what that Philadelphia militia was?"

"I saw," the big man nodded, and then asked fatalistically, "How many desertions?"

"Only three hundred."

The Virginian sighed with relief, nodded, and swung his horse after the retreating army. Riding behind him, Greene demanded, almost savagely, "What are your orders, sir? Or are there no orders? What am I to do now?"

"Nothing, Nathanael, except to take hold of yourself."

"But what are you going to do?"

The Virginian shrugged. "Cross the Delaware, I think."

"And then, sir?" Greene asked shrilly.

The tall man smiled, rode on without answering, and then when Greene spurred desperately up alongside of him, said, "When there is only one road, Nathanael, you don't need maps."

"For God's sake, sir, don't talk in riddles!"

"Then without riddles, Nathanael, we will go on retreating. How far?" The Virginian shrugged. "Do you think the British are patient? Will they follow us across the mountains? Then we will fight them through the forest. Beyond the forest—I don't know. No one has ever been there. Perhaps we will be the first, Nathanael."

They left their signature for all time. It was snowing lightly as they marched down to the Delaware River, and suffering from cold, from hunger, from fear, they left their trail of blood in the snow. Cornwallis would need no hounds to follow; to his dying day he would remember, without exultation, how he knew where the Continental walked.

"If the fishermen were here," the Virginian thought, watching his freezing men awkwardly and hopelessly try to ferry themselves across the swift-running river. They stumbled and struggled and fell into the icy current. They rolled the guns onto boats, and then shed tears of futile rage when the boats overturned and tumbled the guns to the bottom of the river. They soaked their powder and their muskets, and if the British had come on them then the revolution would have finished quickly and painlessly. They cursed and whimpered, and even Knox, up to his waist in water for hours, became a raging two-hundred-and-fifty pound blob of anguish.

Yet they moved across, slowly, painfully, bitterly; somehow they dragged most of their guns across, some of their wagons, some of their few remaining horses, and most of their pitifully small stock of food.

This time, the Virginian needed leeway and rest too desperately to take any chances. The Delaware was not fordable at this time of the year for a good distance; if he removed all the boats for twenty-five or thirty-miles in either direction, he might hold the British back for a while—for how long he didn't know, yet a week would be redemption and two weeks would be grace from heaven. With this in view, he sent small parties of men up and down the river, and wherever they found a boat, they took it across, or if that was impossible, destroyed it.

They got over the Delaware, and this time, as on the Raritan, they escaped only by a hair's breadth, for the last boatload had hardly left the Jersey shore before they heard the skirling of the Highland pipers. The freezing militia built fires on the west bank, and crouched around their fires, they saw Cornwallis' redcoats, kilted Highlanders, and green-clad Hessians marching down to the spot they had just quitted. For the cold, hungry, half-naked, completely frightened Continentals, it was a terrible and awesome sight: the thousands and thousands of brightly uniformed regulars, the wonderful precision of their marching, the matter-of-fact way in which they deployed along the bank, the hundreds of pieces of artillery that rumbled down after them, black and ominous under that cold and cloudy winter sky, the seemingly endless train of supply wagons, the white tents rising up everywhere like mushrooms, and the pipers strutting along the bank, skirling defiantly and mockingly:

"Yankee Doodle went to London, riding on a pony."

And then, as the sun went down, the clouds broke open, and a long, slanting ray of light filtered through onto the massed British, making the whole brilliant picture impossible and unreal.

Knox, standing with the commander, with Greene and Putnam and Mifflin and Mercer, remarked, "In all my life, I've never seen anything like it."

"It's very beautiful," the tall man said quietly.

"Yet we go on," Mifflin mused.

"I never realized before what they meant," Knox said, a good deal of awe in his voice. "It's so long now that we've been fighting with them and running away from them, but I never realized before what it was. I never knew it was so big and so terrible. I didn't think about it."

"It's no good to think about it," Mercer said sourly. "They've a canny way, to put themselves like that in front of us, but it's no damned good to think about it."

"It's not a cheerful thing for them to see," Greene remarked, nodding at the men, who had left their fires and crowded forward to the bank.

"No," the Virginian agreed. "We'll encamp at least a mile back from the river."

"Yet I'm glad I saw it," Knox said thoughfully. "I think it's better to know what you're fighting — or what you're running away from."

The next morning, Greene and the Virginian rode up the river about ten miles, paralleling the path of British patrols in search of boats.

"They won't find any," the tall man said, with some satisfaction.

"No, but if they march up to Frenchtown?"

"That's a long march. They don't like the cold any better than we do."

"Still, they can't go away and leave us alone."

"Some of them might, and some of them might not."

"They can't cross," Greene reassured himself, and then added uneasily, "But God help us if they do."

* * *

The Unvanquished

The Philadelphia patriots, those who had supported the revolution, either by word or deed, were becoming frightened. This city of brotherly love had been anything but that for a long time now, and in spite of the fact that the Continental Congress sat there and the Declaration of Independence had been signed there, the city was far more Tory than rebel. The Tories, with some exceptions, ran to two extremes; on one hand the wealth and aristocracy, the people of family and blood and substance, and on the other the dregs and scum, the useless, the vile and degenerate. The Quakers remained aloof or were—again with a few exceptions—Tories; and holding for the revolution, in between, were the middle class, the artisans, the smiths and masons and shopkeepers and printers and sailors and small merchants and wheelwrights and cabinet makers and plumbers and glazers and drapers and millers and carpenters and brewers—and along with them, smugglers, pirates and privateers, a swashbuckling, hard-drinking, hard-speaking blot on the Delaware waterfront.

Until now, the Tories had quietly waited their moment, knowing that it was only a matter of time before the British swept away the Continental rabble. They were without organization, while the rebels had their militia, whatever it was worth. But now Mifflin came from the Virginian's beaten army, exhorting, threatening, and finally carrying away with him fully half the militia. And that was all the Tories needed.

Suddenly and boldly, knowing that their time was approaching, they proclaimed themselves. They barred their doors, closed their shutters, armed their servants and all of the dregs and scum who would sell themselves for a mug of rum and a silver shilling. The disorganized militia, bereft of half their number, realizing that the Continental army was crumbling, were afraid to take any definite stand against the Tories. If, as rumor had it, the British fleet sailed up the Delaware and took the city, what then would become of them, their homes and families? Thus, the city split into two armed camps, each unable to attack or dispose of the other; and the members of the Continental Congress, looking at each other, saw nothing but condemned men and mass hangings. Suddenly, they reversed the procedure; they had been importuned constantly by the Virginian, and now they turned and sent him frantic appeals for help.

"What can I do?" he asked Putnam. "I have no men to send them. You must go there, Israel, and see what you can make of their militia."

Putnam was old and tired and sick; at night he dreamed about his farm and groaned in his sleep.

"Who else can I trust?" the tall man demanded petulantly. "I know you're tired, Israel. Perhaps in the city you can rest."

"It won't be a rest," Putnam said morosely. "I know what it will be — it will be hell. From what I hear, they are all crazy with fright, and what can I do?"

"Whatever you do, it will be better than nothing."

"And if the British come?" Putnam asked sourly, already giving in.

"Take what men and supplies you can and retreat."

"I'm tired," Putnam complained. "You have troubles, but you haven't got rheumatism."

"I wish to God things were brighter," the foxhunter said gently. "For your sake, Israel. You're not as young as the rest of them. I'm not so young either. I know what it means, that feeling when your body won't listen to you any longer."

"It started so easily," Putnam said ruefully.

"It always begins easily."

Putnam rode away, sighing and grumbling, but he had hardly arrived at Philadelphia before the Congress loaded what government remained into a wagon and left for Baltimore. Putnam sat down painfully and wrote to his commander in chief.

Greene found the Virginian sitting in front of a fire, a woolen muffler around his neck, his glasses perched loosely on his nose, and an old stocking cap on his head. It was almost impossible to warm the shack he had turned into his headquarters, and the tall man, eyes red and nose even more brilliant, sneezed constantly.

"Sit down, Nathanael," he said, motioning to a battered ladderback chair, which with a rickety table composed all the furnishings of the room.

"Flip, sir, is the best thing I know for a cold," Greene said.

"How much flip can a man drink? I've had a quart, and it hasn't helped."

Greene nodded his sympathy and sat gingerly in the chair. He was very cold and sat so close to the fire that the frayed threads on his knees began to singe.

"You'll burn yourself," the tall man warned him.

"Thank you, sir. The winter in these parts is uncommonly wet." He sat with his knees close together, his hands clasped on them, waiting to hear why he had been sent for.

"Congress has gone away from Philadelphia," the tall man told him.

"What!"

"They did right. The revolution exists only so long as a government exists. It's better for them to flee than to be taken."

"Where have they gone?"

"To Baltimore, I think. It isn't that—" Greene had never seen the Virginian look so old, so tired, unsure even, his big hand trembling a little as it groped in his breast pocket for a letter. "I don't know how to tell the others—Congress has changed things. Sometimes, God help me, I'm afraid they've given up."

He had never spoken like this before; every last vestige of authority, of aristocratic pride was gone from his voice. Greene asked hoarsely, "Who, sir?"

"Congress—"

Greene shook his head stubbornly.

"They've given it all over to me," the tall man said miserably.

"Given what, sir?"

"The government. I never asked for that, never wanted it. How much can I carry on my shoulders alone?"

Greene stared at him.

"This is the way it is," the tall man said, peering through his glasses at the letter and reading: ". . . until they should otherwise order, General Washington should be possessed of all power to order and direct all things relative to the department and to the operations of war. . . ."

"If it were anyone else I would be afraid," Greene protested. "But it's you, sir. Don't you see?"

"No—" The tall man shook his head miserably. "What's the difference who it is? What are we fighting for—for one man to rule a people?"

"I'm not afraid of that, sir, I swear to God, believe me, but why did they do it?"

"They think it's the end and they are grasping at straws."

"Do you think it's the end?" Greene asked softly.

"I don't know," the tall man said. "I don't know."

They were sitting around him in the cold room for a council of war: Greene, Mercer, Knox, Mifflin, Stirling, and John Cadwalader, the last a young man of Philadelphia who had come under Putnam's sour but strangely moving influence and had marched up from Philadelphia with a band of volunteers, and who was still shaken by what he had seen on the banks of the Delaware. Aside from Cadwalader, whose suit was fresh from a Philadelphia tailor, their clothes were threadbare, patched, their uniforms, once carefully made in imitation of the

167

commander's buff and blue, now mostly replaced by old breeches and second-hand, ill-fitting homespun coats. Cadwalader had seen the horrible, dirty, broken thing they called their army, and it was like a grotesquely humorous dream that they should sit here in what they called a council of war.

The Virginian had just finished explaining the situation that had turned him into a dictator, and now humbly, almost pleadingly was was saying:

"Gentlemen, I never looked for this, believe me: I never wanted it. I consider our Congress a noble and courageous body, to whom I am responsible for all my actions." There was no hint of mockery in his voice. "I remain responsible to them; nothing can change that. The splendid purpose to which they are working can only command our respect, and their army, which I have the honor to command, must be worthy of that purpose. Yet there are certain actions which I must embark on of my own account, for the time only, since it is almost impossible now to have our Congress consider them.

"We have been retreating only for one reason, to preserve our army, and through it, our country; but we have come to a point where further retreat will only destroy the little that remains to us. We must strike back, and whether that blow will be the beginning or the end of all we have fought for, I don't know. But strike we must, for in a little while it will be too late."

They stared at him, as though he had gone suddenly mad; they looked at each other; he went on:

"Our country and Congress, unfortunately, has little money; most of what they had is spent. Perhaps if more of the wealthy families of this land were inclined toward our cause, the situation would be different; but most of the people in our ranks are poor in worldly goods, and many have given all they can. I am counted a rich man, and I believe I can find some money; some of you, perhaps, will be willing to help, although I know only too well how little you have. Nevertheless, we must offer bounties and rewards of various kinds, so that men will be persuaded to enlist. I do not have to impress on you how unfortunate our situation is; even with the timely arrival of Colonel Cadwalader, we may, in another few days, have less than two thousand men. I don't think, gentlemen, that is a reason for despair, but rather evidence of a need to exert ourselves to even more strenuous effort — "

He paused and looked from face to face. Mercer was staring at the table. Knox's eyes were wet, and Greene was making a dogged effort to keep his face set and purposeful, while Stirling gazed blankly ahead of him. In Mifflin's eyes there was the dull despair of complete frustration.

"You are old comrades in arms," the tall man said softly. "I thank you, each and every one, for all the dark days you have borne with me." And then he rose and walked out.

Greene came to Knox, bursting with the first news of Lee's capture; and after the initial shock, Knox said, "For my part, it's good riddance to bad rubbish. I hate the swine."

"Are you going to tell him that, Harry?" Greene asked.

"I couldn't tell him."

"And where's the army, five thousand men, good men, the fishermen—Christ, Harry, you remember what the fishermen did at Pell's Point. It's all we have to remember. Where are they?"

"Didn't the express say? Wasn't he from Sullivan, if Sullivan's left in command?"

"He said Sullivan was going to try to cross the river, north of here."

"How long ago was that?"

"A few days. They should have been here, unless Cornwallis cut them off. If that happened—" Greene shrugged.

"Who was with Lee at the inn?" Knox asked.

"A filthy little wretch called Wilkinson, one of Gates' men. I know him. He's just a boy, but no good. He says he tried to fight, but I'll swear it's a lie. If he was there with Lee, I can guess why."

"How did he take it?" Knox wanted to know, nodding toward the Virginian's headquarters.

"How do you think, Harry?"

"I don't know—he was worried about the army, I suppose."

"No," Greene said bitterly. "He was worried about Lee, not only worried, but broken, you hear me, broken, Harry. Broken up because he had lost a comrade in arms, a noble leader, an unselfish patriot. He sent an express off immediately to Cornwallis demanding that Lee be exchanged, offering almost every prisoner we have, offering anything and everything and threatening God only knows what if Lee is hanged."

"Why?" Knox asked simply.

"I don't know. I've given up trying to understand him. If I were in his place—"

"Do you suppose they'll hang Lee?"

"They may. He was a British officer, you know."

* * *

Four days later, on the twentieth of December, the tattered, suffering remnant of Lee's army arrived at the encampment on the Delaware Less than two thousand were left of the five thousand Yankees Lee had commanded at White Plains, and even the poor beggars who made up the foxhunter's army were moved to pity at the sight. Blue with cold, their clothes in rags, their feet cut and bruised and bleeding, the Yankees dragged themselves into the encampment, some stumbling blindly toward the fires, others dropping down and going to sleep almost instantly. For a week they had dodged the British in a stubborn, twisting flight, and it was more than a miracle that they had got through at all. The only sign of order or hope among them was the company of the Marblehead fishermen, still together and some six hundred strong, their blue jackets worn threadbare, their shoes gone, but their lean, long Yankee faces grimmer and harder than ever.

Sullivan, swaying from weariness and lack of sleep, a week's growth of whiskers on his face, his eyes bloodshot and staring, stumbled over to the Virginian and said, "I must ask your forgiveness, sir, for certain men of faint heart who dropped out along the way."

16

AND HOW HE CROSSED THE DELAWARE A SECOND TIME

ONCE again, at long last, Glover and the Virginian sat opposite each other, a pitcher of hot flip between them with full glasses on hand, Glover rested and shaven, the foxhunter leaner than ever, hollow of cheek, with deep, dark circles under his eyes. Each man saw the change in the other, and each accepted it with new and humble awareness. Some of the down-east cold had gone out of Glover; he had seen men stripped bare to the soul, and it was harder to take, even, than what he had seen at Pell's Point. As with the foxhunter, he had chosen his road and was determined to walk down it for as long as it went. Both of them the same age, they were as alike in some ways as they were different in others; Glover saw that the aristocrat was gone, and he accepted the fact, sensing if not realizing the strange new pride and purpose in the man sitting across the table from him. They were both lonely men, and even from each other they could take no comfort to ease that loneliness; but in their loneliness they comprehended each other.

The foxhunter, sipping at his glass, said, "I'm glad to see you, colonel. It was a long time."

Glover nodded and smiled a very rare smile.

"I never considered fishermen," the foxhunter mused, half humorously. "I never thought that my life, my army, and my country's cause might depend upon them so much."

"That's good of you, sir," Glover said, a trace of a flush creeping into his wrinkled, weathered face.

"We owe you much."

"Very little, I would reckon," Glover remarked uneasily.

"At any rate, the point is that you're here. I am not much good at compliments."

"Nor I at holding on to them, sir."

The foxhunter drained his glass and said, "I had a plan in mind —"

The Yankee leaned forward.

"Cumbersome, insane —" He poured new flip for each of them, and staring at the hot, strong rum, said, "I needed you; it was no use to think about it otherwise."

"Crossing the Delaware," Glover said softly, not incredulously, but with matter-of-fact awe.

The foxhunter nodded.

The Marblehead man, smiling, murmured, "I reckoned that. It had to be that. What else could it be?"

"The British went away," the Virginian said, speaking with singular rapidity for one usually so slow in marshalling his thoughts. "They went away to the firesides of New York and left the Germans sitting on the bank. That's how they despise us. It's just as well, and we owe the Jagers a great deal!" It was the first time Glover, or indeed any of the others had seen this side of him, a gush of passionate eloquence. "They left the Jagers, men who fight and kill and murder, not because their country is at war, not because they have anything to defend, not because they hate or oppose hate, but because they are hirelings and mercenaries! Knyphausen is there, and we have a score with Knyphausen!" He broke off suddenly, the effort leaving him spent and coughing.

"When do you want to cross?" Glover asked.

"Christmas Day," the tall man answered quietly, the spell broken, his old, calm, almost rigid self come back again.

Reasons were not something Glover cared to discuss; he leaned back, eyes half closed, considering the execution of the matter, as if for a beaten, half-starved, half-armed rabble to attack an encampment of

171

Prussian-trained mercenaries was the most commonplace occurrence in the world.

"How many men?" he asked.

"We should have almost five thousand by then."

"In one night?"

"In a few hours, I hope," the tall man said.

Glover whistled softly, closed his eyes entirely, and sipped at his rum. His fingers drummed on the table, and with his eyes still closed, he asked, "How would it come out, actually, sir?"

"I want them embarked, taken across, re-formed on the other side, and marched from the landing places to Trenton, and I want the attack undertaken, from beginning to end, in darkness."

"It might be done," Glover speculated. "At the same point?"

"At three points, as far as I've planned it, one nine miles upriver, another a mile below here, and the third at Burlington."

"That makes it harder," Glover said. "What kind are the boats?"

"I'm not seaman enough to judge," the foxhunter said. "They're up and down the river for miles, but all on this side. There are enough, I think, for we took every boat on the river that we could move." He stared anxiously at Glover, who leaned back again, eyes closed, fingers drumming nervously.

"How do you think?" the foxhunter asked him.

"I think we can do it," Glover answered slowly. "If you want guns, it will mean barges; we'd be all night working them across in dinghies. But I think we can do it."

"I can count on you?"

"You can count on me, sir." Glover said, and then they shook hands, each leaning his long length across the top of the rickety table.

Things were a little better. The Virginian ordered a count, and it showed almost five thousand men, although not the full number were actually fit for duty. General Gates had come down from Schuyler's army in the north, starting off with four regiments, but losing half his men along the way from desertions. But when Gates heard about the plan that was brewing, he went to the Virginian and said, "I should like to have leave—to go to Philadelphia, sir."

"Philadelphia?"

"I find, sir, that there is a certain degree of madness I cannot fall in with."

"To Philadelphia or to hell, you are welcome, sir," the tall man said quietly. "It's one and the same with me."

172

"If that's your attitude," Gates replied, "I think you understand mine."

Wilkinson had come along with Gates, and now he strutted through the camp, telling, with much embroidery, how with a pistol in either hand he had stood off a whole company of dragoons when they came to take Lee. He talked endlessly and incessantly; he let hints drop that perhaps the commander in chief himself had connived at Lee's capture. Grinning knowingly, he let it be heard about that soon there might be a new commander in chief, and it would not be surprising if the name of the new leader was Gates. He pointed out what a great many letters had passed between the foxhunter and Howe, and how certain disaster which had befallen the army might not have been either chance or circumstance; but rather a part of a plan.

Captain Hamilton sought him out one day. "I want a word with you, Wilkinson."

"Major Wilkinson," the boy said.

They were the same age, both of them nineteen, Hamilton a little taller, a little slimmer, his violet eyes glowing strangely, a crooked smile on his face. "Major Wilkinson," he agreed.

"What do you want?"

"I want to kill you," Hamilton smiled. "But I don't think I will — not yet."

"Are you crazy?"

"No, I'm very sane, major. You'd better go away. Go to Philadelphia with General Gates."

"If you want to duel — " Wilkinson began furiously.

"I don't want to duel, I want to kill you," Hamilton said, turning on his heel and walking away.

The following day, Wilkinson left for Philadelphia with Gates.

"If this is insanity," the Virginian was saying solemnly, "It will be our last insanity, gentlemen. I haven't come to this decision easily; it has cost me many hours of thought and struggle with myself. I haven't lightly considered and used those powers which our Congress gave me, but only after much resolve and equal necessity. How urgent the necessity is, I don't have to point out to you. The game is up. I said once that if needful I would retreat a thousand miles to the west, so long as that would keep our army intact and our Congress in existence. But we have broken faith with our Congress, gentlemen; because we cannot defend them they have had to leave their city and run as we have been running; and were we to retreat not a thousand miles, but a hundred miles, there would be nothing left of our army."

They were all there, facing him, Glover and Sullivan and Knox and Mercer, Stirling, Putnam, Mifflin and Glover. Reed and Cadwalader were at Burlington, but they had already been informed of the plan. The men who were left with the commander listened gravely to what was, for all purposes, a summons to destruction.

"I have chosen for the time," he went on, "Christmas Day at night, one hour before the next daylight."

They stared at him curiously.

"Because the Jagers will be drunk," he explained in a matter-of-fact way.

"Can you count on that, sir?" someone asked.

"We can't count on anything, nor can we hope; we are moving, gentlemen, because our need is desperate."

"Cannon, sir?" Knox asked.

"You have sixteen pieces?"

"Eighteen, sir. General Putnam found two twelve-pounders that could be spared from Philadelphia."

"You will try to put them all across, Harry," he said. "Colonel Glover here has found barges that you will begin to embark the guns the moment the light fades. That will be soon after four o'clock. We will try to take across horse as well, and if possible will mount a group of men on the other side. General Putnam will return to Philadelphia, where there are signs of an insurrection, but the rest of you will be with me. Tomorrow, you will set your watches with mine, so that even if we are apart in the night, we will be able to operate in accord."

They nodded gravely, their fear gone, their faces set, not with hope, but with the realization that this was either a beginning or an end.

"Colonel Cadwalader," the foxhunter said, "has been good enough to present us with some Madeira. I will have it broken open, gentlemen, and we will drink a toast."

By noon on Christmas Day, the whole camp was stirring, the Continentals, wrapped in every rag or piece of blanket they could lay hands on, nervously forming into files, the officers glancing at their big, round watches, everyone stamping, moving, clapping hands to keep warm, the vapor of their breath steaming into the air.

It was a sharp, grey day, clouds banked up in the sky, the still air promising a snowfall before long. It was not very cold, but cold enough for the poor devils, who with all their rags piled on were still half naked. Even now, they did not know exactly what they were going into, except that it would be with the Jagers, a word that rose and fell like sounding notes though their ranks, in anger, in hatred, in sudden terror, a band of south-German volunteers from the Pennsylvania backcountry sickening at the thought of going to face the Prussian devils, all they had fled from and feared, their dread baked into them through countless generations, the New Englanders thinking of that raucous battle cry, "Yonkee, Yonkee," of how it might feel to be pinned by a bayonet to a tree or to go into a Hessian jail, poked and prodded along like beasts, the Jersey Dutch remembering a terror that had always loomed over the low country across the sea, the Pennsylvanians recalling stories of eight hundred other Pennsylvanians stabbed and cut and butchered as they fled up Harlem Heights to the poor security of Fort Washington. They were not brave, but mixed with their fear, there was an aching and terrible determination.

Hamilton was a tonic for Knox. He wouldn't leave the battery of eighteen guns, not giving the gunners a chance to think, but keeping them busy greasing the axles, cleaning the bores, chipping rust off the sighting screws, and making careful packages of the loads. Knox thought back to the time, not so far past, when they were twenty thousand strong in New York and when they could count the guns by the hundreds. Things had changed, just as he had changed from a bookseller who had once dreamed of being a publisher like Ben Franklin. That was gone and out of his life, left behind and somehow already too far behind to ever be reached for or regained; and he would never sit and gloatingly correct manuscript for a book that might sell a hundred or even a hundred and fifty thousand copies. He had liked comfort and ease so much, the good things of life, a house tastefully furnished with imported Chippendale, the best books by the wittiest English writers, the round comfort of his wife in bed at night, children he could look at always, mold, filling them with the good, civilized smell of printer's ink. He was only twenty-six, but he felt old, washed clean of every purpose but one, to stalk along with the Virginian on a lonely road that led to nowhere.

And Hamilton scampered around the guns like a thin-faced, violet-eyed imp.

Looking at the woefully scant ranks, the foxhunter asked Mercer, "Have you the count?"

"Twenty-three hundred and seventy-two."

"And about eighteen hundred with Cadwalader," the foxhunter said, almost to himself.

175

And then he and the little Scotsman looked at each other.

Greene came over to the fat colonel of artillery and asked him, "What do you think, Harry?"

"I don't know; it's better not to think. If he wanted to go into hell and bait devils, I suppose I would go along with him. There's nothing else, is there?"

"I suppose not."

"What time have you?"

"Twelve-twenty."

Knox wound his clumsy, silver-shelled timepiece, and then set the hands. "This isn't much good," he complained. "It goes off about five minutes on the hour."

"So long as you know if it's fast or slow."

"Slow, sometimes more, sometimes less."

"I hope it doesn't snow," Greene remarked.

"It will."

"I hate to think of those poor devils in that water."

Knox shrugged and grinned.

"When are you going to start the cannon?"

"Soon."

"There's ice in the water," Greene said.

"There would be," Knox agreed ruefully. "There would be every damned filthy thing today."

"Well—good luck, Harry."

Ice, breaking from the shelves and shallow creeks in the north, was fast filling the river, big, nasty slabs, not very thick, but sharp and like knife-edges in the swirling current. Watching it gather through the white veil of his breath, Glover shook his head ruefully.

"I don't like it," he told Captain Purdy of Gloucester.

"We'll have to count on poling."

"If the bottom don't fall away."

"At any rate, we'll slip downstream more than we thought. I figure we ought to look for a likely spot up about a mile."

"It's too late, and we can't get the guns into the boats without the ferry landing. We'll do what we can."

The foxhunter, now mounted on a bony chestnut, galloped along the freezing, shivering line, calling, "General Greene! General Greene!" His big cloak was threadbare and flapped loosely about his

176

long figure; his nose was bright red, his eyes watery; and he coughed and sneezed as he demanded, "General Greene!"

"What is it, sir?"

"What time is it?"

"Just about half after one."

"Well, what are you waiting for, Nathanael? Start the men for the ferry. Can't you see they're freezing cold?"

"I thought I would wait just a while longer."

"No, start them off now?" And then he wheeled away and was spurring his horse down to see how Knox and Hamilton were doing with the artillery.

It made Greene's heart ache to watch the half-frozen men shuffling along on their way to the river. They had known an hour of dreadful anticipation, but by now their fear had been whipped into a stolid, dogged determination. Their cockiness was gone and their boasting was gone, but in its place had come a silent, somber intent. Many of them believed that this was the end of their tragic, short-lived revolution; arguments and reasons had vanished; they were men going forward to die because they had committed themselves to freedom, and now, when everything else was gone, there remained only that commitment.

They did not sing nor did they talk as they moved along; they gripped their big, clumsy flintlocks with deadly earnestness; and their eyes, for the most part, were set straight ahead: and they did not know that the cold shuffling sound of their steps would echo undyingly.

And Greene, also treading a blank path, thought to himself: "They are brave, and that is something I will remember. Even if they run away, I will always remember that they were brave at this time."

Greene had once fought a battle with himself; he was a Quaker, and the edict was stern and straightforward: Thou shalt not kill. But if ever there was vindication, this was it, on Christmas Day, the day a man came into the world to preach Peace on Earth, Good Will toward Men — and incongruous as that was, strange as that was, Greene knew that he was not defiling the day, that he was keeping a rendezvous with men of good will. As faint of heart as the rabble that marched beside him, he was nevertheless proud and humble.

Leaning over his saddle, the foxhunter asked Glover, "How are things now?"

"As well as can be expected, sir."

"You have the boats ready?"

Glover nodded, but point to the spinning ice cakes.

"You can get us across?"

"We'll get across," Glover said. "Maybe a little more time than we reckoned on, but we'll get across. When do you want to start?"

The tall man looked at his watch and then at the sky. He thought that in about twenty minutes it would be dark enough to veil their movements from the other shore.

"Men first, then the guns?"

"A little of each," the tall man smiled.

He rode along the line of his men. They were crouched on the cold ground, and as he went past a succession of white faced turned in the dusk to look at him. He thought that it would have been the right thing to say something to them, but looking at their faces, there was nothing for the life of him that he thought mattered enough to put into words. He wondered whether they felt, as he did, the crashing insanity of this last desperate move. And what did they think of him? Did they hate him or did they love him, or did they follow him as sheep follow a leader? Was the stake, the intangible something called freedom, big enough? Was it worth the suffering, the starving, the cold and the hunger?

He didn't know. Once he had been sure of many things, but now he was sure only of the dark, singular path he must travel. He was lonely, and he knew that regardless of what happened, regardless of what came out of this, victory or defeat, glory or ruin, there would never be compensation nor relief from that loneliness. Still, he was not unhappy; often, he had said and written that he would not undergo this again for any reward on earth, but now he was quite certain of that fact. He had learned something terribly difficult for an aristocrat, for a foxhunter, for the wealthiest man in America; but now that he had learned he would not have been willing to unlearn. Wanting more than anything else to be loved and respected by others, he had found a strange peace in giving out of his own troubled heart.

For hours and hours the infantry had been standing and crouching motionless in the cold; now, at last, the order came to move. Their limbs were stiff and their joints creaked as they walked; they clapped their hands and beat their knuckles against their muskets. They stumbled and fell and got up again, feeling their way in the darkness; and they laughed, somewhat hysterically, at the way the Marblehead fishermen sang out, "Step smart there! Step lively! " They jostled against each other, and some of them slipped and fell into the icy water, and then were fished out shivering and cursing. The grinding crunch of the ice cakes and the constant thud against the frail sides of the boats made their throats contract, but they didn't hold back. They went into the inky blackness slowly but certainly.

For all the cold, the artillerymen poured sweat as they put their shoulders to the cannon, and strained and heaved them onto the barges, some of them standing waist-deep in the ice-cold water, others fighting the cannon on the rocking boats as if the big, insensate pieces of metal had suddenly come alive, others staggering under the weight of cannister and iron balls. And the fishermen, groaning at the clumsy, butter-fingered landsmen, cursed and directed and pleaded. Knox, his huge voice drowning out all other sound, roared commands.

"Come at it there! Stand to it! Put your shoulders to it, God damn you! Put your shoulders to it!"

A barge overturned, spilling three horses into the water, creating a sudden maelstrom of confusion as the frightened beasts fought the current, neighing shrilly. Sullivan, whose horse was among the three, shouted, "Get them! Get them! For God's sake, don't let them drown!"

The foxhunter, stumbling through the dark, looking for the harried, tireless Glover, came up with Knox and grasped both his shoulders, demanding, "For God's sake, Harry, it's past midnight! Why can't you get the guns loaded?"

Knox was soaked with sweat and river water, alternately feverish and chilled, his boots full of icy slush, his hate gone, his coat split down the back. He looked at the tall man pleadingly, shaking his head, "I'm doing my best, sir, I can't do more than that. It's the ice. The boats can't go across to where they want to go; they have to float downstream and then be dragged up. And I've been trying to get powder and shot across, sir—in case we want to use the guns in a hurry."

"Well, get them across, Harry! Get them across! And call for Glover. My voice is gone—call out!"

Knox roared and bellowed like a bull, but when he turned around again, the Virginian had gone off into the dark.

At two o'clock in the morning, most of the army had already been ferried across the river. Working like demons, the fishermen had once more accomplished the impossible; they had pushed the army and guns through the black night, the ice and the current, to a point on the other bank some nine miles distant from the Hessian encampment at

Trenton. Glover coming to report, found the foxhunter standing with Knox and Greene.

"I think that you had better go across now, sir," Glover said. "The worst part of it is over."

Washington nodded, and Greene took his arm to help him down into the boat. But he stood aside and said, "Get in, Harry. I'll feel safer once you're set."

For Knox, the reaction was close to hysteria. He climbed into the boat, bellowing laughing until the tears ran over his cheeks. He sat down, and Greene followed him, and then the Virginian, helped by the steadying hand of Glover, stepped in. He looked around for a place to sit, and then poked the fat colonel of artillery with his toe, telling him:

"Shift your weight, Harry, and trim the boat."

The fishermen pushed off from shore, their hard laughter breaking for once the wall that had been between them and the tall Virginia farmer; and Knox, still shaking with mirth, felt a great happiness and a great pride, for next to him, on the same seat, and close against him, was the man he loved more than any other. He looked at Washington, and saw how the light grey eyes were searching the darkness; and Knox knew, and Greene knew, with fierce joy, that this was not the end, that for their kind there could never be an end, but only new beginnings.

AN AFTERWORD

SOME books end with the last page; this one does not, for the sound of the bleeding feet that marched on Trenton rose in a crescendo that echoed and re-echoed across the world, and that today is not lost, and that will not, God willing, be lost for all time to come. How the poor shivering rabble came on to Trenton and captured the place, taking over a thousand prisoners, is too well known to need retelling here.

But the man who had set out across the Delaware as a Virginia farmer, as a foxhunter, became on the other shore something else, a man of incredible stature, a human being in some ways more godly and more wonderful than any other who has walked on this earth. For he became, as with no other man in history, the father of a nation that was to be peopled by the wretched and the oppressed of every land on earth.

CONCEIVED IN
LIBERTY

A NOVEL OF VALLEY FORGE

FOR MY WIFE

AND HERE
IN THIS PLACE
OF SACRIFICE
IN THIS VALE OF HUMILIATION
IN THIS VALLEY OF THE SHADOW
OF THAT DEATH OUT OF WHICH
THE LIFE OF AMERICA ROSE
REGENERATE AND FREE
LET US BELIEVE
WITH AN ABIDING FAITH
THAT TO THEM
UNION WILL SEEM AS DEAR
AND LIBERTY AS SWEET
AND PROGRESS AS GLORIOUS
AS THEY WERE TO OUR FATHERS
AND ARE TO YOU AND ME
AND THAT THE INSTITUTIONS
WHICH HAVE MADE US HAPPY
PRESERVED BY THE
VIRTUE OF OUR CHILDREN
SHALL BLESS
THE REMOTEST GENERATION
OF THE TIME TO COME

— HENRY ARMITT BROWN

Inscription on the Memorial Arch of Valley Forge

PART ONE

THE VALLEY

1

WE STOP, and the word comes down the line to bivouac. It's early; there's a good hour of daylight left. We are used to march until the light is gone, stumble into camp in the dark, wake up in the morning before the light and go on.

There is a faint sound of a bugle, far up the line, dismount. Jacob Eagen drops his pack. Charley Green sits down at the side of the road. His round, bearded, elf's face attempts a smile. His little form is a punctured bubble of weariness. I look up and down the line. Toward evening, the line is four, five, maybe six miles long.

I crawl out of my pack, say: "Ah, Jesus, I'm tired."

All up and down the road men are dropping to the ground. Their muskets clatter against the frozen road. That's the first idea; get rid of your musket. It weighs twenty pounds. It's twenty pounds of hell with a rusty bayonet.

"Why do we stop?" Jacob asks, but of no one. He alone is tireless. He stands stiff and grim, his dark eyes questioning. He probes face after face, and desires to know why we don't go on. He's a tall, spare man, bearded, his long hair falling loose to his shoulders, his large hooked nose thrusting forth from his face. His lips are a thin line, almost hidden by the hair on his face. He might well have no lips at all, and when his mouth parts to speak, I see his uneven, tobacco-stained teeth. There is something fierce and animal-like about his mouth and teeth, about the sharp, wide-spaced yellow fangs.

"What difference so long as we stop?"

"This ain't a place to stop. You don't have to be a general to know this ain't a fit place to stop." He waves a lean arm to indicate our open, unprotected position.

We are in a great flat space, with a roll of hills to the north of us. The hills mean shelter. We think of what it would be for six miles of army to be caught in this open space. But not too much thinking, because most of us don't care.

I saw down at the side of the road, sighing, stretching my feet, calculating how long I could stay that way, rest without my feet freezing. It was a cold day; half an hour, and my feet would freeze.

Next to me and around me were the men of my regiment. There were eight men besides myself who made up the regiment. We had no officers. You don't need officers for nine men. We had a shred of flag until Ely Jackson covered his feet with it. We were the Fourth New York Regiment. There were three hundred of us at one time, Major Anton, of White Plains; he died at White Plains near his own house. Eeden Sage had been a captain, dead. Lieutenant Ferrel died of dysentery. Now, some day in December in seventeen seventy-seven, we had no officers. I don't know what day it was. When you retreat, the days blend themselves together. Maybe it was the thirteenth of December, or the fourteenth. The thirteenth and Friday, perhaps, which is a rare black day. Charley Green had a song about Friday thirteenth, about witches dancing on Boston Common —

The army spilled off the road onto the fields, a haphazard sort of bivouac. I remember that there was one house, a stone building set back against a fringe of forest. The windows were shuttered; no light and no smoke. We were in a country that hated the rebels.

We climbed off the road, a sunken road. We climbed up to the flat of the meadow. Ely Jackson stopped to fix the cloths on his feet; his feet were always bleeding. A pet staff officer rode by us, a boy in a blue uniform. Jacob Eagen stopped him.

"Tell us, son," Jacob said. "We camp here?"

Jacob Eagen, bearded, filthy, a fringe of ice around his mouth, was not nice to look at. None of us was. The boy shook loose his reins.

"We encamp tomorrow. We're resting the troops."

"That's damn nice of you and the General," Jacob said bitterly.

The boy spurred away, and Jacob laughed. Jacob hated officers. God knows, none of us loved them, but there was something of madness in Jacob's hatred. He was a rare man for feeling the revolution, not the way the rest of us felt it, hunger and cold, but as a living, burning thing made by the people. He would argue of the officers, If they're of the revolution, they're of us. It's a war of man by man. I'll call God my superior, but no damned man on a horse. Talking that way now, but we didn't listen. Talk of Jacob's was like wind sighing; we had listened until the words meant nothing — only the bitter growl of his voice. We walked on. We buried ourselves in the troops. There was no army left now, only five or six miles of rabble strung out over the countryside. It was better to be inside than on the outskirts.

We passed the Pennsylvania line. Their general, Wayne, held them in some kind of order. They were camped in brigades and putting out sentries. A sentry stopped us, a tall southland farm boy. We laughed in his face and pushed past him.

He said: "Who the hell are you? What call you got pushing through Pennsylvania land?"

Edward Flagg said gently: "This land deeded to you?" He was a slow man, Edward, a big farmer, slow to anger, but long-burning wnen his ire was roused."

"We don't want fights," I told the boy. "We're a New York regiment." We walked on. He called after us, "You're a lousy-low regiment, all right."

We got off the Pennsylvania land; we didn't want trouble. You give men guns and drive them mad, then there's hell to pay. "I'll tell you 'bout this war," Kenton Brenner said. "It'll be north fighting south, and east fighting west. I don't hold with no low German Pennsylvania sonovabitch. I don't hold with no German who takes a gun when it ain't no more use. Where, I reckon, they been at Breed's Hill and White Plains?"

"You hold on, Kenton," Moss said. Moss was just a boy. He was eighteen years old, and next on the list. The list was an idea of Moss'. That we were named off to die. Sometimes he would sit for hours, trying to recall the names on the regiment's first muster. A long list, and there was no moving the names. Anyway, he talked about it so much that we got to believe him. You only had to look at Moss to know he was next. He had a cough that kept flecking his lips with blood. When he said something, we all looked at him. Now we were quiet.

The officers' tents were rising, dotting the brown, frozen fields. The brigades were scattered all over the fields, no order, and some of the last ones to march up were set right on the road. You could see brigades sprawled on the hard ground as far as the edge of the woods, and north and south until the fields touched the horizon.

"A lot of men," Jacob said.

"Ten, eleven thousand," I nodded.

"They'll go."

"I'm tired," Moss said simply. "I been thinking of going along home."

We came to where there were a few fruit trees, and no brigades nearer than thirty paces. We dropped our packs and slumped down on the earth. Kenton Brenner began to stack the muskets, working automatically and moving slowly. We watched him with quiet curiousity. We were very tired.

The kind of weariness that comes from too little food and no real rest. It goes into every joint and every limb of the body. It eats deep. It saturates and brings a vision into the mind, and the vision persists above everything else. That's a vision of a bed, a broad down bed. The down would take you into itself and eat the weariness out of your bones. Sometimes, too, you think of a trundle bed, a child in a trundle bed. Or a hot Dutch oven with bread cooking. Things of home.

We stretched and crouched on the cold ground. Someone would have to start the fire. We looked at each other, but nobody moved. Then Charley Green got up and walked away. We followed him with our eyes, but didn't call him back. I stood up, took a hand axe out of my pack, and began to hack at the fruit tree. It was an apple or plum tree; I don't remember. It was hard wood.

They watched me with deep, significant pain in their eyes, pain that understood the decades of anticipation that made up the growing of the tree. Someone had planted it and watched it grow. Someone had picked the ripe fruit in the heat of Indian summer.

Clark opened his mouth to speak, then stopped himself. They waited until I leaned on the branch and tore it down. They Ely Jackson stood up and began to break it apart.

"I call to mind the wonderful fruit of a summer," Moss whispered.

I paused; I was hacking on a second branch. I filled myself with the single impulse that every man in the army had. One more summer. Only one more summer with hot sun to make the sweat pour from you. Only one more summer with the juice of fruit bursting its skin.

Then I beat the branch down.

Ely was working with flint and steel. Ely was the oldest, older than Jacob even, and Jacob was a man past forty. Ely was our voice, when a soft voice was needed. Ely was water on fire when we fought in anger among ourselves, and God knows we fought enough of late. He had a loose fleshless body and big hands. I watched the hands now, their sure, tireless motion. Tinder was rare and precious. Kenton shredded it from the inside of his hat. I looked at them and told myself that I had probed deep. I was twenty-one years old. But there were eight men whose souls I knew and whose bodies I knew.

An officer galloped up, reined in his horse, and told me to leave off the tree.

"No pillage," he said. I thought I recognized him. He was bearded and wore no uniform. I thought I recognized him as an aide of Washington. He spoke with the slur of a Virginian.

Eagen got up. He walked over to the stacked muskets. The rest of us rose. We stood in a circle round the officer. Our clothes were filthy and torn. We were all bearded, even Moss Fuller who was only eighteen and whose beard was a patched map on his face. We were filthy and lean, our feet bound in sacking. The sacking on Ely Jackson's feet was a mass of caked blood. There was something wrong with his feet, and they wouldn't heal. They bled all the time, draining the lifeblood out of him.

"Who's in command here? What brigade?"

"Fourth New York."

Kenton Brenner took his musket. Jacob too. There was sullen light in Jacob's eyes. The officer noticed that, and he said to Jacob:

"You're in command? Where is the rest of your regiment?"

"We're all," Jacob said. "No officers."

He leaned over his saddle, pointed to the tree. "You're killing that tree."

We laughed at him. I raised my axe. The officer drew his pistol, aimed it at my head. "There'll be no pillage," he said.

I brought down the axe. I didn't think he would fire. Maybe I didn't care. As in a dream, I heard the pistol roar, and it tore off my hat. I walked forward, the axe in my hand, but Jacob was ahead of me. He struck the pistol down with the barrel of his musket and tore the man from his horse. I saw Jacob's clenched fist lash into the officer's face.

The officer lay on the ground, and we stood there, watching him, not speaking, but just looking at one another. There were Boston men camped near us. They came over, attracted by the shot. They made a crowd around him, and they didn't love officers, not southern officers.

"Oughta killed the swine," one of them said.

"You oughta killed the dirty slave-driving bastard."

The officer groaned and stumbled to his feet. He mounted and rode off. The Boston men left us, and Eagen sat down and put his head in his arms.

We had the fire going. We tore down most of the fruit tree to feed it. Fires were springing up now, gleams that mingled with the twilight. The staff officers rode past, the big form of Washington bulking above the rest. We saw them ride across the fields to the house and hammer at the door. Then the door opened. The shutters were flung back and lights appeared inside.

"A house like that," Moss whispered.

187

"Quakers. By God, they're warm in their houses," Jacob muttered.

Ely Jackson laughed. We had some potatoes in our packs. We laid them out and roasted them on the points of our bayonets. Ed Flagg had stolen the potatoes the day before. They were a rare thing for men on a diet of corn.

We heard singing. Charley Green walked up to the fire with a woman on his arm. She was a stout, blonde woman, wrapped in a dirty blanket. Her feet were in sacking. She had a broad smile. We watched her hungrily; you watched any fat person with fascination.

"This is Jenny Carter," Charley said. "She's a fine fat piece of women." Then he began to sing again.

She dropped down by the fire, her fat legs spread toward it. She moved her hands, anxiously fixing her hair. We began to laugh.

"Where did you find her, Charley?"

"I took her from the Pennsylvania men. A sight of women, too many for stinking Dutch farmers. I reckon they have a hundred women there. I took Jenny and told her we were from the Mohawk. I told her a fine, tall lot of men from the Mohawk. I told her men to love a woman, eh, Jenny?"

He sat down next to her and put an arm around her shoulders.

"A filthy lot of beggars," she said, and spat.

"You won't mind a little dirt."

"I won't mind a little bit of money."

Jacob took a fistful of Continental paper out of his sack. He dropped it into her lap. She scattered it and the hot flame of the fire drew it in.

"None of that!"

"Ye're a haggling Dutch skinner," Jacob said.

I tossed her a shilling and she thrust it into the sacking that covered her feet. We broke the potatoes and added a few shreads of salt meat. We ate slowly, hoarding the food. It was quite dark now. Against the western sky, the dull mass of the brigades was still visible. But in the east, all had blended into the forest and only the fires made spots of light.

North of us, where the fields sloped to a hill, the fires were a pattern, haphazard. As if fireflies had settled themselves in the field and would soon lift away. The glow in the west died out. The wind rose to a whine.

"A cold, bitter night," said Clark Vandeer.

"A night for a woman —"

"For a fat, round woman."

Jenny was giggling and stuffing a piece of potato into her mouth.

Then she rolled back in the arms of Charley Green. Some of us watched, but not with too much interest. We spoke in low tones when we spoke at all, but we could hear the woman heaving and sighing. Far over, from where the New Jersey troops were, there came a confused roar of sound.

Ely Jackson fussed with the bindings on his feet. Sometimes I suspected that there was little feeling left in his feet. But no more than that. I couldn't associate death with Ely. I remembered a time, perhaps ten years ago, when the Hurons came down to the Mohawk. They burnt and killed. Ely came to our house. Then we went with him, from house to house, gathering families. We went to the Patroons' fort, an old rotten place, and Ely and six men fought a hundred Indians for two days. He was a great, strong man, Ely.

"They say there'll be shoes along with the army in a time of days," Ely said wistfully.

"The lies of fatback swine in the Congress."

"There's no hate in me for the British as for the Congress," Clark said.

"There's hate in me for both," Jacob said. "For the rotten, guzzling liars who call themselves our Congress—" He stared into the fire a moment, then went on, "Time for Congress—understand me, Clark—time enough for Congress—after the British. After the British," he repeated. His eyes traveled over the sparks that marked the position of the sprawling, defeated army.

"After the British," he said dully.

"They say we'll be going home," Moss Fuller muttered plaintively.

But there was nothing to go to. The Indians had burnt out the Mohawk. If my people lived, God only knew where they were.

"I'll not go back to the Mohawk," Jacob nodded. "There'll be no safe living in the New York Valleys. They'll fight us from Canada for a hundred years.

"You won't hold a musket a hundred years, Jacob," Kenton laughed.

"I hear of a rare beautiful land in Transylvania, a place they call the Kentuck. A Virginian named Boone sought it out—"

Jacob cried: "Ye're fools—all o' ye. The British way is to play the red men against us. Where is the power of the Six Nations but in Joseph Brant? An' Brant's their tool. Didn' they have him in England, making him into what he is? Mark me—I'll tell you the power an' scheme of the British, to play one force against another. But we're a free people an' no plaything for a King's hand. There'll be peace in the west—when we drive the last King's man back to his dirty hole?"

189

From where he was with his woman, Charley groaned: "Peace here, Jacob. Let be and damn the British."

Jenny had rolled over. She lay flat on her back, and Charley Green sat up, shaking his head wearily.

"You've used her up," Kenton said.

Jacob's mood changed. He got up and went over to her. He slapped her back and pinched her cheeks. "Look at a real man."

"You'll kill her," Moss Fuller complained. He wanted his turn. He wanted the little pleasure he could squeeze from her. He was trembling and anxious, with the fear of death in him.

Jacob lay down next to her. We crouched close to the fire. From the New Jersey troops there came a great uproar, shots fired. We stayed close to the fire, hardly moving. With the heat, inertia had come over us.

"Attack?" Ely asked.

No more shots now. It didn't matter whether we were being attacked. Two officers galloped past, their sabres bare and glistening in the firelight.

"More hell to pay."

Silence and Jacob's hoarse breathing. I glanced at them, the man and the women together. Only a glance. Moss Fuller had buried his head in his arms. He was coughing softly. Ely hummed a lonely French tune of the Valleys.

I tried to think of a time when it had been different. I tried to think of a time when there had been shame and humility. I tried to think of the fire in our hearts that had sent us out to fight in the beginning.

I speak my name. My name is Allen Hale. I am twenty-one years old. I am a soldier with the Continental army of America. I have come great distances to fight for freedom.

The fire burns low, and Kenton rises to hack at the fruit trees. He comes back and drops the wood on the fire. He says:

"I wouldn't think to destroy a fruit tree. For a matter of ten years I saved the seed of cherry and plum. We thought to make a great planting in the Lake country when we moved westward. After the war we'll move westward—I'll save the seeds again."

The fire burns up. The brigades are quiet; perhaps they sleep. Moss lies with the woman, and his deep, regular breathing tells us that he sleeps. We none of us would take the woman now and rouse Moss from his sleep.

Some Massachusetts men come and stand about the fire. Most of their brigades are without fire. They crowd close to the fire and break the wind from us. One is an officer, a bearded boy in a tattered field dress of grey homespun, carrying a rusty sword at his belt.

The talk is soft, because some of the men sleep.

A Massachusetts man says: "I hear the retreat will be in a great circle. I hear the General has in mind to strike south around Philadelphia and march across the mountains. They tell of a rare fair land there in Transylvania, a land surveyed by a man called Boone. We can live there and take our food from the ground and defend the land."

"And our wives — children?"

"A man with bonds is no man for an army."

"There's no army now," Kenton muttered.

"If there are five thousand men here with bonds, will they lay down their arms and go back for hanging?"

"There won't be hanging after peace."

"There'll be no peace so long as George Washington lives. And there's a hell's broth in Wayne and his Pennsylvania brigades."

Vandeer said, softly: "At Haarlem, we held while Wayne's men ran."

"The ground's fallow two years now. When the army's gone, they'll take the ground. If there were women in this land of Kentuck —"

"Where do we march tomorrow?" Eagen asked.

The Massachusetts officer answered: "A place to the north and east called the Valley Forge."

"We camp there?"

Later, the Massachusetts men went back. The fire burnt aown. There were sparks of dying fires all over the fields.

I tried to sleep. Ely Jackson rose and took his musket.

"Ely?"

"I'll stand guard awhile," he said.

Green began to laugh. It was that strange for a man to stand guard. For what was the point in guarding? Any blow would crumple us. We were no army. Once we had been an army — but not now.

It began to snow, large, dry white flakes. Ely stood there, holding his musket with bare hands. He became a lump of white, motionless, the flakes floating past him.

2

I SAY to myself, oh, give me a long sleep with an end in the hot sun of the long morning. I yearn for a fire, all of my body stretching toward where the fire had been. There is no fire. I realize that my sleep has been broken, on and off through the night. A bugle is trilling. I sit up and the snow falls from me, two or three inches of snow on the ground, Green and Lane and Brenner and Eagen—piles of snow.

I stand up, trembling with cold, my body half numb. The men are dead. I glance around. The brigades are covered with snow. Ely Jackson stirs and Jacob Eagen climbs to his feet, trembling with cold. We blow on our hands, slap them against our sides, dance up and down.

"I had a wild, terrible fancy," I say, "that all the brigades are dead."

Ely smiles. His beard is all white with ice and snow.

"Ye're a strange being for thinking such thoughts," Jacob tells me.

The rest of us wake. We've slept close together, yearning toward each other for the body's heat. Only Moss Fuller still sleeps, the fat woman clutching him close.

"A woman's a good thing for a sleeping man," Edward nods.

Figures of ice and snow: we try to build a fire, but it's a hopeless task. We give it up and crunch the dry corn, chew on the salt meat enough so that we can swallow it. All the time, we move for warmth. The brigades are up, and the broken sound of voices carries over the fields. Officers canter by. Everywhere men are stamping for warmth. Here and there, a fire that was nursed through the night is built up.

"We'll go into camp soon, or we'll die," Vandeer says.

I nod, trying to rub the chill out of my arms and legs. One or two nights like this can be endured, but no more than that. I have never wanted anything so much as I desire heat now.

Ely points to a fire over among the Pennsylvania brigades. "I can get a brand," he suggests. The bugle blows, to arms.

"We march soon."

"To hell with that!"

"I am thinking hell's a rare cold place," Kenton Brenner smiles. His face is blue and purple with frost, the dead flesh breaking on his nose. I wonder how men endure it, how I endure it. But I keep stamping around. Only get warm, I think. The idea of warmth, any warmth, possesses me.

"Wake Moss."

With the toe of his boot, Jacob prods the woman. He says: "High time to be moving, Jenny."

Charley Green grins, standing feet apart, his face dull with sleep, his hands in his armpits for warmth. Ely walks toward the Pennsylvania men, slowly, stiltedly, as if each step pained the bottom of his feet. I can understand how his mind is set only on fire; he'll bring back the fire. He'll talk to them gently; he has a way with him.

We stand round Moss and Jenny. The woman moves and stretches her arms. The cold bites, and her hands seek out Moss. Then she screams and sits up.

"He's cold," she whimpered.

Vandeer laughed. Her nose had turned bright red during the night and her hair had spread all over her face. She was an ugly, fat, gross creature. We were all of us filthy and ugly, broken in one way or another. But I hated her because she reminded me of things that had once been and brought them back to me, because she was a mocking caricature of a woman. The kind of woman I had known, once.

I dragged her to her feet. I held her, her dirty blanket clutched in my hands, shaking her back and forth. The others watched me. Henry Lane was smiling stupidly, but the others didn't move. They just watched.

"You'll kill me!" she cried.

Then I let go of her. "Get out of here," I whispered.

She arranged her blanket, turning round and round, patting the loose strands of her yellow hair into place. "I'm a good woman, I want you to know," she said. "I'm a good, respectable woman."

Vandeer was laughing again. He was a little man; he had been a minister before the war. He had had two brothers who were killed at White Plains. Lately he had been like this. I could understand that. He was forty years old, yet he had become as lightheaded as a boy.

"Better go," Jacob Eagen told her.

She stumbled away, turning every now and then to swear at us and to scream at us that she was a good woman. Jacob bent down next to Moss, shaking him gently. Jacob was hard and bitter, but now with Moss he was gentle as a woman. He took the hair away from Moss' face, and we saw blood clotted and frozen above his thin beard.

Jacob stood up, said: "He's cold." When he said that, we knew.

The boy's eyes were open. Vandeer had stopped laughing. I bent over Moss and pulled off his thin cloak, scattering snow. I forced my hands to go to his eyes and close them.

"It's a hard man needed to stand many nights like this night," Brenner said softly.

"He's dead?" Jacob asked me, and then demanded, querulously: "Where's Ely? This is no time for Ely to be away from us."

"Ely went for fire," Edward said, dully.

193

"Why'd he go for fire? It's too late for fire, ain't it? There was a time for fire before, but it's too late for fire now. The fire will not bring Moss alive."

"He went to wheedle a little fire out of those Pennsylvania men—he has a way, Ely—"

"Shut up!"

"We couldn't be starting a fire with flint. Ely'll come with a burning brand. Cold hands can't hold flint."

"There's nothing Ely can do now, Jacob."

Jacob knelt down by Moss. I went over to the fruit tree and sat down with my back against it. The cold was all through me, but it was not such a cold as Moss Fuller knew, nowhere near such a deep and silent cold.

"You're sure he's dead?"

"He's dead," Jacob said.

The bugles were blowing, and all along the line, brigades were picking themselves up and starting to move. The sun came up, showing through the stretch of forest east of us. Along the forest, men were moving in a thin line. They wore the shapeless grey smocks of Virginian riflemen. The officers were prancing their horses, shouting orders. In a long file, McLane's cavalry rode from behind the grey stone house and paraded across the fields. The Massachusetts men were laughing with their women while they formed into ranks.

"He's dead," Jacob said again, covering over Moss' face with the cloak. He said to me: "Come and give me a hand, Allen."

I stood up. The broken branches of the fruit tree brushed my face. Past Jacob, I saw Ely Jackson coming back with a piece of burning wood in his hand. It was a wonder how Ely got things, how he could work men.

"A fine fire soon!" Ely called.

Then he came up, saw how we were standing. He glanced from face to face, puzzled, meanwhile kicking the snow off the ashes of last night's fire. He said:

"Take an axe, Allen, and bleed the tree a little. Just a little, Allen—it's a fine tree."

I didn't move. He said: "Moss is sleeping? Wake him—or he'll not be able to march."

"Moss isn't sleeping," I said.

"He's dead," Jacob said. "The boy's dead, Ely."

"It was a fierce cold last night, and too much for him," Kenton muttered.

194

Ely stared stupidly, shook his head, and let go the torch. It fell into the snow, spluttered a little, and then went out. Nobody moved to pick it up. Ely went over to Moss and uncovered his face. He knelt there for a while, and I could see Ely's feet were a frozen mass of ice and blood. The thought came into my mind immediately: Moss had shoes. They were worn thin now, but they were boots nevertheless. Jacob had pulled them off a dead Hessian a month before and given them to Moss. I wondered who would speak about it first. I couldn't understand that Moss was dead; only his shoes mattered now.

Looking at Ely's feet, I told myself: "Ely will have them." I glanced down at my own feet. I told myself that Ely had seen his youth already and that Ely would die soon. That was not true. Ely would live. His feet could become rotten stumps, and still Ely would live. I cursed him, and then I hated myself for cursing him — for his strength.

Ely stood up, but said nothing. He looked at me.

"He was a fine, tall Valley boy," Edward Flagg said. "I wouldn't have thought him to die so soon."

"He had a cough—"

"He died for wanting home. It's a long distance to the Valley country."

We nodded. We stood around, striking our hands together. Clark Vandeer came and stood above Moss. We watched him.

"You'll bury him and I'll say a few words," Vandeer said. His face seemed to be remembering.

"The ground's uncommon hard," Lane muttered.

Ely said: "Go to the Massachusetts men, Charley, and ask for a bugler to sound a call."

We took our bayonets and jabbed at the ground. I chopped with my axe. The ground was frozen, hard as stone. Once Jacob stopped, and I saw him looking at Moss' boots. I knew what was in his mind.

We dug a foot deep, and it seemed to exhaust us. We stood back and waited for Green to come back with the Massachusetts man. We stood there thinking, and maybe we were all thinking the same thing.

Finally, Jacob said: "The boy has an uncommon fine pair of boots—"

"We won't bury him naked," Ely said. "Two years together, so we'll not bury him naked."

"I was thinking only of the boots."

"Let him wear his boots."

"You need a pair of boots, Ely."

"I said he'll wear his boots. I swear to God, Jacob, I'll kill you if you

195

HOWARD FAST

take off his boots."

"There ain't no call to rage, Ely," Jacob said. "He's dead and no more feeling heat and cold. He don't need the boots, and you need them, Ely."

Ely said nothing, only staring at Moss' figure on the ground. Jacob went over and pulled off his boots, every so often glancing back at Ely, but Ely didn't move.

"I'm sorry, Ely."

Now Charley was back with a bugler from the Massachusetts brigade. A good many of the Boston men came with him, out of curiosity. They stood round in a circle, while we lifted Moss' body into the grave. A Massachusetts man said:

"They plough this land come spring. That grave's not deep enough."

We pushed the dirt, and Vandeer said a few words. Vandeer's voice clogged up.

"A long way home," Ely said.

The bugle call drifted up, fine and clear in the morning air. It was what I would have wanted, if I were in Moss' place. There was a drummer, and he rolled several times. That was nice too. The brigades were moving now, and many of them stopped to watch what we were doing. But it was too common a sight to keep them for long. They marched on. The whole army was moving.

Jacob took Moss' bayonet and thrust it into the head of the grave. The bayonet was rusted and bent, and not much good. We gave the musket to a Massachusetts man. None of us was in any condition to carry two muskets, and a good many of the Massachusetts men were without arms.

The Massachusetts brigades were moving, and their men drifted away. We stood awhile, watching Washington and his aides come out of the grey stone building, mount and ride away to the head of the army.

We walked to the road.

"A long march today," Lane said.

"I don't remember knowing a place called the Valley Forge. An iron smithy, perhaps. This has the look of iron country."

"Why march north, if he plans a march southward after?"

"They say he's a rare quiet man to tease the British in his own way."

"He's a great fool if he thinks these an army."

Clark said suddenly: "Where's Moss?" He had forgotten.

We are on the road again. It is the sort of day when the sun makes a mirror of the snow, and after a while the snow can blind you.

196

The whole army is moving, slowly, but moving nevertheless. I wonder how that is and what makes us move. I seem to lose myself in the common soul of beggars strung out for six miles.

We march behind the Pennsylvania men. And behind us the Massachusetts brigades. Twelve lumbering wagons pass us by. From inside, there is the squalling of women, of the whores who are almost as many as the men. One of them puts her head out between the canvas curtains, and sticks her tongue out from between her teeth.

Charley Green calls: "Come and walk with us, lassie!"

"She's a pretty little wench," Edward nods.

We walk along and we don't think of Moss. There's no use thinking of Moss. We're too near to him. The veil between the dead and the living has been drawn too thin.

The Massachusetts men are singing, and we join in. The song runs, rocking the line, mile after mile:

> *"Yankee-Doodle went to London,*
> *Riding on a pony—"*

3

WE'VE COME, and there's a feeling now that we'll go no farther. We're not resting; I understand that vaguely, but still I understand it. There is no rest.

Ely Jackson says it. It's a terrible thing to see a strong, proud man die slowly, bit by bit. Ely says:

"There'll be no march to the south. He was a wonderous strong man, that Daniel Boone, to go on all his journeys. But we won't follow over his wilderness road to Transylvania. We're no more an army."

"A tired feeling," I said. "I can't march."

Kenton says: "We make a stand here—to meet the British. I call to mind how it was at Breed's Hill, with their red coats flashing. A proud lot of good men. Moss cried. He was sixteen of age."

"Not a thing for a boy to see," Ely says. "A bitter thing, the way they marched the hill—to be blown to bits. I recall there was a boy drumming for the British. He was shot in the belly, and still he tried to drum. Just a boy—"

That was Breed's Hill—Bunker Hill, they call it now.

"A boy like Moss," Ely went on. "It put iron into his soul, and he was too young, too young."

197

We sit around a fire, this time a great, roaring fire. But it has no power to warm us. The cold is in our bones. The cold beats down the flames and adds up on itself.

We are camped on the top of a hill, forest to one side of us and a sweep of meadowland on the other. All over the hill and down into the valley fires burn. Westward, in the bed of a creek, the valley drops to the Schuylkill. The place is called the Valley Forge. There was a forge once where the creek enters the river, a few houses there. It goes that the officers are taking up quarters in the houses.

East, across eighteen or twenty miles of the same rolling land, is Philadelphia. We glance again and again in the direction of Philadelphia. We try to picture a British army, correct, uniformed. They sleep in warm houses. At night, they gather in the taverns and toast each other with warm ale. Philadelphia — men, women, and warm beds — is theirs.

We try to understand that this is the end, that we go no farther.

Clark Vandeer shrugs his shoulders. He is crouched close to the fire, so close that his beard singes without his seeming to be aware of it. He has become an old man since Moss died, and many of his former parson's ways have returned to him.

"I'm afraid," Edward says. That's the way with Edward, who was a strong man once, a heavy farmer man, not dreaming and not fearing.

Ely Jackson shakes his head.

"If our orders are to march tomorrow?" Edward says, anxiously.

In each face is the same fear, that we march. We are too worn to march, too tired. We try to see the way out of the place. The slopes are covered with snow and bright in the moonlight. We crowd up to the fire.

Below us, the Pennsylvanians have built their fires in a wide circle. Each fire is an ember. Between half-closed eyes their encampment might be a crown. My mind is full of fancy, caused by hunger. Jacob sought out the commissary at nightfall. He came back bleeding, with a hatful of corn — for eight men.

"You're too quick for blood," Ely said gently.

Jacob is silent through the evening. A strange, deep man, Jacob, hard. When he was a boy, he fought in the French war. He was a revolutionist then — and no halfway man. In his mind, the revolution began with the French war. It was all one and the same — drive out the French first, then the British. A land for the people. That was what Jacob preached — for the people, all of it. The Indian must go. But first the French, then the British. Both had played along with the Indians, played them against us. He had fought to destroy the French, and now he was fighting to destroy the British. He would always fight. The land was not for him, but for them who came after. Jacob would fight until a shot found him; then he would rest. But the land would never be his.

"I call to mind," Ely says, "how Moss spoke about home. They say four brigades of Maryland men walked out of the line with fixed bayonets."

"It's only the beginning."

"They're a strange bad breed, the Maryland men. Pope-crawlers and sons of thieves," Jacob muttered.

"Only the beginning," I said. "The army's falling to pieces. By God, when I think of that stinking Congress, talking of united states, filling their fat bellies and letting us starve. We fight for Maryland and Maryland walks home. What did Moss die for this morning?"

"Leave him in peace," Clark Vandeer says quietly.

"He spoke of the Mohawk—"

Ely says, simply: "Where would you go, deserting, Allen? We're all of us used up."

"Afraid?"

"I'm not afraid," Ely said. He looked at me. His swollen feet were stretched out towards the fire, his thin hands trying to grasp the heat. His dark eyes looked at me and through me.

Vandeer says, fretfully: "Why—why, Ely? You don't believe any more. There'll be no peace with Virginians hating the Boston men, with the New York brigades feared and hated. Even if we win, there'll be no peace—only battle and more battle."

Ely didn't answer. Jacob raised his dark, shaggy head. Above us, against the forest, shreds of song floated down from the New Jersey line. They were singing a plaintive Dutch melody. I lay down, closed my eyes and tried to sleep. Kenton was talking. He was explaining the thing I had heard a hundred times before, how the colonies could send an army into the New York Valleys and destroy the Six Nations. He was explaining why England would never permit the colonies to overwhelm the Indians.

"The moment we become strong," Kenton says, "we become a nation. It's our destiny." More of abstract destiny. What has that to do with a defeated rabble?

Jacob joins in, his bitter voice marking time to the nodding of his shaggy head. "Ye're right, Kent, and the strength is here—a strength of many. Look you, we could go back to the Mohawk where they're burnin' and killing, so God only knows who lives an' who's dead—but our strength is here. The Indians depend on the British, so it's our fight with the bastard King's men. After we rest, only one more blow. We'll gather strength an' hit them—hit them—"

I try to sleep, my coat drawn up over my face. I think of a woman; I think of little Moss Fuller with Jenny. I finger my beard and scrape the dirt from my face. The cold eats in and I turn my other side to the fire. For a moment, my eyes are open to the sky, and I see the broad stretch of stars. My hunger becomes a gnawing pain. I say to myself, sleep—don't think.

"—or Six Nations—or ten nations. If this man Washington sets himself up for king with his Virginia brigades behind him?"

"You mistake the man," Ely Jackson says.

The stars become sparks in a morning sky, and I lie awake watching the dawn come. The fire still burns, a low smouldering fire. I have slept on and off—a long night. Why have the nights become so long now? Rolling over, closer to the fire, I realize that someone fed it during the night. Wondering who, I think that it might be Ely or Kenton or one of the others. Charley Green, who was a printer in Albany; he was alien and strange for a long time. In the beginning he had been fat and round, but his fat had gone. Edward Flagg, born out of farmers. Or Jacob and Ely, strong men and different. Someone in the night, feeding the fire and making a great sacrifice in the cold.

I stood up; the others slept. They were curled for warmth, and they looked like bundles of rags. I remembered once, years ago, seeing a man dying of a cough, fleshless, but here were men as lean as he and living.

I walked toward the forest for wood. The snow had a crust of ice over it, and it crunched under my feet. As the morning advanced, there was no sign of sun in the sky, only a quilted grey that might turn to snow later on.

In front of the forest, the Jersey brigades lay, men sprawled about their fires. They had flung out sentries who slept now, all huddled over their muskets. I walked past, and the sentries didn't move. The Jersey men were worse than we; bare feet showed and bare skin through their coats. Almost no blankets and only two tents in all the brigades. They were tight, uncomplaining men, Dutch stock, not like the Pennsylvania German.

I gathered wood, went back and built up the fire. The heat of it woke Jacob and Henry. Then the Pennsylvania trumpets shrilled away the morning. The scene was old now, half-naked beggars coming to life, a great rush of movement back and forth to drive off the cold. The brigades were assembling.

"There's to be a review of the brigades today," Jacob said. "A grand review with a flag parade."

Charley, sprawled out, sang, "The beggars are coming to London Town, London Town . . ."

"We'll need a flag—"

"A great white flag with a smoked ham painted on it—a roasted ham with gravy dripping for a border to the flag."

We had no food; we stood and looked at the fire. Edward Flagg slowly munched a handful of snow.

"I wouldn't," Ely said. "The snow'll burn yer mouth and belly."

"The Jersey men are eating," I said. I could see a few camp kettles boiling over their fires.

"I'll go to the commissary," Ely said.

"They'll want an officer's requisition."

Ely stumbled off. "He'll not wear Moss' shoes," I said. "His feet are fair gone and shapeless, not to be put inside shoes."

"There was a good coat gone to the grave with Moss. The dead don't feel cold."

"The shoes shouldn't go to waste," I muttered. I sat down slowly untied the bandages over my feet, holding them close to the fire. Finally, they were bare, blue and frost. I let them warm by the fire. They were covered with sores, unhealed cuts, dirt.

"Rub them with snow, Allen."

I said, laughing: "They'll rot before I make them colder."

Vandeer said: "I call to mind a tract of Bishop Berkeley's I read through. A rare fine philosopher who holds that pain and all material things vanish with the mind that knows them."

"Well, Moss is dead, and we're here. I'd as leave be here as dead and stiff."

"But no cold for Moss," I said. "We can draw for the shoes, Jacob."

"They won't fit me," Edward said sullenly. He was a big man, big hands, big feet. I think he had the largest hands and feet I've ever seen on a man.

Kenton found a pair of dice and rolled them on a crust of snow. Henry drew the shoes with a double six. He held the boots between his knees, fondling them and feeling their softness. Then he unwrapped the bandages from his feet. The bandages clung, and he told us it was the first time in eight days he had bared his feet. When he got to his socks, he found they were crusted with blood. His feet were swollen out

201

of all shape.

We tried to force the boots on. Henry lay down on his back, his feet stretched out, his hands clenched with pain. I had a little tobacco left, and I broke off a piece of it, gave it to him to chew while we worked on his feet. He broke up the tobacco, chewing desperately, his face twisted with pain, the brown stain running over his beard.

When the boots were on, he made no move to rise. "I can't stand it," he whispered. "Take them off."

We bound up Henry's feet after that. Jacob insisted that we wash them, but Henry refused. I wanted the boots. We rolled again, and Kenton drew them. I told Kenton I would fight him for them: I told him man to man, I would stand against him and fight for the boots.

Jacob pushed me away. "Keep yer head, Allen," he said.

"They're Moss' boots," I said. "Where's Moss?"

I sat down on the ground, put my face in my hands. I was hungry and my head was light. I felt a great strength, as if I could fight Kenton and all the rest of them. I felt that I could walk with strides yards long.

Then I began to cry, easily; I kept my hands over my face. When I looked up, they were standing round me. I could see how Clark Vandeer's lower lip trembled. Vandeer was a little man with children of his own. Maybe he was thinking of them now.

"Easy, Allen, easy," Jacob said.

Kenton was still holding the boots in his hand. "I'm not needing shoes, Allen," he whispered.

I cried: "I know what you're thinking—me next! Moss and then me."

"We'll eat soon, Allen."

"Moss wanted to go home. There's no one of you got nerve enough to desert and go home! Jesus Christ, there's nothing left inside of me."

Ely came up. They walked away when Ely came. Only Kenton stood there, still holding the boots in his hand. He said, dully:

"We rolled the dice for Moss' shoes."

Ely didn't answer. He had a piece of fatback in his hands.

"You brought food," Jacob nodded. "Ye're a wonderous quick man, Ely." He walked back slowly and put himself between Ely and Kenton. "Ye're not angered about the shoes, Ely?"

"There will be hell and murder at the commissariat. There's no food to feed ten thousand men. He asked me for papers, and I wheedled the fatback outa him. I said for a regiment. I thought he'd have a little corn. There were Boston and Pennsylvania men there with loaded guns."

"I don't hold with Pennsylvania men," Jacob said. "But I hate the guts of those damned Virginians, lording it over the food."

"They're a quiet, strange race."

I rose and walked away. Inside, I was heaving, and my throat burnt. Beyond the heat of the fire, the cold bit in, through my thin clothes. I resented Ely's way, avoiding mention of me or the shoes. When I turned round, they were grouped over a kettle, cutting up the fatback. Jacob poured the last of his cornmeal into it. The brigades were beginning to move, swarming round the forest and over the brink of the hill.

I went back to the fire. Ely put his arm through mine.

We ate quickly and in silence. We stood our muskets and wiped them carefully. That was habit; we didn't love the muskets. We walked along with the brigades, Massachusetts and Vermont men, Pennsylvanians, tall, light-haired Jersey Dutch. The talk was all of the spot we were camped in, of its virtues for defence. There were hills all round the Valley Forge. It was a natural fort.

I heard a man way: "If they attack on the Philadelphia road, it's another Breed's Hill." Apparently he didn't remember that at Bunker Hill we were fresh and new to war. There had been no other victories since then.

We moved in no order. Occasionally you heard an officer's voice, but for the most part the brigades stumbled along as they pleased. A great hatred had grown for the officers, and they were afraid. All aspect of an organized army had disappeared. We had not been paid in weeks; we had not been fed. I think we were kept together only by the fear of the cold spaces that lay between where we were and our homes. It was said that the British ringed us in with their patrols.

We moved around the forest, over the hill northward, and down onto a great open meadowland that stretched to the Schuylkill. Afterwards this became known as the Grand Parade. The brigades streamed over it, slowly forming into a rough kind of order—the Pennsylvania Line, north, the New Jersey Line, the New York Line, and Virginian Riflemen.

Round the field there was a scattering of people who lived in the neighborhood, mostly Quaker boys, hooting and screaming at the soldiers. The Massachusetts and Pennsylvania brigades still had drummers, and gradually their roll increased, until we were moving to a steady beat of drums. There were old habits hard to break.

The eight of us stood at one end of the Pennsylvania line, near the New York brigades. We leaned on our muskets, speaking little. And the wave of sound all up and down the brigades seemed to be dying away.

We could hear women's voices, and we saw officers driving them out of the Pennsylvania troops. The camp followers were formed in a rough line behind the brigades, the women making a pitiful attempt at colour.

"Nigh a thousand women," Jacob said.

"It's hard understanding what a woman'll take to be near a man."

The clouds were piling up, dark grey and white tumbled together. A battery of artillery rolled across the parade.

"Knox's cannon," Ely said.

There must have been almost ten thousand men on the field then. That was before mass desertions had reduced us to half that number, then to less than half. There were a mass of men.

I close my eyes and try to see them as an army. If I close my eyes, look between the frost on my lids, I can forget that half of them are without guns, and all them in rags. There are no uniforms except among the Virginian troops, who wear grey, homespun hunting shirts. There isn't a decent coat or a good pair of boots. Parts of the body show through, bare, blue buttocks where a man's pants are worn away, bare knees, legs bound in stripped blanket, feet in any material that can be made to cover feet. The feet are most important. Even if an army can't fight, it must be able to march—march day and night or forever.

But if I close my eyes, I can see them as an army, haggard, bearded men who will fight the way wild beasts fight. Only I fear we'll never fight again.

I laugh aloud.

Ely looks at me. Kenton says:

"You're not holding Moss' shoes against me, Allen. We've been together too long for that, Allen. I swear to God I'll never wear the shoes—"

"It's all right."

The trumpets blow a call to arms. We stand on our muskets. For an instant, we are no longer men, only a part of living revolution. We are a force. We are beyond men—only for an instant. The wind is blowing itself into a shrill shriek, and cold and hunger return.

A Pennsylvania man says, stubbornly: "To hell with their parades! Why don't they pay us off?"

Wayne and Scott ride down the Pennsylvania front. Wayne has a cloth bound round his head. His coat is shredded with use. He stoops in his saddle and rides close to Scott. There is a ripple of cheering, because they are both favourites with the Pennsylvania brigades. But neither man takes any notice. They sit on their horses in front of the line.

The flags go by. We don't salute. Very few men salute. We keep shifting about in the cold.

The officers press us together and finally we are in a line about four or five deep. Washington rides out to the center of the field. He sits big on his horse and he seems oblivious to the wind. He's a strange man whom none of us understand and few of us know. Sometimes, we can build a great hate for him. He's a man without fear.

Hamilton is next to him, sitting the horse like an aristocrat, the lace cuffs of his uniform showing, behind him a little cluster of officers.

The voice of the General doesn't carry; it rises and fades out entirely in the wind.

". . . have come a long way . . . a bitter cup to drink . . . to endure . . . the British suffer equally, without our faith . . ."

Someone shouts: "Where do they suffer—in Philadelphia?"

"We must endure all wrong—hate . . ."

"Where is our pay? By God, your stinking Continental money—"

I glance at Jacob. His dark eyes are burning. His face, blue with cold, working—in pain—in anger.

"Soon, there will be food enough . . . rations of rum . . . a petition to the Congress . . ."

"Lies while we starve!"

A Pennsylvania man says: "He's got his fat bit to sleep with, I'll swear."

"A house and enough food to stuff him like a pig."

". . . when we march out of here—to victory . . ."

His voice is drowned out by a deep refrain: Pay us and disband the army! It comes to the thud of rifle butts being stamped against the frozen groups. A thud to the rhythm of a beating drum. Pay us and disband the army! I watch Wayne and Scott, who sit on their horses without moving. Neither does Washington move. His officers crowd round him, but he pushes through them and rides toward the line. Then, close to us, he sits on his horse, motionless. I can see how his face is blue with cold, his lips purple, thin and very tight. I wait for a gun to go off. I can understand how men would kill him now.

Jacob whispers: "There's a man. No officer, but a man to lead men."

"A rare, strange man," Ely agrees.

Then the noise dies away. The General's head drops forward, and his face is twisted with pain.

205

"A play actor," Charley murmurs.

"You are still my men," he says simply. "I want no more from you than to believe I am still one of you, not your General. We must build houses here — live and endure. We must."

Then he rides away. The brigades break. The parade becomes a seething mass of men, a roar of sound. The women flow forward and mingle with the brigades.

The Pennsylvania men hold some kind of order. Wayne rides down the line and stops in front of our little group. We stand apart.

"You're not my men," he says.

Ely replies: "We're the Fourth New York, sir."

He takes a little book out of his pocket and thumbs through it. The pages flutter in the wind and try to tear loose. "Disbanded?" he asks Ely.

"There are eight of us left."

"I'll list you with the Fourteenth Pennsylvania. You'll take orders from Captain Muller."

"We'll not become a Pennsylvania regiment," Jacob says sullenly.

"You'll obey orders!"

"To hell with your orders!"

"Who's in command among you?" Wayne says coldly.

"We have no officers," I say. "They were killed."

"You'll join the Fourteenth — or you're under arrest."

Jacob raises his musket. Ely tries to hold him back, but Jacob shakes loose. He says to Wayne: "You're not talking to a German farmer. By God, I'm half-dead already, and I'd be all dead as soon as to crawl for an officer."

The Pennsylvanians had gathered round us now. An officer pushed through them, and Wayne said to him: "Captain Muller, have your men cover him, and shoot him if he fires."

I felt a single spark like that would set the field on fire. I felt that I was looking then at the finale of the revolution. But Ely put his arms around Jacob and forced the musket down.

"They're your men, Captain," Wayne said. Then he rode away, and I stood there with the rest of them, feeling all sick and hot inside. I felt sick the way I had been sick at Breed's Hill, and not since then. I pushed close to Jacob.

The Pennsylvania men were laughing. There were some women there, giggling and making eyes at us.

"I'll have no mutiny in my ranks," Muller said. "You'll take orders, my fine beggars, or you'll stump along."

"You can go to hell, sir," Ely told him, gently.

He couldn't fight Ely's eyes. He turned around, bawling for them to form their ranks.

We form to march back. Jacob is still trembling, and his face is black. Ely holds onto his arm. Kenton has his arm round a tall, thin woman, whose face is a mockery of any decent woman's face. A Pennsylvanian pushes through and claims the woman.

"She's my wife," he said.

"She's a slut and I'm paying her," Kenton says.

"She's my wife —"

The other women are laughing. Kenton's wench spits in her husband's face. A deep roar of laughter goes up.

"A rare lot of women these Pennsylvanians have," Charley Green says.

We march back. The sky breaks open, and it begins to snow. We stumble on through the snow.

4

A DEEP peace and a great stillness, and a wind to wash clear the skies and show the stars. There is a great silence over the face of the world, and it is Christmas Eve.

We have been here days — or weeks. We lose count of days until the word goes round that Christmas is a day away and there will be extra rations of rum. The word goes round that there will be chickens, that Captain Allen McLane and his foragers captured a British convoy train with a thousand chickens. But nobody believes and nobody is very much excited about Christmas. Another lean day. There are enough officers to take care of a thousand chickens.

It's night now, and I have sentry duty. It has snowed three times since we got here. There is six inches of loose, sandy snow on the ground. When you walk, it swirls up and seeps into crevices in your foot-coverings. As long as anybody can remember, there has never been such a winter as this.

I walk one hundred and twenty paces and back — for two hours. I walk slowly, dragging my musket. At the edge of the forest, where the beat ends, I have a clear view of the frozen Schuylkill, of the King of Prussia Road and of the road to Philadelphia, blue rolling hills that sweep away until they are lost in a mystery of night. A fancy of lights on the horizon—perhaps Philadelphia. Philadelphia is only eigtheen miles away.

I wait there for Max Brone. He's a German boy, a weed of a back-country lout from the hills around Harrisburg, who has the beat with me this night. He speaks only a few words of English, and his face is twisted with pain and homesickness and cold. He's better than no one at all. The silence can drive you mad.

I reach the limit of my beat and stop. The moment I stop moving, the cold eats in. It seems that we are here at the edge of the world—with no barrier between us and the cold of outer space. I wear two coats, my own and Kenton Brenner's. But both are worn thin. The snow has crusted around my feet, and they are balls of ice. My hands are wrapped in a piece of blanket; with them and with my elbows I hold my musket. But no keeping out the cold; I try to kick the ice off my feet.

As I wait there, I see Brone toiling up the slope. He is bent over, almost crawling on all-fours. He doesn't see me until he is quite near, and then he starts back.

"All's well," I say.

He straightens up and sighs. His breath comes out in a cloud of frozen moisture. He leans his musket against himself and beats his hands against his sides.

"I vas feard," he says. "*Gott*—it's lonely."

We stand together for a while, silent, only moving in little jerks to keep the cold off. A wolf howls. His howl begins with a quiver, strengthens and climbs into the night. A dog's bark answers. I feel little shivers crawl up and down my spine, and Brone's face drawn taut.

"I'd like to get a shot at that one," I say. "I'd make me a nice cap and a pair of mittens out of his wool."

Brone answers: "I tink—ven I valk alone, dey're vaiting."

There were no wolves here when the army first came. Farming country that has been farmed for years doesn't have wolves. Eighteen miles away, there was a city of twenty thousand people.

"There are more every day," I say.

"At home, tonight, dere vud be a fire. A roasting pig. Ve drink all night—and dance."

We stare at each other, and I nod. I look at him and try to see him, a thin, short boy with a frost-bitten face, a sparse yellow beard and wide-set unintelligent eyes. No imagination and no hope. I say to myself, why? I say to myself, what have you ever dreamed to follow a terrible nightmare of revolution?

208

He's the same blood as the Hessians. We don't hate the Hessians. But the Pennsylvania Germans do; they bear hate for the Hessians as I have never known men to bear hate. I've seen them torture dying Hessians, kick at them, prod them with bayonets, and taunt them in German.

I turn round and walk back. No words of parting. I glance over my shoulder and see him toiling and sliding down the slope. I see him as a picture of myself, and I try to forget the picture, closing my eyes and stumbling forward.

At the other end of my beat, I stop and stand for a while, leaning heavily on my musket and gradually dozing as I stand. I am falling asleep. A delicious sense of parting with the world creeps through me. Bit by bit, all sense of cold vanishes. Through half-closed eyes I can just make out the half-buried dugouts of Scott's brigades. This night merges with other Christmas Eves, and I hear my father's slow, monotonous voice reading the story of a Man. With that, the whir of my mother's wheel. The lulling hum of the wheel puts me to sleep. Outside is the great flat forest of the Lake country, the mysterious kingdom of the Six Nations where we have made our home. All that is mystery and dread, but foot-thick log walls close it out.

My father's voice: "Allen—" And my mother, gently: "You wouldn't sleep while the Words are being read, Allen?"

I come to myself with a terrible, heart-stabbing fear that I am freezing. I try to move and I lack all power of movement. The fear runs through me and exhausts itself. I give way, and the delicious apathy creeps over me.

Then a hand, stabbing from the far outside, beats down my shoulders. I give way and crumple forward in the snow, bruising my face on the hammer head of my musket. The snow in my face brings me awake. I roll over and Edward helps me to my feet. He's big and strong, and it's a relief to feel his wide hands under my arm.

"I was sleeping," I say.

Edward spits on his sleeve, and we watch fascinated as the bit of water freezes.

Edward shakes his head. "A cold wild night—get in to the fire." He shivers and shakes himself, like a huge, tired dog. "Get in to the fire," he repeats.

I nod and stumble away. He stops me and gives me my musket. Mechanically gripping it, I make my way toward the dugouts. Tears come easily; I feel them on my lids, freezing.

The Pennsylvania brigades are quartered on the hilltop facing the road to Philadelphia. A first line of defence; the attack will come from the direction of Philadelphia. We built the dugouts the second and third days at the encampment, half in the earth and half of logs, log fireplaces lined with mud. Ten or twelve men are crowded into each dugout. The doors face the forest, and the forest offers some shelter from a west wind. But the storm winds blow from the east and bite through the spaces between the logs.

I came in and stood with my back against the door. I let go my musket, and it crashed against the dirt floor. The water began to run from my feet in little puddles.

Ely was sitting on the edge of his bunk, watching me. Jacob picked up the musket, wiped it carefully, and put it in its rack. Ely poured me a drink of rum.

"The last, Allen."

I gulped it eagerly. It burnt my throat and warmed me inside. I started for the fire, but Jacob pushed me back.

"You're frozen, Allen."

I dropped to the floor, stretched out my legs before me. Slowly, feeling came back, darting pains in my hands and feet. Ely bent down and peeled the outer layer of bandages from my feet.

Charley Green lay in his bunk with his woman. Charley was no man for fighting; he was the sort of man who is only half of himself without a woman. God knows what took him away from his Boston printer's shop to this hellhole where we were. When I think of Charley, I think of a small, fat man with children round him, of a small fat wife. But the fat had gone. His skin hung in loose folds. Now he lay in his bunk with his woman, and they must have been asleep, because they didn't move when I came in. Kenton sat on the edge of his bunk, his woman curled behind him. She was a Pennsylvania woman, thin, with light hair and pale blue eyes, speaking a Dutch dialect. She was free with her attentions; it's hard for a woman to be anything else in a dugout with ten men. Vandeer stood in one corner, older than ever, hardly speaking and never smiling, dreaming of a little log parish-house, where the Sabbaths came regularly with six calm days in between. Henry slept. Brone was still on sentry beat. The last was a Polish Jew, a thin, strange man from Philadelphia, tall, hollow-chested, his brown eyes deep sunk in his head. He had been in America only a year, and he spoke no English. But he spoke Dutch, which most of us could understand. He sat next to the fire now, his head bent, his lips moving slowly.

"Praying," Kenton said. "He has no understanding of what night this is." Kenton had never seen a Jew before, and I think he was afraid. "A heathen," Kenton said.

"Edward spat on his sleeve," I said. "It froze before you could count three."

"I call to mind a gypsy at Brandywine—before the battle. He said a winter to freeze the marrow from the land."

Ely had bared his feet. Now, as he knelt over me, his long, grey-streaked beard brushed my hands. He worked my feet slowly. I had to turn my head away, but Ely worked them as if they were his own.

"Feeling, Allen?"

I nodded.

Jacob stood over us, watching with a professional eye. The dugout was hot and close, but draughty, full of body-smell, thick heat and stray curls of cold air. The chimney drew badly, and the log roof was shielded with a layer of blue smoke. The rank odour of bad rum pierced through everything else.

"The foot's a small part of a man," Jacob said.

Kenton's woman sat up and said: "A stinking filthy pair of feet—ye're no more men than pigs!"

"You shut up," Jacob told her. "You Goddamn slut, shut up!"

"Kenton—Kenton, hear his foul tongue?"

Kenton shrugged and smiled foolishly. Kenton was a peaceful, easygoing man.

Charley Green woke up, leaned out of his bunk and looked on, mildly curious. His woman shouted:

"A fine lot of men—to curse a poor woman!"

"It ain't none of your matter," Charley said.

"I'm sicka seeing that slut," Jacob muttered.

"Hear him, Kenton!"

"I'll not have you speaking of that, Jacob," Kenton protested, mildly.

Jacob turned round, his fists tight clenched. I watched them, too drunk with warmth to move. Ely went on kneading my feet, as if he had not heard. The Jew kept his eyes on the ground.

"I speak as I please," Jacob said.

Kenton stood up. Vandeer pushed them apart. "Ye're no men, but beasts," Vandeer muttered. "There's no love or fear of God left in you."

Jacob went to the fire, opposite the Jew, and crouched down. Kenton relaxed on the bed, and when the woman tried to caress him, he pushed her aside. Ely bound up my feet.

"A cold night. I pity Edward," Ely said simply.

Vandeer stood in the middle of the dugout, his arms raised, his mouth half-open, the skin creased loosely in folds about his eyes. Then, abruptly, he dropped his arms and went to his bunk.

Jacob poured some thin corn broth from a pot next to the fire and offered it to me. I drank it slowly, enjoying the warmth of it.

"It's a hard thing to get the cold out of yer bones," Ely said.

The Jew looked up and said, in Dutch: "The cold of Siberia bites deeper—"

"Siberia?"

Green understood no Dutch, but he caught the word. "A frozen land in Asia."

"You were there?" I asked the Jew. "What great journey took you such distances?"

He groped for words, for space that was the length of the world. "Two thousand of us went there—the Czar's prisoners."

"From what land?"

"Poland."

"I knew a Polish man," Jacob said. "He died on Brooklyn Heights."

"You escaped?" Ely asked curiously.

"I escaped—" He opened his coat and shirt, showed us a cross burnt into his breast. "They branded the Jews—said we made the revolution. But I escaped."

I closed my eyes; I tried to see a journey across a world. When I glanced up, the Jew's head was bent over, his lips moving slowly.

"Why were you fighting?" Ely said in English.

The Jew didn't answer. Kenton said: "Tell us, Ely, why are we fighting? I swear, by God, we'll be an army of corpses before this winter's out. I keep saying to myself why—why? I didn't have no call against the British. I never seen a British man before the war that did me a mite of harm. We had two hundred acres clear, and we would have cleared a thousand two years come. We never paid no taxes. All right, I did it. I was a damn-fool kid. I told my paw there was a sight of Boston men making an army to war on the British. I told him I was going, and he laughed in my face. He said he knew Boston men and he'd seen the British fight. He gave two months before they'd hang Adams and Hancock."

"Why'd ye go?" Jacob demanded

Kenton put his face in his hands.

Jacob said, bitterly: "By God—there's no army to be made outa swine like you."

"Easy, easy, Jacob," Ely whispered.

"On a night like this—Christ was born," Vandeer said tonelessly. "In the name of liberty you're ridden with whores and scum. Ye're a stubborn, hard-necked people, and God's hand is on you."

"To hell with your preaching!" Charley cried.

Kenton's woman screamed: "Shut yer dirty mouth! You ain't no men—ye're a pack of filthy, rotten beggars!"

Jacob rose, took two long strides to the door, and plucked his musket from its rack. He faced Kenton's bunk and said:

"Another word outa her and I'll kill her, Kenton! No damned whore can make mock of me!"

Ely sprang in front of him, pushing the musket to one side. Vandeer said, shrilly:

"If you need to shed blood for the black hate in you—kill me, Jacob!"

Kenton's woman was sobbing hysterically. Ely took Jacob's musket. In Ely's hands, Jacob was like a baby, mouth trembling. All the terror of the past week had come to a head in him—and finally burst. Ely led him to his bunk.

"We're a long time together, Jacob," Ely said softly.

Now there is silence—as if we had used ourselves up for the time. Only the sobbing of Kenton's woman, and Kenton makes no effort to quiet her. He sits with his head in his hands. The Jew is motionless by the fire.

We hear the wind outside. A wolf howls—mournfully. I look from face to face, bearded faces with long, uncut hair, men who have lost all pride or consideration for their bodies, men in rags, huddled together for warmth. The women are not women any more. I tell myself that there are beautiful, clean women somewhere, beautiful, clean men. I think of a woman's body the way I used to dream of a woman's body, white and perfect—

Kenton's woman sobs: "We come along with you—you go to hell, but we come along with you."

Nobody answers. We listen for something, the way men listen when the silence is deep and lasting. We hear steps outside in the snow—to the door.

"It's the German lad," Ely says. "Why won't he come in?"

We wait, and then I get up and fling open the door. A rush of snow, and then a figure stumbles into the room.

"Who the hell are you?" Jacob demands.

I force the door shut. She lifts her head, and we see a woman, wrapped in a blanket, barefooted, her feet blue and broken open from the cold.

"Jesus Christ," Green whispers.

She lets fall the blanket; she's half-naked, wearing only an old pair of men's breeches under the blanket. Blue with cold, thin, her breasts the small breasts of a girl, her face sunken, long black hair, curious thin features that might have been lovely once. I stare at her the way we are all staring. Henry Lane wakes and stumbles out of his bunk. He moves toward her, a haggard, bearded, sleep-ridden figure, and she shrinks back against me. I pick up the blanket and cover her shoulders. She gropes toward the fire and crouches next to it.

"Who are you, lass?" Ely asks her.

"Leave me alone," she says. "God's sake—leave me alone."

Kenton's woman says: "I'll tell ye who. She's a fair whore of a Virginian brigade. Her name's Bess Kinley."

"Leave me alone—"

Jacob gets up. He goes to her directly and takes hold of her blanket. "Get out," he says hoarsely.

Vandeer joins him. "Get out—there's enough of rotten women in here. You'll make blood flow between us and the Virginians. Get out."

"Leave her alone," I tell them. I force myself in front of Jacob.

"Boy—get away. The woman's no good!"

"She'll stay," I tell Jacob. "Her feet are bleeding. Let her stay and warm by the fire."

Jacob grips my shoulder, raises his hand to strike. Ely's sharp voice stops him. He stands there, watching the girl.

"They're drunk," she says. "They'd kill me. Look at this." She opens the blanket.

Kenton cries: "They're drunk—drunk. That swine Quiller swore there was no rum, but the Virginian brigades are drunk!" Quiller is the commissary.

"Lead her out," Vandeer says tonelessly.

Green's woman says: "You stay there, honey. Let them try to put me out! A man wouldn't put out a dog on a night like this!"

The door opens, and a man stoops through. He wears the long grey hunting shirt of a Virginian. He's bareheaded, panting. There are others behind him. Some of them carry their long rifles. They hold the door open and the cold eats into the room.

"Close the door," Ely tells him.

"I'll have her—she's our woman."

"She's a Virginian woman!" someone behind him yells.

"Close the door."

"You can go to hell!" I say. "You can get to hell out of here!"

He starts across the room, and I fling myself on him, bearing him back. His fist crashes into my face, and then I hear Jacob's roar as he beats the Virginian through the low door. Ely follows with Kenton and Vandeer. I get up and stumble after them, Lane and Green with me. I catch one glimpse of the Jew, sitting by the fire like a figure out of time.

Outside, there is a mad tangle of figures. I direct all my hate and resentment into the fight. Voices break the night's quiet, and the Pennsylvania men pour from their dugouts. Muskets are clubbed— knives.

The cry goes up: "Virginians!"

There aren't many of the Virginian—a dozen perhaps. They're beaten back. They're overwhelmed by numbers. We stand panting— warm even in the cold.

"Drunk," a Pennsylvania man says.

"We're rationed on rum—and those damned Virginians drink."

We go back to the dugout, grumbling, but feeling that the fight has kept us from madness. We crowd in, close the door; body heat and heat of fire. The Jew stares at us, as if we were things beyond his understanding.

"Ye're Pennsylvania men?" the girl says. "You'll let me stay tonight?"

"We're no Pennsylvania men," Jacob says.

"What's your name?" I ask her.

"Bess Kinley."

"Sit by the fire and warm yourself," I tell her. " No man will drive you from the fire."

I look at her, and something passes between us. I feel bigger than before, different.

"She'll stay," I tell them.

"She'll stay tonight," Ely agrees.

I sit close to her. She doesn't speak. I look at her face, and for once try to read the mystery of a woman who follows the army.

Finally I say, sullenly: "Why don't you get out of the camp? Why don't you get out of here?"

"Where would I go?" she asks me.

Kenton's woman sobs softly; silence takes hold of us. Occasionally, someone puts a piece of wood on the fire.

"I'm hungry," she says.

215

We give her some gruel, and she holds the wooden cup with both hands, drinking it slowly. Nobody speaks. Henry Lane is sleeping again. Green and Kenton crawl into their beds. Already they have lost interest.

Edward comes in, blue and cold, shaking off the snow. He stands and looks at the girl.

"She's Allen's woman," Jacob says. Thus our morality. Thus our years of prayer on the hard floors of hard wooden churches. She was mine without marriage, without the word of any man of God. Because I took her, she is mine.

The girl turns and looks at me, her dark eyes biting into mine. I say nothing. Ely tells Edward what has happened.

"They're hard, bitter men, the Virginians," Edward says. "The girl's a slut. Did she expect them to nurse her?"

"Shut up!" I cry.

"I'm not holding for the Virginians, Allen."

"Where's Brone?" Ely asks Edward. "He should have been back already."

"I didn't see him," Edward says. "I thought he was back."

"I forgot," I mutter. "The boy was sick with cold. I forgot and I had no thought for him."

Ely stands up and puts on his coat.

"Ye're a fool to go out," Jacob says.

I crawl into my coat. I'm sick with weariness, but I know about Brone. Deep in my heart, I know.

I followed Ely out. Jacob came behind me. None of us spoke. We walked across the hillside, away from the dugouts, and then down toward the Gulph Road. It was easy to find the path Brone had beaten in the snow, and follow it. When we came near the end, two low shapes shot away across the snow.

"I should have brought my gun," I said miserably. "You should have known to bring a gun, Ely."

We came to Brone. Jacob knelt down. "Wolves," he said. "Wolves," he repeated bitterly, his voice rising, "and the lad was too weak — too weak."

"He was telling me tonight — "

"He didn't know," Ely said. "He was asleep." We knelt around him, our breath making a cloud, as if from candles. I had to look. Ely tried to hold me away, but I had to look.

"We'll bring him back," Ely said.

"The women — "

216

"We'll bring him back to the fire," Ely said, and he looked at Jacob and me in a way that made us nod and bend to Brone.

We come into the dugout and put the boy down.

"By the fire," Ely says grimly. "Lay him by the fire."

The Jew stands up, his face full of the pain of the world. He bends his head, touches his head simply with his hand.

The girl is crying, as with pain.

We gather around Brone. Vandeer kneels down. He says:

"God—forgive us. Forgive us tonight." He kneels down, and he prays. He prays with words that we haven't heard for a long time. He prays simply, gently, compassionately.

PART TWO

THE WINTER

5

IT IS the time of the great hunger, in the middle weeks of January, seventeen seventy-eight. The hunger has been on us three days, and for those three days we have eaten nothing. We have eaten nothing that is food.

Snow has drifted up to the roof of the dugout; snow in the valley in drifts twelve and fifteen feet deep. There are no parades, no drills. There has been no parade for two weeks. There is a rumour that much of the army has disappeared, but we have no check on rumours. As our strength goes, we move slowly, fretfully, the way old men move. A path is cut through the snow for sentries. We hate sentry duty, curse it, but it keeps us from going mad.

Today, we lie in bed, huddled close for warmth. The fire gives out no heat. Only Kenton sits close to it, painstakingly carving a rhyme on his powder horn. His big hunting knife glints in the light, his large hands guiding it with difficulty. On and off, for months now, he has been working on the carving of the rhyme and the picture of a child with arms clasped about the end of the horn. He can forget things with his carving, remembering only that he began it in the warmth of the summer. Now and then he asks Charley the spelling of a word. Kenton is not much for writing words or spelling them out.

We wait for Ely, who has gone to the commissary. The light from the fire lingers in the centre of the dugout; the bunks are in the shadow.

With Bess beside me, I lie in a broken dream. Sometimes I speak aloud, and then Bess says: "Allen—Allen, what are you saying?"

I don't know. I try to explain a figment of a dream. I try to explain that my mother's name was Anna, that if we have a child, her name will be Anna too.

"A girl?" Bess asks me.

"A boy and then a girl."

I sleep again; I wake and my hands grope for her body, frantically. I say: "You slut — you God-damned little slut, you'll go back to the Virginians. You're no fit woman for a man."

"Allen — what are you saying?"

I close my eyes, and my lightheadedness takes my mind away. I am at all places at once. I am out in the snow, pacing a sentry beat. I am in the deep lush, bottom valleys of the Mohawk. With her hands, Bess tries to reassure me. Her hands travel over my torn clothes, seeking out parts of me. Her hands unravel my beard.

I sink into sleep, and I dream, and I dream that I am child. It is the morning of a hot, sunny day, and we are moving westward. Where we came from is not very clear to the child in the dream, from some place many marches to the east — Connecticut, perhaps. There are four wagons, four narrow, old, swaying wagons. Brown canvas covers them, stretched over bent hickory hoops. The road is bad, and the wagons surge and rock and threaten to fall apart with every step the horses take. But somehow the wagons hold together. They've held together a long time.

I sit at the back of the first wagon, my feet hanging over the tail-board. The hot sun is in my face. Mr. Apply, driving the second wagon, keeps grinning at me. Now and then he snaps his long whip and cries:

"Gotcha then, Allen!"

We both laugh. It's a standing joke between us, the whip. Mr. Apply is a lean old man who sits on his high seat with a long musket balanced across his knees. Somehow, no matter how the wagon sways, the musket never slips from his knees.

My mother cries: "You, Allen, come in or you'll take a fall under Mr. Apply's horses!"

The whip flicks out again. Half-asleep, I cling to the dream. I want the hot sun. When I know that the dream is over, I close my eyes and still try to feel the sun on my face.

When I awake, I turn to Bess with deep, childlike love. A love that's different from the love of a man for a woman. She's warmth for me; she's something for a weak, dying man to hold onto. She doesn't complain. She has never complained. I know she is dying, but I know she won't die until I am gone.

She married a Virginian farm boy at the outbreak of the war. She tried to follow him to Quebec, in the expedition of Morgan's riflemen.

219

She dropped out, went to Boston, and later heard that her man had never reached Quebec. She fell in with a group of Maryland militia — became a camp follower. It was not difficult to understand.

She tells me about it in a slow, truthful voice. "I don't hide anything, Allen. But I was a good woman once. I swear to God I was a good woman once. I'm nineteen years, Allen, and I'm a slut already. You don't have any call to love me, Allen."

Our tears came together, slow tears of weakness. We cling together, and she clutches desperately at my filthy body. I cry the way no man would cry. Each successive wave of sleep is relief.

What she says, she has said before. We dream about it day and night. "You can desert, Allen—"

I think of Edward. Eight days ago, he walked out. He said, simply—he was going to the Mohawk. He stook his gun, and nobody answered him, or tried to stop him. He was a great, strong man. "He'll walk through," Ely said. Jacob raged like a madman. Nobody believes but Jacob. We hate the revolution; we hate our officers and each other. Jacob believes. That you must keep in mind. A man can be parts of many things, or a man can be only one thing. And those who believe in only one thing are like torches; they don't burn forever. That you must keep in mind to know how Jacob is—without weakness, without fear. He hates officers because they are a contradiction. He is not a man for thinking too deeply, and what he believes he believes instinctively. And he believes this—that the people are one. Officers are not of the people; they separate themselves: so he hates them but endures them because they lead the revolution. Yet he refuses to believe that they are part of the revolution they lead. But more than that, he hates weakness. A man is nothing, and the revolution is all. Edward was his friend; for years Edward had been his friend; yet Edward was weak, putting himself before the revolution. For that he cursed Edward—who was dead.

He raged like a madman, and then when he had used himself up, he sat by the fire, sobbing hard, dry sobs for hours.

I would have gone with Edward, but I was afraid. I was afraid of the great distances in front of me.

Some of McLean's foragers brought Edward back. He had gone only a mile. They found him in the snow. Captain Muller came to us and said: "Did he desert?"

"He's dead, isn't he?" Jacob muttered. "What does it matter now? The man's dead."

"He was hunting," Ely said, lying. But even Ely could lie for a man who had died that way—alone and in the snow.

We went to bury him. He was huddled up, his limbs hard and fixed.

"He was sleeping," Ely said. "I thank God he was sleeping. He didn't know. It's an easy way to die, when a man's sleeping . . ."

I ask Bess: "Where would we go?"

"I'm not dreading dying, Allen. But if you go away without me—"

Ely enters the dugout. He closes the door and stumbles over to the fire. The strength of Ely is no thing that can be measured, it's not the strength of a man's body.

He sits by the fire and stares into it.

We climb out of bed and crowd round him. Our faces are sunken death's-heads. Bones stand out through the clothes. Ely looks at us, but he doesn't speak.

Jacob said: "You brought food, Ely?"

"I walked to his house," Ely said. "It's a wonder to see the fine stone houses the officers have. You go in and you hear no sound of storm outside."

I try to visualize it. The houses where the officers are quartered are a mile away. I try to understand a man beating his way there and back. Ely hasn't eaten in three days. Edward walked a mile in the snow and they brought back a dead man. Ely is here by the fire.

"God damn them," I said.

"They told me a food train comes tonight. They took the name of the regiment and company."

Jacob cursed them. He paced back and forth, screaming his rage until it seemed to fill the dugout full and overflowing.

"Enough—enough!" Clark yelled. "The fruit of sin—do you hear me! You're no men, and you reap no fruits of men, but the fruits of sin! As ye sow, so shall ye reap! You lie with your women without shame. You sport and you have no shame for your sporting. You curse God, and in turn you are cursed by God! You made an idol of freedom, and now the idol's smashed open. Allen there—with a slut in his arms. Kenton sharing his woman among the lot of you. Charles who would look from the face of God to the face of women! You whore and murder among yourselves! I call God to blast you for your crimes—I call God!" He fell on his knees; he stretched out his arms. His face grew livid and then deathly pale. Then he crumpled up on the floor.

Ely tried to pick him up. He said: "Help me, Allen." We put him on his bed. His eyes were closed, his chest heaving. Jacob tried to make him hear; Jacob was calmed suddenly.

"We're taking yer words to heart—Clark, you hear me?"

I went to Bess.

She was crying softly, without hysteria, but in an agony of pain. She said to me: "Allen, I'm not a bad woman. He laid a curse of God on me."

"You're not — you're not," I said.

"Allen — I'll sleep no more. Even if I die, I'll not sleep in peace."

Bending over, I tried to kiss her. She pushed me away. "Don't kiss me, Allen."

Charley Green's woman cried: "Who's he to curse me? Who is he, the rotten mock of a man?"

"Ah — be quiet, Annie," Charley groaned.

I took Bess' hand. I turned it over, put it to my lips. "You sleep," I said, "sleep."

I turned to Clark. Jacob had dropped onto his bunk, a mass of helpless bones. Ely stood by Vandeer's bed. The Jew stood just behind him, a bent figure for the ages, as filthy and ragged as any of us — but different.

Ely said: "I'm afraid for him, Allen. We need a doctor."

I looked at Clark. He lay in bed, breathing hoarsely, sweating, his eyes wide open.

"There's no doctor in the Pennsylvania huts. A leech won't come here from the hospital."

"We'll bear him down there," Ely said.

I shook my head. "I can't, Ely. There's no strength left in me."

I watched Ely's eyes pass round the dugout. His shaggy, bearded head turned slowly: Jacob of no use, Charley Green sick and unable to move, Henry Lane with great festering sores on his feet, Kenton by the fire, as if he heard nothing of Clark Vandeer's raving.

"You'll come?" Ely asked the Jew.

We took clothes wherever we could find them. Charley's woman gave a blanket, a petticoat. She lay in bed half-naked, clinging close to him. She called me over.

"If he comes to his senses — plead him to take back the curse."

"There's no curse," Ely said uncertainly.

We picked up Clark, the three of us. Ely, myself, and the Jew. He was skin and bones and he couldn't have weighed more than ninety or a hundred pounds, but he was more than enough for us. We could barely hold his weight.

We went outside and tried to go through the snow. There was a sleet blowing; it was like moving through a morass that sucked in our legs. Sometimes we couldn't move, had to stand still waiting for our bodies to gather the strength to go on. I tried to picture Ely going through this for two miles, to the commissary and back. Coming back empty-handed. Now going out with us again. What is it in Ely? I look at him sometimes, and try to understand. Where is the strength? All of us are thin, but Ely is thinner. Our feet are wretched,but Ely's feet are stumps of mangled flesh. Yet Ely walks without showing the pain. When there is work to be done, Ely does it. When a strong man is needed, Ely draws strength from somewhere. Yet he isn't like Jacob. Jacob is fire, but Ely is spirit. Jacob is hate, but Ely is love. I think, sometimes, that when this is over, Ely will endure. Jacob will burn out, but Ely will endure.

It is about three-quarters of a mile to the hospital, around the shoulder of the hill and down into the valley. Where we stand now, on the top of the hill, we are unprotected, open to every blast of wind that crosses the countryside. I look back and see the dugouts as heaps of snow. No life. Even the smoke is torn from the chimneys and dissipated. I think of how it would be if the British attacked us now, marched from Philadelphia and walked into our dugouts. No one to stop them or challenge them, only half-naked beggars who would sacrifice pride and honour for a bowl of stew. There would be no shots fired. We would be fed. Then we would go back home.

I look down the white slope, half-imagine it. Why don't they come and make an end?

We went on slowly. It was on to late afternoon now, growing dark already. I kept my head down, but Ely led us; and whenever I glanced at him, his head was up, seeking the way. The Jew was a white, inscrutable figure. I had a feeling that I was walking into darkness — made up of white snow, buried deep in white snow. A sense of lightness overcame me, and I no longer felt my feet or the weight of Vandeer.

We stopped once again, taking strength. Across the road, on the slope of Mount Joy, I saw a sentry. He stood in a lunette, a white cannon showing its head beside him. He stood without moving.

"A short way," Ely said.

We pushed up the winding path that led to the hospital. It was a long log building. The sentry by the door scarcely glanced at us. I guess he was used to parties carrying men.

Ely pounded at the door. An officer opened it, a tall, shaven man who wore epaulettes. I didn't know him.

"Who are you?" he demanded.

"We're of a Pennsylvania brigade. We have a sick man."

"You've a doctor there, haven't you?"

"You know damn well we haven't?" I cried.

"Use a little respect when you speak, sir — or that tongue'll be whipped out of you."

"You can go to hell," I said. "By God, you can go to hell, mister!"

"Take no offense," Ely begged him. "We're half-starved. We're not fit to walk."

I could see the officer calculating how far he could go with us. Lately, they were beginning to wonder about the half-beasts they led.

There had been no parades, just a few inspections by lieutenants and captains, and long days between inspections. A sentry on a hill, huddled over his musket, wrapped in all the clothes his comrades could spare him. They were beginning to have doubts when they saw us come out of our holes, like beasts. Only a sense of fear of the greater cold outside kept the beasts together. That and their weakness; their weakness made them afraid of the great distances between this place and their homes. But they had their guns. If they turned the guns on the officers and went off together, that would be the end of it.

He measured us, saw we were unarmed. "The hospital's full," he said. "No beds are left. Try Varnum's hospital at the redoubt." Varnum's hospital was a good mile away.

Ely said nothing; the breath came in thin steam from between his lips. The Jew said, in his curious Amsterdam Dutch: "Give a comrade a place to die. We gave our enemies that. Put a little warm food between his lips."

The officer didn't understand Dutch. "Speak English," he snapped. "The army's too full of your kind."

"We can't walk a mile to the redoubt," I pleaded, hating myself for pleading. "We can't walk that far—"

The two sentries were looking on, dulled by cold, their beards full of the froth of their breath. I wondered whether they would make any move; I wondered how long it would be before each of us in turn came there, like Clark. Clark was groaning now, talking. His words didn't make sense.

"We can't walk a mile now," I said. "We can't walk that far."

"Give him space on your floor," Ely said. "Give him six feet of your floor. The man'll freeze to death if you keep him here."

"Six feet on a gibbet would do the lot of you." He was a New York City man — or English-born; he had the whining, rising inflection.

"We're going in," Ely said. I caught Ely's eyes; I had a rush of sickening fear. I knew that when anger came on Ely, it would destroy him and whoever stood in his way.

I cried: "Ely, damn the swine, and we'll go to the redoubt!"

Ely started forward, bearing Vandeer and the two of us with him. I tried to hold back. The officer wore a sword, and his hand was on the hilt now.

Then a little man pushed the officer aside, crowded him out of the doorway. The little man wore a long grey apron, splattered with blood. He wore spectacles, and he was clean-shaven, his thin hair gathered in a neat bun at the back of his head. He had a long, thin nose and remarkably full red lips.

"What's this?" he demanded. "A sick man out there, Murgot?"

"The hospital's full."

"You'll keep your God-damn nose out of my hospital. Bring him in."

I could see the officer trying to face down the little man. The doctor ignored him, turned his back and walked into the hospital. We carried Vandeer in. The place was a log cabin, thirty feet long at the most, but there must have been more than a hundred men in it. They lay close together on beds built the length of the place.

Some of them slept; most of them moved restlessly, the place was cold. There was a continual groaning; after a while, you ignored that.

"We're a little crowded," the doctor said briskly. "They come and go. About even. We're no warmer here than good mother earth." He led us to a tiny place in the back, partitioned off, and he motioned for us to lay Vandeer down on the bed. We put him down and unwrapped his coverings. There was a small iron heater there. We crowded close to it.

"Filth—my God, it's a wonder to me there's any of you left. Filth, filth—why don't you shave off those beards? Let's have a look at him. Tell me about it."

Ely told him—slow, hard words as he brought the scene back to mind.

"I know—I know," the doctor nodded, before Ely was through. "I know, men go mad. Well, there's a cure I know of for that. What can you expect? It's a wonder to me there's a sane person left here. If there is, I'm the one. I won't be that way long. What do you expect? Can I breathe reason back to him? Am I God?"

The Jew said, softly: "You're God. You see, all of us—we're God. We have to believe that, in the God in us. The nearer we go to the beasts, the more we have to believe. I've starved before. I've seen two thousand men die as they walked to Siberia. You have to believe in man in God. You lose your fear of death; you fear only that the God will go out of

225

you."

The doctor took off his spectacles, wiped them on his apron. "Who are you?" he asked the Jew—in Dutch.

"He's a Jew heathen out of Poland," I said.

"You read Spinoza?" the doctor asked him.

"You'll let him die?" He pointed to Clark.

"All right—give me that basin." Ely held it. The doctor bared Clark's arm, whistled softly at the way the veins showed through. He took a piece of cloth and washed the arm as well as he could. He grumbled: "Can't bathe—give me a hell-hole of an icehouse and call it a hospital. I'm as filthy as you—nice on top, but just as filthy underneath." He picked a tiny object from Vandeer's arm. "See that? Lice—all of you lousy with them. What can you expect?"

He took a lancet and opened a vein in Clark's arm. Then he held out the arm, so that the blood drained into a basin slowly. The blood was dull red. The way it came, so slowly, made me think there was little enough left in Clark. The doctor asked Ely:

"How long since he's eaten?"

"We haven't eaten in three days—any of us."

The doctor whistled again.

"He's weak—he'll bleed to death," Ely said.

"What can I do? I'm not God, in spite of your Jew here. I'll bleed him until his reason comes back. He'd die anyway."

We stood there, grouped round the bed, fascinated by the blood welling out of Clark's arm. Clark began to speak. He asked for Ely. Expertly, the doctor stopped the flow of blood. He pinched the vein together with his fingers, and then quickly bound it over with cloth.

"I'm here, Clark," Ely said.

"Where's Jacob?"

"He was broke by yer words. He had no strength to come. We bore you to the hospital, Clark."

"Who came?"

"Allen and the Jew."

"A great load. Allen's loaded with the blackness of his sin. You'll plead him to give up the wench, Ely?"

Ely didn't answer.

"You'll plead him, Ely!" Clark cried. "I'm a dying man."

Ely nodded. I said: "Clark—you're putting a dreadful black curse on me. I love her."

"Promise me, Allen!"

I shook my head.

Then he closed his eyes. Ely turned away.

"Let him sleep," the doctor said. "Come with me."

We went into a room in back. He had a table there, a bed, and a heat box. The coals in it were dying. He put a wooden plate on the table, took out a pot with a few slices of cold meat in it.

"We don't have much—"

I yearned toward the meat. Ely didn't move. The Jew was smiling sadly.

"That won't feed the army," Ely said.

"Don't be noble," the doctor told him. "It will feed you." Then he saw the Jew's smile. "You can go to hell," the doctor said. "You're a filthy pack of beggars. It's a wonder if the English lay hands on your filth to swing you from their gibbets."

We stood there.

"Drink some rum," he said. He poured three small cups. "Drink it, or by God, you'll die before you reach your quarters."

The rum warmed us up, but made us dizzy. We stood there, sucking in the heat and the comfort of the rum burning our insides. The doctor was sitting on his chair, regarding us as if we were some curious specimens he had picked up.

"You and me," the doctor said, speaking to the Jew and in Dutch, "we're the only civilized men here. You and me—in a land of savages, of filth and ignorance and superstition. They know one thing. They want to be free to cheat themselves and kill each other. They want to be free of the English. They want to be free to cheat and lie and hate. They want to be free to plunge a land into ignorance and misery. I'm here because I'm a fool. But why you?"

The Jew shrugged.

"You came with a great dream of a land for your kind."

"A land for all men."

"It's big enough. But men are the same—here or Europe. If they win—and they won't—but if they win, they'll drive you out. You're a Jew, a heathen."

"They won't drive us out," the Jew said softly. "We've come the length of the world—"

"Driven!"

"No—we've come here. We've come for a dream of a place for all men. This is a new world. The day of the old world is over. A long time—maybe two hundred, maybe three hundred years. But it will make the men who live in it. This is only the beginning. This army is nothing—nothing, only a dream. Do you understand? The army goes;

the dream never goes. I stayed at the home of a man in Philadelphia who is making this revolution. His name's Haym Solomon. He came out of Poland too. Poland was a school for us. Poland will go on fighting, but Poland won't be free. A school. Here's the land for the dream of God in man."

The doctor glanced at us. "Not a clean god. Come and talk again. Man can't live by bread alone or without it. No bread. I won't last the winter. If you make your land, tell your children about a man of science who wouldn't believe. Damn lies!"

We went back to Clark. He was still sleeping. His face, where it showed through his beard, was white as snow.

"Will he live?" Ely asked.

"How do I know?" the doctor snapped. Then: "It doesn't make any difference. He won't be far from any of you."

We take the clothes that Clark was wrapped in, two coats and a petticoat. I give a coat to Ely and the other to the Jew. I wrap the petticoat round my neck and face.

We go out, and the cold hits us in the face, like knives ripping. Out of some forlorn curiosity, I spit on my sleeve. The others see me, and watch fascinated. I count, only once, and then the little balls of spittle snap with the frost.

"My God," Ely whispers.

We have never known such cold as this. Ely has been to Canada. I have been, in winter, in the highlands of the upper Hudson. I have seen bitter cold weather, but never such cold as this. Neither had Ely. It is a cold that has come on the face of a planet stripped bare of all protection. It is a cold living and malignant. It is a cold that has become a force to destroy soul and body. In all the memory of men in America, there has never been such cold.

We go on slowly, forcing our way through snow that is like dry sand. We move a step at a time, bringing one foot up to the place where the other has been. It is night already, no moon, but stars that glitter like bright jewels. The snow is a sheet of white — no sentries, no living thing except ourselves.

To go back to the Pennsylvania dugouts, we must climb a hill — not very high, no more than two hundred feet. But the hill is the difference between life and death. The hill is a slope that leads to hell. We make a step, stumble, and slide back two. We roll over in the snow, feel it slide into every crevice of our clothes. We spit it out, and our lips freeze and go numb. We stand up and go on.

I don't think any more. My mind is gone. Only my body moves, and my body is a machine apart from me. It will go on until the spark of life in it flickers out.

I turn round once, and the Jew is lying in the snow. He doesn't move. Ely calls to me, but his words are lost in the rush of wind. I stand above them and watch Ely go back to the Jew. Suddenly, my mind comes alive. I think to myself, ten steps down, ten steps back. I keep thinking that—ten steps down and ten steps back. The words rush in my mind. I begin to cry, and the tears freeze on my lids.

I go down to Ely. The Jew says: "Leave me. They'll find me soon."

We help him up, and the three of us go on together. We go on into endless night and endless distance. I lose all conception of time and all conception of movement. Someone must be leading us.

Then we are at the dugout. We drop on the floor. The Jew is senseless. Ely stares at the fire with wide, terrible eyes. I cry bitterly.

Bess is rubbing my hands, kissing me, trying to work the cold out of my limbs. She drags me toward the fire. I hear, as from far away, Ely telling Jacob of Clark.

Then I am in bed, and Bess is trying to warm me. I know how little strength she has, and I wonder how she can work so desperately. But the cold won't leave me. I tremble and my lips flutter. My lips are broken and bleeding.

She says: "Rest—rest, my darling."

I feel for her warm face, for her hands, for her breast. I want life desperately. I cling to her for the sense of life.

Then I sleep.

I wake out of my dream, and speak with it: "Clark put a curse on me—he's dying. I should drive you away. He made me promise."

Her cry of terror was the most terrible thing I had ever heard.

I try to soothe her. I whisper: "No—I was dreaming."

But she lies there, awake, and I can feel her fear of the cold night, of being away from me.

6

WE KEEP alive. Days pass, and days slide into one another, days and nights mingling to form a grey. But we keep alive. A strange knowledge comes to me, a knowledge of the strength in men. I can see how layer after layer of life may be taken from a man; take all the strength that is any man's, and still there is strength underneath.

So we keep alive. How many days pass, I don't know. A new man is in the dugout. His name is Meyer Smith, and he was an innkeeper in Philadelphia once. The Jew is sick. We think of Moss Fuller. The Jew has the same racking cough.

Ely said: "A bite of frost. His lungs are frozen. Maybe in the place he calls Siberia. When a man's lungs are frozen, they never heal."

We sit round now trying not to notice that hacking, incessant cough. When we look at the Jew's face, the bony features rising out of the shadow of his bunk, we are forced to think of something we don't want to remember.

"I call to mind Christ was a Jew," Jacob said—strange words for Jacob.

The Jew's name is Aaron Levy. We are very tender with him. With us, it is different: we are born and bred to the land. But the Jew has come great, shadowy distances. The distances keep us away from him, and he is alone. His loneliness oppresses us. In his sleep, he talks in a language we don't understand.

Smith was in the dugout two days when he learnt that Levy was a Jew. He said:

"I'll not sleep with a bloody Jew. I'll not sleep with any Christ-killing bitch."

Jacob almost throttled him. We had to tear Jacob away, and the marks of Jacob's fingers were on Smith's throat for a week after. Jacob pleaded with us to let him go to let him kill Smith. Jacob cried:

"His death won't sit with me. I've seen too many better than he go."

Smith was afraid. He leaped for the gunrack, tore out a musket and faced Jacob. "I'll kill you!" he screamed. "Stay off! I'll kill any man who lays a hand on me."

Ely walked up to him and wrenched the musket from his hands. "You're a low, bitter creature," Ely said quietly.

Smith crawled into his bunk and lay the rest of that night in silence. We pitied him; we were beyond hate. I could see the madness coming in Jacob, in myself, in Smith, in Henry Lane. I began to fear Ely's death. One day, I pleaded with him not to die; I pleaded with him hysterically. We lived in him. Ely smiled; he was the only one who could still smile.

Now we sit and talk a little. Bess crouches by my side, her hands touching me, feeling for me always. They tell me that when I go out on sentry duty, she lives in an agony of fear.

"You'll go out once—and not come back," she told me.

"There are other men."

"No other man," she said.

She sits by me now. We talk of the British attack and what holds it. We are all of us here but Kenton, who is on sentry duty.

"There'll be no attack," I say. "The war's over. In two months, there'll be no army. Why should they attack?"

"Ye're wrong, Allen," Ely says.

Green says: "It goes that there are only five thousand men left in the encampment.

"Lies!" Jacob says bitterly.

"Ye're a crazed man, Jacob. Is John Adams or Sam Adams here in this camp? Is Thomas Jefferson here? Is Dickinson here? Is Sherman here, or Hancock here? They're safe and nursing their fat bellies."

"They'll nurse to a different tune when we've won. By God, they'll sweat blood."

Charley said: "Ye're crazy. It'll be King John Adams—King Sam. I knew Adams—a filthy beggar who never did a day's work in his life. He'd come to my store and say, Charley, I've written a fair beautiful pamphlet—blood and revolution. Print it for the cause, Charley. What cause? Hancock's cause, a dirty cheating pirate. If I'd ask him ten shillings to buy paper, he'd foam and curse at me. I'll tell you about Hancock. He was a smuggler, he and his friends. Ye're back-woods men, and you'd not know about that. All smugglers. Let us be forced to buy British goods and they'd run no more contraband from the Indies, from the Dutch. But who bought ours? England, I tell you. So Hancock and his friends made a war, with Adams for their man. I went. I had a fair pretty girl who put a tune in my head. She set me off singing Yankee-Doodle, God damn her. She's not sleeping alone now."

"I'm not fighting Hancock's war," Jacob said. "By God, we've learned what to do with guns, and Hancock's no better than British men I've seen dead."

"All right," Charley nodded. He was flushed now and happy. He was a man of words, for words—a little Boston printer who had read Voltaire and Defoe and Swift and Plato, who knew Paine. Now he was happy, baiting Jacob, driving Jacob's words into his teeth. "All right," he nodded, "make an end of Paul Revere too. He's a great hero. We rot here, but the newspapers make a great hero of their Paul Revere. I'll tell you something about Revere. He made a famous ride and saved the revolution; but where's he now? With Hancock, filling his fat belly, I'll swear. Hancock the pirate and Revere the business man. Revere wanted copper. You damned backwoods louts wouldn't know that, but

231

there's a fortune to be made in working copper. But before Revere could smelt, he had to have a revolution. Drive out the British and their smelting laws: drive out the British and their customs men. Then Hancock becomes an honest citizen, and Revere becomes a rich smelter. But mind you, they only started it—cleverly. You're doing the fighting. God damn you, Jacob, you're a fool. When you're rotting a foot under Valley Forge, they won't talk about Eagen. They won't write in newspapers about Jacob Eagen. They'll write about Paul Revere's ride and they'll dress Sam Adams up for a god. Mind me."

"We're making a land," Jacob insisted sullenly. "There's a great, rich land to the west, and it'll never be ours so long as England holds the country. There'll never be peace in the Mohawk or in the Lake country while England lets the Indians kill and burn. I'm a backwoods lout, Charley, with no learnin' for yer city ways. But by God, it seems to me yer city's a middlin' small thing in a land like this. All outa size, you Boston men are swelled with yer glory. You have no sense of the land to the west. I knew a French trapper once who had walked westward. Come spring, summer, winter an' fall—he had walked westward; a great lot of walking, always with his face to the setting sun, an' still there was no end to the land. A land bigger than all o' Europe with their rotten little lies an' deceits. That's a mistake the Boston men make—to think we're fighting the war for them. They have no knowledge of the land, but we're fighting the war for the knowledge of the land that's ours. All the time of the world, all the years and hundreds of years, men looked for a land to be free. Ask the Jew of that, an' you'll understand the forces in men that make them die or be free. Give Hancock his dirty ships an' Revere his pound o' copper. This land's ours."

"Two years we're gone," I said. "The Valley land's raped. I hear no house stands."

Then we look at each other—with dumb, senseless longing. And even Charley longs for the comfort of Boston town. We look at Ely's feet, and we turn our eyes away quickly. We sit in silence until the door opens.

The doctor enters. He wears a greatcoat and a woolen cap. He stands at the door, stamping his feet and peering at us through the smoke of the fire. We haven't seen him since we were at the hospital. For a moment, I don't recognize him. The others stare.

"He's a doctor from the hospital," Ely says.

"No air," the doctor says. "Even the beasts seek air. This place stinks. It's the fifth stinking hole I've been in. Ah, there's my Jew." He walks forward gingerly, stands in the middle of the room and glances from face to face. The women watch him with hostile fear. The Jew smiles a little. Jacob's face is dark.

"Sullen, silent beasts," the doctor says. "If I were to paint pictures for an Inferno made glorious in the verse of Dante, I would come here. Hell holds no fear; sometimes I envy you, my friends. You have tasted all; you have searched the bottom. You have become beasts—"

"Hold yer tongue," Jacob growls.

"A beast of beasts. There's murder, my friend, in what part of your face shows through that beard."

"The hell is ours! Get out of here!" Jacob cries.

"Easy—let him be," Ely says wearily.

"I wonder why I came up here," the doctor says. "Maybe to speak with my friend the Jew. He's a creature of another world, and that cough may journey him there swiftly. Did he get it from the deed of bringing a comrade to me?"

He saw the hate, the burning resentment in us. He had no fear. I don't think he understood fear, or maybe he was only dulled beyond fear? He grinned at us.

"The man's dead!" he said suddenly, "I walked a mile and froze my hands to tell you he's dead. There's a lot I don't do that for."

"Clark's dead?" Jacob asked, unbelieving.

"You let him die!" I cried. "You let him die!"

"God and me. Jesus Christ, I'm sick of the lot of you, sick of filthy, whining beggars. That Jew there—he and I are civilized. If I trimmed his beard, I'd make him into a pretty Christ. One of Rembrandt's." He went over and spoke to Levy in New York Dutch:

"You've a fine cough, my Jew friend."

The Jew smiled at him. He watched the smile, and felt the smile's meaning, a deep understanding that the doctor tried to brazen off.

"You and I know," Levy said. "We've seen men die."

"And you're not afraid," the doctor insisted. "Tell me that you're not afraid, my Jew friend." He took off his glasses, wiped them carefully, and put them back on again. He pulled off his gloves.

"Tell me you've conquered fear of death," he insisted.

I listened, and I couldn't take my eyes from the Jew's face. In the back of my mind—Clark Vandeer, who had been a preacher once. Clark was dead. But we had known—we were used to death of others. But death in ourselves . . .

Even Jacob—whose face was a mask of pain that reflected Clark's death—even Jacob listened. Bess was holding tight to me. Mechanically, my hand covered her ear, as if I didn't want her to know.

"Is there a fear of death?" Levy asked the doctor.

"An Oriental way, always a question with a question,"

"I wanted to stay," the Jew said. "I wanted to see the spring come. All my life I dreamed of a day when I'd come to this land. It would be beautiful —"

"Here?" the doctor snorted.

"Here in this place — beauty beyond man's conception. A land of milk and honey."

"You're a dreamer," the doctor smiled.

For the first time, deep anger in the Jew's voice:

"Not romance. You make a mockery of this — to find romance here."

"I'm sorry," the doctor said shortly. "Christ, when you see them come and go — all day long. You can't bury them — the ground's like rock — so you stack them like wood. All day long. You don't want me to pat your head. It's no use bleeding you. You and me, we're civilized. We're not like these beasts. We don't have to lie. There's a line in Pope, I think — the men who grope and grope. We're past that. You're dying, why should I lie to you?"

Jacob cried: "By God — hold your tongue!"

At his deep, black rage, the doctor turned. The Jew was lost in thought, his eyes half-closed. The doctor smiled. He crawled into his coat and went out.

Panting, Jacob walked to the Jew. But he could find no words. He stood there. Smith said: "He stinks to hell of rum. They have it, but we've had no drink for weeks now."

We sit in silence, and outside, night comes. The light in the cracks of the door fades and vanishes. The days are shorter now. We wait for Kenton. There is no other event, nothing else to look forward to. Kenton will come back from sentry duty, his story the same: cold — freezing feet. When he bares his feet, perhaps a toe from which all life is gone.

We wait — and we hear Kenton's steps, running. He bursts in, and there's blood on him, blood on his face and hands and all over his coat. A knife in his hands. He stands there, panting, his eyes like a madman's. He says:

"Two buck deer, great, beautiful bucks. I heard their horns clash. They fought on the Philadelphia road, locked with each other. I killed both."

Henry shakes him, frantically. He touches the blood, tastes it. "Deer? Deer?"

"He's lying," I say to Bess. "He's lying."

"By God, the wolves'll have them before you." Kenton brandishes his knife. He's a horrible, grim figure of a man.

We scramble for clothes. We put on whatever we can find. We have forgotten about Vandeer, about the doctor, about the Jew.

We go outside, and for once we are unaware of the cold. Kenton starts off, running, and we string after him. Then he goes down. We stop, and our breath steams; we are weak, sick. We move more slowly. The women are with us. They run with short, hard cries. Bess' arms and head are bare.

Ely warns us: "Slow—slow, you'll have no strength to return."

We are laughing hysterically, laughing and crying at the same time. Then we see the deer, two large buck deer, locked in the snow. Kenton shows us; he cuts fiercely with his knife, drives it to the hilt in one of the deer.

"Like this—they fought and I cut the life from them"

Ely cries: "You'll go mad—leave off the deer." I try to touch the blood, taste it. Ely strikes me, a hard blow on the side of my head. The tears come to my eyes, and I plead with him to forgive me.

We dragged the deer back. Men and women, we fought through the snow, dragging them. Somehow, the word had spread, and men poured out of the Pennsylvania dugouts. We had a hundred hands on each animal, men laughing and singing.

We got the deer up on the hill, and Kenton stood over them. The rest of us formed a little ring to keep off the Pennsylvania men.

"Food for all!"

"You'll not keep it to yourself!"

"We're dying for the want of a bit of fresh meat!"

"There's food and plenty for all!"

Jacob's deep voice rang out: "It's Kenton's spoil—let him say!"

They caught the name. Women tried to break through and reach Kenton.

"Ah—Kenton!"

"He's a fine, good man!"

"You've got the light in yer eyes, Kenton. You'll not keep the meat!"

"I've rum to go with it—meat for rum, Kenton!"

Kenton took on dignity. A lean, bearded wretch, his yellow hair all stained with blood, he took on dignity nevertheless. He waved his arms for silence.

"A haunch for us," he cried. "You'll grant us a haunch. Roast the rest. By God, build a fire—a great, roaring fire!"

They screamed for Kenton. Haggard, death-stricken women clawed through our line to touch him. We cut a haunch from one of the deer, and Henry bore it into the dugout. They were gathering wood for the fire. Weariness gone for a moment, the wood grew into a pile. We strung a log from the top of a dugout to a tree for a spit. Eager hands skinned the deer. We took out the entrails and divided them up for separate roasting. Kenton was drinking rum. Hoarded bits of rum came to him from every side. He did not work; he stood close to the crackling fire, drinking rum and getting good and drunk. A dozen times over, he had to tell the story of how he had killed the deer. He called me over, said:

"Ah, Allen—they're noways such bad men, these Pennsylvania. I got a little bitch for you who speaks a round, fine German. No arguments."

I laughed and tasted the rum. I was in a mood for laughing. Bess stayed close to me.

"You'll be with me, Allen—all night. You'll not leave me go, Allen, for a German Pennsylvania woman?"

"For no woman," I said.

The deer were pierced by the spit and set to roast. We spread the fire, so that it would give out more heat. We laughed the way we had not laughed for long. Even when the officers' horses sounded on the hill, we laughed.

Muller was there, with two others—Lieutenant Colby and Captain Freestone. They dismounted and pushed through us.

"What's all this?" Muller demanded.

Jacob answered him: "You've eye enough to see we're roasting deer."

"All plunder goes to the commissary. Take that meat down. Colby—have a dozen men carry it to the commissariat."

"To the officers' bellies!" Jacob roared.

"You fat bastards!"

"You bleeding, dirty swine!"

Kenton cried: "Since when's deer plunder? I killed them, free beasts of the open." He held his knife in his hand. "I've good fair use for the knife—better game than deer."

The officers wore small arms. Some of us had muskets. We were a hate-maddened bunch. The women egged us on. They hated the officers not so much as they hated the officers' wives, the well-dressed, well-kept women who lived in the stone houses of the Quakers near by, along with their men. They didn't come to the camp very often; but sometimes they came halfway, to look curiously. To look at beasts, male and female. Our women hated them.

One screamed: "Go on, Kenton—show them the killing of deer! Show them a swift killing of deer."

They had courage, those officers. They stood there, in the middle of us, eying us one by one. Muller smiled a little. Ely went up to them.

"You won't be fools," Ely said quietly. "You won't see murder done."

Muller turned and walked through us. The other two went with him. They were followed by hooting, laughter. I felt that they would remember.

"They're no men to lead us," Ely said to me. "They don't know us."

"They're fools," I said.

The meat was being turned by a half a dozen men, roasting slowly, dripping fat that burnt with blue and yellow flame in the fire.

We cut it down when it was still half-raw. We stood close to the fire, gulping the meat. Charley Green sang a parody of a Boston song— "The Jolly Sons of Liberty."

We joined in. It took our fancy, and we sang:

Come jolly sons of liberty, come all with hearts united,
We stink so high we scare the foe, not easily affrighted,
Our angry bowels we must subdue, now is the time or never,
Let each man prove this motto true, and droppings from him sever.

We sang it to the tune of "Glorious First of August." We sang it again and again until the words had no more meaning. We were drunk with fresh meat in empty stomachs. Some of us were sick. Finally we stumbled back into our dugouts.

I go out on sentry duty. It is night—a clear, still night. The Pennsylvania brigades have exhausted themselves; the dugouts, small lumped huts, are quiet.

The cold had eased itself a little; there is almost no wind at all. I walk up and down slowly, and sometimes I turn and look at the glow in trees behind the huts—the embers of our fire. I think of how the Jew's lungs froze when we carried Clark Vandeer to the hospital. But Ely and I are still alive; we are two strong men.

Clark is dead, not even buried. I take my bayonet, and thrust through the snow at the ground. It's hard as rock. I go down on my knees, try to dig, and manage to turn up a little earth.

I must get rid of my fear. I look over the country, and try to see it as it will be in the spring. The Jew's words stay in my mind; he never saw the spring in America.

I attempt to rid myself of the fear that this will be our grave.

There's no sound. Are we all dead? I cry out, and my voice comes back, a plaintive echo. I want to fire my musket. It's a great desire, and I have to use all my powers to hold back. How many men on sentry beat fire their guns for the same reason? Break the silence. The day before, a man had been whipped half to death for that.

The moon shows above the far hills. It shows a curved rim of yellow ice. It lights up the countrywide, gives a weird, unholy beauty. The moon rises until it looks like half a mouth, laughing.

7

THE JEW is dying. Smith suffers from scurvy, and we can do nothing for him. To some degree we all have it, but Smith's face is like a rotten apple, and his teeth have fallen out. He lies in his bed, groaning with pain and cursing the Jew. Or calling back memories of roasts in the kitchen of his inn.

His voice grows stronger as he talks. "—a roast of beef, a prime rib roast of beef. Give it fifteen minutes to the pound, and turn it slowly. Turn it slowly and catch the drippings. Drippings for gravy—"

We can't stand that. We tell him to close his God-damned mouth.

The doctor came twice. Once he brought a slice of potato for Smith. It helped a little, but potatoes are rare. The second time, he asked the Jew if he'd go to the hospital.

"Good mother earth has relieved us," the doctor said. "There's a place to spare. They squabble like chickens—give it to a New Jersey man, give it to a Massachusetts man, give it to a Vermonter. God, a stinking breed, those Vermonters, cold as their mountains and ignorant as pigs. Can I say I'm holding it for a Jew? Can I tell them that? I threaten to walk out, and they let me do what I want with the place, save it for the Jew. They listen to me. I tell them eighteen miles away—in Philadelphia—there's ten golden pounds a week waiting for an army doctor. I take their Continental money and use it for bandages. It doesn't make good bandages even."

"How long have I got?" The Jew asked him.

"Any day now."

"I'll stay here," the Jew said, his smile curious.

The doctor looked at him oddly. He seemed to be really regretful. "I thought we'd talk," the doctor said. "You can go mad, not having anyone to talk to."

"You won't go mad," the Jew said.

Then they looked at each other; there seemed to be a sort of under-standing between them.

We sit, now, waiting for the Jew to die. We fear his death, more than he does himself. Of that I'm certain. We know it won't be long. He bled for a long time through his nose and mouth, and after that he lay quiet, hardly breathing. His face is like yellow parchment, old skin stretched over bones. But he can't be very old.

I ask Ely what guess he'd make of the man's age.

"There's no age to him," Ely says slowly.

"He ain't seen thirty winters," Jacob guesses.

"He never spoke of wife or children. He's a strange, silent man."

I say, fretfully: "Why won't he die? He's been a week dying."

"A black magic that struck me," Smith says. "The scurvy comes from the heathen Jew."

I crawl into my bed, and Bess asks me: "He's dead?"

"No—not yet."

"Allen, I can't stand any more of this. I tell you, I can't. Only take me away, Allen. It's better to die outside than to die here. I wake up in the night, sweating—thinking that the place has closed in on me. Only take me away."

"There's no fear," I tell her, "no fear."

"But take me away, Allen."

"It's a long, weary five hundred miles to the Mohawk," I say. "It's a road we could never travel. And the British hold all the country in between."

"We don't have to go to the Mohawk, Allen."

"Then where?"

"The British in Philadelphia pay a price and keep for information, Allen. Food and housing—"

"Christ, you slut!" I cried. "You turning, crawling slut. You'd have me sell Ely—you'd have me sell them all."

"Only for you, Allen, only for you—only for my love of you, Allen. Only for my deep, abiding love of you."

"You're not a fit woman to love a man—to be loved by a man. You're not a fit woman to hold a man's body—"

"Allen, what are you saying?"

"I'm saying the truth! Clark Vandeer put his curse on me when he lay dying. He predicted true. You're a little filthy slut, and you're not a fit woman for a man."

"No, Allen—only my love of you to make me say it. Only my love

239

that put thoughts in my mind. Loving and sleeping, sleeping half the day and night from weakness, dreaming all the time, you dream fancies, Allen. Like I dream I'm not here, but in a place where men and women are real. God forgive me, I think of a dress, Allen, almost go crazy making a dress in my mind, a dress of fine white flax, spun. I spin it myself, Allen. Day and night, I spin the flax. I can spin; I can card and weave and spin. I'm a fair, decent woman, Allen, and no bad woman could card and weave and spin. I make the cloth and cut a dress for myself, and sew it. Like the snow outside, Allen—a dress of snow, clean and spotless. No marks on it, Allen—all over it not ever a mark. To make me good, Allen, only a dress of white to make me good. You wouldn't have to tell them truth, Allen. It's said the British are fair stupid beings. They'll believe you, Allen, whatever you tell them. They'll give us food and shelter to keep the winter—"

"You're no fit woman—let me go!"

"Allen, I'm good—stay by me, Allen. Allen, I could grow strong and round with a winter. Come spring, Allen, we could go to the southland and over Boone's road into Transylvania. There's no war there in the south, Allen, and I would be strong—a fit woman to weave for a man, to clean and to work for him. You wouldn't have to love me then, Allen—only let me work for you. I wouldn't be holding you down, Allen—only to work for you."

I climbed out of bed, stumbled, and almost sprawled into the fire. I heard Bess' little cry of terror. I stood and watched the flames. Our wood is almost gone—a low fire. I tried to see something in the small flame.

Ely is by the Jew. He says something, and then over his shoulder to me: "Allen—come here."

I go and bend over the bed.

"You've had schooling, Allen. You've read books."

I nod. "You've come on a fair prayer for a Jew in your reading?"

I shake my head helplessly.

He says a few words. The Jew sighs, and Ely closes his eyes. Ely says: "I'm not a man to think a lot about heaven and hell—but I'll go where he went, and content with that."

I can't speak.

Ely says: "Come and cut a few sticks of wood with me, Allen. The fire's low."

I take up the axe, and we go outside. Ely leads the way into the forest. I cut down a small tree, and then I rest while Ely lops off the branches. The work is good; it takes my mind off things.

240

We come back loaded with wood and build up the fire. Jacob is kneeling by the Jew's bed. We both look at him, but neither of us speaks.

I go to my bed. Bess touches my face, timidly. I put my head on her breath and sob convulsively.

8

WE'VE decided to desert, Kenton Brenner, Charley Green, and I. Not at once did we come to the decision, but slowly, working our courage, and giving ourselves all the arguments we needed to leave the army. First Kenton and I—then Charley.

Two days after the Jew died, I walked on sentry beat with Kenton. The fresh meat had lifted us, brought back little fires of strength that were all but gone. I came on Kenton at the end of my beat. He leaned on his musket, looking northward over the hills.

I said to him: "I was watching you—you were silent and unmoving here wondrous long. I thought to myself, you're frozen and sleeping on your feet."

"I'm thinking a strong man could walk through the snow."

"Where to?" I asked him. "Where would you be walking?"

"North—a great stretch north to the Mohawk. I'm sick to look at the Valley land."

"For five hundred miles? Edward froze. Stiff as a log of wood. They brought him back and laid him down, and he was all ringed over with ice. I don't forget the sight of Edward, with the ice sealing his lips."

"Edward was alone."

Then I looked at him, and I could feel how the hope was tearing inside of me. "We're like rats in a trap—and lacking all courage," I muttered.

We asked Charley that night. Charley a Boston man, a city man. A curious man who had read many hundreds of books. He had a round face, tiny blue eyes, and a stoutness that days of starving wouldn't rid him of.

"We're enlisted three years," Charley said.

"For three years, and three hundred men in our regiment," I said. "Six of us left. There'll be none of you left for ripe rewards at the end of three years—not enough to hang from an English gibbet."

"I've a woman here," Charley muttered. "I'd be sleeping alone many

241

a night."

"You've a dirty slut who won't hunger for you once ye're gone."

"I'm sick to be home."

"There's food on the way," I told him eagerly. "There's a country full of food on the way. Rich, good food for our taking."

"We've no money. Our Continental paper wouldn't buy a loaf of bread to the thousand dollars."

"We don't need money. We'll take our muskets. Men with muskets can find food "

"I'm no thief,' Charley said stubbornly. "By God, I've become a rotten mock of a man, but I'm no thief."

"No plunder. I'm not meaning plunder, Charley. Old soldiers could find a little bit of food."

Then we sit close to the fire, looking at each other, looking around the tiny smoke-blackened dugout. Ely is out on sentry duty. I try not to think about Ely; I try to think only of freedom—of an end to the awful monotony that's rotting my soul. Jacob lies in his bed, a cloud drawn over him, his feet protruding—ragged, bandaged stumps. His eyes are closed, and he lies without moving. Smith groans softly. Henry Lane is sick with the French disease. He has been sick and silent that way for weeks now—a living dead man lying quietly in his bunk.

We three look at each other and measure each other.

I say: "How long? I'm afraid to die here. Outside—anywhere outside. I'm not afraid to go to sleep in the snow, not wake up—just sleep in the snow. That's easy. There was no pain in Edward's heart for his dying."

"We'd start without food," Charley says.

Kenton grins. "We're used to that."

"You'd go to the Mohawk?"

"Or to Boston until the winter's over."

"No women—"

I stare at them, and they both look at me, and I glance over my shoulder; if Bess is awake.

"No women," Kenton says dully.

I get up, and I go to my bed. Her arms are round me. I watch the fire, pretending not to know that she is awake. I lie there for a long time, not moving, watching the fire, until I think she is asleep.

Ely comes in. Slowly, painfully, he gets out of his clothes. He is very tired; his face is sunken and drawn. Each step he takes draws a grimace of pain from him. I had thought of pleading with Ely to come along with us. But his feet wouldn't carry him a dozen miles.

He puts wood on the fire. He stands there for a little while, wiping the smoke out of his eyes. Then he walks to Jacob's bed. He and Jacob are both older than the rest of us, both of them apart from us. He watched Jacob, draws the cloak up to Jacob's neck. Smith groans. Ely takes cup of the thin corn-broth that we keep by the fire—when we have corn—and holds it to Smith's lips. The man drinks a little.

Ely takes something out of his pocket. "A bit of onion," he says to Smith. "I got it from a Massachusetts man for a few Continental papers. A rare good thing for the scurvy."

Ely sits down by the fire, puts out his legs in front of him. He closes his eyes and leans back, his hands spread on his thighs. I look at him until he blurs in front of my eyes, and then I say:

"Ely—"

He turns to me. "Allen? I didn't think you were awake."

I don't say anything now.

"You wanted something, Allen?"

"Nothing—nothing, Ely."

I turn round. Bess is awake. I see her wide-open dark eyes.

She whispers: "When will you be going, Allen?"

"Going? Where would I be going?"

"Allen, when I came to you that night, and my feet were bleeding, like a pain all through me, and you bound them up, Allen, and said that I was your woman—"

"I said it to keep men from putting hands on you."

"However you said it, I swore I would make no claims on you, Allen. I swore I would love you as long as I lived, Allen, but make no claim. What they were all thinking—that I was a bad woman and a slut. But it didn't matter about those Virginian men, Allen. It didn't matter, their having me. After you, there's nobody else, Allen. When you go away, I won't live."

"What do you want me to do?" I demanded hoarsely. "If we were man and wife, you could make a claim on me. I'd not part from any wife of mine."

"I make no claim, Allen."

"I could go mad, staying here—making my insides rot out."

"I don't want you to stay here, Allen. I wouldn't ask you to stay here. It's two years now of bitter fighting, and I cannot make out yet what they're fighting for. Only I've come to hate war, Allen. What is there, Allen, to make a man give up his life and bring an abiding sorrow in a woman?"

"I don't know," I said miserably.

243

"You're a northland man, Allen, and cold in the way of the north-land men."

"I can't take a woman with me—"

"But tonight, Allen. I'm not holding it against you. Put your arms around me and love me tonight."

I lay without sleeping. Half the night, I lay without sleeping. Finally, I said: "I'll not go without you."

The next night, we were ready. When I told Kenton that Bess would come, he shook his head. I argued with him. I told him that having a woman with us would make it easier to get food.

"She won't walk it."

"She's a lean, hard woman," I said.

"But ye're a fool, Allen. She's not fit woman for a man. She's a slut. So why would you be nailing yourself to a slut?"

"You can go to hell without me," I said.

"We won't be fighting over the matter of a woman. If you want the wench, take her with you, Allen."

Now that we are ready to go, Kenton's woman and Green's woman sit and watch us, but say nothing. Kenton's woman is already glancing at Jacob. There are more than enough men for the women.

Jacob hasn't said a word. He must have known before that we were going, but he doesn't speak. He sits on his bed, a ragged, bearded man, hair streaked with grey, watching us. I try to avoid his eyes.

Henry Lane watches wistfully. He says: "When you come to the Mohawk country—if you see kin of mine, you'll not tell them of my sickness. You'll tell them I had a fair, clean death."

Kenton says: "Ye're not a dying man, Henry. It's just a slow spell of weakness."

"But you'll tell them a quick, clean passing?"

We try to smile at him. We wrap our feet carefully, feeling all eyes in the place upon us. Ely is standing in one corner; he doesn't look at us.

"You won't hold it against us, Ely?" I say to him.

He doesn't answer. We go on with our preparations. We load our muskets carefully. We have about ten rounds of ammunition apiece— no food. If we pause for a moment, the entire hopelessness of our enterprise appears to overwhelm us. When we are ready, we stand round and look at each other. Nobody moves toward the door. We look round the cabin we have lived in for so many weeks now, the smoke-blackened timbers, the beds built against each wall, the dugout floor which has become as hard as rock. Out of our own hands.

Where are we going?

Kenton says: "Time to go—"

I say, desperately: "Come along, Ely. We're not doing any wrong, Ely. There's been no pay for weeks, no rum, no food. Two years we've fought for them. Come along."

Ely shakes his head, doesn't answer.

Jacob cries: "Christ—what are you waiting for? Get to hell outa here! A blessing to be rid of a spineless swine. For once I thought there was the making of a man in you, Allen, but ye're one with that bloodless Boston printer. Kenton's mindless, senseless, but I never thought it of you to follow that Boston man."

"Jacob—"

"I want no words with you. Why don't you go?"

"We're going," I say dully.

Charley moves to the door, opens it. The cold air rushes in. Charley waves to his woman. Kenton follows him. I take Bess' arm, and we go out after them, closing the door behind us.

We go a few paces into the night, and then we stand and look back at the dugout. As if we expect movement, as if we expect some sign of life. The dugouts stand in a long row, and we walk past them.

I glance down at Bess' face. It's lit with happiness. She walks apart from me, as if she wishes to prove that there's enough strength in her. She says:

"I can walk, Allen. Don't fear for me. I'm a strong walker, Allen."

I try to feel glad. We're free; and there's no going back.

"If we're stopped," Kenton says. "What if we're stopped?"

We grip our muskets. We've passed the Pennsylvania dugouts. On our right is the encampment of General Poor's men. We push through the thin strip of woods and come out into the open. A sentry standing on the hill sees us.

"Shall we make a run for it?" Green asks.

"He'll fire if we run," Kenton says. "He's no officer. We'll talk to him."

"He'll listen to reasonable talk," I say hopefully.

Bess shrinks against me. We go on more slowly. When we come up to the sentry, we stop and stand there. We don't know what to say.

"Where are you going?" he demanded.

"We're Pennsylvania men."

Then he sees that Bess is a woman, and his eyes open. He's like us, bearded, ragged. He can't mistake us for anything but what we are.

I say, desperately: "We're deserters. We won't go back. If you want

245

to die—we'll die along with you." Green is covering him with his gun.

"Deserters—" the man says, oddly.

"Which is it?" Kenton demands.

"Go ahead—Jesus Christ, I'll keep no man here."

We go on, and when I glance back, the sentry is still standing there, where we had left him. We cross the Gulph Road, string out over the parade ground. A moon is in the sky. We throw long shadows in the snow.

Bess is limping, and I see that the wrappings on one of her feet have come undone. I stop to fasten them. Green mutters:

"I told you—about a woman."

The moment I bare my hands, they get numb. There's no wind, but it's mercilessly cold. I fumble with the wrappings, finally manage to fasten them. We go on. A grey stone house looms ahead.

"Varnum's quarters, I think," Kenton says. "We'll go round."

We go back, avoiding the redoubt. We skirt a row of dugouts. At the end, we come across a sentry again. He stands blocking our way, but he makes no move toward us.

"Go on,' Kenton says.

We walk past him, and he follows us with his eyes; but he makes no effort to halt us. We begin to run, enter the woods panting, and fling ourselves down. Bess clings to me, sobbing hoarsely.

"How'll we cross the river?" I ask Kenton.

Kenton shrugs. He said: "It's better to die this way, better to be shot clean. We'll freeze to death from the river."

"I made you go, Allen," Bess sobs. "You'll hold it up to me that I made you go."

"Christ—shut up!" Green whispers.

We go on, falling, rolling over, clutching at trees and tearing our clothes. Our muskets are useless, clogged with snow, the powder wet in the firing pans. Our strength is pretty much gone, but somehow we manage to stagger through the woods down to the bank of the Schuyl-kill. At the bank, we lie in the snow, panting hoarsely, unable to move.

"The bridge is guarded," I mutter. "We can't cross the bridge—it's guarded."

"You damn fool, the river's frozen."

Somehow, none of us had realized that. We laugh like idiots. Bess hugs me. She says: "Allen—Allen, I don't care—we're out of it."

It's terribly cold. As we lie there, I can feel myself growing numb, sleepy. I close my eyes, and almost instantly a deep rush of relaxation overtakes me. I want to sleep. I draw Bess close to me.

Kenton is gripping my shoulder. "Allen—we have to get out of here. Sentries patrol the riverbank."

We stumble to our feet. There is a great drift of snow against the bank, and we flounder through it. Bess almost disappears. Then we are out on the river. Some of the ice has been swept bare by the wind, and we go sprawling. We have no strength left for directed action. Green drops his musket, claws at it, and then creeps after it. And all the time we are in an agony of fear that we will be seen from the bank we left.

Finally, we gain the shore. It takes all our strength to scramble up onto the bank.

We go up slowly, panting, breathing heavily; then through the forest. It's black in the forest. We fall, bruise and cut ourselves. Finally, we come out on a stretch of open fields.

Kenton says: "Ah—I'm used up. We'll make no distance tonight.

"We have to keep going," I pant.

Bess looks at me; her face is drawn with an agony of weariness. As we walk, slow as we are going, she falls being. She can't keep our pace. Forcing herself to run a little, she'll catch up with us, drop back.

"I told you not to bring the woman," Charley said.

"She's here—leave her be. It was a fair hard run out of camp."

Bess says: "Allen—I'll stay with you. It's easy for me, Allen."

She falls once, lies in the snow. We turn, and I can see her straining to raise herself.

"You shoulda known," Kenton nods.

I go back and lift her up. She clings to my arm, and says: "Forgive me, Allen. I'm no fit woman."

We walk on. More and more, I feel Bess' weight on me. We've been half-starved for weeks—sick. None of us has shoes. Our feet are bandaged, covered over with cloth, and then bandaged again up to our knees. Our breeches are torn. Our coats are thin as paper. Kenton wears a forlorn cocked hat, two of the cocks down and flapping. Charley and I have no hats. Our heads are bound like Turks'.

We come to a little dirt road, walk along it. I seem to sleep, even while I'm walking. Suddenly, I come awake. Kenton is walking on ahead. Charley has stopped; he stands looking at me. I turn around, and see Bess crumpled in a heap on the snow. I go back to her.

"Go on, Allen," she says.

I draw her up to me, and she clings close, sobbing into my coat. We go on, with Charley and Kenton ahead of us.

We made camp. We couldn't have been much more than a mile or two from the Schuylkill. How far, I don't know, because half the walking was a nightmare. But we couldn't have been very far from the river. Half-frozen, we stopped and tried to build a fire.

All I could think of was Edward Flagg, the skin of ice over his lips when they brought him back. He was a great, strong man, Edward; but they brought him back stiff as a log.

We break branches and gather bits of wood together. Bess crouches close to the ground, trembling.

Charley tries to make a fire. He uses a handflint. For minutes he tries, striking again and again, until the flint drops from his numbed hands. He tries to rub life back into his hands.

I tear a bit of cloth from my leg bindings, drop some powder onto it. Kenton takes the flint, and a spark ignites the powder. We feed the fire carefully, nurse it and blow on it. It grows larger. We build up a great, roaring mass of fire.

"They'll see it," Kenton says.

"We need fire. We'll never live the night out unless we have fire."

As the fire grows, we gather around it and absorb the heat. Bess crowds close; her thin, white face lights a little. Kenton grins. He says:

"Edward made a great mistake, walking alone. It's a wonder to me how any man could think to win northward, walking alone."

"Don't speak of Edward."

"You can speak of a dead fool," he says lightheadedly.

"My belly's tight and empty," Charley says. "By God, I'd give ten years of my life for a steak to feed that fire with."

"There's food—we'll feed well enough tomorrow."

We stayed close to the fire. We arranged for a watch through the night to feed the fire. We wiped our muskets clean and reloaded them.

Kenton stood the first watch. I lay down with Bess in my arms, Charley sprawled by the fire a little distance away. I could see how Charley envied me the having of a woman to spend the night through.

In my arms, Bess still trembled. I couldn't make her warm. I tried to soothe her, tried to tell myself that we wouldn't freeze. But if Kenton slept and the fire went out—

"I'm no fit woman, Allen," Bess said as if repeating a lesson she had learned. "You made a mistake to bring me along, Allen. I'll be nothing else but a drag on you."

"We'll go together," I told her. "We'll find a place where we can rest and warm ourselves. Then we'll go together. It'll be nowhere as hard as tonight."

"You're a good man, Allen. You're a strong, good man to be so tender with me."

"I said you'd go, and I'll care for you," I told her proudly.

"I won't ask any care of you, Allen. I'll fend for myself—"

"I'll fend for you. It'll be like you were wedded to me. I'll fend for you."

"Some day, Allen—you might wed me?"

"There's a fair lot of things I'm thinking to do," I said.

Then she slept. I held her close to me, and I lay looking up at the stars, watching the slow rise and sway of sparks against the dark sky. I thought of Ely and Jacob, and tried to understand that I would not be with them again. For the first time, I recalled how Ely had been when we left.

I must have slept. Kenton was waking me.

"Your watch, Allen," he said.

I got up, feeling the cold eat into me as I moved from Bess. She murmured my name in her sleep.

"You saw anything?'

"Nothing," Kenton said.

He curled up by the fire. I leaned on my musket and watched the flames.

9

IN THE morning, I awake to the sound of bugles from the encampment. We can't be very far away. The bugles are thin, but they sound clear in the morning air.

Bess, opening her eyes, looks at me and smiles. Her smile is deep, happy awareness of my presence. She touches my face, passes her fingers across my beard.

"You're better?" I ask her.

"Better. A hunger inside of me, but I can stand hunger, Allen. I've no fear of hunger."

Charley is feeding the fire. A moment later, Kenton comes across the field, holding a few frozen ears of corn.

"We'll break our fast on this," he calls.

"I wouldn't think of breaking fast, but of getting out of here," Charley says. "We're too near to the encampment, and far enough away to be deserters."

"They'll not stop us any more," I say. "After last night, they'll not stop us."

"We'll go north and east," Kenton says thoughtfully. "There are good roads through the Jersey bottoms."

"If we had horses—"

Charley looks at us.

"It's horses—or dying in the snow," I say.

We toast the corn over the fire. It's not fit food for a pig, but we eat it eagerly.

"I dug it under the show," Kenton says. "It's a wonder it stayed so long. The ground's scraped clean of food."

"We can go east—to Norristown. It's a good farmland over that way."

We finish the corn—close to the husk. We take our guns and look at the priming. Then we start off.

We walk slowly in the direction of the King of Prussia Road. Last night was a lesson. We know how little strength we have, and that we must husband it. It's cold this morning, but not so cold as last night. The sun comes up, clear and bright, making long blue shadows on the snow. The snow glistens, and each crystal shoots a tiny beam of light into our eyes.

A sparkle in Bess' eyes. She turns her face to me, showing me how long her steps are.

"I'm a good walker, Allen—a fine good walker."

"A fine walker," I agreed.

We're all of us eager. Kenton steps out ahead, long strides, and confidence in the way he swings his heavy musket. We're content that Kenton leads. He's four years older than I am, a powerful man. Bess is like a boy, thin, her long dark hair twisted into braids. Charley sings snatches of song.

Bess keeps glancing at me. She says: "You've no regrets, Allen?"

"No regrets—"

"I think of Ely," Charley says. "I was never understanding men like Ely. A fearfully tolerant man."

"He might have come—"

"He wouldn't come without Jacob. There's a deep bond between the two of them—for all the black murder in Jacob's heart. There's no other man Jacob ever loved, unless it was the Jew. I cannot make it out, but I've never seen such sorrow as Jacob had when the Jew died."

"I'm fearful of Jews," Bess says. "I had not seen a Jew until I was fifteen. My mother said she'd show me a Jew some time, so I'd have a

250

deeper knowledge of the Book."

"There were a pretty lot of Jews in Boston," Charley says. "Sam Adams was a great one to bleed them. He'd spin them a fine tale of revolution and take their last shilling, and there was more respect for him for bleeding a Jew than for all his wild talk."

"It's said Hamilton's a Jew—"

"He has the look in his eyes."

We're near the road now. Kenton waits for us. He's standing there, listening.

"What is it?" I ask him.

"We're too near the camp. I'm thinking we should bide a while longer in the forest. Ye're safer in the trees."

"We make better time on the road."

"It's Quaker country hereabout. I'd put no trust in any Quaker."

"Or fear them—" I said confidently.

We walk out on the road, Bess close to me. Now, again, seeing the stretch of open road before us, we realize the distances. Distances pile up for hundreds of miles to the snowy mountains that bind the Mohawk. Bess presses close, looks up at my face. I understand now that she knows, as I know, that she won't go that great distance. There is no strength in her for that. She stands like a small, frightened boy, half-grown.

She says: "Sometimes I'm afeard, Allen. Hold me."

"You hear anything?" Kenton demands.

I shake my head. We walk on, along the road towards Norristown. We walk very slowly, feeling the cold more than before. A hundred yards more—we stop.

"I hear horses," Kenton says.

"Not from the camp." I can hear it now—a thudding muffled by the snow.

Bess looks at me, shaking her head.

"Not from the camp," Charley cries. "It's up the road."

"More than one horse."

"Farmers don't ride like that."

"Get out—for the trees!" Kenton shouts.

But there are fields on either side the road, trees only in the direction from which the sounds of horses are coming. A heap of snow on the side of the road suggests a stone wall underneath. Long shadows on the road, and a glare from the snow, it makes a scene to stay in my mind.

We stand there like people who have lost all power of movement.

251

Bess says:

"I brought it on you, Allen. God forgive me—"

Kenton leads the way off the road, Charley after him. Kenton stumbles, and Charley bends to help him to his feet. I take Bess' hand and drag her through the drift against the stone wall. We climb over the wall. Kenton is stumbling along, like a man who has been shot.

I turn round, see a dozen men on horse coming down the road.

"McLane's raiders," Kenton sobs.

A man pulls out in front, and I hear him crying for us to halt. They begin to gallop, and the thud of their horses' hoofs is like a drumbeat in my ears. I drag Bess along.

Kenton and Charley are waiting for me. They see that with Bess I can't reach the woods before the cavalrymen, but nevertheless they wait. They hold their muskets before them.

I cry: "Don't shoot—for God's sake. Run for it!"

We're almost at the trees. I think that we'll make it. I sob with pain of the running.

Some of the horses are floundering in the snow. The man out in front cries: "Stop or we'll fire!"

"The hell with you!" Kenton screams. "Keep a run, Allen! They're lost in the snow!"

I glance back once more. We're almost up to Kenton and Charley. They've lowered their muskets and are starting toward the trees. But the men are dismounting, dropping from their horses.

A blast of musketry crashes behind us. Bess is torn from my hand, crying.

Kenton sees; he runs toward me, cursing, Charley after him. I face round and the cavalrymen are closing in on us. I see it all in a red haze, and I fire. Kenton and Charley too; like machines, their muskets go off. I notice one of the cavalrymen falling, so slowly that the picture is impressed permanently upon my mind. I look at Bess, and try to understand what has happened. Bess lies in the snow in a little heap.

They close in on us, and there's no fight left. I wonder why we fired. They're like us, bearded, ragged, their feet bound in blood-stained cloths. They're like us, thin, worn.

They hold onto us. I strain to get away—to Bess. I say: "Let me go to her! God damn you—you've got us now. Let me go to her!"

McLane stands in front of us. He's a young man, clean-shaven except for a small moustache, wearing white breeches and a good blue coat, sword, pistol, a cocked hat. As he stands there, panting, his breath steams out.

"Deserters?" he asks. Behind him two men are carrying the one I saw fall. McLane whirls round. "Who is it?"

"Dave Seely—"

"He's hurt?"

We all see it. The man is shot through the head. Vaguely, I wonder whose bullet it was—thinking of Bess. Whose bullet there?

"You filthy swine?" McLane says to us. "You damned, cowardly swine! You'll hang for this if I have to gibbet you myself."

Kenton stares sullenly. Charley says: "Let him go to his woman. You shot his woman"

I try to tear loose. Some of the men are turning Bess over. I scream: "Hands off her! Christ, leave her alone!"

"It's a woman," one of them says.

I plead: "Let me go to her. You have us now. That's enough, isn't it? Let me go to her."

"Hold your damned tongue!"

"Let me go to her—" I pull loose. I don't know how, but I pull loose, and nobody tries to stop me. I run over to Bess, and the men who are bending over her stand aside. I kneel down next to her. She's shot somewhere in the body, because all the front of her clothes is stained with blood.

I rub her cheeks. She opens her eyes, and I keep rubbing her cheeks.

"Allen," she says.

I can't say anything. You fight in an army for two years, and you know a death wound; you know the sign of it in a man's eyes. She knows; the deep knowledge of it is in her eyes. What can I say?

She says: "Allen—I brought a wrong on you. I'm no fit woman for a man."

I shake my head. Maybe it seems to her that I'm going away, because she whispers:

"Bide with me, Allen—for a while."

Very slowly, I stand up. I say aloud: "I should have known—it was such a distance for a woman to walk."

The cavalrymen take hold of me and lead me back. McLane is watching me, oddly. Kenton's face is despair and nothing else. When I come close to him, Charley Green reaches out a hand for my arm.

"Allen?"

I say to myself, in all the crash of shooting, it might have been someone else. It might have been. I tell myself, We're going back.

"It's no great horror—a dying like that," Charley says softly.

"I'm not sorrowing for her," I say desperately. "I'm not sorrowing

253

for her."

"Easy, Allen."

"Easy, sure—you'll be with her soon enough," McLane says.

Kenton cries: "Leave him alone, God damn you! Leave off taunting him!"

They march us back toward the road. I look round, and see that it's still morning, a glorious cold morning. As we reach the road, we see a brigade coming on the run, panting. They must have heard the shooting in the encampment. The brigade gathers round. They keep telling the story.

"Pennsylvania deserters—"

Two men carrying Bess. They walk alongside of me.

"It's Wayne's boast he has no deserters."

"He'll take off some of his pride, Wayne will."

"We were walking to the Mohawk," Kenton laughs. "God—we were walking to the Mohawk."

McLane hands us over to the officer of the brigade. "Take them to the redoubt," he says, "and hold them. They've murdered one of my men. I'll charge them myself."

"We're no murderers!" Green cried. "We shot after your men fired on us."

"Take these swine away," McLane says.

They marched us back slowly. He was no hard man, the officer of that brigade, a young man whose name was Captain Kennedy. They were Massachusetts men. There were a few there whom Kenton knew, and they made things easier for us.

Their officer saw how weak we were, and he marched us slowly. But it was a long way back, a weary way. Kenton came up and put an arm round me.

"It was a good run last night, Allen," he said. "I didn't think it to end so soon. I didn't think of no cavalry to find us out right away."

"I'm not blaming you, Kenton."

"The lass is dead. You'll be blaming me for that, Allen? Her blood's on my hands."

"No—I'm not putting the blame on any man."

We marched down the King of Prussia Road to the crossroads, then turned right toward the redoubt. As we passed between the dugouts of Varnum's brigades, Kennedy stopped and had them send out a drummer. The men, part of the Pennsylvania and New Jersey line, flocked out of their huts to see us pass. The drummer beat a low, monotonous roll—for the condemned and dead. Some of the men dropped their heads. We went through slowly; I heard one man say:

"Poor, damned devils."

All the time moving—the cold air, the sunlight glinting from the snow, half-blinding us; I didn't think much. I understood that Bess was dead, but she was already part of all my memories of the army. They come and go, like the doctor had said, like Moss Fuller had died. I can't think.

We march into the redoubt. Into a cold, bare log hut, where Colonel Varnum sits at a camp table. Kennedy salutes. The guard stand at attention. But we're used up. We stand limply, our hands hanging at our sides.

"Deserters, sir," Kennedy says. "Taken by Captain McLane. They resisted arrest, and one of Captain McLane's men was killed. I have their muskets, all fired. McLane's man had a ball in his head. They had a woman with them, and she was shot in the breast. McLane's men fired a volley."

"What regiment?" the Colonel asked tonelessly. Too many incidents like ours had occurred for it to matter a great deal.

"Fourteenth Pennsylvania."

"Wayne's men?"

We nodded.

"Your names?"

We gave him our names.

"Ragged, filthy beasts, Kennedy. I'd tame a few of them. Maybe we'll tame these."

Kennedy stood without answering.

"Put them in the guardroom."

They took us into a room about six feet square. It had no windows, but there were chinks between the logs. It had a dirt floor, low roof, no fire.

They barred the door. I heard Kennedy say: "Poor devils—"

We sit on the floor in silence. Light comes in thin bars through the cracks between the logs. It splatters us with gold, gold on Kenton's yellow beard.

We're cold. Unconsciously, we move toward each other. But we don't speak.

My feet pain me. I stretch them out before me, to ease the pain. I find myself trembling, perhaps from the cold.

"I never thought to hang," Charley says—like a child would say it.

10

THE light goes; the bars it made throughout the guardhouse vanish, and a deep dusk replaces it. A slow afternoon, and then quick falling of night, with increasing cold. A wind that blows through the spaces between the logs The floor is cold as ice. Our arms and legs stiffen. We try to find some relief in movement.

Three times the guard outside changes. We can look through cracks in the door and see him, a ragged, lean soldier.

We are given nothing to eat. At first, the pain of hunger drives us half-mad. That's the way hunger is at the beginning. It eases off afterwards. The dull gnawing in your stomach becomes desire, desire for all things. it's not so hard to bear at the thirst.

We pound on the door. "Guard — guard — for Christ's sake, bring us a little food and water!"

He comes close to the door, looks at us curiously.

"A drink of water — "

He says: "A waste of good food."

"Anything — a little water."

"Do you think I've been eating fine today?" he asks us. "Do you think I've tasted meat in a fortnight?"

"Bring us some water."

He brings us a pot of water, watches us as we drink it. " A sight of wretched men you are," he says. "I heard it was nowhere so bad with Wayne's men."

"Why are they keeping us here?"

"I haven't asked them."

Night comes. I lie on the floor. Kenton's close to me for warmth. Charley stands up against the door, a dark blur. Closing my eyes, dozing, I can imagine the body next to me as Bess. I can imagine the place as the dugout, and I wait for Bess to make a movement, to touch me, to put her hands on my beard. I wait for Bess to speak, her voice breaking through my slumber. Bits of her voice at first, and then more and more.

I shake Kenton, and ask: "Bess? Bess?"

"Allen — you're losing yer mind."

"No — no, I dreamed a little. I'm hungry, Kenton. You don't suppose they'll bring us food? Men can't live long without food. If they're meaning to hang us, they'll bring us some food."

Charley growls: "I'll not hang. By God, Allen, I'm meaning to take my life before I let them put a rope around my neck."

"We shouldn't have fired," Kenton groans. "They were well on to take us, and we shouldn't have fired."

"They shot Bess," I mutter.

"A poor fool to think she could walk through five hundred miles of snow and ice. She was no woman to go walking the length and distance to the Mohawk. I wonder to think that you shoulda brought her along, Allen."

"A man 'comes attached to a woman, sleeping with her night after night. You can't bear away the cold, bitter nights without a woman."

"I had a woman," Kenton says, "but she was no legal wedded wife of mine. If I made my mind to go a great distance over the snow, I would not take a woman to drag on me."

"Leave off Allen," Charley snaps. "He's got sorrow enough. The woman's dead, isn't she?"

"She's dead."

"Then leave off Allen."

"I'm holding no hate for Kenton," I say wearily. "I wouldn't be sorrowing over the woman. She was no lawful wedded wife of mine, and she was no fit woman for a man—" I can't say any more. I put my face in my hands, and in the awful, complete silence of the place, I know they're listening to my sobbing.

There's a long while of silence after that. A crunching in the snow outside where the sentry paces up and down, a wash of the wind over the top of the redoubt. A wolf's howling from down the Schuylkill.

I grope back for a time when we were not in the encampment. There was a battle at Brandywine, where three men of the Fourth New York Regiment were killed. That left nine men. Moss Fuller and Edward Flagg and Clark Vandeer. Six men. Allen Hale; Charles Green; Kenton Brenner. Henry Lane was dying. Clark died, and he put a curse on me as he lay dying. Jacob burning like a fire, a black fire. The Jew had died in peace, with knowingness in his eyes. Suddenly, I hate the Jew, envy him. I make a picture of Jacob kneeling by the Jew's bed. Ely is left, only Ely.

I groan aloud.

Charley says: "Be easy, Allen. There's nothing for men to fear who've seen what we've seen."

"Nothing," I repeat.

Kenton says: "I've no fear of dying—only of hanging. They put a man on Mount Joy to hang, a man who went mad and killed his lieutenant officer. They put him there to hang, and I swear to God that when I stood on sentry duty I saw the wolves leaping for his body."

257

Charley laughs. "You're a man to see things, Kenton."

"As God is my witness, I saw them—wolves leaping high in the moonlight."

"You don't have to talk about it!" I cry. "You don't have to talk about it."

The silence after that makes a tension; I can see how it is: if they're thinking the way I'm thinking—every move since we left the dugout. Kenton's idea—but without Bess we might have gone miles farther from camp. If her blood is on Kenton's hands, then his is on mine.

It comes to me that if Bess were here this night, she wouldn't be afraid. She'd have no fear; she'd only want to abide with me. Her face would be calm, and I would only have to pass my hands over her face to realize the calm.

I say to Kenton: "Did she die with pain? You saw her fall, Kenton. Did she die with pain?"

"There's no pain in her now," Kenton says.

"I couldn't rest again if I thought she died with a great pain in her heart."

Charley says: "I had a brother die—I was twelve years then. He died of the pox. He said there was no pain to dying—he kept saying there was no pain to dying."

"It's different on the gallows," Kenton says bitterly.

There's a movement at the door; it opens, the sentry and another man bulking against the lighter darkness outside. We watch—wondering who it is. Then I know it's Ely. I don't doubt any more. I feel a restfulness that I haven't felt since I left the dugout. My muscles relax. I sit there on the cold floor, my arms hanging limply by my sides; I feel tears come into my eyes.

Kenton knew. I guess we all knew. Kenton said: "Come in, Ely." His voice was lighter.

"Only a while," the sentry said.

Ely came in and stood by the door. "Allen's here?" he asked.

"All of us, Ely," Kenton said.

It was dark where I sat. I got on my feet and went over to Ely. I went close to him—tried to make out his face. I touched his coat. I said to him:

"Ely, I'm glad to see you. You're not hating or despising us, Ely?"

"I was hoping you wouldn't be brought back," he said slowly.

"Give me your hand, Ely? You won't hold your hand from us?"

He put out his hand, and I clung to it. I put it between mine, and tried to feel the flesh under the mitten he wore.

"It was good of you to come," Charley said. "A long walk through the snow. It was mighty good of you to come, Ely."

"I thought I'd see how you were faring. It's no matter of a walk."

"How'd you know?"

"They brought word that you were taken—one of you shot."

"They shot Bess."

"She's dead?"

"She died out there. She never knew what would happen. She died in my arms, Ely."

"She'll rest easy, poor child."

Kenton had stood back. Now he stood against the further wall. "Ely," He said, "did you come in hate?"

"No—"

"If you came in hate, Ely, I'll tell you that I was the leader. I made Allen a plan to desert, and the woman said she'd die if Allen didn't take her, and Allen had given me his word to go. The woman's blood is on my hands, Ely."

Ely said, softly: "Don't burn yourself, Kenton. The poor girl could not have the peace she has now."

"We shot a man, Ely. They're going to hang us."

"They say we murdered a man, Ely," Kenton went on, dully, no heat or feeling in his voice. "There was no murder. We fled across a field and McLane's men loosed a volley at us. Charley and I turned to wait for Allen and the girl. I saw the girl shot, and I saw her fall. Then I killed one of McLane's men—"

I forced myself to say: "He didn't—we don't know whose shot it was killed him."

Kenton went on as if he hadn't heard me. "You know, Ely, I draw a good bead with a musket. There was no man in all the Mohawk country could outshoot me. You've seen me take my mark and bring down my mark, Ely. I shot the man, Ely. I want you to remember that. I swear to God."

"He's lying," Charley whispered.

For a while, Ely stands there and says nothing. I can feel what's going on inside of him, how hard it is for him to make the effort to speak. He takes a few steps toward us.

Finally, he says: "I brought you a few bits of salt meat—I had it from the meat Kenton killed when we built the fire—you'll remember that?"

"I remember," Kenton says mechanically.

Ely puts the meat in my hands. He stands a moment, as if he's trying to see my eyes in the dark. Then he turns around and goes out.

We divide up the meat and eat it slowly. We sit down again, with our backs to the log walls.

Charley says: "You didn't aim to kill, Kenton. You shot from your waist. There's no man can aim to kill shooting from his waist."

Kenton doesn't answer. I reach out, put my hand on his knee. His hand covers mine.

11

SOMEHOW, we endured through the night. Man's power to endure pain is only exceeded by his ability to forget. We had some water left in the pot; it froze into a solid block. The guardhouse was like a sieve; we lay on a cold floor, close to each other for warmth. The morning came, and we were more dead than alive. We tried to rise off the floor, but we couldn't. Our limbs were as stiff as if death had already laid hold of us. We crawled to the door and hammered on it. But nobody answered, and after a while we stopped. We lay there, making the least noise we could of our own pain.

Charley said: "A night more of this—and we won't fear the gallows."

Finally, the door was opened. A guard stood there, and a strange officer. He told us to get up.

"We're fair stiff—we've eaten only a bit of meat in two days."

We managed to crawl to our feet, and they took us to the same log building where he had spoken to Varnum the day before. We could barely walk. There were some chairs there, and we slumped into them. A fire was going, and the heat of it was like nothing we had ever experienced before; the heat was new and wonderful. We were afraid to go too near the heat at first; we went to it slowly.

"You don't look like you'll wait for the gallows," the officer said. "God, what a sorry mess—" He stared at us. "How long since you've eaten?"

"We had a little meat—"

"I'll have some stew sent in."

The stew was of corn and potatoes, in wooden bowls. We gulped it eagerly.

"I've tasted no food like this in many days," Charley said. "They eat well here."

"It warms you."

We crowded up to the fire, stretched out our feet to bake. We opened our coats.

"A rare, fine fire," Kenton said. He seemed more at ease now, hardly worried.

"They'll hang us today, do you think, Kenton?"

He shrugged. Charley stared into the fire. We sat that way, without talking, until the door opened. A young officer came in, not much more than a boy. I thought I recognized him, but dulled as my mind was, I couldn't recall his name. He came in and stood at the table, studying us. He was remarkably well dressed: some of the officers were as ragged as we. He wore a blue uniform greatcoat with black facings, a silk scarf, a black cocked hat, brown leather breeches and good high-boots of black leather. He held a riding crop in his hand; and hooking one leg over the table, he beat the crop against his thigh.

He was tall and thin—deepset dark eyes. He had a way of staring from under dropped lids.

"You're the Pennsylvania men?" he asked us.

Kenton stared at him sullenly. I could see he didn't like the young swell. I didn't have much interest in him; I was forcing myself not to think—not to think at all. I was trying not to see a gibbet on Mount Joy. Charley Green hummed a song.

He asked us again: "You're the three deserters?"

"Colonel Hamilton?" Charley asked. He hated officers the way only Boston men can hate. He smiled a little as he spoke. He had nothing to lose. Not even fear. It made me sick at myself to see how little fear he and Kenton had. As if they had lost all human quality that related them to me, leaving me alone.

The boy nodded, still looking at us curiously. I recognized Washington's favorite, Alexander Hamilton. I might not have hated him in another situation. As it was, I despised his smug, well-dressed complacency. I looked at his fine black boots, and I thought of how we had taken the boots off Moss Fuller when he died.

"If I have the story right," Hamilton said, "you're three deserters from the Fourteenth Pennsylvania. Deserted with arms and killed one of Captain McLane's men. By God, you're a pretty, filthy bunch of beggars. I'd let you desert; I'd see you all in hell before I'd have you in my army."

"You can go to hell, sir," Charley said.

The regular motion of the quirt against the boy's thigh didn't stop. As if he hadn't heard Green. He shifted his gaze to the chimney over our heads.

"You'll be court-martialed this afternoon," he said. "You've raised a fuss. You'll be a shining example of a gibbet on Mount Joy."

"All right," Kenton said. "Get out of here."

Hamilton got off the table; he had control: he walked up to Kenton, and I waited for the quirt to cross Kenton's face. Then the boy shrugged.

"I'm to defend you."

Charley laughed. His laugh was more than words.

"We don't need anyone to defend us," Kenton said.

"My orders are to defend you."

Charley kept on laughing. I stood up and walked to a window. Beyond the walls of the redoubt, I could see the snow stretching away to the trees that lined the bank of the Schuylkill. The morning sun made colours on the snow, delicate colours of yellow and violet, tints of brown, stray bits of green, colours of life and of spring. I thought of the Jew's words before he died. Spring like an awakening; spring like the hand of God reaching down and caressing the earth, spring with a softening of the earth, so that a man could die and go to the bosom of the soil.

When I turned round, Hamilton was lighting a pipe, a long-stemmed, Dutch clay pipe, the kind the burghers smoke, sitting in front of their shops at Albany, the kind you see racked round the wall in any small up-country village tavern. He had bent over to take a burning twig from the blaze, and now he was blowing clouds of blue tobacco smoke toward the ceiling.

It must have been in my eyes, on my face, all the longing of a condemned man for tobacco. For weeks we had not smoked; for weeks we had not tasted the odour of tobacco.

He looked at me, that curious smile coming on his face again. Impulsively, he offered me the pipe.

I hold out my hand. Kenton and Charley are looking at me. Whatever they thought before, I'm open to them now. I take the pipe in my hand. I go forward a step or two, and offer it to Kenton.

He doesn't move.

Charley whispers: "Christ!"—his whisper hoarse, loud, breaking up in his throat. He takes the pipe and puffs on it. He watches the smoke, passes his hand through the smoke, smiles childishly. He gives the pipe back to me.

I smoke slowly, just a puff or two. Kenton nods, and I give it to him. He puffs; then, suddenly, he throws the pipe across the room, shattering the clay bowl and stem to bits.

262

Hamilton, still smiling, watching us. Kenton with his face in his hands. Charley Green walks back and forth. I say to Hamilton:

"They'll hang us today?"

He shrugs.

"We don't want any pity!" Kenton cries. "By God, what do any of you know, tight in your houses, eating, drinking?"

Hamilton says, slowly: "I had dry bread this morning—two slices. I had a little meat yesterday. It was the General's dinner. He forced me to eat it—"

Charley laughs.

"You don't believe me?"

Kenton says: "Why don't they hang us? Why don't they hang us and get it over with?"

"They'll hang you," Hamilton says. "They'll hang you high enough—"

He goes back to the table, hooks a leg over it, remains there, watching us. I stand by the window. Kenton gets up, awkwardly, painfully, goes over and looks at the shattered pipe.

Hamilton says: "Tell me what happened."

"We deserted," I say. "We're Mohawk men, and we had it in our minds to walk to the Valley country."

He looks at me, at Charley and Kenton. He sees three men who are as thin as men can be—and remain alive; bearded and ragged, none of us wearing shoes. His eyes go to our feet.

"You were going to make that journey?"

I nod. I walk over, sit down, try to hide my feet from his gaze.

"You had no food to take with you?"

"We are used to that."

"Were there any more—only you three?"

"There was a girl with us—who was shot by McLane's men."

"A girl," he murmured. "That's a point against the dashing Captain McLane. Something to remember. Who was she, a wife to any of you?"

"She was no fit woman to be a man's wife," I say. "She was a follower of the camp."

"Whose woman?" Hamilton asks.

"She was my woman—"

"She was killed instantly?"

"She died in my arms—"

Kenton cries: "Can't you see the pain in him? Leave us alone!"

"You killed one of McLane's men," Hamilton says, ignoring Kenton. "Who fired first, his men or you?"

"We fired after he killed the girl."

"And which one of you killed the man?"

"I did," Kenton says.

Charley breaks in: "We shot from our sides without aim. There's no saying who killed him."

Hamilton stares at Kenton. Again, he seems to be a boy, not more than half-grown at that. The smile goes out of his face. He goes over to Kenton, and holds out his hand.

"You'll take my hand?"

Kenton stands stiffly, not moving. Then Hamilton walks out.

12

We WAIT, without knowing what we are waiting for. We stare at each other with lifeless eyes. We sit close to the fire, but we don't speak. As if we are used up and all of our words are used up.

Kennedy comes in. Beyond him, through the door, we see a guard of eight men. Kennedy has a long leather thong with him, buckles hanging from it. He avoids our eyes, and he stands by the table, staring out of the window.

"Stand up," he says.

He comes over to us, buckles the strap from neck to neck. When he comes to me, I tear away.

"We're to be drummed like beasts?" I cry.

"My orders—"

"Christ!—I'll not be saddled like a beast. Why don't you draw your sword on me? Why in hell don't you draw your sword on me? You God-damned filthy-bellied swine, why don't you draw your sword and kill me?"

Kenton grips my arm. "Allen—Allen, there's no use making it worse."

"I'm sorry," Kenton says.

I try to cover my face with my hands. Outside, it's biting cold, but clear, and the snow has the glowing sheen of cold sunshine. The men of the guard move restlessly, trying to warm themselves. Two drummers stand just beyond them. As we come out, they break into the roll for condemned men.

The guard walk behind us with fixed bayonets. They have no identity as men—eight beggars like ourselves, their bayonets rusty and bent. The drummers are in front, beating out their roll. Once, Charley falls, and we all go down in a heap; the band is tearing my neck, choking me.

The guard help us to our feet. One of them is a grey-bearded old man. He says:

"Walk easy, son. We've time."

Kennedy is out in front. He doesn't glance back at us, even when we fall. He walks slowly, his head bent over. We pass the rifle pit, and the men on duty stare at us, but not with too much curiosity.

We go through a line of dugouts, and some of the troops come out to watch us.

"You'd make right fine eating," someone calls.

We march on, until we come to the stone house where Washington has his quarters. It's a fine, tall two-storey house, with a long stable next to it. We go round to the front, and the guard stop before the door, beat their roll to a mounting crescendo, and then rattle their sticks into silence. Kennedy takes us in.

He takes us through the house to the rear righthand room on the first floor. Inside, there are six officers, seated at a large round table near the fire. Hamilton is at a camp table near the window, writing. When we come in, he glances up, nods at us. Another officer stands next to a tall clock. By the door, chairs are placed for us, and Kennedy motions for us to sit down. We sit down awkwardly, the straps drawing us together.

One of the officers stands up. I recognize Anthony Wayne. He says: "Why are those men lashed together?"

"Colonel Varnum's orders, sir," Kennedy replies.

"And who in hell is Varnum? By God, they're Pennsylvania men! Tell Varnum to keep his damned fat nose out of my men."

"But it's customary," one of the men at the table breaks in.

"To hell with your customs. Untie them."

Kennedy unties us, goes out. I glance at Hamilton; he sits by the window, wrapped tight in his coat, smiling. Wayne sits down and stares at the table. I watch the officers; some of them I recognize: Greene, Lord Stirling, Colonel Conway, General Scott. There's an empty chair in the centre; they seem to be waiting for someone. They drum impatiently with their fingers on the top of the table. Wayne fidgets with a sheet of paper he holds in his hands. None of them look at us.

It's cold in the room, in spite of the fire. The rustle of the fire intermingles with the dull ticking of the clock. For a while, I listen to the ticking; then I stare at the clock. It's half an hour past one. I look at the clock curiously, time has disappeared for so long, the time that moves on the face of a clock. It moves with short, nervous jerks. I bring time back; I try to watch the hand move.

Outside the frosted window, a ragged sentry paces back and forth. The clock tinkles out the half-hour.

I look at Charley, at Kenton. They are staring straight ahead. Neither of them has spoken since we left the guardhouse. I feel childish, lightheaded, full of interest in the clock, in the shiny table, in the bits of lace at the officers' throats. I stare at a hatrack in one corner, all full to overflowing with cocked hats. One of them has a cock loose, and I wonder whose hat that is.

An orderly enters, bearing a pewter pot of water and some pewter cups. Everyone glances at him. He puts the stuff down on the table, salutes, and goes out.

It was fifteen minutes later on the clock when Washington came in. He came in wearing a long, loose blue cloak, his hat under his arm. The officers rose as he entered; he motioned them back to their seats. He went to the rack in the corner, perched his hat there, and began to unknot the collar of his cloak. Hamilton was next to him; he smiled a bit as Hamilton helped him off with his cloak. Hamilton whispered a few words, and the General nodded. Then he went to his seat at the table.

The presence of Washington seemed to fill the room—a tall man, broad, a big face. He appeared years older since that last time, when he spoke to us on the parade ground. His face had fallen in.

After he had seated himself, Hamilton went to the table and placed a sheaf of papers in front of the General. Washington thumbed through them, took out his glasses, then wiped them slowly and put them on. He read a little—then looked at us.

General Greene said: "Sir—it's damnably cold in here. If we're to get this business over with—"

"I'm aware of the cold, General," he said shortly.

He kept his eyes on us. We had risen when he came in; we were still standing. He studied us carefully; his eyes rested for a long time on our feet. When he spoke, his voice was very low:

"You are here before a military court of your superiors on charges of desertion and murder. If you are found guilty, you will be publicly hanged before the assembled brigades. I want you to understand the gravity of the charges and of the sentence that may be imposed upon you."

We nodded.

He turned to the officer who stood by the clock, and said:

"Read your charges, Colonel Mercer."

Mercer was a tall, bearded man, with small grey eyes. He walked over to the table and began to read:

"A charge brought forward by Captain John Muller, of the Fourteenth Pennsylvania Regiment, that on the night of February sixteenth, seventeen hundred and seventy-eight, three men deserted from his brigade. The names of these men are as follows: Charles Green, Kenton Brenner, and Allen Hale. That they willfully deserted is proven by the fact that they made their way out of the set boundaries of the encampment without reporting their action, taking with them full arms and ammunition, bayonets, and muskets, and being in uniform—"

Kenton laughed. His laugh was hoarse and loud, and he swayed back and forth. I gripped his arm.

Wayne rose, glaring at us. The General stared at us, his thin mouth set tightly. Hamilton rose and went to the table. "Your excellency," he said, "I beg you to ignore this. The men are half-starved, certainly not in uniform."

"We're none of us overfed," Washington said.

"Will you grant them the court's pardon?"

"A dozen lashes would cool that laugh," Conway said.

"Or a gibbet," Lord Stirling added.

The General nodded. He said to Mercer: "Go on."

"In the following order, they confessed the fact that they were deserters to Captain Allen McLane, Captain Kennedy, and Colonel Varnum."

To Hamilton, Washington said: "Have you anything to say, Mr. Hamilton?"

"Nothing."

"If you desire," Colonel Mercer said, "I can call any of the officers I have mentioned. They hold themselves at my disposal."

"That will not be necessary. Do you wish to call any witnesses, Mr. Hamilton?"

Hamilton shook his head.

To us: "Do you dispute the truth of these charges?"

We stood as we were. There was no heart in us to say anything.

"The prisoners will answer the court."

Kenton said, shrilly: "The muskets were ours—mine from my father, and Allen's from his. We had no uniforms and we had no money to buy clothes for our backs or shoes for our feet. We were noways doing a wrong thing. There's no war, and we thought of the Valley land . . ." His voice died way.

Charley said: "He has no thought to offend these men, Mr. Hamilton."

Wayne said, coldly: "You will address your advocate as Colonel Hamilton."

We stand there, silent again. We feel helpless. We move our feet uneasily, glance down at the filthy wrappings that cover them.

Washington said: "Mr. Wayne, do you have anything to say in behalf of these men? They are in your command."

"Nothing."

Hamilton said: "Your excellencies, may I ask the court to extend its mercy?"

Washington tapped the top of the table with a quill. Greene was whispering something to him. He said a few words to Wayne, softly, and Wayne shook his head. Finally, Washington said:

"The court finds you guilty of desertion with arms. Out of respect to Mr. Hamilton's request, the court withholds a decision of desertion in face of the enemy. The court sentences you to twenty lashes each before the assembled brigades of the Pennsylvania Line."

Hamilton stepped forward and said: "I thank you for your leniency, sir."

We wait there, still not moving, the strain of standing so long on our feet beginning to tell on us. I glance at Kenton and Charley, and both their faces are set in masks. I wonder what my face is like. I touch my beard. I look at Kenton again. There is a certain dignity about him. His thin yellow beard juts out from his chin; his moustache droops. I say to myself, "He's seen twenty-five winters, only twenty-five." But he has become ageless, old; a marvellous mesh of little lines is etched about his eyes.

We wait, and I wonder what is meant by the first sentence. A sort of hope wells up inside of me. I have no fear of lashes, no fear of pain added to pain: only of a gibbet on Mount Joy, with the wolves leaping for my feet. I never felt life more, wanted life more than I do now, standing here.

They are talking among themselves, heatedly. Wayne rises, kicking back his chair. Across the table Colonel Conway stands facing him.

"I'll have no slurs on my men, sir!" Wayne says.

"I meant none."

Washington says, coldly: "Gentlemen, we are trying men for their lives." He says to Mercer: "Continue."

Mercer reads: "A charge brought by Captain Allen McLane of the

First Continental Light Horse, that on the morning of February seventeenth, seventeen hundred and seventy-eight, returning from a foraging expedition, his party intercepted three deserters, who later gave their regiment as the Fourteenth Pennsylvania, and their names as follows: Allen Hale, Kenton Brenner and Charles Green; that these men were in uniform and under arms, and that they ignored repeated commands to halt for examination. That as they were about to be taken, they opened fire, killing one of Captain McLane's men, David Seely. That they were taken on the King of Prussia Road, a mile and a half north of the Schuylkill. That there was a fourth member of their party, a woman, shot and killed by the fire of the light horse."

When he had finished reading, he placed his papers on the table. The officers handed them round. Washington took no notice of the papers; he kept his eyes on us.

He said: "Mr. Hamilton, do you wish to deny any point in the charges?"

Hamilton answered: "I should like to question Captain McLane, sir. I should like to call at least two of Captain McLane's men, who were with him on the morning in question."

"The last will not be necessary. Colonel Mercer—will you have Mr. McLane in here?"

Hamilton said: "As a point of justice, your excellency, I ask the court that it summon two more men to testify along with Captain McLane."

"The court denies your request. Captain McLane's word is enough."

"Sir, I demand this. Captain McLane is prejudiced. Any cavalryman is against the foot."

"You forget yourself, Mr. Hamilton."

"I apologize. May these men be seated until the court calls them to speak?"

"They may."

"I thank the court."

We drop into the chairs gratefully. We stare at our feet. Then our eyes go to the window. We sit there, men dumb as beasts, staring out the window.

I feel an awful resentment at the whole business—at the trial, at the mockery of their reading our charges, at the well-dressed, warm officers sitting at the table. Who are they? What have they to do with us? What of the weeks when we lay in the dugouts, like diseased animals? How is it that they materialize now, to take hold of our lives, to hang us, as murderers and thieves are hanged? I know that they will hang us; I have no doubt of that. Only to draw it out, to play with something called justice, to make an example.

We desert with arms; whose arms? We desert in uniform. I look at Kenton's uniform. His coat is cut from a blanket, sewed with strips of cloth, shredded all round the bottom. The blue skin of his knees shows through his breeches. His mittens are made of a piece of blanket. His neck is bound with a strip of our old regimental flag. But we desert in uniform.

McLane comes in. He never suffers for food, the dashing Captain McLane. His men plunder the British food trains, the produce that the Quaker farmers haul in to the Philadelphia market. They eat well and they eat first. He comes in with a brisk stride and salutes. He wears a hunting coat of grey felt with red facings. He wears high, polished kneeboots and doeskin breeches. He wears a cocked hat of grey kid.

He wears his sidearms, a sabre and a pistol, a bunched hand of lace where his coat opens. He walks up to the table, salutes and stands at attention. Hamilton has dropped into his chair by the window. He leans his elbow on the window-sill, and lazily rubs away the frost with his fingers. I watch, fascinated, as the scene outside comes into view — a sentry passing, a picket fence coming out of a mound of snow, two women picking their way along the road. Then Hamilton turns to us, watches us a moment, and smiles. His smile is reassurance. He's slight as a girl, but the story goes that he is fearless. He doesn't like McLane; the smile is casual contempt of McLane.

Washington glanced at McLane fondly. "You may be at ease, Mr. McLane," he said.

Hamilton rose, walked across the room slowly, staring at a few sheets of paper he held in his hands. He paid no attention to McLane. He walked across the room to the farther wall, and there he turned, resting against the wall. He never looked directly at McLane; his eyes were shaded by long, girlish lashes.

He said, "Mr. McLane, will you describe to the court the incidents that led up to your intercepting these men? Will you tell just how you happened to be returning along the King of Prussia Road at that hour? I believe it was early morning."

McLane said: "Your excellencies, I resent Colonel Hamilton's implication. I was in the line of my duty."

Hamilton: "There was no implication intended."

The court: "You will answer his questions, Mr. McLane."

McLane: "Your excellencies know the work I have done in providing forage for the army. Lately, I have had information that the Quakers are given to travelling at night. They form their produce wagons into trains, start out at sundown, and trust to reach the British outposts, near Philadelphia, before dawn. I make it my practice to range during the early hours of the morning. On the morning of February seventeenth, I was damnably unlucky. I was returning with forty horses along the road from Norristown, when I noticed four persons on foot, bearing arms. I rode forward to investigate, crying for them to halt and stay where they were. They ran across a field, but luckily were bogged in a drift of snow. My men rode them down, but at the last moment, when they saw that escape was cut off, they turned and deliberately fired into my men, killing a trooper."

Hamilton said: "Thank you, Mr. McLane." He walked over to us, turned his back on McLane, and asked softly: "The girl bore arms?"

"No, sir."

He walked back to the table, rested one hand upon it, and faced McLane. "Mr. McLane," he said, "you speak of four deserters. Were they all men?"

"No, sir. One was a woman."

"Then there were only three deserters. To my knowledge, there are no enlisted women in this army."

"Yes, sir — three men."

"And you spoke of four persons on foot, bearing arms. Did the woman bear arms?"

McLane seemed to hesitate.

"Mr. McLane, I call you to answer! Did the woman bear arms?"

"I don't recall."

"Mr. McLane, what is the weight of the average musket?"

The court: "Mr. Hamilton, will you keep to the point? You are not here to dramatize, but to help formation of a just decision."

Hamilton: "If the court will permit me to go ahead, I can prove this all to be to the point. Please answer my question, Mr. McLane."

McLane: "One stone — more or less."

"Or in pounds — fifteen, or twenty. Wouldn't you say a musket could easily weigh twenty pounds, Mr. McLane?"

"I don't make a practice of weighing muskets."

"But I do. Here is a woman, half-starved, weighing eighty or ninety pounds, and you don't know whether she was armed."

McLane said: "Your excellencies, I object to being baited this way by Colonel Hamilton. I am not on trial here."

"Then you'll admit the woman was not armed?" Hamilton asked.

"Your excellencies —"

271

"Answer Mr. Hamilton's question."

"The men were armed."

"And the woman wasn't. And the woman is dead, shot by your men. You omitted that from the story, Mr. McLane. Will you explain why you omitted that fact—why your men shot an unarmed woman who was certainly not a deserter?"

"We had no knowledge that she was a woman at the time. She was dressed as they were."

"But unarmed. How many of your men fired, Mr. McLane?"

"I don't know—a dozen perhaps."

"Did you give the command to fire."

"I did. It was in the line of duty. They were armed men, resisting arrest."

"Yet the one shot that took effect brought down an unarmed woman. How do you account for that?"

"I can't account for the marksmanship of my men, and I see no reason why I have to. They were on horse, firing at moving figures—"

"Mr. McLane, you indicated that the man in your brigade whom these deserters killed was shot before you opened fire. You admit that when twelve moving men, on horse or on foot, fire at targets that are not stationary, one hit out of a dozen attempts is a reasonable score. You indicate that your return fire was given immediately after these deserters opened fire, and that at the time the deserters were moving. Let me make myself clear: three moving men fire at your brigade, and one of their shots takes effect. Does that suggest anything to you?"

"That General Wayne's men are better marksmen than mine? My men are cavalrymen, not marksmen."

"Or that your men fired, killed the woman—that the three men halted and fired from a stationary position."

The court: "Mr. Hamilton—you will not attempt to influence the court by conjecture."

Hamilton turned to McLane, said quietly: "Mr. McLane, who fired first, the deserters or your men?"

McLane said: "Your excellencies, do I have to answer that question?"

"You will answer."

"I gave the order to fire when I saw the men were about to escape in the forest."

"And who fired first."

"My men."

"Yet you stated, Mr. McLane, that these three men returned your fire simply to resist capture. You said that they returned the fire when

272

they saw their position was hopeless. Also, your implication was that they had fired first. Deliberately, Mr. McLane, you portrayed these men in an act of treason and murder."

"Your excellencies, must I be baited like a common criminal?"

Washington said: "Mr. Hamilton, you have no right to ascribe intentions to Captain McLane. He is not on trial."

"But these three men are on trial for their lives."

Wayne said: "Your excellency, an act of treason reflects upon my command. I demand that it be substantiated."

Hamilton: "Mr. McLane, did these three men fire deliberately, when about to be taken, or was their action simply a burst of fury at the killing of the woman?"

"They killed one of my men. They were deserters."

Conway leaned across the table and said: "Colonel Hamilton, what are you driving at? We are not trying officers or gentlemen. We are trying three deserters. Look at them. You profane the name of soldier when you call them soldiers."

Wayne cried: "If Colonel Conway desires to indulge in personalities at the expense of my troops, he can answer to me. Whether or not these men are soldiers—"

"Gentlemen," Washington said coldly.

Wayne stood up, trembling, facing Conway. Washington said: "Be seated, General Wayne. You forget yourself."

Hamilton said: "If Colonel Conway wishes to make any remarks, I'll answer them personally. There are five thousand men like these in camp, and if I can't address them as troops of the line, I'll resign my commission."

Washington's voice was like ice. He said: "Mr. Hamilton, you are not here to engage in personalities. If you are through, you have the court's permission to leave."

Hamilton stood there, biting his lips. For a moment, I thought he'd walk out. Then he said:

"I beg your pardon sir, humbly. I have no interest in these men. I was asked to take up their rights. That's my duty, I think."

Wayne said: "Your excellency, I add my voice to Mr. Hamilton's. I beg your pardon."

"Go ahead, Mr. Hamilton," Washington said shortly.

Hamilton said: "Mr. McLane, if your wife were shot down and you had a loaded gun in your hand, and the man who committed the crime were before you, what action would you take?"

McLane stood in silence.

273

Washington said: "Captain McLane will not answer. If you can't confine yourself to facts, Mr. Hamilton, I'll dismiss the witness."

"But, your excellency, what are the facts? I have proven that Captain McLane's men fired first. These men could have escaped. Mr. McLane himself has admitted that they might have escaped. They saw this woman shot—"

Lord Stirling said, wearily: "Are you making out a common camp follower as someone to be compared to an officer's wife? If you are, sir, I am not the only person at this table who will take offence."

"Sir, I made no such comparison. If Lord Stirling wishes to pick a quarrel—"

"I shall not warn you again, Mr. Hamilton," Washington said shortly.

"I'm sorry, sir. I beg you to allow me to go on."

"Very well."

"Mr. McLane, did any of these deserters show signs of sorrow at the death of the woman?"

"I believe one of them did."

"Would you describe his actions?"

"He tore loose from the men who were holding him and ran over to the woman."

"Could you say which one?"

"I couldn't."

"Would you look at those three men, Mr. McLane? Colonel Conway remarked that they profane the name of soldier. Obviously, they are half-starved, half-naked. They don't look strong enough to tear loose from two or three men. Only a fit of intense feeling could impel them to such strength. You would grant that the feeling was intense, Mr. McLane?"

"I don't know."

"But you must know. You saw it happen."

"Then I grant it."

"Thank you. That will be all, Mr. McLane."

"Have I the court's permission to go?" McLane asked.

Washington asked: "Do any of you gentlemen wish to question Mr. McLane." There was no answer. "You may go," he said.

McLane stalked out. Hamilton walked to the window, walked back slowly. The room was very silent. The ticking of the clock sounded like a beating drum.

Washington said: "Have you any other witnesses, Mr. Hamilton?"

"Have I the court's permission to examine these men?" Hamilton asked, nodding at us.

"You have."

"Allen Hale," Hamilton said. I stood up. Kenton and Charley were looking at me curiously.

"Come forward," Mercer said.

I went up to the table.

"Your name is Allen Hale?"

"Yes, sir."

"Your regiment?"

"The Fourteenth Pennsylvania."

"Are you a Pennsylvania man?"

"No, sir. I was born in New York."

"Where?"

"The Mohawk Valley."

"And you lived there all your life?"

"There and in the Lake country."

"Where is the Lake country?"

"Westward, near the Finger Lakes. We call it the Valley land."

"How old are you?"

"Twenty-one."

"And when did you enlist in the army?"

"At the end of May, in seventeen seventy-five."

"You've served two and a half years. How long was your enlistment?"

"Three years—"

"And what made you desert, when there were only a few months left to serve?"

I shook my head; it felt heavy, clogged. As out of a dream at the dugout, to find myself standing here, the round table of officers, Hamilton watching me with violet eyes from under long lashes, playing a game.

"I thought I'd desert," I said.

"But why?"

"I thought to desert—I had no thought of living out the winter. I was fair in hell, and sick for the sight of the Valley country. I thought to go away. There were a good lot of men deserting, and talk went that there'd be no army in the spring."

"And you expected to reach the Mohawk Valley?"

I nodded.

Expressively, Hamilton looked at my feet, at the clothes I wore. He said:

"When you enlisted in the army, did you enlist in a Pennsylvania

275

regiment?"

"No, sir. There were few Pennsylvania men outside of Boston. I enlisted in the Fourth New York Regiment."

"Where is that regiment?"

I answered: "Dead."

"You mean there's no one left of that regiment except yourself?"

"Five more men."

"Was there any desertion in the Fourth New York?"

"Some few men. The rest sickened or died in battle."

"I see. When you deserted, three men, why did you decide to take a woman with you? Did you think a woman could make the trip you were planning?"

"I had no thought that a woman could go the distance. She was noways a strong enough woman."

"Then why did you take her?"

"She pleaded to go along. She said she'd take her own life if I left her behind."

"Was she your wife?"

"She was no fit woman to be a man's wife," I said dully. "She was a woman of the camp."

"But she loved you enough to take her own life if you left her?"

"Yes."

"Now, on the morning when you were taken, where were you?"

"On the highroad to Norristown."

"And you saw Captain McLane's men. Did you recognize them immediately?"

"We knew they were part of the army from their number."

"What did you do then?"

"We made across a field — to run for the shelter of the forest."

"Were you together when you crossed the fields?"

"Bess fell, and I was helping her to rise. Charley and Kenton were a dozen paces beyond."

"Then they could have escaped?"

"They might, had they not waited."

"What happened then?"

"Some of the cavalrymen took the ground. They fired a volley at us. They had a bullet in Bess, and she fell from my hand —"

"Some of the cavalrymen dismounted before they fired? They took time to aim?"

"I don't know — they weren't much at shooting."

Hamilton smiled. Then his face sobered, deliberately. He said:

276

"What did you do then?"

"When I saw Bess shot, I guess I went crazy. I guess I didn't care much about anything, and I let go with my gun. Kenton and Charley fired. I guess we were all crazy—thinking about going back."

"And when you fired, did you aim?"

"I reckon no. I shot as I held my musket, at my side. They did too."

"Your friends?"

"Yes."

"Thank you. That's all." I walked back to my chair, slumped into it. Kenton and Charley were sitting like stone figures, staring straight ahead of them, but looking at nothing. They didn't look at me.

Hamilton turned to the table. He said: "Your excellencies, there's nothing I can say more. These men are deserters; but they are not murderers; they did not commit treason. They fired in a fit of passion. Their crime was not premeditated or deliberate. I don't have to tell you what they suffer. God knows, you're aware of it. This is a winter of hell. We're quartered in stone houses; we eat and drink and sleep and wear decent clothes. But you've seen them crowded like beasts in their huts. You know."

Washington said: "Mr Hamilton, we are not in a civil court. We are trying these men for a military offence. They opened fire in an act of mutiny, and killed a man."

"But their act was self-defence. By all the laws of humanity, they're innocent. They had been starving for weeks. They were half-insane."

"Nevertheless, they killed a man."

"Your excellencies, I am not the court. All I can do is to plead a case you have given me. But I know that in the place of these men, I would have done the same."

He walked to the window then, dropped into his chair, and stared out. The men at the table were talking in low tones. I heard Wayne say: "You're not dealing with soldiers, sir, but with beasts. No discipline. You'll touch off a powder keg."

"Then touch it off I will. If there's one man left, he'll be under my command."

Lord Stirling: "I'd have them drawn. I'd teach them a few of His Majesty's lessons."

"Sir, His Majesty is not commanding my army," Washington snapped.

Kenton and Charley both sat motionless, like men in a dream; they seemed to have no interest in the court-martial. They sat staring at nothing at all. I listened to the clock, watched the pendulum. I counted each movement. I felt drowsy, tired. I felt that I would like to sleep. Gradually, the room had become warmer. There was a rug on the floor. I thought of stretching out full-length on the rug and sleeping. I half-closed my eyes. The drone of voices was like bees humming.

Then the voice of Washington broke through: "Mr. Hamilton, will you inquire which of the three men killed McLane's trooper?"

Hamilton turned to us. Kenton lurched to his feet. He said hoarsely: "I did."

I heard Charley's voice, as from far off: "He's lying."

I found myself saying: "He's lying—"

I find myself crying: "What difference? You want to know who killed him? There's no life in this place—only death, nothing but death! You don't bury us; you pile us in the snow, like logs of wood—" I find myself laughing, sitting there and laughing like an idiot.

Kenton's arm is around me, his voice whispering: "Easy, easy, Allen."

Charley says, clearly: "God damn you—you can all go to hell!"

I sit there, feeling away from them now, beyond any pain or power of theirs. They sit around the table like dolls, a little bewildered. Hamilton's face is drawn and twisted; he doesn't look like a boy any more.

"Take them out, Mr. Hamilton," Washington says, his voice cold, tired.

We stand up. Hamilton moves through the door with us. The guards form around us, and Hamilton leads us into the next room.

"Sit here," he says. "There's no need for you to stand. I'll go back, and maybe they'll let me talk some more. I don't know—" He takes a pipe out of his pocket, a small bag of tobacco, and drops them on the table. "You can smoke."

He goes out. We sit and look at each other. Charley says: "A fair lot of talk—"

"I'm afraid," I whisper. "Christ—"

"It's an awful bitter thing to hang," Kenton says. "I can't call to mind that I ever thought to hang. It's a bitter thing to be out there in the cold, hanging from a gibbet."

"It may be that we'll not hang."

"No. It's in their minds to hang us."

"That man Hamilton made a good plea for us. It's a wonder to me that he spoke so long for us."

"I'm thinking, he hates McLane."

"It was fair talking."

278

We stare at each other, keep staring, then abruptly turn our eyes away—anywhere. It seems to me that I can hear the clock ticking in the next room. I say:

"Strange to see a clock beating out the time."

The room we sit in is shadowed with twilight. Outside, the early winter night is beginning to call. A low fire burns in the room. We look around curiously, at the fine furniture, at the rugs on the floor.

Kenton remarks: "They live well, these Quaker people."

I reach out toward the pipe. "He was meaning for us to smoke it," I say.

"I'm sick for food, not for smoking," Charley mutters.

"We could draw on the pipe a spell, pass the time."

"They'll sentence us."

"I'm thinking so."

I stuff the pipe with tobacco, go to the fire and draw a spark to it. The smoke makes me dizzy. I hand the pipe to Charley.

Charley looks at it and says: "Ely was a great one to be puffing on a pipe. Night and day, when we had tobacco, he had a pipe in his teeth. You recall?"

"It seems like years past."

"He could take a quiet enjoyment out of tobacco like no other man I've seen."

"He could."

"It's a strange thing that Ely should watch us die. I think back to how Ely watched me grow," Kenton says.

I say: "If we hang, Kenton, I'll be no man. I'll be sick with fear."

"It's a dreadful thing to hang."

We sit and we smoke. It grows darker in the room. The fire throws mottled shadows over us. We seem to tremble and waver in the firelight.

"God—I'm hungry," Charley whispers.

My throat is dry and numb. I think of drinking a glass of clear water.

"They ought to be through with their talk," I say nervously.

"They're making out to hang us."

"Christ, Kenton, leave be," Charley mutters.

Kenton has the pipe. He says, sadly: "I did a fool's thing to smash the other pipe. He was noways mocking at us, giving us the pipe."

We hear steps outside, and we turn to the door. Hamilton stands there, the guards behind him. "You'll come back with me now," he says tonelessly.

279

I think we know, all of us. We follow Hamilton back into the room where the court-martial is being held. There are some candles on the table. The faces behind the candles waver, change colour.

"Stand at attention," Mercer says.

Hamilton goes to the window. He stands there, back to the room, hands clasped behind his back. I see Washington's big face. It seems to me that the muscles are relaxed, that the compact coldness has given way to loose lines of pain. Wayne stares at the table. Greene looks over our heads. Lord Stirling bites his nails, his face vacuous. Conway has a sort of smile.

Mercer reads: "It is the decision of this court that Allen Hale, Kenton Brenner, and Charles Green be found guilty of high treason and murder. It is the decision of this court that they be paraded before the assembled brigades of the Pennsylvania Line, drummed out of their regiment, be publicly stripped of arms and insignia, and then be hanged by the neck until dead."

Kenton laughs softly. Charley Green's hand grips my arm, fingers biting into my flesh. I cry out, in spite of myself, and then my throat chokes up and I can say nothing. The guards press out of the room. They stand round us while the officers file past.

Hamilton says: "God help us all for this. I'm sorry. You believe me?"

We can't answer. He goes, and we fall into step between the guards.

13

WE SIT in the guardroom at Fort Huntingdon. The room has no fire, no window. Four log walls and a flat roof. A space between the roof and the walls for currents of air. No lack of air. The cold of the night seeps in, the eternal, awful cold of this winter.

The commandant had a firebox brought in. He said: "You poor devils'll freeze tonight otherwise. No damned sense letting you freeze before you hang." The firebox is red-hot with glowing coals. It may hold its heat for three or four hours.

We sit round the box. Through a crack in the roof, we can see a bit of the sky, a narrow bit with a single star. I look at the star first, and then the others, and then we sit with our eyes fixed on that single star. We sit, and our dumb longing fills the place; senseless yearning in the cold of outer space.

"Tomorrow—" Kenton starts to say. Then his voice and his thoughts drift from him. Words are an effort for us now, each word a distinct and separate effort. We shiver; close to the box, its heat scorches our skins, leaves our backs cold. Kenton says:

"That was a great lot of talk—"

"I had in mind that we would go back northward," I say. "I had no thought in mind that we'd be taken. I had in mind that spring would come on us in our journeying."

"I had that in mind," Kenton agrees.

"I shouldn't have spoken up to them the way I did," Charley mutters. "I lost hold of my senses."

"It's no matter."

"I'm sick with the thought of going to the gallows. I call to mind that as a child my mother would warn me I was born to be hanged. As a way of joking."

"Your mother's living?" Kenton asks Charley.

"She's an old woman in Boston—if she's living. If she's dead, she'll curse me when I come off the gallows. She had no way with war. Christ, how she hated war! She took a stick to Sam Adams one time when he came to my house to leech me on a matter of printing. She took a stick and beat the dust out of his dirty back. He says, All right, my fine Tory. She answers, All right, my fine beggared bastard. Only keep off from my son and keep your dirty feet outa my house!"

Kenton laughs; he says slowly: "I'm not thinking there's aught after death—no matter for a man to fear, no matter of starving and freezing and whoring."

"I can't," I say. "I had no thought of dying. Now I tell myself, I'm twenty-one years, and I'm going into a blackness."

Charley says, gently: "There's no matter of going alone, Allen. Look, boy, there's no matter at all of going alone. There's Kenton and me and a fair lot of good men all the way down."

I cover my face with my hands; I feel the chill in my heart. I feel a terror so awful that I want to scream and scream again.

When I look up, our faces glisten dully in the glow of the firebox. Kenton and Charley are regarding me strangely.

"You think I'm afraid—" I whisper.

They shake their heads. I put my face in my hands and stifle my sobs.

It might have been an hour or less after that that Hamilton came in. He stood by the door, wrapped in his blue greatcoat, his breath steaming in a red glow.

"I brought you some meat," he said, holding out a wooden bowl.

Kenton took it. Kenton said:

'You made a fine plea for us. We're not ungrateful."

"I'm sorry," he said simply.

"We had no thought that we'd be made free by officers."

"You're not dead. The General said he'd speak with me tonight." He looked at us oddly. "One of you come along. He's no hard man, the General."

"Go along, Allen," Kenton said. Charley nodded. I shook my head.

"Better go," Kenton said gently.

I stood up, holding onto Kenton's shoulder. He stared at me, his thin face old and drawn, his beard ruddy in the light. Charley was nodding, whimsically.

Outside, the sentry stopped us. "I have orders to keep these men, Colonel Hamilton."

"I'll stand for him," Hamilton said. He had a curious way of speaking, as if he wasn't to be doubted. Then he walked on. I followed him, his orderly behind us.

At the door of the stone house, he told the orderly to wait. The sentries came to attention. He walked in, and Hamilton said to me:

"There's no need to fear him. He's a strange, hard man, but there's no need to fear him."

Hamilton tapped on the door of the same room that the court-martial had been held in. Then he went in. Washington was there alone, sitting at the table, writing. He didn't look up when we first came in. He was wrapped in a woollen jacket, a small cap on his head. There were a few candles on the table. I could see how slowly his hand moved writing.

"Who is it?" he asked.

"Colonel Hamilton."

"Come in, my boy. And close the door. There's a draught."

Hamilton said: "Thank you, your excellency." He closed the door softly. We stood there, in front of the door. I could see that Hamilton was nervous, biting his lips and staring down at his hands.

Washington was all intent on his writing, squinting through his spectacles. He looked like an old man in the jacket and the cap. The large spaces of his face were filled with shadows. Finally, he laid aside the quill and looked up, half a smile on his face. The smile went, and a sullen, rigid coldness replaced it.

"What is the meaning of this, Colonel Hamilton?" he demanded.

"I thought, your excellency—"

"By God, you go too far, Colonel Hamilton! What do you mean by bringing this man before me? Where is your authority?" He had risen from the table, his whole being rigid with sudden fury.

"I have none, sir."

"Then take him out of here!"

I moved to go, but Hamilton stood where he was. He had dropped his head. He spoke softly.

"I will, your excellency. I wish to resign my commission at the same time. I no longer have a place here."

I thought for a moment that Washington would hurl the table aside and fling himself on Hamilton. His rage was awful and terrible. Then, in a sudden, it collapsed, like a pricked bladder. He dropped back into his chair, limply, staring at us, his face old and tired. He leant his elbows on the table and put his face in his hands.

"Resign your commission?" he said, unbelievingly.

"I must."

His face was broken. I had never seen a face so broken all in an instant. He spread his hands hopelessly, murmured: "You too—I might have known. Stirling spreads his tales, and Conway plots, and Varnum mocks me, and Wayne is half-mad—and now you too. God, I'm alone. It's too much for me."

I didn't know whether he was acting; if he was acting, then he was a marvellous actor. His hands spread wide on the table, his mouth open just a bit, his eyes staring at Hamilton and unseeing at the same time, his face trembling, he whispered:

"Go on—get out—leave me alone. God knows, I'm alone. Always alone. You're no different. I thought you believed—but you're no different."

I glanced sidewise at Hamilton. His face was a reflection of the General's, pain and a deep sorrow in his half-veiled violet eyes. He stood stiffly, his hands a little in front of him.

"Get out," Washington said hoarsely.

Still Hamilton stood there, for moments; and then he stepped backward toward the door, slowly.

"Wait—" Washington had wilted; he was an old, old man. He said, tonelessly: "Why are you resigning your commission? Why do you want to leave me?"

"I don't want to leave you, sir. Believe me, as sure as there is a God in heaven, I don't want to leave you, sir. After I leave you, there is no reason for me to live. Sir, I have no other reason to live than you and our cause."

A sort of hope in Washington's face, love and a groping toward

Hamilton. He stretched out a hand.

"You won't leave me," he said.

"Sir, if one life is taken unjustly, if one man must die because of jealousy and hate, then a cause is already dishonoured. The cause exists no longer. Men can suffer for it no longer. It marks the limit of all suffering, all—"

Washington rose to his feet, crashing his hand down upon the table. The change in him was sudden and furious, like the change in a man gone suddenly mad. We recoiled from him. I felt suddenly that the room was too small for us. He wrenched out from behind the table, stood panting, cried:

"You talk of suffering! My God, you talk of suffering! What do you know? What have you suffered? Does anyone believe in me? Can I trust anyone? Do you know what it is to be alone—always alone, feared, hated? Whom do they come to? They come to me pleading, crying! Men are starving! Have you see me touch food today! Do I sleep? Do I rest? Is there any peace for me, ever—until the day I die? Is there anything ahead of me but a rope and a gibbet in England? They talk about ambition, about King Washington. Christ!—don't deny it. I'm cold—I'm ice waiting for a throne! Look out of that window and you'll see my throne in the ice on Mount Joy! Howe swore I'd hang there! Who'll be with me then? Whom can I trust? Can a man go on alone, always, endure—"

He stands there, a pitiful giant, used up with his own fury. His arms drop limply to his sides. His cap has fallen to the floor. He fumbles at his glasses, puts them on the table. He reaches for his chair, then walks across the room to the fire. Trembling, he tries to warm himself at the fire, seemingly unaware of the fact that we are still in the room. Hamilton murmurs:

"Sir—I'm sorry."

"We'll endure," he says quietly. "We'll endure." He has taken hold of himself. He walks back to the table and sits down. He says:

"I'm sorry, Colonel Hamilton. I owe you an apology. If you wish to resign, that is your affair. I can do nothing."

"You can, sir—only say you need me."

"God knows, I do."

"You'll hear me?"

"Go ahead, Colonel Hamilton."

"Sir, this man is condemned to death. You know that. He and two more deserters were condemned to hang for shooting one of Captain McLane's troopers. Sir, I didn't bring him here to mock at your decision; I brought him here to appeal to your mercy. I want you to see what war and suffering can do to a boy of twenty-one. I say that he has already atoned for his crime, that the others have atoned."

"There's no place for mercy in an army."

"But there's a place for justice."

"They confessed to the crime."

"But, your excellency, their act was an act of passion, of self-defence."

"I told you, Colonel Hamilton, that civil law cannot apply to an army in the field. The British hang deserters."

"But we're not the British."

"No—we're a rabble, a caricature of an army. But so long as one man is left, that man will be under my command. If he's naked and without arms, he'll still be under my command."

"Then one man can hang. One is enough. Only one of McLane's men died."

The General shakes his head slowly. He says: "Colonel Hamilton, the only justice I know is the justice I have kept an army together with for three years. We're in hell, and hell is not gentle."

"Sir, we are human beings in hell. Once we are not—then where is the use in going on?"

The candles are burning low. I stand there wearily, trying to keep from hope, trying to forget the pain in my feet. The General becomes a blur in the light of the candles. There is a long time of silence. He sits behind the candles, a bewildered man away from the world, unable to be part of the world, staring ahead of him and looking at nothing. Finally he says, uncertainly:

"I'm writing to the Congress for shoes, Colonel Hamilton. The Congress have shoes. They have a thousand pairs, but I can't plead humbly enough. I can't. You'll write it over for me, Colonel Hamilton?"

"I'll write it, sir."

He looks at me, stares at my feet, at my face. It seems that he is trying to break me apart from five thousand men. "Which one of you fired the shot?" he asks, not ungently.

I shake my head. "We don't know, sir," I say.

"Decide it." He turns to Hamilton. "Write an order for the release of two, Colonel. Have them flogged and sent back to their brigades."

Hamilton is unable to speak. He sits down at the table, takes up a quill, and begins to write. When he is through, he says hoarsely:

"You'll sign it, sir?"

285

Washington signs, drops the quill. He seems hardly able to hold up the weight of his head. Hamilton goes to the door. As he opens the door, Washington's voice stops him.

"You'll come back, Colonel? I can't sleep. If you come back, we'll talk a while."

"I'll come back, sir. I can't thank you now. I'll come back."

We go outside. Hamilton doesn't speak until he hands me over to one of the sentries, with orders to return to the fort. Then he says: "Try to know before morning. I wish it could have been different."

I want to speak. I'm choked inside. He gives me his hand, and I hold on to it. Then he goes back.

I walk across the snow with the sentry. The air is cold, sharp. I think of life. I feel the the bite of the air, the cold of the snow. I try to think of life, not that one of us must die. I think of going back to the dugout the way I would think of going home.

14

THEY keep staring at me, trying to make me out in the dark, and I don't know how to tell them. I stand at the door. I keep in the shadow.

Kenton says: "Come over and sit, Allen."

Keenly aware of the pain in my feet, I go to the firebox and sit down. Only the pain is life, more an evidence of life than of pain.

Kenton tells me: "We saved a part of the meat for you, Allen. It's good salt ham. I have it warming."

"I'm starved," I say. "I'm starved for some meat." I take the meat, eat it. Kenton hands me water to drink. There's more than enough meat for a man. It occurs to me that they ate little themselves, saving the bulk of the meat for me. They look at me while I eat, but they don't ask questions.

"It's good meat," I sigh. "It's ripe salt ham."

Charley says: "They have a ham called Boston round; it melts like butter in your mouth."

"They have a hickory cure in the Mohawk—"

"I'll pledge Boston ham against backwoods pig. It makes me fair sick to hear a backwoods man talk like he knew the way of living. You take a grown man who can't write his own name, and he's no better than a red savage."

"Allen here has learning, and he's a backwoods boy for all that,"

Kenton says. "It's no matter of trouble to learn to read and write. Only I had a hatred for it."

Charley laughs. I finish eating, and put the bowl away. They look at me, still asking no questions. I wonder how they can sit that way, talk, laugh, as if there was no gibbet waiting. I'm afraid to tell them; I don't know how to tell them.

A red glow falls upon us out of the firebox, mottles us, burns in Kenton's beard. I touch my own beard nervously, short curly hair; I tangle my fingers in it.

Charley puts a hand on my arm, says gently: "We had no thought to joke with death, Allen, only to drive off fear."

"We shouldn't have sent you," Kenton says. "God damn them, can't they send us to a gibbet without playing with us?"

"It was Hamilton's thought to save us," I say. "He did what any man could do to save us. He made an honest strong plea to Washington."

"I can't abide a man so stone hard as Washington," Charley says.

"He's a hard man."

"I had no great hope when Allen went —"

"What came of it, Allen?"

I look at them.

"We're to die?"

I say, slowly: "We're to choose among ourselves for one. The other two go free with a flogging. But the one man dies on the gibbet."

They stare at me. "One man?"

"He said he would noway spare the three of us."

"One man," Charley whispers.

I can't stand their eyes; I shake my head, cry: "It was not my doing! You think I had no courage to die along with you!"

"We know, Allen," Kenton says. "We're grateful to you, Allen." His voice had a tone of complete relief in it; he smiled a little as he spoke, almost contentedly.

Charley asks, querulously: "How was it that they came to spare two men? How was it that way, Allen?"

I try to tell them what happened in the room. I try to tell them how it came about. I find myself sobbing hoarsely.

"It's all right," Kenton says. "It's no matter to sob about, Allen."

"You're thinking it's me. You're thinking I had no thought to be the one. Only one of you. You're thinking I had no courage to stand up on a gibbet. I took a way out that was easy—I told them one of us would die for the other two. You're thinking that. Why are you looking at me like that?"

"Allen, Allen — be easy."

"I'm not fearing."

"Allen, we had no mind to give you pain."

"You're despising me."

"Allen, it's better two of us should live. It's a horrible bad thing for a man to die on the gallows. It's a dreadful thing to think about and dream about."

I say weakly. "Which one? Which man of us to die?"

We sit there for a moment, watching each other. Then Charley Green tears himself up, walks over to the door, and pounds his fists against it. He pounds until the door shakes under the impact, and then he leans against it, panting.

"You'll beat yer hands sore. Come away," Kenton begs him. "Come away, Charley."

"God damn them, are they playing with beasts? Are we no longer men, but beasts to be tortured?"

"Come away —"

Charley whispers: "I'm oldest. I'm a man of thirty years."

He turns round to face us. The coals in the box are almost gone — a dim glow. At the door, Charley is a black figure without form. I look at a black figure that is nothing of a man — a fear in form, groping for death, afraid and unafraid. I think of a man who joined our regiment in Boston, a fat, short man with printer's ink staining his figures black. A small moustache and red cheeks. A black cocked hat and a black coat. Blue eyes. A man in a round happy form who became a butt for our jokes and contempt. A man fascinated by backwoodsmen who wore green hunting coats. He carried a musket with an ivory stock, a treasure of a musket, small, beautiful. He carried a silver snuffbox worked by Paul Revere. He wore lace cuffs. He tried to be a dandy, but he was more a troll than a dandy. I try to think of him that way, making such a figure out of the black mass at the door.

"I'm a man of thirty years," he says again. "I'm the oldest man of you all." Then he comes toward us, sinks down on the floor, and stares at the firebox. A small man, thin and bearded, filthy.

Kenton's voice is soft, curious, a world of curious wonder in his voice: "You'd go to a gibbet for us, wouldn't you, Charley? You'd have no fear to die for us?"

"I'd have a dreadful, awful fear to die on a gibbet," Charley says simply.

"You're a brave man," Kenton says.

"There's a way of being brave, and I'm noways brave. I'm thinking that if Ely were here, he would see no younger man die in his place."

"Ely is a strange creature—a creature out of fear."

A smile tries on Charley's face; a smile takes his mouth and moves it slowly. He reaches out and touches my hand. I'm afraid to look at him. He holds onto my hand. "A long way," he says. "A great length of marching. Christ, we're like brothers, all the three of us."

Kenton says: "I've no matter of fear any more. I'll be in company, good company. There're no men who've gone already to hold back from me with contempt, to say that a man dead on a gibbet is not a man for their company."

"We'll draw lots," I say desperately.

"We'll draw no lots."

"Why? I'm not afraid! I swear to God I'm not afraid. I'm not afraid—"

"It's no matter of fear, Allen," Kenton said gently. "I couldn't go back to the Mohawk and say that Allen Hale, a boy of twenty-one years, had died on a gibbet so I could live."

"But I'd go back—"

"Allen, I shot the man. Allen, I swear a holy oath by God and Jesus that I shot the man. I aimed with my gun and killed deliberately. The sin is on my soul and the taking of blood was by my hands. Can there by any peace for me, if another suffers for my sin, Allen?"

"You're a liar," Charley whispered. "I stood by your side and you took no aim."

"Would I go to death with a lie?" Kenton asked.

Charley took a coin out of his pocket, a tarnished shilling. He turned it over and over. He said: "You're a strong man, Kenton. You're a rare man for loving and hating. We'll not argue."

"We'll not argue "

"The King's head is life for you."

"Agreed."

He threw the coin, so that it would fall on the firebox, but Kenton caught it midway. He fingered it a moment, then tossed it over to one side of the room, where it fell in the dark. I sighed deeply. Kenton was smiling.

"You shouldn't have done that," Charley said.

"This tossing a coin for a life is play for children. If a man has it in his mind to die—"

"I can't let you."

Kenton said slowly, thoughtfully: "I made a scheme to desert and go northward. I said to myself, no other man'll pay for my scheming."

I couldn't stand any more of that. I put my face in my hands an sobbed. They didn't stop me. I went away from the firebox and thre myself down on the floor of the room.

Finally, Kenton came over to me. It might have been an hour after wards, two hours. I don't know. The coals had about burnt out, an the firebox glowed dimly. Kenton knelt down by me and put an arn about my shoulders.

"Allen," he whispered.

I didn't answer.

"Allen, I'll have no fear. I swear that to you, Allen. I'll have no fea or shame or remorse to die on a gibbet."

"Leave me alone!" I cried.

He went on talking, his voice soft and easy: "Allen, a time ago, maybe twelve, thirteen years, you stood up to me and I beat you down. I had it over you by a foot of height, and you swore you would not for get the beating—"

I didn't move. Kenton was far away. I groped for him and held onto his arm. I saw a shadow move across the room; Charley Green came up to us, sat down.

"I had in mind to ask your forgiveness. I had in mind to give you my powder horn—for a thing to remember me by."

Then we sit together. There are no more words. We lie close for warmth.

15

KENTON says goodbye to us. A grey morning with big flakes of snow dropping slowly. Charley's face is all twisted up, and the tears wash the dirt from under his eyes. He won't look at Kenton. He stares at the floor, clenching and unclenching his hands, moving nervously, shivering.

The care is gone from Kenton's face. He puffs on Hamilton's long clay pipe, blowing clouds of blue smoke between us. Kenton says:

"If you're the only man to go back to the Mohawk, Allen—then they won't know I died on a gibbet?"

"They won't know—"

"Not for my shame, Allen: I think it no shame. But they might consider it a matter of shame."

I nod my head; I wipe my eyes and hold a hand over my mouth.

We go out. Kenton stands in the centre of the room. He waves his hand.

Outside, Hamilton and the commandant of the fort are waiting. Hamilton avoids our eyes. A guard of four men forms behind us, and a drummer goes in front. The drummer beats a slow roll. I see how the flakes of snow fall on the drum, splatter under the sticks. Charley plods along next to me, his feet dragging. I feel a wild, insane impulse to run back to Kenton, to stay with Kenton. I look at Charley, and see the same impulse in his eyes. He shakes his head. He keeps on shaking his head, dumbly.

We march up the Baptist Road, and then onto the Grand Parade over to the whipping posts. The snow is falling more heavily now. The men of the Pennsylvania brigades bulk like shadows out of the snow. They march along with their heads down and form into their lines.

They curse the snow and they curse us.

"Did you bastards have to pick a day like this?" they cry. "A hell of a thing to drag men out for!"

They stand round us, not too interested, knowing only the cold and the snow, shivering in the snow. They hold their muskets close to their bodies, their hands in the armpits for warmth. They bend their heads to break the force of the wind. They don't look like soldiers; they don't look like men. I try to find Ely, but there are too many bearded, ragged men. they all look the same, their identities lost in the swirl of snow.

The officers come riding up, close together, bent over on their horses. They ride up and down, beating the men into formation. Wayne sits on his horse, wrapped tight in his cloak; the snow gathers all over him, over his horse.

The drum beats up a crescendo. It dies, and the stillness is broken only by the muttering of the men. The parade stretches away, a plain of snow with walls of snow. A man's voice reciting: "— twenty lashes to be delivered on the bare back, in dishonour —" Charley is a little to the front of me, rigid. He shakes his head. Kenton is sitting in the guard-room, alone. Kenton deep in his loneliness. The drum again, slowly, a beggar's dance, a beggar's ball. I dance with Bess. They are a great company on the other side of the veil of snow, Bess with her husband. Is her love for me or for her husband? Like Kenton's love? The love of a man or the love of a woman?

They strip off our clothes. I stand very still. The fear of cold and pain is a monstrous lump, swelling my heart. The same fear that brought Kenton death. — If I were in Kenton's place?

291

I'm watching Charley. They peel off his rags. In Boston, Charley was a fat man. A round, fat man. Something to be laughed at by a regiment of backwoodsmen. Tall men in green hunting shirts come out of the Mohawk. My mother sews on the shirt, cloth she wove with her own hands, pleading with me not to go. The planting is done; come winter I'm back. The war will be over. The whole land will rise in arms, and then the war will be over. Four, five months, ten months.

They bare Charley's back; they bare my own. I tremble with the cold, and my skin crawls together. I feel that my blood is freezing.

"The whip will warm you —"

The bones stand out of Charley's flesh, bones with skin stretched tight over them. A winter's filth on the skin; but the snow will wash us. I clench my teeth and bite my lips. The snow melts on my skin; the wind on the wet surface is like knives cutting into me.

They bind us each to a post. Hands bound together and then tied to an iron ring at the top of the post. Charley is stretched like a drawn chicken. I feel an impulse to laugh. Kenton feared the cold; he stayed in the guardhouse.

I strain around to see the brigades. Warm in their clothes. Warm —

The first lash. Charley wilts. I feel a knife drawn over my skin. But no real pain; nothing to compare with the cold. The cold makes a wall round me that nothing can come through. Bess could lie up against me and warm me with her body. Bess is in the dugout — or dead. I could have Kenton's woman, because Kenton is good as dead. Back in the dugout, I'll have Kenton's woman to warm me.

Another — third, fourth: I stare in wonder at the red marks on Charley's back. Too cold for blood to flow.

Are there marks on my back, open spaces on the skin with red in between? The fourth lash brings a cry out of Charley. A low animal cry; his strapped hands wrench back and forth, spasmodically. The fifth lash brings blood flowing over the dirt. Blood to wash him — washed in the blood of lambs.

A sense of pain comes to me, pain out of the distance. The wall of cold around me has been broken. Pain with fire; heat and cold at once. The scream from between my lips comes from another, not from myself. I lose count of the lashes.

Maybe the eighth — or the tenth. Charley's back is no longer human flesh. If I see it clearly? I see a writhing figure; or I see nothing. We tried to desert — a long trip back to the Mohawk Valley. Three men plodding through the snow, and the fourth figure is Bess. A fair good walker for a woman. The strength in a woman is the strength of the earth. She clings to me, crying:

"What did we do? Allen, for the love of God, what did we do?"

I realize that it's Charley's voice, and I'm sane enough to hear and understand. I would tell him, a just punishment, meted out by officers sitting round a table. A big man with a big face talks about an army. Men in dugouts talk about Washington's purpose. He plays for big stakes. No other reason for it. He's put his head in a noose—because he's playing for big stakes. A kingdom, a wilderness stretching away for thousands of miles. Jacob knows, and Jacob has explained it to us again and again. Washington sits at the table in a nightcap. Does he love Hamilton? Who is Hamilton?—eyes like a woman.

The fifteenth lash—or more? Much more. They're giving us twenty or thirty. The pain is gone. A thudding hammer on my back and a cold pain in my lungs. But I stand on my feet. Charley hangs by his hands and feels the pain no more. He's at liberty. A word to make songs of. We're scared boys at Bunker Hill, and we try to strengthen ourselves by saying liberty. Always liberty. The British march up, rank upon rank of scarlet-clad men, the drummers beating a mocking parody of Yankee-Doodle. Yankee-Doodle went to London, riding on a pony. They keep on marching. A bugle pipes up the tune of "Hot Stuff." The officers flash swords in the sunlight. I'll throw down my musket and run away—to Boston, hide in Charley's house. Old Putnam says, Fire and give the red bastards hell. Then we're at liberty—free.

A crisp voice says: "Twenty—cut them down."

Charley first. He falls in the snow, a little mound of human flesh, all cut up and bleeding. He falls there and he doesn't move. But I stand up. Oh, dear God—the strength of me! I stand on my feet. I move my arms and spread them apart. Kenton, look at me, cut and bleeding and standing on my feet, the guts inside of me freezing!

"Brigades—at ease!"

I keep moving my arms.

"Brigades—march!"

I move over to Charley, step by step, until I am right above him. The snow is stained with blood.

"Charley—"

He doesn't move.

"Charley—we've done our punishment. Get up!"

"Charley—get up!"

I say: "Oh—Jesus Christ."

I see Ely walking toward me. Ely is an old man. He walks toward me, and more pain than I ever knew is on his face.

I turn to him. "Ely—"

He begins to clothe me. He picks up my rags, bit by bit, and forces me to get into them.

"I'm noways cold, Ely."

He helps me into my coat. Then he goes to Charley. I don't follow him, only stand where I am, looking round curiously. Some of the men have stopped, and they're watching us. The officers force them on; it doesn't matter a damn if deserters die in the snow. An officer spurs over to Ely. Ely glances up at him, and whatever the officer might have said is left in his throat. I walk to Ely.

"We'll help him back," Ely says.

Charley looks at me and tries to smile. I take hold of one of his arms, Ely the other, and we help him to his feet.

"I should have stayed—not Kenton," Charley whispers. "I'm no man to live out of this."

It was an endless distance to the dugout. We walked slowly. Ahead of us, the brigades disappeared into the wall of falling snow. We plodded on, and always there was more of the grey snow wall ahead of us.

We have to carry Charley. He's a limp thing in our hands. Every few feet we stop to rest.

"I'm sore afraid he'll die of the cold," Ely says.

We climbed the hill. There were some Pennsylvania men there, and they helped us along. They looked at me with wonder. Indeed, it was a wonderful thing that I could still move and talk.

"It's a rare man who could stand a flogging and walk afterwards," one of them said admiringly.

"A rare strong man."

"A freezing bitter day for a flogging. It's a wonder."

They carry Charley into the dugout, lay him in one of the bunks. Ely enters and I come in behind him. I was never gone. I see Jacob standing in one corner, avoiding my eyes. The two women are still there, Smith sitting limply on a bunk, his face a haggard mask from the scurvy. Henry Lane is gone—dead, I suppose.

A Pennsylvania man says: "The blond lad who brought in the deer, where is he?"

I begin to laugh. I am cold suddenly. I stumble over to the fire and huddle close to it. In front I am cold, but my back is burning with pain.

"Where is Kenton?" a woman asks.

I crawl into one of the bunks, put my face in my hands and cry bitterly. Ely approaches me, bends over me.

"Allen — I'll go get the doctor."

"It's no matter."

"I'll go get him."

I move from side to side, trying to ease the pain. I kick at the wooden bed until my toes are bruised and hurt. One of the women brings me a cup of water.

"Here — drink."

I drain it down. I try to sleep, to forget myself, but there's no escaping the pain. I whisper: "Ely — Ely."

"He's gone out, boy."

"Jacob — "

I look up, and Jacob is standing where he was when I entered the dugout.

"Jacob — we've suffered enough to ease your hate for us."

He doesn't move, and his face doesn't change.

"Only forgive me, Jacob. Kenton's to die."

"We're a people at war. A just punishment — "

I groan. I put my face in my hands and sob bitterly.

A long time passed then, or perhaps only a short time made long by pain. Ely came back with the doctor. I must have slept, because they were taking off my clothes when I knew things again. The doctor was saying:

"Civilized — here's their civilization. Here's what they fight wars for. Look at that back."

"They were deserters," Jacob said.

"Deserters? Would any sane man remain in this place? Are any of us sane? Eight hundred men in my hospital, piled up like meat in a butcher's. Naked, frozen, starving. I cut off arms and legs. I'm no doctor; I'm a butcher, a barber, a leech. There are no doctors. False — it's all false, a rotten fabric of lies. I know nothing, nothing. I bleed them. I cut off frozen limbs. And they die — they die like ants. What's your cause worth when men die like ants — like savage beasts — ? I'm no better than the rest. We're living in a world of ignorance. Let them die. I don't try to save them. It's better if they die."

He washed my back with warm water, rubbed some sort of fatty paste into it.

"He'll be all right?" Ely asked anxiously.

"This one's strong. By God, it's amazing what a strong man will stand. I don't know about the other. Let me have a look at him."

I twisted my head and watched them go over to Charley. The doctor

295

worked with strong, sure hands. Only his hands were the same. The rest of him had changed. He seemed older than when I saw him before, not so clean. Nor was he shaven.

"He'll be all right?"

"How do I know? You expect me to be God, to give life. Well, I don't know. Doctors are fakes. None of us know anything. And it doesn't matter. There's plenty of room in mother earth — plenty of room for all. Don't give him anything but broth. He has a fever."

"Thank you —" Ely said.

"Don't thank me. This does me good. I'm learning. I'm learning the secret of man. Pain — pain. Eight hundred men in a log cabin. I go back there, and they want me to be God. Christ, I'm sick and tired of the lot of you."

Then he went out, and I called Ely over to me.

"Don't fret now, Allen," he said. "Try to sleep."

"I have to tell you, Ely."

"Tell me later."

"No — now. Of Kenton. They said they'd spare two of us, but that one man should die for the shooting of McLane's trooper. Kenton would have himself the man." I grasped Ely's coat. "I was afraid. It was my doing, my bringing the girl along that got us taken."

Ely looked at me oddly; then he shook his head. "If Kenton wanted it. A man's life is his own."

"Kenton had a fear of the gallows — a bitter, awful fear. He was in no way wanting to die on a gibbet."

"Ye're hurt enough, Allen."

"No —"

"Sleep now."

"No — when the brigades march out to see Kenton hanged, I must be there. I want you to swear to it, Ely, that you'll wake me to be there."

"I'll wake you, Allen."

"You've no hatred of me, Ely?"

"No hatred, Allen."

"When the brigades march —"

I slip away — a long way down into darkness. Sleeping and walking. When the brigades march — to dishonour a man.

A long way back, a surging backwards and forwards, and Bess lives and dies. Bess comes and drifts away. She whispers the secret of her death. Why did I die, Allen? Why did I die? Fair, beautiful men die. Why do men die, oh Allen! What is the making of this war? For the poor to drive out the rich, for the rich to crush the poor — for a freedom that makes no man free? What is the making of war, Allen?

She goes and I wake and I see the fire burning; and Jacob feeding logs onto the fire. Jacob is a man with dreams, but men with dreams lose all semblance of humanity. What kind of dreams has George Washington—dreams of a throne? I try to see the big, hurt face underneath a crown. No dream of a throne. A man groping. Jacob wants the wilderness; he's a wilderness seeker. A new land out of a wilderness. A man with one purpose: drive out the British. Men may die; nothing matters so long as the purpose is left. Drive out the last Englishman. Take the wilderness for ourselves. Drive women into the forest to be killed by savages. Women like Bess. All women like her.

I drift into sleep again, dreaming that Bess is with me: but this time I know she's beyond the veil of death. With the others who died, with the great company who know why we fight, why we struggle, and what will come of our fighting and struggling. She asks me no questions. She's thinking of Kenton. Kenton wakes. One more to a company of men who have gone.

A dream of pirates, of Massachusetts men who made a war so that their ships could rule the seas. Virginian planters who would get better than English prices. Fur traders who would break the great English companies. Only why are we here, farmers, dying and becoming beasts? What have we to do with all that? We were farming men, and we would live in peace so long as we could turn the soil and bring food forth from the ground. What had the Jew to do with it?

I sleep, a troubled, feverish sleep. A sleep broken by the faces of living men and dead men—

The brigades marched out the next day. They marched out to see Kenton hanged. The snow had stopped. A blanket of snow, two feet deep in some places, lay all over the ground. The sun glistened from the snow, made the highlands a place of bizarre, incredible beauty. On every side, away from our encampment, the countryside rolled, a white sheet spread on hills.

The order came to assemble for parade. We knew what it meant. Charley Green lay in his bunk, the pain of a feverish man in his eyes. When I went over to him, he said to me:

"You'll go out on parade, Allen. You'll watch him and honour him."

"I'll honour him."

"He was not meaning to humble you, Allen. He did it out of love."

"I know," thinking only that I hadn't guts enough to die for another.

"I'm thinking it should have been me. Allen, and that I'll never rise out of this bed. Kenton would have lived. Kenton is a strong man. He would have endured the whipping and lived."

"You'll be better, Charley."

"Try to look into his eyes, if they leave them bare."

"Yes — I'll look into his eyes."

I went out of the dugout slowly. It was still an agony of pain for me to move. My back felt like flesh pressed against hot iron bars. Ely begged me not to go.

"It's no sight to see, Allen. They'll not expect a man who was flogged to get out of his bed."

"I'll have no peace unless I go."

We formed for parade on the road, the pitiful remnant of the Pennsylvania Line. There were some eight or nine hundred of us left, poor, tattered wretches. Wayne's pride. The pick of the army. We bent under the weight of our muskets. We dragged our feet through the snow. We blinked like owls at the light that flashed from the polished surface.

The drums beat out their monotonous roll. Wayne rode a nag with ribs prodding out, a half-starved, broken horse. Most of the officers walked. Their horses were dying from lack of fodder.

Ely and Jacob walked in my rank, Jacob still wrapped in the same stony silence as before. Ely bore the weight of my musket.

We marched down into the valley, past the hospital. The doctor was standing on the steps, watching us, a curious, sardonic smile on his face. We turned up and were drawn into ranks near the fort. On the slope of Mount Joy, a gibbet had been constructed. Kenton stood before the gibbet, a guard of four men round him. He was bare-headed, his yellow hair like gold in the sunlight.

I was weak and sick from the marching. Once I had looked at Kenton, I could not take my eyes away. Yet I felt that I would collapse in the snow if I watched the thing.

I whispered to Ely: "He's not guilty. The three of us shot in a passion. There's no knowing who killed McLane's man."

"God help him," Jacob muttered.

"He'll not be fearing God," I said.

The brigades were sympathetic towards Kenton. No one of us had any love for McLane's raiders. They foraged food, but we saw little enough of it. The brigades were muttering and talking among themselves. They remembered the time Kenton had slain the two deer.

I thought of myself up there with Kenton, three gibbets instead of one. What sort of fear was in Kenton's heart? How could he stand like that — and bear it?

I thought he was looking at me. Then I realized that the sun in his eyes would show him only dark figures of men coming out of the glare on the snow.

I thought of Charley, who would have died instead. Only I was always outside of it. Never had it occurred to either of them that I should be the one to die. I had known it. The moment Washington agreed to Hamilton's request, I had known that it would not be I; I had known that I would live.

I thought of how there had been no word of hate out of Kenton's mouth, no word of resentment, only regret for something he had done to me when we were both children, something I had forgotten already. I thought of the Kenton I had always known; this man —

"He's godlike," I said to Ely.

Ely was crying, unashamed. It was the first time I had ever seen tears in Ely's eyes.

The brigades were muttering with resentment. "Let him live — he's a fair good man — he's guilty of no crime —"

Muller walked up to Kenton, tore a piece of cloth from his ragged coat, turned on his heel and walked away. The act signified the defacing of a uniform. But Kenton wore no uniform. There had never been a uniform for any man in the Continental army. The uniform business was a conceit of the Congress and the officers. Now, for the first time, I took a pride in our rags, a great pride in the fact that we were men together, no soldiers, only men in our own right — beggars with guns.

Watching Kenton, watching Muller striding away smugly, watching the men on either side of me, I had a picture of the revolution as coming from us, part of us, part of the awful resentment against forces that destroyed man's pride in himself. Part of men born into a new world.

It rose like the growl from the brigades, a growl of dumb fury and hate. I wonder whether Muller saw it — saw a new world in us, a world groping blindly to find itself. Kenton saw it; I swear to God that Kenton saw it. I swear to God that Kenton died with that vision in his eyes.

I cried to Ely: "He'll not hang! We'll take him back!"

A moment the brigades surged forward, a moment during which Wayne's ringing voice shouted:

"Brigades attention!"

We fell back, men in arms and in rank. We fell back into the years of war that stretched before us, how many years no man there knew.

They stood him on the scaffold. When they wanted to blindfold him, he shook his head. He stood bareheaded, the rope around his neck, his hair golden with sunlight. Then they shot the trap, and Kenton died.

There was a great sigh from the brigades. Men slumped visibly. Men stood with their heads hanging over, holding their muskets limply.

"He's dead," I whispered.

The drums beat out into the morning air. The brigades began to move. Wayne had become a figure of stone; he rode ahead and looked at no man.

Jacob's face was grey, his eyes black hollows.

I said: "You bear him no hate, Jacob. leave the hate for me. Hate me, Jacob — but not Kenton."

"I bear him no hate —"

Ely muttered: "The love of a man who gives his life for a man — "

We marched back to the dugouts. I went in, and Charley Green was waiting for me, his face flushed hot.

"Kenton's dead," I told him.

"How? — he wasn't afraid?"

"No. He was smiling."

Charley cried. He lay with his face in his hands, crying bitterly. I went to the fire, sat down close to the flames, and stared into them. I tried to get back what I had seen when Kenton went to the scaffold.

16

I SHAKE my head. The hand I hold the cup of water with trembles, spilling some of it. My hand is a frame of bone with yellow skin stretched over it.

"I've seen a lot of fever," Ely says. "It comes, goes, and leaves you weak. It leaves strange thoughts."

"How many days have I been here, Ely?"

"Six days — "

I consider it thoughtfully — six days. Six days without food. Yet I'm alive. I say:

"Have you ever thought, Ely, about a man's lot after he's died?"

Ely shook his head. 'I'm no religious man, Allen. It's a thing for preachers."

"Kenton died for me. He'll hold no hate for me?"

"I'm not thinking he'll hold any hate."

"You'll stay by me, Ely?—When I go, you'll hold me, Ely? I'm afraid."

"I'll stay by you, Allen."

"You're a great, good man, Ely. You're the best man I've ever known."

Ely shakes his head. He wets a rag, wipes my face with it. He covers me. He sits by me, washing the heat from my face.

I relapse into a stupor. The cold and heat alternate again. The fire in the dugout fills all the space taken by my eyes, a roaring blaze of fire that consumes me. I cry for Bess. I wake, sweating, and reach out desperately for her. The days and nights blend into the even smoke-filled grey of the dugout. The dugout is eternal; and we are men doomed to it.

The doctor comes once more. The fever has broken itself, and I lie in bed, weak as a baby. Charley is sitting up already, a thin, wasted figure.

The doctor is different red-eyes, a straggling beard over his chin, thinner. His smock is dirty with blood. His voice has lost its sharp bite. He comes into the dugout, and Jacob helps him out of his coat. He shakes his head.

"I'll climb that damned hill no more. Doctor's no good here. Let me rest."

He sits down by the fire and stretches his legs. He glances at Charley, then at me.

"Both of you sane again," he says. "I wouldn't have thought it."

Charley laughs. "They'll not pile me in the snow."

"Give them time. I've a thousand men in my hospital. Do you believe me? A thousand men in that shack—a full thousand men between the four walls. No room to walk, and it doesn't matter if you walk on top of them. There's no hell hereafter. Hell's here. Hell's in my hospital. A thousand men and no one of them will walk out of the place. better that they don't. It's not a thing to remember. But the women live. God knows how, but they live and hold on. They won't put the women in—to hell with the women. But the women live. Look at those two."

Mary says: "You'll not drag me into your charnel house. You're an evil man."

"Am I? You'd both make a fortune in Philadelphia whoring for the British."

"You're a bad man."

"I'll have a look at those two now. Thought they'd be dead and

301

spare me the trouble."

He examines us wearily, shakes his head. "You'll live—it's a wonder."

Jacob says: "You've news? We march soon?"

"March? Where? How? There's no army left—maybe a thousand men with the strength to walk out of this place. Maybe less. Three thousand deserted. Maybe half the Maryland line, two New York regiments, a Massachusetts regiment. God only knows how many dead. I've cleared a hundred bodies out of my hospital in one day. I can't stand much more. Drives a man mad. I spoke to Washington—a stubborn, ox-like man. I told him, There'll be no man alive in this encampment, come spring. No one man living. You're sitting in a valley of the dead. He said, Doctor, I'll be alive. I asked for medicine—bandages. I said to him, Here's a fair rich country of two million people. A Congress sitting. What the hell is the Congress sitting for? I don't know, he said. They give us nothing. They complain I demand too much. Then he cried like a baby. I said, Your excellency, I've seen a sight of tears—they won't bring us food. He said, I know—I know."

Jacob shook his head. "No—you're lying."

"I'm lying. Look at me. I don't give two damns for your suffering here. I don't give two damns for your cause. I'm no patriot. I'm a doctor. In the beginning I took it. I said, let them be damned. I'll do my leeching, and I'll learn. Maybe I'll help a poor damned soul. Well, I'm broken."

Jacob said, plaintively: "We can't go back—there's no going back now."

"Why not? General Howe would take his surrender."

Ely said: "If it's like you say, why don't the English attack and make an end of it?"

"They're noways discontented in Philadelphia. Why should they waste a man? Two months more—there'll be no army for them to attack. They'll win the war by sitting on their behinds in Philadelphia and begetting children on the good Philadelphia women."

"There'll be men to fight," Jacob muttered.

"Dead men."

Then he went out. We heard, a few days later, that he had shot himself. A Pennsylvania man, back from the hospital, brought us the news. He said: "The little doctor's dead now."

I remember how we stared at him, shook our heads.

"Blew his head open with a pistol."

Jacob whispered: "He would not do that. He was a good, strong man."

"Well, he's dead. There's no doctor left to care for Pennsylvania men."

After that, we sat around the fire. Each of us was afraid to speak.

Finally, I asked Ely: "What now?"

"I don't know," Ely said.

Jacob takes his musket and goes out for relief sentry. But his steps are slow. Charley Green crawls back into bed, his woman with him. She has taken him back as naturally as if he had never gone. Kenton's woman is looking at me. She smiles.

Ely bends over and begins to unbandage his feet. I go to my bed, and Kenton's woman follows me. It doesn't matter — Kenton is dead. Bess is dead.

A long time later — and Ely still sits by the fire. What does he think? Ely Jackson is a farmer man out of the Mohawk Valley. A simple farmer man; there's no great depth to Ely. What drives him?

I turn over — back to the woman, and try to think that she is Bess. I am getting a strange answer to my longing for Bess. More and more often, she will come back to me. I feel her growing inside of me, becoming a woman. I think of the boy Allen who took the woman from the Virginians. That was long ago. She was no fit woman to be a man's wife. She was a camp follower, and a prize for any man who was strong enough to take her. She was a prize for me. She was a rare, good prize, a slim girl with a body to keep a man warm at night. I took from her, and she wanted nothing, and finally, she died.

I lie with Kenton's woman, and I feel a curious grace from Kenton over me. I would have hated the woman, but I don't hate her now. Somehow, hate has gone out of us.

We heal slowly, Charley and I. At first, Kenton's death hangs over us. I can't get out of my mind the picture of Kenton as he stood in the sunlight, in front of the scaffold, Kenton with his bare head golden in the sunlight. I am as close to Charley Green as one man can be to another.

Finally, I speak of Kenton. I tell Charley how he died, word by word. I watch Charley cry, unashamed. It is a curious thing how strong men come to find a relief in tears.

One day, I go to my musket. A man from the Rhode Island brigades brought back our muskets, Kenton's and Charley's and mine. I clean it carefully and rub off the rust with sand.

I go out on sentry duty. We must fill a quota from our dugout, and it is too much for Jacob and Ely to do alone. I go out on a cold, clear night, when there is a new moon in the sky. I walk slowly, thinking how many times before I've walked this same beat, looking over the snow-covered meadows and hills.

When I meet the Pennsylvania man whose beat intercepts mine, we stand together for a while, talk a little. I have no hate left for Pennsylvania men.

"A cold night," he says.

"The back of the winter's broken, I think."

"It's noways different with the cold."

We stand and listen to the wolves howling. There are more wolves than ever near the camp now.

"I can't call to mind such a lot of wolves in farm country."

"They come after the dead. It's said a wolf in winter can scent meat on twenty miles of wind."

I think of the German boy. I glance down the slope, and in my mind's eye, I can see him crawling up, falling in the snow, stumbling to his feet and crawling on again. A German boy thinking of his home in the Pennsylvania highland. We are a strange lot, Dutch and German, and Puritan men from the seaboard, and Jews from overseas in Poland, and men from the southland, Scotch and Irish and Swedes, men from the Valley country in the north, black slaves from the Virginias.

I spoke to Ely and Jacob the next night. Jacob had come back from the commissariat with a little rum. We had a gruel of cornmeal. We sat around the fire, eating. Some Pennsylvania men had come in to ask news and to have a little talk.

I said to Ely: "It seemed to me that Kenton knew something when he died—"

"How was that?"

"He was noways afraid."

"He was a strong man," Charley said.

"Not only strength. Why do we go on, Ely? We're not paid. They starve us. We're sick for sight of our homeland."

"We'll be free men," Ely said.

"There's nowhere free men in Europe."

"There'll be free men here," Jacob muttered.

"But we can't win the war. It's said the British have twenty thousand men in Philadelphia. A thousand men can't fight twenty thousand—"

A Pennsylvania man said: "There's a wilderness road over the mountains into the land of Kentuck. It's said that Washington has sworn to take that road before he lays down his command. Beyond the mountains, he can fight on for years."

"For years?" we asked incredulously.

"For years," Jacob muttered, almost to himself. "For years."

"I'm sore tired," I said.

For two days, there is no food, a roaring cold wind out of the north. No sunlight. A sleet that forms a coat of ice over the ground. We crouch in our dugouts, staring about like trapped animals. We eat the leather straps from our muskets, boiling them for hours in water. We tear cloth into fine bits, cook it and eat it. Bark from the trees. The few trees left in the forest are stripped bare of their bark.

We fly into rages easily. A word from Charley has Jacob at his throat. Ely and I tear them apart, while the women fill the dugout with their screams. Charley is weak as a baby. His woman has left him. He's too sick to satisfy her. She goes to Pennsylvania men in other dugouts, and Charley demands her back. She comes into the dugout, and they spit at each other like a pair of cats.

"Let the woman decide," Ely says.

She says: "Ye're no men for a woman to want—filthy, rotten beggars."

"You'll come to one of us—"

"As I please. I'm a free woman."

"A dirty slut."

"You don't call me a slut. I was a good woman once. I had no wish to be dragged around by a rotten rebel army."

Finally, she goes back to the Pennsylvanians. Charley lies in his bunk, sobbing weakly. I offer him my woman, Kenton's.

"No, no—keep her, Allen."

I fall into an insane temper of rage. I threaten the Pennsylvania men. I tell Charley that when my strength comes back, I'll kill them, every one that's had his woman.

Ely cries: "By God—we're no strangers! We're men together through hell. We're no men to be at each other's throats."

Ely keeps the fire going. Ely cuts wood in the forest, goes out into the sleet by himself. Ely nurses us the way he'd nurse children. He humors us . . .

He sits at night, and tries to bear the pain in his feet. He no longer uncovers his feet.

A parade is called on the day of March seventh. The troops crawl out of their dugouts. The brigades assemble. Less men than ever. We march out to hear a message from the Congress read.

Rumours go about. A rumour that we retreat southward.

"They're going to break camp."

"It's over now—"

"A British attack, and we're to defend the forts of Mount Joy."

"Congress would know nothing of a British attack. Congress knows nothing of anything. God damn their souls—"

We stand shivering, waiting. At last, Wayne rides up with his staff. He dismounts and walks up and down our line. He says: "Attention, brigades."

We try to form ourselves erect. He shakes his head, and walks back to his horse slowly. He stands there, looking over the grey hills in the direction of Philadelphia.

A young officer comes forward to read the message. We stand tense, waiting. He reads:

"From the Continental Congress to the Army of the Republic: In recognition of the men's courage in bearing their privations, we hereby appoint a day of fasting and prayer—"

We laughed. By God, we had not laughed like that in days and weeks. We laughed until we were trembling and weak. Then we turned round and marched back.

I remember how Wayne had not moved through all the reading. he mounted his horse slowly, like an old man, and rode down the hill to his quarters.

PART THREE

THE BATTLE

17

IT HAS been raining all morning. We sit in the dugout and try to understand that rain is falling—not snow but rain. The fire burns low, but we put no wood on it. The dugout is warm. The rain on the roof is like a corps of drummers beating out a roll.

Mary cries. She sits on the edge of a bed, sobbing, her lean figure swaying back and forth.

Curiously, Ely asks: "You've a sorrow, Mary?"

"No—"

"Then why are you weeping?"

"The rain—do you hear? I thought the world was lost in the cold."

"It's rain—"

"Rain," Jacob says, nodding, "rain out of the sky—a beautiful, fair rain."

Anna lies in my bed, her head swaying a little to the beat of the raindrops. Near the bed, the roof is leaking. She holds out a skinny hand and lets the drops splash off it. "I mind," she whispers, "how it was when I was a girl. We clung to the kitchen in the rain. It was a special day for kitchen work. Baking and sewing and weaving cloth. If I had a loom, I'd weave out a fine cloth to make coats."

I go to the door and open it. Trees are like shadows. Clouds hang low to the earth, and the rain pours out in a great downpour, each drop biting a hole in the snow. Already, the snow is giving away.

When I turn back, I can hardly speak. I say: "Ely, what day is this?"

"A day in March—I can't think of the exact day."

Jacob said: "I call to mind how the Jew spoke of the spring coming. He had no sight of the spring in this country."

I whisper: "We're alive—Charley, me, you—we're alive to see the rains."

"A fair land in spring."

"But we're alive. We're talking, moving."

Ely nods. He walks around aimlessly, toughing the rough frames of the beds, reaching up and touching the leaks in the ceiling. He sits down by the fire.

Jacob goes over to him, says gently: "You're disturbed, Ely?"

"I'm noways disturbed. I'm thinking."

"We'll go back to the Mohawk some day, Ely — a free land for people to live in, a green, beautiful land."

"We'll go back," but with no faith in his voice.

I go to the door again. I'm like a child. I cry: "Ely — Ely, the snow melts!" I take my bayonet, stand out in the rain and dig through to the ground.

I come back into the dugout, dripping.

"You'll take cold," Ely says. "Don't be a fool, Allen."

Charley whispers: "You were digging in the ground, Allen. It's not soft so quickly."

"We'll bury them," I say. "They'll lie in peace. All those who died — they'll be no longer unburied and prey for the wolves. We'll dig in the ground and bury them."

"In peace."

I sit down on my bed, laughing.

Jacob says: "I call to mind how it was in the Mohawk, April — a month of rain and soft skies. The blossoms would come out on the apple trees in the month of May. I'll never forget the blossoming of the apple trees."

"There are apple trees in Valley Forge," Charley says eagerly.

The rain is dripping through the ceiling with a steady patter. We sit around and look at it, let it drip from our hands, watch the little puddles of mud it makes on the hard dirt of the floor.

"The cold is in my bones," Charley says sadly. "Come years — I'll never get the cold out of my bones. I'll never get out the cold they flogged into me at the whipping post."

"I dream of a hot sun —"

"I have a dream," I say, "to lie down in soft green grass with the sun on me, with a bit of cloth over my eyes, with a breeze overhead."

"With a lass?" Mary asks.

I shrug my shoulders.

"A hot sun," Charley nods.

Jacob, looking into the fire, says: "The army will come back — there'll be new men. Militia will gather. We'll march . . ."

The door swings open, and Kirk Freeman, a Pennsylvania man, bursts in. He stands there panting, dripping wet.

"What is it?"

"The ice on the Schuylkill—it's breaking up."

We follow him. All along, men are out of the dugouts, standing in the rain, listening. From far off, a dull booming.

"The ice!"

"It's thunder—"

A ripping crash. Someone laughs shrilly.

"Get back into shelter!" Ely calls. "We're not fit to stand out in the pouring rain!"

We go back inside. Some Pennsylvania men come in, and one of them has some rum. He tells a detailed story of how he came by the rum. Eight Pennsylvania men were on guard at the commissariat. Coming off duty one evening, they intercepted two McLane raiders, with a tub of foraged rum slung between them. The sergeant of the Pennsylvanians signed for the rum, as a captain, and they took it to their brigade and got drink. For that, the sergeant had ten lashes, the others four apiece. But it was worth it.

The Pennsylvania man has what is left of the rum. There's a long drink for each of us We heat it over the fire, drink it slowly.

There's a toast of liberty—"To John and Sam Adams, may they be hanged!"

"To the Continental Congress, may they rot in hell!"

"May they have dysentery until their bowels rot out!"

We sit around the fire, tasting our rum, listening to the rain. We are lulled by the steady, even beat of raindrops on the roof.

The Pennsylvania men talk of Kenton. "He was a strong man—a bright flame of a man."

"He was a man to fight and to win—never to know pain or sorrow."

Charley is already a little drunk from the rum. We are not used to hard drink, and there's not enough food inside of us to sop it up. Charley says:

"He died for us. There was no man had such a fear of the gibbet as Kenton. But he died for us."

"God damn Muller's soul. He remembered the deer. He took it out on Kenton."

"There are good Pennsylvania men who won't be forgetting a gift of two fine buck deer."

"Something for Muller to remember."

Ely said: "Let Kenton rest in peace. There's no score in the encamp-

309

ment but has been paid out in blood.

"There's no peace for a man who dies on the gibbet."

"Peace enough."

Some of the Pennsylvania men brought in their women. The women shift from man to man. There's no hate. A man dies, and his woman is left behind. We have suffered too much to be jealous. They're a strange race, these women of the camp. Many a camp follower was a good woman once. Her man was going to war; they married and came along together. Then her man died, or he deserted, leaving her behind. No place for her to go; she fell into the life of the camp. These women went from man to man. what a man needed — They had seen how we were like beasts, but still men. Maybe they kept us being men.

We lie in front of the fire, and we sing sad Dutch songs, songs that were sung along the New York and Pennsylvania rivers for a hundred years.

And the rain beats on the roof.

It rained for two days more, and then, on a grey, wet day, the order went around for a grand review of the entire army. Muller brought the news himself. He came into the dugout and said:

"Come out of your hole — clean up!"

He met our eyes and smiles. He had courage, that man. "Parade with fixed bayonets. Stump!"

"The army moves?" I asked Ely.

"I don't know."

A while later, General Wayne stepped into the dugout. We stood at attention, in spite of ourselves. There was a simple, natural dignity in Wayne, a spark of fire in his light blue eyes. For Muller we had not moved.

He walked round the hut without speaking, took up our muskets, looked at the flints. He nodded, said:

"You're soldiers. A man may go to hell, but he keeps his musket in firing condition." He looked at our feet, man to man — stopped at Ely's. "You can walk?"

"I can walk, sir," Ely said.

"I pleaded for shoes, God knows. Maybe we'll have them soon."

"Yes, sir, I trust so. But I'm fair afraid no shoes'll fit my feet again."

"I'm sorry," he said softly.

He stopped at the door, said bluntly: "You're New York men, but my troops now. We've all seen hell. I pleaded for you at the court-martial." Then he walked out.

310

We assemble outside the dugouts in brigade formation. The snow is a slush, and with each step we sink into it, ankle-deep. The drummers stand around, trying to tighten their drumheads. There is movement, new life in the air. Finally, the order comes to march — eight hundred of the Pennsylvania line.

We go through the trees, the slush falling into our faces. At the Gulph Road, we fall in behind the Massachusetts regiments. The Virginian men join in behind us, cursing in their soft drawl. We curse them back.

We march out onto the parade. Across the meadow, the Rhode Island men face us, next to them the Maryland brigades, then the long stretch of the New Jersey line. Thin, white-faced, bearded, filthy, no man with a whole, decent suit of clothes, we make a strange, nightmarish picture of an army. An army come back from hell, crippled beggars collected from the ends of the earth.

The drummers march out to beat their roll, but the noise is dulled. Their drum-skins are wet. Clouds hang low overhead. We can hear the cracking and rushing of ice in the Schuylkill.

Washington rides out, with his staff. They canter to the centre of the parade, draw in their horses and dismount. The men stand in the slush — waiting. With Washington there is a stranger, and all eyes are on him. He wears a blue and white uniform, gold-trimmed, and a white cocked hat, high black boots. We ask each other who he is. Nobody seems to know.

He walks toward the Pennsylvania brigades, Washington behind him. Wayne comes out, takes his hand, and they stand in a little group, talking. They are too far away for us to hear what they're saying, but suddenly the stranger breaks out into a roar of laughter — real laughter, the kind we have not heard for months. It takes effect. We look at each other.

He walks toward the brigades, stiffly. He's a stocky man, a broad flat face. He kicks his feet out in front of him, splashing the slush. When he is a few yards from us, he stops; his eyes widen. He walks along, his head turned sidewise, staring at man after man. He comes to one man who has no breeches, who wears an improvised sort of kilt instead. Then the stranger stops. For a moment, he stares straight ahead of him, then turns his head slowly — warily to look at the man. The head goes back. Still warily, it seeks out General Washington — then back to the man with the kilt. It takes us. We begin to smile. The brigades smile. A flurry of rain comes — and still the brigades smile.

Wayne says: "You must understand, Baron — we have suffered a

311

winter of hell."

The stranger answers in German: "Ja — Ich versteh'."

"You must allow."

"Ja —"

He turns his head again. Then, slowly, he walks toward the man. I know the man, his name is Enoch Farrer. He's a tall thin man. As the stranger approaches him, he backs away, stooping down to hide his knees.

The stranger stops. "Come here!"

Enoch knows no German.

"Come here and turn round."

I know Dutch well enough to make out the German. Most of the Pennsylvania men can speak a Dutch or German dialect. Farrer is a north Pennsylvania man, of English stock. He backs away from the German, making an effort to draw his kilt down over his knees. Then he drops his musket.

"God-damn thing's wet," he snaps, fumbling for it. "Who the hell are you, mister?"

The stranger roars with laughter. His whole body shakes with laughter. He sways from side to side, clapping his hands together. Washington, Wayne, Greene — they stand and regard him with indignant silence. He turns to them, stumbling through the snow, shaking his big head.

"I'm sorry — sorry — but in Europe I hear of an army. An army that stands the English nation on end. An army they chase all over America —"

"We have muskets, sir," Washington says stiffly.

"I know — I'm sorry. Forgive me." But he stands there laughing. He can't stop laughing.

It was the first time we had seen Baron von Steuben. He came to the Pennsylvanians first. He came to us when we were almost finished.

That day, we stood in the rain for three hours, half-frozen, soaked through and through. Nothing else could have kept us there — nothing but the fat German who stamped up and down, cursed us furiously, and then roared with laughter at our blank expressions.

We began to remember. Maybe our thoughts went back to that day at Bunker Hill in Boston, when a rabble suddenly became an army.

He walked up and down our lines impatiently. He would tear a musket from a man's hands, grip it with his own, roar in German: "Like this — God damn your cursed peasant soul, hold it like this! It's a musket — not a log of wood! Like this!"

He would thrust it back at the man, a Massachusetts farmer, and the man would hold it limply — as he held it before.

The Baron would snatch it back, become livid with fury. "Like this — like this — pig — peasant — fool!"

The blank face and a sheepish smile. The Baron would groan, give him back the musket, walk back and forth, groaning and shaking his head.

"An army out of this! God — to make an army out of this!"

Or else he would break out laughing, great, animal-like bursts of laughter that echoed across the parade. Then he would try again.

"A manual of arms — one — two — three — four."

A blank, wondering face.

"Ah, God — God, why can't I speak their accursed tongue? Why can't I speak their miserable, savage tongue?"

He marched us back and forth. He stood in the centre of the parade, roaring out his orders. When we began to march, he mounted his horse, rode up and down our lines, cursing us, trying to keep the brigades in line.

"In line — in line — eyes right! Wayne — God in heaven, come and speak for me!"

The rain grew harder. For hours we marched back and forth, while Steuben roared and cursed. I could see Washington pleading with him to let us rest. He shook his head, drove us.

Weary to death, we staggered back to the dugouts, through the rain. We built up the fire and crouched close to it, trembling with cold and fatigue.

But Jacob was smiling. He stood by the fire, staring into the flames, smiling. Jacob had found a man and an officer.

18

RAINS — a ray of sunlight darting through — a sky of rolling black and grey clouds, an eternity of rain that turns the snow to slush and the slush to black mud. The dugouts leak. The floors are muddy. We become creatures of mud and slime.

Some day, the sun will come out.

Baron von Steuben drives us. It seems that the German is working against time. Who is he? What does he expect? Does he hope to make an army out of the few hundred of us that are left? The army of revolution is learning to laugh again—at itself, at the few hundred pitiful men who make up the ranks.

Eleven thousand men came onto the Valley Forge encampment in December. Today, half the dugouts are empty, their roofs fallen in. In the Pennsylvania line, two and three men make up a regiment.

And Steuben drives us. Out into the pouring rain, onto the grand parade, a mockery of drumsticks threshing over wet skins. Form brigades. We drag our bandaged feet through the mud, back and forth, back and forth—drill. We understand the German for one, two, three, four—manual of arms. Men drop out of the ranks, sprawl on their faces in the mud. Bayonet charge—a thin line of tattered men stumbling against the rain. Re-form ranks, charge back. Back and forth until we can no longer stand. Our beards run water. We stand limply, look at one another—then laugh. We have reached the bottoms of misery, of filth, of wretchedness. We can go no lower—we are beasts of the earth.

Steuben roars his orders, more, more—but we stand limply. You can't ask more of a man when he has no strength left. Steuben pleads with us.

"My children—once more."

He stands in the rain, bareheaded. His uniform no longer sparkles with gold lace and braid. His white breeches have become a dirty grey and brown. He stumps along, man to man, pleading with us, losing himself, roaring out in wrath—and then becoming gentle as a woman. He takes a musket and goes through the drill.

"My children, listen to me. I am not making an army out of you. I am making a nation out of you. You and I, we will march across this country—victorious. You understand?"

We stand limply, beggars.

"All right—go home."

Jacob and Ely and I come back to the dugout. Charley has a fever, perhaps the same fever that took him after the flogging. He coughs continuously, and sometimes there's a splatter of red on his lips.

Tired, wet, we come in and crouch close to the fire. We build it up into a great roaring blaze. The rain is harder, like a steady flow of pebbles onto the roof.

Charley calls to me: "Allen—"

I take a rag and go over to his bed. I sit there, wiping the mud and water from my musket. His woman no longer sleeps with him. But sometimes she comes into the dugout to sit with him. In a way, she must still care for the little printer. Now she sits at the opposite side of the dugout, watching us.

"You're better?" I ask him. "You don't look so bitter hot today, Charley."

"I'm used up, Allen—all used up."

"That's no way for a man to talk—that's a foolish way for a man to talk."

"Allen, I want you to swear that you'll bury me. Deep in the earth, deep as the height of a man standing. I have a great fear of lying out in the cold. I want to be below where the ground freezes—far below."

"You're talking foolish."

"But you'll bury me, Allen?"

I nod, stand up and put away my musket. When I turn back, Charley is lying with his eyes closed, breathing hoarsely. I go to the fire.

"He's no better," Jacob says.

"He's used up by the whipping. Kenton would have lived."

"The rain will stop soon—after that, he'll gain strength."

"We should bleed him."

"Or take him to the hospital. They say there's two new men there, doctors from Boston."

"Not to the hospital," I mutter. "There's no man coming out of that hospital."

"I wouldn't want to live—coming into that hospital."

The next day, Ely went to the hospital. He came back, wet and tired.

"There's no doctor would come up to the dugouts," he said.

"You asked them?"

"They said bring him there. It's like going into hell to go into that hospital. They have the beds built one layer over another, with the men lying so close they can't move. The doctors are Boston men, not caring much one way or another."

"We'll bring him there?"

Ely shook his head. We went over to Charley's bed. He lay there, his eyes closed, speaking softly.

"Bleed him," Mary pleaded.

"I can't bleed a man," Ely muttered. "I don't hold with bleeding."

"Can't you see he's far gone? Bleed him—"

"You'd better," Jacob said. "It will relieve him of the evil sickness in his blood."

Ely nodded. I brought a pan. Jacob sharpened his knife on a stone, and then cut into a vein on the inside of Charley's arm, just above the elbow. Charley didn't seem to feel the pain of the cut; he went on talking to himself, talking nonsense. Jacob found the vein, but he wasn't very skillful at bleeding; he cut almost all through the vein, and the blood poured forth in a thick, red stream. It frightened me, the gush of blood. It didn't seem that a man could lose blood that way and live.

"Give over!" I cried. "He'll bleed to death."

"Till he comes to his senses, Allen," Ely whispered. "Otherwise he'll die in madness. Let him come to his senses."

The pan filled with blood. The flush passed from Charley's face, and his skin became the color of dirty parchment. He sighed and opened his eyes. He glanced from face to face, and he knew us. Somehow, he managed to smile.

Clumsily, we bound us his arm, but we were unable to stop the flow of blood completely. It still seeped through the bandage. For a while—and then he bled no more.

"You'll be a new man in a few days," Ely told him.

"In less time than that," Charley whispered. "Tonight, the rains stop, Ely. I have that in mind. A peace on earth."

We nodded. Charley's woman went to a bed, lay down. We heard her lips moving in a soft prayer.

"I'll be near Kenton," he said. "I should never have taken myself away from Kenton . . ."

I went out on sentry duty that night. A wind from the west had blown the skies clear. There were stars spread in a great circle over the land.

I walk back and forth slowly. The earth is different, a new land. Most of the snow is gone. In the lee of hills, in places where the drifts were, there is still snow; but most of it is gone. The wind is cool and gentle.

My feet sink into the soft earth. Once, I bend over to touch a patch of withered yellow grass. A blade of the grass, I hold in my fingers.

I come to my contact and two of us stand there. We wait for the third sentry. He walks up, shaking his head like a man in a dream.

"On the wind—the smell of the seasons."

"Spring—"

"There'll be green grass and warm winds. There'll be wheat in the meadows and tall corn."

"It seemed like there would never be a time for growing things again, a time for planting."

"A time for breaking the earth—a time for hitching a horse to a plough. A time for the smell of new earth turned."

"I call to mind how the locusts bloom first. We had a spread of

316

locust trees at home, all along the bank of the river. A good Pennsylvania tree."

"You're a Mohawk man, Allen. Is there good crops and good planting in the Mohawk land?"

I nod. My enlistment will be over soon—mine and Ely's and Jacob's. Three of us left.

"You'll be going home, Allen?"

I look at the Pennsylvania men wonderingly. I say: "It's a great distance for a man to walk—alone."

"There be none to go with you?"

"I don't know . . ."

"There'll be war again with the coming of the flowers," a Pennsylvania man says. "There'll be armies marching."

"They say Howe will attack the camp."

"It's not to my thinking that the old man will keep us here. He'll be out—marching."

"There's little enough army left."

"Mark my word—there'll be more. After the planting, they'll come by the hundred."

"I put no faith in militia."

"There's the German baron to train them."

"Feel the wind—"

"It's warm. It's got a deep, strange warmth in it. It's a wind out of the south and the west."

"There'll be a fair sun tomorrow."

"A ripe sun."

"The ice knocked the bridge out of the river. The Maryland men were in cold water up to their necks, putting the bridge back."

"I've no love for Maryland men. Swedes or Pope-crawlers—"

"Or envy—for men in icy waters."

We separate. We wave our hands and plod back on our beats. My feet make a sucking sound as they part from the earth. At the lunette, I stop and lean against a fieldpiece. Its cold surface feels good to my hands, so much has the change wrought in me that I can enjoy a chill after the cold of winter.

I think about going home. Ely and Jacob and myself. I try to picture the soft green fields of the Mohawk Valley. The realization that it will not be the same forces itself upon me, the realization that we are no longer a part of that life. I picture myself behind a plough, breaking open the land. Then I shake my head. The unrest inside of me won't die. Horror can't kill it—or hate—or suffering. We'll go on and on.

Jacob relieves me. He walks slowly, and he doesn't look at me.

"Go back to the dugout, Allen," he says.

"A clear, beautiful night, Jacob. You feel the wind out of the west?"

He nods.

"A warm breeze. I picked a blade of last summer's grass, Jacob."

"There'll be more grass, new grass with fertile soil to feed it."

"Blue skies, Jacob."

I walk back to the dugout. When I come in, I feel that something has happened. Then I see Charley's woman kneeling by his bed. I go over to the fire and sit down. I look into the curling flames. A fire like this—night after night, all through the winter.

Ely says: "We'll endure, Allen."

I remember Washington's words. How much can a man endure? I stare around the dugout curiously, as if I had never seen it before— smoke-blackened logs, packed dirt on the floor, a double tier of beds, built onto the wall, a few rags hanging from wooden pegs. A musket rack. Moss Fuller's musket is there, Clark Vandeer's, Henry Lane's, Aaron Levy's, Kenton Brenner's, Edward Flagg's, Meyer Smith's, Charley Green's—

A roll call—the muskets answer, each one an individual. Charley has a musket with a silver-inlaid stock, the work of Paul Revere. Clark's is a French piece. There are three long-barrelled Valley-country muskets.

I say to Ely: "The rain has stopped."

"I know," Ely answers softly. He is looking at the muskets, too. His big grey head is bent over.

He comes over to me and sits down. He says: "Best not to keep the women here tonight."

"I'll stay here," she says, not moving from her place to Charley's bed.

I nod to my woman, and she goes to the door.

"Tell them you're Allen Hale's woman. They'll keep you."

She's anxious to go. After she's gone, small as the dugout is, it seems curiously empty.

"Ely," I say, "there were three hundred of us come out of the Valley country."

"I know."

"Will any go back?"

The next day we buried Charley Green. We laid him in the hillside, just away from the abatis. We put a wooden cross as a marker on his grave. We laid him where he could see the blue hills, off to Philadelphia.

19

JOB ANDREWS, a Massachusetts man, crying for us to come and see. He's run up the hillside, laughing like a child. We make a circle round him, and he shows us what he has, a delicate purple flower.

"The first," he ways. "A winter flower."

It goes from hand to hand until it falls to pieces. Men hold it close to their noses, trying to sniff its perfume. We handle it tenderly.

"Only one," Job says.

"More later."

"I seen these blossoms come in great banks."

We go to the grand parade under a blue sky that's rolling with clouds. The wind out of the west is cool and clean, and brings a fragrance of spring. We are without our ragged greatcoats.

The brigades form, and the drums beat out their roll. Steuben rides onto the field, and we smile. We've found a man to love, a man like ourselves, coarse, hard, living with the earth, but patient and gentle as a woman.

He dismounts and walks toward the brigades. He has mastered a broken Enlish, which he delights in using.

"Mine children," he says.

We laugh. He's taught us to laugh again. We're a few hundred broken soldiers, but he respects us. It's a new thing with us.

"Mine children—ve learn to march dis day. Ja—ve learn to march vere ve vant, ve take—ja?"

We imitate him. "Ya—ya, Baron."

We march back and forth, across the grand parade. We have learned to lift our feet, snap them forward in the Prussian fashion. We have learned to march in close order, ten men moving as one. We have learned about bayonets.

He pleads with us: "Mine children—you vill not use der bayonets to cook food? Please. You vill clean der bayonets?"

He tells us to sit down. The staff officers protest. They tell him that he is mad. These men are beasts—and he is destroying what discipline is left in the army. Men on parade do not sit down.

He doesn't understand, and he shakes his head. "But a democratic country—I thought things would be different," he says in German.

"We are at war, Baron."

"I know, I know—I've seen a little of war. But my own way. Let them sit down."

We sprawl about, watching him curiously. He says: "I make mit der bayonet vat you call a show — ya? You vill vatch." He walks through the brigades, seeking a musket and bayonet to suit him. As he walks, his rage mounts. Musket after musket, he examines and throws aside in disgust. Finally, he cries:

"Vat pigs — vat svine! Vy did I come to dis accursed country — to dis land of peasants?" He stamps back and forth in a fury of rage, and we watch him without heat. The rage will cool. We know enough of rage. We were penned up like beasts for a winter; some of us went mad.

He cools. He selects a musket and bayonet, and goes out before us. He salutes us, says:

"Vatch careful, mine children."

A short, fat man, he moves awkwardly as he goes through the drill. Beyond him, a cluster of our officers observe with expressions of mingled amusement and resentment. Steuben walks back, whirls, and runs toward us with fixed bayonet presented. He thrusts at the air, wrenches, and plucks back the bayonet.

"As dis, ja? Der British are clumsy fools — ja? Der virst — brezent, barry — t'rust!" He lunges again. We roar with laughter. We call out:

"More, Baron!"

"Give us one for General Howe, Baron!"

"Give us the whole thing — over again, Baron!"

He doesn't resent our laughter. He joins in himself, laughing and panting at the same time.

"Now — mine children, mit all. Attention!"

The brigades form. The endless drill goes on again: present bayonets, four steps and lunge. Parry, four steps and lunge. We march up and down the parade. We march endlessly, eternally, until our heads are whirling. We lunge at the air, again and again, long lines of tattered men.

Steuben is tireless. He seems to know only one thing — drill. Morning, noon, and night, he drills us. He comes up to the dugouts alone, examines our muskets. He tells us how to clean our bayonets, how to edge a musket-flint to make it spark, how to divide powder into the proper amounts to make a sure load.

He comes into our dugout once. It is toward evening, and we are resting from the drill, lying in our beds.

He enters, and we stumble to our feet. He says in German: "Be seated — I pray you. You understand German?"

We nod, and he looks round the dugout curiously.

"You lived here all winter?"

"All winter." He turns to our musket rack, and his lips move as he counts the guns. He says:

"Where are the rest of the men who live here?"

"They're dead."

He shakes his head, walks to the fire and stares into it. "I have seen some terrible things," he mutters. "I have seen men suffer—"

The drills go on. The sky turns a shade of blue taken out of our dreams. The locust trees along the Schuylkill bud green. The brown dirt on Charley Green's grave sends up little shoots of growing things.

20

I AM out with Ely on sentry duty—a cool, clear night. We meet each other and walk slowly toward Charley's grave. I bend over and pick a bit of grass from it.

I hold it out to Ely. He takes it in his hand and stands there looking at it.

"I had in mind that Charley would be with us," I say. "I had no thought that he would die . . ."

Ely says, thoughtfully: "There will never be another winter like this. When you were born, Allen, I stood outside your house with your father. It was a bitter, sad thing to hear your mother scream. All night long, she screamed out in pain. You were born in the morning."

I listen; it comes to me that Ely is an old man, part of a past.

"There'll be something out of this winter, Allen—something from our suffering. I don't know what, I'm not a learned man. But we've given birth—do you understand?"

"I don't know—"

"You're only a boy, Allen. You're making something for yourself. It's not for Jacob or me."

"What, Ely?"

"A way of life—a new world for men. The Jew who came from Poland, a great distance, seeking it. The men who died—"

"For whom?" I demand. "They let us starve here, while they filled their fat bellies."

"When your enlistment's over, Allen, you'll go back?"

I shrug.

"You're looking for something, Allen. Only find it. It needs a strong man."

I'm thinking, a man like Ely, a strong man to take things and hold them. I'm thinking of all who went — Moss, Kenton, Charley . . . My turn sooner or later.

I say to Ely: "God — I'm sick for home."

He nods. "I know how that is, Allen."

"You'll come home with me, Ely?" I ask him eagerly. "You and Jacob — the three of us back to the Mohawk?" I take his hand.

"There's too many died here, Allen," he says, shaking his head.

"But why — why must we keep on? Ely, I'm afraid."

He says, gently: "Go back, Allen. If you wish to go back — then go."

We walk apart, and I turn again and again to watch the lean figure of Ely, Ely an old man already, Ely with a knowingness that frightens me because it's away from me, out of my world.

The next day I go to General Wayne's quarters. I try not to think of what I'm doing. I try not to think of how the green shoots are pushing themselves up through the dirt on Charley Green's grave.

Wayne is sitting at a desk, writing, when the orderly brings me in. He glances up at me, and his brow puckers. I can see that he remembers me.

"What do you want, sir?" he asks me.

"I want to sign papers for re-enlistment."

He stares at me. The orderly leaves me alone, and Wayne sits for what seems a long time, staring at me, looking at my torn, filthy clothes.

He says oddly: "Your name's Allen Hale — "

"Yes, sir."

"What regiment?"

"The Fourteenth Pennsylvania."

He takes a paper from his desk, and looks at it thoughtfully. Then he says to me: "That girl you had with you when you deserted — you loved her?"

I don't answer him; I am strangely aware of myself. I don't want to speak of Bess; she is too close to me now; she will be closer.

"Why are you staying with the army?" Wayne asks.

I can't tell him; I can't put it into words to tell him.

"Haven't you suffered enough?" Wayne demands, his voice rising.

"I haven't suffered," I say quietly. "Those who suffered are dead. I haven't suffered."

Wayne stands up and comes over to me. He holds out his hand, says: "You know me, sir."

I take his hand.

I walk back to the dugouts slowly. As I climb the hill to where the

Pennsylvania brigades are encamped, I notice the new grass. New grass—its color the faintest, purest yellow-green. Tiny blossoms of violet.

I come to the top of the hill and look round. A faint illusion of green all over the countryside, rolling hills, a blue sky almost near enough for you to reach up and feel it.

I come into the dugout. I say to Ely: "I've been to Wayne's quarters."

"You'll be going home soon?"

Jacob is watching me, curiously. His long, dark face has a trace of sadness on it. For once, the hard, inherent cruelty of his tight mouth has relaxed. He has the dignity of a silent king as he stands in the little dugout. It seems that into him—not into Ely or myself—has gone the force of all the men who died there. He stands there alone. There's nothing to endure about Jacob: I see him going out in a magnificent flash of black fury; sooner or later, he'll go that way. Now, as if he had suddenly realized himself, he's alone. As much as on Washington's, the force and weight of the revolution is upon his shoulders. The stiffness of his shoulders makes it all the more marked. All during the winter, those shoulders had never once bowed, never once moved from their tense, upright position. Then I see him as the Jew, and I realize for the first time how close together they were in force and understanding.

"I'm not going home," I say. And dully: "I enlisted again—for a time of three years."

Jacob shakes his head. It is the first time I have ever seen pity for any man in his eyes.

"You shouldn't have done that, Allen," Ely says.

Jacob sits down on the edge of one of the beds. He's terribly alone there—the double row of empty beds behind him. His eyes wander around the dugout slowly, from Ely to me—groping for others when he knows there are no others. His eyes come to rest on the musket rack, and it seems to me that he is counting the muskets.

"You shouldn't have done that," Ely says again, sadly. "It's my fault."

"There was nothing for me to go back to."

"Your people Allen—come spring planting, they'll be watching for you. It's on me, your enlistment—and my words that kept you here."

I try to explain. And then, suddenly, I'm tired, and I don't want to explain. I want to go outside and lie down in the sun. I say: "All that's gone. None of us can go back, Ely."

Jacob nods. "There will be war for years—God only knows how

long."

I go outside, feeling that I am leaving behind me two old men who are strangers. I feel bitter—sad. I'm left alone.

I walk through the trees, and find a little space of meadow where the sun beats through. I lie down there. The ground is cool, but not too cold. The sun is a beating pulse in my eyes.

I lie there for a long time, watching the small, bundled clouds drive through the sky. I think of Bess, not of a person who is dead, but of a woman I will meet again some day. I think a little sadly of the boy Allen, who despised her—but there is no feeling of hate or resentment in me, not for her nor for the boy I was and whom she loved.

21

We SHAVE our beards. A great amount of hair going away. One man lies flat on his back while another shaves him. The knife scrapes and cuts the skin.

We bare our feet. Bandages fall apart as we unwrap them. Feet that are black knobs of filth. We bare our feet and walk gingerly—barefooted.

About two or three hundred of us lie naked along the Valley Creek—Pennsylvania, Virginia, and Massachusetts men. We wash our clothes with sand and ashes, hang them on the trees to dry. All along, up and down the creek—a beggar's wardrobe, tattered breeches, paper-thin coats. We roll over and over in the icy-cold water and then come out into the sun to dry. We can't get enough of the sun. First it burns us red, blisters our backs; we turn brown slowly. We've become a cult of sun-worshipers. The cold is in our bones. We take long hours in the sun the way we'd take a tonic. The hot, salty sweat is good as it runs into our eyes and our mouths.

We sit on the bank, our feet dangling in the water, and scrub ourselves with curiosity. We pick the lice out of our hair. We investigate each part of our body as the winter accumulation of dirt disappears. We're a curious lot—thin, bony, hollow-eyed. We curse the Virginia men goodnaturedly. The spring has washed away hatred, washed away the differences between the north and the south—the east and the west. We've suffered together for too long.

I wash Ely's feet—and then he stares at them curiously. Somehow, they are healing. Long, raw scars are ingrained with dirt, but the bleeding has stopped. The poor, tortured flesh is knitting itself together once more. Soon the scabs will fall off. The dead white skin will be replaced with new flesh, and new blood will flow through the blue veins that stand out so sharp. He stares at his feet as if he had never seen them before. He takes a few steps through the water—then goes back to the bank and sits down. He attempts to say something to me, and his words choke up. He moves his feet back and forth, watching the water wash over his toes. Finally, he asks me:

"You'll shave my beard, Allen? I'm longing to feel my face clean and smooth."

He lies on his back while I shave him. It's strange to watch his face emerge from under the whiskers. The wind is sighing through the trees, and dogwood blossoms fall over us.

I lie down for my turn. While the knife scrapes over my chin. I close my eyes. I feel the bite of the blade as Ely plucks at my whiskers. Every so often he dips the knife into the cold water to wash it. When it touches my face again, it is chilled and clean. Bit by bit, Ely removes my beard. The years drop from me. I'm a boy again. My skin is firm and clean and hairless. Ely's fingers wander over my face, kneading what's left of my beard to soften it, so that it will come off more easily. Under the lulling play of his fingers, I doze. When I open my eyes, he is finished, looking at me and nodding his head.

Later, we play in the water, lean white men, childish. We throw handfuls of water at each other, duck each other. We find deep holes where we can paddle round. We find two wooden buckets, and a couple of Massachusetts men appoint themselves a bucket squad. We line up and pass between them, and they douse us with water. It's a rare treat, and we keep up until the Massachusetts men are dog-tired. Then we lie in the sun, drying ourselves, telling stories, exchanging the latest jokes about the British, about our officers and their wives.

We put on our tattered clothes and walk back barefooted. We rub our feet into the lush, green grass. When we see flowers, we stoop over to pick them, and then stand and look at them. We put the flowers in our hair and prance round. We become pagans and children: we do foolish things and we are not ashamed.

In between drills, we lie out in the sun. That, we can't get enough of. Our bodies are like sponges. As much sun as we soak in, there is always need for more. We lie about, talking, laughing, rolling dice: but we say little of the winter. It's too near us.

The women try to make themselves pretty. There's no whole dress or hat among them, but they fill their hair with blossoms. They parade

back and forth — smiling at us. They even wash, and once we surprise a
lot of them bathing in the creek. They try to hide their nakedness in
the shallow water, and we stand on the bank laughing at them, like
gangling boys. Finally, they seize their clothes and dash away. We
chase them, laughing wildly, roll over in the woods, plaster wet bodies
with dead leaves.

Recruits are coming into camp, along with food. A great wagon
train from the north brings thousands of pounds of meat. The militia
come and sign papers for three-month terms. We have no love for the
militia; and for their part, they're awed and a little afraid of the regulars. They stand around and watch us. On the parade, they blunder
about, while we go through Steuben's Prussian drills like well-trained
troops.

Baron von Steuben is losing weight, but he delights in us the way a
father would delight in his children. We're his men. Half of the
Pennsylvania line he knows by name.

We let the fire in our dugout go out. Ely stands in front of the empty
fireplace, poking at the ashes with a stick. The door to the dugout is
open, and a breeze from outside stirs the dry ashes. It is the afternoon,
toward twilight, and the two of us are alone in the dugout. The two
women are gone. They went after Charley died, and afterwards I saw
Anna with a Massachusetts man. It doesn't matter.

"A forlorn place without a fire," Ely says. "I'm not bemoaning the
cold, but there was life in the fire."

"A dull, lonely place."

"I hope we march soon."

"I hated this place at first," I say. "I don't hate it now."

The brigades build fires outside. I ask Ely to go out with me, but he
shakes his head. I go out alone. The Pennsylvania men are roasting
meat over the fire. We sit round in a circle, drinking, singing.

I find myself with a woman, a round young girl with light hair.
Three or four men are playing for her attention, but I manage to draw
her off. I take her back from the fire, where there's a bit of grass, and
we lie down there.

"Your name's Allen Hale," she says.

"How do you know?"

"I seen you around. I heard tell you deserted and were whipped nigh
to death."

"Yes —"

"My name's Bella."

"You've no man?"

"I had a man—he deserted without me. I never heard word of him."

"I'm a fit, fair man for a girl to love."

She giggles, and when I put my arms around her, she comes to me willingly. We lie there, watching the blaze of the fire, the dark figures moving in front of it. I pass my hands over her body.

"They say you're no man to be without a woman," she says to me "They say you took a fair woman away from a Virginia brigade—"

"Yes."

"What was her name? Tell me her name? You're not thinking of her now—in my arms?"

"Her name was Bess Kinley."

"Did you love her? Were you pained to see her die?"

I cry, suddenly: "Be quiet, God damn you!" Then, as she draws away in fright, I told her back. "I'm sorry—I was not meaning to fright you."

I come back to the dugout, and Ely sits where I left him, next to the empty fire. He says:

"Allen?"

"Yes, Ely."

"Allen—make me a promise."

"What?"

"You'll have faith in the revolution. There'll be no peace for many years. There'll be strong men needed."

"You'll be with me, Ely."

"No—you'll be alone, Allen."

I go to my bed, and for a long time afterward Ely sits motionless. I can't sleep—and I watch him.

I sleep, and I wake later and still Ely sits there. The door is open, and a vague moonlight seeps into the dugout. Jacob's long form is stretched out in his bunk.

"Ely?" I say.

He looks up at me. "I thought you to be asleep, Allen."

"You'll not sit all night, Ely, not resting?"

"For a little while, Allen—I'm noways tired."

I go back to sleep, but even in my sleep I see Ely's form, bent over the ashes, stirring them with his stick. A man with a deep knowledge—a knowledge that comes out of his heart. A man with a great heart.

The next day, a May day that is like a benediction. An order comes to the brigades for a grand parade—a review of the entire army. A parade, and then a day of rest and celebration. To celebrate . . .

327

All sorts of rumours; but Melrose, a Massachusetts man, says that he carried dispatches to headquarters. He says that it's an alliance with France.

The brigades form, and we talk about it eagerly.

"A great country over the water. A country that has warred with England these many hundreds of years."

"It's La Fayette's doing—it's said that he brought about the alliance himself."

"Mark me, Ben Franklin's the man who had a hand in this. Old Ben himself."

"An army they'll send—an army of ten thousand men."

"Washington in tears, crying like a child. That, I saw myself."

Wayne is laughing like a boy. He has rum served out while the brigades are forming. We stick blossoms and green leaves into our jackets and our hair. The drums beat out Yankee-Doodle, and we sing it as we march down to the parade.

> *Yankee-Doodle went to Boston,*
> *Riding on a pony,*
> *Gave all hell to old man Howe,*
> *Called it macaroni.*

> *Yankee-Doodle keep it up,*
> *Keep the lobsters running,*
> *Let the bastard redcoats know,*
> *Yankee-Doodle's coming!*

We roar it out, and it echoes back from the parade. We cheer Wayne as he rides up and down our ranks. We sing verse after verse.

> *Yankee-Doodle went to hell,*
> *Claimed it was right chilly,*
> *Take six months in Valley Forge,*
> *Hell is willy-nilly.*

> *Yankee-Doodle keep it up,*
> *Keep the lobsters running,*
> *Let the bastard redcoats know*
> *Yankee-Doodle's coming!*

We form on the Grand Parade. Washington rides up with La Fayette and Baron von Steuben. Washington sits on his horse, smiling, his eyes wrinkled up with tears. He waves his hand, awkwardly, and begins to dismount. We break ranks. We press around them, half-mad, trying to touch Washington, to touch Steuben. Steuben is crying, frankly the tears pour down his face. Washington nods his head, like a man in a dream. Steuben says:

"Mine children—mine children—"

We go back to our ranks, staring around us, at the trees, at the green spread of the Grand Parade, at the cloudless blue sky. We are men out of a dream. The winter was a dream. More than one man is weeping quietly as he walks.

On the edge of the parade, the officers' ladies stand; a little away from them, the camp women. They wave at us and nod. They make little splashes of delightful color.

Steuben puts us through a parade drill. Bareheaded, he marches at the front of the Pennsylvania and Massachusetts brigades, waving his sword. He's as happy as a child. He beats his sabre against the ground, in time to our marching. He runs down the line of men, glancing along the ranks, nodding his head with approval. Winded, panting, he stands in the centre of the field, smiling.

He calls Washington at the top of his voice: "Mine commander, vatch—der bayonet movements!"

He walks towards us on his toes, his hands spread out. "Ja—mine children, you vill do it for me! Like I teached you."

He calls for the bayonet charge, names out brigades for flank attack, marshals in the brigades one after another as covering bodies, pivots us, rearranges brigade formation, and laughs like a delighted child.

"Such troops—vere in der vorld do you find such troops? Gott—dey're splendid!"

Washington speaks a few words. He says: "We have made an alliance with France. What we suffered this winter, you know and I know. Nor shall we forget. I thank you from my heart."

He sits on his horse, nodding at us, swallowing hard. He takes off his hat.

The rest of that day we sprawled over the parade, drinking, eating, or lying quietly, soaking in the heat of the sun . . .

The days go slowly, warm days. Lazy days with blue skies overhead. The heavens are a bowl of blue, and Valley Forge is in blossom. The apple trees are like balls of snow, and under the trees the white blossoms make a carpet for the ground. We walk through the woods and try to understand that this is the same place we came into in December.

We have buried the men who died during the winter, and the crosses make long rows along the Schuylkill. I go there with Ely, and we pick out seven of the graves—mark them for our men. Most of the graves are nameless. We mark a grave for the little doctor, and I carve the rhyme on it very painstakingly.

> *He did his work,*
> *He healed the sick,*
> *He did not shirk*
> *To keep men quick.*
> *God rest his soul,*
> *Forgive his sin.*

"They're fair words," Ely says. "A good rhyme for a man to leave behind him."

"He was a strange, hard man."

Charley's grave is a mat of green grass. I am glad that he lies where he does, looking over the gentle hills toward Philadelphia.

One night, we sit and talk. We sprawl outside the dugout, around a fire, Ely and Jacob and myself and half a dozen Pennsylvania men. It is a warm, cloudy night, and a mist rests in the valleys.

"They won't remember long," Ely says. "They'll forget how this winter was."

"It's something to forget."

"It was a hard, cold winter—no such winter before in all the memory of man."

"My father and my grandfather—take back a hundred year—I can't call to mind that men ever spoke of such a winter as this one."

"It's something to forget—to have no bitter memory of."

"The chill is in my bones yet."

"There'll be no getting the chill outa your bones."

Ely says, thoughtfully: "I puzzle sometimes to make out what will come of it."

"War's not a thing for simple men to understand."

"It's like death. There's no thinking of war or death."

But I wonder whether I understood it then, long past when Kenton died, with a vision in his eyes. I have enlisted again—for three years. I can't think of that, only believe; whether or not there is anything to believe, I must believe.

The days go on—a lush heat flowing over the land, until men predict a summer as hot as the winter was cold. Valley Forge is ripe

330

with beauty—a grand, flowing beauty, as soft as the hills. The hills are green, except where the Quaker farmers are turning over the land with their ploughs, and there the red-brown furrows make warm gashes.

Rumours come that we will march soon, but nobody knows where.

The British will leave Philadelphia. They won't attack us. Four or five thousand militiamen have already poured into Valley Forge. Our position is too strong.

We drill and drill and drill. We who have stayed through the winter, the battered Pennsylvania and New Jersey and Massachusetts brigades, are Steuben's pets. He makes soldiers of us. We were never soldiers before. We were a rabble of farmers, retreating all over the country before the British, defeated in every battle we fought. For the first time, we drill until we are like machines. Steuben is tireless; we must become men of iron; he is a fanatic about that.

He says: "Soon, soon, mine children. Ve strike dem vun blow—and den der var is over. Vun qvick blow. Soon—soon."

It comes sooner than we expect. A rider on a lathered horse pounding up the Gulph Road. He rides through the sentries, screaming out something. The hoofbeats echo through the camp. He reins up wildly before headquarters.

Word of the rider goes through camp like fire. Nobody knows what word he brings, but it's taken that he comes from Philadelphia. We gather in groups, talking, guessing.

"The British march on camp . . ."

"They've burned Philadelphia—pulled for New York . . ."

"They've sailed down the Delaware . . ."

Night comes. We build our fires. For the first time, I wonder how these fires appear to the Quaker farmers down in the valleys. Strange men-beasts, who call themselves an army; they came out of the night, in the snow. They'll go back. The Quakers will live on, the way they've lived for a hundred years.

I wake in the night, and I grope for Bess. I mutter: "If we leave here—where will you come back to?" I think of three more years with no woman, three more years. I cry out for Bess, childishly, longingly. I am afraid to be alone.

The next day, the camp is curiously uneasy. In the morning, Steuben drills us. But he's a sullen Prussian for once, and he puts us through the drills mechanically. The sun is a hot red blister in the sky. Steuben marches us back and forth until we are wringing wet.

We lie about the dugouts, discuss rumours. It is certain by now that the British troops have left Philadelphia. For a winter they lay there at their ease, filling their bellies, twenty thousand of them. Twenty thousand men, while three thousand sick beggars starved in the hill country, eighteen miles away. now the word comes that the remaining British troops, ten or twelve thousand, have left Philadelphia to march overland through the Jerseys to New York. The officers say nothing, and we try to piece things out for ourselves. Half the British forces have sailed away. If Washington attacks those who march through Jersey . . .

We look at each other. Only once have American troops defeated the English in battle—that was in Boston, in seventeen-seventy-five, at Bunker Hill, and then we could not hold our ground. Since then, we have been defeated continuously.

"We'll know soon," Ely says. He is oddly calm, as if he had been waiting for this.

"We'll know," Jacob agrees.

The next morning, the order comes for the brigades to march. The order comes to break camp—a place where we have lived for six months.

We are very quiet about it. Working in the dugout, putting our few belongings together, we try to understand that we have lived in this place for half a year. The calm is like a blanket over us. We are breaking camp—going into battle.

I stood in the dugout after Ely and Jacob had gone. I walked around, felt the beds, things we have built with our own hands. I leaned against the low, log walls. I kicked at the few ashes in the fireplace. It was very hot in the dugout then. The morning sun beat down on the roof.

It might have been years ago that we had built it—Clark Vandeer, Henry Lane, Edward Flagg, Kenton Brenner, Charley Green, strong men hewing the life out of trees.

Inside, it had been hell and inferno; inside, I had lain with Bess in my arms—loving a woman. How does a man love a woman and not know?

If I had carved inside, along the logs: Here a soldier of the army, Allen Hale, lay with a girl who was no fit and decent woman—a follower of the camp . . .

The musket rack is empty. One day we had brought the muskets to Wayne, eight muskets. Wayne looked at them. Ely said: "You'll need arms, sir. There's a fair lot of men in camp without arms." Wayne answered, dully: "They belong with the men who used them—they belong—I'll take them. We need arms."

Ely called to me now, and I went outside. I closed the door, threw the latch. It would stay closed; it was a place of the damned, and nobody would molest it. Maybe, after years, a pile of rotten timber covering a mudhole. Men of the revolution lived there—half a year. People would look at it curiously.

"Allen—come," Ely says gently.

We join our brigade. It is a hot day, a burning hot day. The sun is a globe of yellow liquid in a sky of cold blue fire. Wayne walks his horse along our line, smiling, nodding—ragged, lean men, but men drawn fine with suffering. Men who will follow him into hell; men without a fear of hell. No fears left.

He calls out: "Brigades—forward!"

The drums pick up the tune. No other tune. A doggerel and a fit song for an army of beggars. A trumpet joins in, pricking shrill notes at the sky:

> *Yankee-Doodle went to London,*
> *Riding on a pony . . .*

The Pennsylvania brigades step out with the Prussian stiffness Steuben taught them. We march past the assembled Massachusetts and New Jersey lines. We walk past a mass of militia. Sitting on his horse, Steuben nods and nods; his face is twisted up; he can say nothing.

We take up our positions at the head of the army, directly behind Washington's life guard of Virginians. The tall Virginians look back at us and grin:

"Come on, farmers—there's ploughin' tu be done!"

We pick up our song.

> *Yankee-Doodle went to hell,*
> *Claimed it was right chilly . . .*

I look back, and the hills of the encampment are like a lush garden in the summer sun. A little cluster of Quaker farmers and their wives watch us from the parade.

Ely is on one side of me, Jacob on the other. I don't look back again.

22

A CLOUDBURST soaks us, and we march on through the pouring rain. The army is sprawled like a great snake over the hills, each end lost in a mist of rain. When the rain is over, the sun comes out again, stronger than ever. The mud on the road is turned to ripples of hard earth, which gradually powders into a fine dust under our feet. Many of us walk barefooted, and the crumpled dirt of the road feels good to our feet.

The rain soaks our clothes, plastering them to our backs. A film of dust forms all over them; it's unbearable. We drop our coats into the road, then our torn shirts. The musket straps bite into our backs. We strip to the waist, become a strange sight, an army of the naked.

We toil on, and at noon, throw outselves down wearily. We can't eat much. We're strung too fine, nervous, waiting.

Talk is of the enemy. Where are they?—when will we meet them? We hear that the militia is uneasy with fear. We begin to understand why the Pennsylvania brigades march at the head of the army.

"I put no faith in militia," Jacob says. "Whatever comes, we'll drive into it first. If we stand, the militia will stand. But I put no faith in militia to meet an attack."

I feel a curious chill of fear. Life was never so precious or good— after the winter. I lived; all through that winter I lived.

"There'll be a battle, Jacob?"

"There'll be a battle. He cannot keep the militia with him for more than three months."

"The last battle," Ely says oddly.

We both look at him. Ely says, slowly: "I have no love for battle. There's been enough death. I'm sore tired, and wanting to rest. You and me, Jacob—we're no more young. We'll be wanting a long, quiet rest."

"Time for resting," Jacob says. "There'll be time enough afterwards for rest."

We march on—a forced march. The wagon train and the camp followers are left far in the rear. We're chasing something. We drag along, and the drum-beat seems lost in a fog of dust. Blood begins to speckle the road—from the naked feet. When a rest is called, we drop in our tracks, too weary to talk.

It rains again the next day, a solid wall of water, drawn out of the sodden heat. We cross the Delaware River, and come into a country of tall pines and barren sand dunes. The pine smell is heavy and sickening. The mosquitoes buzz in thick droning flocks, biting us until we are covered all over with welts. Sweat drips into our eyes, into our mouths. We are coated with dust.

Wayne laughs and says: "You'll scare the enemy. There'll be no need to fight."

We're not pretty. We've become haunted by a spectre of battle. No rest until we come up with the enemy. We begin to long for the enemy, for anything that will relieve us.

We camp that night in the dunes, build our fires between the pines. We cook, and then sprawl away from the fires. It's cool nowhere. The sand itself is hot, and it doesn't lose any heat during the night. The heat is burnt into everything.

It's difficult for us to breathe. The heavy air, clouded with pine smell, is like a solid thing. It clings to our lungs.

One of the men, a dispatch rider for Wayne, comes over to where we are lying. He was stationed outside the tent where the staff officers were at council.

We ask him for news. Do we march? Do we ever leave this godforsaken Jersey land?

"They're fighting among themselves, the officers. They've been squabbling for hours. Lee wants no battle."

"He's a fair wise soldier, Charles Lee."

"He's no man for leading; he's a sickening man to look at."

"Washington's nigh mad—sitting and muttering that he's alone—no man but Hamilton and Wayne and Steuben to follow him. He's like a man in a dream, Washington, sitting there and muttering, Why aren't you with me? Do I have to be alone? It's too much to be alone."

"Where are the British?"

"Somewhere in the Jerseys. It's said there's a train of them fifteen miles long—half the people in Philadelphia with them, maybe two thousand Philadelphia wenches to lie with them each night."

"Wayne wants battle—"

"It's Wayne's story that he'll go into battle with Pennsylvania men. He says the whole army can go to hell and be damned—he'll go into battle with his Pennsylvania men."

"He's no man to plan a battle—too hot."

"He's sits muttering, Fight—God damn you, fight. God-damn cowards, the lot of you. Lee says he'll take no words like that, and Wayne says he's a lying bastard if he'll swallow any words of his for Lee. Washington tries to soothe them, and Hamilton swears the lot of them are playing treason. Lee calls Hamilton a Jew—and Hamilton's fair ready to kill Lee. They fight like cats and dogs."

"There's no man among them with his mind made up?"

"It's Washington's idea to fight."

"He can't hold the army together for another battle. We're eight — nine thousand strong now. He'll fight now — or come a month there'll be no army."

We march again the next day. Wayne dismounts and walks with us. He's a man burning with rage — tireless, pacing up and down the line, spurring us on. There's no sign of rain, no cloud in the sky, only a blue fire with a concentrated red fire in the centre of it. We trail between the pines, drag outselves over sand dunes that give under our feet, curse the swarms of mosquitoes, fight blindly through the dust that rises the length of the army.

There's no rest. Hour after hour — forward. The men who started out barefooted have raw, bleeding feet now. The sand blisters our feet, burns them. Between the sun and the dirt, we are burnt black, our faces stubbled with beard again, our skin welted all over with mosquito bites.

Ely is taking it hard. Jacob, a thin wraith of a man, marches with the smouldering fire of a fanatic in his eyes. Jacob is the soul of the revolution, uncomplaining, tireless, fire that will burn steadily until it is blown out. But Ely's feet are cut to pieces again, swollen. They have never fully healed from the winter. They bleed steadily, in spite of our bandaging.

Once, when dropped to rest, Ely gasped: "This is the last march, Allen."

"No — you've been through a lot worse than this, Ely. We rest soon."

He said, not bitterly: "I'm tired. I've carried a load, Allen — a great deal of a load."

Job Andrews, sitting near us, said: "It's hard, tired marching for an old man."

"An old man," Ely nodded, smiling a little.

"You're noways old."

"Old enough, Allen. I'm thinking to give these poor feet of mine a rest soon. A long rest."

We stumble on. Night, and we drop in our tracks. We have no strength to build fires. We fall asleep in brigade formation, toss on the hot sand, gasp for breath. With dawn, we're up and fighting our way north.

Men drop out of line. They clutch at their eyes, reel, stagger a few steps, and crumple to the sand. They lie in huddled bundles and the brigades crawl past them. We're caked with dirt—horrid black, sunburnt figures.

We come to a Hessian's body. A man dead with heat. What with their seventy pounds of uniform and equipment, the heat is more than they can stand. They die like flies. His bright green uniform is streaked with dirt and slime. He lies on his back, eyes open, face swollen shapeless by mosquito poison. He's a strange, lonely figure, a reminder of the enemy we haven't seen for six months. Some of the men pause to drag his boots off.

We go on, and now we know that they're fleeing from us. It's a fantastic, bizarre thing. For six months they could have wiped us out with a single blow. Now they're fleeing from filthy, naked beggars.

We see more and more Hessians dead of the heat. They sprawl directly on the road, or they lie crumpled to either side of it. Their green uniforms make splotches of colour on the sand. It's difficult to understand how they could have marched even a mile with those heavy uniforms. We tear off their boots. We laugh, and some of the naked Pennsylvania farmers wear the high Hessian hats. But not for long.

We see a Fusilier. We stop and stare at his red coat, at the gold facings. A uniform fit for a king.

"But warm," somebody says. "He could noways carry such a warm coat. Poor fellow's dead of a little bit of heat."

"He should have been at Valley Forge. He'd not be minding a spot of sun."

"I could have used such a pretty red jacket this winter. It fair breaks my heart to pass it by."

Things break out of the haze of dust suddenly. The drums have stopped. We appear to be crawling through a sea of dust. The Virginians have spread out to scout the advance. Their voices come hollowly from nowhere.

"All's well—all's well—all's well—"

"A ravine—a dozen feet deep."

"A ridge of sand."

We come to an overturned cart, one of the British wagon train. A broken axle threw it on its side, and two broken trunks spill women's clothes onto the sand. We hand the clothes round, lace petticoats, lace and silk jackets, a gown.

"My Annie could wear this."

"Your Annie's back with the militia. They're no men to demand lace petticoats."

More men dead of the heat, horses whimpering as they die in the sand. In one place a dozen Hessians lie together, their glassy eyes rolled upward, no longer afraid of the sun.

The pines are endless, tall bare pines that in some places make a complete roof over our heads. There will be an open space, a hundred paces across, rolling sand dunes grown with weeds, then the pines again. There is no forgetting the hot, languid smell of the pines. The sand has no grasp for our feet. It burns them up. Our feet slip, we sprawl, we pick ourselves up. Next to me, Ely is a dogged machine, his eyes glazed. I give him an arm to help him along. He thanks me in a hoarse whisper.

We camp for the night. A thunderstorm drenches us, puts out the few fires we attempt to build. We lie like animals, dumb in our misery.

Word goes round that the British are near us. Faintly, the sound of a trumpet comes to us. Wayne stalks through the Pennsylvania brigades, putting us in a position to resist an attack if it comes. We drag logs to make breastworks, sleeping on our feet, stumbling over the logs and falling prone.

Not far from us, Washington pitches his tent. We watch the officers from other brigades riding up to the council—Varnum, Steuben, Charles Lee, Greene, Lord Stirling. They crowd into the tent, and their figures move against the light as shadows.

For what seems to be hours their tired voices bicker back and forth. We hear Wayne crying hysterically: "Fight—fight—for the love of God, can't you see it's all over if you don't fight? We'll never have this chance again—fifteen miles of half-dead soldiers and whores strung out across the country! We strike one blow—and the war's over! Only one blow! Look at my men out there! Do you think they'll suffer another winter like the last? Do you think you'll have an army a month from now if you don't fight?"

Washington's voice, soothing him, like a weary father.

And from Hamilton: "Sir—I'm sick of this, sick of this. You can have my commission."

Lee's shrill tones: "You'd ruin everything! Sir, is this an army commanded by children—or by men? I'll have no young whelp like Hamilton instruct me—"

"Sir, you'll answer for that!"

"Please—please—for the sake of your brigades, gentlemen, quietly. There's no need to roar."

Their voices drop to a murmur. We come closer to the tent. We lie in the sand, listening, listening. On and off, I doze. Each time I open my eyes—the voices from the tent. La Fayette's broken English:

"Can eet be? Can anything be so shameful? I weel not weesh to live, sirs, eef we don' strike."

"Strike—strike! By God, with what? With those broken beggars out there?"

"Sir, I'll answer for my brigades?" Wayne cries. "I'll answer for the beggars! I'll go into hell with those beggars! Only give me a chance."

Steuben: "Dey're goot men—by Gott, dey're goot men to fight mit."

Finally, the council breaks up. The officers come out of the tent, mount their horses, and go back to their brigades. Washington stands at the entrance to the tent, talking softly with Wayne and Hamilton. His face is years older, thin, a face of large bones with skin stretched tight over them.

Washington shakes hands with the two officers—goes back to his tent then. Hamilton stands there, his deep violet eyes looking at nothing at all. Wayne walks over to the breastworks, sits on the stump of a tree and stares at the ground.

Captain Muller goes over to him, waits expectantly. "Tomorrow, sir?" he asks.

"Tomorrow will answer a lot of things."

"We fight?"

Wayne nods—without glancing up.

I am on watch with Ely. We walk a little way from the breastworks and stand there, looking into the dark. The night is deep and silent, a hot, windless night.

"A strange forest," Ely says. "A forest of the dead with its roots in sand. I was thinking to look at the Mohawk again, to walk between green, soft trees."

"Maybe we'll go back soon. Maybe after the battle tomorrow . . ."

"You're afraid, Allen," Ely says gently.

I nod.

"You're thinking of Kenton and the rest of them."

"Of Kenton. If Kenton curses me for the shame of dying on a gibbet—"

"Kenton's dead. It seems to me, Allen, that the dead rest in peace. A deep peace back there on the hills where we left them. There's no shame. It's peace and a rest for a tired body."

"When I look forward to it—to battle and more battle, to more winters like this winter past, if the war goes on for years. I'm fair sick of war, Ely. I'm fair longing to have one day come after another without the beat of drums. I think of that little girl who came running to us from the Virginian men. She was no fit woman to be a man's

339

wife, Ely—but that's what she wanted. It seems to me, now, that I had a full love for her, and that I wouldn't have hesitated too much to make her my wife. It would have been a peaceful way of things to make her my wife, Ely, to look for the sun-up as a day of planting, to see brown dirt turn up under the plough and to come back at night to a wife who doesn't ask too much of a man."

"There'll be none of that," Ely says. "I wouldn't hurt you, Allen— you're all to me. I never had a son, Allen, and I think sometimes that you're a son to me. But there'll be none of that—no rest. I deny you rest, Allen, and I'll be resting soon. But you can't rest. My day is over. Yours is beginning."

I look at him, shaking my head.

"You'll come out of the war, Allen, with broken pieces to put together. There'll be years of war for strong men—and you'll be strong. Then you'll put broken pieces together, and there'll be no rest—no peace."

"What then?"

"Maybe a belief sometimes that the dream is coming true. We're not fighting the British. We're fighting for a great, fair stretch of land—out to the west. A different kind of people on that land, Allen. A free land."

"I don't know," I say. "I'm tired, Ely."

"Believe me," he says.

I try to sleep that night. I try to find Bess and draw her to me. But there's nothing—only a struggle without end, a groping for ideals that are empty. I try to believe, the way Ely believes, the way Jacob believes.

23

WE WAKE with dawn. Wayne seems not to have slept at all; he is walking up and down our line, nodding, looking at our guns, whispering to us, though there is no need to whisper. He's nervous, and the sweat rolls off his face.

We strip for battle—naked to the waist, many of us barefooted and without stockings, many of us wearing no breeches, only a tattered sort of kilt. The brigade captains call monotonously:

"Measure loads—measure out your loads. Dry your powder pans and keep them dry. Any man with less than twenty rounds of ammunition report immediately. Try your guns and see that they spark."

Files are passed up and down, and men put edges on their flints. I spark mine, and it seems to fall dull. My hands are wet and shaking. I take a file and attempt to edge my flint. Ely takes it from me and sharpens my flint with two deft strokes, roughens the steel. Ely is wonderfully calm, his face sad and a little puzzled. Jacob's eyes are hot and burning; he seems to have a fever.

Wayne can't stop moving. "Bayonets," he calls. "Fix your bayonets—bolt your bayonets!" He tries a gun and then throws it aside. He acts like a man gone mad.

We count our loads. I measure the powder in my horn, mechanically. I sift some of it through my fingers. It's dry, but my fingers are wet. I'm wet all over, my breeches plastered to my legs. A film of water covers my body.

I finger my musket nervously. "Load," Jacob says. "Load her careful, Allen. It's the first load that measures a man's life. If she don't spark the first time, she won't spark."

I load the musket. It's an old musket with a large bore—my father's. I load it with a heavy charge and three balls. I say to Ely anxiously: "Three balls—that's not too much?"

"She's a strong musket, Allen."

"I'm sick, Ely—sick and gone. I feel like sitting down and just resting. I'm in no way to move, Ely."

"It's not your first battle," Jacob says shortly.

"It's seven months since we've been to battle—"

"Easy, boy, easy," Ely murmurs.

"Three balls is a fair heavy load for a musket," I say doubtfully.

We form our lines. The word is still being called: "Dry pans and measure loads . . ."

Some of the men are munching on salt meat. I feel empty, terribly hungry. I go to my pack and get a piece of meat, but Jacob strikes it out of my hand.

"You'll be thirsty enough."

"I'm bitter hungry."

"You don't want to eat," one of the men tells me. "It's a rotten thing to have a bullet in your belly after you eat."

The officers are clustered around Washington. Wayne is arguing. Charles Lee stalks away in a rage; they are going into battle against his advice. Then Washington calls him back. Hamilton is sulking alone by the tent. Steuben can't keep away from the men.

"Mine children—you vill remember . . ."

The sun is just rising. A splatter of light fans the tops of the pines. No wind. Even at that hour of the morning, it is unbearably hot. The smell of powder, of sweating men, mingles with the odour of the pines. We move uneasily and stare at our muskets as if we had never seen them before.

Suddenly, Wayne goes to his horse, mounts, and rides to the head of the line. La Fayette follows him. Lee is calling something after them. Then Lee mounts too, and the order comes down the line to march. Wayne is leaning over his saddle, talking anxiously to a tall Virginian scout. Washington watches us, his face clouded. Lee rides off to one side, speaking to no one, his strange, ugly face contorted in anger. An ugly man, his ugliness burns in him. A professional soldier, he was respected at least for his professional advice until Steuben came. Now Steuben advises battle, and Washington has overruled Lee's plea not to fight. His hatred for Hamilton, for La Fayette, for Wayne is plain enough.

We march quickly, as if Wayne were eager to get into whatever lies ahead of us. It's damnably hot. We thread our way through the pines and then through woods of birch and maple. We go down into a ravine, form again on the other side. Wayne wheels the brigades, and now we march spread out like the broad end of a fan. We are in a wood. As yet, we have made no contact with the enemy.

We go through the wood, a distance on a road, and then down and out of another ravine. The bottom of the ravine is mud. We sink into it to our knees, suck our feet out, claw through. The mud splashes us from head to foot. The brigade commanders call out to each other, and Wayne waves his sword, trying to keep us in battle line. Lee's white horse, streaked all over, is struggling through the mud. He rides without looking back at us, sitting in his saddle wearily and indifferently.

We have been marching for at least an hour now, maybe more than that. I have no sense of time, but when I look up, I can see the sun through the trees. The bottom of the ravine is less hot than the road; the road was a furnace.

I stumble, and Jacob helps me up. He says: "Stay close to me, Allen—we'll get by. Stay close to me."

Wayne's voice, crying: "Powder dry—powder dry—for God's sake, keep your guns out of that mud."

As an echo: "Watch your powder pans—keep your flints clean—"

Our brigade is climbing out of the ravine, men wet to their waists with mud. We stumble up through the trees, and hear a flurry of shots.

342

It means that our scouts have come into contact with the British rear-guard.

As we are, on the slope, with the ravine full of mud to our backs, we're in a trap. The body of the army is beyond us, perhaps a mile to the rear. It comes like a flash of red fire in our brains; we stop; we stare at one another, our mouths open. I think of getting back out of the ravine—only out of the ravine. I guess we all think of that.

Wayne spurs his horse along our front, screaming madly for us to go ahead. "To the top!" he screams. "Climb to the top!"

I wonder dully how we could have come here, who placed us in a trap like this. Like cattle—to be caught in the mud and shot down.

Ely is shaking his head, like a man in a dream.

Jacob is cursing and screaming along with Wayne. He is ahead of the rest of us, clawing his way up. He seems to slide up through the trees—no volition of his own—slide up through the trees.

We go ahead—as if Wayne were drawing us. Stumbling, falling, we climb the hill, come out on top, drag ourselves forward with our muskets and make a line. More and more men. We make a line, and then we see the Virginian scouts running back through the trees, beyond them a glint of red.

The British drumbeat wakes the morning air into waves of heat. It throbs into our heads, pulses through the ground. It turns over and over, like wheels rolling, beats our thoughts into oblivion, seems an incarnation of the heat. Wayne, dismounted, dashes along the line, pleading:

"Hold them here—hold them here!"

Charles Lee, on his white, mud-splashed horse, reins up, cries: "We have to get out of here, General—we have to get out of here. We're like rats in a trap. We have to retreat."

Wayne screams: "Sir—you can retreat—you can retreat to hell, sir!"

"I'm in command!"

"You can go to hell, sir" Wayne sobs.

The British are less than a hundred yards away now, marching in three columns, their muskets presented, their bayonets glittering in the sun. The drums waver from a marching beat to a light, rippling rhythm, a rhythm of heat laughing at us. They come on steadily.

I try to count them—how many? Their lines are endless. The entire rear of the British army is marching to attack a few Pennsylvania and New England brigades. Where is the army? What kind of fools' sacrifice are we?

We don't know what to do. Lee is in command. Lee has given an order to retreat. La Fayette and Wayne are raging like madmen—screaming for us to hold our lines. Down the line, Scott stands and shakes his head. We are under the spell of the heat. We are still in a dream of the hell at Valley Forge—heat for cold. Hell is hot; hell is cold. Some of the men drop their muskets and bolt back into the ravine. Some of the men let go their muskets and stand watching the British—dumb. We have forgotten how to be an army, how to do anything but suffer.

We suffer now; we suffer in retrospect. We're bound up in ourselves. As a parade across our eyes are the days and nights in the dugouts, the nights in the freezing cold when we stood on sentry duty, the days when we lay like sodden beasts, starving. The dead who were piled like logs in the snow—unburied. The weight of a nation unborn on the shoulders of men—who are no more than men. We have not the power to suffer as women suffer, to give birth out of agony and rise full and new from the bed of pain. We have not the power to see beyond our sufferings, to make dreams from pain. There are no dreams from pain; we're lost men, conquered men.

The British come on, and we hear the officers speaking commands in sharp, clear voices. Strange voices. Accents of another land, another world. They're on parade, the British soldiers, men without fear, men marching to victory.

And a sobbing voice, the voice of Wayne—who understands now, who will no more ask giant deeds from men who are not giants. The voice of Wayne who sees a spectre of Valley Forge rising to overwhelm him. Wayne grows; Wayne is a man without fear, a madman without fear. But bigger than Wayne is a picture of men becoming beasts, men trying to drag themselves out of hell.

We're in hell, Wayne with us, Lee cursed by the doom he brought on himself, the men leaderless.

Fifty paces from us, the British form for the bayonet charge. We can see them very clearly now, each face under the high, pointed hat, the gold on their red uniforms. I can see one man's mouth move as he chews a wad of tobacco. I can see the drummers, spraying their roll. I can see their powder cases flap against their sides as they march. I can see one man's yellow hair waving from beneath his hat.

We begin to fire. Men let off their muskets wildly, without aim, without reason. A few of the British fall to the ground. I see one man clutch at his belly, stagger out of line and sit down with his back against a tree. The rest of them begin to run toward us. Their bayonets flutter like a line of fire, and their red coats are fire beyond their bayonets. Their muskets roar, and they smash out of the smoke.

I fire my musket. For some reason I am surprised at its recoil against my shoulder. Suddenly, I am alone with Ely. Jacob lies on the ground, on his back, a hole in his head. In that instant, I see and understand Jacob. Jacob who lived like a torch, who went out like a torch. Jacob, who was beyond men, beyond Wayne, beyond Washington, Jacob who was the single purpose of the revolution. I see others beyond Jacob, there must be others. What Ely meant when he spoke to me, told me there would be no peace, no rest . . .

Ely is pulling me away. The English are almost up on us, their bayonets sweeping like a scythe. A Virginian scout, ahead of us, is cut down, four bayonets in him while he swings with his clubbed rifle. They have no bayonets, the Virginians—only their long, small-bore rifles.

With a great strength, Ely is pulling me through the pines. We run together, blindly, falling, picking ourselves up. There are other men in front of us, naked men, running, crying out like frightened beasts, falling, hurtling into trees—bruised, bloodly, panic-stricken men without thought and in the grip of only one idea—to get away from the merciless line of English bayonets, to get out of the path of the scythe.

We come to the edge of the ravine, stumble down into it. There, on the edge, I have one brief picture of Wayne, a man on a horse—sobbing. He cries out: "What does it mean? What does it mean? Where are my troops? My men?"

We roll down the slope, crash against trees. We struggle through the mud. The morass is full of men—filthy, panic-stricken wretches. They mill around blindly. I am as blind as any; I try to make for the farther bank, but Ely pulls me back.

The British have formed on the top, and they are shooting mercilessly, picking off the men as they come out of the mud and try to scramble up the farther bank. In spite of that, hundreds of them break through. I point, I cry to Ely:

"We'll go that way, Ely!"

Ely drags me through the mud, down the ravine. I see one man, just ahead of me, pitch forward, as if struck by a hammer blow on the back. He tries to steady himself, wavers, falls, and sinks into the mud. I watch fascinated as bullets strike the mud, splash. I know this place; I have been in Inferno before.

Down the ravine, a few hundred men stand waist-deep in the mud, Pennsylvania brigades. Somehow, they've gathered there, and the officers are trying to beat them into a sort of order.

We go toward them, merge ourselves in their ranks. It gives me a feeling of security and order to see men standing around me and firing their muskets.

The rout goes on before our eyes, as if we were an audience and a stage of fear-maddened men were set before us. Step by step, we retreat down the ravine, our steps to the tone of the brigade commanders:

"Load—wipe your pans—clean your flints—load easy and fire."

I ram my musket. All of a sudden, I am calm, as if a great fire inside of me had stilled itself. I stand there, wondering why I should have run before, why I should be afraid of anything. What can hurt me? What can bring me pain? Death is rest. There's no other rest for me. Inside, I am cold as ice, in spite of the hellish heat.

Ely says to me: "Jacob's dead." He says it dully, as if he didn't quite understand.

"He's dead," I say coldly. "He wouldn't have lived through this. It's the way for him—to be dead."

"God rest him . . ."

"There's rest for Jacob now."

I load carefully. It's almost terrifying, the calm that has come over me. I load as if I were on parade. We are still moving down the ravine, close—I don't know how many of us, maybe three or four hundred. Muller is there—two more officers. Muller stands out in front of us, cool. The man has courage.

The British attempt to cross the ravine, but we sweep them with our flanking fire. I see the red coats stain with mud, fall, bubble down through the mud, try to crawl out of it. The ravine fills with smoke, and men move through that smoke like ghosts. From above, the British snipe us, but they are not good shots. Here and there a man groans, falls in the mud, struggles to bring himself up, struggles against the mud that is choking him.

I load like a machine, aim carefully, trying to find a target in the smoke, trying to pick out a red or green uniform. I wonder about the army. Have they deserted us? Forgotten us? Have they lost us? Don't they hear the sounds of the battle? Where is Wayne? Where is La Fayette—Charles Lee? Where are Steuben and the artillery? Where are the thousands of militiamen?

Was it too much for Wayne and La Fayette to see that they had made a mistake, that men are only human, that men are not beasts to kill one another without fear, without compulsion? Was it too much for them to understand what Valley Forge did to us?

346

We fight our way down the ravine. Time has no meaning any more. For an eternity, we draw our feet out of the clinging mud, put our feet down again, load until the muskets burn our hands. The heat is unbearable—a clinging, a solid wall of heat, heat taking form.

The sniping goes on. The British hang onto us like flies, and their bullets patter into the mud. Muller is only a few feet from me when a bullet strikes him. I see Ely go to him, attempt to raise him. He shakes himself loose, cries: "I'm dying, damn you! Can't you see?"

I watch him settle into the mud, thinking vaguely that there will be no burial—no stone or bit of crossed wood to mark his place. No rhyme to tell his virtues, whether he lived a good or a bad man. Nothing. After a while, not even a memory in the minds of others. He went alone.

We keep on, desperately, guided by the strange, purposeless drive that animates men sometimes. We come to the end of the ravine, make our way out onto solid ground. The firing has fallen off round us. Some of the men wander off, aimlessly. I call them back—surprised at the sound of my voice. I beat them into line, and they obey my commands. Ely stares at me, oddly. I tell him:

"Keep them together! Can't you see we have to stay together?"

He nods, dully. I lead the men through high grass, along a hedgerow. The roar of the battle is off to our right—a huge sound, rising and falling, nearing suddenly and then retreating from us, a sound interspersed with the booming of cannon. The cannon are sharp and clear, the roaring of angry beasts.

It's hot out here, much hotter than it was in the ravine. Nothing to shield us from the sun; the sun is part of the enemy. I look behind at the men trailing after me, a few hundred exhausted men—hot, filthy, listless. I wonder why I'm leading them. Where are the brigade commanders? I saw Muller fall; Muller is dead. But there should be others. I look for them. I ask Ely:

"Where is Captain Dean—Marcy?"

He shakes his head.

"Gainbroe?"

He keeps shaking his head.

There is an orchard ahead of us, an old barn and an apple orchard. There are men there—half-naked men like ourselves, hundreds of them, crouched over their guns.

"Rhode Island men," Ely says.

"They're waiting for the attack," I think to myself. "They're waiting like that. They don't know what an attack is—so they're waiting."

347

I see a man come riding toward us, a man covered with mud and blood. I tell the men behind me to halt. They stand there, dazed, staring at me, their mouths open, their breath coming hard.

I cry: "Sit down—damn you, sit down and rest! Talk! You're not dead!"

The man dismounts, and through the mud I recognize Wayne. He says: "What men are these? Who are you?"

"The Fourteenth Pennsylvania, sir—what's left of it. The rest are Pennsylvania men too, I guess,'"

"How did you get here?"

"We fought through the ravine—after the retreat. We came out there—through that wood."

"Where are your officers?"

"Dead—"

"Who led you out?"

"After they died, sir? I led the men. There wasn't a lot of leading to do."

Wayne stares at me, nods. He says brokenly: "You're my men—all my men. You fought out of there alone—alone. Christ! I rode off with a retreat, and you covered it. Where are your officers, sir? Tell me."

"They're dead."

"What's your name?"

"Allen Hale."

I can see him searching his memory. He's sick with heat. He keeps rubbing his eyes, and his hands are full of blood. He shakes his head. "Allen Hale—you were tried for murder—"

"I was tried for murder."

"I know," he whispers. He looks at the men, sprawled out behind me. He says: "Take the brigade—"

"I don't want the brigade, sir."

"God damn you, do you think I want you for an officer? I said take the brigade. I brevet you captain. You'll lead those men—or I swear to God, I'll kill you where you stand."

I looked at him, stared into his bloodshot eyes for just a moment; then I nodded.

I said: "I'll lead the brigade, sir. I'll lead them into hell, sir."

He repeated it, tonelessly: "You'll lead them into hell." He said: "Form them behind that stone wall at the edge of the orchard. Go over their guns. They'll address you as Captain Hale—you'll command that. Prepare to resist any attack, as long as you have a man left."

"Yes, sir."

348

He held out his hand, but I didn't take it. I stood there watching his cold, blue eyes.

He looked at me a moment, turned on his heel then and walked to his horse.

I went to the men. They had heard Wayne. They were studying me curiously. Ely kept his eyes on me. His face was the face of a man who is in a dream—who knows that he dreams and that he'll never wake out of that dream. I said evenly:

"You're to form as a brigade. I'm in command of you. You're to address me as Captain Hale."

Nobody answered. Some of them nodded.

"Brigade—attention! Form in fours!"

They climbed to their feet, formed in line, dragging their guns. I marched them over to the stone wall and showed them their places behind it.

"You will load—prepare to return fire. I'll give the command to fire."

I go over to Ely and sit down on the wall. The rocks are hot. The sun is dropping pellets of flame. The sweat runs off me, grooving lines in the dirt that covers my body. I look out over the field to where the battle is going on. Our main army is still behind us. The British will have to sweep us out of the way. I think of all that, and yet my thoughts are something apart from me. Inside I am cold and empty; my thoughts come out of that emptiness.

Ely says: "So they've made you a captain, Allen."

"They've made me a captain."

There is no emotion inside of me, but I find that I am crying. I taste the hot salt tears with my tongue.

24

THE morning passes, and we wait. They will attack some time—or never. Behind us, across the Wenrock Brook, General Greene has massed the army to throw off any attack. But meanwhile we are to hold off the British. We are to hold them off until they have exhausted themselves upon us, and then we are to let them roll over us—to be defeated by the massed Continental army, when it forms. We are a thin line of men behind a hedgerow and a stone wall. We have been fighting all morning—fighting in hell. We have sweated out all the water that is in us. We are bone-dry, fleshless, naked men. We are weary to death. We are three brigades formed into one, and God only knows what we will be tonight.

We lie behind the stone wall, in the burning sun. The men crouch close to the wall, seeking shade, but the sun is almost directly overhead, and there is no shade. They plead with me to let them go to the brook and drink.

I hold my musket and say: "I'll kill any man who moves from this wall." Yet I wonder who is saying it. Who is Allen Hale? Ely looks at me, almost with fear; but had he expected anything else? Hadn't he known? Hadn't he formed me for this, destroying himself? Now Jacob was dead. At the beginning—with a bloody round hole in his head. There are two men left, Ely and myself; and there is no rest for me.

The battle rolls toward us. We stare at the long lines of redcoats, at the Hessians in their green uniforms. A play that we are watching.

I count the cannon shots. I try to study the field. I don't allow myself to remain still, to fall into the dull apathy that precedes sleep. I walk up and down the line, looking at muskets, feeling the powder pans, warning men to keep their wet hands from their flints. I speak out, and the words are strange to me as they come from my lips:

"Don't handle your flints. Keep your muskets in the sun. Keep your muskets dry. Let your powder bake in the sun. Hot powder is better than cold. Loosen your ramrods—loosen your ramrods."

Ely watching me—always watching me—his eyes never off me for a moment. I have an impulse to say to him: "Why, why don't you understand? For the love of Christ—if you don't understand, who will? Must I be alone—like Jacob, like Washington, men crying out in their loneliness, men impelled by fire and letting no man touch them for fear they will lose some of the fire? You're left—you're the only one! You planned this for me! Jacob's dead."

But I say nothing to him, and it comes to me that I'll never speak to Ely again. I've left Ely. I've left him behind, and there's no going back to him. As Wayne understood us this morning, when he saw his picked corps—his beloved Pennsylvanians—melt away like a pack of frightened deer, in that way I understand Wayne now. I understand Washington. There's no joy in that, no achievement. I'm cold inside—and empty.

They form for attack. Afterwards, I learn that these are the Royal Fusiliers who are attacking us. That they are picked men, the sons of the noble families of England, the finest soldiers in the world. That they are men without fear.

I don't know that now. I see a column of English soldiers marching to sweep us out of the way. They have detached themselves from the main body, and they come across the fields, boldly and bravely. They hold their muskets at salute, and they march the way men march on parade. I have never seen such marching, and I recognize the perfected thing which Steuben tried so vainly to teach us. But we are not soldiers, and we will never march like that. We are farmers, naked, filthy man-things. I cry it to myself; I speak it to myself the way I would sing a song I loved: we are not soldiers. We will never march as they march. We are farmers. We are free men, and we know fear—we know hate and suffering. We are weak the way men are weak. We can fight only for what is ours, only for what is ours.

I notice how the men are staring at the English column. It has a fascination for them. It is unreal, lifeless. It has no association with life. We are a part of life, and we know only things that are a part of life. But this is no part of life, this column of men marching into the face of our guns with perfect precision, with drums beating and with fifes playing. I recognize the tune they play—"Hot Stuff"—the tune they played when they marched up Bunker Hill.

For myself, I destroy the fascination, the illusion. There's enough ice inside of me to destroy it. These are men—men out of the other world—to be destroyed. Ice inside of me to destroy them. I walk up and down our line, speaking softly:

"Hold your fire—hold your fire. No man is to shoot until I give the word. I'll kill any man who leaves the ranks. Keep down; keep out of sight. Don't watch them."

I see a boy, no more than a boy, a lean farm lad, rising to his feet, staring with his mouth wide. I crash my open hand into his face.

"Get down! Behind the wall! Don't watch them! Keep under the wall."

Wayne is behind us, sitting on his horse, smiling a little, a man of ice—a man who is all ice. He bends his head at me, but I don't want his praise. I turn my back on him, stand behind the wall watching the English.

They are very close to us now, still they have not moved their muskets from parade position. With each step, the long line of bayonets sways, a crop of shining, shimmering steel. A drummer walks at one end of the line, his hat pushed back on his head, his head moving to the rhythm of his drum. He carries a high, English military drum, gold bands at top and bottom, a crown and lions on the side of it. He has a broad grin on his face, and he struts as he plays his sticks.

351

Their officers march out in front, sabres bared. They turn some-times, glancing back at their men, as if they were reviewing the column on parade, swinging on their heels.

It seems that for a moment the battle has paused—to watch this, to watch a single regiment of young, fearless fools sweep a lot of farm louts out of their way.

I say to myself, This is England—this is all of Europe. This is what we are fighting, this crass contempt of man, this laughing contempt of the life of man, of the soul of man, of man's right to live, to know sim-ple things and to be happy with simple things—to have no man over him. I say to myself, This is what we shall be fighting always, time without end. The fight will go on, and there will be no rest. We are life. Naked, starving, dirty farmers are life. They, out there—they are a laughing contempt for life. I tell myself that.

They are very close to us, none of them much more than boys—laughing, flinging jokes at each other with a twist of the head. They show their teeth, hold their heads high. Their clean-shaven, clean-cut faces laugh contempt at us, contempt at death, contempt at life. They've lost life; they've lost fear. They've lost the power to suffer and endure and exist. They're of the past. They are magnificent, but their magnificence doesn't touch me. What is that to me, who have spent a winter in hell, who have seen men die, men who were the blood and soul of me?—Kenton Brenner, who died in shame so that I might live; Charley Green; Aaron Levy—a Jew who had come five thousand miles to die with a dream that some day men might be free; Jacob Eagen, a man of flame and selfless in that flame; Edward Flagg, a farmer who went because he believed in something. The Fusiliers are to be pitied, but I don't pity them. How can I pity them? I walked into the log hos-pital at Valley Forge and saw a thousand men dying in hell; and the hell was theirs before ever they were dead. I saw nameless men piled in the snow, because the ground was frozen like iron. They were meat for the wolves that roamed the camp, and they didn't die smiling. They died clinging to life, wanting life. They were the blood of men who had always clung to life, who recognized the life of man, the free, beautiful life of man as the only holy thing on God's earth. They died crying out for life. They didn't throw life away.

One of the officers, marching in advance, turns, shouts a command. The field of bayonets sweeps to a horizontal position. The laughing boys break into a run . . .

I cry out: "Now—now—give them hell!"

The Pennsylvania farmers rise up—naked, mud-streaked figures.

Their wide-bore muskets belch fire. The hedgerow and the wall burn with a sheet of fire: A blasting, crackling sheet of fire that mingles with the screaming of men. The red line of Royal Fusiliers is a tangled mass of screaming, dying men. Their laughing voices are hoarse with the agony of death. They claw at their bellies and retch blood. They stumble, try to run. Their line is broken, shattered. They give back and back, distorted broken figures through the smoke. Or they crawl forward to the wall where the Pennsylvania farmers brain them with clubbed muskets.

I scream: "Load—load again! Stay behind the wall and load again! Stay behind the wall! Load again! Dry your flints!"

I hear Wayne's voice, as from far off: "Reload—prepare to fire!"

The smoke lifts. They are standing out there on the field, beyond the wreckage of shattered bodies. Their officers form them into ranks. The drummer, half his drum shattered, beats a dull roll. Their courage is beyond reason, beyond life. They form calmly, and again they are on parade. One of their officers walks towards us, stepping backwards until he is no more than thirty yards from the stone wall. He addresses his men in clipped English tones, his voice trembling between rage and pride.

We hear his words clearly: "—peasantry—do men of blood turn their backs?"

They come toward us again. The sun is burning down. We run sweat. I can see how our men are sweating. There is no moisture left in their dry, lean bodies, yet they sweat.

I beat them down under the wall. "Don't look—don't look. No man show his face!"

They are on parade, forcing themselves to smile. They swing their feet and kick up the dust. They laugh. They are glorious, but we have seen death that is not glorious—too much.

Their officer walks ahead of them until he is within ten yards of the wall. Then he stands there, his sword at salute, looking at me and smiling his contempt. I don't hate him. I feel a thrill of savage pleasure in that—in the fact that I am beyond hate. He is part of what must go. I know only that, that he must go. He and all his contempt of life and suffering must go. Their insane, stupid courage must be destroyed. They must be taught that life is good, not to be laughed at.

They advance as before—thirty paces, twenty, fifteen. Their bayonets flash for harvest and they dash toward us.

I cry again: "Now—now!"

The farmers rise up, and the fire rages through the Fusiliers. They go down as before, men screaming in the contorted agony of death. But the Pennsylvanians can't be held now. They've seen what they have never seen before — British regulars shattered to pieces by their fire, on the open field.

They are over the wall, playing Steuben's game. They drive forward with their bayonets, slashing, thrusting, destroying with all the pent-up fury of the winter months of hell. They are hell now — all the slow, kindling hate in them let loose. These are the men who took their city, who kept them in the snow, starving.

I am with them. Life doesn't matter. Death doesn't matter. Nothing matters but that we should clear them out of our path. Destroy them. They were sent to destroy us. They laughed at us. They laughed at country bumpkins hiding behind stone walls. They laughed at a rabble without uniform. They laughed at naked men, filthy, emaciated. Their laughter still burns in us.

I drive my bayonet into a fleeing man, tear it free and leap past him. I am a machine to kill — ice inside. I am no longer a man. I have discovered Jacob.

We stand, panting. Bloody, grimed spectres. We have destroyed the Royal British Fusiliers. We have destroyed the picked troops of Europe, wiped them out in hand-to-hand battle. They are strewn over the rocky field, dead, dying — the blood of England wetting the ground of America. There is an America born out of blood and out of death. They are our blood — but no longer us. A world is ours, made here, made out of a winter of hell and the blood of the Fusiliers.

For a moment we stand that way, weary, victors on a field of battle. We look around us and wonder at what we have done. We are not soldiers. Maybe it comes to most of us then — that we are not soldiers, that we have done this thing once. Forget. A cool place to lie down and sleep. A long sleep to forget. A long, long sleep.

Wayne is riding among us, calling for a retreat. I stare at him dully. Some of the men drop where they stand, their bodies tired beyond endurance. We look at Wayne. Haven't we done enough — held them?

The British army is advancing. We stare at that great horde of men moving down on us, and shake our heads. We are a few hundred men in the path of an army. They come in long lines of green and red, Hessians to the front, bayonets set. A field of bayonets. We try to retreat. We stumble out of the way. I call the men to follow me, call my body to run. My feet move slowly, as in a dream. I fall once — pick myself up. The musket fire is a raging blast in our ears. Nothing can live in that, nothing can exist. It is an eternity before we reach the stone wall, climb over it. I look round, and half the men are gone. Somewhere back there—with the Fusiliers. Dying in a moment that encompasses all the sorrow of winter.

The musket fire of the advancing British seems to sweep the world clean—clean of life. We try to run, twist, get out of that musket fire. We reach the brook, and the men fall flat into it, soak their heads, gulp the water.

It's like a wave of life, the water. I gulp it in, feel it run through my body. I stand up and order the men to go ahead. Ice inside of me. I walk through the water and give commands calmly, coolly, as if this moment the world were not going mad. The men file past. Greene's regiments are lying ahead of us, waiting behind their entrenchments. Waiting.

One of the men remains in the brook. I say to him: "Get up there, you damn fool!"

"My brother's back there, Captain Hale."

"He's dead. Get out of here."

"He's not dead. I saw him move when he fell."

"I tell you, he's dead. Get out of here."

He walks on, looking back over his shoulder, shaking his head. Wayne passes me, his horse grinding water from the brook. Wayne is lost in the battle, a madman shrieking his battle-cry.

I look for Ely. He didn't pass me by with the men. I look for him to come, and I see only the rolling mass of the British attack.

I say to myself: "Ely's dead. He's back there—somewhere, and he's dead."

Walking toward our lines, I hear men shrieking in warning. The attack is coming—behind me. I try to think, to cut the rushing, blasting sound of fire out of my ears. I must think. I must kill the emptiness inside of me and think about Ely. I must understand what has happened to Ely—who was with me all my life, who stood outside my house with my father when my mother gave birth to me, who heard my mother scream with agony. Where is Ely? Why have I lost him?

Ely's dead, and why does his death mean nothing? They are all dead—and I am the last. I'm alive, and all the rest of them are dead.

I'm running. I must live. I can't rest.

I break into the Continental lines. What's left of the Pennsylvania men are there, sprawled and half-asleep over their muskets. It's a New Jersey line, men fresh for the battle and waiting. It's hot. It's too hot to think, but not hot enough to kill the cold inside of me. I'm in command of men. I must tell them to load and shoot, to dry their flints.

My head is aching, bursting with pain, but I must tell them to dry their flints. I wake them. They want to sleep, but I won't let them sleep. I drive them into a battle line

The British are attacking. A great wave of them roll down to Wenrock Brook. My voice is lost in sound, a solid wall of sound. I see the Hessians sprawling into the brook. They die in the brook. The American front is one solid wall of flame, thousands of men shooting together. A wall of sound and a wall of flame. A pain in my head—bursting it apart. The brook runs red with blood. The British officers, horses shot under them, roll on the ground. The attack falters and gives back. Grapeshot tears the front to pieces. The brook is red; the whole world is red. The blazing sun of day is beginning to set, leaving a red world behind. The Pennsylvanians sleep over their guns. They are no more a part of battle. The crash of sound does not awaken them. A long, long sleep.

A long sleep—to forget. Sleep to forget about Ely. Ely is dead. A good company—a great, fair company. They sleep in peace. No sound can wake them, no sound that the world makes can ever wake them. A deep peace and a deep sleep, without heat and without cold, without trouble, without longing. A rest as sweet as the heart of Ely—a great golden heart.

A heart for man. Man is a holy thing, and his body is a holy thing. Man is made in the image of God, in the holy image of God.

Smoke out of the battlefield and a sighing that is not sound. They have turned the water of the brook red.

The British retreat. Their retreat turns into a rout, and broken columns flee the field. The Hessians, who bore the brunt of the first fire, can no longer endure the weight of their heavy uniforms. They stagger, sprawl and roll over. The field is dotted with little green heaps of their bodies. They lie in and out of the brook. We stop firing, but the dull booming of the cannon goes on. A wall of grapeshot between them and us.

They splotch the field with red and green patches. They try to form as they retreat. They leave their dead behind them. They leave us the field, the dead and the dying.

Time has been lost. The only measure of time is weariness, and how long have we been weary? Tonight, we'll sleep.

The sun is low. There is almost a breeze, a movement of air that sends the powder smoke into curling tendrils. A curl of smoke from the muzzle of my musket. Like a machine, I have been loading and reloading, firing. The musket is hot as fire in my hands. The bayonet is bent.

I try to think how I bent my bayonet. I touch it gingerly. Dry blood—
the life-blood of man.

Like the blood of Ely. Ely sleeps. All round me, men are dropping
to sleep over their guns, dropping to sleep where they lie. The officers
try to wake them. Why? Why? The battle is over. They've earned their
sleep—a long sleep and a deep one, a sleep to forget.

But I can't sleep. The pain in my head increases, a beating, rushing
pain.

I stand up and watch the retreat. The haze of twilight has fallen
over the fields. The British columns are moving slowly, dragging themselves off a field they lost. A cannon booms, again and again. From
somewhere in the distance, there is the crackle of musket fire.

There is a wisp of white cloud in the sky in the east, and the setting
sun stains it—a pink and then a blood-red. As if the groaning pain of
the battlefield had gone into the sky.

The cannon booms, again and again. Gradually, other sounds die
away. The cannon booms out in a great stillness.

Why don't they stop firing?

The British columns lose themselves in a haze of twilight. Green
and red merge with the brown and green of the ground. I wait for the
cannon, but it doesn't come.

The sun has set.

The army sleep. Sprawled over their guns, sprawled in long lines
behind their breastworks, the men sleep. The dead sleep beside them,
but they are not afraid of the dead. It's a long sleep.

A sighing wind in the trees. I stand there, staring at my musket,
which lies at my feet.

I step over the breastworks—begin to walk. Each step in pain, but I
have to walk.

A man challenges me.

I say: "Captain Hale—the Fourteenth Pennsylvania."

The man says: "It's hell on guard. Let them have the dead. I'm
going to sleep."

I walk on. Wounded men are groaning. A doctor and some stretcher
bearers pass me by. "A man needs some sleep," the doctor is muttering.

A wounded man clutches at my foot. I call to the doctor.

"Christ—I'm one man! How much can one man do?"

The dead and the living lie together, naked, sleeping. I stumble on.
Cold inside—cold as ice. Ely knew.

I walk through the brook, walk among the bodies of the British

357

dead. It is quite dark now. How long ago was it that we fought a battle?

Somewhere—out there—is Ely. I could explain to Ely. He would
understand. He understood how it was with Jacob.

I walk toward a tree. There are two men sprawled under it. They
are speaking. I make out the voice of Washington; I would know that
voice anywhere. The other is La Fayette's.

I walk toward them. I walk on until I stand under the tree where
they are.

"Who are you?" Washington asks.

I am laughing in spite of myself, laughing while my head bursts with
pain. I answer:

"A deserter—a murderer. But Wayne made me a captain. The
brave General Wayne made me a captain—to lead my men into hell.
Do you know what hell is? I was there. I led my men into hell today.
Ask Wayne. Ask him. He made me a captain."

"Mad," Washington mutters. "No wonder—the heat and what we've
seen today."

"I'm not mad," I said calmly. "I know when a man is mad. I'm not
mad—only tired and wanting to sleep.

"Then go and sleep."

"I'll go and sleep," I say.

I walk through the apple orchard, looking at the faces of men. I
find Ely at last, lying near the stone wall. Even in the dark, I know
him.

I bend over him and whisper: "Ely—it's Allen Hale."

The wound is in his breast. I try to fold his hands over it. I close his
eyes. His face is not tired any more. His face is the peaceful face of a
man who has given out of a great heart.

I lie down next to him. I whisper: "I'll sleep now, Ely. I'm fair dying
to sleep. You know how it is with me. You have a heart for understanding."

Sleep comes slowly, but the hot pain in my head goes. I lie there,
next to Ely—listening to the sighing of the wind through the trees of
the orchard.

25

THE NEXT morning, I bury Ely. There is much burying to be
done—British and Hessians and Americans. Most of the Americans are

naked, and we wrap them in the green coats of the Hessians. It's not good that a comrade should go into the earth naked. Stripped and dirty, the Hessians lie in a row. They go into a trench, and no stone marks their graves.

I bury Ely where he fell, in the apple orchard. Close to the stone wall, where there will be no ploughing. And when the sun is low, the wall will shade him. Grass grows greener in the shade, and the grass will grow over Ely's grave.

The farmer who owns the orchard stands there watching us. A tall thin man, he curses under his breath and speaks of money to be paid for damage done. He stops his cursing to stare at his apple trees, stripped and shattered by the rain of shot. Then he begins to curse again, yelling:

"Bury them deep! I'll turn them in my ploughing!"

Some of us look at him, and then he's quiet. We haven't washed; we are bloody, filthy figures, but victors . . .

I want a sword for Ely. A sword to place by his side, and regimental colours to cover his face. Our regiment is gone and there are no colours. Ely never wore a sword, but there are swords on the field.

I walk among the Fusiliers. They have not been buried yet, and some of them lie on their backs, their eyes open. Most of them are boys, and even in death they manage to look gallant in their red coats. I would pity them, but there is no pity in me for anything, not even for Ely.

I find a slim dress sword. I find a blue flag. Blue is a good colour, cool. I cover Ely with the flag, and the sword I place by his side. Dirt falls on the flag, and then there is a little mound to show where Ely lies. I mark the grave with a bayonet—a rusty, bent bayonet that is no use to anyone. It will stand for a little while.

Ely is dead. Jacob is dead.

I walk aimlessly. The field is death, but death doesn't move me.

It is not so hot as yesterday. The sky has a few scudding clouds that throw shadows along the ground. I sit down under a tree and stretch my legs out. A long rest . . .

A man comes over to me and stands waiting.

"What do you want?" I ask him

"I can't find my regiment, Captain."

"Why do you call me Captain?"

"You led us yesterday."

He stands waiting.

"Well?"

359

"You led my brigade."

"That was yesterday."

"Shall I report to you, Captain?"

"That was yesterday," I whisper.

I go to the brook and wash. There are other men there — naked, rolling in the cool water. I lie in the water with them; I lie on my back and let the water ripple over my body. It is very cool and very pleasant. I watch the clouds tumbling across the sky.

There is talk about what we will do now, where we will go. They talk as if the war were over. The British have been defeated; France is our ally.

They talk of going home, and the talk makes me uneasy. There is no place for me to go, no life for me except this. What was my home once is a dream now; the reality is here — with the revolution.

I dress myself. No shirt; a pair of torn breeches and my musket.

I walk back to the orchard, and I see Wayne. He is sitting on the grass, and Steuben stands next to him. Wayne is talking eagerly and quickly, smiling, and Steuben, frowning, tries to follow his English.

I go up to them and stand waiting. Finally, Wayne looks at me; as he looks at me, I see that he remembers, and he smiles.

"Allen Hale," he says.

"Yes, sir."

He nods at Steuben. "This is the man —"

In German, Steuben says: "You are a very brave man."

I shake my head. The brave men are dead. I say to Wayne: "My brigade is gone; my regiment is disbanded."

"Who disbanded them?"

I point to Ely's grave.

Wayne rises and gives me his hand.

"You refused my hand once before," he remembers.

I nod.

"Where are the rest of you — the New York men?"

"Dead, sir."

He is silent for a while. Then he says: "I brevetted you captain. You commanded a brigade."

"There is no longer a brigade, sir."

"Nevertheless, I'll have your rank confirmed."

I nod, salute, and walk away. I pass Ely's grave. Already, the bayonet has lost its grip in the soil. It will not stand long.

We paraded before we marched away. We lined up on the field of battle. Front and centre, there was the Pennsylvania line, militia

360

mostly, but in every company of militia a few enlisted men who had been through the winter. But only a few.

We stood in our ranks with the hot sun over us, with green twigs in back of our ears, with our hot muskets in our hands. The generals reviewed us and praised us. The beggars were an army, standing on a victorious field. The beggars had proven their right to exist.

That is written.

Ely lies on the field of Monmouth, with Jacob. The others are at a place called Valley Forge.

In the summer, Valley Forge is green and lovely. In the winter it is never so cold as that winter — never so cold that the ground will freeze deep to where they lie.

THE PROUD
AND THE FREE

*To the memory
of the brave men of the Pennsylvania Brigades,
and of their still unrealized dream*

PART ONE

Wherein I describe how it came about that
I am telling this tale, which no other has told.

IT IS AN UNCERTAIN thing when an old man sits down to write a
tale of his youth, in the long ago; for even if he remembers well, his
memory will be cold with time; and no matter how well he remembers,
he is making a drama in which the players are dead and the scenes
have been shifted . . .

I remember not so long ago that we were in New York and saw a
production of *King Lear,* where Hammond Drice played the old man
so well that I was moved to return the next day to tell him how much I
understood, and how much I was touched by him. I would perhaps
have gone backstage that same evening, but I was awed at the thought
of the grand and glamorous personality of the actor—since we have no
theater in York in Pennsylvania, where I still live—and I put it off until
the next day. But the next day, my wife urged me to it and I went; for
even if I was not at ease with large city things, I was twice representative in the State House, and never playing a stick of politics to get
there, and once in Congress too, and the law I practiced was law in
which I tried to find justice at least as much as I tried to find a living.

. . . But you see that already I am off and drifting, the way an old
man drifts when he sets out to put down a simple sequence of events,
and I mention this simply because the show had finished the next day.
The flats were taken down and piled around the big, bare stage, and
the costumes had that awful, deflated and lifeless look which comes to
old-fashioned dress cast off and aside. Thereby, I lost all desire to meet
any of those who had looked so gallant and fine under the bright lights
of the evening before; and I went away as I had come, only a little
sadder.

I said that was not so long ago, but it was six years, the way time
passes, and in those years my wife and many other good friends passed

364

away; so that more and more I get to feel that I, Jamie Stuart, have overstayed my leave. For that reason, with what strength I have for concentrating on so exhaustive a task, I would write down the one tale I have always meant to tell: the tale of the foreign brigades of Pennsylvania in the faraway days of my youth. I would write it down as nearly as I can in a truthful way; for I know of no one else but myself who remembers what took place in those old and trying times, and the story is one which should not be forgotten.

Well may you ask, Who is Jamie Stuart, that we should listen to him? And why should we be bored with the ramblings of these ancients, who will not consider that the world moves on?

It moves on, that I know; but a little from the old along with what is new, and there is the taste. Like those good Pennsylvania housewives who could never tolerate food wasted. In the corner of the stove they kept a pot of soup—and very good and peppery soup it was—and each day's leavings went into the next day's pot. So there was ever fresh soup for eating, but always a taste of the old as well.

And of myself, when my wife died and left me an old and lonely man of seventy-seven—I am past eighty now—I had little desire to live any more. It was less grief than a sort of absolute hopelessness. Day in and day out, I sat and counted the passing of time. Life is like a moment, and you can sit in the gathering cold and eat your heart out, if you are so minded; and that way I was sitting one night, filled with a sort of senile pity for myself, when there was a quick and angry hammering at the door. I went there and asked who it was.

Does Lawyer Stuart live here?

He lives here. He does live here. And this is Lawyer Stuart; and who the devil are you at this hour of the night?

Well, open the door and see, by God! We're on quick business, so would you yammer with us all night long?

I opened the door, because there was nothing much that I had to be afraid of, and if they wanted to rob an old man like myself, or break my head, why that was as good a way as any to put an end to the fright of sitting alone and waiting for death. Six of them there were altogether, two white and four black men, and the two white men carried guns. They were young, hard, quick-talking men who laid it right out in front of me that they were a part of the underground line for taking black men out of slavery in the South, and this was four of a group they were running through to the border of British Canada. Their regular contact was Pastor McGilcuddy and the manse of the

Presbyterian church was their regular station; but a band of armed men from below the Virginia Line had broken a link of contact at some point and now were waiting for these at the manse; and what would I have? Would I have a bloody slaughter here in the peaceful village of York — for, as they said, they were determined not to give up their cargo without laying down their own lives first and making a real price of it — or would I grant them shelter for the night, a stable for their horses, and a chance to bind the links of their chain together again?

Come inside, I said, and don't stand outside there yelling, as if this were the first pot of tea you ever tipped over.

And all the while I was trying to straighten out in my mind the fact that the gentle and soft-spoken Pastor Lyton McGilcuddy was one of the Devil's brew of Abolitionists, and here were two more of them right in my own hallway, the first I had ever seen or spoken to in the flesh — that is, not counting the Pastor.

Who told you to come to me? I asked them, looking them up and down now and seeing that they were not much different from other men — dirty in boots and overalls and cotton shirts, with three days of beard on their cheeks, but otherwise plain-looking lads, and the black men behind them were tired and dirty and frightened too, but no menace in them; they brought back to me memories I had not dabbled with this long, long while — memories of other lads who had had a wild venture in freedom; and this you will see if you read through the tale I set down here.

. . . The Pastor, they answered; the Pastor, he said: When it comes to a pinch, go to the old man, Jamie Stuart.

Well, you have come to me, I said, so leave the black men here and go out and stable your horses . . .

It was that way that I fell in with them, and became one of the underground chain, a way station on it, a stopping place for men who fled through the nights for their freedom; and it is that way too that I, Jamie Stuart, an old man in the twilight of his life, have become a part of the little, hated — well-hated, well-loved — group of men and women who call themselves Abolitionists.

There is a tale — but for others to tell. I have a little bit of it, but I am an old, old man, and when I see the young ones come in and out of my home — when I see the black men, whom I see only for the moment, coming and going and bold for liberty — I am filled with a different kind of sadness than I had before. I want to know the end of this, and I realize that such knowledge is for others, not for me. Little use I am to them, crouched by the fire in the cold days, trying to warm the ache from my bones; but my house is theirs and all else that I have. In another way, I am joined to them, and it is of this other way that I would tell.

It has often seemed to me that while man cannot look into the future, he can make a good deal out of the past; and in my own past, there is an adventure not wholly without meaning. How many lies have been told about those times! But how many lies have been told about the young men who call themselves Abolitionists today! So it may be that if I look back, it will not only be the rambling memories of an old man, but a clue to that which lies ahead. Or so I tell myself.

In any case, there is no other left alive today—of whom I know— who can tell the tale of the great revolt of the foreign brigades.

They are all dead, my comrades, scattered like leaves to the four winds, and their time is dead with them. They were not men eager for growing old, for the winter of their lives came with the springtime; and the fruit I have tasted was not for them, but a more bitter fruit indeed. What a strength they had, that wasted away and went sighing off; and sometimes it seems that their cold bodies were filled with honey, such a swarm of activity and wealth arose from them!

They were soldiers, you know: the men of the Pennsylvania Line of the Continental Army, a rock for those strange and troubled times. I was one of them. Eleven regiments of us there were, hard soldiers of hard times; and I myself, Jamie Stuart, was master sergeant in the 11th Regiment. Originally, I was part of the 1st Regiment, and then I was only seventeen years old; but later on, when the 11th and last regiment was formed, they took me and Danny Connell, and made us sergeants in it; and there I was when the great rising took place.

Often enough, as time went past, as the war slipped into the faraway and everyone tried to forget and wanted to forget, I brooded over the circumstances of our revolt, so that I might extract some meaning from it. But the meaning apparently became more and more difficult to grasp. I found a way of life; I worked and studied and became a lawyer. Here, I said to myself, you have done this, Jamie Stuart, and therefore you are an outstanding man and unlike that devilish rabble that fought in the brigades—for where are they? Scattered like chaff, they are. But you, Jamie Stuart, you have reaped a real harvest and you have married your own sweet Molly Bracken and made a home and watched your children grow and blossom, and buried some children too, and tasted a little of this honor and that honor—and therefore what is right is right.

Could you also say that what is wasted is wasted, and that the dreams and the pains of the men I once knew were wasted? For when I was left alone in my old, old age, my life was bereft of meaning as well as companionship, and it was not until those two young men came to my door, and with them the four black men in flight, that I had a glimmering of a story unbroken and continuous.

That is why I have determined to set down my part in it, and the adventures which befell me in the year 1781, so that you may see some of the meaning of the eleven foreign brigades which stood for the country of Pennsylvania in the old times, before there was such a union as we have today.

I must tell something of myself first and of my beginnings, so that I may establish a part of the logic I believe in; for I believe that neither in the lives of men nor in the lives of nations is there a lack of reason. This is a matter I once discussed with a very wise man, a physician in Philadelphia, Benjamin Rush by name, and it was he who first said to me that given sufficient facts and a truthful method to apply them, almost anything is knowable. And this I intend to do, putting down a narrative of our adventure as well as I can recall it.

Of myself, I must say to begin that I was born here in this same place where I will, in all probability, end my life—in the village of York in Pennsylvania. I was born in the year 1759, out of a mother and father who had been bound over as servants from Glasgow in the old country. I am not ashamed to state this, for my mother and father were good and honest people, for all that they were held in chattel slavery for a matter of twelve years. Nor am I ashamed to say that I was born out of parents who were slaves. It is the habit of thinking today that only black men are slaves or fit for slavery, such a proud and arrogant fetish have we made of our own freedom. But we know little enough today of the purchase price of this freedom, and, in my childhood, many of white skin were slaves, as well as those whose skin was black.

My mother was a MacAndrews of the Highlands, the daughter of a poor crofter; my father was a weaver by trade and a free man until he took sick with a condition that made it impossible for him to use his fingers for some months—nor did he ever regain the full dexterity of them. Because of this, to avoid death by starvation for my mother and himself, they both of them sold themselves into bond slavery in America for a sabbatical, or seven years. But when costs and sick charges and birth charges were added, it came to twelve years that they labored for their freedom on a Virginia plantation, and in that time, a boy and a girl were born to them, both of whom died. When they gained their freedom, they came to York, where my father thought he would set up a loom and go back to his trade of weaving, and there I was born; but my mother's labor over me gave her a lesion which killed her in two years. For the next eight years, my father raised me as best he could, which meant that without a mothers' care I ran like an animal in the woods and the streets. Then he died of smallpox, and, ten years old, I was an orphan in the world.

So I was an orphan, without father or mother, and all the wealth I got from them you could press into a thimble. Nor had I letters or anything of that kind, for this was before Pastor Bracken took a fancy to me and taught me to read and write.

My father was in the church, so the Presbyterian elders had me before them and they said: Well, Jamie, here you are, alone in the world by God's mercy, without kith of kin to lend you a hand, and what do you think of your future.

I'll be a robber, I answered, which seemed to me to be the only practical way of keeping body and soul together, and already I had had some indication that unless a little thievery was mixed in with an honest man, he did less than well in the world.

The elders, however, were unimpressed. They pointed out to me that this was hardly the attitude for me to take, if I hoped to be adopted into some good, God-fearing home, and they also pointed out that the likelihood of such was not too great, considering how my father had let me grow up. I stood in front of them, my toes coming out of my shoes, my knees coming out of my pants, my elbows coming out of my sleeves—a ragged, bony, unprepossessing little boy, I suppose; and to this day I remember well my bitterness and resentment against them, those pious, hard-jawed, sharp-nosed trustees of the Almighty who were sitting in judgment upon a lad of ten summers. A Scottish pout, they were thinking of me, no doubt, a wild one, an animal like all the young of the miserable Highland beggars and gillies who thought that gold was turned up at every step in the new country. My speech in those times was thick and broad and their own was sharp and narrow. So they looked at me as at some insect, and my own heart was full of repayment in kind.

369

Do what you will with me, I said to myself, but never will I rest with what my mother and father had, going to their graves in such sorrow! Do it and be damned!

I went home and lay down alone in the little shack my father had rented, with his loom and his bench and the two or three sticks of furniture he had in the world, none of it mine but all of it in pawn for back rent. And the next day I was called to Stephan Dobkin, the church head; and with him was Fritz Tumbrill, the cobbler, a monstrously large and fat man, pig-eyed, with a rolling collar of his own flesh in which his head sat like a pudding in gravy.

Here is good Master Tumbrill, and he has agreed to take you in and keep you for apprenticeship and teach you the trade, said Stephan Dobkin. Such is the charity of Jesus Christ, our own Master, he said, and God help you if you should ever prove ungrateful.

My father's trade was weaving! I cried. I'll be a weaver and no damned shoemaker!

So I learned my first lesson in the weight of Fritz Tumbrill's hand and the nature of his ethics. From the floor where he sent me with his blow, I listened to his instructions on language to be used in his presence and in his household.

Thus I went to serve him to learn cobbling, and a full sabbatical I served before I threw his leather apron in his face and walked out to join the 1st Regiment of Pennsylvania, then being raised to march north and help the farmers in the siege of Boston town. I mention this because in the narrative I propose to tell, concerning what befell myself and my comrades in the winter of 1781, you may be moved to ask, now and again, How does one account for these men? What made them and what moves them, and why do they endure what they endure?

Also, you may ask, What of this one who writes the narrative? What of Jamie Stuart? He is native born in the American land. What kind of bitter cud does he chew over and over again, retching the acid into his teeth?

But it is not my intention to make such a compilation. If I at twenty-two was no lad, then I was little enough of a lad at ten. Childhood is for those who can afford it, and my own purse was light from the beginning. In the years I sat crouched over the bench in the workshop of Fritz Tumbrill, particularly before that day when Molly Bracken walked into the shop, like sunshine coming into a dark well, in those years I thought often of my father's lean and tired face.

A word about that face before I go into the tale I must tell; for I think that before you are finished you will have some curiosity about my own look, and if you see my father, you will see me too.

I remember him best at the loom. The light was poor in the shack where he worked, so when the weather was good, he took half a dozen shingles out of the roof, and through the opening a broad shaft of light fell upon the loom and upon his face as well. I would play on the floor facing him. Sometimes I would glance up and meet his eyes, and his whole face would smile, for I was all he had in the world. But at other times, he would be unaware that I was watching him, and I would note the incredible sadness of his face. Ah, what a sorrow was there! What grief for the thin crust of bread he handed to his child! A Scotsman is dour, they say, but the quality is not born into a man but comes rather from the soil he scratched.

My father's face was a long one, as mine is too. A narrow one. His brows arched, and on either side his forehead there was a slight indentation of the bone—as there is on mine. The nose was long and well-shaped, the curve of the head high, the hair a tarnished sand-color, and the eyes gray-green. The chin was large yet gentle, long and narrow, and the neck was lean, as the man was, a tall, lean, long-muscled man; and taking away a quarter of a century it is a fit description for myself, Jamie Stuart, when I signed my name to the enlistment papers and became a soldier in the army of the Revolution for the commonwealth of Pennsylvania. An ugly lad I was, to a way of thinking, but I had qualities that I little knew of, myself, until I was rubbed like a sword on a grindstone, and then because of those qualities men gave me a post not without honor for a lad of twenty-two, as you will see.

So I have told you a little of my life in each direction, a little of what was in the old days, when one day was not so different from the other while I learned the best way to ease my back so that Fritz Tumbrill's blows fell as lightly as possible, while I learned how to bevel the leather for the sole and how to sew it for the upper, how to cut, shape, trim and awl, how to drink and coddle and roll—and some of what came after, when I grew old and away from the memories of my youth.

But Fritz Tumbrill never made an animal of me, or I would have become like him. Instead, I hardened and I became something else, and through Molly Bracken—of whom you will hear more—I learned to read and write. So I was able to read in a newspaper of the incident that happened in Massachusetts in April of 1775, and I was able to read as well that they were raising a regiment of Pennsylvania men and all others who would enlist for pay, bounty and glory, to strike down the tyrant. I knew what to do and I did it, because the answers to my questions were written on my back and on my memory too.

That is enough of Jamie Stuart to justify this narration which I will set down. He was like the other men, of whom I will also tell, and he loved them deeply and came to know them.

May they sleep well, do I say, myself. They reached up for the stars and they made a crude key to unlock the gates of heaven. This, other men will do, and the key will become a better one; so I will not weep for them or have you weep, but only give them their due.

PART TWO

Being an account of the death of Tommy
Mahoney, and the Congress we held and
the pledge we made on the eve of the
New Year of 1781.

THE FACTS which I am about to set down in a narrative to do
honor to my dead comrades—for no other honor has been done to
them—had a beginning somewhere; but the more I ponder the inter-
connection of things, the more I come to understand that the beginning is not traceable—which is all for the best: for then a spark of
hope burns in my heart, and I ponder the possibility that the end is as
little traceable as the beginning. And if that is the case, then I for one
believe that there was a meaning and a purpose and a final chapter
still to be written out in life to what we did.

But however that may be, there must be a starting point, and for
that I have chosen the death of little Tommy Mahoney, the Protestant
drummer boy from Dublin town, who died on the eve of the new year
of 1781, in the encampment outside of Morristown, New Jersey. I will
also tell you that I choose the death of this poor, damned little lad
because our first Congress of the Line followed; but there were other
places for the beginning. Even before the war, there was a beginning
to what we did, and even before any man there was born, and even
maybe so long ago as when Christ led men not so different from ourselves, and no more poorly clothed and fed.

It is something we know and which doctors cannot explain, that a
man will not go on living if he has lost the desire to do so; and it was
plain to everyone after we had marched from Totowa to Morristown
that little Tommy Mahoney was not long for this earth. It was not the
cold winds that blew so cruelly from the northern forests; it was not the
fact that we lived on a little parched corn with never a taste of meat; it

373

was not our nakedness, our lousiness, our sickness—for all of these things we were used to, and these things we had lived through before and had a ripe belly of, when we lay at Valley Forge. It was because we had stopped hoping, and because we were bereft and betrayed; and the little lad knew better than some of us who were old enough to be his father what the situation was. His beardless face became gray and the sparkle went out of his eyes. When he beat on his drum, it was a new rhythm, a sad and hopeless rhythm.

I beat because my heart is breaking, his drum said.

There was a time when such a drumbeat with such a sad and frightened rhythm would have angered us, and then some of us would have said, Twelve on his backside, that drummer lad needs. And others of us would have said, Stop your chopping dirty sticks, if that is all the kind of a tune you can beat out. And there would have been many a clip alongside the head and chin for little Tommy Mahoney as a reward for the devilish and persistent means he took of beating that drum.

But we were changed too, along with the lad, and nobody clipped Tommy Mahoney and nobody shouted at him; for inside of us we knew that the tune he played was the truth and nothing but the truth. We had all of us, all of the men of the ten infantry regiments and one artillery regiment of the Pennsylvania Line who were marched from Totowa to Morristown to go into winter encampment, become gentle. We were soft-spoken; we were quiet; we were sad. And as we set to work to repair the little log huts that stood in various stages of decay from the encampment of the year before, it seemed to many of us that there was never a time but when we were what we were now, such homeless, lonely, lost men as the world had not seen before. The heart had left us; we did not fight; we did not beat our women; we did not sing—and one time when big Angus MacGrath strode forth to play on his pipes, the music that came forth in spite of himself was such cursed and lonely music that he laid his pipes away and vowed never to play upon them again, so long as he lived.

For that reason, we did not clip Tommy Mahoney when he beat his crying rhythms. The lad is not for this world, we said. He is making a requiem for himself, and who will deny him that privilege?

He was undersized, the way most of us in the Line were, coming as we had from foreign soil, or out of bondage and poverty. When Massachusetts or Connecticut had first marched alongside us, they made many a joke of it, shouting things like, Ho for the dirty little runts! Ho for the little men! Are you going to war now, little men! But the

Yankees sang another song when the grape opened up, hissing like a great kettle boiled over, and when the muskets balls whistled from the British volleys. Then they ran away but we stood and died, even as we stood and died on every field, New York, White Plains, Trenton, Monmouth, Stony Point — how many there were, and we in our line stood with our Irish and Scotch and Germans and Poles and French and Portuguese, our black men and our Jews and our Romans — we stood and they stopped calling us little men!

Yet Tommy Mahoney was smaller than most. His arms and legs were like sticks; he had a pinched face, pocked and tired and sad, but for all that a little boy's face. He had sandy hair, close-cropped, that stood straight up from his head, and he had a dainty alto voice that was the sweetest thing men ever heard. How he loved to sing once! But he sang no more now. We urged him and urged him, thinking that music would be like medicine, but only when Christmas time approached did he lift up his head and sing, *On the first day of Christmas, my truelove sent to me, a partridge in a pear tree. On the second day of Christmas, my truelove sent to me, two turtle doves and a partridge in a pear tree . . .*

And then he sang on and on and we joined in the round, and made a real ringing roundelay of it; and that was the only real roundelay we sang in all that Christmas time. The women kissed him and petted him; and Handsome Jack Maloney, of whom you will hear much more, beat time with the tears streaming down his face and said:

Sing more and more, my lad, with old tunes of the old country, so you will make my rotten old heart crack with the joy of it all.

I can sing no more, the drummer boy answered, for I remember the beauty of Dublin city, before me uncle sold me to go overseas into bondage.

But ye're not in bondage now, me lad, the girls pleaded.

I can sing no more, he said, for me heart is breaking, and I want to lay me down and die.

They went on with their persuasion until big Angus MacGrath roared, Now let the lad be, for will ye make music out of a broken lute, like the officers make war out of our own lifeblood?

He withered, did little Tommy Mahoney, like the apple that is picked too soon and then goes uneaten, and when the last day of the year 1780 came, he laid himself down and he died.

We were hutted up then with our own bitterness, and because you should know to understand what followed, I will tell you what our huts were like. This one of mine will serve, for I was sergeant over the drummer boy, and apart from myself, fifteen men were hutted here in my house. Also, in this same house, the first Congress of the Line was held, and also in this same house there came into being the Committee of Sergeants.

The hut was twenty feet long and sixteen deep, fronting on the parade — which made it somewhat bigger than most of the others. It was made of logs, and chinked with clay, and had a dirt floor and a bark roof, no windows and a clay and log hearth. We bedded in threes, one atop the other, and there was a sawbuck table and two benches down the middle, at which we ate when there was anything for eating. The bunks were split logs with straw bolsters, only it was years since we had sewn the last of the bolsters into shirts and the last of our blankets into coats, so that now we slept on the straw and under it too. Such were our hutments.

In this hut of mine, Tommy Mahoney breathed out his last; and we laid the little lad out on the table, and Katy Waggoner and Olive Lutz came in to wash him and make him ready for the ground. We took off all his clothes and washed his poor skinny body clean, and then we washed the few rags he wore, dried them by the fire, and dressed him over again. Katy Waggoner went to the quartermaster general to beg a winding sheet, but for her pains all she got was a curse and a slap in the face — which was no way to treat her, for all that she was a loose and slatternly woman. But even if she had gotten a winding sheet of the purest linen, I do not think that what followed would have been noticeably altered. I start this narrative from the death of Tommy Mahoney, only because I must have a starting point somewhere and not because I believe it was the death of the drummer boy, from sadness, starvation and bleeding lungs, that caused what followed. Nor do I believe that the beating of the two Kelly brothers, John and Dobie, made any decisive difference. The two of them were Romans who had come to us as replacements, signing in for what they and theirs had suffered in the old country from the British and from their own tyrants; and not knowing that the boy was a Protestant lad, and not knowing that in such a village as Morristown there could be no Roman priest, they now set off, without leave, to fetch one.

They were men out of the 2nd Pennsylvania, in which there were many Polish and Irish, and particularly eleven Jews, which gave the officers a singular reason for hatred. It is such a long time back that I may have a name twisted here and there, but I think it was Captain Sudburry and four or five of his fellows who stopped the Kelly brothers, demanding of them:

Now where are you going, my lads?

We're off to Morristown to fetch a father for a little lad who died unshriven, John Kelly replied.

The hell you are! And where are your papers for leave? the officers said ungraciously.

We have no papers, John Kelly answered, courteously enough as we heard of it, but his brother spoke up and asked, Now would ye want papers to enter into the gates of heaven, or hell also? Here is a little lad from the old country, from Dublin town, from which me blessed mother came, and he wasted away into his death all unshriven, and we only seek a holy father to give him a little unction.

Whether they knew what either Kelly brother spoke of, I know not; but they fell into a fury and cursed them out.

Now to hell with ye, for ye talk like a damned Englishman, said one of the Kelly brothers.

That was all that was needed. The officers, of whom there were at least four or five, drew their swords and set about to belabor the two boys with the flats and backs. One of the officers was armed with an espontoon, a weapon like a pike and much in favor by officers in those critical days, and this he drove into the stomach of Dobie Kelly, while the other was brushed and cut all over the face and head. Then both of them were taken under guard, and when we heard about it, early on the eve of New Year, Dobie Kelly was already dead.

You can imagine how it was. We were sitting in a wake around the body of the littler drummer lad, and the word came to us, brought by Stanislaus Prukish, sergeant in the 2nd. Already, there were grouped around the boy, in the flickering firelight, small delegations of one or two sergeants or corporals who had come from each of the ten infantry regiments and from the artillery company too, for the lad had been much considered for his singing and the good spirits he once owned. Prukish told us what he knew of the incident of the Kelly brothers.

There it is, he said, in his thick Polish accent, which I cannot reproduce. We are not fast enough dying, so they have begun the killing. We are the enemy instead of the Lobsters.

If there was a drop of rum in this cursed encampment, I would be howling drunk this evening, said Sean O'Toole of the 4th Regiment. I would spin my head like a top and go out into the white snow and howl like the devil at the stars. But there is no rum, and here we are sitting at the wake of two good lads, with never a little bit of a drop to wet out throats.

Be damned with it! I have not been paid these eleven months, not even in the lousy Yankee paper; I have not been clothed; I have not been fed. The cold is in me bones.

Silence fell, and in the next half-hour it was only interrupted when someone said to throw another handful of faggots on the fire. I don't know what would have been that evening had we been drunk, the way soldiers have a right to be on the eve of the New Year; but apart from the officers' quarters in the fine and genteel houses, there was not a dram of spirits in the camp. Sober we were, sober and moody and angry. Nor were we cold, for one by one, men entered to pay their respects, and women too, until more than fifty of us were packed into the one cabin, on the floor, on the bunks, sprawled, squatting, standing; and those who came stayed. Sergeant Bily Bowzar of the 10th came in, and with him Jim Holt, the black man who was corporal in the 2nd. The two Jews, brothers in the 2nd, Aaron and Moses Gonzales, entered, and with them was Danny Connell of my own 11th. Connell had been a minstrel in the old country, and when I saw him first, in 1776, he was as fair a lad to look upon as you would find in all the tidewater countries, twenty-three years old then with black hair and black eyes and a swagger and a dash, and as ready for a fight as a cock with spurs. But now, in his rags, he looked fifty if he looked a day; his hair was gray, as was his big, bushy beard, and his eyes were deep-sunk into his head, and he was as dirty as we all were, and as smelly and as lousy. He had his lass, Mathilda, with him, a mountain girl from the buckskin folk over westward; she was faithful to him and stayed with him from year to year, so thin a breath of wind could blow her away, yet with spirit in her. To look at her made my heart yearn for my own sweet Molly Bracken in York village, but I would not want her here to share my own misery and dirt.

Connell had been to look at the Kellys, and he said as he entered:

It was a wanton thing they did to the boy, and if I had ever raised my voice, they would have done as much to me. For it is in me head that they are stricken mad and that this is the end of everything.

If it's the end of everything, said Freddy Goulay, a black man and corporal in the 6th Regiment, it's an end they made. The only gift they got is to lead us to slaughter. They are whipping men, like overseers, and each of them would be a king. They fill their cup with hate, they do. The people hate them and the land hate them, and we hate them too. Now they don't come near us, they don't touch us, they afraid.

Each had something to say of that sort, but it was surprising with what little anger they said it, and how slowly and regretfully. Our tone was gentler than our appearance, for crammed into the hut, sitting almost one on top of the other, with the little lad's mortal remains stretched out on the table square in the center of us, we looked like something that man had never made of himself before. It was a long, long time, yes many, many months since we had been given money or clothes or a blanket to shelter us from the cold. Put a man in rags, feed him on cornmeal until his teeth are all loose in the sockets, and he will not look after his body as if it were a thing to be precious about; we had stopped shaving because we had stopped caring, and our hair was long and wild and knotted. When we had fought, we were taken into battle like cattle into a slaughter pen, and when the battles were lost, as almost every one was, we were left to hold the field while the Yankees fled.

. . . So I went into the fine house of Thomas Hardwick, continued Danny Connell, still telling of his journeys to know why and how the Kelly boy had died . . . and the officers of the 9th Pennsylvania Regiment—may it be glorious in battle, this heart and soul of the Revolution—they sat at dinner. And on the eve of this New Year, when there is no eating or drinking or dancing or singing, would you like me to spin you a tale of the officers at dinner?

You should be sitting with respect at a wake, with respect and sober sorrow, said Olive Lutz.

And have I no respect in me voice? And is my heart not breaking with sober sorrow—me, Danny Connell, who sang such songs of gladness when he was a lad? If ye don't recognize that, you dirty bitch, it's because you got the soul of a slattern!

To hell with that, I told him. If it's the Roman way to have foul talk over the dead, you swallow your tongue, Danny Connell. For this is a Protestant lad laid out on the table.

Then would ye have a theological discussion? asked Connell, combing his beard with his fingers and looking at the ceiling. Here we are Jew and Protestant and Roman and heathen too, but I do not find discrimination among our officers. They hold with equality, me dear Jamie Stuart . . .

I was on a top bunk, perched with my head against the roof beams; I was bent over—a taller man than the foreigners—chin on knees, staring with smarting, watering eyes.

. . . Me dear Jamie Stuart, ye are not the only lad in the regiment can read and write, and I got in me head here four hundred songs.

Tell me I'm lying, ye scut.

When our anger rises, we fight each other, said the Jew Aaron Gonzales, so sadly that the tears ran down my cheeks; and Connell cried too, and said more gently:

I got in me head many things, and I don't know how to use them, like ye take me who was a minstrel and set me to coopering. Me father was struck down by the tyrant's hand when he led the march of the starving folk on Dublin town, and I was just a lad when he lay there, with a bullet in his chest and dying in me arms. Danny, he said to me, ye must not take it amiss that a bullet strikes down yer father and lose yer taste for freedom. We are a downtrodden folk, Danny, me lad, and we got no taste for the finer things; but we got a taste for music and a taste for freedom, and these are from the olden times. So he died out his life there, and for the sake of me poor mother, for ten pounds in her hand and passage for me, I bind out to Pennsylvania for two years. But I got this in me head: *We hold these truths to be self-evident—that all men are created equal; that they are endowed by their Creator with certain unalienable rights; that among these are life, liberty, and the pursuit of happiness.* In me head is all this, when I come into the Hardwick House tonight to see if I can find a smell of justice for the Kelly boy. I am a free man. I am no peasant sod, but a free man in the army of the Revolution, in which I enlisted of me own free will out of hatred for the Union Jack and for the rich tyrant who murders the poor. So I come into the Hardwick House, pushing aside Frank Meyers, the stinking orderly who is lapdog there, and there are the gentlemen of the 9th, fifteen of them sitting at this long table, with white linen and candles as bright as the sun, and all of them in their finest buff and blue, and all of them shaven clean, and all of them wigged, and all of them with lace at the cuff and lace at the throat, and all of them with wine in the glass and wine in the bottle, and I am standing there when in there comes a roast of mutton with the very smell enough to break me poor heart. But not even to smell it am I permitted, for I am rushed out of there like I am the plague, which maybe I am from the look of me, and as for Kelly, they said to me that the dirty dog got what he deserved. . . . So there it is, Jamie Stuart, who is not like myself, a dirty foreigner, but native born out of Pennsylvania. Where have we been and where are we going? . .

They looked at me, all of them fanciful people—some good, some bad, some bright and some dull—but all of them fanciful folk or they would not have been there, and I looked back at the thick of their upturned faces, half seen in the dim firelight, with passion and anger wiped out through the mood of Danny Connell's tale, and only a question left. But the question was not new. With high hope and high heart, we answered the call to come to Boston in 1776 where the Yankees had hemmed the British tyrant into the tidewater town; and each and every one of us came with that curious, unspoken, unformed dream that is in the heart of every man with a foot on his neck. They were farmers around Boston town, but we were a different crew, and I came with a dream that no more would an apprentice work for grits and beatings; the sailors came with the dream that free men would sail ships with no lashes on their backs; and the Scottish buckskin men came with a dream of land, so that they would no longer hire out as hunters and pack animals, and so that some day they would wear woven Christian cloth instead of animal skin. The Jews came with a dream of standing up as men free, and so did the black men; and in the bellies of the Irish estevars and ropewalkers was a hunger ache a thousand years old and a hate almost as ancient. And the Poles and the Germans came with their heads bowed, but they would hold them upright now, and all of it because the British were hemmed in Boston town. We did not reason it out. Here was talk of freedom and we knew what side we were on, and we had nothing to lose. But then the years went by, and the question began to burn in us; still we were the poor led by the rich, the disinherited led by those who did inherit, and here were curses and whiplashes and blows from those who spoke the pretty words of freedom. Here was worse hunger, and we knew hunger; here was worse cold, and we knew cold.

The others went home; they came and they went, did the Yankees, which is something that is forgotten now, but the Pennsylvania Line stayed: the foreigns stayed. They had no place to go, and now the foreigns looked at me out of the shadows and out of bloodshot eyes, and I looked at Handsome Jack Maloney, who sat as I did on an uppermost bunk, his small, sharp face the only clean-shaven one among us, his little black eyes observing me narrowly, his mouth twitching a little, as it did in the excitement of an engagement—he who had been a master sergeant in a British regiment, and had deserted and had come to us and our hell with the cold logic of a man who chooses between two sides. That he was, cold and logical and hard as rock.

The first to do, Jamie, he said, is to lay poor Tommy out in the cold, for the lad is beginning to stink, and then we will talk it over until we get it out of our systems.

I am tired of talk, growled big Angus MacGrath.

It helps.

If we talk in a straight line then it may help, said the Jew Gonzales. If we talk in a circle, we come back to each other where is no solution. We must lift up our heads.

And our eyes, I agreed.

Jim Holt picked up the drummer lad in his arms, and the women wept.

When you return, said Jack Maloney, bring with you men from the 1st and the 3rd and from the artillery company. Tell them there's a Congress sitting in the hut of Jamie Stuart, and they should not send any damned navvies, but good men in respectful standing.

That was how our Congress came about.

We let the fire die to embers, for — the way that hut was packed with humankind, their smell and their breath and their warmth — we wanted no other heat; and on the table we lit a tallow lamp. The year turned. We had no watch among us, having long ago bartered away the last for food and drink, but the sound of the New Year came up, fretful and uneven, with a huzza here and there through the encampment, and then with the tolling of the bells from the village church. The door was opened to let us have a breath of air, and as the swirling snow eddied in, we saw a man or two run across the moonlit parade, in a grotesque imitation of what a New Year's Eve should be.

The tallow wick lashed and flickered, and in a voice as sober as a parson's on Sunday morn, Jack Maloney spoke and said:

By the rights invested in me by the race of mankind — to which I have tried to do some good, for all the whoring and drinking I have done — and by a part of that holy right which made me, a deserter from the tyrant George III, master sergeant in the army of this republic of Pennsylvania, in the name of the Line and the 6th Regiment, where every lad is a comrade of mine and calls me by name, I do call into being and session this Congress of the Pennsylvania Line. . . .

No one laughed. Our being there and our listening to those pompous words of Handsome Jack's had already committed us, and our necks were inside of fifty nooses and our hearts were beating faster.

Representing *who?* someone asked.

The Line.

Not enough.

The people of Pennsylvania.

We lie in Jersey now.

Is there a Jersey lad here? asked Jack Maloney.

There arose the Dutchman Andrew Yost, who said, That I am, and my father before me.

Then what in hell are you doing in a Pennsylvania regiment? asked Sean O'Toole.

Pulled in by my neck, by God, with a promise of twenty-dollar bounty I never got, a promise of a suit of clothes, I never see, a promise of a pint of rum a week I never even smell, and a promise of twelve-dollar-a-month pay I never get paid, not even once, you hear, not even once, God damn it to hell!

And are ye fit to speak for yer land and folk?

Maybe yes, maybe no, the Dutchman answered slowly. What we do will make me able to speak later.

That's good enough, nodded Jack Maloney, and if it's yer pleasure, I will put the Congress in your hands to elect a board and a president. But I would solemnly advice ye first to choose a protector, and let him beat up a corporal's guard of honest lads, so that we'll have no gentry walking in on us.

This was done. Angus MacGrath was made protector of the Congress, and he left to find a dozen true lads who would patrol the hut, watching for any dirty informer with his nose in the eaves or any of the officer gentry with a nose in the door. Then we set about discussing form and shape for the Congress, everyone trying to talk at once, until Danny Connell roared us down, and Chester Rosenbank, the pinchnosed German schoolteacher from Philadelphia, advised:

You must have a chairman *pro tempore*.

And what in hell is that?

It is Latin and means "for the time being," and how else will you have each one talk in turn instead of together?

Then let it be Jamie Stuart in whose hut we are, said Maloney, and if ye talk, make it cutty and sharp.

So I was chairman, and then for an hour, instead of turning our thoughts to what we intended to do, we debated the point of what we were and whom we represented and what our form should be. Maloney and Rosenbank and the Gonzales brothers, and the black man Goulay, and three buckskin men from the 1st Regiment and a handful of others all held that we represented the people, and that therefore we were a Congress of the people; but the rest of us opposed this, pointing out that aside from the officer gentry, there were none the people hated more than the foreigners of the Line, as witness the way they let us starve and die in the midst of their plenty.

After we were set on to rob their trees and pilfer their stock, said

Goulay.

Be that as it may, we do not represent them, and it will be our burden in the future to see if we represent them or if their own guns are turned against us.

Then who do we represent?

The soldiers of the Line, said Danny Connell, and then only if they follow us.

When we ourselves don't know where we be going, but sit here quacking away?

Then let us get to where we are going and the hell with the shape of it, whether we are a Congress or a Committee or a Board, Jack Maloney said. And if ye want a president to sit over it, Jamie Stuart is as good for me as any other.

No, no, I said. Give it to some other.

Dwight Carpenter is Pennsylvania man, said Prukish slowly. So is Jamie. So is Button Lash.

Carpenter I remember well—a long, bony man, with a great hatchet chin and a somber way of speech. He had been a powder maker before the war, and he went as powderman for the first cannons we rolled from Philadelphia. Now he was a layer and a sergeant, but always to follow and never to lead; and, knowing this, he shook his head and made the point that linemen would want no cannonmen over them.

Nobody is going to be over nobody, said Jim Holt. Over us is too many and too big.

Then let it be Jamie, said Jack Maloney, and I said:

To hell with that! Let it be you, for I tell you it shouldn't be any man of the 11th, which has had ten whiplashes for what any of you had—and tell me different!

But they looked at me out of the dark, hairy faces and said never a word.

. . . And ten wounded for each of yours; so they'll say, It's a good grievance the 11th has, but why should *we* thraw for *them?* And that's why it shouldn't be me, and maybe Jack neither, him being British; so what about Billy Bowzar, who can read and write to boot?

They agreed to that. Bowzar was a native man, quiet and not looking for a fight, but a good soldier and a way of talking that made folks listen. They voted him, and he climbed up onto the table and said:

I accept and I call you to order in a sober way, my good comrades. Now I say to you that we must bind ourselves together here and become like one man, for it's the way old Ben Franklin said now, and maybe now for the first time. If we don't all hang together, just as sure as there's a God in the heavens above, we will all hang separately.

He stood with his head under the peaked roof, his head all dark and somber up there, but the edges of his red beard catching a glint from the tallow wick.

I pledge you together, he said. Take the pledge.

And we all of us raised our right hands and pledged that we would stay together and see this thing through, come what might, even if it meant that we must die together.

Then who wants the floor to speak? he said.

But since we were committed now, since we had all of us already done a thing for which many of our comrades had died in the past — spoken and plotted and organized against the gentry who led us — we fell to brooding upon our position instead of giving voice to thoughts and plans. Silence and cold crept over us. Rum would have loosened our thoughts and our tongues, but we had no rum; and thereby arose at that moment a danger point, where the whole thing might have simmered out, each running to unbraid the particular piece of hemp he wore as his own collar. Sensing this, I began to speak without having any clear orderly notion of what I would say. I only knew that someone had to talk, ease them out, start their own tongues. I knew no more than they did where we were going or what awful road we were preparing to explore; but I did know that as soldiers we had things in common, and soldiers we were, and maybe the best in the whole damned world, if the truth should be known; and I also knew that, as with so many of them, the whole of my grown life had been as a soldier and discipline was in my bones and mutiny was a dreadful thought to entertain. Yet I spoke, telling them:

It'll be me first, if you tolerate it, and I welcome you here to the magnificent hut I live in. Anyway, you know me, all of you: Jamie Stuart, sergeant in the 11th; and Danny Connell and Moses Gonzales have watched me since I was a little shaver of a lad, and now I'm a man grown, and all the years in between right here in the Line as a regular soldier. The others of you know me too, and you know what is true and false in me. If the gentry look on us as dirt — and dirty we are — I say the best thing in my life is the comrade in the Line, and I'm here because I want to be here. We joined up in York village before they ever wrote out the fine principles of independence, and I said to myself, shaver that I was, the fine logic of my life is the army of the Revolution. Where else was I to look for logic? Born out of slavery I was, my mother and my father in bondage, like so many of yours, and when I was six, turned into the fields to pick. And apprenticed at ten.

And beaten, starved, driven, mocked at. I know not why the Yankee men fight, but I know how it was with us in Pennsylvania, and I know that when I fell in love with a sweet young lass called Molly Bracken, my master beat me and told me love was for the gentry. The devil it is! Love is for us There are land and woods and iron in this place for all of the world, and this is what my musket says, me, Jamie Stuart. But where am I now? They sold me. My mother and father they sold, and they sold me, and here I sit, ragged and hungry and worn out with the wild battles they made me fight out of their vanity and stupidity and their fear lest the Revolution should turn itself into something against the officer gentry. . . . And that's all. I've had my say.

Then it was Andrew Yost, the Dutchman, who rose ponderously and told what his father had said to him, one day when the Line encamped nearby to his land.

We hold on quits from the patroon, said Yost, and all his life my father dream of freehold. If we hold land in New York Colony, the patroon goes with the British. Instead, we are lucky. We hold land in Jersey, and the patroon has to go with the Revolution or lose his land. So he goes with the Revolution and they make him colonel. Now patroon is colonel, and the rents go up. On my father's land, every year since 1776, rents double, and when I go home to my father last spring and ask for food, he just look at me. He just look at me and say, you think I'm not starving too, God damn you to hell, and the Revolution with you. That's what he say, with barns empty and larder empty, and all the officers of the 4th, 6th and 10th quartered with the patroon and living on the fat of the land. Then he say to me, Lend me your pay. Make me a loan of your pay. I say to him, *Pay?* My God, old man, you're surely crazy as hell!

Then there spoke Freddy Goulay, who said, his voice singing like a drum softly beaten:

You all know me, I am Goulay, black man, African man whose daddy was sold into slavery for Quenten Soames, the Lord Schofield, who I never seen — only his name I know. But I know that, sure enough. When I eight year old, they put me in the field under the whip, and whip me in the sun and whip me in the rain. Whip me in the sun and whip me in the rain, and I ain't got no back at all, only the whip marks. Then there comes war for freedom, we hear, war for freedom, sure enough for us, for who need freedom more. Sixty-two of us work the fields out in Blue Valley in Virginia, and when news come, we rise up and slay the overseers. Seven of them, and us do like the Bible say, and put to death them who hold us in bondage. Cold and cruel we put them to death, for they whip us and hold us in bondage, and we brake the muskets over their heads. Then we go across to Pennsylvania, for them in Virginia would be wrought for what we done, and we enlist us here. Sixty-two black men from Lord Schofield's lands, and only me, Goulay, and Jim Holt and Kabanka is left. We is left, but the other all perish, for the gentry put them in front. All right — the gentry put them in front in Monmouth and eighteen of us is slain right there, and that all right, I tell you. You going to slay for freedom, you going to pay the price. We know that — but we know too that the gentry is turned around, and they don't want no freedom. Otherwise they don't take men who fight the war and make beasts of them and slaves of them, and starve them, and let them die away of the plague while they fill their bellies, and whip them and hang them, and gut them in, like so they did to Kelly, and make a mockery of them, and steal their pay and spend it on wine and women . . .

Like a drum, his deep voice beat, and the rhythm caught the upturned, haggard, dirty faces of the men, and set them to nodding a rhythmic agreement; for who was not hot with the memory of the fourteen thousand dollars pay money stolen and spent by Lieutenant John Bingham of the 5th and the four others who were with him, and the three thousand dollars spent and squandered by Captain Silas Greene of the 3rd, and how he said, when they tried him — not believe me, as they tried us — that it was better spent than on the lousy Irish and the heathen Jews? Who did not recall that his fate was neither death nor whipping, but six strokes of the cane and then a disgraceful removal of his name from the regimental rolls, a disgrace that paid him well enough? And who was not bitter with the memory of four thousand dollars more of commissary money — hard money and not the worthless paper — appropriated to the Philadelphia tailors to make fine winter woolen uniforms for the officers when all the while we starved in our nakedness? And more and much more; and the memories flooded over us and stiffened us and hardened us as the black man spoke — we who had once hated black men and had then learned to die with them and eat with them and live with them, which was more than our gentry could learn.

There then spoke Lawrence Scottsboro, master sergeant in the 1st, a bent, gnarled, bitter little man of fifty years — old, woefully old that was, in our ranks — toothless, professional soldier all his life, from the French wars; dirty profane; such a man as I would have shrunk from once, but whom I knew now — and knew also the core of hope and fear within him.

387

Naked, he said, naked into the world and naked out of it, and where will I lay my old bones when the time comes? A bounty of twenty dollars they promised me, nor paid it. Christ no! Nor paid my wages! I see them a nation! Gentry they are, but where is a tot of rum to warm my aching old bones? A shred of meat? A man wants a woman, a sip of wine, a bite of pudding! A man's entitled to his wages — I tell you so. What in hell's name else has he?

Else, much else, said the Jew Levy, in his piping voice with its Spanish accent, a skinny little man with black eyes and a thin, ragged beard. He has in him a soul which can also be whipped, and that can be whipped to death even if the body lives. We here — we are like huntsmen roving the world for some flowers to smell, but the smell, it has become a stink in our nostrils. For you it is the cane and the whip; but for me and my kind, it is dirty Jew bastard from dawn to nightfall.

Talk, talk, talk, said Emil Horst, chief carpenter in the train, but what does it lead to? It leads to the gallows, you benighted fools!

Will they hang all of us?

How many scaffolds have ye built, Emil? Will you carve us one?

Now who is that? Who is that? roared Horst, a powerful and bitter man, short and broad and powerful.

He leaped onto the table top and roared, Come up here with me! Come up here with me, you dirty outland rat, and stand up to me, and say it to my face!

Ah, quiet, quiet — or they'll be hearing us over in Morristown, soothed Bowzar.

Do I have to look of gentry? Has sense no place here? Are you all mad with hunger and the want of a little rum? I'd be a rich man and gentry myself, if I had a dollar for every lad who died mutinous! And frightened I am not — we pledged the oath, I hold with it!

And how many scaffolds have ye fashioned?

I'm a soldier, and I was ordered to build, and by God in heaven, I'll build a staircase to hell if they order me.

Then Jack Maloney leaped onto the table alongside the carpenter, and they stood there in the center of that stirring, murmuring, packed body, like two wolves centered in the circle of the pack, the one great and gross, the other small and dapper, and Jack Maloney, grinning, asked:

Will you call yourself a better soldier than me?

Shaking his great head, the carpenter answered seriously, No, no, there be no better, Jack, but you have betrayed the King what fed you.

Betrayed? For what pay? For what reward? For what gain? So that I will never lay eyes again on my bonny land and my native Yorkshire?

You have never seen a pretty land, Emil Horst, until you look upon the green sward of England, but it's bitter for a man whose eyes open and who says, Only a butcher kills for pleasure or pay. From that, I move one step. One step! How many times have I told the raw recruit that fear is a matter of one step; the second comes easier. When I had said to myself, I will not fight against the rebels, I had to ask myself: Then will ye not fight alongside them? Only if I stayed in the pay of King George would I betray, and now if I bend my head to this mockery the officer gentry have made of good men who fight for freedom, then I betray. Don't betray me, Emil Horst! Get out now, and go to the Hardwick House where the gentry are swilling, and tell them that over here in a hut of the 11th, a lot of dirty curs are making a mutiny—or stay here and hold your peace, for they will never hang the Pennsylvania Line! Who will hang us? Who?

He addressed this to the crowd, and a low, animal roar of approval answered him.

Who? Who? Five years ago, when the Yankees ran like frightened hares in New York, their war would have been over if it were not for the foreign brigades—and it hasn't been different since. You ask who is the Revolution? We are the Revolution—we are! And if we should cast out the gentry who have made this noble thing into a pigsty, who is traitor to who?

No answer now, but a deep and thoughtful silence, now that the thing had been formulated, worded, made plain. Whatever thoughts are, whatever thoughts we had been keeping inside us, no one had ever spoke like this. My heart matched theirs; well I remember the stab of fear and pain and excitement and wild exultation that ran through me, as if a new sky were seen beyond black clouds, a sky that was more of a mystery than the secret of life itself, but glimpsed a moment. All the years I have lived since, all the pain and sorrow I have known, have not served to take away that one single glimpse I had that night, in that crowded, body-warmed, stinking hut.

Now stay or go, Emil Horst, said Jack Maloney, in a voice that was gentle and awful. And after moments, the carpenter answered:

I stay.

Do we all stay? asked Jack Maloney.

Then the Revolution is over, a voice spoke from the dark corner of the hut.

Ye are mistaken there, for it has just begun.

Then clear your heads and fuzz the cobwebs off your brains, said Billy Bowzar. The night is half over, and we have a matter of work to do.

PART THREE

Being an account of the events of New
Year's Day, observations on the mood of
the men, and certain details concerning
the preparations for the rising of the
Pennsylvania Line.

Dawn CAME, and still only the barest essentials of our work were
complete, for we were trying to remake not only the Pennsylvania Line
of the Revolutionary Army but, in a fashion we only vaguely understood, our lives and our destiny and the lives and the destinies of all
folk within our land; and that, you will agree, was no small undertak-
ing for a handful of wretched and hungry soldiermen. So when it
comes to what we made and what we failed to make, you should measure the target we shot at as well.

One of the first steps we took was to appoint a Committee, to act for
the Congress of the Line, which had come into being spontaneously
and without plan or direction, but simply out of grief and anger over
the death of the drummer lad, of the soldier Kelly, and of our own
tired hopes. A Congress of fifty or sixty persons could hardly accomplish what we needed to accomplish before dawn broke, and that was
readily agreed to and understood; so we created a Committee of Sergeants, which would have a sergeant — or in some case a corporal, since
many of those were good men, held back by the hate they had earned
from the gentry — to represent each of the ten infantry regiments, with
an eleventh to speak for the artillery company. A twelfth was added to
the Committee, and that twelfth was myself; the purpose was to ensure
discipline and protection. First, I was designated provost, but the name
itself was compounded out of such hate and fear and terror and
misery, that it sat uneasily with me and with them as well.

We could not do as the provosts did. If we were not all of us hanged or shot down by noon of the next day, we would begin to bring something new into being; it would be a new army with a new discipline and a new law and a new hope, and it would have no officers, but a discipline out of itself—which was not a matter we understood too well, but somehow felt in the marrow of our hopes. All that long night and morning, we were changing, and somehow we had the assurance that all the soldiers of the Line would change too. Yet for all of that, we knew that in the first stages at least, there would be an iron hand needed—not I but a group, a Committee, to enforce decisions; and if they chose me first, it was because I was Pennsylvania and Scotch too, free but born in bondage, native yet bound blood and body to the foreign brigades. And another thing, if I say it—I was a soldier, and I would know my work. If they chose me, it was because the pattern of toil and trouble was rubbed into me—and they knew I would not leave them in the lurch.

So my committee was given the title Guard of the Citizen-soldiery, and I myself was called President of the Guard.

It may seem strange to you that everything we did was done through committees and you may have heard folk who malign us say that we took not a step or an act without making a committee first; but it should also be remembered that, before the gentry took over, the Revolution arose from committees of the plain people; and for five years, the lesson had been driven home that war is not made by heroes or by gallant officers in blue and white uniforms, but by the men of the Line, standing shoulder to shoulder. It is true that we created committees for care of the women, the children, the ammunition, the commissary—yes, and we even had a Committee of Moral Purpose for Citizen-soldiers, and a Committee of Propaganda, and a Committee for the General Good of the Common Weal; and it is also true that few enough of these committees ever functioned; but that is not to say that what we did was wrong. We did only what we knew how to do, and that was little enough.

First the Committee of Sergeants was formed. Names were raised; they were discussed—some at length, some hardly at all. Billy Bowzar was elected from the 10th, Danny Connell from the 11th, Lawrence Scottsboro from the 1st. These were all unanimous, but there was a good deal of discussion over Leon Levy on the 5th. Many held that it was not right for a Jew to stand for a whole regiment, even as they held again that it was wrong for the black man, Jim Holt, to represent the

2nd Regiment. It was Jack Maloney, who was elected from the 6th over protests that a British deserter could not be wholly trusted, who said:

What kind of a mockery is it when we make foreigns among the foreigns themselves?

They were elected, as was Bora Kabanka, the giant African-born Bantu of the 9th Regiment. There was Dwight Carpenter from the artillery and Abner Williams, the gentle Connecticut-born scholar from the 3rd Regiment. Sean O'Toole stood for the 4th and Jonathan Hook for the 7th. Some thought it proper to have someone stand symbolically for the 8th, but since they were hundreds of miles away, guarding Fort Pitt, and since we had heard nothing of them for so long, it was decided better to let them be apart from us, until they could come to a decision of their own.

Before the Committee of Sergeants sat down to build an agenda and deal with it, a Commissary Committee was appointed by Billy Bowzar and myself, with Chester Rosenbank as its president, and they adjourned to his hut in the encampment of the 2nd, to begin to deal with the various and complex questions of supply.

Most of the night had gone by now, and most of the lads of the Congress had staggered sleepily away to their hutments. Built red though the fire was, it could not drive off the cold that crept through the chinks in the logs, and our tallow wick had burned out and we had no fat to replenish it. Katy Waggoner was huddled on the floor, close to the fire, with Mathilda's head in her lap, and as the mountain girl slept, Katy gently stroked her yellow hair and sang to her, so softly that it came as a kitten's purr: *Long is the night for sleeping childer, goblins dance in the redwat snow . . .* In the bunks, men huddled in the straw snoring hoarsely, for our heads were heavy and thick with constant sickness; and on either side the long table the Committee of Sergeants sat and planned, their bearded faces weary and gray. Billy Bowzar had a writing pad that he tilted to catch the fire gleam, and Jack Maloney was advancing an argument for speed and precision in getting under way.

Or you'll find a traitor among you, mark me, said Katy Waggoner, breaking her sad song and then picking it up again.

Angus MacGrath came in, beating the cold from his blue knuckles.

How is it? we asked him.

Caller, and much so. Cold and deeply so. But quiet.

Have ye a good guard of lads?

Twenty of the best. I took me the Gary brothers, who are tight on a

392

scent as hellhounds, and I put me one at the Hardwick House and one at the Kemble House, and there they crouch in the snow for a whisper among the gentry. But they sleep the sleep of the just this New Year's, even if no other time, with bellies full of wine and pudding. And if I may trouble ye, Jamie, I'd be the better for a crust of bread in me to stave off the cold.

And wouldn't we all, smiled Danny Connell. Just tighten yer belt and come another day—we'll all of us be eating sufficient, or without any appetite to trouble us.

Jamie here—and heed me, Angus, and get it into your thick head—is now President of the Guard . . . said Billy Bowzar seriously, his broad, flat face solemn and judicious . . . and it's him we will thank for staying alive. We are a Board of Sergeants to deal with a rising up of the whole Line, so that from this moment on, we will fight a war for ourselves and for our own, and not for the God-damned officer gentry. . . .

The big Scot's jaw fell, and he rubbed his beard and looked from face to face among the twelve stolid members of the Committee.

Well?

Give me a chance to swallow.

Are ye with us or agin us, Angus?

What in hell kind of a question be that to ask a man? Do I have the look of the fause?

True or fause, each man pledges here.

Be damned to ye, and I pledge, said the Scot sourly. Ye would mistrust your own mother, and me that has never been corporal even, for I would not put my head where some will!

And I'm a better man than you are, Danny Connell, he added. Or any other black Roman! Would you make something of that?

If I were not this tired, answered Connell wearily.

Button yer lip, MacGrath, said I, putting my arm through his, for you are my man now. We need a hundred more to the twenty fine lads ye have found, and then we will figure out the putting into action of all the fine plans they cook up here.

And I turned him to the door—

Come along, and if yer head rings a little, and if ye find your belly rubbing your backbone, it's but a temporary nuisance; for it seems to me that we're on the wildest jig a man ever danced.

And it's no pleasure dancing when the ground is four feet below ye, MacGrath said solemnly. Ye do not intend to go into that cursed cold at this hour of the morning, Jamie Stuart?

393

Indeed I do. There is no more sleep for us, Angus, until this is finished.

There is sleep for me, the Scot said stubbornly. I have done my round of this mad duty.

I slid my musket from the rack and looked at him. Then I said:

Well now, Angus MacGrath, this is a new hitch for me, but the skin of my neck is tight enough for me to play it out, and to tell you the truth, I don't much give a damn at this point. I have lived in hell too long, and I will not see my sweet Molly again, and the whole fact of it is that I'm past caring for anything but the one chance in a thousand we are playing for. So what do you say?

I leveled the musket at him; and from me he looked to the eleven grim-visaged men who sat at the sawbuck table, all of them watching us, but no one of them saying a word, and still Katy Waggoner in front of the fire, keening her plaintive lullaby.

What will I do? I thought to myself then. What will I do? Will I shoot down this great brave man, this large ugly Scotsman who is like a brother to me — or will I back out? And if I do back out, what then? What sort of a wild venture have I embarked on, that every step of the way it comes to a crisis that must either be driven home, like the peg into its wooden loin, or left to triumph on the ashes of our insane hopes? Are any of us sane? Or are we all mad with hunger and cold and humiliation?

Yet for all these thoughts, I knew that I was sane — saner indeed than I have ever before been, in all of my life, and I also knew that I would slay Angus MacGrath or any other who stood in our path from here on. Something had happened to me, just as something had happened to the eleven at the table; a new fire had been lit, and the heat of its flame was still untested.

Well, I will be damned, said MacGrath. Here is Jamie Stuart, with the pap still wet on his mouth, and he holds a gun on me. By all that is holy! Well, it will take the gentry to slay me, not such a skinny lad as you, Jamie Stuart. So let us go out into that cursed cold night and do yer crazy business.

And I went out arm-in-arm with Angus MacGrath, and when I returned, as I said, there was dawning in the smoky air, and still hardly a beginning had been made by the Committee. I brought them an accounting of the Line, which was three thousand and fifty-two enlisted men, as near as I could reckon it with no access to the officers' records.

394

Just for a moment before I entered the hut, I paused and looked across the silent, flat parade ground, with its lines of huts and its tracked-over, dirtying snow. It slumbered in uneasy peace; but what, I wondered, would it be like a few hours from now? Would that pale, cold sun, nudging the mist so timidly, look down upon a sanguine plain of fratricidal horror? And would this be the end of all the best hopes that the ragged band of us had ever entertained? Yet I was committed, so what did it matter? And as for nightmares — had I not lived long enough in the midst of one?

The Committee listened as I made my report on the number of soldiers we had in the encampment. I spoke and blew on my hands alternately, edging to the fire to warm myself. Now Danny Connell rose and spread his ragged coat over the two women, who lay sleeping before the bed of coals, and old Scottsboro shook his head sadly, commenting:

A sight of men is three thousand and more, Jamie, and has any of us the head to lead them?

Cut that grumbling, said Jack Maloney. . . . How did you and Angus make out with the Guard, Jamie?

I reported that we had enlisted at least sixty more lads who pledged to stand by us; but that it was no easy work, crawling into bed with a man in the dark and persuading him with whispers. The call for the Guard was the refrain of the Yankee camp jig, to be sounded three times on the trumpet; and whenever that came, if there had been no further instruction, the men pledged to us would lead their hutments out onto the parade, with arms and bayonets fixed. But so far we had nothing to speak of among the 4th and the 2nd, and were particularly strong in the 10th and 11th.

And where is Angus?

Seeing to the guard over the Kemble House, and then to sleep, which I must have too, otherwise I will not be able to set a foot in front of the other.

I would sell me own sweet mother for a pot of steaming hot coffee right now, said Sean O'Toole.

Then heed me, Jamie, Billy Bowzar nodded, marking the words with his quill, and then you can turn in for two hours but not a minute more. We have made certain decisions, the main one being that a man on a gallows trap had best get off it or prepare to dance in the air. There is no more turning back from what we decided, and no more delaying it either. So we have chosen sundown this day to expel the officers and take the Line, and the Revolution too, into our own hands. There is our commitment; either we succeed tonight, or we will pay for it tomorrow.

But it ain't humanly possible to convince all the men before this evening, I protested.

And we don't want to, said the black man, Holt. If they all know of this, they will set to pondering it, and they will coddle right and wrong until they're tight in it as a worm in a apple. Let them do what they feel when we hail them. They do right—and we win. They don't do right . . .

It is the only way, Jamie, insisted Dwight Carpenter. Either the men are with us or they are not with us, and there is no persuading them with words, not if we had a fortnight to plan and plot. This is the only way.

Like casting dice . . .

Ye see it wrong if you see it that way, Jamie, for the hopes and dreams of men are not dice to play with. We have been too much played with already, and if this was just a wild adventure for our own hope and glory, why then there would be somewhat in your say. But we got a simple and unclouded stake in freedom, not in wealth and property and power as the gentry do, but for the right to hold up our heads a little and taste some sweetness in living, and don't you think that every lad in the line has a similar stake?

I don't know.

You are overweary, Jamie, and Billy Bowzar, and it's truly a miracle you wrought out there in the darkness. So turn into your straw and rest your head for a time.

This, I did. I was past thinking or caring, and the moment I had covered myself with straw, I slept.

It was that morning, during my short rest, I think—for I kept no journal then, being more concerned with remaining alive than with telling the tale someday—that I dreamed so sweetly of my lovely lass, Molly Bracken. I make note of this because I believe it helps somewhat to show the simple, ordinary nature of folk we were; which might be taken for granted, as you might take for granted that most men are wrought out of the same stuff as you yourself, were if not for the slander that every learned scholar places upon the great rising of the foreign brigades. But the learned scholars sit snug and warm; they never took a barefooted march of thirty miles in a day, and they never went hungry for weeks on end, and they were never called forthright with the earnest, Come and enlist in the army of freedom, for ten dollars a month and eternal glory! So they never took that glory apart to see what it was made of, and less they care what the men who found that glory were made of; and the most they give thought to is how passing strange it was that the great land of Pennsylvania, with its three hundred folk and all its great resources, could never call more than fifteen hundred native born to its colors and had to enlist the remainder out of the foreign scum. But the native born and the foreign scum both dreamed, and I dreamed of the future and the past.

And in my dream of that past that morning, I sat at the cobbler's bench of Fritz Trumbrill once more: I, Jamie Stuart, an apprentice lad of sixteen summers, and for the grits and greens and fatback he fed me, and the patched shirt and trews he lent me, I cobbled all day, from the dawn to sunset. I swept the shop and blacked the boots and cleaned the panes and weeded the garden, and for all of this I never saw a minted penny. My reward was in blows from the huge, hamlike hand of the enormously fat half-German, half-Yankee master cobbler. And I stood it because until I had my trade, I was no part of the world of men. I gritted my teeth and stood it until they nailed up the first enlistment bill, and then I stood it no more, but flung my apron in the fat pig's face and told him:

I've a new trade now—and when I and the other lads have driven the British back into the sea, take care, take care!

And I walked off to the tune of his curses and abuse. But it is of before then that I dreamed, of the first time I saw Molly Bracken. I sat at my bench, alone in the shop, for Fritz was out for a pint at the tavern and Tibby, the junior apprentice, was over at the tannery, picking up a hide. In my dream I worked at a set of buskins for a little boy, awling the high uppers, when there came a tinkle from the bell at the door. Come in, I called, and there entered a slim reed of a girl, with hair so black it startled one, and eyes so blue they fair frightened one—until one saw how direct and open they were, how wise and knowing they were. And those eyes looked at me calmly and appraisingly as she said:

I have come to be fitted for a pair of walking shoes. I am Molly Bracken, the daughter of the new parson at the Lutheran Church.

To that point, my dream matched in a fair way with reality, for it was much in that same fashion I had met Molly Bracken. But in my dream I rose up and took her in my arms and kissed her, for I knew her well and nothing held me back. But in life itself, four months passed before I dared to take her hand and set my lips to it. And in those four months, she taught me to read and write and she taught me to know the flowers of the field, the stars in the sky, and some of the noble things men have done which are greater than either—in a certain way. Her father was a wise and humble man, and he took a liking to me and made his house my house. He unlocked his bookcase for me; he fed me, and he was as much a father as I ever had.

What a hunger I had for the things he gave me! As you will see, there was much apart from me in Pastor Bracken when I grew to manhood and had become proficient in the one trade I knew aside from cobbling, the trade of killing; but at that time of which I speak now, when I was a tall and stringy lad of fifteen years, he was the best and wisest person who had come into my life—the more so than my poor father, who had loved me but could give me naught.

In my dream, I dreamed among other things of my coming to the manse for the first time, where Molly Bracken brought me as she would bring a wild animal into a tame pasture, saying:

Never in all my born days did I see the like of such a boy as you.

Well, let me be, then. Let me be as I am. I ain't asking to be no different, so let me be.

You're a creature, not a boy, she said.

Well, you can go to the devil and be damned then, calling me a creature!

We were outside the manse, and she stopped and turned to me, wide-eyed and horrified.

Jamie Stuart!

What you asked for you got.

Then I'll leave you alone to your dirt and your nasty mind. You're a miserable little boy!

And she stormed into the house and left me standing outside alone, and there I stood, first on one foot and then on the other, and then on both feet, but unable to move, unable to go and unable to remain—in that wholly ambivalent condition that only a boy of fifteen, deeply and wholly in love for the first time in his life, can experience. And there I remained until Pastor Bracken came along on his way into the house, cocked an eye at me, prepared to pass on and then paused to question.

Waiting for someone? he wanted to know.

Nope.

You're the Stuart boy, aren't you?

Uh-huh.

Trumbrill's apprentice.

I nodded, feeling shame cloak me and run all over me. Evidently, he sensed what was going through my mind, and in any case there was visual evidence in the way in which my toes crawled for cover into my broken shoes, the way in which my elbows crawled from their holes, my knees from the gaps in my breeches. But mostly my toes, writhing over each other like terrified snakes, for what could be more incongruous or humiliating than a cobbler's apprentice shod as badly as I?

Why don't you come in, he said, and meet my daughter?

I know her, I answered, staring at my toes as I manipulated them.

Oh.

She don't like me, I said.

No? Well, maybe she could learn. That happens, Jamie Stuart. People start out disliking each other fit to tie a cat, and then they change. So why don't you come in and have a cup of tea with us? How about that now? Won't you come in? Come along now, won't you, Jamie Stuart?

And Jacob Bracken put his arm through mine and took me into his house with him, and of this I dreamed and of other things as well. How he made Molly my teacher, I dreamed; for he gave me a book to read and I pretended to read it. Yes, one fine day this happened, as I sat with them in their unbelievable kindness, and the man who wrote that book was a poet called Milton. And there in it was a picture of the splendid and awful turmoil of heaven and hell, so that my very heart ached to know what it meant.

Read it aloud, Jamie, said Pastor Bracken.

My head was bent and I would not raise it.

What is into the boy? asked Pastor Bracken. Molly, what is into the boy, do you suppose?

Leave him alone, she answered, God bless her. Then and there, I said to myself, God bless her for her kindness, for she is the best and sweetest lass in all the world.

Jamie! cried Pastor Bracken then, in the thunderous voice he used on a Sunday morning in the pulpit. Jamie! he cried.

And I raised up my head all covered with tears, and answered that I was as ignorant as a pup just whelped, and not a word of the English language could I read or write, and here I was, fifteen years and better.

So Molly taught me, and I dreamed of her teaching me. I dreamed of the ABC as I, big gawking lad, learned it out of a hornbook, and I dreamed of the first little verses I put together. But such is the magic of words that I dreamed also of the first book of depth and beauty that I was able to make out for myself, and how eventually I lay before Pastor Bracken's fire, reading like a cat gone mad in the catnip, first from one book and then from another, all unconcerned with the beating these late hours away would earn me when I returned to the shop.

So I dreamed of this and that, of one thing and another, of my meeting Molly Bracken, of seeing her, of learning from her, of defending her once from a mad dog, holding the dog at arm's length, both my hands flexed around its neck until it strangled like that, and conscious for the first time of the strength in my long, lean body, and proud—proud as when I said to her:

There was a spark inside me once, which I always knew. But now it will burn, and you will not be ashamed of me. . . .

But the dream placed all together, and in the dream, after I kissed Molly Bracken, I took her hand in mine and we walked down the street through York Village and out to the meadows beyond. And as we passed along the street, everyone whispered:

See there, it is that worthless orphan lad, Jamie Stuart, but we must honor him now, for there is by his side the loveliest lady that ever lived.

We walked into a meadow all carpeted with daisies, and suddenly we were ringed around with fragrant pine woods, alone under the sun and the breeze. Oh, my true love, sweet Jamie Stuart, she said to me, and I answered, For all eternity, I will be true to fair Molly Bracken. We stroked each other's face and hair, and our happiness was so great that it seemed we must surely die of it, for it was too much to bear.

And then Jack Maloney was waking me, with:

Time's up, Jamie lad. Would you sleep away your whole last day of grace?

Let me go back to my dream, I begged him.

There is no going back to dreams, Jamie, he said, with strange tenderness. As a matter of fact, it seems to me that there is no going back ever, whether in dreams or out of them.

I resisted him and closed my eyes and tried to slip back into the pool of sleep. Weary enough I was, but he kept shaking me, and as he shook me the dream dissolved and I knew I would never regain it.

You have lost me the fairest maid in all of Pennsylvania, I said.

How, Jamie?

You have never loved, so how would you understand?

And do you think there is a man who never loved, Jamie, even a soldier of King George III who was put into the camps with the pap still on his lips? Let that be . . .

I crawled out of the straw and dropped to the ground. The hut was dark, as it always was, with just one narrow bar of light through a crack in the door.

Close the damned door! I cried.

You're mighty mettlesome, Jamie, nodded Maloney, closing the door. Then he said:

There are some of us who have had no sleep, Jamie, so sit on your temper. You've got a day's work ahead. The Committee wants a check on every hut in the encampment, and at least one member of the Citizen-soldier Guard should be chosen from each hut, if that is possible. Then, tonight, when we issue the order to stand to arms and parade, the guards can lead. We have also heard gossip that a ration of rum has been allotted and will be issued out in honor of the New Year—which is something, for all the officers' crying that they had no rum or food either. Also, it is a piece of madness, for that rum on empty stomachs will drive the men crazy. All the more reason for the guards to be good men and to keep their heads. Also, keep your foot down on powder and shot. The hotheads will want to load muskets, and to the Committee's way of thinking, there's more danger in that than in anything else; for if we pull this off, bayonets will be ample to deal with a hundred and fifty officers, and if we fail, there will be nothing gained by turning it into a blood bath. We have had reports from the Hardwick House and the Kemble House and from three houses in the village where gentry are quartered. They stuffed themselves last night and most of them are still sleeping, and unless I mistake their temper, they'll give the encampment a wide berth all this day. But if any officer seems to get wind of what we're up to, Jamie, you are empowered to place him under arrest, binding and gagging him. The old hospital hutment will be turned into a guardhouse. Both barbers have joined us and taken the pledge to be true to the Line and the enlisted men.

I was out of my sleep and my dreams now, and I noticed that Billy Bowzar and Jew Levy still sat at the table, scribbling away on paper in the light of a tallow wick they had obtained from somewhere. While Maloney gave me my instructions, two men entered the hut, spoke softly to Bowzar, received slips of paper, and left. And as the door opened, I noticed two other soldiers on guard outside.

The men of my command, who shared the hut with me, were all of them awake, which was strange since they had missed most of the night's sleep. Curled in their straw, which was the only place they could find warmth when they did not have parade or drill—neither of

401

which would be given us on New Year's Day—they were oddly grave and quiet. From somewhere by some means, an organization was shaping itself, and the wild venture of the night before, which should have been revealed for all its lunacy on this cold, clear morning, managed to maintain itself.

Well, then, I said to myself, swinging my feet down to the floor, here you are, Jamie Stuart, twenty-two years old, with a little reading and a little writing and a little cobbling, making a great uprising. And I bethought me of Jimmy Coleman of my own regiment, who was hanged here on this same parade in Morristown only May past. Nothing had Jimmy done or said that could match the distance we had traveled since the evening before; he had only talked openly and publicly of the gap between the punishment and food issued out by the officer gentry. He had written down in charcoal across a posted order of the day, *When Adam delved and Eve span, Who was then the gentleman?* And it was also charged that he fomented plots and had made insulting remarks to Colonel Chickering, of the Connecticut Line. For this, he was put on the gallows and hanged by the neck until he was dead. But I remember well his behavior there, how he was calm and easy as any of the gentry might be, fingering the rope as he said: A little bit of freedom is not enough, my friends, so mind you treat us better or you will find the tiny spark you struck a mighty flame—and it may be that flame will even singe an officer or two. So the officers cursed him and he swung out of this life, and the officers said: Good riddance to bad rubbish. When an apple is rotten, you pluck it from the barrel.

Well, here I was, Jamie Stuart, and that was that, and there was no use thinking about it any more, and Jack Maloney was saying:

Hop to it, Jamie. There is much to be doing, and after we have made an army out of ourselves and driven George's men into the salty sea, we'll clean house. So there'll be no rest for a long time to come, and you might just as well put that in your pipe and smoke it.

I had slept with my shoes, and there were needles in my feet as I moved across the floor to the musket rack.

As I passed the table, Levy caught my sleeve and said, A moment, Jamie. I am writing you our credentials, and you had best wait for them.

Credentials? What in hell's name do I want with them? Is there anyone in this Line who don't know me?

Know you or not, said Billy Bowzar quietly, every Committee man will have credentials from here on. And no order need be obeyed unless a man can show his credentials and his warrant from the Committee.

Yet if it peters out, I reflected, a man carries his death warrant in his pocket.

That's right, Jamie, said Billy Bowzar, regarding me evenly from his bloodshot, fatigue-ringed eyes. We are all in this together, you know.

But Levy smiled slightly as he handed me my credentials, a slip of paper I still have here beside me as I write, so many years later, the paper less mortal than the men who made and wrote upon it. On it, it says, in the fine, cultured script of the Jew Levy:

> To all men who may examine this: Let it be known that this warrant empowers Jamie Stuart, Sergeant in the 11th Regiment of the Pennsylvania Line, to carry out all and sundry orders, desires, needs and complaints of the Committee of Sergeants, which is now and until the enlisted men of the Line shall rule otherwise, the supreme authority and the commanding power in the army of Pennsylvania — which power was invested in them by a representative Congress of the Regiments of the Line, notably as follows: 1st, 2nd, 3rd, 4th, 5th, 6th, 7th, 9th, 10th, 11th and Artillery.
> *Enscribed this Day of the 1st of January in the Year 1781, by* LEON LEVY *and signed by . . .* WILLIAM Z. BOWZAR *sec.*

This I took and wrapped in oilskin with a profile I had sketched of Molly Bracken, a testament of bravery given to me after the New York fighting and signed by Reed, three letters from my Molly, my Bill of Apprenticeship, and my enlistment and bounty papers. These constituted all that Jamie Stuart had gathered in twenty-two years of living, and for what they were worth, I carried them wherever I went.

Then I left the hut to undertake my duties as President of the Citizen-soldier Guard.

That day we began, after midnight struck, as a rude and unruly Congress; by dawn we had created and put into operation our Committee of Sergeants and certain other committees; and by nightfall of the first of January half the Pennsylvania Line was organized and prepared to move; and except for one incident, which I shall relate to you, not one breath of this came to the ears of the officer gentry. On that day when we worked to prepare the uprising, the feat we accomplished seemed not one half so remarkable as it does now, all these years later; but on reflection it seems passing strange that we, the enlisted men and noncommissioned officers of the foreign brigades, despised and reckoned as so much dirt, so many filthy animals, could have carried out in so short a time an organizational scheme never matched in all the history of the Revolution. It is a matter of record that no permanent encampment of the Continental Army was ever broken with so little preparation as we had for our uprising; and it was part of our plan that once we seized power to ourselves, we would break camp immediately and march through the night to another place. This was through the urging of Jack Maloney, who insisted that the only way in which we could consolidate ourselves and impose our new discipline was in the motion of a march.

Marching men, he said, are soldiers. Encamped, they are something else.

But that morning when I came out of my hutment, only the most tenuous threads bound us together. A credential in my pocket which was as good for the hangman as for anyone else; a few loyal and true comrades scattered through the encampment; and a musket in my hands which held one shot to smooth the path to glory. But I was young, and my earlier despair was transmuting itself into a mounting excitement, and my dreams of fair Molly Bracken gave way to dreams of a new army, an army which would sweep across the land, calling thousands to its banners, an army which would brush the British into the sea as a new broom flicks the cinders, an army which would call upon all of those who worked by the sweat of their brow and the strength of their hand to create a new kind of republic. . . . Yet there my dreams halted, for I knew of no way in which men could live except with the gentry above and such people as myself below. However, I shrugged that off, deciding that I was better for the doing, leaving the planning and the thinking to such men as Billy Bowzar, the Jew Levy, Jack Maloney, and Abner Williams, all of them men in their thirties, wise in all the ways of the world and full of the bitter wine of experience.

As I began to cross the angle of the parade, to a hut of the 1st where there were four good lads to start work with, a little group of officers, mounted and cloaked, came into sight on the road from Morristown. Strangely enough, I was the only one on the parade at the moment, except for a handful of men at the other extreme, a half mile away. There was no reason for me to be afraid, even though I carried a loaded musket—for I could bluff through that with a tale of guard duty—but the very sight of officers threw me off balance. They were the first I had seen since the day before; then they were my officers, the men who led me; now they were something else. Now they were ranged against me and I was ranged against them, and I carried a warrant in my pocket which would give any one of them justification to shoot me down like a dog.

I forced myself to walk along without changing my pace, yet I couldn't help glancing at them, and I noticed they slowed from a canter to a walk and that they were engaged in conversation—in the course of which one of them pointed to me. They must have come over from Kemble; for Wayne, the brigadier general, was among them, and it was he who nodded the agreement that detached one of them to my direction. The rest picked up their canter and went down the Hill Road toward Mendham, and in a few minutes they were hidden by the huts and the rise of ground toward the parade. The one who rode toward me, I recognized as Lieutenant Calvin Chester of the Artillery, the arrogant, pimply-faced son of a Philadelphia merchant.

He drew his horse up within arm's length of me, prancing it as was a habit with them, so close that I could smell the toilet water from his lace and see the brown drip of snuff from his nose. He wore a splendid greatcoat of brown, with yellow facings; his riding boots had yellow cuffs and he wore gauntlets of yellow pigskin.

Stand to attention! he shouted at me. What's your name and rank?

I presented arms, clicked my heels where there would have been heels had my torn boots owned any, and staring straight ahead of me, answered, Jamie Stuart, sergeant in the 11th.

From the corner of my eye, I watched the bobbing heads of Wayne and the others disappear beyond the hutments.

Sir.

Sir, I said.

And what are you doing on the parade with a musket?

Relieving guard, sir.

Now that's a damned lie, said the lieutenant, for I never knew a sergeant to stand guard where there was a private to do his work for him, and much less one of you damned, dirty scuts from the 11th. Let me see your pan.

I leveled the musket.

Primed, he nodded, and—with his affected, imitation-English lisp—'Od's blood, but we'd be better off if every one of the damned 11th was hanged from the hill. You're under arrest, Mister. Make an about-face, and we'll stroll over to the provost.

Oh, no, I smiled—hitching the musket around and dropping it on the middle button of his fine greatcoat—You are under arrest, and don't reach for a pistol, or I'll blow your fat ass out from under you. Just climb down from your horse and hook an arm through the reins, and lead it like you and me was out for strolling, and never a thought of who is gentry and who is dirt.

You'll hang for this, he began wildly, but I cut him short, telling him, I have no desire to converse with you or any of yer damned brethren. Just walk ahead until we come to the last of the 1st's hutments, and then knock at the door.

There was something in my voice that told him I meant what I said, and he did as I ordered him to. He led me and his horse to the hut and knocked at the door, which Sammy Gruen opened, rubbing the sleep from his eyes and staring in wonder.

We have a breakfast guest, I smiled, so make him welcome.

That was all Sammy needed, and the lieutenant entered the hut quicker than he warranted, and dropping the reins of the horse, I followed. There was an oil-paper window in the hut, and by the light I saw the dull, hopeless expression on the lieutenant's face as he watched the men tumble from their straw and gather round him. Dennis Sullivan, a good lad, but wild and marked for some sort of foolish fate, fingered the greatcoat, stroked the lace, and then pinched the pimply cheeks.

Do you plan to kill me? asked Chester hoarsely. For if you do, you will swing for it as sure as there's a God in the heavens above.

Now will we? grinned Dennis.

Pack that! I snapped. He was going to arrest me so I arrested him instead, and you can take off those nice clothes of his and gag him and tie him up, but no manhandling and no taking out grudges here and no talk. Tie him up and put some sacking over him, and we'll bear him to the hospital, where they're making ready for the sick.

This they did. We trussed him, wrapped him in sacking, and bore him to the hospital like a sack of potatoes, only of less use in any way. Sullivan and Gruen and a Pole named Krakower came with me, after I had warned those left in the hut to stay in the straw and keep their mouths shut. Two others, Kent and O'Malley, unsaddled the horse and then led it to the Artillery stable, with a story of a stray mount.

The old hospital hutment was supply dump and dispensary for the 4th, 10th and 11th Regiments. No doctors were assigned to it, since at that time we had only three doctors for the whole Line, and two of them were fine gentlemen with Philadelphia practices, which at the moment they were attending. The third doctor, a Jew from Charlestown in South Carolina, was brigade officer at the General Hospital, which was at the further end of the encampment. Some thought we might trust him, seeing that he was a Jew, but others said, Jew or not, he was an officer and gentry and would therefore best be left alone. Here at the dispensary were two barbers from Edinburgh, Andrew MacPherson and William Hunt, and they tended the odds and ends of hurts, distempers and minor sickness that took the three regiments. For all that theirs was a rough-and-ready practice, picked up as porters at the medical school and as staunchers on the battlefield, I would rather have had them than the cruel and offhand gentry; if you died, you died at least with a warm hand on your shoulder—and when one of our lads stopped a large-bore ball from a British gun, it was short odds that he died whether you had a physician or a barber to bleed him.

MacPherson opened the door for us. He was a tiny, wizened imp of a man, clean-shaven, a sharp, filthy tongue in an ugly little head, a randy goat of a little man and never without a woman, whether in camp or on the march. And not an old bag either, but the fairest lass in camp would be his, and how that was none of us could ever make out; except that his was a joy in life not matched in the grim and sorrowful encampment. Hunt, on the other hand, was a dour, unhappy Scot, dark and humorless, and slowly dying away with longing for the streets and taverns and fog of Glasgow.

Now welcome, Jamie Stuart! cried MacPherson. You would not think business to be this good when we have only set up some few hours past, but already the lads of the 10th have brought us two white-livered sergeants, and that's not bad for the first of a darg. Now what have ye there? . . . Not Chester, the dirty little dog!

Chester it is, sang Dennis Sullivan.

Then roll him in and make him snug and warm.

And like a sack of potatoes, we rolled the lieutenant to where two sergeants, trussed and gagged, sat against the wall. Already the hospital was crowded, and the day had only begun—and it was hot. A huge blaze roared in the hearth, and six women crouched before it, so close that the loose ends of their hair crackled, melting lead and spooning it into bullet molds. The hutment being supply depot as well as dispensary, a good third of the space was taken by bar lead, stacked as high as a man's head. Only the two barbers had sleeping quarters there; but in addition to them, the six women, the three prisoners and a white-faced lad from the 4th who was being bled for the shakes, there were Arnold and Simpkins Gary making a high bid for the girls, and with me and my four lads and the heat, and the sharp smell of molten lead, the bitter smell of medicine and the sweet odor of blood, the air was

407

never unbreathable. But no one seemed to mind that. The women gave the Gary boys as good as they took, telling them, Now why don't you take over this molding, if ye're so bright and strong and free with affection? And as she worked, MacPherson's lass sang: *The Bishop's wife, she looked me down, ye're either fine or common, I got what ye can never match, and sure it's far from common.*

And how is a man to treat the sick with this stinking lead boiling? . . . Hunt wanted to know . . . Already, we are cursed with committees, for the first Committee man comes and turns this into a jail, and then comes the second snooking for supply. The lead he spies, and orders it to be bullets before nightfall come.

Come out a ye tout, laughed MacPherson. The less sick we meddle with, the more will survive, and this is a fine piece of organization. I tell ye, we got a natural bent for committees.

But my heart was heavy as I left there. Suppose Chester should be missed and a search made? And didn't all this activity indicate that the gentry had a whiff of something?

From the hospital, we started a check of the hutments, but already the thing was in motion of itself, and every third or fourth hut there would be a black, cold silence until I had shown the warrant the Jew Levy wrote out for me. The men were in the straw and the encampment was dead — a silence and withdrawal that would have been suspicious on any other day than New Year's.

Because it was New Year's Day, much went by that would not have passed muster in the normal course of things. There was no parade and no drill; and until midafternoon, aside from Wayne and his orderlies, no officers approached the hutments; Lieutenant Chester was not missed, which was not so strange, for we learned afterwards that his mess had thought him to be with Wayne and Wayne had thought him to be back by now at the Kemble House. In any case, though the officers neither knew nor cared what we did that New Year's Day, the hutments were full of talk about how the gentry passed their time, once they had slept off their drunkenness of the night before. And they could not have better confirmed us in what we had decided to do.

There was, around our encampment, a ring of great holdings of the gentry, some of them patroons, some of them British quality, and all of them loyal to His Majesty, George III. We learned well the year before, when we encamped at this same place, to respect that loyalty, for eight men of the 4th Regiment who broke into Peter Kemble's grain bin were docked their pay and given thirty lashes each. The pay was nothing, for we never got it anyway, but thirty lashes is a cruel and terrible thing, and one of the lads, a boy of fifteen, died from the beating. Peter Kemble held over four thousand acres of land, with three manor houses upon it and sixteen barns, and for all that he was open and brash and defiant with his loyalty to the King, never a step was taken against him; instead, our own gentry snuggled up to him, for he was a true gentleman and hunted his hounds day in and day out, and in return for their respectful consideration, he quartered our officers, lent them his hounds to hunt with, and fed them at his board nightly. It was one of those things—as I came to know later—that are understood among gentlemen, even though they fight on different sides; but it was not understood by the buckskin men in our ranks, those who came from the Western counties, Scottish men with a century-old dream of an acre of land for their own, bound out to America to realize their dream—and discovering then that, far from their having land, they could never get enough hard money to own woven clothes or an iron tool.

So when word passed through the hutments that four musicians had come up from Philadelphia to play for a New Year's minuet at the Kemble House, and that two carriages of Philadelphia ladies had followed them—and that there were hanging for bleeding on the Kemble sticking rack two beefs and five fat pigs—you can imagine that our mood was not eased.

Angus MacGrath and I were going among the huts of the 7th, passing out instructions and arguing with faint-hearted men and family men, when we came into a hutment with a stew cooking, the first stew we had smelled in a long while. Chicken heads, they told us: a stew of two dozen chicken heads scrounged out of the garbage at the Kemble House; and did we want a pan?

I would die first, said Angus MacGrath. I am a simple man and not a prideful man, but I will see myself damned before I scrounge in garbage for the leavings of the gentry.

It was no way for him to talk, for these were hungry lads and hunger is a great leveler, and a man wants a taste of meat after he has lived a month on corn mush.

Toward midafternoon, there was a flurry of alarm in the hutments, for we beheld a company of at least thirty officers coming toward the parade at a smart canter. Angus and I were at a hut of the 7th then, and we and the men inside it charged our muskets and determined then and there that if this was a stroke to cut the head from the rebellion, we would go down under bullet and bayonet and not stand trial for any shameful hanging. But the crowd of officers turned off down

409

the road to Whippany, and we learned later that they were guests for a great dinner given that evening at the castle of the patroon Van Beverhoudt. Van Beverhoudt was a mighty Dutch lord who held two hundred black slaves and lived in peace with both the British and the Colonials. In '76 and '77, when the flame of the Revolution burned hot and fresh, one of his barns had been raided and burned, but after that he went to Philadelphia and had certain dealings with certain folks there, and from then on he was not molested.

So with one thing and another, the men became more sullen, more bitter, more willing to attempt some wild and foolish enterprise, and their bitterness increased as midday passed and the promised ration of rum, the one note of joy for the New Year, was not dispensed.

I recall how Angus and I faced at least forty of them, packed into a hut of the 7th, answering their questions, fighting their wild, random moods.

By now, I had spoke to hundreds of men, and I came to realize that the dream I held, the dream held by Billy Bowzar and Handsome Jack Maloney and the Jew Leon Levy—the dream of turning the still, stagnant current of the Revolution into a mighty new stream; the dream of a whole population of farmers and artisans and bond servants, serfs and slaves, rising up and sweeping the handful of redcoats into the sea like so much rubbish, and then making a true new land where there was freedom and equality for all—I came to realize that this dream was no commodity for sale or conviction. The men were with us; they were for the Committees; they hated the officer gentry as much and more than we did; their cup of sorrow was so full that they no longer cared for the consequences of some wild venture—but they could not be lured with dreams.

We must be paid, they said. That's a simple matter, a plain matter. If a man enlists him at ten dollars a month, he deserves that money, not in paper, but in hard metal. If a man is promised a bounty, he has got to get it. Now what of that, Jamie?

It is not a matter of money, I tried to tell them. There is a reason why you have not been paid, and the reason lies in the very nature of how the gentry lead this struggle. That is what we must change.

But how will *you* pay us, Jamie? How will the Committees pay us? It is all very well to have a fine dream, but a man wants a dollar to send home to his wife and kids. And whatever you say about the gentry, it's them as has the hard money, not us. Not any of us. Can you deny that?

I could not deny it. There was a simple truth in the fact that the gentry had the money, the wealth, the food, the forges and the looms. That they had it out of our blood and sweat, I knew, but what other way there was, I didn't know.

Now me, says a lad out of the German country along the river, I enlisted in '76, and they told me for three years, but I cannot read nor write, as you know, Jamie Stuart, and it seems I put my mark on articles for the whole of the war, with the right for them to hang me, just as they hanged Hans Forst and Emil Guttman. If the war lasts twenty years, I got to fight and grow old and gray and get my death of a wound finally, and all for a twenty-dollar bonus they swear to pay when peace is made.

And how many a good lad is dead and never lives to see the peace! . . . cried Johnny O'Brian. . . . And the dirty militia cowards that come up now for a six-month enlistment, they get a bonus of one hundred dollars in hard cash, while the heart of me at nineteen years is worn out with fighting and marching and starving. If Jack Maloney and Billy Bowzar are making a rising, I will follow them to hell and be damned, for I care no more for this kind of living. But I will not go on fighting. For what, Jamie?

For the Revolution, I answered.

Be damned with the Revolution! It's one set of masters for another, and that's the way it has always been. In the old country it was the chief of the clan, and here it's the cursed squire; and it will always be that way and no different, and if you think otherwise, Jamie Stuart, ye're just a feckless young idiot. You know what they say in the old country—for a dog there be always a shangan, and we are dogs. Look a-here at Johnny Burke, sitting beside me. Eleven years old he is, and already two years in the ranks and not knowing of anything but foul language and blows . . .

I lot more I know, and the hell with you! the child squeaked.

Now shut your damn mouth, Johnny Burke, and let me speak. When they bring up their whores from Philadelphia, they are lasses and ladies, but the women who bore our bitterness and our children in the camp and on the march, they are whores and are whipped monthly for the morale of the regiment. No Jamie Stuart, we have had a stomachful of the Revolution! We will drive out the officers with you; but then, down arms and go home!

Where is home? a tall, broad-faced Pole asked slowly.

I was racking my brains for what to say, when Angus MacGrath rose and told them:

If I thought living that dree and no hope but to be a lousy gillie all

411

my days, then I'd blow out my brains and be done with it. Give it up, Jamie. I will not argue with these scuts. To hell with them!

We left together, but there was no comfort in the Scot's words. We walked along the hutments, and already the early winter evening was upon us, cold and dreary.

At the houses of the 10th, rum was being poured from two hogsheads on a cart, an ounce to a man, and the muttering of the soldiers began to grow like a drum beaten heavier and heavier. White-faced, the two rum peddlers sat on the seat of the cart, their lips trembling, their eyes cast down. Captain Oscar Breddon of headquarters straddled a hogshead, pistol in hand, glaring his hatred but keeping his mouth shut, while the sergeants measured out the ration.

As we reached the cart, a soldier, his rum in his hand, walked forward to the driver and said: You profiteering Yankee bastard, look at me!

And when the driver turned his head, the soldier cast the rum in his face, spat in the snow and walked off.

PART FOUR

Being a true narration of the great rising
of the Pennsylvania Line, with details and
incidents not hitherto revealed.

W HEN I REPORTED to my hutment an hour past sunset, it was
like the heart and brain of an army in battle. Candles and two lamps
had been found, and the hut was filled with light. Five of the Committee of Sergeants sat at the table, each engaged in some separate task,
and there was a steady stream of men coming in and out from the
various regiments. Messengers delivered messages and sped away with
the answers. Also, food was being found and stored, and already the
bunks were crowded with sacks of grain and corn meal and frozen sides
of pork and lamb.

Most of the food had come from the central commissary, for the
whole guard there was with us and were already removing whatever
could be taken without arousing the suspicion of the officers; but
somehow, already, news of the rising had leaked out to small farmers
nearby, and the meat was a gift from them — and this heartened us
more than anything, since not only were most of us foreign brigades
but even those of us native to our country's soil were foreign here, to
the land of Jersey. The years of our compaigning over the roads and
fields of Jersey had wasted much of the country, and those who had
suffered most were the tenants of the patroons and the great lords.
They were filled with hatred for the army, so it was a wonder now that
they too should make a separation between us and the gentry and that
they should aid us instead of betraying us to our officers.

I had to push my way into that hut, for at the first glance it was like
a madhouse; it was only when you looked a second time that you found
a scheme in the madness. A giant, yellow-haired German shouted at
Levy, who ignored him and went on speaking to the black man, Holt,

413

and to Prukish, who loomed over the table, a pistol in each hand. A delegation of women demanded to know what Jack Maloney expected to do with the children, while he strove to give a messenger an answer and to dispatch him with it. Bowzar roared for quiet every so often, and Sean O'Toole, in his high-pitched voice, screamed across the table at Levy:

Ye damned Jew, if ye will not give me warrants for the two hostlers, how in hell's name am I to find horses to move the four cannon I have already laid hands on that are standing exposed like a cake of ice in the pit of hell!

And background to this was a wild hammering which came from my own bed and berth, where the hated Captain Jack Auden of my own 11th—and how many marks I bore from his cane I cannot count—lay trussed like a turkey for roasting, his face in a side of pork, his heels drumming madly on the wall. I saw him, and the strain I was under snapped, and I stood there in the doorway roaring with laughter fit to break a gut.

Shut up, ye Dublin dung digger! cried Jack Maloney at O'Toole, and to hell with yer cursed hostlers!

And at me:

Jamie! Jamie—have ye gone mad or maybe gotten the pint ration of rum we was promised? Get in here and make a disposition!

Now here is Jamie, shouted Billy Bowzar. Will you shut your mouths or get to the nation out of here!

But three more men crowded in behind me, calling for Connell.

We were sent to see Connell, they insisted, and that we will. We will see him or be damned. We will not be taking our orders from a black Nayger man, and here we stand until we see Connell, or you can take yer rising and be damned with it!

So you see, Jamie, said Bowzar, when I stood over him finally, the Romans and the Protestant lads and the Naygers and the Jews are all at one another's throats; and this is what we have, with two hours left before the rising . . .

He had not slept, and his broad, flat face was lined with fatigue, yet the square cut of his curly red beard and the bald spot on top of his skull gave him a whimsical turn of humor, and there was a blaze of suppressed excitement in him, the more unusual for so stolid a man. From somewhere, he had obtained a big silver watch—it was a wonder, the things we discovered about ourselves now—and it lay ticking in front of him, while alongside of it there was a big sheet of foolscap entitled *General Orders and Instructions for All Regiments on the*

Night of January the 1st.

So make a disposition, Jamie, he said. Have you covered the hutments?

The noise dwindled. We were like that, with waves of confidence, and then with waves of fear. We were sure of ourselves, and then our certainty went away, and we stood in terror. We had been beaten and starved too long; we were criminals or madmen or heroes or wild adventurers who were embarked on a road no man had traveled before: and do not imagine it was easy for us to know, or that we were all of one mind or one piece.

Talk up, Jamie. And where is MacGrath?

He went over to the old Connecticut huts where the 5th and the 9th lie, and that is where we will have trouble as sure as God. They took the Nayger Kabanka, because he was asked to polish the boots of Major Quenton, and Quenton was in the boots and said, Kneel down, you black dog. And Kabanka answered, That I will not do, nor be called a black dog again. So they put him under guard, and now MacGrath is over there to see how bad it is.

A plague on this bloody pride! snapped Maloney. Are their noses up?

At those regiments, I answered. They have turned out all the lieutenants of the two regiments, and they are in and out of the hutments, filled with fury that they should not be swilling with the others; and if a man turns up from another regiment, they drive him on his way. Angus is on it now, and as for the other brigades, they are secure, or as secure as anyone can hope with a day to prepare, and they are sitting now with knapsacks strapped and bayonets fixed — not with one mind, but our lads have the better of it in the disputes. And all I would say is, for Christ's sake, do this soon, for a man can go mad with waiting!

Ye wanted much more waiting before.

Well, I don't want it now.

His neck itches for the rope . . . a pock-marked buckskin man remarked.

The lot of ye shut up! cried Danny Connell. Christ, to make a rising with this lot!

And I never saw an Irishman that wasn't expert on matters of rising! — I shot back at him — But to put two and two together, yer land is under the redcoat heel and never was else; and I'm sick of the talk of them that think this is a tea party. Ye sit here, but all this cursed cold day, I was in and out o' the hutments —

Now, easy, Jamie lad.

In and out o' the hutments, and this one wants wages and that one wants to go home and this one wants his bounty, and is Billy Bowzar going to pay it, and is the Jew Levy going to get gold from the Philadelphia Jews, and they've all had enough of the bloody war and want no part of it again, and they've heard there are Nayger men on the Committee and will not be led by Nayger men . . . and here ye sit like Jesus Christ was going to walk on the earth and make a miracle!

And it may be that He is, Jamie, answered Billy Bowzar — quietly, but heard because all the rest were so quiet now; and in that deep silence the Jew regarded me quizzically, his narrow, pinched face puckered up, his dark eyes probing as he said:

Now, then, Jamie Stuart, you are an impatient lad who wants a thing answered that can't be answered. But since the olden times men have risen up like we are rising up to throw off their hurts and sorrows.

But in the hutments they tell me, *There have always been gentry, and always them who are bounden under.* Will Bowzar be gentry now? Will the Jew Levy or the Nayger Holt?

No.

What then?

I don't know, answered the Jew. Maybe the Almighty God knows, and in time He will reveal to us what to do. And maybe not so. But there is a will on our part to assert ourselves and to cast out those who make a mockery of our dreams, and that we must do — because if we turn back now . . .

Flatly and matter-of-factly Billy Bowzar said: Go to work and stop this business of trying to be a gypsy, Jamie, which no Scot is any damn good at. There's not much time left, so get out in the cold again, which is better for your hot head, and turn out your guard. Let each man committed and pledged tie a white rag around his arm above the elbow. The left arm, Jamie. Rouse them up, and when Andy Swain begins to sound the camp jig on this trumpet, all files are to parade before the hutments, bayonets fixed, knapsacks on, but no powder in the pan. I don't mind if they load them their guns, but keep the powder safe from hotheads. We want no killing of the officers, Jamie — and you others too!

Now Bowzar rose and looked from face to face.

No killing, no murder! This Committee stands as a court of military citizen justice from here on, and every crime will be punished. Before tomorrow night, we will have arranged and set down the discipline of this new army; meanwhile, we will make it a simple and elementary justice, such as anyone can understand. When the officers come running, cast them off! Drive them away! Tell them we do not want them in the sight of our eyes! But no one retorts and no one speaks unless he carries a properly executed warrant of this Committee. We will be no rabble tonight, Jamie, but a credit to the honest folk of this land. And if shameful things are done, we will hold you accountable. Mark me, Jamie Stuart.

I mark you, I said, and then I saluted. It was the first time a sergeant of the Committee had been saluted. And then I went out to prepare.

I saw Angus coming across the parade, a dozen lads with him, and I joined him. We tore cloth from our shirts and neckcloths, and made our badges, and the moon rose and lined our shadows out across the trampled snow. Low lay the huts, like sleeping hounds, and fanged like hounds too, and far across the white expanse of the parade were the bare trees and the belly hills of the fat Jersey land. Here and there, a light gleamed as the door of one or another hut opened, and, dim on the other edge of the parade, we saw the shadows of men running but could not make out who they were or what they ran for. The sentries were out, and in their cold loneliness they paced back and forth, wrapped in God knows what dreams—for that was a cold and uncertain night, a night for dreams and fears and the inner coldness that freezes the heart of a man who cuts the ropes that bind him to his past. For whatever it was and however it was, this army was our life, and many of us knew no other life or remember another life only vaguely and indistinctly. We were parts of a body organism that was mother and father, and the tissue of our lives and the logic of our lives was the army of the Revolution. So I do not recall that we had a great and burning certainty; there were forces that moved us and drove us, and there was a spark of glory somewhere; but in the cold matter-of-fact, we moved because it was intolerable to remain as we had been.

We formed the lads in twos, Angus at the rear and I to the fore, and I smartened them and whipped for a marching gate and fancy arms. We went from hut to hut, checking the mood of the men and passing the word at the time, and the way the sentries walked their beats and saw us not at all gave us a strange feeling of disembodiment. At one point there, two officers galloped their horses madly across the parade, but either they saw us not at all or wanted not to see us; and after that a hutment door flew open and men poured forth, but back they went as if the hut had blown and sucked in one spasm. And the minutes passed and the moon traveled; and then the time was upon us, with

417

the shrill, taunting call of the Yankee camp jig.

Now the two officers came riding back, whipping their horses madly; and as they reined up near us, I saw that one of them was our regimental commander, a bitter, sallow-faced man, and one of the very few human souls I have known who never showed one spark of warmth or graciousness. He had a high-pitched, rasping voice, which shrilled out to know why the cursed damned trumpeter was playing that fool tune.

To awaken the dead! roared MacGrath.

I'll have your hide off for that, MacGrath, he screamed back. And you, Stuart, what in the devil's name are you doing with that file?

Drilling them! I shouted back.

With him was Captain Purdy, who claimed to be the first son — and a bad one, he always added — of Lord Purdy of the County Mayo, and he spurred on us; but Angus fired a musket over his head, and his horse bolted with him. Meanwhile, the trumpet kept on shrilling, and all up and down the regimental hutments, doors popped open spilling light onto the snow, and men poured out and began to fall in. From the area of the 6th, a rocket hissed up, and a roar of sound greeted it. The colonel whipped out his sword and spurred his horse at the 11th's hutments, screaming a string of foul oaths, the only printable words of which were *Back to quarters! Inside with you!* But the men laughed at him, and Katy Waggoner flung a handful of snow at him as he went by.

I ordered my men on the double with bayonets for attack, and we made a smart sight as we ran down the hut fronts, with Angus and me shouting:

Fall in! Fall in! All troops out on parade! Fall in! Fall in!

It was amazing how much discipline was shown there, for hardly had the bugle finished its call when at least a thousand men were forming in parade order, muskets in hand, knapsacks on back. A ripple of musket fire came from the direction of the redoubt; and then, square down the center of the parade, hanging for dear life onto a big white horse, came Sean O'Toole with four fieldpieces and their ammunition carts thundering after him. A wild roar of cheers greeted this, and O'Toole, for all his difficulty in maintaining his seat, managed to wave back and grin and bow his head. Most of this, and most of what followed, I saw in only the most fragmentary fashion — for I was moving on from hut to hut, shouting at stragglers, calling them out, and putting the parade into marching order as I went along. What became of the colonel after that, I do not know, but at least twenty minutes went by before any officers appeared on the scene, and then it was too late. By then, better than half of the Pennsylvania brigades were under arms and in marching order, with the Committee of Sergeants as the acknowledged authority.

It was our plan to march across the face of the hutments and over to the separate quarters of the 5th and the 9th Regiments in the old Connecticut huts. From where I was and in the darkness, it was impossible to see what had happened over there; possibly they too had gone out — possibly not. In any case, we felt that the moral force of our own column of men, in perfect discipline, with fifes playing and drums beating, would sweep them along with us.

In the telling, and more so in the telling after so long a retrospect, what happened up to now seems simple indeed, as if the men had moved with one mind and one heart; but things are not done in that way, even though the wise scholars of our Revolution would have it that the rising came about of itself, born and executed in that same evening, as if three thousand men all at one moment felt the need to rise up and cast out their officers. But in my mind's eyes there is a memory of that chaotic night, of hundreds of men running here and there and shouting all at once, of little clumps of men locked in struggle, of a five-year-old child standing in the snow and crying, of the disorganized groups trying to maneuver the cannon into position to cover our advance, of the frantic fool who touched a match to one of the cannon, and the roar of grape as it screamed across the parade, of O'Toole beating the man into insensibility, of the twitter of the fifes as the drummer boys and the fifers from all the regiments formed at our head, of the group of Germans who barricaded themselves into a hut of the 6th Regiment, screaming that they would die there before they joined the rising, and of Andrew Yost standing before the hut and addressing them in Dutch in a mighty voice that carried over all the noise and tumult.

We had reached the space between the huts of the 1st and 2nd Regiments when the baggage train appeared, led by an ox-drawn freight wagon, with the Gary brothers riding astride the lead oxen. The freight wagon was filled with the youngest children, and women and older children were perched all over the baggage carts. I recall that moment well, for it was then that the magazine was broken into. I heard the flurry of musketry and wondered whether we were already engaged in a fratricidal combat with troops who held back, but the shooting stopped as suddenly as it began, and I learned later that we had taken the magazine easily enough and that only one young lieutenant had been hurt with a bayonet wound in the thigh. But the children in the big wagon began to weep in fright, and Arnold Gary had to shout at the top of his lungs to make himself heart, as he called:

Well, here we are, Jamie, and where in the hell do you want us to put these brats and sluts?

Olive Lutz climbed down from the wagon and ran up to him, crying, You big oaf, sitting there so one cannot tell which is ox and which is man—there's children behind you and keep your tongue decent. We're not in this to take from you what we take from the gentry!

She's right and this is no rig, said Angus. So shut your dirty mouth, Arnold Gary.

Where the baggage train was to go I had not been told by the Committee, but it seemed obvious that the best place for them would be somewhere in the middle of the column; and acting on that, Angus and I led them along between the huts and the parading men. The men cheered as the women rode by, and the older children watched everything open-mouthed, this being such excitement as they had not experienced before.

Now, for the first time, I ran into Billy Bowzar and Jack Maloney, and they seized me and pulled me outside the line of men.

How is it, Jamie? asked Bowzar.

There are still men in the huts, but each one needs a great argument and persuasion, and I would say, To hell with them.

I am with Jamie, agreed Maloney. We want to march.

While we spoke, our committeemen ran up and down the files, trimming them into order and dressing them up. Never before in the history of the Continentals had a permanent camp been broken thus swiftly and with such dispatch, and there was a new air about the men, a smartness in the way they addressed their lines and ordered their arms.

By now, the musicians had arranged themselves into one compact group, and the two dozen or so little drummer lads were stiff and proud as peacocks, not wholly understanding what had come about, but knowing well enough that they would no longer be sport for any officer who wanted to exercise his cane. Chester Rosenbank started the music, leading the men so that they would all play together, and the first song they struck was that sweet Pennsylvania air, *Oh, lovely hills of Fincastle, for thee my sad heart yearns.* Afterwards I asked Chester why he had chosen that air instead of marching music, and he answered that marching songs were only partly ours, but this song of the buckskin men something all ours and calculated to take the hot bitterness out of the men, yet leave them their resolution. The fifes played sweetly if somewhat raggedly, and the drummer boys tapped their sticks lightly.

The shouting had lessened and now with the music it halted entirely. At least fifteen hundred men were on parade now, and Sean O'Toole had finally arranged his cannon to flank the column head. Angus was laying out the baggage carts alongside the center of the line; and there, but outside the men and facing the expanse of the parade, I stood with Bowzar and Maloney. We were joined by the Jew Levy and Danny Connell and the Nayger Holt; and it was then that we saw a body of mounted men sweep up the road from Morristown and drum across the parade toward us.

So here are our officers, said Danny Connell.

We stood side by side, waiting, and the Line dressed like grenadiers. The music finished and there was no other sound than the drumming of hoofs as the officers rode down upon us and drew up their horses a few yards away. I counted them; there were seventeen of them, many of them regimental officers, with Anthony Wayne, brigadier general of the Line, among them and voice for them. He, with Colonel Butler, stepped his horse forward and demanded:

What in hell's name is the meaning of all this?

As if he didn't know—and that was to be the way it was, at first, as if none of them knew. Billy Bowzar glanced sidewise at us, and his look said, Keep your mouths shut. Let me talk. If more than one talks, we'll be talking against one another. . . . So Billy crossed his arms and looked at the general a lot more coolly than I felt; but I stepped back and waved at Angus, and when he ran over I told him to dress up ten lads of the Citizen-soldier Guard directly behind and alongside of me, and for them to prime their muskets. While this went on, Butler reared his horse, a trick our gentry knew better than the leading of men, and roared out at the top of his lungs at the Line:

Undress! Stand at your ease!

I think of all the moments we faced, that was the hardest, for it was in us and in the marrow of our spine and our bones to obey a command hurled at us that way; so that while my mind said, Keep cool and stand still, Jamie Stuart, the muscles in my legs twitched of their own volition. I looked at the Line, and a good half of them had dropped their muskets to butt the ground and were falling out of

421

parade position. But their sergeants and corporals were snapping, Dress it, dress it, ye dirty white scuts! And once again the Line pulled itself into tension.

Who gave these men the order to parade? Wayne demanded.

The Committee, answered Billy Bowzar quietly, yet loud enough for much of the Line to hear. He was square and small and rocklike, and to this day I recall the pride I felt as I watched him that night. There was a solemn, unruffled truth about him that few of us matched. He had been a ropewalker before the war, in the Philadelphia cordage house, and, as with the ropewalkers in Boston, he and the men who worked with him had formed a Committee of Public Safety and armed themselves, and when the question of independence hung in doubt, the whole shop laid down tools and paraded a show of strength before Carpenters' Hall.

What Committee? Wayne wanted to know, his tone high and disdainful. Many of the other officers, I could see, were afraid, but there was no fear about Wayne, only a wild anger he could hardly keep from dominating him. The man had courage and little else; and courage was not enough to make us love him; for along with the courage went a cold streak of contempt and disdain and unmitigated cruelty that had earned the undying hatred of all too many in our ranks. A general they loved or a general they didn't know might have won over many of them right there, for what he had done was yet unresolved, and the light of fear had begun to burn in us — and we had no certainty, even now, that an army could remain an army without officers; but we did not love Anthony Wayne, and we knew him all too well, and what we had done for him in the past, to give him such glory, we did because his gut was the gut of a reaver. His gut won no respect for him here.

The Committee of Sergeants, answered Billy Bowzar, still in the same tone.

The Committee of Sergeants, said Wayne. The Committee of sergeants!

And he raised his voice, hurling it into the cold and rising night wind:

Disband, I tell you!

But it was too late, and we stood on our ranks, and we stood silent except for the wail of a little child that lifted over and above the men and mingled with the winter winds.

Butler said: I know you, Billy Bowzar, and I know you, Jack Maloney, and I know that dirty Jew and that black Nayger Holt, and you too, Jamie Stuart, and well indeed do I know that slaister Connell who was swept up with the dung from the streets of Dublin—and I have a long memory!

We are not hiding our faces, answered Billy Bowzar.

Then well you should, cried Wayne, for this is the dirtiest picture of a mutiny I have ever seen, and I'll go down to my grave if them that fixed it don't swing for it!

We are not mutiners, spoke Bowzar firmly, but loyal and good soldiers, as you should know as well as the next man, General Wayne, and it is not for the sake of any mutiny that we stand here in the winter cold.

And what are you loyal to?

To the name of freedom and to the deep hopes of Pennsylvania folk.

Enough of this sanctimonious gibberish! cried Butler. Either disband or prepare to take the consequences!

We are well prepared, for this is not anything that we did lightly, and we are no strangers to your consequences—

What kind of damn fools are you? cried Wayne. How long will this rabble last when we bring the brigades up against them?

What brigades? said Billy Bowzar softly.

I tell you, cried Wayne, loud enough for the whole Line to hear him, that if you go back to your hutments now and lay away your arms, and go to sleep as honest men should, then no more will be made of this, except the punishment of the rascals who lead you! I tell you this now!

There was a mighty urge in me to turn my head and see how the men of the Line took this, but Bowzar and Maloney and Levy and Holt and Connell stood as still as though they had become a part of the frozen ground they occupied, and, for all the cold that seeped now from my skin into the marrow of my bones, I would not do otherwise. But when I heard not even the crunch of a lifted boot, I was filled with a heady pride, as if I had suddenly become drunk, and my earlier dreams of a great movement and rising returned. Now Butler sided his horse to Wayne, and moments went by while they whispered to each other. Then Wayne dismounted and walked over to us, so that he, in his elegant, booted, spurred, cloaked height, his thin, handsome, clean-shaven face thrust forward, stood almost up against the square and ragged rock of Billy Bowzar, yet a whole head higher—like some chief facing a bearded, work-hardened crofter. It was later that they came to call him "Mad Anthony," but even now there was a touch of madness about him, and fame and glory had touched him, so that he would never forget what it was to wed either. He was imperious, but

423

without the humility that could have made him a great leader whom men would love as well as fear; and when years later I watched Junius Brutus Booth play out Shakespeare's tale of *Richard III,* I thought immediately of this young, wild, arrogant general officer who crunched toward us through the snow so fearlessly; but again it was only years later that I could place myself inside him and understand that much of the courage came from hopeless desperation; and that, for all of his proud and violent talks, there that night his world crumbled about him, and all the vainglory of his belted boots, his fine doeskin trousers, his powder-blue coat and his deep blue cloak surrounded a crushed man. No better picture of the relationship of this officer gentry to us can be shown than through their surprise at our rising; not only did they not anticipate it, but, now it was here, their only means of treating it was as another cause for caning or whipping. But you do not cane or whip a line of the best and hardest troops in the New World, standing motionless to arms in the bitter cold of night.

Yet Wayne carried it through in the only way he knew, and he walked up to Billy Bowzar and faced him boldly and asked more quietly:

What do you intend to do?

We intend to march away to our own encampment.

Where is your encampment?

That is in our own orders, General Wayne, and not for the knowledge of you or any other officer.

Are you the leader of this mutiny?

This is no mutiny, and it doesn't profit you to call it that; but I am spokesman for the Committee of Sergeants.

And what does your Committee propose to do?

To reconstitute the army of the Revolution.

That is talk, said Wayne, and you know that as well as I do. Tell me what you want, and it may be that I spoke hastily before. But if you will state your demands and I can satisfy your demands, I am willing to forget that tonight ever happened and no measures will be taken against any man—including your Committee—and you can go back to the hutments and sleep out the night. Things will look better in the morning.

We can never forget that tonight happened, said Bowzar seriously and reflectively. If I did as you say, I would be hanging from a tree in the morning . . .

You have my word!

. . . But it is not the hanging that stops me. I am not so almighty fond of life that I can't look at a rope, even the way my good comrade Jimmy Coleman looked at a rope last year when you hanged him until he was dead; but tonight is something you can't blow away like a handful of snow. Look at them—

He turned and flung a hand at the Line.

When have you seen the men stand to parade that way—with the cold so bitter that it freezes the juice in the bones? They would not heed your command, and I have little doubt that they would less heed mine if I ordered them back to the hutments.

What are your demands? insisted Wayne stolidly, but biting his underlip until the blood smeared through, his fists clenched, his cheek twitching. I have given you my word as an officer and a gentleman. What are your demands?

We have no demands for you, General Wayne. There is nothing you can do for us. Our demands are to the people, and the Congress.

If I can right them—

And can you right them, my general? asked Billy Bowzar, grinning bitterly at the handsome young man before him, taking a fold of his cloak between his fingers. Will you cover all our rags with this? Will you feed us with the slop from your New Year's dinner? Will you pay us, who have not been paid these six months past? Will you bring back our children, who died of disease and hunger? Will you put shoes under our bleeding feet?

His voice raised; he still held the fold of Wayne's cloak, and Wayne stood rigid as steel while Bowzar spoke, even more and more loudly and bitterly, with a passion I never knew the man to own.

Or will you scrape together our bloody tracks over five thousand miles of road for five years? Will you give us back our honor, we who have been beaten and lashed as foreign scum—or will you take one man out of the ranks, one man who talks the English a little less finely than you do, one man without property and wealth, and raise him up to be an officer over us? Will you honor us with even one of our own to lead us? Will you stop the ache of hunger in our bellies, so that while you fatten yourselves in the houses of the God-damned patroons and the cursed British gentlemen, we must watch our little drummer lads die for want of a shred of meat? Will you march us against the British enemy, instead of leaving us to rot in these cursed encampments— because you have not the guts to risk a fight that might bring a frown from that rotten, betraying Congress? Will you bring all the Lines together, so that they will stop plotting against each other and go against the enemy? Will you make the Declaration of Independence

425

the law of this army? Will you give us equal bounty and equal pay? Will you have every officer who kills one of us in his anger, who cheats us, who sells our food, who gambles away our pay, who speculates in the Philadelphia market with our clothing, who insults our women, who kicks our children? Will you do that, General Wayne? Will you declare that the Jersey and Pennsylvania farmers who hold their land in tenancy from the patroons and the lords now have it in freehold forever? Will you tell them that if they give us food, we will fight to the death for the freehold? Will you guarantee a hundred acres of land for every man in this army? You can do that, General Wayne—for there is land without end or limit in Pennsylvania, and no one owns it but the lords in London. Will you take it from them, and give it to us? Will you give us a stake in this? Will you now? . . . Come now? . . . The Line is standing to arms in the bitter cold, and you would not have them stand in the cold the whole night through! You would not have that—for then they would think that this is another evidence of the ways of the gentry and the disregard they have for what a simple man feels. So speak out, General Wayne!

In a fury, Billy Bowzar finished, and he flung away the general's cloak as if it were dirt. But Wayne didn't move, and there came a sigh out of the paraded men; and then Wayne said softly:

These are not demands I can satisfy, as well you know.

Then you can satisfy one other demand of ours, said Billy Bowzar. Get on your horse and ride out of our sight, and take your damned staff with you. The lot of you are like an abomination!

Now Wayne was rage incarnate, his face flour-white and every muscle along his cheeks trembling and quivering, and like a man made out of clockwork, tight springs and bent metal rods, he mounted his horse, hesitated just one moment, and then walked his horse toward us—with the other officers following him—spitting out words that were like molten spots of metal.

I command this Line! Do you hear me? All of you! This is an order: Break your ranks!

It was just before and during this that Angus MacGrath returned and whispered to me. For Christ's sake, Jamie, there is hell to pay in the old huts—and breaking into the Scottish—an' a deil gaed o'er Jock Webster, and the situation is dour, I tell ye, with the 5th and the 9th standing to arms, all cosh with the officers; and will ye tell the Committee to get us to hell out ö' here before we shed our blood and die in this damned place?

Where are they? I asked him.

Parading over yonder, behind the Connecticut huts.

But then Wayne was riding his horse down on us, and his officers less confident, less brave, but with him at the moment, and as the Committee was pressed back, it was touch and go; so I did what I felt should be done; I addressed the citizen soldiers and told them to let a volley into the air. The muskets roared over the horses and a harsh shout went up from our men, and the horses broke and bolted, the riders not fighting them but letting them bolt across the parade and into the darkness in ten directions, riding with relief to be away from that long file of grim and bitter men. But the truth must be told that Wayne alone fought his horse as it reared and beat it back onto the ground, his face contorted, tears running down his cheeks; and then he ripped open coat and vest and shirt, ripping the clothes and buttons, tearing at his undershirt to bare his breast and revealing it with the red marks of his nails across it. And he screamed at us:

Then kill me! Here is a mark, if you want a mark, you dirty, mutinous bastards! Then kill me here and now, and have it over with! God curse your souls, kill me!

There was a trumpeter standing by, and Bowzar ran to him and had him play the advance. We left Wayne screaming and weeping, alone on his horse, while we ran down the Line to its head, where the drummer boys had picked up the beat, and Rosenbank was already marching and keeping time for the shrilling fifes. As we ran, I told Bowzar and Maloney of the news Angus had brought, and they questioned Angus as we ranged ourselves across the head of the Line. Somehow, we had failed with these two regiments: the officers had got there first, and now five hundred men were standing to arms and ready to bar our path—yet the way they had remained behind the Connecticut hutments, out of sight and sound and a good half mile away, it was plain that they would avoid a struggle and leave us to march out of camp if we wished to.

And they got six cannon, said Angus, by grace of Emil Horst who sold us, the dirty smaik . . .

We will go up against them, nodded Billy Bowzar wearily, for this is either all of us or no part of us, and it's better to die here than to split the Line. If we split the Line, then it will be civil war and not war against the enemy, and I would rather hang now than have it that way.

Then it's war now, muttered Danny Connell.

Is it? If our brothers will cut us down, we are damned wrong, and we should know it.

And Billy Bowzar waved his arm and swung to the left—and the whole long Line of the Pennsylvania regiments moved across the moonlit parade toward the Connecticut huts. We marched slowly, four abreast, a long, dark ribbon across the entire parade, and the shrill of our fifes and the beat of our drums woke the countryside for miles around.

It was a wonderful moment, that in which we crossed the snow-swept expanse of parade, for the beat of the drums was matched by the beat in our hearts; and when I ran down the Line and back, I saw in the faces of the men, cold and reddened and wrapped in rags, an indication of the fierce exultation of our strength—our power, inevitably— for nowhere on the whole Western continent was a force that could come up against us; we were the heart of the Revolution into ourselves and our hopes and our angers. Many, many times before, I had seen the Line go out, sometimes on parade, sometimes on one of those interminable marches up and down the Jersey pine barrens, sometimes against the enemy, sometimes in the lonely, broken way of retreat; but I never saw the Line as it was then, like a fierce old eagle whose clipped pinions had suddenly discovered once again the power of flight. The men could not keep still, and they picked up the march, so that their voices rang out with:

In freedom we're born, and like sons of the brave, will never surrender, but swear to defend her, and scorn to survive if unable to save. . . .

One deep, rich voice picked up the verse—joined then voice by voice, while the fifes lifted it and shrilled like a wild and savage Highland fling. It was then that the two regiments came forth, marching in an opposite direction to ours, so that the two files crossed and faced each other, while a thousand throats roared their defiance in a song we had not sung these many months past—and were heard in every house and hamlet for miles around, and heard by the men of the two regiments as we chanted:

The tree which proud Haman for Mordecai reared;
Stands recorded that virtue endangered is spared;
The rogues, whom no bounds and no laws can restrain,
Must be stripped of their honors and humbled again!

The 5th and the 9th moved to cut us off, their officers riding behind them and shouting at them above the wild chant we maintained; but as we continued, the two regiments halted, and then a field gun was pressed through from behind, officers straining at the big, iron-bound wheels that men would not move, and Emil Horst holding a lighted match. Billy Bowzar and Jack Maloney and the Jew Levy ran toward them, Bowzar waving both his hands for silence, and Angus and I ran after them, and the lighted match waved back and forth like a torch. The singing died away, and the sudden silence was cut by a shrill voice screaming:

Fire on them! Fire on them!

We halted before their ranks, but MacGrath ran on, his musket clubbed, and as Horst dropped the match, he struck him on the side of the head and felled him like an ox.

Fire on them! Fire on them! The voice shrieked.

Now what in hell's name are you doing there, Bowzar cried at them, when the whole Line is marching?

This was heard, and a roar went up from our ranks, and our men called them out by name, and suddenly a thousand voices were calling:

The Line is marching! The Line is marching!

The two regiments broke; they went mad and wild, and when their officers cursed them, they pulled the officers from their saddles, beat them; and some they bayoneted; and the rest ran away, whipping their horses through the night. Two officers were slain there, and many more wounded, whereas in our own rising there had been no bloodshed at all. But it lasted only a few minutes; then it was over, and Bowzar's great voice was heard, crying:

Make room for the 5th! Make room for the 9th!

The Line parted to allow the regiments to form in their places, soldiers embracing soldiers, laughing, crying, shouting—and presently the drums picked up the march again.

I saw fleetingly Emil Horst staggering along, his hands bound, his face covered with blood. I saw Bowzar running toward the head of the Line, the tears streaming down his face as he ran. I saw Captain Oliver Husk lying face down in the snow, in a pool of blood.

And then I joined the Line, which was marching off to its own strange destiny.

PART FIVE

Being an account of our first march, and
of the fate of Emil Horst.

WE MARCHED only four or five miles that first night, to a place nearby where two Virginia brigades had encamped the winter before. What huts they had built were made slovenly, in the way of some Southern folk, and they were rotted and of no real use, but there was cleared space and a stream for drinking and plenty of firewood; and the only tactic we had worked out for that first night was to get away from the Morristown encampment. Once we did that, we felt that sleep was the first item on the agenda; although all in all it was little enough sleep that we of the Committee got ourselves, then or later.

In this march, there was only one incident of any importance, and that happened when we came to the first fork of the road; but already Billy Bowzar and the Jew Levy and Jack Maloney and Danny Connell had dropped out of sheer exhaustion, and they lay on a baggage cart, sleeping the sleep of the just, for all the rocking and lurching of the cart. A platoon of the 1st Regiment had intercepted a herd of cattle, a gift or a bribe or a sale from a wealthy patroon of Amboy to the officers; we left six beasts for the officers, and the rest, almost a hundred, we drove with us, and though they milled around the cart where Bowzar and the others slept, all their mooing disturbed them not at all. In the same way the women and children slept, but the little drummer lads stumbled along, keeping their rhythm going, and the men swung out their legs and sang as I had never known them to sing before.

Abner Williams and I led the column, and directly behind us marched Angus MacGrath and the Citizen-soldier Guard, which now numbered about one hundred men, and which was finally stabilized at exactly one hundred, in ten platoons of ten each with a platoon leader

430

who bore the title of citizen-protector. Many of these names might appear pompous today, for it is a different time and a different era I write this in, but they were neither strange nor pompous to us; and we were filled with a mythology and a folklore of freedom, in which such names loomed like giant symbols. Each member of the Citizen-soldier Guard had a white rag of some kind knotted around his left arm; and later these became white arm bands, six inches wide, sewn into the sleeve above the elbow—and to this day I have the band, sewn onto my old, ragged coat, yellowed with age, but not the least, I think, of the few honors I retain from that ancient Revolution. Also, the members of the guard carried primed muskets, held at advance position with bayonets fixed.

Behind them, Chester Rosenbank led the musicians of the Line, the fifers and drummers and trumpeters, and now two Scotsmen from the 5th Regiment, who had unearthed from somewhere kilts and pipes and who marched along, one on each side of the drummers, making the night awful with their wild Highland music—nor would they desist or keep time with us for all of Rosenbank's pleading.

It is a night for the pipes, they said, and if you want harmony, tell yer damned drummers and fifers to hauld off!

Behind them, came the regiments, flanked by the guns and interspersed with at least two hundred carts and wagons, and at the very end, a dozen of the citizen-soldiers to whip the stragglers into position.

I do not know of any other occasion during the entire war when a camp was broken like this, during the middle of the night, with no prior preparation; yet for all of that, we marched well and the discipline was good. We had cast out all of our officers, but the sergeants knew their jobs; and the long and short of it was that we were, almost without exception, tough and hardened soldiers who did not have to think twice about doing a thing.

When we came to the first fork in the road, the only incident of the march happened. There was a clearing in the woods with the moonlight flooding through, and on the branch of the road that led to the coast and toward the British, Wayne and a handful of the officers had stationed themselves, mounted, their haggard white faces set in desolate determination. We had planned to take the other fork anyway, but when I saw them, I halted the column, and Abner Williams went forward to speak with them. In the course of this, they asked him his name and rank, and that was how it came to be that in so many reports of the rising, Williams was mentioned as the leader. But in all

431

truth, the whole Committee led the rebellion, and if credit should be given, Bowzar and Maloney and the Jew Levy deserve more than either Williams or myself.

My rank is sergeant, answered Williams, and we are in no mood to stand here in the night chatting with you.

Can ye stop that cursed skirling? Colonel Butler demanded.

We have little to warm ourselves with, other than the music, said Williams, and if you would talk, talk over it.

We have come to hold this road! shouted Wayne. Here we are, and you will have to shoot us down before you march here!

Why should we march there?

To join the British!

A roar of anger went up from the men who were listening. Now the drummers and the fifers stopped, leaving only the skirling pipes; and MacGrath, all in a rage; advanced toward Wayne, crying:

A plague on yer foul dreams! Ye would bespatter all with yer own dung!

Grasping his arm, I pulled him away, telling him, Easy, easy, Angus—we have no truck with them and we have no words with them, and they will go their way and we will go ours.

And I waved my hand for the march; the musicians picked it up, and the column went down the road toward Vealtown—and we marched without another halt until we came to the old Virginia encampment. There we made a quick, rough camp, letting the women and children sleep on in the carts, building a few fires for warmth—for the cold broke that night, and it was almost balmy outside—and raising tents only for the sick and wounded. I divided the Citizen-soldier Guard in half, and placed them on two-and-two sentry duty, and then, like most of the Line, I scraped the snow from a bit of ground, wrapped a cloak about me, and fell asleep so quickly that I have no clear memory of the process.

I have a better memory, though, of being awakened in the sad, wet fog of the early dawn, with the feeling that I had only slept a moment, and with the feeling too of a day lost somewhere; for here it was but the morning of the second day of January in the New Year, yet in twenty-four hours I had lived lifetimes; and the old Jamie Stuart, the lad from the Western hill country, the cobbler's apprentice, the gawking, freckled lad who had dared to love the Parson Bracken's daughter—all of them were gone, and I was something else who was

432

awakened by Billy Bowzar and told, as he shook me:

Now come awake, Jamie — come now, Jamie! Would you be sleeping the whole blessed day away?

Just an hour of it, I pleaded.

You have had five good hours, Jamie. Come, lad, there is much to be done. We have a tiger by the tail, and it will be dancing and prancing all over us — and maybe a little bit of clawing too, and we on the Committee have become such theoreticians and such great ones for planning and scheming that it will do my heart good to know there's a soldier standing by to do a soldier's work, if it need be done.

So spoke Billy Bowzar, who was a better soldier than I ever could be, and a better man too, as he showed in the end. But that was his way, and he could make you love him as I loved him that morning, standing up with every muscle in my body aching and throbbing. Yet the cold had broken, and the morning breeze was soft and mild, and from far off across the meadows came the screech of roosters and the doleful *caw, caw, caw* of the crows. The mist lay low in the valley where we had bivouacked; its smoky tendrils shifted over the men where they slept, and on every side, as far as one could see in that gray morning, the men of the Line lay haphazardly, a clump here, a single man there. The few tents raised the night before floated like strange boats on the sea of mist, and the cattle wandered among the men, nosing in the snow for grass. Far off, the sentries moved like ghosts, and somewhere a baby whimpered with that plaintive insistent sound that seems to have more of the crux of life in it than any other.

Now come along, Jamie, said Billy Bowzar again; and I followed him, picking our way among the sleeping men to a large brigade tent which had been staked directly in the center of the encampment. The Stars and Stripes had been raised over it, for it seemed more fitting to the Committee that we should use this new banner, which had only come to us during the November of the past year, than any of the old ones, marked as they were with memories of whippings and hangings and the shame of our eternal retreats from the enemy; the two striped flags we had were never flown before, and, unless my memory fails me, this was the first occasion that Pennsylvania troops ever flew the flag of the United States.

As we entered the tent, we were saluted by two members of the Citizen-soldier Guard, who were stationed on either side the doorway. I had a moment of shame, for while I slept much had been done; yet I realized that there was still enough for the doing. In the tent, three

433

camp tables had been set up in a row, and a crow's nest of candles ringed the tent pole. Around the table sat Jim Holt, Abner Williams, Leon Levy, Danny Connell and Jack Maloney. This time, it was Williams who was writing a long document, and as I entered, he laid down his quill and smiled wanly.

Greetings, Jamie, he said, in his mild and cultured voice.

He was a slim, soft-voiced man, college-educated, the son of a Protestant minister, strangely out of place among us, yet strangely liked and respected by the men. About thirty years old, he was a thoughtful person, holding matters inside himself, not easy to know, but coming out occasionally with strange statements indeed. He was a nonbeliever, not passively as so many were in those times, but militantly, as if God were a personal antagonist of his. At a later time we had a long talk, which I will put down in its place. Now he went on to say:

Here are the orders of the day, Jamie, which we have decided upon. It will be up to you and the Guard to see that they are carried out.

Read it aloud, said Jack Maloney.

Billy Bowzar dropped into a chair to listen, and Jim Holt stuffed a corncob pipe with a mixture of grass and dried sheep dung, with a little tobacco to flavor it. Levy seemed to be dozing, and Danny Connell sat with his eyes closed, his legs sprawled, rubbing and scratching at his beard. I remained standing as Abner Williams read:

The first General Orders of the Pennsylvania Line, issued by the Committee of Sergeants on this date of January 2nd, in the year 1781, in their names and also in the names of the citizen-soldiers of the Line . . .

So it began, and when it was all finished, as you will see, Abner gave me a copy which I have preserved. Not the paper I took then, which fell apart from usage, but a copy which Abner gave to Billy Bowzar, who held it until we were together in York village and which I left with my sweet Molly Bracken and which I have before me today. Thus I am able to copy the words exactly rather than from memory, yet they are the same as Abner read in the tent that morning. There were twelve Orders as follows:

1. The expulsion of Officers shall be maintained, and all authority is vested in the Committee of Sergeants, until a representative Congress of the regiments shall decide otherwise. However, any regiment shall have the right to recall its represen-

tative sergeant and appoint another in his place. No member of
the Line is to hold any converse with an Officer, and such converse shall be regarded as grounds for expulsion from the Line.

2. The Committee of Sergeants shall have the power of court-
martial in all offenses against the security of the Line or the People of the United Colonies.

3. Any foreign regiments of the States of the Confederation
shall have the right to join the Pennsylvania Line. Upon such
action, they are entitled to representation upon the Committee of
Sergeants.

4. All soldiers of the Line are to conduct themselves in manner
becoming a citizen-soldier and worthy of the aims of this Line of
musketmen, that is, the Freedom and Welfare of the peoples of
this Continent. They shall strive sedulously to win the affection of
the inhabitants, so that we may look forward to a future where we
become one with the people.

5. The following offenses are punishable with expulsion from
the Line and with whatever additional measures short of death
the Committee of Sergeants shall see fit to impose: Looting;
inflicting of damage upon any property other than enemy property; the use of vile language to any comrade citizen-soldier or to
a woman or to a child or to a civilian citizen; neglect of weapons;
infractions of general disciplines imposed by these orders.

6. The following offenses are punishable with death upon just
and considerate court-martial: Dealings or converse with the British or any of their agents; rape; murder; desertion in the face of
the enemy.

7. All citizen-soldiers of the Line shall regard their appearance
as a part of their solemn duty. All citizen-soldiers are to shave
daily and to see that all extremities of their bodies present a clean
and wholesome appearance. All arms are to be cherished. All sergeants and corporals will be held solemnly accountable for the
enforcements of these regulations.

8. All pay shall be equalized, regardless of rank. But bounties
shall be determined by length of enlistment and battle service. All
citizen-soldiers who present to the Committee of Sergeants ade-
quate and sworn testimony to the expiration of their enlistments,
shall be released from further service ten days from the date of
such presentation. All enlistments and re-enlistments shall be
voluntary.

9. All food and liquors shall be divided equally among all

ranks, but first preference shall be given to women and children, and then to drummer boys and other enlistments under the age of thirteen years.

10. All citizen-soldiers shall have absolute freedom to practice the religions of their consciences. No measures shall be taken to discriminate against Jews, Romans, or Naygers.

11. All foodstuffs and beasts for slaughter shall be turned in to the central commissary. The commissary shall allocate the food and the liquor to the extent of four ounces a day when available.

12. All disputes in the practice of these General Orders shall be referred to the Committee of Sergeants or to a duly authorized Committee to be set up for that purpose. The only authority in any and all instructions and commands shall be the authority of the Committee of Sergeants, through a duly issued and inscribed warrant. This authority shall be binding until such a time as the Committee of Sergeants disbands itself or is disbanded by the regiments of the Pennsylvania Line.

Such were the first General Orders, which Abner Williams read that day in the tent. What discussion had gone into the making of them, I do not know, but they were plain and clear and simple, and they expressed well enough what the men wanted.

But where does it begin? I wanted to know. Look at us here now, dirty, unshaven —

And here it begins, Jamie, answered Billy Bowzar, smiling gently. We are still in the manner of rubbing our necks, but it has come off, hasn't it, Jamie? And for some of us it is like a dream, with an army on our hands . . .

His voice trailed away, and weariness and wonder passed across his face; so that looking at him and looking at the others, I began to realize the enormity of what we had done; and we were so immersed in our own thousandfold detail that we had never paused to think that the sound of this was rocking across the world, that the great Pennsylvania Line of the Americas, those same soldiers whom Lord North had called "The ragged watchdogs of the gates of Hell," those same soldiers who were not only the heart of the Revolution but the Revolution itself — those same soldiers had taken the power and the glory into their own hands, and, for what it was worth, the American Revolution now sat in this torn tent, black man and cursed Roman and hated Jew sitting down with the Protestant to go where no one had ever been before.

So I folded the General Orders, put them in my pocket, and went out once more into the foggy morning, waking those who had a white rag around their left arms, until there were six of them, and while they still rubbed the sleep from their eyes, told them:

Now we will shave ourselves and clean ourselves, and begin to make a new army.

Yet the words were as strange to myself as to them, and the affronted wonder in their eyes must have been matched by the doubt in my own. However, we shaved; without mirrors and without soap, we cut off our beards and scraped our skin and scrubbed our dirt away with the melting snow; and those of the soldiers who woke and saw us laughing, and then crying with pain as we cut our flesh, thought we were mad—as perhaps we were.

The encampment was coming awake, but I could not wait. I was eager, like a boy again, and it made me feel like a boy to finger my smooth face. I ran through the sleeping men, shouting for the trumpeter, and after me ran the six guards, whooping and laughing. Then the trumpeter sounded and the camp came alive, and there was never such a reveille as that one. The sun was breaking, warm as a winter sun rarely is, and everywhere the snow was becoming slush and dirty pools of water; but to me it was all beautiful; and it must have been beautiful to the men as well, for never before in all the history of the Line had they laughed this way, romping with each other as if they were children again. We picked up the guard as we went, and I found Angus sleeping under a caisson, and I dragged him awake and told him to shave and clean himself up, so that he would not be a disgrace to us.

Are ye daft? he asked me.

But then his eyes opened wider as he noticed that seven of us were shaven already.

Pawky, pawky, he grinned. And what in hell are ye up to, Jamie? Women?

Angus was well onto forty, which was old for me and old for most of us, so I told him:

Shut your mouth, you dirty old goat! I want them paraded in the brigades, like they never was before!

The men were crowding around us, and they doubled over laughing with what I said to Angus. Old goat, roared Stanislaus Prukish, old goat—and Angus caught him by the shoulders and threw him like a tenpin. That was how we felt that morning. I sent Angus to lay out the

437

order of the parade with the guards, and then I was off to find the
Gary brothers, so that they might organize some sort of scouting line
for our march. I saw none of the Committee, but I felt that if they left
it to me, it would be well done; for this was my own meat and not one
of those fine theories of where the Revolution was off to — a bone they
chewed day and night, filling paper with little script and burning every
bit of tallow in the Line.

To hell with theories, I thought. I am twenty-two years of age, Jamie
Stuart by name, and the blood in me runs quick and free.

Already, the commissary was disturbing mixed grits of buckwheat
and corn, and here and there a pot was bubbling. Voices followed me
with:

Hi, Jamie, what goes today?

We did not do bad, eh, Jamie?

Stop and have a bit, Jamie!

The smell of porridge touched my nostrils, and I realized all in a
moment how famished I was; so I sat in with a group of lads from the
4th, and they filled a great bowl for me, a spoon of molasses upon it,
and the whole topped with a fine lump of gribbled lard.

Now this is eating like I haven't seen in a nation of days, and where
in hell did it come from?

From the Dutch crofters, and before God, I think me they broke
open the bins of the stinking patroon!

Ye don't say?

I do say it. They must know of this rising now in China, for before
the sunrise the woody-shoes were clumping in with the provisions. We
ask them why? Because ye will burn down the patroon's castle, they tell
us, and hang him high as Haman.

So see that ye do it, Jamie, another added.

Laughing, I stuffed myself, and the sun rose and splashed us with its
light and warmth, and the sparrows sang as foolishly as if it were
spring already. The women of the brigade were primping and cooking
and scolding the children and singing: *The squire came along the
road, he saw the huntsman's bloody load, and Mary Jane will weep but
sing no more. Heigh-ho, heigh-ho . . .*

I wanted no better than this, to be here with my comrades all
around me to see the love in their faces because they trusted me. So I
ate my breakfast and finished my rounds and went back to the command tent to make my report. By then, the parade was forming and
Chester Rosenbank was marshaling his drummer lads and his fifers to
beat to station; but the two Highland pipers were walking their bags in

a circle of delighted men and children, skirling the Devil himself awake.

Entering the tent, I saluted; but here was more than I had been prepared for. The candles were gutted, yet the weather-worn tent gave light enough. At one end stood Emil Horst, with Sammy Green on one side of him and Dennis Sullivan on the other, each standing like a ramrod, with musket in line from navel to chin; and Emil Horst looked like the very Devil, his face all stained with dry blood, his head swathed in cloth, his lips as white as the skin around them. A few feet away, the Reverend William Rogers sat upon a camp stool, his long, thin face fixed on the ground in somber meditation. At the camp tables were the Committee, shaven and cleaned and somber as the Reverend Rogers, but starker in their look and grimmer in their aspect.

So you are here, Jamie, said Jack Maloney as I entered.

Is this a wake?

A court-martial, he said flatly. And how is it outside?

The men are parading for a reading of the Orders. We will have them read up and down the Line, so that all may hear. And then?

And then we march, answered Billy Bowzar. But wait here, Jamie, for you are a part of the Committee, and it's fitting and proper that you should have a vote.

So there I stood, while Abner Williams arose and spoke, apparently continuing what he had been saying before.

We have seen a peculiar treason, he said, for this man Horst has betrayed his comrades and nothing more, and when has there been a punishment for that? He claims loyalty, and I must defend him, for it would not be fitting that he should have no advocate.

You are his advocate, Billy Bowzar nodded. He needs no accuser since we have all seen what he did.

Yes, he did an awful thing, Abner Williams agreed, more thoughtful than angry. . . . He had a lighted match in his hand, and he would have fired a cannon loaded with loose grape, sending his own comrades to their deaths. For this he should be slain, which is what the men would ask if we brought him before the Line and demanded their will. That is what they would ask, but he must be defended.

I did what a loyal soldier does! cried Horst. I stood by the colors when you all had betrayed them! That's what I did!

Ye had better shut up, said Dennis Sullivan, or it will be me duty to tie a bayonet atween yer God-damned teeth.

This question of loyalty, said Jack Maloney tiredly, is the strangest of all questions. I have thought about it too much—too much to know the answer.

He rubbed his bloodshot eyes with both clenched fists, shaking his head as he did so; then he laid his hands, so small and dainty that they might have belonged to a woman, flat upon the table in front of him, staring at them and examining them as he spoke. He and Billy Bowzar and the Jew Levy were the only ones among us who seemed to have been marked for greatness; but Jack Maloney more than the others, for he was a man racked in perpetual combat with his destiny; and because he struggled against wrong, as he saw it, as if it were embodied like Lucifer the Devil, he had a great and sometime splendid dignity. To the very end, he had that dignity, as you will see; for it is my intention to pursue this narrative to its ending, making a whole thing of it.

Now, however, he spoke searchingly and painfully:

What is one loyal to? he asked. That German—and he nodded contemptuously at Horst—is loyal to the colors, as he puts it, but there are other colors too, and the blood of all men is tinted the same. When I wore a red coat, I read a book by a man called Thomas Paine, and I decided that I had been loyal to the wrong things. I was born a bastard and weaned on gin, but I was told to be loyal to my sovereign liege, George III, for that mighty privilege. And when an officer of the King took me as a drummer lad and did terrible things to me that are best not even spoken of, I was told to be loyal to him. I was in the regiment the half-witted Howe marched against the fishermen at Pelle's Point, and only I and eight others lived from the regiment; but we marched, because we were loyal—the way a whore is loyal to her pimp. But after Pelle's Point I said, Since I am destined to die with a bullet in my belly, let it be for freedom; not for Wayne, not for that cold Virginia farmer, not for that craven Congress in Philadelphia, not for the fine Pennsylvania ladies in their silks and satins, not for the property of every dirty lord and fat patroon in Jersey, not for the tobacco plantations and the merchant fleets of Boston and the warehouses of New York—not for that, but for freedom and a little bit of dignity for them that was born like me and raised like me. For this, do you see. I talk pretty and sweet, but I not only can dance like an ape—I got an ape's ear to mock the talk of the British officer gentry who turned me into a servant to black their boots and shine their metal. So there's a variety of loyalty, and a complexity to it also, and sometimes I think we are all the accursed, who are loyal to a dream and no more. But I take no talk of loyalty from him!

So spoke Jack Maloney and without bitterness, but only tiredly.

Yet I must defend him, said Abner Williams stubbornly, and the Reverend Rogers raised his head and nodded.

That is so. His is a different kind of loyalty. Don't scorn it, Jack Maloney, for some of us are loyal to God as we know him, and others are loyal to a piece of rag—and some are loyal to the Devil.

At this point, the reading of the General Orders began, and through the open tent-flap we could see the Line drawn up on parade, and though we could not see him we could hear plainly the booming words of Angus MacGrath. Five or six little boys and girls, flaxen-haired Dutch children from the neighborhood thereabout, raced past to see this great wonder of men and guns and wagons that had come down upon them during the night, and I bethought me of how strange it was, the way life and death mixed themselves; for we who were subjects for hangmen so shortly past were now debating the life or death of this dull and obstinate man, Emil Horst, and still children played and laughed under our noses—and soon they would be listening to the great lies and tales of the children of the camp, and thus were legends born and thus would one of these children someday remember how the Pennsylvania Line, the terrible, savage foreign soldiers, had come into their valley and drawn up on parade, so that documents might be read to them.

. . . To ask for his death, Abner Williams was saying, would be an evil thing. We are not such an army as the officer gentry would have made us. Somewhere in him, fat and dull though he is, there is a streak of the gentry, so let him go to his own kind without stripes and without caning.

And anyway, I said, without any by your leave, this is one thing that was not in the General Orders. We made no provision for those who betray us.

Horst stood still and eager, mouth open, for somewhere in the words he scented life and freedom; and he cocked his head as the Jew Levy said:

True—true. You can see the gentry in him.

Ay—ay, and that you can, said old Lawrence Scottsboro, twisting his wrinkled neck and spitting over his shoulder. And Danny Connell broke the spell for fair, leaning back and laughing as he said:

Gentry or me eyes have never seen it.

441

But on no grounds of loyalty, said the Jew Levy softly and meaningly. He is loyal to nothing, that animal.

There was no courage in Horst. He stood there and hung his big head and stared at the ground.

Remember, cried Sean O'Toole, that the blood in you is blue — blue blood of gentry! Go to them and tell them that you are like they are — and if ye doubt it . . .

Like a flash, like an animal, the little Irishman was out of his chair, knife in hand, and the knife flicked and left two crossed cuts on Horst's cheek.

Damn you, O'Toole! Billy Bowzar cried; but O'Toole stood in front of the cringing Horst and laughed, and then wiped his knife on Horst's overalls, sheathed it, and spat on the floor.

Do it yer own way, he told the Committee. Me own gut is too sick with him.

Yer gut is like your head, said Jack Maloney, and you're too damned quick with a knife to satisfy me. But get Horst out of here because he stinks the place.

Sure, get him out, said Jim Holt, and Bowzar nodded and the others of us nodded too. But still the man stood where he was, cringing and weeping as the blood ran down his cheek. The Reverend Rogers rose and took his arm and led him out, and as he went past I severed his bonds with a stroke of my knife; but I felt sick, sicker than I would if they had killed him, and my sickness increased as he walked across the fields, away from the parading soldiers of the Line, across the fields and into the woods.

PART SIX

Wherein we discover that roads must be
made before men may travel.

IT IS SAID that certain officers remained near us, and others watched us in great danger of their lives; but of all that I know nothing, and until the sun set on Wednesday night, we saw not hide nor hair of any officer. It is true that late on Tuesday afternoon, we had word that one hundred and twenty officers were massed ten miles away with two thousand militiamen, but that proved to be nothing but a wild rumor, and so did every other rumor of militia being massed against us dissolve in smoke. For the militia could only come out of the countryside and the town, out of the crofter on shares and the tenant farmer and the little freeholder, out of the artisan, the carpenter, the cobbler, the weaver and the ropewalker, out of the hatter and the barber and the saddler and the cooper and the soaper and the tinker and the staymaker and the vintner and the silker and silverer—and they were with us, and would make no militia to go against us and shed their blood and our blood. And how much they were with us we learned on this very morning.

I must tell you of the weather, for unless you have lived in the Middle States, you will not know how it is that so often, early in January, winter turns into summer for a spell; the sun shines warm and sweet; the snow melts and the ground dries, and the foolish birds come out and sing as if there were no long and dreary months of cold ahead. The sky is bluer than even in the summertime, for there the cold, metallic sheen of winter persists, and when the sun sets, there is a riot of wild color, as if nature were upset and distraught at this topsy-turvy inversion of the seasons. This was the weather we had on Tuesday and Wednesday as we slowly marched through the Jerseys, with our fifes playing and our drums beating, but with more than that too.

We changed. It wasn't merely that we had new General Orders and no officers, for the change was as much inside of us. I felt it in my heart, in my stomach, in my limbs—and the others felt it too. For the first time in the five years since 1776, the regiments of Pennsylvania shaved themselves and cleaned themselves in the wintertime, and that was done on that Tuesday morning before we moved out of our bivouac. I remember well the camp that Tuesday morning, for it was different from any camp we made before that, or after that either. For one thing, it was alive—and in a manner of speaking we had been dead for a long, long time. The cold of winter was gone, not only from the air but from our hearts, and we exploded into life and noise and song and heady exuberance. And the women caught it, and the children too, running and laughing and shouting. There was such a time of cleaning and mending and patching, and rubbing the bayonets and muskets with lye and soap until they gleamed in the sun, and polishing the cannon and scraping the mud from the carts and carriers, and more mending—for we had a sudden lust and frenzy to look like an army and we carried this on until we were strangers to ourselves, and I remember how men stopped to look at each other and to grin or hoot or laugh until their sides shook.

And we had an audience. First, when the Jersey folk began to gather around our bivouac from all parts of the countryside, we were reserved and wary—for we were still the foreign brigades, and this was the land where winter after winter we had starved and sickened and died on all the endless miles of road we had marched, from Morristown to Newark to Trenton to Princeton to Basking Ridge to Chatham and Pluckemin, north and south and east and west, year after year, and here too we had fought and fought, on the Palisades and in the lonely reaches of the flats and at Monmouth in the pine barrens and along the rivers and on the coast; and always we were strangers and always we were hungry.

But not now. Let those who lie about us and malign us explain how, on Tuesday morning, the farmers came from all over the countryside with their gifts of food, with grain and pigs and sheep and sides of beef and chickens and bags of apples and potatoes. More and more of them came, until our commissary wagons were loaded full and piled high, and still the people came until a solid circle of them ringed our whole encampment. I doubt if there was one man or woman or child for ten miles around who was not of the gentry and not bedridden who did not come that morning to watch us and cheer us and bring us some gift.

444

They came out as if it were a holiday occasion. There were fat Dutch housewives holding little children, who shuffled uneasily in their wooden shoes, Dutch farmers with their clay pipes, Westphalians in their colorful costumes, the women with their high hats, the men with their blue vests and silken tassels, Saxon peasants who yawked open-mouthed at these terrible foreigners who had cast out their officer gentry, even the way it was whispered their own ancestors had done so long ago in their own revolt, which ran away in the distances of time in a river of blood. There were tall, rawboned Yankee tenants, Connecticut men from the paper works, wagon drivers, bearded, dirty leather-clad men who for years had driven their Jersey produce to the coast, where it was picked up by fishing smacks and sold at the wharves of British New York. And there were children of all ages and all kinds babbling away in all tongues, so that it occurred to me again, as it had so often before in Jersey, that we of the brigades were no more foreign than this strange assortment of folk who lived in the land. Little enough they had of Scotch and Irish, but sufficient of everything else—although today you would never know it to travel through the Jerseys as they are now. But it was different then, and the folk were simpler, and in their simplicity they saw much in us that we did not see in ourselves. Many of the women came with loaves of bread and baked herrings and potato pudding, and if we were wary of them, at first they were warier of us; for even their own hatred of the gentry could not entirely overcome the legend of our wildness and wickedness. But in a little while, all of these fears broke down. The drummer children were fed as they had never been before; the fat Westphalian women clucked and sighed over our skinnyness, and the wagon drivers handled our British muskets, which we had taken from the enemy in the course of the years, our long British bayonets and our shining bronze cannon. Children worshiped open-mouthed at our strutting pipers, who had such a wind as was never seen in America before, and tirelessly went on and on with their outlandish Highland music. Farm girls giggled as they helped our lads to patch their clothes into some sort of order, and reticent close-mouthed farmers became loquacious and snorted over the condition of our animals.

And for our own men, this was the strangest thing that had ever happened in all our years of warfare; for we were the foreign brigades without home or kin; we were soldiers without discharge; we had been whipped and beaten and herded like cattle; and for us there was no discharge—as there was among the New England and Southern troops. Where would one of us go if he deserted? Never before had we known such a sense of the people for whom we fought, and never before had the people known us—except as ragged, ugly strangers who marched endlessly up and down their roads, who stole their stock and broke their fences, and who did the will of our officer gentry. Long ago, in the first flush of revolt, they had welcomed us as we marched north to Boston, but already when we fled from New York, in 1776, their doors were closed against us; and never thereafter had either party done anything to endear him to the other.

With Abner Williams, I watched this that morning, after Emil Horst had been driven from the camp like a leper; and I was filled with emotion and sadness and joy all at once, as a cup is filled with water that laps over the edges—and I felt above all things a loneliness and wanting for the one maid whose lips had been sweet to me; and as I watched Abner Williams pick up a little child and pet it, I tried to make some order out of my thoughts. I pointed to the loose, eddying throng of our men, and I asked Williams:

What has happened?

I don't know, he answered, stroking the hair of the little girl as she laughed at him.

But you see that something has come over us.

I see it, but I don't know, and he put the child down, and it ran between his legs and then onward, twisting this way and that way.

Why did they hate us yesterday? Why do they love us today?

If I knew that, I would know much more, answered Abner Williams.

And what has happened to the men?

What has happened to you, then, Jamie Stuart?

What has happened to me? How should I know what has happened to me when I am sick a bittock and mighty a bittock, and I want to put my head to the side and cry, and I am filled with shame for every time I was drunk or wild or laid with a whore, and I feel pure and close to all these hard and godless men. But I am only Jamie Stuart who knows a little cobbling and a little bayoneting and you have had yerself education and college and learning of all kinds.

Of all kinds but the kind that would tell me what has been done here in our awful despair of yesterday.

And were do we go?

I don't know, Jamie, he said, and I said nothing to that, but stood in the warm sunshine, looking down at my broken boots, my torn, mud-stained leggings, my coarse overalls, so big and rough over my bony knees and legs—and I remembered back to the springtime after Valley Forge, when we came out of our stinking clothes and all of a sudden became thin-shanked lads frolicking in a brook. So we were young again now, and there was the strange and frightening discovery of youth in all we did.

A woman came to us and asked was there anything she could do?

Do me a favor of sewing, I said so softly, and took the rag from my arm.

They had come with needle and thread. Here were men who wanted glory. She was a woman of forty or so, buxom and round and yellow-haired, and Dutch I would say, from the manner of her speech, with little blue eyes like buttons; and just to look at her made the man in me rise up and beat against my stomach and chest. So she stood by me and sewed and asked me:

What is your name, son?

Jamie, I said. Jamie Stuart.

A foreigner?

I was born in Pennsylvania, but my folks were bound out from the old country.

As were mine, she sighed. And will you be going home?

I have no home, I answered, my voice all thick with emotion and longing. I have no kith and no kin.

You are an orphan boy?

That I am, I told her, but I am not so much of a boy as you think.

And I moved closer to her and touched her round, full breast, not boldly and wantonly, but so timorously that she smiled instead of being angry at me. But fires raced through me and all over me, and she saw in my eyes what I was thinking, and asked me:

How old are you, boy?

Twenty-two years, if you count the years. But if you measure the sorrows I have seen, I'm older than you are.

And all the while I stroked that fine, full womanly breast of hers, and she did not tell me nay, or make any other kind of play with me, but kept looking straight into my eyes.

I'm old enough to be your mother, she said.

That, you are not!

What do you want of me, boy? Marching in you come, and then you will go marching out, and you are hard as nails and strange as the moon, you men of the brigades.

Why am I strange to you, when you are nohow strange to me?

What do you want of me, boy? she asked.

And I knew what I wanted. I wanted to go where she was and lie next to her and put my head on her bosom and soak up the fullness of

447

her and the warmth of her and feel the comfort of a bed and a woman and an end to this marching into nowhere.

Marching in, marching out, she said.

Put your arms around me, I begged her.

With a thousand folk to see?

Let them see and be damned to them! Put your arms around me!

And that she did, holding me tight and tender. And then she let me go and began to sew with quick, nervous stitches at the dirty rag that was my badge of rank, saying to me:

It's a bitter thing to be a soldier.

Bitter indeed, I nodded.

But now we are sib, she smiled, using a Scottish word as the needle raced.

Sib, I nodded, sib, and the tears rolled down my cheeks. She finished the mending, and Williams returned and said harshly:

Blow the horns, Jamie, and get them to marching! What in hell are we doing here?

He was right. Without looking at her again, I left and found the trumpeters and had them blow; and Chester Rosenbank rounded up his drummer lads, their bellies so full they stuck out, and while the drums rolled and the fifes twittered, the men ran from all over the broad meadows, falling into ranks.

It was a heady thing, the way the men moved; it was full of pride and confidence and strength — and never did a sergeant or a corporal have to raise his voice. Regiment by regiment, they fell in, until the regiments and the artillery company were lined up across the meadow. It has been said often and too often that through all the time of the rising, we were drunk; but if we were it was not with rum but with this fine new freedom we had found for ourselves. Drunkenness was made a reason and excuse for every action we took, and it was said that the whole countryside sold us rum; but we were men without a bit of silver coin among us, and I do not remember any case of drunkenness in the first days of the rising — nor did we have rum to drink.

And drunken men never paraded and marched as we did. We set off down the road to Pluckemin with our drums beating and our flags flying, and we raised our voices to sing:

> Captains, once more hoist your streamers,
> Spread your sails and plow the wave,
> Tell your masters they were dreamers

When they thought to cheat the brave.

The Committee marched in front; then the band; then the first six regiments of the Line; then the artillery; then the wagons with the women and children and sick and wounded; then the last regiments of the Line. We covered a good deal of road, and often the head of the column was out of sight of the rear, but we never broke pace or order; and all along the way, the road was lined with village and country folk who cheered to see us pass.

The hundred men of the Citizen-soldier Guard paced the files and skirmished the front and rear, and I ordered the head of the column with Angus at the end of it. The men were in fine spirits and as proud as peacocks, and at every halt they did things to give them a uniform appearance. Though some regiments of some states had uniforms, we of the Pennsylvania Line never had more than our yellow canvass overalls and our brown coats to mark us as soldiers; but all the uniforms in the world could not have made any other troops on the continent march as we did. How well I recall it, when I ran up and down the files, the shoulders backed, the lines of four rigid and holding, the muskets swinging in tempo and unison—and there a wild longing came on me that we could meet the enemy as we were, in this mood and this heart.

Yet my courage was threaded with fear and born out of the sick loneliness I had after leaving that woman. She stayed with me and inside of me, and my stomach was sick and tight until finally I had to go to the roadside and retch out the morning meal. Now where would we be going, if all the men were like me? I knew how I was. Home, I wanted, and that more than anything else, and my home was in the town of York with the lass I left so long ago. And what kept me here, I wondered. What kept any of us here?

But you, Jamie Stuart, I said to myself, are a man, and they have given you the trust of a man.

That, too, is a damned lie, I said to myself, as I marched on. . . .

When we halted for our midday meal, two of the guard brought us a deserter who had stolen a chicken from a widow woman in the neighborhood. I mention this, because this was an incident that became known in many places, and when more than usual lies were told of us, sometimes someone might say, And what of the chicken of the Widow Brennen? So it became the case of the chicken of the Widow Brennen, and of fame too; for of all the chickens and hogs and lambs that had been stolen in the Jerseys in the course of the war, this was the only one that became a symbol of something.

The looter was Dennis Finnigan of the 3rd regiment, a man who was full of tales and with a talent for setting one of his comrades against another; a great one for talk of rising, he had run away when the rising actually came, as some two or three hundred men did, going over to the officers or going into the woods and the back lanes to watch their own skins. Already, he was something apart from the rest of us, bearded, dirty, frightened and cursing the fact that two men of the Line should drag him along for doing what any Pennsylvania soldier would have done had the opportunity come his way. He twisted and struggled and swore, and the two guards had practically to carry him, and behind them came the Widow Brennen, a mild and anxious little woman who was bewildered by this great turmoil she had raised, and would have stolen off and dropped the whole matter had we not insisted that she remain.

Then and there, the Committee of Sergeants convened themselves as a court-martial. The road was sunken in that place, between two stone walls, with an apple orchard on either side and a big stone barn making a backdrop for where we set our stage. We of the Committee seated ourselves upon the wall, and the men of the Line packed into the sunken road, and children climbed the apple trees and hung over us, and the people of the neighborhood pressed in to find places where they could listen and watch. The farmer who owned the place and his friends climbed into the big open loft of the barn, and our own women and children stood on top of the baggage wagons.

The guards told their story, briefly and to the point: They had heard someone scream, and they met Finnigan running with the chicken.

The Widow Brennen held the chicken now, a bedraggled little bird, and she said, I have my chicken, so let him go. I hold no grudge against him. The man was hungry—

And what are ye, dragging me around in this damned way? cried Finnigan. Are ye so damned virtuous now?

There are two counts, said Billy Bowzar. You have deserted from the Line and you have looted from the people.

Are ye the law now—you that are mutineers? What if I stole a thousand pieces of gold! I need no thief to read me the morals of me own thieving!

There was a roar from the men, and they surged toward him and would have taken him and done badly with him, if it weren't for the guards holding them back. We waited for silence, and then Bowzar went on:

The morals of our thieving are something for you to ponder, Dennis Finnigan—we don't stand alongside of you. When we cast out the gentry, we became like the people. We are not bandits. If we take one ear of corn out of a field, we have nothing left, nothing—and then we are truly bereft.

There was a whole and absolute silence now; you could hear the breathing of those packed men; you could hear the wind in the leafless trees; you could hear the beating of your own heart, too, as I did, as Finnigan did the way he stood there staring open-mouthed at the Committee. And Billy Bowzar sat on a rock of the stone wall, a little man, smaller now that his beard was shaven, swinging his feet and contemplating them seriously and troubledly. His square face, his snub nose, his broad full mouth all reflected the inner conflict and doubt that beset him. When he spoke, he chose each word carefully and slowly, and marked them out with his hand, saying:

You make a great mistake, Finnigan, if you think of us as thieves. I think you are not much good as a man, and I don't give a damn what you think, but it is a mistake all the same; and the people all around here and back where we were encamped made no such error. We are a mighty force, for we are good soldiers and hard men, and I would lay the Line against any troops on earth, be they equal man to man or five times our number, and we could fight anywhere in heaven or hell or in between, and sometimes it seems that we have too, God forgiving me, for I mean no blasphemy. But what kind of force would we be if the people were against us? Just look around you, my lad, and tell me where all these folk have grown from—since all the winter days we marched this land and saw no soul are fresh in my memory. And how did they know that what we did was right? It is a staggering thing we did, to rise up and cast out the gentry who led us so long—and not to become bandits or thieves or animals to blunder the fields, but to hold our ranks and to make a better discipline than the gentry ever forced out of us. And this is what the people knew, before we ever knew it ourselves. Even before we rose, they knew it, and they came to Mt. Kemble with food, so that we should not march away hungry—and this morning they came to our bivouac and embraced us. Do you hear! They embraced us! How was that? We are the dirty, outland foreign brigades, and even our officers are afraid of us and paint us as devils, but the people are not afraid, and that is why we will not take a blade of grass out of their fields or a grain of wheat from their bins. We are no rabble; we are their army and their shield, and you brought dis-

451

grace on us and you deserted when we faced the gentry. So what do you say to that?

I did no worse than you did, muttered Finnigan.

Worse ye did, God damn ye! cried Connell. If ye looted, that was one thing, but ye crawled away into the darkness when the little drummer lads stood and beat their drums and faced the gentry!

Ye got no right to punish me! Ye got no right to whip me!

Bowzar looked from face to face and so did Finnigan, but there was no hope to be found in the Committee.

We are going to hang you, said Jack Maloney.

Jesus Christ, have ye gone mad?

The Widow Brennen fell to the ground and lay there sobbing as if her heart had broken, and here and there a man expelled his breath like a windy sigh of pain, but there was no other sound except the high-pitched screaming words of Finnigan:

Then what are ye hanging me for? For me poor belly that hungered? Four years I served in the Line, and did I run away when we battled? Is me hunger different from yer own hunger? Is a chicken exchange for a man's life? For Christ's sake, what are ye hanging me for?

For betraying yer own comrades, said Sean O'Toole.

And did ye hang Emil Horst who tried to fire a cannon at ye?

He was loyal to the officers, but what in hell were you loyal to?

Ye are not going to hang me! Ye cannot hang me! Me old mother in Ireland would know, and she'd die of the shame of a son who went to hell on the gallows! Ye look at me like I was a dirty traitor, but I swear to you by the holy Mother of God that I never betrayed you! Ye must not hang me! Four years I walked in this Line, and took with ye the bad and the good, and ye are not going to take my life away from me for a chicken — ah, Christ, Christ . . .

He put his face in his hands and wept, and here and there through the crowd a woman wept too, and the Committee sat like stone.

But after a long moment, the Nayger Holt said, Let him live. We that strong, we can let him live, and I never going to sleep if I see a man hanged by my hand. Make him go away, and we can spit in the dirt where he walks.

Billy Bowzar looked at me, and I nodded. Let him go, said Scottsboro slowly. I seen many a man hanged, but we don't need to hang men for crimes the gentry only whipped us for. Let him go.

Let him go, said Levy, and Jack Maloney nodded too. No whips, no canes, let him go. And Abner Williams said, Let him go. . . . And let him go far away from us, said Bora Kabanka.

So the press of people opened and Finnigan walked through, his head hanging, still weeping, and he climbed the stone wall and went away across the fields.

Then the trumpets blew, and we put on our knapsacks and marched away.

This was the chicken of the Widow Brennen, and while it is not much in the telling, it was much indeed to us and to all the folk in the countryside. It became something apart from the details of what happened, something that wholly transcended the simple fact that a chicken was stolen, and that the rank and file of the Line had dealt justice to thief and plaintiff. For no one who witnessed that strange and brief court-martial was not influenced in some way, and the men who marched away from that resting place were not the same as when they came there. And even to this day when I write, among the whole welter of lies and bitterness and awful accusations, it is still remembered that on this matter the Line was just.

Yet we were just on other matters too, and day in and day out the Committee met to pass on the slightest infraction of our General Orders; and if the truth is known, no army of that sort marched in America before then — or since then either.

But I must take up the tale of how we left our resting place and marched on toward Princeton. For the first time since the earliest days of the war, there marched along the Jersey highways an army that was light in heart and ready in spirit; for all of our doubts and fears, we marched as though we were returning victorious from some decisive battle. All morning and all afternoon the skirling of the pipes mixed with the drums of the fifes, and over and above it we sang every song we knew. With all good heart, we sang the Yankee song, *Come out, ye Continentalers, we're going for to go, To fight the redcoat enemy, so plaguy cute, you know.* And then our fifes picked up, *Why came ye to our shores, across the briny water? Why came ye to our shores, like bullocks to the slaughter?* But soon we had enough of Yankee songs, and all up and down the Line the regiments began to sing a strange and wild melody, the old Scottish air which was sung, they say, by the clansmen in the long past when they marched south against the false kings of England, and which was called by us "The Song of Revolution," but by others "The Song of the Foreign Brigades," for only we of the Line sang it. It is a low and moody song, mounting and savage and bitter:

453

And his fate is now sealed and his power is shaken,
As the people at last from their slumber awaken!
For their blood has run freely on green grass sod,
And no power now rules them save that of their God!
Death to the tyrant, torture and shame!
Death to the tyrant, faggot and flame!

Thus it was that we marched through the Jerseys and let our voices sound, so that the people would know that the Pennsylvania Line was coming; and as I said, in all that time, we saw no officer — and when we came to one of the manor houses of a patroon or a squire, the windows were barred and shuttered; the stock was driven away and the fields were empty.

Yet that day, too, it began to dawn upon us that men did not march without going somewhere, and again and again it was thrown at me:

Where are we off to, Jamie?

Where is our destination?

What is the Committee thinking? Where are the officers? What are they up to? Where are the other Lines? Where is the British enemy?

It was only curious now and only inquiring, for the men were still flushed with the ease of the revolt and with the rare sense of being their own masters, and with the knowledge that each and every one of them could become a part of the general flux of committees that we spoke of setting up. Also, the march was southward toward the Pennsylvania border, and that was as good a way to go as any other, and they were led by good men whom they had trusted before — but whom they worshiped with a singular reverence now that the revolt had come off so well and cleanly. Still, they had to have answers; so I took my place with the Committee, between Billy Bowzar and Jack Maloney, and told them:

The men are asking where we're off to?

Are they, Jamie? And is there a man in the Line who doesn't know every lane and bypath in the Jerseys?

That's tomorrow, and what comes the day after tomorrow?

And what do you think, Jamie? asked Billy Bowzar.

I've had no time to think. I've been on with the Citizen-soldier Guard since my waking hour — and that damned music takes the sense out of my head.

The music's good for the men, said Maloney. What are they saying and thinking?

This and that and everything. Some of them think that we should march straight into Philadelphia and put our demands to the Congress.

As if the Congress did not know that we are a bitter and angry file of men?

They might know it better if we stood on their doorstep.

And then what, Jamie? asked Billy Bowzar, as much to himself as to me. Do we take back our officers for the promises of Congress? Or if we get no satisfaction, do we take over the power of the Congress? Then we fight the country, eh, Jamie? And we fight the British enemy, and the country fights us and the enemy—and what will the people say, Jamie? And what of the men who enlisted for three years and served for five? Do we let them go away, Jamie? And then where do the foreign brigades recruit from?

If I knew the answers—

If *we* knew them, Jamie. . .

We walked on then for a time in silence, and then I said, Then why did we rise up?

Have you forgotten, Jamie?

Christ, no! But you have forgotten, it seems to me!

Go slow, go slow, laddie, said Jack Maloney; we've been eating our hearts out with this.

I say again, why did we rise up?

Because it was intolerable to remain the way we were, answered Jack Maloney.

But this is madness, I insisted, and the more you turn it in circles, the more insane it becomes. We have cast out our officers; the men are with us; we have the best line of troops in all this continent—and we are citizen-soldiers who have felt the whip enough to know better than to pick it up ourselves. All the dreams and hopes of men who were fed on dirt and scum for a thousand years add up to this. And when I ask you two where we are going, you can only tell me that you don't know!

Because we don't know, Jamie. We will sit down with the Committee tonight and talk about it.

And talk and talk and talk.

That's right, Jamie.

We talked for five years, but in one night of action those of us who know a little about doing and less of gabble turned the world over.

Not the whole world, Jamie, said Billy Bowzar gently, taking my arm as I strode along beside him. Not the whole world, but just the Pennsylvania Line. And meanwhile we are marching to Princeton, where we will rest awhile and patch our boots—

And you'll have use for a cobbler, since I have no brains in my head to match yourself and the Jew Levy!

Easy, Jamie, and cork your bung a little. We got a great appreciation for what you did. I am no general that I can pin a medal onto you, Jamie, but I also have no crystal ball to peer into and find the answers. Maybe if we had waited a month or six months before we rose up, we would have known. But if we waited, we would have lost our guts, for we are still like men in a dream, and it was only last night, Jamie, that we did what we did.

Then Danny Connell drew me aside into the drain of the road, so that we stood against the hump of hedge and rut while the columns marched past. The men came swinging by, grinning at us, and one and another said:

Ho, Jamie! Ho, Danny!

What bird pecks in you? asked Danny Connell, his pinched, drawn face anxious and warm, an old man in a lad's body, like so many of us.

No bird.

But the answer was fear, I knew; and I was asking myself, *Why, Jamie Stuart, why?* even as the 10th marched past, singing *Erin's sons are weeping sadly, they will see her sward no more . . .* I wanted to know *Why? why?*

They got an affection for us, said Danny Connell, and me damned heart is glad for that. We lead them, and they got an affection for us, Jamie. There is the whole world turned upside down.

And again, we stood and watched. Across the road, on a shoulder of a hill, was a wooden stake fence, and a family of nine or ten children were there, German or Dutch from the look of them, all of them like peas from the same pod with corn-thatch hair and blue eyes, a dog next to them—all of them staring open-mouthed and silent at this endless line of men, marching four abreast, playing drums and fifes and pipes and singing outlandish songs.

Then the wagons came, and on one of them was Connell's Mathilda, and when she saw him, she dropped off and he caught her up in his arms, laughing as he rocked her back and forth.

To hell with that! I cried at him. We are on the march, and you are of the Committee, and this is a hell of a thing to do!

What pecks in him? asked the Irishman.

But I ran off to catch the head of the column again.

We bivouacked that Tuesday night in the old encampment at

Middlebrook, where we had hutted for a time two years before. That was the way it was then in the Jerseys—for you will remember that for five years we had fought and marched over this ground. There was almost no stream of clear water where we had not bivouacked at one time or another, if not the Line, then one or another regiment of the Line, and there was no lane or bypath with which we were not familiar. And all over the country were our huts, or the huts of the Jersey men or the Connecticut men or the Massachusetts men, the abandoned parades, the forests we had clipped for our warmth, all of it brief, a quick erection that began to rot almost as the sound of our drums vanished; and I know of nothing more melancholy than an old encampment, filled with the ghosts of dead comrades and dead dreams—and in the same way have our deeds and sufferings vanished in the rush of years, to be replaced by a pleasant fairy tale for little children and old women, with no little memory of what the flesh and blood men were and what they wanted and what they died for.

So we came back to Middlebrook as the sun was setting on that mild, uncommon winter afternoon, and we encamped ourselves on the parade. We had no desire to put the hutments to use, for they were filled with all the old wickedness and suffering of the past—and dirt and refuse and the foul smell of long disuse. The weather was mild enough for us to be comfortable in the open. We raised up all the tents we had, built our fires foursquare, twenty to a regiment, and laid triple pickets around the place; that is, at no time in the night did we have less than three hundred men standing guard, and our cannons were loaded with small grape and short powder and set to sweep every approach. This was the trust of Angus and myself, and it was amazing how, in the short space of a few hours, the hundred men of the Citizen-soldier Guard had become expert at the business of organizing and provosting a bivouac. I can say without boasting that though I have seen many a display and bivouac of soldiers since then, I have never seen the discipline or the co-ordination that existed in the Line during the time of the rising. Each Committee we had created was functioning in the part at least, and small though that part might be, it was better than the bitter hatred which had prevailed under the officers, the discord and resentment.

Meanwhile the Committee of Sergeants, augmented with other committee heads and leading men from the regiments, had begun to meet in an old stone barn which stood at the end of the parade.

MacGrath and I, and the Gary brothers with us, did not come to the barn until well after nightfall; by then at least forty people were present in the big, drafty room, which had only half a roof and was lit with pitch torches. Two logs had been dragged in for the men to sit on; the rest sat on the floor or on the old feed trough. It had turned cold with nightfall, and the men were wrapped in scarves and in their threadbare blankets, bulked up with shoddy goods and looking strangely small now that their beards were gone, like sheared sheep. When Angus and I entered, old Lawrence Scottsboro was speaking, and it took a while for us to get the drift of what had gone on. Sometime — my memory lapses here, and I cannot recall whether it was after or before we came — they raised the thought of a march westward; yet it was on that the old man spoke, that ever-present dream and refuge and last stand of the army of the confederation, ever since the confederation had come into being. Always in the past, when matters were so low that no one believed they could sink lower, when our nakedness was past nakedness and our hunger was past hunger, when the other Lines of the other states had shrunk into skeletons of a few hundred men each, when no army and no resistance was left but the foreign brigades of Pennsylvania — when that came to pass, the last card was brought from the deck and it was said that we would march westward over the mountains into the wild and lonely land of Fincastle, as we called it then, and make a new republic there, and war on from there if need be for a hundred years against the British enemy. But this was always the kind of dream that desperate men make for themselves, and it was like smoke, blown away by a close examination or even a puff of wind. Yet this was being spoken of now, and the old man Scottsboro was recalling how he had marched with Braddock in the great destruction that the Frenchmen and the Indians had brought upon them, and this and that about how it was to fight in the dark woods. And as we listened, a colder chill than the weather crept over us.

You may not understand now what a deep horror we had in those times of the dark and awful forest, where the trees were seven feet through the trunk, and where a man could walk a fortnight and never see the sky or properly know when it was daybreak or nightfall — and where a child could go out of sight and never be seen or heard of again, and a grown man too. You are town bred and country bred. But we had with us in the Line many, many of the lonely Scottish buckskin men from Fincastle, who had been driven there because not an acre of open land existed but was pledged to a man of property who had the King's guns to shoot down those who poached on it; and yet these men shook their heads somberly at talk of a retreat across the mountains.

Yes, we could lose us, said Scottsboro, choosing his words slowly and painfully, and the nation would lose us too. And we would not set up a republic, but only a company of lost men who would turn bandits in that bitter land.

Lawrence Scottsboro was an ancient among us, a small, knotted man, wrinkled, with only four teeth in his whole mouth, and on and off racked with the rheumatic pains which were the special reward to each and every one who followed the soldier's trade. He, like Jack Maloney, had no father, no mother, no kith or kin. He had licked and scra[ ]ed from a camp kettle when he was seven years old, and he had not the slightest notion where he came from or who he was or of what blood. Scottsboro, as you know, was the old wooden fort the British built on the upper reaches of the Hudson River, so long ago — and now not even a stick of it remains — and that was the name he took, since it was the first place he could root out of his memory. And he had grown up in the camps of the British regiments, lickspittle at first, serving and scrounging and running to heel with a fist at his forelock — until he was old enough to beat a drum and then to carry a gun. Often I have heard him remember the endless marches he made, the uncounted miles from garrison to garrison, fort to fort, post to post — in the dirty, miserable, meaningless life a redcoat Regular lived, the cane on the shoulders, the filth, the loneliness, the depraved practices among the ignorant, hopeless, undersized men who sold their souls and their lives for the mess of pottage King George served out. He became a corporal and a sergeant and then a master sergeant, and you would have said that there was never a thought or a dream in his obedient head; but the bitterness had made a score, and when the farmers beat the British into Boston in 1775, he and two others cut off a redcoat captain's head and brought it to the Yankee farmers as enlistment papers. But he was an army man and nothing else, and in the great rout of 1776, when the Yankees ran away, he saw that the foreign brigades remained to fight, and he joined the 1st Regiment of Pennsylvania — which was my regiment then, until they took me out to be sergeant in the 11th.

This old man, such a hard and bitter old man, now spoke with gentleness and wisdom and said:

Because we are not a folk, but an army. We be soldiers, and of soldiers and soldiering I know something, laddies, for I was under the weight of a gun before the lot of ye were born. There is no good in soldiers except what comes from the folk they soldier for — and if you

459

soldier for that bastard King, as I did so long, what are ye but a
buffer, a pimp, a bruiser, a blower, a hooker, a prigger, a whipjack—
and it don't matter ye wear a red coat on your back. Now, what virtue
is in us? I been rolling that round and round in this old head of mine,
for we are as hard-bitten and scraggy a lot of men as there are in this
whole world over, and I know, I tell you. I seen hard men a-plenty,
but I seen harder in these foreign brigades. But I look around at my
comrades, and I find them gentle, so gentle I got to go and put my
cloak over my face and cry, which a grown man shouldn't need to do.
I ain't but a simple man, as ye know, but I think there is a deeper virtue in freedom than we sense—and that is why the country folk come
with food. That is why. We are their soldiers for freedom, but we got
no virtue apart from that. I don't know how to say that to make it
plainer, because it ain't too plain in my own head. But if we go away
from them, from the Jersey and Pennsylvania and York and Connecticut and Massachusetts people, we become something else, and all what
is bitter and hard in us will erupt like a boil that breaks. When ye
come down to it, that is why we let the gentry cane us and whip us and
starve us these five years—we got a deeper attachment than them. But
if we do like Connell and Carpenter says and go into the deep woods,
then God help us indeed. I don't know what we can do, but not that.

He's right, said Billy Bowzar then. We are in a war because people
have suffered and people struck back. If we go to a place where there
are no people, we are all through. It would be better to lay down our
guns and go home.

And where is home for the foreigns? asked the Jew Levy. Here is my
home.

Me thought is this, said Danny Connell, that Scottsboro is an old
one, and the heart is out of the old ones. Me old father he said, If ye
are going to make a rising, then go through with it and be damned!

Christ, when I hear an Irishman talk! cried Jack Maloney. Do ye
make a rising for the sake of a rising? Then ye could rise all alone, ye
damn fool! We made a rising because the men wanted it, and now we
have cast out the officers—but what the old man says is right, and
don't make mock of him. I tell you, I will not run away to the mountains! I will lay me down and die first! I will crawl first to Wayne and
tell him, come back and lead me again!

I am sick to me belly of hearing ye talk about the Irish, began
Danny Connell, but Billy Bowzar cut in and held them.

You have neither of ye the floor, and hold your peace. This is a
Committee meeting, and that it will be. If you want the floor again,

460

put up your hand and ask for it, and when your turn comes you can speak. But I'll not have us shouting back and forth like a gabble of red Indians.

He then recognized Abner Williams, who remained silent for a while before he began to speak. There had always been a little of mistrust in our attitude toward Williams, not only because he was a Yankee with the long, narrow, aloof face that so many of the Yankees have, but because he was a man of college education, strange with our women, apart from our jesting, and had made such remarks as to the effect of his believing as little in God as he did in King George III, except that one was there and you could put a hand on him and the other had a residence unknown. While this wasn't taken well by the Protestants, it went even worse with the Romans, who pointed out that it was logical for the Yankees, who had cast out the true God, to make the next step and defame their own false God as well. Also, he spoke a different tongue from us, a different way of the English; yet he stood for us, and from him the officers took much that they would never take from us. He too had come to us in the great rout and had remained with us, and we knew that he, like the Jew Levy, was full of many books and many mysteries. So we hearkened when he spoke and studied his words, always conscious that we were ignorant men, most of us by far knowing no letters and few numbers. And for all our dislike of the Yankees, they were like the Jews in this matter of reading and writing, scrounging for it, even if they were just common folk like ourselves.

We are a people of committees, said Abner Williams. It's in the blood, and for ten years we've made a Committee for everything, and everything we have done has come through a Committee, even the Revolution itself—and my father used to tell me that more hours than he slept, he spent at committee meetings. I say this because perhaps a Yankee is more patient with the Committee way than someone who has not bitten his teeth on it. When I first began to hear and speak, a Committee of Resistance met at our house, and then a Committee of Liberty in the church cellar, and then a Committee on Stamps and then a Committee on Tea and then a Committee of Correspondence— only we couldn't run our army with committees. We tried, but it didn't work. Well, here in the Midlands, it is different, and you have a gentry of a kind we don't have in Connecticut, or in the Bay Colony either— or I should say that those of them we had, some we hanged and some we tarred and feathered and the rest we drove away on the British ships. Not because we are more knowledgeable about gentry, but because it is a different world in the North than here with the patroons

461

and the lords and the squires—and the cheating of a man out of his little bit of land to make him a tenant, and binding men like slaves to apprenticeship, and the kind of officers who rode a saddle on us, and the kind of a war they are fighting. But they're not all of it, and that's why I want to talk as a Yankee, as a stranger among you, although I've eaten and slept and marched and fought with the foreign brigades for five years—and never seen my own home or my own blood in all that time. I lived under the officers as you lived under them, and to me they and what they represent and what they believe and hold are like a disease—and here for a moment the disease joined the body to cast off a greater danger; and sometime—a year, ten years or a hundred years from now—the disease must go or the body will die. That is why I rose against them and that is why I will do whatever you do and go wherever you go, even across the mountains—although I hold with Scottsboro that such a way is wrong and bad. But I've brooded over this and brooded over it, and I know no way, no other way. If we turn out the Congress in Philadelphia—and they have no force that can prevent our doing so—then we will plunge our confederation into civil war, and there is still the British enemy sitting among us and waiting. If we call for the other Lines to join us, some will, but some will march against us. Jersey is with us, and I think Pennsylvania would be with us—but I don't know what the Yankees would do, and I am a Yankee. And what would Virginia and the Carolinas do, where the gentry are worse than here, and where their own slaves have run away to fight in our brigades? And if we lay down our arms and go home—where is our home? Shall I go back to Connecticut and say, This is no more for me, this Revolution, for I hate the Midland gentry worse than I hate the British? *But I don't hate the British. I love liberty*—and not a word, but a way I've dreamed where there would be a little dignity to men, and not for the most to be like beasts driven by a few. And that we've won, here in the Pennsylvania Line; and we've had twenty-four hours of it, and, God help me, I don't know where we are to go with it!

Then Yankee, take the damned gentry back! Andrew Yost snorted. Or go to them!

Fairly—fairly: ask for the floor, several shouted.

I had the floor—all I want to say. I ain't got words like him! cried Andrew Yost.

Keep your order! shouted Billy Bowzar, pounding the floor with a stick of wood.

And I can tell ye where to go, cried Angus MacGrath, though I no be one of the Committee. Has a kemp a right to speak, Billy Bowzar?

462

I have not enough of the Scottish to know if that's a good man or a dirty scoundrel, but say your piece, MacGrath. This is a forum for the regiments. Say your piece.

I'll tell ye where we can go, providing ye got a little bit of courage. We can go up to York city and dad them — if ye got the guts — march north, and cross the river, and hit on them!

The British!

I mean no others, answered Angus, standing straight and proud, throwing his deep voice against the back wall of the barn.

There are fifteen thousand of them in York city! someone cried.

And when there were fifteen thousand dirty redcoats on the border, was it my own father afraid to come down and faught? The hell he was!

Ye got a fine notion of the Scottish, and too little of the English, a lad in the hayloft laughed.

I got a notion of the Line. And if ye want to fight for that notion —

Angus! cried Billy Bowzar, spreading his arms. I gave you the floor, and you said your piece. Now keep a still tongue! There is no doubting your courage or the courage of the Line, and I'll have no fighting unless you want to fight with me. And I'm no Scottish and no Irish either and half your size, but I'll take you on, thick head and all. Now listen . . .

We were laughing now, and wrapping deeper in our rags; for a cold night wind blew through the openings in that ruin of a barn; and the laugh was all surface, for there was a memory of the cold of winters past, and there was the beginning of a realization that we were embarked on a road no one had traveled before.

Now listen, said Billy Bowzar, if you are so short of memory that a day of sunshine can wipe the winter from your mind. Today we marched in the sunshine, but tomorrow the snows can begin again, and our tents would not even make good foot wrappings. That is why the Committee chose Princeton as our destination. The college buildings there are empty and waiting, and we can make something in them and in the hutments the British set up there. So Angus MacGrath says, *March on York city where the British are. . . ?* With enough leather on our feet to sign our tracks in blood? With twenty thousand loads of powder to the whole Line? I am not impressed with the fifteen thousand of the King's men, laying with their whores in that rotten city — give us the support of the country and the people, and we can take the Line against *them,* and cut them up too, and drive them shrieking and screaming and howling from York city the way they drove us out of there in '76 — but I don't live in dreams. We have food for three or four days, and we will have more here when that is eaten, too, because the Jersey folk know us — but who will feed us when we march into the doxy-hole of New York? Who will shelter our wounded? Who will give us powder when we have shot away what we carry?

The British, someone called.

Ah — yeah? And if it snows, and we must wait five days to feel the bottom of the roads before we can march?

Let me speak a word, Billy Bowzar, said the Jew Levy, standing up and walking over to where Bowzar sat on an old cider keg. He put his hand on Bowzar's shoulder, gripping it — and Bowzar smiled self-consciously, pulling off his woolen cap and running his fingers through his curly red hair. He nodded and pursed his lips, and the skinny little Jew said:

We are lucky for having Bowzar. Such men there aren't too many of.

No one's against Bowzar, said Simpkins Gary.

That's right — no one's against Billy Bowzar; but he hasn't slept for two days. He's never stopped for two days. It shouldn't be thought that this revolt just happened. It had to be organized and led, and it still has to. And if men should lead it, they got to see over the heads of the soldiers of the Line. A thousand times since it began, we said to each other, What will we do next? Where do you go with a thing like this? What is the rest of the army doing? What is Washington doing? Does he know about this? Does Congress know? And if we elect new officers — can we fight alone? You heard Billy Bowzar: Who will feed us? Who will arm us? Today the Jersey folk, but what about tomorrow? The people will not trust foreign bandits who have cast out their officers — this is not what we are, but this is what the officers will say. I know — I know what the people think about Jews and Romans and black men. Ask Jim Holt!

He is right, said Jim Holt. My God, we ain't criminal — we be good men, but who going to believe that unless we show it? And how we going to show it? The Nayger should be no slave, because we fight for no man to be slave, but if we sing out *No Nayger slave,* the whole Southland going to turn against us! We say, *No rich man, no man with a million acres.* But how you going to live without rich man? You hang them all, and then it just take a little time: there be rich man again. You going to turn them against George Washington, who is rich man with many Nayger slave. . . ?

Thus it went, on and on, with one and another and then still another speaking, and round and round and round it went — in a weary, awful circle, with the wind blowing colder and colder through the open gaps in the barn, with more and more men from the regiments coming to listen and shiver and watch our leaders butt their heads against a wall that had no openings.

Guns we had, and powder and shot, and almost three thousand of the best troops in the world—but we had nothing to fight for except what we had fought for under our officers.

It was the tail of the evening—well on and well under, when sleep had mixed with cold and many had gone and I no longer heard words but only voices—when MacPherson came and shook me from my doze, and said softly, Come outside, Jamie.

I went out with him, and there was Allen Gutton, a barber from the 3rd Regiment who had dropped away in the rising, as men had here and there—and what with one thing and another, we were not able to brood on those who were gone.

So ye lost yourself, Allen, I said.

No, Jamie: I chose to stay.

Like similar filth.

Say what you like, Jamie. I followed my own conscience.

None of ye got one; but, anyway, what in hell are you doing here?

I come with a message from the general.

I would have kicked him to the ground and driven him from the camp on his hands and knees, with a stick across his shoulders, but MacPherson was watching me out of his somber eyes, and I nodded and said, I will get someone to talk with you. My own stomach is too delicate.

Go to hell and be damned, Jamie. I come with a message from the general, and I don't have to take your gabble.

Not now, you don't!

I went into the barn and called Billy Bowzar aside and talked to him. He turned the chair over to Danny Connell, and then nodding at the Jew Levy and Jack Maloney, he motioned for them to follow. We went outside, our feet crunching the hard ground, and Gutton handed him the letter, which he read in the moonlight then and there. I had wanted to make a copy of that letter, but I neglected that, and it is gone and lost now, but I remember that it stated matter-of-factly enough that Wayne and two of his staff would appreciate a conference with the Committee of Sergeants of the Pennsylvania Line. It was polite and gentle and somewhat coaxing, not the way gentlemen talk to dirt, but the way one gentleman talks to another.

He wants to meet with us, said Bowzar.

He looked at me and I stared at him emptily, and then he looked at Maloney and Levy—and they made no move nor gesture, but they did not have to.

Tell him to approach our pickets at Princeton tomorrow, said Bowzar tonelessly. The Committee will discuss any matters he wishes to bring before us. Now take him through the lines, Jamie.

With that, I escorted Gutton through the sentries and onto the road where he had left his horse. When he turned to mount, I kicked him in the butt and then ground his face in the dirt.

That's reward for your conscience, Allen Gutton, I said.

And something to remember in the future, Jamie Stuart, he answered, rising and climbing on his horse.

Remember and be damned! Geck on ye!

With no other word, he mounted and rode off; and I went back to the barn. The meeting was over now. The Committee and the Reverend William Rogers remained; the others had gone.

Well, Jamie? asked Danny Connell.

I sent the little rat on his way. But I been thinking to ask you something, you gentlemen of the Committee. What in hell have we got to say to the officers?

We don't know, Jamie, Bowzar answered.

Well. . . , I began, but Dwight Carpenter interrupted me with:

Close your yap, Jamie, and let us get to bed.

To hell with them, I thought. To hell with them and their theories and their wisdom; and I turned around and walked out. But before I had taken ten steps, Jack Maloney was after me with an arm around my shoulders.

Jamie, hold yer hot head. We are in a profound and frightening thing, and we got to feel our way.

And take back the officers!

We are not taking them back, Jamie. We are going to look at this and that, and try to understand what we have done. That is all. We got to find a future, because, as sure as God, there is none facing us now! Then I went to my blankets, rolled close to the fire, and slept. And once more the morning was warm and sunny, and as we marched down the road to Princeton, the men of the Line singing as they paced, the drums beating and the fifes shrilling and the pipers blowing with all their might and main, my fears of the night before went away, and I knew only the great and massive comfort of the Pennsylvania Line, the strong and tried men who alone of all the armies in the world had no officers, but ruled themselves and marched for their own freedom.

PART SEVEN

Being an account of the events at Princeton.

ON WEDNESDAY, the 3rd of January, about two hours after the sun had set, I was summoned by one of the Citizen-soldier Guard to Nassau Hall, where the Committee of Sergeants had established the general headquarters of the Pennsylvania Line.

In those times, the Prince Town, as many of the native Jersey folk still called it, was a village of some thirty or forty houses, almost all of them built on the main pike that ran southward and across the river to Philadelphia. It was a pretty and quiet little village, which Jack Maloney said reminded him of the Sussex towns in the old country, and it was dominated in its center by the hall of the college, which was not in those days called Princeton, but the Old School of the Jerseys. We were no strangers to Princeton, for one or another regiment of the Line had marched through there at least a hundred times since the war began, and at least four times the whole Line had made a bivouac in the broad meadow behind Nassau Hall, and so had the British on one occasion or another. And at least four regiments of the Line recalled well and vividly the wild and terrible battle we had fought with the British, hand to hand, butt to butt, knife to knife—when they first tasted the difference between the foreign brigades and the Yankee militia. Four years ago to the day, that was, on the 3rd of January—yet how many lives had we lived since then, and how many good comrades had died, and how many things had changed!

In more ways than one had things changed, for Nassau Hall, which had been such a fine and lovely building, was gutted and wrecked, with not a window left in it and not a stone in reach that wasn't defaced by those gentle advocates of culture, the British enemy, who had stabled their horses in one part of the hall, while the German mercenaries used another part as an outhouse. Also, the war had raged closer to this village than to many; some men had fled to York city; others had died or gone into the Jersey Line; and here and there among the houses was a little tyke who would never know that he or

467

she had been sired out of the foreign brigades, and was none the worse for it either. So it was a good welcome the regiments found in Princeton, with the news gone ahead of them that they had thrown out the gentry, and with the brigades marching down the street between the houses like redcoat grenadiers, and with the two Scottish pipers taking their place on either side the big hall and skirling us around it onto the camp grounds.

My own work, along with that of Angus and the Gary brothers, was to lay out and order the encampment, and this time we set to work to repair the old huts and get them fit to live in, and it was from this that I was summoned by the Committee of Sergeants.

They were already at work around a long, mutilated table that had been rescued from the debris of the ruined hall. It was set up on the first floor in a big room, lit with candles and hastily made as habitable as possible. Old shutters and boards had been nailed over the smashed windows to keep out the draft, and a good fire was roaring in the hearth. Odds and ends of boxes and kegs had been put to use as chairs, and the tavern keeper from the crossroads had presented to the Committee as his own peace offering, a big pewter jug of hot flip, which now filled the whole room with its delicious smell. As I entered, Danny Connell dipped into the flip and poured me a measure.

Drink hearty, Jamie!

To the Committee of Sergeants, I said sourly.

What pecks in ye, me lad? grinned Connell.

My whole lousy, worthless twenty-two years of life, and my one glimpse of glory.

Then hold onto it, Jamie, nodded Jack Maloney, for I wish to God that I was twenty-two again, glory or no.

And when this evening is done, added Dwight Carpenter, go find a village lass, Jamie; for ye are a fine, upstanding Pennsylvania lad and winsome too—

The devil with you!

Old Scottsboro here, he is sour and old, but it is not natural, Jamie, to be sour and young.

Leave the lad alone, said Bowzar sharply. It's one stinking taste of flip, Jamie. Tell me, how are we covered?

It would not be covered at all if it was left to the great discussions of the Committee. At least, what I do, I do.

Jamie, Bowzar broke in, stop yapping of that. We gave ye a task because we thought ye could do it—and do you want a certificate for every time ye leak? Now, Jamie, how are we covered?

I got forty men of the Guard out, and another fifty beside.

That is not enough, Jamie. We want a picket around this place that a rabbit could not squirm through—and no picket is to yap—and I mean no gabble whatsoever. If anyone comes up to the guards, they are to turn him over to you or MacGrath. Turn out three hundred men on two hours—

They have had a day's march.

We know that, Jamie, and let them go guard tonight, and we want them out and on parade in full gear at seven o'clock in the morning.

I have no watch, I said.

But I have, and I'll turn you out, Jamie. So get that under way and leave Angus to do it, and then take one of the Gary lads and ten of the best and most likely lads you have got in the soldier guard, and go across the road to the inn, where you'll find the general and two of his staff waiting. Bring them here.

How do you know they'll be there then?

Because they there now, said Holt.

They are there, Jamie, but let them cool their heels a little.

They'll be raging.

Then let them rage, lad. They have done their share of raging, and it should not take too much out of them. Bring them here gentle, but very firm—very firm, Jamie. Polite, but very firm indeed.

Drums? asked O'Toole.

To hell with that, said Scottsboro. They have drummed us sufficient, and we'll not drum them back.

I saluted.

That's a good manner, to salute, Jamie, said Levy. This is not the end, son.

I went out thinking of what the Jew had said, and I was thinking of it as I repeated to Angus MacGrath the instructions for guarding the encampment.

I want it proper, I told Angus, with a devil of a lot of rigmarole and saluting.

But I chose my ten soldiers for the honor guard out of sheer bitterness, five white and five black, knowing how the officers hated to see a Nayger or a Jew do more than die—or less. Three of the white were Roman, with the Irish thick on their faces as well as their tongues, and the other two were the Gonzales brothers. The black men were big Bantu, none less than six feet tall, big-muscled as well. From here and there, we scraped together the best clothes we could find, and I set the drummer lads to scurrying among the huts to turn up cocked hats,

469

since the scarves and home-made woolen caps we wore were hardly of a soldierly appearance. Katy Waggoner and Jenny Hurst showed up at the command hut of the 11th, where we were, and set to work with needle and thread, sewing on the men as they stood around, self-conscious and grinning; and meanwhile a drummer lad blacked their broken boots and the toes as well, for I considered that in a dim light that might give the appearance of a whole shoe. When they were done up as well as they might be, I formed them in two columns, and we marched smartly across the road to the inn.

The Hudibras was kept by a Dutchman named Jacob Hyer. I knew him from the past, a big-bellied middle-aged man, with a gift for gab and a fund of stories of battles he had never seen. Like a thousand others from the Jerseys and Pennsylvania, he had once paraded with some local folk, and that made him a colonel of militia or something of the sort, but he was a smart man and a born diplomat, and he blew the way the wind blew. When the British were in Princeton, he, like the others, became as loyal to the crown as a man could be, and the half-dozen barmaids he employed for other purposes than drawing beer served the King with all their will and might and main; but when Continentals marched in, he was a mighty patriot indeed. But we of the foreign brigades now occupied an uncertain category in his mind, and when he opened the door for me, after I had smacked it once or twice with a pistol butt, his face, usually so pink and pleasant, was dead white and earnest and apologetic — as he said:

Why now, it's Jamie Stuart, it is, and welcome here to the Hudibras.

It is indeed, I answered him, and where is the officer gentry?

Now, Jamie, I always been a good friend to you, and I never have no trouble in my house. You come in by yourself, huh?

The hell I will. I come in with them — motioning for Gary to lead the guard in, and standing there as they filed past.

And if there's one little bit of dirty play, Jacob, I added, I'll ram this pistol up your fat ass.

Jamie, you know me as a good friend . . .

We went into the taproom, and from the blazing hearth, the smell of roasting pork and lamb, and the fullness of it, the steam of smoking flip, and the way the wine and the beer and the rum were flowing out of the taps and into the well-padded bellies of well-clad travelers from Tory New York to rebel Philadelphia and back again, you would never know that there was a war and a few thousand men in rags and bare feet trying to fight it. There were tradesmen there, and commission

470

men from the shipping and corn agents and meat speculators and military contractors and subcontractors and overseers from the big holdings and prosperous farmers, and quiet, sharp-eyed men in black broadcloth who asked no questions and answered none, who minded their own business and did it with both sides in lofty impartiality—and there were women serving and having their behinds pinched and giggling; but the giggling stopped and the talking halted and the motion froze as the dozen of us stalked into the room.

They were afraid. How many times in the past had I come into this same inn and walked past the taproom to the kitchen, because officers were here and fine gentlemen in fine clothes and I was a dirty sergeant of the Line in my patched overalls and my broken shoes? And as I moved through the taproom, close to the wall, no one had even looked up from their roast or beer—since I was something they paid no mind to, only one of the rabble that was foolish enough to carry a musket in the war. They looked up now; they looked up with terror and their chairs scraped and the scraping stopped—and there was silence until a barmaid dropped a pewter mug.

Where are they? I asked Jacob Hyer.

Even the motion of the candle flame seemed to have halted, even the reflection in the copper pots and mugs that lined the walls and the polished pewter trays and pitchers behind the bar.

Now, Jamie, my lad . . . began Jacob Hyer.

God damn it to hell with *Jamie my lad!* Where are they?

Let your boys go into the kitchen and wet their throats, and I'll take you along, Jamie.

Where I go, my men go—and we want none of your stinking brew!

He sighed and shrugged and nodded, and we all went up the staircase, and every eye in the place followed us, but no word was said. We marched up the stairs, the great Bantu Naygers bending their heads to fit themselves to the place, and down the short hall to a door, upon which Jacob Hyer knocked timidly.

Come in, a voice said.

He opened the door and entered, and I followed—Gary behind me, and then the ten men crowding into the room—and there was Wayne with Stewart and Butler, two colonels of the Line and men close to him.

In full uniform, they sat around a small mahogany table. Two candles in silver sticks burned on its polished surface, and a bottle of port stood there too. Each had a partly finished glass which he held and fingered, but the ease of it was too contrived even for the unknowledge-

471

able lad that I was. I realized very certainly that they had been waiting for us impatiently enough, and had only taken up this pose when they heard us downstairs. The gilt was gone off them, and not now and never again would I see in these uneasy gentry even a touch of the greatness that I found resting so simply and softly in my own comrades. So I stood there calmly and deliberately, while the ten men marched into the room and around the table.

Whatever Wayne and Steward and Butler thought, to see us, they concealed well enough. They looked at me and my men coolly, sipped at their glasses, set them down and flicked their cuffs. They were turned out in buff and blue without a wrinkle or a speck of dust—only a little fall of powder from their wigs onto their collars. Butler and Steward were florid men, fleshy and healthy and big of head; in my mind, men, as against the lad that I was; well-turned out, well-cared for men who had always enough to eat and drink, always a bed between sheets, always a woman for their assured, commanding manner, always an arrangement to take care of any contingency—except this one. They were not, perhaps, identical with the old-country gentry, but they were very close to it nevertheless, good horsemen who had callused their asses driving over honest men's fields to kill a fox, good drinkers, good eaters, not overconcerned with politics but only with what they liked to call a soldier's task, and seeing nothing at all wrong with lying down in a Tory or patroon house, as long as it was with men of honor that they consorted.

Now they faced no men of honor at all, and they remained stiff and silent as Wayne demanded:

What is all this?

A guard of honor for you, Mr. Wayne—which I said deliberately, the lad in me playing it loose, which was something I paid a fearful and terrible price for, as you will see. Yet I do not know if I could have done it any differently, even if I had known well ahead what the accounting would be. I was a wild and headstrong animal—and not ashamed of that, even now, for the piece of truth that was in us was a firm thing.

Since when do you address me as Mr. Wayne? . . . he asked quietly, for all that his voice trembled with anger.

I have no orders to address you otherwise.

And who gives you your orders, Sergeant?

The Committee.

He didn't answer that, although he made to, and I realized that he had swallowed down what he intended to say. He sat in silence, and the two colonels with him were silent too. Now I noticed from the corner of my eye that the landlord still lingered, so I said:

Get to hell out of here, Jacob!

The door closed behind him, and still the three officers sat grimly silent around the table. Anthony Wayne was never a very brilliant man; courage he had, and loyalty to his own lights, but not the rapier mind that belonged to Hamilton and Burr and Reed and some others. His inner conflict was visible to us who watched, and when he spoke again his voice was hoarse and dry.

We will go along with you, Sergeant. We need no guard. Dismiss them.

My orders are that the guard takes you into our lines.

Damn it, Sergeant, he cried, his voice rising, you seem to forget who you speak to!

I have not forgotten.

To hell with you and be damned! We will not walk among you like dirty criminals!

Very well, I shrugged—and started toward the door. But he called me back, as I knew he would.

Wait a minute, Sergeant.

Without turning, I halted. Wayne spoke like a man with a bullet in his lungs.

Are these your orders?

They are. I'm not in the habit of lying, Mr. Wayne.

Very well, he said softly, so softly that I scarcely heard it. I never turned around—and this they remembered well, and for this too I was repaid in their own peculiar coin. The cobbler's apprentice led them out, and the guard formed on either side, and Gary brought up the rear. Into the corridor we went, down the stairs, through the taproom, outside into the night, across the road, through our lines, and up to Nassau Hall—and never a word was spoken.

Angus MacGrath was in command of the guard there. Ten of the citizen-soldiers, their white armbands showing in the night, their bayonets fixed, were lined up on either side the doorway. Angus opened the door, and inside were ten more of the Citizen-soldier Guard, a good, solid show of discipline and strength, a better show than they had ever managed themselves.

It made an impression on them, all right, even as the pickets had made an impression, standing so tight that a rabbit could not crawl through. We brought the three officers into the ruined and desecrated hall and led them over to the long table, where the eleven men of the

Committee of Sergeants sat. Three seats had been left in the center of the table, and as we approached Billy Bowzar rose and said:

Will you and your companions be seated here, Mr. Wayne?

I think, sir, answered Wayne, we had better clear up this matter of address before we go further. I demand that we be spoken in our military rank.

Your military rank is in terms of the Line, sir, Bowzar said quietly. We admit you no rank in the Line now. Let me be square and clear about it. We are the Governing Board of the Pennsylvania Line, and no officer holds a commission here today.

I hold my commission from the Congress, Wayne said.

Is that your feeling?

That is my feeling, Sergeant, answered Wayne, his fists clenched, the knuckles white, his whole body rigidly under control.

Then we'll address you as General Wayne, but we'll give no title to these two men — nodding at Stewart and Butler — who were regimental officers and are no longer. You can take that or leave that, General Wayne.

This time, I had a feeling that they would walk out; but they must have agreed in advance that under any circumstances, they would enter into discussion, and after a moment of silence, Wayne nodded shortly. They removed their hats, opened their coats without removing them, and sat down in the seats Bowzar had indicated, each with his big three-cornered hat in his lap. In their heavy, faced regimentals, wearing epaulettes and dress swords and large powdered wigs, with their ruddy, well-groomed faces, they made a strange contrast to the eleven men of the Committee. It is not only that five years of starvation and exposure will take their toll — a toll had been taken from us long before, and placed against the gentry we were undersized, as well as undernourished — wizened, with gaps where our teeth should have been, and the lasting marks of scurvy and the pox planted well upon us. A wig is a master's thing, for it sits on the head like a great crown, snow-white and beyond the damage of years, making the face and head very imposing indeed — as against little Jack Maloney, or Bowzar, who was five feet and three inches tall, or the Jew Levy who was a tiny, skinny man who could blow away in a good breath of wind — or as against Lawrence Scottsboro, a wizened gnome of man, or Danny Connell and O'Toole and the rest; all of us shrunk, except the Nayger Kabanka; all of us patched — all of us, except the Yankee Abner Williams, separated from the three officers by a thousand years of demarcation between the squire and the crofter, between the merchant lord and the broken-nailed laborer, between the white master and the black slave, between the English Protestant and the Roman Irish, between the Christian world and the hated Jew. And we felt it and they felt it too.

Yet with all that, Bowzar was fine and soft and easy as he introduced each man in turn.

These are the representatives of the regiments, he explained. We speak for the men, and every man in this Line who executes any task or gives any command carries a warrant from us. So when you speak to us, gentlemen, you are in a way talking to the whole of the Line, and we can answer for them too.

During this, I dismissed the guards, telling them to wait outside, and then threw a few logs of wood on the fire, which blazed up bright and cheerful — but no real warmth against the winter wind, which crept into the broken room from twenty different holes and openings. The table was well lit with candles in sticks and bottles, but the corners of the big hall stayed in darkness, and every now and then one could hear the scurrying of a rat.

Instead of seating myself, I stood at one end of the table, near the fire; and even with that measure of heat, it was pleasant enough, and I would find myself becoming drowsy now and then. For that reason, my memory may not be too exact on these conversations, but I recall well the tenor of them, and the picture of Wayne and Butler and Stewart as they sat there will remain with me as long as I live. How different it was from any pictures I have seen of that almost forgotten war!

Billy Bowzar finished speaking and waited — and there was a long silence until Wayne said:

Concerning the uprising and all that has happened in the past three days, I have the power to say this. If you agree to a return of the officers, no soldier will be punished. I give you my word on that.

We rose up against the officers, Billy Bowzar reminded him. Why should we take them back?

Because you are no army without them, Wayne said shortly.

Were we an army with them?

That's neither here nor there.

But it is, said Jack Maloney, because as sure as God, we are an army now.

Looking straight at him, Wayne said, You deserted out of one army, and now out of another.

Damn you, whispered Maloney, I am a truer man to the republic of Pennsylvania than ever you were.

Shut your trap! cried Stewart, and Bowzar broke in, cold as ice:
You come here as our guest, Mister.
You make a great score for yourself, Billy Bowzar.
Yes, and I have made great scores in the past, and paid them too,
Mr. Stewart, and if I have to pay for this one, you render the account
when the bill is due. Until then, you sit in our house at our table—and
however such things are ordered with the gentry, they are ordered
decent with us. We did not ask this meeting. We cast you out—every
damned one of you—and you beseeched us this meeting. If you cannot
sit and talk as gentlemen, then go back to Jacob Hyer's whorehouse!

I had never seen Billy Bowzar like that before—his face dead white
against the red hair, every freckle standing sharp and prominent, all of
him in a cold, awful anger that had its effect on the Committee as well
as on the officers. His nostrils dilated with fury; the muscles bunched
all over his square face; and his tiny blue eyes became narrow slits. If a
bird pecked in me, it pecked deeper in him, closer to the soul of him
that had been scarred by God only knows what. He reached in his
pocket and drew out the silver watch that had become the official timepiece of the Line, and laying it on the table before him, he said:

You have one minute, gentlemen, to decide whether you will stay
and talk decently—or whether you will go.

And then there was silence, the watch ticking away the second in a
large and painful silence—louder and louder it seemed, or perhaps
only in the memory is it that way; for I have often recalled those
seconds and wondered whether our lives and the lives of many others
would have been different had Wayne waited through the whole sixty
seconds and then left. But that is idle fancy; the matter was a matter
of power, and we were the Line and the power—a sullen, proud,
angry, aware power that no force on the Continent could challenge,
and Wayne was a general without an army, even as Stewart and Butler
were regimental commanders without regiments, and all of them had
gone through three terrible days—each of them no doubt contemplating a pistol at one time or another and debating a question of blowing
out his brains. For the whole fabric of the thirteen states was hinged on
the Pennsylvania Line, and whatever the result, they would have to
answer; we were the power, and they were, at the moment, only three
men alone. So they stayed, and Wayne said:

We will stay and talk.

As you desire, gentlemen . . . Bowzar nodded shortly, and then
waited—as we all waited.

Wayne groped with his thoughts; Butler leaned over and whispered to him; Steward sat stiffly and proudly, the bitterness congealing within him like a souring curd.

Well, said Wayne—well, we must discuss this. I recognize how hard it was for the soldier in the Line. War is not a gentle practice, but it may be that it was too hard. On the other hand, I have stood for the men: I pleaded for food; I pleaded for clothes; I pleaded for money . . .

His eyes traveled from face to face, but none of us said anything. He placed his three-cornered hat on the table in front of him, as if that was a symbol of concession, but a muscle near his mouth twitched and twitched and his back was like a ramrod. Swallow and chew, I said to myself, as the scene blurred before my eyes and then returned again to focus—swallow and chew, my friend, my general . . . And then I held my own conversation with myself: Ask him for my youth, Bowzar, before you sell me. I am wise in the ways of men who lead; they are all alike, men who lead, and the tears were in my eyes for the woeful, lost hopes of my comrades back in the huts. But, I said to myself, leave them here to discuss, Jamie Stuart, and back to the huts and sound the trumpets, and march off.

Myself—said Butler, speaking for the first time—am in agreement with the general. The patience of the men was tried too sorely, so they rose up and hit out at what they could see, the officers. We are agreed that this is not a criminal matter, but an orderly and peaceful disposition. But under all, there is a fervent faith in my heart, and in the heart of the general and in the heart of each and every one of my fellow regimental commanders, that we and the men are of one mind and one heart concerning the basic principles and program of the Revolution, as set forth in that document we have lived by, the Declaration of Independence.

That we are, answered Bowzar.

Then it is possible that we should make progress.

Ye sit facing the men, said Danny Connell suddenly, which is not a common thing, and every word brings up another matter of reality. Ye make the Declaration a blanket to cover both of us; and we, who are such ignorant clods, by and large, that we cannot write out our own names, nevertheless know that document by heart—which is more learning than the gentry have studied lately. Therein it says, word for word, that when a long train of abuses and usurpations, begun at a distinguished period and pursuing invariably the same object, evinces a design to reduce them under absolute despotism, it is their right, it is their duty, to throw off such government and to provide new guards for their future security. Have I quoted correctly?

We do not deny that the men had certain just grievances, Wayne said.

But you deny that those grievances were in the province of the officers, countered Bowzar.

We have laid aside our pride—said Wayne—to come here and discuss these matters for the common good. If you would lay your grievances before us—

You know our grievances, Billy Bowzar interrupted him. Look around you here at the leading Committee of the regiments, and see how we are clad and how we are nourished and how we are provided. Out there in the hutments, the men are fed and their bellies are full for the first time in months. Have you fed us? But you fed yourselves. Did you share what you ate? You clothed yourselves, and we went naked. Without pay we went, without drink, and our share was blows—blows until we cringed like a pack of dirty dogs instead of free soldiers of the republic! And even dogs have rights, for dogs are loved, and if they get a kick, they get a caress too; but our lot was unbroken by any consideration, and you abased us until we were worse than any dogs ever were. And when an officer shot down a man of the brigades, there was no court-martial for that officer, no trial, no demand that cause be shown—yet how many of our own good comrades have been hanged by the neck because provoked beyond all reason, they struck back? How many, General Wayne? How many, Mr. Stewart? How many, Mr. Butler?

The three officers looked at him, their handsome, ruddy faces controlled now, their anger stowed in the proper compartment, wherefrom it would be taken at the proper moment. This bitterness, this recitation of grievance—this was familiar and common and a part of their memory since the war began. This they could handle. This was different from the snarling, defiant anger of before. This was the beginning of something—and this I knew, and I wondered whether the others of the Committee knew it as well.

There is the matter of enlistments, Dwight Carpenter was saying. A man who has made his mark for three years, and served five—he said—is kept like a slave for his lack of reading . . .

But I was no longer listening. It was the end and over, and two days of glory had finished. We had marched through the Jerseys and become something noble if brief, but now it was something else again. They went on talking, and I dozed, and some I heard and more I did not hear, but watched the fire and dozed and dreamed of how in my childhood in the warm summertime—so I had been told—I played in the little creek that ran by the house where my mother once served.

I played there because sometimes they gave me a sweet or some cold crust off the roast of the day before, for I was "the little one of Annie Stuart," and what a good, loyal servant she had been, not like those born and bred in Pennsylvania, who knew not their own place and standing!

Sick as my mother was after carrying me, with the seed of death planted inside her and planted to stay and take its toll in two short years after my birth, she nevertheless had gone each day to the house of Elder Simpkins, who was toll agent on all the roads through town and clerk as well, to do the service that his strong wife and his four strong daughters could not do, for they aspired to be quality as the fine ladies in Philadelphia were. All day, day in and day out, she had labored there, and her pay for a day's work was fourpence—fourpence for the price of a life!

So there I was allowed to play after she had paid her full price of one life for fourpence a day, and I was too much of a babe to even think of what was right and what was wrong, but knew only that there was a bit of a sweet or a crust of meat to be had for the memory of the strong Scottish lass who had served them.

One has a debt, said the wife of Elder Simpkins, later on, for me to hear—loyal folk they were, and humane too. Poor lad—she said with such sympathy—poor lad!

Let the poor lad play, he feels safe here, she said . . . One doesn't find girls these days such as his mother was; for now they're born and bred in the Pennsylvania land; they are spoiled, that they are, and not like the ones who had tasted a bond—they were the grateful ones.

You are grateful for charity, Jamie Stuart, she said to me, and the good Lord rewards those who are.

I am indeed, said I, *whose mother was a girl when she died, and a fine, strong worker* . . .

And then back to today I came, and the hall in the college at Princeton and the fire and the fine figures of the bewigged officers. They were finishing their conversations now. I shook sleep off me; I listened to the Committee.

They agreed to meet with these three gentry the following noon, and then my guard and I marched Wayne, Butler and Stewart back across the road to the tavern . . .

Early the next morning, I found Jack Maloney and Danny Connell, as they were going from hut to hut, talking with the men; and when I would have passed them, Connell called out:

How there, Jamie Stuart of the black puss and sour heart—what in hell eats you that you give me a look to make me stomach crawl?

When an Irishman betrays me, do you want me to lick his God-damned ass?

It's mighty quick that ye are for learning the Irish language, said Connell, but it is not myself that has betrayed you, and if ye want to take off that dirty jacket of yours and fight on it, why I am as willing as a lad could be.

I will not fight with a miserable, undersized Hooley that I could break in two with one hand.

Because ye lack the guts.

I said some words that are best not recalled, and Jack Maloney demanded:

What in God's name is eating you, Jamie?

This, your honor—the sweet pledges of the officers and the sweet pledges of the Committee. That's a start, and I can see damned well what the end will be; but I swear to God, I will never go back to be a slave under those dirty dogs, and give my life sooner or later, so that they can preserve their gentry apart from the British gentry, instead of together with it. For that is all this matter comes down to.

How do you see that, Jamie? asked Maloney.

There are two thousand, six hundred and odd men here in this camp today, and they have followed after the Committee for only one reason, not for a bellyful of food and a swig of rum and a dollar in their pockets—but because they are proud and because they would be free. A different kind of pride from what the gentry has, and a better kind for my money.

And where shall we lead them, Jamie?

Into hell, if need be. Into hell and be damned! But not into polite "Our grievances are this and that, and if you satisfy them we will come back and beg you to lead us once more."

Danny Connell was watching me. I hold with Jamie, he said.

Oh, you would, said Jack Maloney. Oh, Christ, you would—my fine lads—for you are both good for a fight, where there is no more sense needed than to pull a trigger. But what shall we do? That is the heart and core of it—what *shall* we do? By now, without question, every body of soldiers under Congress is marching here toward the Line. Shall we fight them all?

No soldiers will ever fight the Line—unless you speak of British troops. I swear to that!

Shall we proclaim "the Republic of the Pennsylvania Line"? Shall we execute the three officers? Shall we march into Philadelphia and imprison the Congress? In the name of God, Jamie, what *are* we to do, now that the Line will follow us? Where? Where? Whatever kind of strange dreams you have, the world has not yet made them real. There is no other way than to come to terms with the gentry . . .

His voice rose now; pitched up and woeful, he cried: For withal it is a bloody Revolution, this is their war! A little crust of the bread is for us, but the slice is theirs, Jamie, and God help us, there is nothing we can do but come to an agreement with them.

I would rather die.

Maybe I would rather die, too, Jamie—but the men of the Line are extremely practical, and they have chosen us, and we will lead them. They have no intentions of dying. They, at least, have certain practical demands for pay and clothes and discharge, and every trust they put in leaders before was betrayed. Shall we betray them too, Jamie?

What else are you doing?

You thank God I love you, Jamie Stuart, and know you well too, or I'd cut your heart out. The devil with you!

And he went his way—and I went mine.

But that afternoon, after their hours of talk with Wayne and Butler and Stewart, the sergeants called me in, and this they said to me:

You take over Princeton, Jamie—every inch and corner of it, and make it secure so that a mouse couldn't creep in.

The taverns?

Yes, the taverns, Jamie, and all the rest; but be easy and gentle with the townsfolk.

Then Billy Bowzar motioned to a bearded, mud-stained man who stood close to the fire, warming himself.

This . . . he said . . . is Sergeant Dekkerholts of the 2nd Regiment of the Jersey Line. They have been ordered . . . he said, his voice becoming flat and toneless . . . to march against us. But they will not march against us, he said—Is that so, Sergeant?

They will not, said Dekkerholts. They will not shed your blood.

He turned around from the fire, a small, flaxen-haired, travel-stained and travel-weary man, his beard long and full, his overalls rent and patched, his feet bound in canvas instead of leather. He looked at me, and then he looked at the sergeants of the Committee, as if he had

481

not seen them before, and then he looked at me again out of his large, bloodshot blue eyes, and he said:

Who in hell are you?

I am Jamie Stuart, and responsible for the safety of the encampment.

I told you they will not attack you, the Jersey men, he said, sullenly and somewhat sadly, for they are going to rise up and cast out the gentry, just as you did—just as you did. And now I want to go to sleep.

And with that, he sat down in front of the fire, his knees drawn up, his arms around them and his head pillowed upon them. I stood there, looking from face to face—and sad, troubled faces they were—until Billy Bowzar reminded me:

You know what you must do, Jamie. I put little stock in what he says, since he has walked too much and slept too little. We also have information that the Light Horse Troop is riding up from Philadelphia to join the officers. So get on.

And if the Jersey Line rose, what is the Committee prepared to do?

We don't know that they rose, Jamie—only that they are intended to do so. We will see. . . .

We will see, I nodded—and I went out, happy at least that I had work of my own that I understood; I found Angus, and together we worked out our plans.

But before I go into that, I must say just a little of the encampment at Princeton, where we now spent a week of our lives. Not that it was a perfect achievement, or any sort of a dreamlike place. Men deserted; men ran away because they could not face the terror of what we had done; men got drunk and men whored: but these were the exception, and by and large, in those seven days, we established a working, cooperative means of living together. In the very first day, we cleaned out the upper floors of Nassau Hall, and established there both a hospital and a school. Two women and three men were found among the regiments who were equipped, some better, some worse, for teaching—and the children of the Line, almost a hundred in number, from the little babes to the twelve- and thirteen-year-old drummer lads, were put to letters; which was a great wonder in an army where not one in twenty could write his own name. More curious still, those classes for the children—short-lived as they were—were packed always with soldiers too, for we had a hunger for some sort of dignity and learning that was almost as great as our hunger for food. Having neither paper nor ink nor crayon, we made slates out of board and burned and shaped our own charcoal. We had no books, but, for the time we were there, the small knowledge in our heads was sufficient, just as what crude medical remedies we owned had to be sufficient for our hospital. There was a wonderful inventiveness and facility in the Line; every trade was among us, and there was nothing we could not make if given a little time and a minimum of tools and goods — candles, rope, cloth, furniture, shoes; yes, and we would have made paper and a press to print books and a newspaper, if it had not all finished so soon.

Maybe there was much more that we would have made — for word that the Jersey Line would rise stirred a brief vision in me of a new kind of republic that might come out of this long and sorrowful war; but, like other dreams I had then when I was young and strong and filled with my own power, this one is unfinished and befogged with all the years that have passed since then. I tell myself sometimes that now I know better what we could have done; yet when I listen to the same, half-formed dreams on the lips of the Abolitionists — of the young Yankee men who will sweep the whole world with their banner of freedom for all — I am none too certain. I see the thread that ties things together, but where it began and where it will end I do not know.

There was a Roman priest who came into encampment at Princeton, a little, round-faced Irish man, who was bitterly poor and much despised, as the Romans were in our land then, and who had walked all the way up from Philadelphia when he heard that the foreign brigades had made a rising. Dusty, dirty and cold, his black clothes worn paper-thin, his wide-brimmed, flat-topped hat perched comically on the top of his head, he was brought into our lines and brought to me, and I asked him what he wanted of us and why he had come.

Sure, he answered, when I heard that the Irish men were in a rising with all sorts of low company, Jews and Naygers and Protestants too, I said to myself, I will go up and share their enterprise and perhaps soften it somewhat.

Because he seemed cheerful, and because our hopes were low and morbid then, I told him:

It will as likely be a hanging as anything else, and if the gentry make a start, I assure you they will hang the Roman priest first.

Then I will not be the first Roman priest was hanged by gentry, he grinned.

To which I answered that it was certainly an odd attitude for a man of God to have, since with the rising every pastor had cleared out except William Rogers, who was not properly a Christian but a Baptist

483

or something of the sort. The rest held that resistance, revolution and such were not becoming to a low type of man unless he was led and instructed by a high type of man.

But among the Irish, said the priest, we have had a lot of resistance, yet surprisingly few of the latter type. Myself, I will stay if you don't mind and if you can trust me. It seems to me that, while I cannot predict where this business of yours will end, I have an inkling of where it began. . . .

I tell this in the way of threads, but I wander from the main tale of how we took Princeton city and made it an armed camp. I pause only to tell you that we did many things in those few days of our new army that are forgotten, and they were things that were good, not only the schools, but discussions in the hutments on such documents as the Declaration of Independence and *Common Sense,* the fine book of Mr. Paine, and we also framed out certain propositions on the rights of all men to speak freely and to assemble and to petition—things that were fanciful then but which came about later, with much additional suffering, in the time of Tom Jefferson. We also made common teams for the sewing of cloth and even for the weaving of it, and for this latter we made looms, although they were never put to use. We put new roofs on the huts and we repaired the bitter damage that the enemy had done to Nassau Hall. So much for that, and more later, but now for how Angus and I turned over Princeton and put it in condition for defense.

There was the town, with the pike running into it across the brook and the gully, so that we were enabled to have the bridge at one end for a boundary and the crossroads at another. We threw a regiment—as we planned it—to the north and another to the south. A regiment could cover the brook, beyond the meadows, and two more regiments could ring the town and block off the two stem roads. This would be a matter of five regiments, leaving five in reserve and one for relief and mobility, and with a light breastworks and concentrations on lanes and footpaths, a cannon at each crosslane and another at the brook and at the bridge—why, it seemed to me that the little place could be held until Doomsday.

It was a fine feeling for me, to have a plan of defense in my own hands, after five years of running, leaping, crawling and scurrying to the plans of the officers; and there was more of that satisfaction when Angus protested that *they* would have done it differently.

I looked up from the paper on which I was sketching and answered:

484

To me, that is a commendation, and nothing else.

But ye have but one man to twenty feet of ground, and no corrie for them to crawl into!

And I want none. And if I had ten men to twenty feet of ground, it would be a thin defense, but the one man is a cleg, and he stings a little while we throw the five regiments where we will. And if we know a little sooner, there is our one regiment of mobility to nibble a bit, while we come at the flanks. We are sick with warfare where one puts up a breastwork and cowers behind it.

. . . In any case, I added from my heart, there is only one body of Continentals in all this land that will come at us—from my heart I know that and surely—and I say that is the Light Horse.

Ye would fire on the Light Horse, Jamie?

On any man that crosses our lines without our will.

God help us if that should be, Jamie.

Something else will be if the Jersey troops come to join us—for something pecks in the Connecticuts and others too, and maybe for once the men who fight for their freedom will win it too.

So we called out the soldiers to dispose them. We sounded the trumpets and had the brigades parade, the ten infantry regiments and the artillery, and we formed them up four square to hear the orders. Jack Maloney and Jim Holt joined me, representing the Committee, and they stood with me in the center of the square and listened as I read the plan. When that was finished, before we disposed ourselves, the whole Committee came and we had an inspection parade. We made a fine, proud, handsome square, and if we were not uniform, we were clean-shaven and we carried well.

We dressed like British show troops, and our bayonets were gleaming and rustless, and every man was smooth of face and sharp of spine, and the forty drummer lads stood across the corners of the big square, ten at each point, beating to dress. Every regiment had repaired its faded and tattered banners, and many regiments—because this habit like so many others had fallen into disuse from neglect—set to work to sew the banners they had not carried since '77, so that now the 1st carried its segmented rattlesnake, the 2nd its clenched fist, the 3rd its wolf's head, the 4th its depiction of Romulus and Remus nursing at the wolf's udder, and so forth and so on—while at each side a color guard of the Citizen-soldier Guard bore the Stars and Stripes. Our cobblers had been busy with every scrap of leather we could turn up, and there was not a man in the Line that day who was not shod with a piece of leather on his soles, even if the uppers were sewn from tent canvas. Overalls were sewn and patched and made presentable, so if you had looked at us from the road, as the townspeople did, crowding there to see our display, you could well have said that this was the prettiest, neatest, trimmest body of fighting men that had ever marched among the Continentals.

The artillery had formed inside the square, where every man could look at the six cannons, four of bronze, two of iron, all shining; and by every gun, stiff and proudly self-conscious that they served cannon which had never been left on a routed field — cannon which had been fought since the first engagement outside of Boston in '75 — stood two gunners, two layers, two caddies and two plungers, while behind them were sixty buckskin men from Fincastle, not standing to arms-parade as were the regiments, but leaning on their long six-foot, snakelike Pennsylvania rifles, dressed in smock and shawl, with a powder horn and a bag of shot girding every hip — these the only riflemen in the entire Line, and snipers from the artillery.

The women and children stood outside the square, some clapping to the drums, some weeping to see what a proud and strong thing we were with every man standing to his place with only a whisper or a word from sergeant or corporal; and indeed I could have wept myself to look at them, and I would have given all the years of my young manhood to march them on York city where the Enemy was and show the British how men could fight when they fought for themselves, for their own soil and their own dreams.

But the evening was coming on now, with its snapping cold wind to chill the unseasonable warmth of the day. The sun dipped down to the trees, leaving a dazzling warp of pink and purple, and there was much to be done. I threw a look at the Committee, where they stood alongside the cannon, all grouped together, their faces filled with pride and sadness and wonder and joy and bereavement, all of it mixed and struggling with the past and the future, the knowable and unknowable, the victory and the defeat; and then I shouted:

Brigades to station!

And the regiments marched away to take their places. I checked with one and another as they left, put the Gary brothers on horse and set them to checking over the perimeter and establishing the easy contact of all the regiments, sent Angus to the inn called Sign of the College, to empty it and close it down, and then took twenty of the Citizen-soldier Guard with me to Jacob Hyer's inn.

486

The Proud and the Free

It would be a lie to say that I did not relish the job. What would you have of a lad who was twenty-two years old and had known nothing but camp and march and battle in all of his precious youth, so that all the softness within had to be compensated for by a hardening of the shell? Hard we were, and I was a little harder than most, as you will see, hard at the beginning and hard at the end too, God help me.

But now it was still a long time from the end, and I led my men over to the inn, kicked open the door, and had them file into the tap-room with bayonets fixed and the winter wind sloshing behind them. Oh, there was good business in the tavern, all right, for the rising of the Line had provoked a great buying and selling, and the commission merchants and the dirty and indifferent traders — who owned allegiance to the hard dollar and the proud sterling and to nothing else — were scurrying over the road between York city and Philadelphia like rabbits, buying low and selling high, spreading every filthy rumor they could concoct, buying what they did not own and selling it before they ever had it, dealing in uniforms unworn, shoes we never saw, food we never ate, guns we never handled, munitions we never shot and bodies not yet dead. They were all there as I have told you, packed in with the warmth and the smell of roasting meat and smoking rum, and I relished what I did, believe me.

What now, Jamie, what now? Jacob Hyer squealed, spreading his arms against me and pressing his great paunch to me as my men crowded into the room. Haven't I been a good friend to the Line? Haven't I sent, noon and night, a gallon of hot flip to the Committee? Didn't I roast up in my kitchen, special, a chicken pie and a hasty pudding? What now, Jamie? Is an honest man not to do his business undisturbed? Is that a way to have folk think of the Line, that you torment an honest citizen?

You're as honest as Judas Iscariot, I said, and if the truth were known, what a dirty spy's nest you operate here!

Not so, Jamie! You got no right to blacken my character. I'm a legal-commissioned colonel of militia, and as ready to serve —

To hell with all that! I interrupted him. I will not touch a penny you own or a stinking cut of beef from your racks, but the whole town is now within the perimeter of the Line and under the government of the Line, and I want every transient person out of here in ten minutes and out of Princeton too.

You mean my custom?

Precisely what I mean.

His face turned white, and then as the blood returned, suffused with an angry blush. I had spoken up and loud, and every person in that packed and silent room heard my words. Then a babel of sound commenced, led by the landlord himself.

You got no right . . . no justice, no right, no warrant! . . . I will not submit to this! . . . Here I stand, and my house is my castle! . . . I will lay down my life first . . . Here I stand, and you go no further into this, Jamie Stuart!

You fat, foisonless man, I said, you shut your mouth, or I will drive a bayonet up your butt and pin yer tongue with it. What a cackle you make! And look at this room here, you damned bugger — look at this collection of scavenging crows! Look at them and you would never know that this is a country at war and that one or another has taken sides and that there's no inch of Jersey soil without a drop of American blood on it! What are they doing, traveling the roads between York city and Philadelphia? Honest work?

At this moment, Wayne and Butler and Stewart behind him appeared at the foot of the staircase. Wayne didn't come forward into the room, but remained there on the stairs for the moment, listening to me and watching, his long, thin cold face composed and emotionless. But some of the guests had risen while I spoke, and now one of them, a lean, middle-aged man with side-whiskers and a mustache and dark, calculating eyes, came over to us and interposed:

Son, how old are you?

Twenty-two winters if it is any of your damned business.

That's a harsh way of speech, my lad, and harsher for your elders. Don't you think it's a little foolish to drive us out of here this winter night? Will that bring you friends? There are many men in this room who would make good friends to you, for they are men of influence and instruction, and it would be better for you to befriend them. Now suppose you sit down at our table and have a glass of grog on this. Hot words and hot heads never accomplish anything constructive.

What do you do? I said. What do you do that you grace this world so?

I buy and I sell, he answered, which is as honest a way as I know.

What do you buy and sell? I roared at him, grasping his cravat and pulling him up to me. Do you traffic in men's lives and men's souls? What is north of here for an honest man to buy and sell? Do you sell a little information to the British enemy? Do you buy the dollars the people have, to make them more worthless than they are? Och, I could spit on all your sweet-tongued kind. Get out of my sight!

And I hurled him from me, so that he went down and rolled over, crashing against a table and then crawling on his hands and knees to be out of harm's way. But Jacob went wild, gabbling and gabbling, running first at me and then to the stairs where he began to plead with Wayne. But Wayne shook him off and pushed him away and brushed the sleeve of his uniform where Hyer had touched it.

All of you! I shouted. Get your goods and be out of this inn in ten minutes! Ten minutes, or a bayonet will prick a little haste into you!

Help them along, I told my men—while the landlord was pleading with Wayne:

Will you let this be? Is no law and order left? Is an honest man to be robbed of his custom?

Standing there at the foot of the steps, Wayne listened to the landlord without particular emotion or interest, and he might have been hearing a dog bark for all the effect it seemed to have on him. When the landlord moved to touch him, he shook him off—and then, as the press of people mounted the stairs, he and the two colonels stepped into the taproom and to one side, from where Wayne watched me curiously.

And out of the village! I shouted after them. Every one of you out of the village. If you came by horse, saddle up and get out. If you came by stage, walk out.

Jacob Hyer stopped gibbering, stared at Wayne for a moment, and then walked weakly over to the bar and leaned against it. But then he recalled that customers were leaving without paying their score, and prudence overcame grief as he dashed past me and outside, calling them to pay up. Meanwhile, Wayne sauntered over to me, followed by Butler and Stewart.

What does all this mean, Sergeant? he asked.

It means that we are placing the whole village inside our lines, and that anyone who doesn't live here is to get out.

Why?

I don't know why. I am given orders and I carry them out.

I think you know why, Sergeant. You're making a hard score for yourself, and, as you may have heard, I have a long memory.

That's just as it may be, General Wayne, and if you want to know more I'll take you over to the Committee of Sergeants and you can ask them.

I can wait. I'm a patient man.

As I am also. . . . And then I started to turn away, but he caught my sleeve and said:

Does that order about nonresidents apply to myself and Colonels

489

Stewart and Butler?

It does not apply to yourself and Mr. Stewart and Mr. Butler. Yourself and Mr. Stewart and Mr. Butler can stay here, General, if you wish, or you can go out of our lines or you can go over to Nassau Hall — or do anything you damn please except talk to the men. I will leave six of these men of mine here at the inn, but they are only to see that you can go where you want to go safely, and as for talking to the men — well, you can do whatever talking you have to do to me or to the Committee. That's the way it is.

So that's the way it is, Sergeant.

Yes, sir.

And the news I am expecting from Philadelphia?

Who is bringing it?

The Marquis de Lafayette or General St. Clair or both, with Colonel Laurens, said Wayne — holding onto his temper remarkably well, which was something for him, since he was as hot-tempered as he was arrogant.

When they arrive, I will let you know.

You will not conduct them here?

I will not take them or anyone else into our lines until I have orders to do so.

Said Wayne to that, looking me up and down: We have an old saying, Sergeant, that if you would skip a jig, you must pay off the fiddlers.

Or, among the Scots, I grinned, that he who dances must pay the piper. But the hell with that, with the dancing I've seen these five years, and many a lad who had no ground under his feet when he danced and no breath for song, either. But I must say, General, I added, that we are a sober folk with the gentry, for when you cracked the whip, you were never one half so gentle with us.

We cracked it lawfully, whispered Wayne, and not for a God-damned cursed mutiny.

Ye have always had the making of the law, haven't you, General?

And will have it again, Jamie Stuart.

Then if you know my name, I said, and I didn't think you knew the name of any of the dirt you led, call me when you want something.

Then I turned away and told off the men for the inn. I put Aaron Gonzales over them, who was a lad with a level head, and I told him that if one dram of spirits was touched, I'd see that a court-martial took place. I was burning with anger — for no matter what I said, there was that cold, thin, assured face of Wayne to tell me who would have the last lick—and he knew that I meant what I said. Then I took the rest of my men and went out of the damned place, with Hyer plucking at my coattails and pleading his cause.

Let go, you scut! I threw at him, and marched off past the raging ousted guests up the road to the bridge. The men had done their work well, but such was my mood that I found grounds for complaint wherever I went. The cannon at the bridge was at the further instead of the nearer end; the barrier of logs and branches across the road was not filled in with dirt; the opening was too wide. At the side roads I swore because the men had crowded the roads instead of picketing the fields, and at the Philadelphia direction, there was a little knot of town girls, joshing the men as they made bastions and built match fires.

What are ye? I cried. Is this some damned militia picnic?

And when Button Lash, the sergeant in charge and the first man ever to enlist in the 1st Regiment of the Pennsylvania Line, blinded in one eye with grape at White Plains, without toes from the freezing winters, and sometimes addled in his head with all the woe he had seen, but gentle and dearly loved by all of us, said to me, Ah, Jamie—Jamie, my lad, ye have no call to wallop these boys for taking a word with a maid. They are good lads and working truly . . . I was sick and sore and speechless and did the rest of my rounds in silence.

Then I went past ‘Nassau Hall where the Committee still burned light, found my hutment, pulled off my boots and crawled into bed, overalls and all. I was sick at heart and knotted in the belly and bruised inside with loneliness and frustration and hopelessness—and for that I slept poorly, tossing and turning and dreaming dreadful dreams of my childhood, dreams in which I stood naked in the midst of a circle of bearded, kilted gillies such as my father had told me of, and while an unseen arm whipped me they chanted, *Caper, Jamie, caper, for this is your lot and it will not be otherwise.*

Sweating and grateful, I awoke to someone's whisper and a hand on my shoulder, and there was Willie Hunt, unseen in the darkness but his voice specific enough telling me:

Jamie—Jamie, wake up, for we got some passing strange fish in our net and we don't know what in hell to do with them.

What time is it?

Onto morning, Jamie, but this is a dirty catch and the men will not wait.

Coughing, my stomach all sour and heaving, I crawled from the straw bolster and pulled on my boots and struggled into my coat, and then felt my way out after Willie Hunt. Onto morning it might have been, but there was no sign of that in the starless sky, which was as black as pitch. Benny Clapper from the 2nd was waiting for us with a lit brand, and in the light it cast we followed him over to the bridge. As we walked over there, I asked Willie Hunt:

How did you get into this?

I could not sleep, Jamie, so I stretched my legs over to the bridge, where I thought maybe I could pry a little tobacco out of the lads. And there I am, warming by the fire and gossiping with them to pass the time, when out of the night come these two very strange birds.

What are they?

Wait and you'll see, Jamie. You'll see.

We were at the bridge now, and there, behind the barricade in a circle of men, were two well-dressed but nervous gentlemen, one long, one short, both cloaked in black and wearing fine felted hats. Outside the circle and to one side, another of our lads held their horses, and in spite of the cold of that early winter morning, the two of them were sweating.

Here is Jamie Stuart, someone said, and the circle opened up to let me in; but the two strangers said nothing, only eyeing me nervously and speculatively.

Who are you and what do you want? I demanded.

We want to speak to the authority of the mutiny.

What mutiny?

The mutiny of the Pennsylvania Line.

Who in hell said there was a mutiny?

That is the intelligence we have.

And who in hell is *we?*

Who are you, sir? demanded the taller one suddenly. Who are these men? What security have we that these are Pennsylvania men?

That's the kind of dirty culls they are, Jamie, said Benny Clapper, and they got the white mark of Tory on them, I swear. They been standing here and talking in circles these twenty minutes now. And you know what I say they are? I say they're dirty damned spies, and we ought to string them up on a handy branch and have done with it.

Now that's a hasty opinion to come to, said the smaller man, licking his lips, his eyes darting from face to face. A hasty way of dealing with honest men. Are you the Pennsylvanians?

We are, I nodded.

We must see your commander. We must speak with him.

Now look at them, Jamie, said Michael Omalley. Me eyes have not seen two more honest men.

What do you want with our commander? I asked.

We have a message for him, a most confidential message, and exceedingly confidential message.

Message from where?

That is our intelligence, said the taller man hoarsely. We are honor bound to reveal that only to your commander. To no one else. I am sorry, sir.

All right, I said. All right —

And when they all began to talk, I cried, Shut up — the lot of you. I'll take them to the Committee. Benny and Willie, come along with me. The rest of you mind that road and stop the damned gabble. A fine lot of talkative soldiers you are!

But our horses, sir . . . the tall one began.

Leave your horses where they are. Do you expect to ride through the village at this hour of darkness like a bloody Paul Revere? If you're as honest as you testify, you'll have your horses soon enough.

And with that, we marched these two uneasy gentry down the road to Nassau Hall. By now, the night was breaking, the pitch-black giving way to murky gray, the houses emerging like ghosts from the darkness. The little town had that ultimate quiet that a place has in those very early hours, and the sentries in front of Nassau Hall were haggard and weary, their eyes full of the mysterious weight of the nighttime.

What's up, Jamie? they asked. What's up?

I must wake the Committee.

They bedded down late, Jamie, right there on the floor by the table, and it's only God's mercy to leave them alone.

I haven't much mercy lately, and here are two queer birds who can't wait. I'm thinking this is important enough.

All right, Jamie, go on in.

So we went in, with our two strangers and our torches, and woke up the Committee where they lay, stretched out on their blankets on the floor. It was a shame, a burning shame to wake men who slept so tiredly, such a sleep that it was like the sleep of the dead; but there was something about those two black-cloaked messengers that made my skin crawl, and I wanted none of them on my own. We lighted the candles on the table, and once again that queer, singular, almost worshipful feeling about the Committee of Sergeants came over me; for waked as they were now, at this unholy hour, with the splutter of torches in their faces, they were nevertheless patient with a patience beyond belief and listened gravely to my tale.

493

Very well, said Billy Bowzar when I had finished, we are the Committee which is entrusted with supreme command over the Pennsylvania Line, but we will have no dealings with you, sirs, unless we know who you are and from whence you come. And when you say this, you say it with no restrictions—otherwise go now. This is a military encampment of a Continental Army, and within our own lines, this Committee is the court of law with all powers of martial enforcement. Also, our law is not the law you might be accustomed to, for we make our law to enforce what we believe to be right and just. I say this to offer you due warning.

I think we can do business, sir, and the taller man, so I am ready to accept your conditions. You have been waked out of your sleep and we have gone without ours, so I will get to the point quickly and without further ado. My name is Mason and this is James Ogden, and we come as emissaries from Sir Henry Clinton in His Majesty's loyal city of New York. From the Commander in Chief of His Majesty's forces, we bring greetings and good cheer—and it is our good fortune to be the first to do so. We also bring a message of historic importance, which I will deliver into your own hand.

Roughly and as well as I can remember, the foregoing is what Mason said. He was not an imaginative man, and he appeared unaware as he spoke of how stony and set the faces of the sergeants became. Almost cheerfully now, he took off his shoe, raised the inner sole, and extracted a piece of lead foil. Then, with the same precise motion, he put on the shoe again, unfolded the foil, and took out a small piece of thin paper, laying the foil on the table and handing the paper to Bowzar, and still no one spoke.

Billy Bowzar read it. The writing was exceedingly small and cramped, and Bowzar had to hold it to a candle to read it, and then he passed it to another. Softly, Levy read it aloud for those who had not the learning, and it was short, direct, and to the effect that when the Pennsylvania men entered into accord with His Majesty's government, each soldier would receive a bonus of twenty British pounds, while each corporal would receive thirty and each sergeant fifty. All former deserters from the British Army would receive full and unconditional pardon. All men who desired to enlist would be welcomed. Those who did not could claim transportation to the West Indies, where they would be given land.

Finished, Bowzar looked from face to face. Jack Maloney said, I was once George's man, even more recently than Scottsboro, so let me say this. I say we should hang them now, before the sun rises.

They are dirty spies and dirty traitors, said Scottsboro. I say hang them.

I know what you feel, said Bowzar slowly and thoughtfully. They have robbed us of something. Just in coming here, they have robbed us and dirtied us . . .

We came in good faith, Mason began.

Be quiet, be quiet—Bowzar said quietly, but so coldly!—Be quiet. You did an awful thing when you came into our line. These are the Pennsylvania brigades—the foreign brigades. Do you know what that means? Do you know what kind of a trust we carry? I know you are just a little dog for a big dog, but how did you dare to come to us—who have lived and died these five years for man's freedom—with a tyrant's offer?

While he spoke, Bowzar had folded the message, and now he was wrapping it in the lead foil again.

That was a terrible thing to do, said Bowzar. We will give you to General Wayne, and that way maybe wipe some of the dirt off. There is no other way but that, he said, turning to the Committee. Do you agree?

One by one, they nodded.

Ogden began to plead. He fell down on his knees in front of the table, crying as he pleaded. That he was a family man, he said. He had been paid for this. A man does a job that he is paid for. He emptied his pockets and the coins rolled this way and that way across the floor. Do you kill a man who comes to you in good faith? Turn him over to the officers . . . Hadn't they revolted against the officers? What kind of insanity was that? At least forget it—forget it and let them go. Let the whole thing be forgotten, as if it had never happened . . .

But Mason said never a word, for finally he realized what this Committee was, and the knowledge of the foreign brigades came to him, even if it came too late.

Take them to Wayne, Jamie, said Billy Bowzar.

We prodded them out of the room, Ogden stumbling so that he could hardly walk. Outside, I picked up the sentries for a guard, and we went across the road to the inn. It was dawn now, a cold and cloudy winter morning, and when I rapped on the tavern door, Gonzales opened it to me.

We herded Ogden and Mason in, and I told Gonzales: Wake up Wayne and tell him I must see him here immediately.

He won't like that, said Gonzales uneasily.

The hell with what he likes!

So Gonzales went upstairs, and we stood in that cold and sour-smelling taproom and waited. Jacob Hyer came in while we stood there, but when he saw my face, he said nothing but went about building up the fire in the hearth. One of his women came in rubbing her eyes, a big woolen wrapper coiled around her. Morning, Sergeant Jamie, she said, to which I answered surlily, Go to the devil and begone. Then Gonzales came back with the officers.

They had pulled on their boots and thrown their greatcoats over their nightshirts. With the sleep still in their eyes, without their big white wigs, they were less formidable and less proud, closer to life and closer to death. Death was around. That big, cold, sour room smelled of death that morning.

What does this mean, Sergeant? said Wayne.

Absorbed in himself, he was, but the other two saw Mason and Ogden, and they knew what it meant. I gave Wayne the piece of lead foil, and he opened it and read what was written on the paper. He passed it to Butler and Stewart.

When did it arrive? he asked finally.

A few hours ago.

With these two swine?

With them, I nodded.

White and quiet, they stood there, quiet and dreadful and hopeless — and it ran through my mind what an awful, monstrous thing war is, but more awful than anything the war where men strike for freedom — for there is no forgiveness, not by the masters and not by the slaves; and I knew more than that: I knew with deep finality that my dreams — wherein this kind of hatred and cruel practice would be no more — were not for accomplishment in my time or my children's time, and I knew what it was to be of a Committee of Sergeants which led men into a future that wasn't. Hate went out of me, and I was only tired and forlorn and young, thinking that there are always strange men like myself — and a little of the strangeness in Wayne too — who must chew the bitter cud of freedom and find some nourishment in it. The fruit was not ripe, but it was our sustenance, our only sustenance.

What are you going to do with them? Wayne asked.

What are you going to do with them is more to the point, I said. They are a gift from the Committee to you. Take them and be damned.

And I turned around and walked out.

PART EIGHT

Wherein I tell of the fate of the two spies,
and certain details concerning the Philadelphia
Light Horse Troop and the New Jersey Line.

WHAT WAYNE THOUGHT, I did not care, for I had no desire to
be an honest or loyal man according to his lights. Later that morning,
he wrote a note to the Committee, in which he used a good deal of ful-
some language and said that his heart had been warmed and reassured
by this deed of honor, and he also pledged, in the name of the
Congress, an award of fifty gold guineas to each of the sergeants
involved in the capture of Ogden and Mason. There was a price on the
blood of two miserable wretches, and fifty gold guineas, which made
more thousands of Continental dollars than you could count, was the
kind of money that no solider of the Line ever hoped to have, even in
his wildest dreams. There I was, a rich man, and Benny Clapper
too — but we talked it over and threw the offer back in Wayne's face;
and there's the answer for those scholarly historians who have been so
hard-pressed to comprehend how two such dirty and mean articles as
ourselves could turn away a fortune in terms of gentlemen's honor.
Well, we were not gentlemen and it was not gentlemen's honor, and
nothing is paid for but something is bought. We didn't like that kind
of deal, and when Benny Clapper and I had talked about it for fifteen
minutes, we agreed that Bowzar should tell Wayne and the rest of
them to take their dirty blood money and use it elsewhere. For myself,
Jamie Stuart, this was not so hard, because I had neither kith nor kin
and no lien on tomorrow, but was a wild and headstrong lad; but
Benny Clapper had three kids and a wife in Bristol, and when the gentry boasted to Congress over the hundred guineas they had saved, they
were by no means able to comprehend what it meant to a family man
to give away security and free land and beasts and tools. But the devil
with that, for Benny Clapper was subsequently slain at Yorktown, and

497

no one except myself, an old and feeble man, knows his name today or remembered anything about him; and let the dead sleep, for they will not be awakened or honored in this time.

Mason and Ogden were hanged, but that was later, and I tell it now only so as not to dwell on it. We come to the end of things, and I must get on with my story. . . .

It was Friday, around noon, that the Philadelphia Light Horse arrived, with Lafayette and St. Clair. With them was Laurens, one of the brigade officers of the Line; and altogether there were forty cavalry prancing up the road from Philadelphia. There were building up by now a thousand rumors, the two main ones being firstly that Sir Henry Clinton had moved six thousand British troops across the Bay into Staten Island, and was marching from there to confront us — either to join him or be wiped out by him; and secondly to the effect of George Washington gathering together every Continental regiment to march with against us. As to the first, I think there was no man in the Line who would not have welcomed the release from tension that would follow a British attack, and I myself wanted it, for I sensed somehow that there was no other resolution of our fate than in battle. And as for the second, I knew now, even as Wayne knew, even as every man in our encampment knew, that there was no American soldier north of the Virginia border — except for the Light Horse Troop — who would raise a musket against us; and as for the Light Horse . . .

Let them come, the men said. Let them come, by all that is holy, bring them to us!

And at about two o'clock in the afternoon, as I was standing in front of Nassau Hall with the Jew Levy and Danny Connell, there was a burst of gunfire from the Philadelphia pike. The three of us set off at a run, and as we passed through the village, I saw Andy Swain talking to one of the girls, his long trumpet slung over his shoulder, and I shouted to him to get to hell off his behind and sound To Arms. But even then, the drums at the encampment were beating To Stations, and everywhere men not on duty were racing back to the parade to join their regiments and stand to arms, a remarkable point of discipline when you consider what an urge there was for them to go to the perimeter. As we passed Hyer's house, I saw that Wayne and Butler and Stewart were standing outside, Gonzales and his men around them, and Wayne called to me:

Can we come, Stuart?

The devil you can! Hold them there, Gonzales!

We ran on. There were two more shots, and then silence except for the shouting of men. We turned the bend of the road and came to the barricade, and there was our guard, raging, the cannon shotted up with grape and a lighted match over it. Powder smoke drifted on the wind, and a man of ours lay in the shelter of a tree, stretched out and made as comfortable as possible by his comrades, but spitting blood and retching clots, and dying, as anyone could see. He was a Polish man, Piotr Lusky by name, a broad-shouldered, quiet blond man, flat-faced and slow of speech, having little English for all his years with the Line, and one to be filled with hunger for his own faraway land. Well, he was going there or somewhere now, for he died in the next few minutes; and I saw that and also the cluster of the Light Horse down the road out of musket shot, and also in between one of them whose own horse had been shot under him and who had broken a leg coming down and now crawled on his belly along the road, pleading for one of his gallant gentleman comrades to come to his aid and bear him from our anger.

Next to me, big Andrew Yost, who was corporal over the guard, was sighting a musket on the crawling man; and I watched him, fascinated, waiting, gauging the pace of his finger on the trigger—until some spark of sense made me strike up his gun.

Ah, let him shoot the bastard, Jamie, a man pleaded, and Connell told them:

Och, shut yer mouths, the lot of ye! What in the name of hell made ye fire on them?

They called us names, answered Yost.

Names they called ye!

They fired first . . . someone else put in.

And what did ye call them?

The poor Polish man breathed out his life then, the Jew Levy holding his head and wiping his mouth and whispering to him in his own heathen tongue. Angus MacGrath and Billy Bowzar came running up now with the whole of our own 11th on the double behind them, and it did my heart good to see how those sweet and terrible men of the 11th, whom Angus and I had given our hearts to so long ago, fanned out among the trees without a word of instructions needed, and took up their places in cover. Now all the cavalry on the continent could come up the pike, and all they'd have for their pleasure would be a bloody ruin in the dirt.

A few words told us what had happened. The Light Horse, led by General St. Clair, the Marquis de Lafayette and Colonel Laurens, had

come up the road and demanded that they be let through into Princeton. One word led to another, and when one of the troopers would
have forced his horse over the barricade, Piotr Lusky seized its bit and
turned it back. The horseman drew his pistol and shot Lusky through
the chest. A dozen men fired at him but the horse reared and received
the lead and went down on the horseman, and the rest had clattered
away out of musket range. That was when I came, when Andrew Yost
was evening the score; and now Yost said:

It is a long shot, but you let me try, Jamie—just let me try.

No! cried Bowzar. We'll have no murder!

And was it not murder when they shot down that poor Polish man?

Let him be—let him crawl—let him crawl to them.

And Bowzar, making a trumpet from his hands, cried out, You can
come back now, and safely! Pick up your man! We'll not shoot!

Stow that damn match, Connell said to the man hanging over the
cannon. Ye make me nerves crawl.

And back on the wind came the thin reply:

How do we know you will keep your word?

Ye don't know! Bowzar shouted. Ye can go to hell or Philadelphia
and be damned!

Children from the village were pressing up now, staring goggle-eyed
at the dead man, and we shooed them away, nipped them over their
behinds and sent them running. I did not know what would be, but it
was no place for children; and I wonder now how many of the children
who were there recall that cold, clear winter afternoon as the Light
Horse troop came back, urged on by St. Clair and Colonel Laurens
and the little Frenchman, who was mopping the sweat from his face,
for all of the weather.

*　*　*

They were a pretty lot, that Philadelphia Light Horse, and in all the
Continental Army there was nothing else like them. In those times, all
around Philadelphia were the great manors of the squires. What they
were in blood, I don't know and care less, for I have little taste for this
business of blood and birth; but in every detail they aped the English
squires; and their one passion was to tear up the fields of honest farmers, hunting fox. If a farmer protested, they could prove that they had
the right to ride roughshod over him by law, decree and immortal
grant. When the war came, because they were too close to Philadelphia to be comfortably Tory and because they stood to be rich in the
way of land grants from a free Pennsylvania, they made sounds for our

side and they organized themselves into what they were pleased to call "the Loyal Philadelphia Light Horse." They were rich enough to do it properly. Every one among them turned out a fine chestnut mare. While we wore our canvas overalls into shreds for which there were no replacements, they kept Philadelphia tailors working on what they were pleased to describe as the sweetest suit in all America: brown shortcoat which was faced and lined with white twill, white doeskin breeches, white satin vest. Their black boots were knee-high and cuffed with white, and their gloves were of the best white chamois. White lace at throat and cuff, a little black hat with a stiff brim, all bound around with silver cord, the same silver cord that swept from one shoulder. Their harness was white leather, intricately worked, and the saddle on the horse we had shot down could not have been bought for five thousand paper dollars, so heavy was it with silver inlay and fine relief. They were great ones for parties and balls and dances of state, and whenever some foreign visitor came to Philadelphia, they were turned out to show what a handsome military force Continentals were, and whenever we of the Line marched into Philadelphia, there they were to welcome us with their sedentary gallantry and maybe to reassure the Congress, who were never too easy about the black-hearted men of the foreign brigades; but whenever we marched out of Philadelphia, they remained behind, so that the ladies would not grieve for them. Each of them carried two pistols and a carbine that was a marvel of beauty and workmanship, each imported from the finest Italian house of gunsmiths, and each carried a saber of Toledo steel priced—to quote Jackson Lunt a swordmaker in my regiment—at sixty guineas; but I know of no occasion when their swords drew blood unless it was against the poor crippled, unwanted outcasts of the Line, who in '80 came to Philadelphia where they shook their stumps of arms and legs before Carpenters' Hall, claiming that it was not right for those who lost limbs in the service of the state to die of hunger and be forced to beg in the streets, and who were properly cut up and courageously dispersed by the Light Horse—who received a special regimental insignia for that deed; and I know of few occasions when one of their pistols or carbines had been lifted against a man until they slew this poor Polish fellow.

Now they returned, and they picked up their lad with the broken leg on the way. They sat their horses a good thirty yards from us and would come no nearer, those bold and gallant men of the saddle, and the three officers came on alone, St. Clair to the fore and Lafayette and Laurens behind him. St. Clair was superior to Wayne in Pennsylvania, and the one attitude of Anthony Wayne which we held in com-

501

mon with him was a lusty hatred for General St. Clair of the land of Pennsylvania. But you had to give St. Clair credit for the way he came on up to the barricade and the muzzles of our muskets and the hungry mouth of the shotted cannon, where he said:

A mighty strange welcome for the general of the commonwealth.

Bowzar had been to look at the dead man, and he walked now to the barricade, where he stood with his hands on his hips, staring at the haughty, flushed face of St. Clair.

You come with blood on your hands, General, he remarked quietly. Is this a curse on you? What a history you have of blood and suffering! We are good soldiers. We are disciplined soldiers. If we were not, you would not be alive this minute, you and those dirty Philadelphia barons behind you. How long is our patience to last?

St. Clair did not answer, not because he had no will to, but because his anger clotted the words; his face turned the color of a beet, and his lips trembled and coiled as he sought for proper speech. Meanwhile, Lafayette had advanced his horse up alongside the general's, and the French boy, throwing back his white cloak—heavy wool lined with silk of powder-blue—burst into excited speech:

Clods—what is this! How do you dare! This is Gen'ral the whole Pennzl'vania! How dare you!

But even that is only an indication of how he spoke; I can do no more than to suggest his accent, to give an indication of the babble of indignant sound, high-pitched, his body trembling, the saliva spattering out; until Danny Connell, who was observing him thoughtfully, his head cocked as he contemplatively rubbed his nose, said several things unprintable and told Lafayette specifically where he could go, concluding:

. . . Sure, for me nose cannot tolerate the scent of you!

I will see you all in hell! roared St. Clair, but Bowzar said nothing to this, only standing there in silence with his hands on his hips.

Now Laurens had pushed up his horse, and was speaking earnestly and quietly to the general, plucking his sleeve, and when the general shook him off Laurens said bitterly:

But I must insist, sir!

How dare you insist! You and Wayne! Damn it all to hell, why isn't Wayne here?

Please, said Laurens, softly but murderously, I will not hold this kind of talk here. I will not be responsible.

St. Clair swung his horse around and rode back to the Light Horse troop, Lafayette and Laurens following. There, they conferred again,

Laurens arguing determinedly. Then Laurens dismounted, handed his reins to one of the horsemen, and walked up to the barricade.

I'm sorry, he said to Bowzar simply. I'm sorry as the devil, believe me.

It was a bad day's work, Mr. Laurens, said Billy Bowzar. It was murder, and that's all that it was.

Where is General Wayne?

He is at Jacob Hyer's house and comfortable enough, as are Stewart and Butler.

Are you holding him prisoner, Sergeant?

He's no prisoner. He can leave when he wishes to leave. Of his own free will he came, and of his own free will he may go.

Will you take the general and the marquis and myself to him?

Bowzar thought that over for a while, before he made any reply. Levy had come over to stand next to him, and he looked at the sad, bitter, hollow-cheeked face of the Jew before he spoke, saying:

No—No, we will not. We will not have any dealings or words with that man St. Clair or with that Frenchman. You must understand, sir, that when we cast out our officers, we were in deep earnest. So long as we are in command of the Pennsylvania Line by the edict of the men of the Line, we talk on our terms. You can take that or leave that, Mr. Laurens.

Standing there on the other side of the barricade, his cocked hat tilted back, his hands in the pockets of his greatcoat, Laurens studied us shrewdly and not without respect. He was a very young man, was Johnny Laurens, only twenty-seven years old or so, and a very brave man too, and not long for this earth; for only a year later he was slain in the fighting in the South. He was one of the very few of our regimental officers who had some respect for the men who served under him; and when he fought a duel against Charlie Lee and near killed the wretch, it was not only because Lee plotted and connived and talked against Washington, but because Lee treated us like dirt and dogs, and because that sat poorly with Laurens.

Why do you call me Mister? he asked now, not angrily but curiously.

Because your rank came from us, and now we have taken it away.

I see, he nodded. And you are absolutely adamant about the general and the marquis?

We are that.

Will you take *me* to Wayne, along with one of the Troop?

Connell and Levy nodded.

If you wish, Bowzar said.

Laurens looked back at the Light Horse and the two officers; he sighed, shrugged his shoulders and walked back along the road to where they were. It was at least ten minutes he stood there talking with them, and then we heard him addressing the Light Horse. A word here and there told us he was asking for a volunteer, but there were no volunteers. He stood apart and raised his voice, and still there was no response. Then he returned to us alone.

I have no love for what you've done, he told Bowzar ruefully, but so help me God, I prefer the foreign brigade to those. Take me to Wayne, will you?

Take him along, Jamie, said Bowzar, and then come to us at the Hall where the Committee meets.

So Laurens and I walked back to Jacob Hyer's inn. For a while, we walked in silence; then he said to me:

Well, Sergeant, you have sure as hell stood the world upside down, haven't you?

A little bit of it, perhaps.

Well, he shrugged, I think you will take us back, Sergeant, though God knows maybe we don't deserve it. There's nothing else to it, as I see it. Someday, perhaps, your kind will get angry with the gentry and do us in proper — and when I think of those damned Philadelphia fops, I'm not all regrets. Only there are harder men than those, Sergeant; and that's something to remember.

It is indeed, Mr. Laurens, I answered.

Sweet taste to that *Mister,* eh? But you will call me Colonel, Sergeant, and when the time comes, I'll enjoy the taste as much as you are enjoying your lark today. How is it in the Book? *Ye are the salt of the earth; but if the salt have lost his savour, wherewith shall it be salted?*—or something like that. You need a new seasoning, Sergeant, and you have not found it.

And you're damned arrogant for a man who walks on this road by grace of the Committee.

Let us say confident, not arrogant, Sergeant. . . . And there are my good comrades.

For we were now at the rim, where Wayne and Stewart and Butler stood shivering in the cold, looking down the road and waiting. Laurens laughed and waved at them, and Stewart ran over and embraced him. I left them there talking and walked down to the parade, where five regiments were drawn up to arms with knapsacks and whole equipment, and where the drummer lads stood cold and blue waiting for the signal that would send them into battle—in the strange inhumanity of armies of the time, which chose children to lead grown men to slaughter. Jack Maloney and Jim Holt and Sean O'Toole were in command here, and I told them what had transpired on the Philadelphia pike and of Bowzar's call for a meeting. We dismissed the regiments, and then together we walked over to Nassau Hall, where the rest of the Committee already awaited us. In the other big room, to the right as you entered the Hall, the body of the Polish man was laid out on a bench, awaiting the building of a coffin and burial, and it was covered with the wolf standard of the 10th Regiment. Good-by, I said to myself, good-by and farewell, lonely Polish man. But no one said anything aloud, and we went into our headquarters to hold our meeting. We lit the candles, for night was falling now, and we listened to Chester Rosenbank, who was there by invitation and with no good words.

The Committee, he said—his solemn, German face owlish and regretful, his little blue eyes watering behind his spectacles—the Committee has asked me to report on the state of our supplies; I humbly submit the report.

Speak up, Chester! said Dwight Carpenter, and the schoolmaster looked at him reproachfully as he removed his glasses and wiped them with a rag of cloth. He had for his report some scraps of paper, and now he assembled these in front of him, squinted through his spectacles, cleared his throat and began to speak. He was not quite like anyone else in the brigades, but then, I may ask myself who was? From one or another of the states, they might have been cut from a whole cloth, but we were a union of difference, of distances, of extremes; and this German schoolmaster, who could sit for hours, dreaming over his flute and Johann Sebastian Bach, and would spend hours more teaching our fifers counterpoints and harmonies, was a very good soldier indeed and one of those who had enlisted in the first Pennsylvania regiment organized in Philadelphia in March of 1775. But soldiering had not made him other than he was before, and he spoke to us as he would to a classroom, explaining a painful and unhappy problem.

Considering first the question of ammunition, he said, I can be most explicit. We have at present in the whole encampment two thousand, seven hundred and twenty-two men—that is today. Our previous counts—well, they have not been wholly accurate. In this, I include the drummer boys and the riflemen, but not the forty-three men who are in the hospital; because when I discussed that with Andrew Mac-Pherson, he insists they must be left here if we move. Now we have, all

505

told, fourteen thousand and thirty musket balls, less than five rounds to a man even if you exclude the riflemen and the gunners. With rifle shot, we are better off, with almost seventy pellets to each rifle, and we have gunpowder to the amount of twenty-one hundred pounds. This does not include the contents of the individual powder boxes, since I have no way of determining that. But that is not good either, for until New Year's Day, no regular inspection was made of the powder boxes, and a good deal was used for flinting and for purging sick stomachs too. This, however, we have put a stop to. It is my estimation, nevertheless, that we have not enough powder in the boxes for the balls, unless they are undershot. We have, for the six guns, forty iron balls and twelve stone balls. We also have fifty-two rounds of grape-shot, which makes exactly one hundred and four cannon rounds, and for that, you see, there is plenty of powder for undershotting but not for dueling. But since we have so few balls, we cannot go dueling any-way. The grape can be recast for musketry, but that would leave us open, and the men would not like it. We have neither bar shot nor chain shot. That is the way it is with the ammunition.

This finished the first part of his report. We should have known, but we didn't know, and I saw many a face go pale as we listened.

But I myself, said Levy, counted eight hundred bars of lead. In the hospital alone, there were three hundred bars.

We never finished rendering those—and the rest we left. Just as we left the four dismounted cannon at the redoubt at Mt. Kemble, and two hundred cannon balls and fifty bags of grape with them.

If they are still at Morristown—began O'Toole.

No, No, said Jack Maloney. The Yankee soldiers are already there. If we should raid the place . . . His voice trailed away, and no one else spoke. Once again, Rosenbank cleared his throat.

As for food—he said—we are no better. We have meat and flour for two days and corn meal for a third day. That's all—and what we have is only because the farmers brought it to us and gave it to us. We have no money to buy, and the farming men here in the neighborhood—no matter what they feel, they cannot support three thousand men. If they give us all their food, what will they do then with no money in exchange? We have eleven tents that are any use; the rest we had to cut up for shoes and overalls, but they were no good anyway. All the men are shod, but not for marching. For perimeter duty all right, but not for marching. We have some cows, but if we eat them we can't milk them. But we have no fodder, so I thought I would trade with the farm folk for corn meal. That will give us enough meal for two days more, but then we will have a lot of sickness if we eat only corn meal. We have twenty-three oxen and forty-seven horses, and if we leave the wounded here, we can begin to kill the oxen; then we can burn the carts for firewood, but that is like eating our fingers to feed our bellies, like eating the horses, which would be like eating our feet to feed our bellies . . . Our feet, our fingers . . . I've thought all I can about it, I don't know what to do. There is food on the farms, I guess, but if we should take one grain of it, well, that would be the end—yes? It would be the end?

It would be the end, Levy answered. One chicken, one ear of corn—it would be the end.

Anyway, it's the same, someone said.

All right, Bowzar nodded, smiling. Thank you, Mr. Rosenbank—giving him that term because he was a scholarly man and deserving it—we are very grateful. Will you stretch the food as far as you can? Don't let the men go hungry, but don't waste food.

Food I would not waste, Sergeant Bowzar.

No. That's true. Well, we thank you. We are grateful to you. Maybe someday, if we ever have medals, we will be able to give you a medal.

A medal would be nice, said the schoolmaster thoughtfully as he rose to leave. When I go back to school teaching, it will be nice to wear a medal. Good night, he said. Good night.

He walked out, breathing on his spectacles and polishing them and rubbing his eyes. He will be weeping when he is outside, I thought.

Medals, said old Scottsboro.

Well, gentlemen? Bowzar smiled.

Medals, old Scottsboro mumbled.

If the British—said Levy, almost to himself—are marching on us from the east, and the Yankees from the north and the gentry from the south, all our problems will be solved, no? I won't mind a finish the way a soldier should finish, the way the Polish man finished.

Time for that, said Bowzar. There is the Jersey Line still, and nobody knows what they will do . . .

But before the night was over, we knew that too. All things came to us that day. Johnny Laurens came to us in Nassau Hall, knocking on the door and then smiling as he walked in, his greatcoat open, his youthful, handsome face flushed and healthy. He stood strong and tall and confident, looking at the twelve of us as we sat around the table, never bothering to remove his cocked hat, for we were twelve small, shrunken men who had prodded our dreams too much—whereas he stood there as one who had never overmuch had the need of dreaming.

Forgive the Jew Gonzales, he said, for I talked him into bringing me here, after he had intimated that you might meet all night long. What I have to say will not wait all night long.

What have you to say, now that you are here? Billy Bowzar asked him coldly and bitterly.

Only this: that Joseph Reed, the President himself of Pennsylvania Country, will come here and talk with you and treat with you on the terms General Wayne laid out. I am empowered to say that—your terms and General Wayne's terms. You must take this or leave this.

And what be them terms? asked old Scottsboro.

Three main points—the rest can be settled if you talk with the President. The points are these. *One:* No reprisals to be taken against any member of the Line. *Two:* All soldiers whose enlistment has expired to be discharged. *Three:* All proven bounties to be paid. . . . On your part, you must pledge the discipline and will of the men who remain.

That is very little you give us, said Bowzar slowly.

Or a great deal, depending how you look at it.

We will let you know tomorrow, Bowzar said.

Laurens smiled, nodded, and then, as by a sudden impulse, saluted. He turned on his heel then and left. . . .

The salute lasts in my mind. We were finishing, but a brigade officer of the Line saluted us; and I sometimes wonder whether if Johnny Laurens had not laid down his life so soon, we might not have been remembered a little better—and then I wonder why we should want a better memory. What is the memory for all such things as we did? Johnny Laurens had a smile and a gentle manner and the juice of life ran strong in him, but there was never a moment's doubt where he stood. They stood in one place and we stood in another, and so it was until the end, and I must get on with the end, for I have told much and yet there is much more to tell.

Leaving the Committee to talk, I went out into the night and on my rounds. Filled with a great restlessness, I could not remain there with them and listen to them debating what could not be resolved; for when all is said and done, they were good, brave and strange men, not proud but filled with the sense of freedom, and thereby their debating came to nothing at all. If they had been adventurers, they could have embarked on some wild and terrible adventure; but though they came from all parts of the world to fight in the foreign brigades, they had come to have a deep love for the land on which they fought, for over many a year they had sealed a pact on it in blood. So they who led an army had no place to lead it — and they talked on and on, and at the back of their minds was the thought that surely they were not singular, and if the Jersey Line rose to join him, and then the Connecticut Line, could not the Revolution go on, in terms of the simple folk who did the fighting?

In a sense, they were not wrong; the bird that pecked in us pecked in others — even though we did not know it; even among the Yankees, for the Massachusetts troops had put their names to a petition, laying out the same demands that we had. And their officers responded more cleverly than ours: they marched; men who march have less time for brooding than those who sit still, and though their feet bled and though their limbs froze, the Yankee troops marched on and on through the forests of the North. Southward they marched until word came that the Midland armies had done strange and frightening things. But this we did not know, and we had no way of knowing it until that night, when, in my restlessness and loneliness, I walked from point to point on the perimeter of our Princeton defenses.

What a cold night that was — when a twenty-two-year-old lad walked among the defenses of an army he and a few others led! The curious Midland midwinter thaw had vanished, and the mud had turned into steel, with a thousand knifelike edges. As the cold increased, I heard that snapping, brittle winter sound, the small agony of the land's surface, and I drew closer the blanket I had thrown over my coat. I was out of my thoughts now; I went from fire to fire, exchanging a few words here and there in the easy way of men who have known each other a long time. At each place, it was *All's well*—but well only because no enemy was fool enough to come through those frozen woods and fields at night. And then I came to the bridge, where the two Jersey men were, half-frozen, crouching so close to the flames that they singed the edges of their clothes. Oh, like great, beaten dogs they were, with their dirt and their beards and the misery in their eyes.

As I came into the firelight, they looked up at me, their mouths full of toasted corn bread that crumbed over their beards; it is not pleasant, when your belly is full, to watch starving men eat.

Have ye no rum, Sergeant? one of them said.

These are Jersey men, Jamie, said Prukish, who was in command of the post.

Jersey men — said someone else — and the look of them! But they have had it bitter, coming all the way down from Pompton, where the Jersey Line rose up against its officers.

The Jersey Line rose! I cried.

Aye — one of them mumbled — aye, Sergeant, that is the truth of it. The Jersey Line rose, God help us. . . . A little rum would be a pleasant thing — he said, looking from face to face, stuffing his mouth again with the corn bread — ye have none? No. Well, that's the way it goes . . .

I shook his shoulder. What's this about the Line? I demanded. You hear me?

He nodded, and the tears from his bloodshot eyes ran down over his dirty cheeks.

He's a sick man, Sergeant, said the other.

That's right. I be a sick man now.

Talk up! I shouted at the other.

You got no business shouting at me, Sergeant. I came a long way, a powerful lot of walking with the cold weather on. I seen some bad things too. So I say to myself, with them Pennsylvania lads, I'll just rest easy and sweet.

Did the Jersey Line rise up? I asked softly.

Sure, Sergeant. They rose up and they was put down. They brought down the Yankee men, and the Yankee men shot us. They just stood there, them Yankee men, with the tears rolling down their faces, and when the order was given, they shot our lads. So that was that with the Jersey Line, Sergeant, and we two of us, we think, We'll off and tell the Pennsylvania lads, which is necessary anyway. You wouldn't never shoot us and we wouldn't never shoot you, but who would have thought the Yankee men would have done it? Not the Yankee men themselves, if you ask me, because they stood and cried like children when our leaders was brought out to be shot down. But they done it anyhow.

His partner, meanwhile, had rolled over close to the fire and gone to sleep. So close he lay that I could see the hairs of his beard begin to curl and crackle, so I kicked him awake and pushed him away.

Come both of you with me to the Committee, I said.

We done enough walking tonight, Sergeant.

Come now, come now, I answered gently, and there you ll find a warm place, and maybe a glass of hot toddy too. A blazing fire ye will find, and tallow candles stuck in sticks, while here in the open you can never be warm. So come along now, lads.

Thus they came with me, forcing each step that took them to Nassau

Hall, and while they walked they told me. There was not much to tell, for it was essentially our own tale with all gone wrong with them that had gone right with us. There were many differences, of which I will tell you; for the Jersey Line, while it was a Midland body with many foreign folk in it, was not like our Pennsylvania army, just as no force on all the continent was like ours. There were only two regiments in the Jersey Line, the 1st New Jersey, with two hundred and thirty-nine on its rolls, and the 2nd New Jersey, with just a little less than that—but it was not only in numbers they differed. They had nothing like our Committee and they could not make theirs into something like it, for there were not in the Jersey regiments men who had fought through every engagement from Boston to today, like the grim and knowing veterans of the 1st Pennsylvania, who had been made into sergeants and corporals for our whole Line. Also, while the men of the Jersey Line had dwindled, they were overburdened with officers—one for every four men—and their condition of sickness and starvation was even worse than ours. For all of that, they had driven the gentry from their ranks and were on their own under their sergeants when the Yankee men came down, and that broke their hearts. The leading folk of their Committee were taken out and the Yankee men formed firing squads and shot them down—with the tears streaming, they shot them down; and these two had come on to tell us.

So I took them to Nassau Hall to talk with Bowzar and Maloney and Williams and the rest. There I took them, but I did not go in myself.

I knew what the outcome would be. Regardless of how they talked or how much, we of Pennsylvania were alone—alone we were, at the end of the road. Now we would talk to Reed and make terms with him, and the dreams we had dreamed would be no more than fanciful desires.

It might take days or weeks from now on; but to all real purposes, the rising was finished.

PART NINE

Being an account of the leave-taking of the
foreign brigades, how each went his separate
way, and of what befell Jack Maloney and myself.

T HUS IT CAME about that in time we made our peace with the
officers, through Joseph Reed, the President of the Commonwealth; for
we were alone now, and no place to go and no future of our making
that we could comprehend. But it was no such peace as the Jersey Line
made; even at the end, they took no liberties with the foreign brigades,
but kept their word — all men who had served more than three years
were free to leave if they chose to leave. The terms were our terms, but
they were terms for departure not for remaining. Our terms for
remaining were that we should choose our own officers, and that we
should be clothed like human beings and fed and paid; this they would
not or could not accept, but our Committee had an obligation to the
men and the men were sick to their hearts with service under the gentry
for the gentry's way of fighting a war.

So, still holding the Line intact and under arms, we paraded once
again and formed up foursquare on the meadow at Princeton, on a
cold winter afternoon with the snow clouds building up in the east. In a
way, that was the end, although there is more to tell that must be told;
for there at Princeton was the last time the regiments, the riflemen and
the artillery company of the Pennsylvania Line stood together at dress
formation to listen to the drums beating and see the old regimental
flags flying and hear the order of the day read out. There were tears in
many an eye before that afternoon was over, for the foreign brigades
were something and they had made something, and now they would be
no more. And many a lad was there like myself who knew little else but
the camp and the march, and had no home to go to and neither kith
nor kin. With the cold east wind blowing, we stood to attention, and
then at our ease with our captured muskets grounded, listening to Billy

Bowzar. He had climbed up on top of a caisson, and there he stood, legs spread, hands on hips in that manner we knew so well, his curly red hair blowing in the wind, his square face reassuring and becalming; for you listened to Bowzar and heeded him, in battle or out of battle; he was a calm man and a knowledgeable one.

My comrades, he said, when you chose myself and the others to be the Committee of Sergeants, you had the power to keep us or replace us, as you saw fit. You kept us every one, and for this we are glad. On our part, we tried to serve you in what ways we knew, and we served you as best we could. There were adventurous things we might have done, and if we had done them you might have followed us, but we reasoned that a man's life is not something to adventure with unless the cause is worth while. Therefore, we sought for a way in which the Line could serve your cause and the cause of our country and its folk—and yet remain as we were, with discipline but without the officer gentry. How many hours we sat together seeking such a way, I need not tell you, for that you know. We found no way. When we heard that the Jersey Line would rise up, we thought perhaps the whole of the land would join us; but that is over, and there is no way left without shedding the blood of our own people. That would be sorry business, to turn brother against brother, and that we rejected. We were right in rejecting it—but we did not do so out of our weakness, but out of our strength!

Then there was a roar, and we stamped our muskets on the frozen ground, so that the *thud, thud, thud,* of two and a half thousand guns echoed through the village and across the valley. Jack Maloney stood beside me, and he put his arm about me, tight as a steel vise, and he bent his head to hide the tears as they flowed, and he whispered to me:

Ah, Jesus Christ, Jamie, we have been given a moment of opportunity and a sight of glory, and we failed them.

I saw the Jew Levy weeping, the strange little man of his own council and his own peace whom I had hated two years for his being a heathen Jew, and then loved for three years for his being a patient man who never raised his voice or lost his temper or had anything but a gentle word for a man in pain—but knew him not ever, not in two or five years; and the big black man Holt wept, and old Lawrence Scottsboro wept, since his moment was past and finished. So I knew then that what Jack Maloney said was right and true, that we had been given a moment of opportunity and a glimpse of glory, and we had failed because we knew no better way of things than the gentry could offer.

We still have our strength, said Billy Bowzar, when the stamping of the muskets had finished, and we must use it well and wisely. We cannot remain as an army and have our own officers out of our own ranks, and we will not remain under the officers we cast out. Therefore, they have agreed to discharge every man with more than three years' service, which means the greater part of the Line. The rest will be formed into new regiments, perhaps in this Line, perhaps in another—and this they must do. I would to God that there was a way to hold the Line together, but there is no way. A thousand men have sworn that they will never serve their officers again, and we know of no way they can serve this Committee other than to peacefully go their ways. So that is it; yet we have proved something. We have proved that we, by ourselves, can make ourselves into a better army than whips and canes ever made of us. Someday, other men will remember that. For my own, I will stay with what is left of the Line, for that is the way I feel. I don't put this as a matter for anyone else's conscience, only for mine. Therefore, we will break camp in the morning and we will march to Trenton, where we will disband.

That was it, or something like that; for I cannot recall all of this exactly, and it was a long time ago, and I have no journals but only the pictures that were engraved on my mind. I have many pictures, but the clearest are of winter afternoons when the foreign brigades stood to square parade with the sere, cold sky overhead, with the old banners blowing in the wind, and with the drummer boys beating a roll, their little hands wrapped in pieces of wool, their fingers blue with the cold. And rather than the important it is the unimportant that lingers; so that in the moment when Billy Bowzar finished talking, I saw one of the drummer lads whose name was Harold McClintock bawling like a child—which he was, for he was only thirteen years old and no larger than a boy of ten would be these days—with his blue lips and his blue fingers and his skinny, sunken chest; and I wondered what would become of him and all of those lads who had been picked up here and there along the way in the miles we marched, and taught to beat a drum or blow a fife. Those things I wondered about—and what would become of the blowzy or worn women who had followed us here and there and everywhere; and where would the big Bantu black men go, who spoke hardly any English at all but were runaway slaves from the tobacco fields in the Southland; and what of old Lawrence Scottsboro who knew nothing but soldiering? What of the Poles whom we picked up in York city in '76 when the Polish brigade was shot to shreds, and what of all of us, of all of us?

But it may be that those are partly thoughts of the years afterwards and not of the moment. At the moment, I was one of them—the only difference being that I had some place to go to—and I made up my mind that I would go back to York village in Pennsylvania and to the manse of Jacob Bracken.

So after some time it was sounded to break ranks, and the sergeants blew their whistles, and the men crowded around Billy Bowzar whom they loved. But I got out of it, and walked away by myself; I was not in a mood for farewells and I did not know, then, that we would come together again soon enough.

We marched to Trenton, where we were mustered out. I could tell of that, yet it was without particular incident, and we were not what we were once, the Pennsylvania Line of old. We were nothing at all now, except men of many tongues and ways of speech, ragged and aimless. We stood by the riverbank and watched our cannon loaded onto barges which carried them away to Philadelphia. We saw the Line dissolve like sand washed away, and it was done. Each went his own way, and to some of them we said good-by and farewell forever; and there was many a man there I never laid eyes on again. But there were others I saw soon enough, for it was not easy to break the bond and the habit of what we had been for so long; and of that I will tell in due time.

But now we said our good-bys, and Jack Maloney and myself together walked off down the road to Philadelphia. He had no place in particular to go; and for my part, the road to York ran through Philadelphia. We turned once to look at Trenton and the shrunken encampment that remained there, and then we went on. We were no more soldiers; we were discharged; we were free; but the taste wasn't sweet. We had no money and no future in any particular, and what we owned in the world we carried on our backs—our old knapsacks, our knives, our flint boxes. We had a piece of bacon, a pound of corn meal and a pinch of salt. These were the rations we had drawn, with an oath to go with them, from the plump, healthy commissary sent up by the Congress. We each of us had been given a threadbare blanket, and we had odds and ends of rags that we had held onto; in my knapsack was the banner of the 11th Regiment, which I had folded up and taken for myself, partly for sentimental reasons and partly because I considered its usefulness as a scarf in the cold weather. So we were off on our own, I myself a tall, skinny, rawboned lad, Maloney a foot shorter—Handsome Jack Maloney, as we had called him once.

Two days we were on foot to Philadelphia, and it was a blessing that

this was a mild winter, and not the terror of cold and ice we had
known three years before at Valley Forge. Always the snow clouds
hung in the east and the north, but the snow did not fall until the
church towers of Philadelphia were already in sight, and the night in
between we spent on the roadside with a good fire to warm us. Altogether, it was not bad. The road was fairly empty, except for occasional groups like ourselves, out of the Line and drifting toward the city
without any certain purpose or intent. The only incident worth recalling happened when a patrol of the Light Horse came trotting along.
We stood our ground—perhaps foolishly—and when they saw that we
were out of the Line and without guns, they gave us a taste of their
whips as they cantered past. Well, we had taken the whips of such men
often enough, and we rubbed our faces and went on.

So we reached Philadelphia with a wet snow falling, tired, chilled
and dispirited, and walked through the streets and saw the cheerful,
bright-lit windows, the citizens hurrying to be home to the warmth of
their firesides; and we smelled the food cooking and saw, through the
windows, the children laughing as they went to dinner, the families
gathering together with great certainty that all was right in the world.
We saw the shape and heard the sound of something we had never
known, and the misery of that winter night made it all the more poig-
nant. And it was no pleasure to have citizens cross a street rather than
pass two men of the Line—the same Line which had again and again
made a barrier of its bayonets between this city and the enemy. Right
or wrong, we had given five years of our lives to the war, and those five
years the Philadelphian citizens had spent secure and comfortable.

So you see, said Jack Maloney, what it is to be discharged and a soldier of the Continentals.

Which is why, I nodded, feeling the icy water in my thin boots, so
many come back to the whip and the cane. There are worse things
than a whip and a cane.

Far worse, Jamie, for here I am just like a dog without a master.
Here I am in the cold, wet snow with houses all around me, but to
them in the houses I am a fearful thing. Have you any money, Jamie,
forgive me for asking you again?

None.

Not even a copper penny?

Not even a copper penny, I said.

Well, said Maloney, kicking the slush out of his path, here we are at
the great Carpenters' Hall, where fine words were said and fine documents were signed; and I have two hundred dollars of Continental

paper in my sack, so let's get them out, Jamie, and eat and drink, and then we'll render in payment what was paid to us—if you are game.

Game I am, I answered him. So we stopped in the square, rooted in his knapsack, got out the paper, stuffed our pockets with it, and went straight-away to Josef Hegel's Coffee House, where there was light and warmth and merriment, and all the other things cold, hungry men desire. Hegel's inn, called the Red Cock, two squares from Carpenter's Hall, was not the best place in the town but by no means the worst, which meant that while you didn't encounter the great merchants, neither did you encounter the great thieves; and Hegel closed his doors to street doxies, peddlers, cripples, beggars, if not to footpads, pimps and purse-lifters. It was one of those in-between places where a soldier could go if he had some hard money in his pants, and as we remembered it, there was a good piece of roast meat and good beer and good rum. We had gone there first after the occupation in '78, when we came into Philadelphia as liberators of a town which to a large degree, recognizing the difference between the golden pound and the paper dollar, did not particularly desire to be liberated; and we had come in hard and bitter, and the town was wide open for us in an unvirtuous display of virtue, whereby the women proved their loyalty and there was free beer in every tavern. The welcome had cooled since then, but we had not expected something so chilly as what met us when we turned back the door of the Red Cock, which invited all comers so merrily with its diamond-shaped panes of colored glass.

Well, there was merriment within all right, and the proper smells and the proper sounds, but as we stood in the little hallway, eyes were averted from us, and Josef himself came over, frowning and thinking of the neatest way to turn us out into the bleak wet of a night that had already changed to rain.

Innkeepers, said Jack Maloney, are cut of a mold, by God.

To which I answered that among the few pieces of wisdom I had inherited from my poor father was something to the effect of the selling of food and the other sustenance of man's soul and belly putting the seller apart from the race.

An evil practice, which gives rise to fat, dirty men.

The fat man was upon us, head to foot in his apron; and I thought, this is my own true punishment, for the ghost of Jacob Hyer has arisen against me! This man had a pear-shaped face, little pig eyes of pale china-blue, and an enormous chin which swept, layer by layer, down onto his chest,for all the world like a majestic beard.

No soldiers, he said, short and sweet and to the point.

517

You buggerin' randy reaver!

What's that?

Scots, I said smoothly. And what in hell is wrong with you, Josef Hegel? Is this true German hospitality, that I hear so much of?

No soldiers, he said again. That's that.

Like hell it is, I answered—holding back little Jack Maloney, for I felt the little man begin to shake with anger—Just look at us again. I am Jamie Stuart and this is Jack Maloney, and in our time we spent a pretty penny on your lousy rum. Do you think you're going to turn two soldiers of the Line, two sergeants, mind you, out into that miserable cold rain? Guess again . . . dropping my voice . . . for we'll dance a pretty jig around your place. Now let us sit down quiet, and that will be that.

You got any money? he wanted to know.

I did quick arithmetic and answered him, To the face value of five guineas.

Show it, he said.

Now I will like hell. Sit us down, or—I swear to God—we will take this place apart and break it into little pieces.

Don't shout, he said. Now, all right. Just come with me.

And he took us to a corner through the hard and unfeeling eyes of his guests, who shrank away from two dirty and soaking men in overalls, swearing all the while under his breath at the various curses that plagued him—dirty, worthless soldiers being the first and foremost among them.

What will you have? he asked ungraciously, as we slipped off our knapsacks and sat down.

For each, a noggin of rum and a cut of that lovely meat on your flame.

The meat comes dear.

Well, we are great ones for dear things, so fetch it!

And when he left, Jack Maloney leaned back, sighed, grinned happily and observed that we would probably spend the night in jail, but that it would be worth it. He brought the rum and we took the first hot gulp of it down on our empty stomachs. The second drink went smoother, but already I could feel my nerves tingling. It was a long time since I had tasted rum, especially this thick, brown, syrupy stuff that was better than the best wine of Europe, to my way of thinking . . . especially since I was something of a connoisseur of rum and totally ignorant of the best wine of Europe.

So you see, Jamie, said Jack Maloney, when we had finished the meat on our plates and wiped up the gravy with good white bread—the kind of bread I had not tasted in at least twelve months, good white flour bread instead of the miserable corn pan we ate in the Line—So you see, Jamie, said Jack Maloney, what a queer thing this matter of life is. We have in our pockets two hundred dollars of paper, stamped with the name of the Congress and issued out to us as pay at one time, but since it is not worth the paper it was printed upon, we are thieves and sit here eating stolen meat and drink with a stolen roof over our heads. But you and me—who were a part of the Committee of Sergeants just a while ago—now we are despised, because we wear overalls and carry sacks. But on the other hand, Jamie, those men who remained by the fireside, blessings fall upon them, like little snowflakes from the heavens. Why are we accursed, Jamie Stuart? Is freedom a sickness?

A rare sickness, I answered slyly, my head light and airy. Nor catching at all, like the pox.

Nor catching, agreed Jack Maloney, and added: Except at times. Except at times, Jamie. . . . Except at times, he told the barmaid who had come beside us, putting his arm around her and smiling into her face.

Now what is? she wanted to know.

A sickness like the pox. Now bring us some rum, darling, a little rum. Ye do not hate soldiers?

Not when they look like you, little man, she smiled; and he pinched her behind and she slapped his face and went off with the noggins.

Jamie, Jamie, said Jack Maloney, Jamie, my lad, I am filled with sorrow at myself, for I am just a lonely man with no knowledge of anything but killing, and even that trade is gone. Pride is for the gentry, Jamie—we should not touch it. Pride brings us down. A man falleth with pride. I envy my good comrade, Billy Bowzar, who remained a soldier, which is all that any of us are good for. Will I find me a good, sweet woman someday, Jamie, will I now? And peace? Will I find me contentment, Jamie?

And he stared at me earnestly and drunkenly, his eyes wet with tears for his own sorry fate, his thin-featured, handsome face bemused and inquiring. And as the barmaid returned with our rum, he sang:

> In London Town, in London Town,
> The lassies are so fair,
> That I who wandered off so far
> Am sooth in deep despair.

His voice was high and sweet, but it carried; and eyes turned toward us, and a party of men at a table nearby regarded us with little love and much disgust. Their conversation turned on us, and they spoke, among other things, of the dirty, drunken mutineers of the Pennsylvania Line. Jack Maloney heard them, stopped singing, eyed them for a moment, and then rose up, mug in hand, and walked over to them.

I beg your pardon, he said politely.

They looked him up and down. They were well-dressed, well-fleshed, sober men, sitting over their supper and beer; they were shopkeepers or small traders of some sort.

I drink to the foreign brigades, blessed be their memory for ever and ever, said Jack Maloney.

Ha!

What does that mean, sir? asked Jack Maloney.

Gentility had overcome him, which he had absorbed from the years he served his British masters, and there he stood by the table like the very soul of politeness, delicate and small and very handsome indeed, as only he could be in his broken canvas-topped boots, his big, wet, stained overalls, his coat thrown open, his ragged mockery of a vest, and the old rag he wore around his neck with all the elegance of a ruff. He had raised his brows with solicitude, wrinkling his small, well-shaped nose—and one would take him for the least dangerous little man in the world, which he was not. So I reached out and wrapped my hand around the heavy pewter candlestick that stood on our table, and lay there against the table that way, watching and listening, too drunk to mind what happened now, too unhappy to raise a finger to prevent it.

Ha! It came again.

Shall I take that as an insult, an observation upon the brigades?

Get out of here, you damned, dirty deserter, said one of the men.

Deserter—deserter? asked Jack Maloney. Why? he said gently. Why are we dirty too . . . he inquired . . . unless because we tended to the war while you tended to other things? Five years I have been in the old Pennsylvania Line, gentlemen, and it ill becomes you, I think, to speak so poorly of me. Yes, even if I was a deserter right now—added Jack Maloney—for a man gets a bellyful of fighting and dying and hungering and the cold and the misery and the wet winter nights, and of all those things which you know so little. . . . So apologize, if you will.

I'll see you in hell first, said the man.

I'll see you there, said Jack Maloney cheerfully and emptied his rum in the man's face. Now Hegel was thundering across the room and people were rising everywhere, but the man who had gotten the rum was rising to fight, spluttering and swearing, and so were his companions, and he was with his hand in his waistcoat, looking for a weapon of a kind, so I considered it time for me to stop dreaming and do something. They were to crush little Jack Maloney like a cockroach, but they underestimated their man, as the large man usually will the small one, and he tipped the table upon them and crowned one of them with his mug. Another who would have flanked him, I touched gently with the candlestick—not enough to hurt him but only to deflect him, and then I put the heel of my hand in the face of roaring Josef Hegel, tipping him upon the man who had gone down from the stick.

It's time for the door, Jackie! I shouted, and we fought our way across that room in a fine fashion, sowing devastation around us, until at last, and more sober, we were out in the cold wet night and running down the street with a great outcry behind us.

Now come with me, you crazy damned fool. I told Jack Maloney, grasping his arm and pulling him into a dark little alley, the kind with which Philadelphia abounds; and I dragged him along to an old woodshed, where we crawled in among the shavings and listened to the hue and cry pass.

What a brave thing you've done, I said, for here we are without even our knapsacks.

Yet better than in jail, Jamie, you will admit, he insisted.

I will not admit that, you crazy, drunken Lobster, for there is enough dishonor to be made of the Line without you adding to it.

Did I add to it, Jamie?

That you did.

Ah, Jamie, he moaned, putting his arm around me and weeping on my wet sleeve, there you are, a little bit of a lad of twenty-two summers, and I am thirty-six years old and witless, and you will go off and leave me with proper disgust, and here I will be in this strange, wild land of America, a deserter from the King's army and a renegade to freedom. A renegade, Jamie, do you hear me, for what was our great rising in the end? What was it, Jamie? Naked we came into the world, and naked we lie here, two hunted men. What a kettle of stew the world is for our kind, Jamie—Jamie, my lad, look upon ourselves as those respectable men at the tavern looked upon us, two dirty, wretched soldiers who have turned their backs upon the struggle. I tell you, there was a great and immense rightness in their attitude.

Shut your mouth, I said angrily. You are drunk, Jack Maloney, and

521

to listen to you turns my stomach.

Drunk, I am, Jamie, royal drunk, drunk as quality, but there is nevertheless a deep truth in my drunkenness. I see things clearly. I see Handsome Jack Maloney clearly, and it frightens my immortal soul to see him so. I am a little man walking with a heavy burden upon me, and the burden is freedom. What right had I to make a great blather over those citizens in the tavern?

Every right, I threw at him, for there they sat and swilled while we fought and died.

Yes, yes, Jamie, he answered me very softly. We fought and died. That was the essential of it. The cross we bear is like the cross of our Lord Jesus Christ, when his poor weary feet took him up the hill to Calvary. Did he turn and say, Lessen my burden. . . ? No—no indeed, Jamie, nothing of that he said to the citizens who watched him go past.

And you are not Jesus Christ, Jack Maloney.

As you say, Jamie, but did it never occur to you that we share something?

You talk like a damned parson!

No, Jamie—God forgive me that I should talk like a parson? Drunk I am, but not that drunk. Not with religion, Jamie, but with a little bit of the truth. A little bit. Did it ever occur to you, Jamie Stuart, to contemplate the truth, the immense awful truth of today and yesterday, of the present and the past and the future too, the way a man lies upon the ground and contemplates the stars in the sky in their vastness? Jamie, you are a young lad, so a lot that I say you will thread into one ear and out the other, but some years ago I was stationed at a place called Gibraltar where there is a single rock as high as a mountain and the little monkeys clamber all over it, and we in the garrison there made a mutiny and struck for our freedom, and afterwards forty good lads were hanged up by their necks, and then I climbed me the rock and lay on top of it upon my back, looking up at the soft summer sky which is so lovely in those far parts and asking myself, What is the meaning of a man who dies unknown and unsung and unremembered, with a curse upon his soul from all of the gentry and all of the quality, and all of the kings and their grand commanders, and even his own true comrades are questioning themselves to know whether what he did was right or wrong or good or bad—and who keeps a score, Jamie Stuart, of the whiplashes and the canes and the multitude of other sorrows since time began? Who keeps that score, and what is the meaning of all the ranks of men who stand up for freedom and are then struck down? Always, they are like you and me, miserable and lowly men, with no quality to them and no grand manners and not even a decent shirt on their backs; but it is the essence of this thing called freedom that we should have some understanding of it, while those who sit and swill in the taverns look down upon us. Do you know where the score is kept, Jamie Stuart?

Where? I asked, caught up, in spite of myself, in his drunken outpouring.

In your own heart, Jamie Stuart, and in mine too; and with that he rose up to his feet.

Where are you going? I asked him.

Back to the Line, Jamie, where I will enlist me. And I hope to God that you will go with me.

The devil I will! I cried. I will not return and serve under that cursed crew—never! I will lay me down and die first!

Then I'm sorry, Jamie, because it's a lonesome thing to travel singly. But I am going.

But not tonight, I said, grasping his arm. Not tonight, you drunken idiot. Wait until morning.

He shook off my hand and answered with immense dignity. I will not wait until morning, Jamie and you can do as you damn please. I will go now while the pride is upon me.

And with that he went out of the shed and into the rain.

So Jack Maloney left me, and I did not follow him—and yet I saw him again. I let him go out into the rain and the dark cold night—and for all I knew, out of my life and away from me forever; and there was the last of my good and splendid comrades whom I had lived with and eaten with and by whose side I had fought ever since I was a little lad of seventeen years.

All alone in the world, you are, Jamie Stuart, I said to myself, as I lay there in that woodshed, all alone with nothing to show for the years you carried a musket and bayonet. Alone and alone.

And like a child, I put my face in my hands and wept tears of bitterness and self-pity. Then I heard a noise and a scratching, and drew back in fear, but it was only a bedraggled cat seeking the same shelter I had. I purred to him and he came to me, and I gathered him close in my arms, and that way, sleeping sometimes, awake and shivering sometimes, I passed that unhappy night.

If the commonwealth of Pennsylvania and the Confederation gave me nothing else, I could thank them for a body that was hard as nails and more or less inured to every variety of cold and sickness, and I could thank them that I was able to walk out of Philadelphia the next morning on the turnpike to York village. The clouds had blown away, and it was a clear, cold sunny day, with blue sky and a clean wind from westward. So I said good-by to Philadelphia, which was no town to my liking, and I turned my steps to the only place that had some aspects of home to me. There were my memories and there was sweet Molly Bracken, and there were the old houses, the old church and the old mill—and all the childhood matters that one dreams about.

So there I went; and because I was young and healthy, my spirits soon picked up, and I strode along the pike with long steps, whistling as I walked.

PART TEN

Wherein I tell of my homecoming to York
village in Pennsylvania, and of what took
place until that day when I heard the
beating of the drums again.

I<small>T IS HARD</small> to imagine today how far away one place was from
another in those old times, for as you know there were no railroads
then anywhere in the whole land, and no river stream vessels, and no
smooth surfaces on the highways for fast stages to dash along, but only
the lumpy pikes and post roads, which were for the most part two
tracks grooved deep in the mud, soft and slimy in the springtime, dusty
in the summertime, but murderously hard with knife edges in the
frozen wintertime. The gentry went by horse, but poor folk walked;
and I was just about as poor as a lad could be. So it took me four long
days to walk the distance to York village, and when I came there, the
soles of my boots were worn to nothing; and if I was thin before, I was
thinner now, my cheeks sunken, my belly rubbing lovingly against my
spine.

I ate well on the first day and a little on the third day, and otherwise
I ate nothing at all on that trip. The first day, after seven or eight
miles of the cold winter morning had made me ravenously hungry, I
stopped at a farmhouse gate, with the dogs yapping against it and
longing for a chance to try their teeth on me, and with the wonderful
smell of frying scrapple coming from within. That was a food I had
not smelled or tasted a long, long while now, and I stood against the
gate looking longingly at the little house, with its strange yellow and
blue decoration—which told me that Bavarians lived within—and its
plume of smoke in the chimney. In all the world, there is nothing like
smoke out of a chimney to make a homeless man feel his condition.
There I stood, until the door opened, and a small, neat, motherly

woman appeared, with a veritable horde of children somehow managing to find shelter behind her skirts.

Her corn-colored hair was bound tightly back, and her tiny blue eyes regarded me shrewdly, as she said, *Was willst du, knabe?*

I had little enough German then; I wanted to say something else, something about myself and my homelessness, but I came out with, *Kleine Mutter* . . . and then added, *Hunger ich.*

The children giggled at this very bad speech, but something touched the lady deep to her heart, and she slapped them into silence, called off the dogs and invited me in. How I did eat that morning! An immense platter of scrapple was put before me, and with it I had three bowls of wheat porridge, good and salty, with lumps of fresh-churned butter melting in it. There was fresh cottage cheese and little yeast rolls that were taken out of the oven as I entered and a big wooden dish of boiled potatoes, with cream for a sauce. And for a side dish, for a nibble as we call it, there was smoked duck, cold and sliced thin with sliced hard-boiled eggs. And up and down the table were earthenware pots of jam, peach and apple and crabapple and the marvelous carrot jam that one finds only in this part of Pennsylvania. And to wash it all down, there were big clay jugs of milk, fresh taken from the cows only a few hours before and hot and sweet-smelling and delicious. It was such a breakfast as I had not eaten for years and years, such a breakfast as one could only find in the South Country of Pennsylvania, and I could have wept for the look and the taste and the smell of that food.

I sat at the table with the family, a weather-beaten, work-hardened man of fifty or so, his wife, and five children, the oldest about twelve, the youngest just a babe; and since they had no English at all, I tried my best to talk to them in my bad German, and to answer the many questions they threw at me. First, they let me eat, seeing how hungry I was, and enjoying, the way simple people do, the quantity of my appetite. Seeing that they did not hold against me the fact that I wore a soldier's overalls, I told them what I could about myself in their language, who I was and from where. They listened to every word respectfully and attentively.

Continental, the children said. They knew that word, and they said, Yankee?

No, no, I told them. *Fremden Brigada—brigada.* I spoke with my hands and with English, and the farmer man laid a hand on his wife's arm.

Wir haben einen sohn—he said very slowly, so I would be certain to understand. A tall son, a strong son who had worked with him, but then he went off. And the woman asked me to eat, please eat more, eat until all the hunger was gone. But there were hungers that never go, and suddenly I was sorry that I had come in here. But in German words I shaped the question, Who was their son and where was he?

In dem fremden brigada, said the man.

Du. . . ? the wife asked, and the same question was in the children's eyes. And the man repeated slow, *In dem fremden brigada.*

I was there, I said; but I did not tell them that the foreign brigades were no more, no longer, but dissolved and gone forever. Was the war gone too and dissolved forever? I didn't know, but I asked them the name of their son.

Hans Stuttman.

And I knew. Was there anyone in the brigades I did not know? But it was three whole months since he had run with the bloody dysentery and laid down and died. What was I to tell them?

Das Kann man nicht wissen?

No, I answered, so many men in so great an army. I knew him not at all. I thought and thought; what was he like and what had he suffered and what had he dreamed? But he would never come back to this little brightly painted house, never at all. No, I knew him not, I said. I rose to go and, with questions still an ache in their eyes, they filled my pockets with bread and potatoes, so I had supper that night and an empty belly the next day. The second day I had nothing, and two farm doors were closed to me until my pride forbade me to go near any others or to beg at the kitchen of an inn; for while I had been many things, I was never a beggar and would not turn one now. On the third day, I saw a gypsy wagon camped in a little clearing among the trees, and there I went and ate of a rabbit stew the Romany folk were cooking. Though I was welcomed among them, there was precious little of the stew, and I ate only enough to take the edge off my hunger. But I lay by their fire that night, having no flint of my own to make one with, and I listened to their sad Romany music and looked at their fine-featured maidens—but not with wanting now, because I was on my way to see a maid of my own. The yearning to move was more than I could withstand, and though they invited me to wait and ride with them, I was up and afoot before the dawn, and when the sun rose, it shed its cold light on the lovely foothills of my own land. And that evening I arrived at the village of York.

Ours was a quiet, out-of-the-way little village, with nothing in par-

527

ticular to distinguish it until the Congress was driven out of Philadelphia in 1777 and came there to sit; but long before I returned now, the Congress had gone away and back to Philadelphia, and the one simple straight street of York village and the two simple cross streets that divided it were very much as I had known them in 1775, when first I marched away. I came walking along the pike as the sun was setting, onto what we had called the Deeley Street when I was a boy, but which even then had lost that early name, and there was the house of the master cobbler where I had been apprenticed, and as I passed by I glanced in and saw Fritz Tumbrill, seemingly not one whit changed, even though I had lived lifetimes since I saw him last; and here across the street was the feed store, the chemist's shop, and the Halfway Inn, called that, I think, because it was roughly halfway between Philadelphia and the Virginias. So I moved down the street in the twilight, seeing this and that which was the same and seeing this one and that one, whom I knew very well indeed; but I lacked the courage to speak even one hello, and no one at all knew me, who had gone away a stripling boy with a downy face and came back a tall man with a week's growth of beard upon him.

Not that they didn't look at me, for a soldier of the Line was no common sight in York village, and if nothing else, my big, dirty, canvas overalls marked me surely for what I was; but there were other things too: the beard on my face, the slow aimlessness of my steps — for who else is so adrift as a soldier discharged? — the cut of one shoulder above the other from the weight of twenty pounds of musket I had grown to manhood with, and that wary walk of the man who has learned to use the bayonet. Every face was turned toward me, but none saw in me Jamie Stuart who had gone away once, and none addressed me as I moved down the street to the old church and the ivy-covered manse. For where else would I go but there, and what other friends in the world had I but Jacob Bracken and his daughter Molly? You would think, wouldn't you, that there would be a lot from York village in the foreign brigades? But though once there had been nine from this place, there was only myself, Jamie Stuart, left from them. One of them, Frank Califf, had come home; two others in the 1st Regiment had died at Monmouth, and a fourth at York city a long time back. Three had been taken by sickness, and the last had disappeared, as soldiers do, gone away and no one knew to where. But here I was back, and I could imagine these quiet and home-kept citizens whispering:

Look how he goes to the church, and is it not a sorrowful thing what comes of a soldier!

There walked by me Brenton, the tanner, who had once hided me well for stealing his apples, and though he looked me full in my face, he knew me not, nor did Mrs. Swinson, nor Grandmother Sturtz, who did my mother's wifery, as I have heard said, when I came into the world. So I walked on, my heart filled with wonder and terror that I would see Molly Bracken as I saw them, and that she, as they, would see nothing of the lad she loved; but I did not see her, and presently I came to the manse and knocked at the door.

Himself, Jacob Bracken answered the door in the color-run twilight of that evening when I came home, with the sun setting in the winter west, with one paintbrush of violet across the sky and with the red glow of eventide lighting that wise and gentle man who opened the door to me. But even his eyes were not discerning enough, and he looked upon me gravely, standing there tall and unafraid, his long, narrow face seriously inquisitive of a travel-worn soldier who knocked upon his door, his side-whiskers grayer than I remembered them, but otherwise no different—and all of that was immensely reassuring, for one who is marked and branded with revolution is apt to consider that all the world turns over with his own adventures; and here was this little village and the folk in it fairly much the same as when I had left them. His broad mouth held that slight, ready smile, which told you that here was a man of God not wholly unconcerned with the brown dirt and the folk who stood upon it, and he said to me quietly:

My good friend, what can I do for you?

And he told me afterwards that in this skinny, ragged soldier who stood upon his doorstep there came to him, all at once and like an accusation, the voice of a handful who like men accursed went on without end; but there was no accusation in my thoughts or my voice, and I must have sounded like a little lad when I said to him:

Pastor Bracken, this is Jamie Stuart, come back again.

Dreadful to me was the long, lasting moment of silence, while he stared and stared—and fear came; for how did I know that here was where I belonged, and how did I presume on those I knew so little? To older folk, five years is very little indeed, but the five years from seventeen to twenty-two are a whole lifetime.

Jamie Stuart, he said slowly and thoughtfully and wonderingly. In all the mercy of God, is this him? Come up here, my son.

He held the door open and I passed in and followed him to his study, where a lamp burned. The wick of this he turned up; and then, putting a hand on either arm, he faced me and examined me search-ingly all over, but warmly and fondly.

Jamie Stuart . . . he repeated . . . Indeed it is he. A boy goes away and a man comes back, and I am glad to see you home, my son.

Not being able to talk, I just stood there and faced him and let the warmth of the room, the golden light of the lamp and the curling flames of the fire sink into me.

Then sit down, he said. Sit down and rest, and in a while, you will be yourself.

He led me to a chair close to the fire, and I sat down there and I began to cry, ashamed of myself and hiding my face in the wing of the chair. But I had walked thirty miles that day, and never a bite of food had I eaten, and this was unreal and uncertain; and I wept because it would vanish as dreams always vanish, leaving behind them only the aching memory which in turn grows dim and unrecognizable.

I am ashamed, for a man should not weep, I told him.

And how else will you rid yourself of your sorrows, he answered, and make yourself clean again? How else, Jamie Stuart?

He poured a glass of wine from a bottle on his table and handed it to me. I drank it and felt better and wiped my eyes and sighed, for the generous heat of that place was all over me and through me.

Now I will tell Molly, he said, who is in the kitchen this minute, and what will she think to know that Jamie Stuart is back here, safe and sound and whole!

He would ask me no questions, I realized, but I stood up and begged him, She should not see me this way—and do I know her even? I am afraid.

You know her and she knows you.

Is she married?

No, he said. Why should she marry, when she considered so much of you?

But she should not look at me the way I am! What a sight I am! . . . Yet I could not explain to him in Philadelphia a citizen would cross the street rather than pass by a soldier of the Line. I stared down at the ragged ends of my overalls, at the broken shoes that showed below them, at the frayed cuffs of my threadbare coat. Months had passed since I had bathed, and after the Line dissolved, I never shaved, but let the corroding ruin of it show all over my body.

And I have nothing, I said. To show for it all, I have nothing, not even a copper penny to buy a clean shirt, nothing, and I am here like a beggar . .

Make your heart easy, Jamie Stuart, he said, and come with me. You are right, and she will not see you the way you are.

Then he took me upstairs to his own room, and laid out his own razor and a clean shirt and an old but clean pair of brown britches and good woolen stockings, and then left me there by myself for a little. But while I was still shaving, he came up with a wooden tub and then with a great kettle of boiling water, and a washcloth and soapstone and a dish of oil—for in those days we had no soap such as there is now—and he added to the wardrobe underclothes and a handkerchief, which I had to touch and handle, so unused had I become to the sight of such things.

Does she know that I am here? I asked him.

Now wouldn't she know, Jamie Stuart? Who is this for and who is that for? she asked me, so I told her, and she stood looking at me the way you looked at me before. Is the war over? she asked me, but I did not know the answer to that, and after you have eaten, you may tell us what you desire to, and if you want to speak of nothing at all, well that is all right too.

I nodded, and then he closed the door behind him and left me alone. I finished shaving, and then I stripped off all my clothes, so that I stood naked for the first time since the winter began, and there was a great strangeness concerning the sight of my body, the white skin which turned black at the line of my boots, so that I wore stockings of ancient filth, the knobs of my joints, the long, stringy muscles, and the long lack of intimacy that made me ashamed, as if I were peeping surreptitiously at another. Standing in the tub, I poured the hot water over myself, and then scrubbed and scrubbed, oiling myself where the dirt was heaviest and working it out, scrubbing my hair too, every bit of me, until for the first time in so long I stood clean and fresh and sweet-smelling. Then I dressed myself in Jacob Bracken's clothes, with only my old boots to remind me of what I was once. From my own clothes, I took the few papers and documents which I had saved, my warrant from the Committee of Sergeants and the one or two other things I valued, and then folded the ragged bits of uniform together and placed them in one corner, thinking that the next day I would wash them, since they were all that I had.

Then I went downstairs into the low-ceilinged parlor of the manse. There Jacob Bracken waited for me, and he said:

This way, I would have recognized you, Jamie. You are not so different.

But inside—I thought to myself—there is a deep and profound

531

difference, and how shall I explain that to anyone? And less and less able would I be, now that the events of Morristown and Princeton were so far away. . . .

It will snow tonight, Jamie, said the Pastor Bracken, and it is good that you are here under our roof.

But where, I wondered, would Jack Maloney be when the snow fell, and where Billy Bowzar and Danny Connell and the Jew Levy and all the rest? Where would they be?

Taking my arm, Jacob Bracken led me into the little dining room, where the round table was set for three people, and where Molly Bracken waited.

Here is a man to see a woman, said the Pastor, and I said:

Good evening to you, Molly Bracken.

Good evening, Jamie Stuart, said she.

And then she gave me her hand, which I held for a moment, but more than that I could not do, and what I would say, I did not know. This and that out of the past is unclear and indistinct, but I see Molly Bracken plainly enough as she was on that evening when I came home, with her black, black hair so shining and lovely, and with her eyes so blue, the fullness of her womanhood lessened only a little by the size I had gained in growth; and this was the dream I had over and over for five long years. Well, my throat was big and my voice was hapless, and overgrown and awkward I stood, like a large and hapless lad, until she asked me, simply enough:

And are you hungry, Jamie Stuart?

Never a bite of food did I taste today.

Then sit down and I will bring you my cooking, and you can see what a fine cook I am.

So the three of us sat down at the round pine table, with its pretty painted top and its four pewter sticks, which I remembered so well, and the pewter mugs and the yellow dishes that were made by the Dutch folk in Philadelphia, and the two-pronged forks that had come over from the old country; and the Pastor bent his head and said:

Lord God of Hosts, Who is merciful in His strange ways, we give Thee thanks this night not alone for bread which we eat, but for bringing home to us this lad who, without kith or kin, is dear to us and close to our hearts.

Then Jacob Bracken looked up and smiled and said, Bring in the food, Molly lass, and we'll see if the lad has improved his appetite along with his ways.

But I sat there with my head bent and the tears coming again, hating myself for my weakness, for I had been a strong man and a hard one, hearkened and respected by the soldiers of the Line. Not until Molly had gone for the food did I raise my head again.

In those times, the South Country of Pennsylvania was fruitful, and even a poor Lutheran Pastor set a good table, and if as a boy I ate poorly in my apprenticeship, it was less for the lack of food than for the contempt of men, child or otherwise, that the whole system of master and servant bred. Tonight, there was fresh baking, suet pudding and boiled beef with turnips, with pickled apples on the side and small beer. It was good and filling food and I ate well, but mostly with my eyes on the table, and almost as little as I spoke, Molly spoke; but the Pastor kept up a running history of the five years in the town, who was born and who died, and what had taken place when the Congress fled Philadelphia and came here to sit. In this very manse had sat Peytons from the Virginias and Schuylers from York colony and such other men as Stewart and Adams and Reed and great gentry of like kind, and what would Molly Bracken think of me sitting here now, the orphan child of Scottish bondslaves who did not even know his own grandfather and was owner not even of the clothes that he wore? But Jacob Bracken had no mind for that, and on and on he went; a sawmill had been set up, and with the new loan from France, it was turning out wood for muskets day and night, and it was done on shares so that Tumbrill was no longer merely a cobbler, but held a percentage of stock in the mill, as did Jackson Soakes, who had set up a banking establishment here when Congress came—which bank still flourished; and there was talk of iron molding, since if campaigns were to be fought in the South, why should not ball ammunition be dropped here? Many were the changes that I had never noticed, and he said:

These are new ways, Jamie, but I can't say that I like them. It troubles me that the war, which we never see or feel, brings us wealth so strangely . . .

Father, said Molly Bracken, never a word can Jamie get in when you go on like that.

I am merely filling in the years.

Yes, Father, said Molly Bracken patiently, that you are, and he comes straightaway from where there are things doing and battles fought and grand encampments and cities—but never a word of this will you give him a chance to tell.

When he wants to tell it, he will tell it, said Pastor Bracken. When my son comes homes, I do not ask him why he comes. It is enough for

533

me that he is here. When I opened the door, Molly, and saw a soldier of God's own angry army standing there in the cold winter night, with the ragged overalls that Christ's soldiers wear, I did not think to catechize him on where he was from or where he was bound for, or whether he was coming from the battle or going to it; for who am I here in the comfort of mine own house to question those who freeze in the open wintertime and march all footsore and weary? I think, sometimes, that we are too proud, too proud, and such as we would not hasten to lighten Christ's burden if he came by with the great weight upon his back, but would rather point out that his clothes were ragged and his face unshaven. So if I would give shelter and comfort and confidence to a stranger — which no man is in all truth — should I do less for my son here?

I didn't ask for a sermon, Father, said Molly patiently, but simply for a moment for someone else to get a word in.

Jamie, he said, these are new times, with less respect from a child than my father got from his. Is the war over, Jamie?

No, I answered, and then I told them what had happened. Wholly and completely, I told it, keeping nothing back, and there we sat at the table while the candles burned down, with no interruption except when Jacob Bracken rose to throw a stick of wood on the fire, and all of it came out of me, even to the last betrayal of my comrades. So I finished and said:

That is what I did, and I came home to the only place I knew as home, and as to whether what I did was right or wrong, you can judge.

I cannot judge, said Jacob Bracken, and that is something that only the Lord God can do, so I will not judge, Jamie. Meanwhile, go into my study and pull up a chair to the fire, and while Molly finishes the women's work, I will burn some rum and we will drink a glass with butter and talk as friends, which is what we are, Jamie Stuart. So go on in there, Jamie, and build up the fire and draw the chairs close, and soon we will join you.

This I did. And then with the dry wood spluttering in the hearth, with the little room just as warm and cuddly as a squirrel's nest, I went to the window and watched the first real winter's snow begin to fall. You know when it is the real snow, the deep snow, the abiding snow that comes to blanket the ground and remain. Each flake is large and firm and turns and twists with great assurance as it comes to the ground, and then for a man indoors there is the mighty security of roof and fire, but for a man out in the field it is an awful thing to see the whole world turn white and cold and silent. So for all that I was here, with the fire blazing and the books lining the walls and the stuffed wild goose sitting popeyed and proud on the mantel, I was neither restful nor at ease; for the best of me was elsewhere, and what was I doing by the fireside with all of my good comrades gone away from me?

I was glad when Jacob Bracken came in, for I feared my own thoughts and had no desire to be alone with them. He gave me a mug of hot flip, and we sat down before the fire, and he said:

Well, Jamie, here we are, myself and you too, snug and safe in front of the fire—which in a way is God's judgment for whatever small good we did in our lives. Do you believe in God, Jamie?

It took a while for me to answer that, for in the flames and come to life, as pictures do when you sit and ponder a burning log, were all the troubles I had known in my own young life, and all the little bites of glory, and all the faint heart and fears, and all the marches and countermarches since that long ago time when the 1st Regiment of the Pennsylvania Line had paraded through the streets of Philadelphia and then set out to join the Yankee farmers outside of Boston town, each of us with a sprig of May finery in our hats, each of us with something or other in our hearts. Thus moved the possessed and the dispossessed and we were one together, but I was not one with them any longer; and here was a man of God asking me if I believed in his Master.

I think not, I said finally and unhappily, for I never saw any judgment between the good and the bad which was not either the whim of chance or the working of the gentry. There was a little drummer lad in the beginning of this revolt, and his name was Tommy Mahoney, and while some drummer boys become mean and sly and bad in every way—which is not so strange, when you consider the terrible life they live—this one was good and pure, and he died without cause or reason, as did so many of my comrades in all the years of this bitter war.

And was the Revolution no reason, Jamie? asked Jacob Bracken.

Sure—reason enough, if you say that what we went away to strive for might have been. But soon enough we discovered that the grudge and gripe of the officer gentry was not our grudge and gripe, and it was only to serve their purpose that we existed. There was one class in the Line of the foreign brigades, and there was another class who led us, and never was there a meeting between the two or any kind of understanding. They turned us into dogs; it was the whip and the cane, week in and week out, with no pay and no food and no clothes—and soon that became no hope, which could not be otherwise, it seems to me. We in the Line were Jew and Roman and Protestant and black and white, and we learned to fight and live and work together; so when you asked me if I believe in God, what should I think about the big Bantu Nayger, a slave and unbaptized without grace or salvation, and he came into the Line with blood on his hands and a heathen name, Bora Kabanka, a great black man who had slain his master? What should I think about him, when at Monmouth he picked me up in his arms and bore me from the field under fire, like I was a little babe—and if I had a guinea for every lash he took from the officers because he was a proud black man, then I would be rich indeed? There is dying for a cause, which is one thing, and there is dying for the proud folk who do not give two damns for us. I leave that. I will not go back and serve under them again, and I will not believe in a God who stands firm behind the man with property but has only a curse and a blow for men like me.

Well, Jamie, Jacob Bracken said thoughtfully, there's a way of looking at things, and belief in God is not an easy matter to argue, is it? I don't hold with those who say *Don't discuss religion*—for what is better meat for chewing than the food of one's own soul? Now I believe in God and in the Lord Jesus Christ the way I believe in my own right hand, and I attempt to serve Him, you know; but consider that I who talk of God with such certainty have never ventured in His behalf any more than a little speech and now and then a bout with a sinner, whereas you who deny Him, Jamie, have given five years of your life in His holiest service.

Have I? I said.

Indeed you have, Jamie, and on that point I am completely clear.

Well, I wondered, what of the King's soldiers, who are blessed with the blessing of God when they put on that lobster suit of theirs?

Now, for the first time, Jacob Bracken lost his calm manner; a flush came over his long, narrow face, and the broad mouth roared out:

Who said?

The Archbishop of Canterbury, for one.

The servant of the Devil! he cried. On his lips, the word God is an abomination! Ye hear me, Jamie? An abomination! Every sacred martyr of Protestantism is proof of that! Cursed is the Church of England as the Church of Rome is cursed—

But, I interrupted, a great many of the lads in the brigades were Romans.

Jamie, he roared, have you become a damned theological pettifogger? Do my words mean nothing to you?

He was half serious, half humorous. Jamie, he said, there is not that much obscurity concerning the works of God.

Molly joined us now. Across the village, they could hear you, said she.

And with reason.

That I doubt, she answered him, drawing a chair up to the fire, so that the three of us sat in front of it now, and in this all my dreams were realized. Yet the rum I held was without taste, and Molly Bracken was a stranger to me.

Jamie, said the Pastor, surrender not grace that easily.

But I had surrendered, and staring at the flames, I held my rum untasted and tasteless.

Outside, said Molly Bracken, a great storm is making. And it will snow and snow.

Said the Pastor, Jamie, when you made the uprising, you and your comrades, what was in your minds?

Not God, I said sourly, not anything like that—but only that it was unbearable.

Yet there must have been a thought of what would be afterwards.

How do I know what the others were thinking?

I will not lose my temper with you, Jamie Stuart, said Jacob Bracken. You are under my roof, and under my roof you shall stay.

Molly said, Leave him be. Leave him be. Look how tired he is.

This I was thinking, I said suddenly. I was thinking that we would strike a flame that would ignite everywhere, and everywhere plain folk like myself would join us. And that we would sweep the British into the sea and make a place here of justice and decency.

That's a grand thought, Jamie, said Jacob Bracken.

And look what it came to. Where are the foreign brigades now. . . ?

Consider, Jamie, said Jacob Bracken, that you have given five years, and how many have given nothing!

I have given nothing! I cried. How can I tell you?

But there was no way in which I could tell them, and they were more gentle and good to me than I deserved; and presently Jacob Bracken led me up to the little attic room where my bed was, and I crawled in between the clean sheets and lay there, looking out at the big flakes of snow that drifted past the window. . . .

So it was that I came back to York village and to my friends and to what life had been before I went away, and I picked up this thread and that thread, and presently the numbness in my heart, which had been there ever since Jack Maloney left me that cold and rainy night in

Philadelphia, eased out, and I began to forget the whole violent wash of war that had surged up and down and through the Jerseys for so long. Here, we were a long way from Jersey; life went on here, and in the wintertime, when the roads were closed with snow, this was a world to itself.

The town made no fuss over me; Jamie Stuart had gone, and now Jamie Stuart was back, and it mattered very little indeed. The war was something they had long since become used to; and like most Pennsylvania people in good circumstances, they were only nominally in favor of it. Perhaps a little more in this town than in others, since the war had brought business and money, but the fact that the Pennsylvania Line was no more—a piece of news that came to the village from this direction and that—gave them no great concern. This was a war that had gone on too long. If Jamie Stuart washed his hands of it, that was sound sense from where it was least expected; for what real good could come from a miserable Scottish lad born from parents who had been bondslaves?

I stayed with Jacob Bracken because I had no other place to stay; but often enough I thought to myself that it was time for me to be moving on, and I decided that when the snows began to melt, I would take the road for Philadelphia, perhaps to sign onto one of the sailing vessels, or to get a job in the ropeworks, or even to find a place there as a cobbler. York village was not for me, and Molly Bracken was a stranger, as if she had never kissed me upon the lips, as if we had never exchanged words of love; but she was a grown woman now with the need to think seriously of the future, and what was the future of a soldier out of the army? In no way did I hold this against her, but I tried as much as I could to avoid her; and when they took me on as a hand at the sawmill at half a guinea a week, I saw her almost not at all—for it was up at the dawn and back with the night, and only at the table did we exchange a word or two.

Once or twice I said to Pastor Bracken, I have no right to stay on here like this, and suppose I found a room and board elsewhere?

But his response was always something to the effect of my wanting to drive home a disagreement; and indeed I did not take too much persuasion, for there was nothing in York for me now but the sight of Molly Bracken, if even for a little and without hope. And when, here and there, one of the long-tongued gossips in the village let it drop that they did not approve of the wild and wicked Jamie Stuart living under the same roof as the poor, motherless Bracken girl, Jacob Bracken's spine stiffened like a ramrod.

538

The Proud and the Free

Now you stay here, Jamie, he said firmly, and from his pulpit he thundered at those who carry false witness. . . . Aye, we have a militia, he told his congregation, but a militia waits for the war to come to it, and the good Lord has seen fit to keep the war far distant—for His own purposes—although one gunshot in freedom's name might be a better sermon than all my words. But who else is there except one orphan lad among you who has ventured his life in what we discuss so glibly?

And I squirmed and avoided the eyes of those around me; but Molly Bracken sat with her head up and smiling, and that made me wonder.

But themselves, the townsfolk were a little afraid of me; I was not only different from them now, but the distorted tales they had of the rising made them think of me as a wild and lawless person, and when finally I came face to face with Fritz Tumbrill, he was a meek and a chastened man.

It was when I had my first half-guinea in my pocket that I went to his shop to order a pair of boots, which was my greatest need at the moment. Believe me, it was a strange thing to be back there now, to see how small the shop had become in its insignificant frame building, all covered with snow, so insignificant a reality in comparison with my memories—and I often think now that there is the best sign of maturity, the reality of things instead of the unreal threat of them. My world had been a world of spirits and demons and witches and ogres, but I had faced real fears and found them not so awful as they might be, and death itself is not the worst thing in the world if you can face it with your eyes open. And here was this man I had feared so, all shrunken and old and small, and now he was afraid of me.

But let me tell you how I came in, how I pulled at the latch and how the little bell tinkled, and how a child's voice told me to come in, even as I had once told people to enter. Inside, nothing at all was different; a boy at one bench and Fritz Tumbrill at the other, but when he looked up and saw me, his face became pale; his big jowls shook; and he said to me, almost pleadingly:

Why, welcome home, Jamie Stuart.

Good evening to you, Fritz, I nodded. I have come to have a pair of boots made.

And glad I am to see you, Jamie. I tell you now, they will be the best boots I ever turned out of my shop, and not a penny will they cost you. All the time when you were off to the war I said to myself, There is Jamie Stuart gone with never time to give him a little gift. So this will be a gift in a way of speaking, Jamie.

539

I want no gifts from you, Fritz Tumbrill, I said. I will pay you what the shoes are worth.

Are you holding old scores agin me, Jamie? he asked, cocking his head and looking up at me.

Well, I had been, I had been; but looking at him now and from him to the thin, pale-faced boy who sat on the other bench, his head down, his skinny little hand frozen in mid-air, clenching the hammer, his mouth full of tacks—looking from one to the other, my hatred for this fat, gross man who was now part owner of a mill went away, and I asked myself, What are you doing here, Jamie Stuart? What are you doing here with this fat shopkeeper, in this fat and contented town, living with a pastor who will patiently convert you to God again? What are you doing here, Jamie Stuart? I asked myself, remembering the worst of times I had known—and the worst of them were not like this, not like this in this place, where the Roman was hated and the Jew maligned and the black man considered an ape from dark Africa. Yes, standing there in the cobbler's house, I felt that my soul was shriveling up within me, and all the goodness and greatness that had been mine once when I marched in the companionship of Revolution was plain to me now and made plain too late; and as my heart had never hungered for anything, so did it hunger for the ugly little men of the brigades who were my comrades.

Old scores? I questioned. No, cobbler—no; there are no old scores left. Make me my shoes and be done with it. . . .

So I had new boots and work at the mill and a home with Jacob Bracken, who spoke to me gently of God and of humility and of my future. The month passed and March came, and with March the warm sunshine to shrink the snow—so that by the middle of the month it already appeared that spring was at hand. There was one fair Sunday when I took Molly to church to hear her father preach, and I sat as I always did in the church, stiffly and uncomfortably, counting the minutes until it was over, filled with a turmoil of doubt and unsatisfied longing and hesitation and the brooding wonder that attempted to extract some meaning from my life and from my deeds. When the service was finished, I rose to leave, and Molly Bracken said:

Look at the day, Jamie, with the sun shining like in summertime. Will you walk with me a little?

If you wish, and if you are not ashamed to walk down the street alongside of Jamie Stuart.

What a thing to say! Now I am not ashamed but proud.

And after we had walked a little way, she said to me, Why should I be ashamed, Jamie Stuart?

Because I am not like the others in this place.

Maybe you are more like them than you think, Jamie Stuart.

No, less like them than you would think, Molly.

We passed out of the village and along the road, walking slowly, side by side, and saying nothing until we had gone quite a way. And then it was Molly Bracken who asked what gnawed inside of me, the way I was.

What way?

Like a stranger, Jamie Stuart, like I had never known you before and there was nothing at all between us of any worth or meaning or reason for remembering. Sometimes, you frighten me.

As I frighten other people, Molly?

Yes . . .

Tell me why, I said, as gently as I could, for now I realized clearly enough that it was not the difference in herself but in me; and here was a beautiful and womanly person who wanted myself who was nothing and less than nothing, an orphan and a penniless soldier out of the Line; and the bitter sorrow of it was that he did not want her.

I can only tell you part of it, she answered, but you never made to kiss me or to touch me or even to look at me full in the eyes. When you came home that evening, and my father came down and put a kettle onto the fire, and I said to him *Why?* and he told me that Jamie Stuart was upstairs and would wash off the dirt of marching and fighting before he would come before me—and when I heard that, I thought I would faint from gladness, and there was a song in my bosom that said over and over and over again, *Jamie Stuart is back— he is back to stay, and he will never go away again.* See how shameless I am to tell you all of this—

Not shameless at all, Molly Bracken, but tell it to me only if you desire to.

Why am I telling it to you then, and you ask me how are you strange? The winter is gone, Jamie Stuart, but the cold clings to you— do you know that?

I didn't know that, I said unhappily, and if it is true, then God help me.

How can He help you when you don't believe in Him, Jamie Stuart?

You hold that against me?

Oh, I don't hold that against you, Jamie Stuart, but you hold it against yourself, and you have no belief in the people here or in the

541

war or in me either—but only a terrible hatred that makes me afraid
when I look at you. What do you hate so?

Many things, I answered her, many things, walking step by step and
so slowly, my eyes on the road, kicking stones out of the soft mud as I
went along—and wondering what I could tell her, but wanting underneath not to tell her anything, for what was the use of cataloguing
hatred when nothing I hated could withstand the scrutiny of my
thoughts? It was less the gentry and the village and the pinch-souled
cobbler, and the narrow self-concern of these people here and the
hypocrisy of their lives, and the limit of their vision and the compla-
cent relationship they had in each of their churches to their God, than
the fact that I knew of nothing better than their way. When my comrades and myself took into our own hands the strength of the army, we
marched into nowhere; and that was the way my hatred went—into
nowhere.

So I said many things, but I could not tell her what the singular of it
was. I hated in its wholeness a life that twisted the souls of men, but I
knew of no living that did not; and thereby it had come about that I
was a stranger wherever I went; but that I could not tell her, and I
could not tell her that the only men who were my kind were those men
who had marched with me in the brigades—and less could I tell her
that I felt a closer bond and a purer sympathy to those poor damned
women who had cast in their lot with us, whores though they were by
any of her standards, than I did to herself, so young and fine and
lovely. None of that could I tell her, but only that I hated many
things.

Then God help you, Jamie Stuart, if you do not even know what you
hate.

I have never known Him to help me or any other man.

Because you close your heart to Him.

About that I don't know, I said sadly. It may be.

Then we turned around to walk back, and walked on for a time in
silence. We were almost back at the village, when she took my hand
and held it tightly for a moment.

Jamie Stuart—

Yes?

Jamie Stuart, were you thinking of going away?

I was thinking of that, I answered.

Will you tarry a little while?

If you want me to, I will, I said, but I was afraid it would only make
it painful for you and for me both. In some ways now, I am only half a

man—and I am no good for myself or for you.

For me, Jamie Stuart, you are good.

But even though I answered her that way, the thought of going never left my mind. As Danny Connell had said, a bird pecked in me, and I tired of the work at the mill, the sameness of it, the boys off the farms who worked alongside of me, with their talk of this girl or that one and never a thought of anything else in their heads—and no curiosity either about the boundless world that stretched away in every direction and only contempt for me who was the child of bondslaves and was five years a soldier with never a penny of hard money to show for it. But when I began to think that they were truly like animals, I would remember that I had been very like them before I went away; but I never ceased to wonder that, at one and the same time, a great war could be going on in the same land where these people lived from day to day, with never a thought of the war in their heads or a care for it either.

Sometimes, I went into Jacob Bracken's study and looked at his books; but there were few among them that could interest me. Most of them were heavy and dry theological tomes, written by serious and outstanding Protestant authorities, and there were various editions of the Bible and commentaries upon them. There was all of Shakespeare, but little enough of it could I understand. And in a book of seven poets, such men as Wilmot and Prior and Pope, I found once these few lines by William Collins, which I said to myself until they lodged in my memory and remain there still:

> How sleep the brave, who sink to rest
> By all their country's wishes bless'd!
> When Spring with dewy fingers cold
> Returns to deck their hallowed mould,
> She there shall dress a sweeter sod
> Than Fancy's feet have ever trod.

It made me dream of what a fine, rich thing it would be to write some poetry of a sort about our own Pennsylvania men and what we had done, but not like this, but rather proud and angry; and this thought, I knew, struck only a chord of lament for my own bereftness. But once, I recall, I was looking through a book of sermons that had been published in Philadelphia, for the use and convenience of men of the cloth, as it said; and therein, written by a Yankee called Jonathan

Mayhew, I found something that beat on my mind like a brief flash of light, so that my groping almost found something to hew onto out of these words:

> Tyranny brings ignorance and brutality along with it. It degrades men from their just rank into the class of brutes. It damps their spirits. It suppresses arts. It extinguishes every spark of noble ardor and generosity in the breasts of those who are enslaved by it. It makes naturally strong and great minds feeble and little; and triumphs over the ruins of virtue and humanity. This is true of tyranny in every shape. There can be nothing great or good where its influence reaches. . . .

This above, I read with great excitement, like the key to a door that might open and admit me; and my excitement was such that later I interrupted Jacob Bracken in his work and begged him to listen while I read it aloud.

Yes, he said, that is part of a preachment of Mayhew, and I know it well. It is from a sermon he preached some twenty or thirty years ago. I should have liked to hear him preach. He is said to have been a man with a rich color of speech, but there is nothing new or particularly original in what he said, Jamie.

But there is, I protested. Tyranny *in every shape,* he says. Not one tyranny, not another or this one or that one, but in every shape. Then it means to destroy all tyranny—not only the tyranny of Britain and George III—

It is not to be taken literally, Jamie, he said patiently, for Mayhew himself distinguishes between what is a just and what an unjust tyranny.

How can there be a just tyranny? I demanded. If all men are created free and equal . . .

Created, Jamie; yes, indeed, created, Pastor Bracken said, his long, sober face expressing a mixture of concern and annoyance, but after the creation there is a natural order of things. One must be master and one must be servant. One must be rich and one must be poor. This is not matter of equality but of the order of life, which is another thing entirely, and man was conceived in sin not in perfection, and it is idle to dream that it could have been any other way or even will be different. Here are you who have learned to read and to write, and as an educated man, Jamie, you can have a future in something better than running sticks through a watermill. And if you should find grace,

544

Jamie, the ministry is open to you, and I will do all in my power to help you—and indeed I know of no better calling for a man who believes in justice and right. On the other hand, when this unhappy war is over, this will be a country of boundless opportunity, and many a lad like yourself has started in a Philadelphia countinghouse with no more than the coat on his back and found himself a rich and respected merchant. Such men as these are a mighty bulwark in our struggle against the corrupt and insidious Church of England and the decadent and monstrous King who keeps it in power. And sooner or later—

Who taught me to read? I interrupted.

I know what you will say, Jamie, but I assure you, Jamie Stuart, that if I had not taught you, another would have, for the desire to learn and know was within you, and this desire to learn and know will never be within all men. Some are wastrels and others are thoughtless, dull people, and that is why even in so just a war as this one, we are forced to open the prisons and poorhouses to find men to serve—so that we come to understand that in the highest cause, the lowest of men will find a place, not because they love liberty more, but because they are fitted to take orders and thereby fitted into the eternal scheme of things. This is a wisdom beyond our understanding, my boy, but we must accept it. And when we accept it, we find that it is the best of ways.

I see, I said.

I hope, Jamie, that you do not think I meant any reflection upon your comrades in the foreign brigades.

What difference does it make, I said slowly and strangely, since I have left them and gone away, but they are dull and thoughtless and see nothing else but to go on serving without pay and without reward? What difference does it make?

I hope, Jamie, said Pastor Bracken, that you will come to think differently about many of these things . . .

I came to think less, perhaps; and I did my work, and the days passed; and April came, with the sweet singing and budding springtime of the Pennsylvania hills. Then I would have been far less than human to remain in the same house as Molly Bracken and remain this cold, aloof and self-sufficient thing that I prided myself on having become; for there was a certain bitter perversity in what I did, as if I took some pleasure in my separation from all the natural things of life. And one evening, when her father sat in his study, writing, I entered the kitchen as Molly Bracken was coming out and went head on into

her, and then we were in each other's arms and I was covering her face
with kisses, while she said:

Jamie, Jamie — how long and how much you hate me!

I love you the way I've never loved anyone.

And she pulled away and smoothed her hair and said, How you've
showed me your love, Jamie Stuart!

I could not.

And what now, Jamie Stuart? What is different? Is it the springtime
that scents a bitch?

God damn you! I cried. God damn you to hell!

Why, Jamie? she demanded, standing cool and aloof and apparently
undisturbed now. Because a parson's daughter talks that way? Do you
talk to me like I was a whore because you want a whore?

Shut your mouth! I cried.

No, that I will not do, Jamie Stuart. For long enough I held my
peace, while you lived here, hating us and eating our food and taking
our shelter —

Because you kept me here! And I offered to pay, but you would not
take my pay, so that I would be beholden to you!

And you would not be beholden to anyone, Jamie Stuart? Twenty-
two years old you are, and the heart inside of you is like a flint rock
that nothing can scrape, and what I said before is true, that wherever
you go, the winter cold goes with you! But here I waited five years,
dreaming of my fine lad that had gone off to the wars, because whatever you were — and even that first time when I saw you sitting on the
cobbler's bench, your hammer in your hand and your mouth full of
tacks — there was a purity and a goodness in you. But there's no purity
and goodness in you now, Jamie Stuart, and the man I waited for died
somewhere.

Then I'll go! I cried. By God, I'll go!

Go on, Jamie Stuart, and see if I keep you here. Go on out and see if
you can find the heart and soul of Jamie Stuart wherever you have left
it! You should not have come home for somewhere you betrayed yourself and destroyed yourself!

And wasn't five years enough?

She was weeping now as she said, More than enough, more than
enough, God help me, if you could have kept your own soul. But this
way, Jamie Stuart, you should have stayed where the rest of you is.

I left her, stormed out and paid no heed to her calling after me, and
went straightaway down the street to the inn. It was the first time I
had been there in my ten weeks in York village, and this night was the

first time I was drunk in my ten weeks at York village. But I knew what I wanted, for once; and when Simon Decorman, who kept the place, began to welcome me with, *Well, Jamie, and is it not fine to see you down here with human faces?* I cut him short and told him: I have not come here for companionship or gabble, but for a mug and a pitcher of rum!

Now is that a way, Jamie—

Damn it to hell, do you serve rum or don't ye?

If it's a drink ye want, with no word of kindness or good cheer, why you can buy it and be damned!

As to that, I'll decide, and you can speak to me when you're asked for it!

So I got a table in a corner and the rum, and I proceeded to make myself drunk in a right royal fashion. Gradually, as the supper hour passed, the place filled up, with the lads from the farms and the mill coming in to have a pint of beer or something hot, and many of them were surprised to see me and came over to pass a word with me. What I said to them, I don't remember, but it was not gentle words, and if it had been anyone else but me, there would have been fighting in the inn that night. But there was something in me that made them afraid, and they left me alone.

Of that night, there is little I remember and less that I desire to recall. Even in so small a place as York, there were the necessary forms and places for a man who desired a little taste of hell, and I had my taste and found shelter, finally, on toward the morning, in the barn of Caleb Henry, where I burrowed into the hayloft and slept until the sun was high in the sky. Then I awoke with an aching head and a burning throat and very little desire to live altogether—though the last was diluted somewhat when I got to Caleb Henry's brook unseen, and soaked my head and drank my fill. Then I quartered across the field away from the village and toward the Philadelphia pike. Thus I would go as I came, with the clothes on my back and nothing in my pockets—and nothing in particular in my heart.

Oh, it was a lovely day, all right, and I will not forget that, nor how the wind blew so warm and softly from the west and how the little white clouds sailed across the blue sky. For all my misery, a taste for life would not be denied, and I felt myself expand and yearn toward this mighty and beautiful and limitless land of mine, with its hills and its valleys and its triumphant and unmeasurable spaces; it sang a song for me as I walked along, unshaven and unwashed, my cotton shirt

547

covered with the filth of the night before, and in that song were the echoes of my own unborn poetry of the good struggle I had fought, side by side with the good and brave companions I had known. I was leaving all that I had, but there was a merciless truth in what Molly Bracken had said to me, and all that I had was nothing and less than nothing. And if I was miserable now, it was that misery of youth that is never complete and never unmixed with something else. So it was in that mood, as I neared the pike, that I heard the beating of the drums, that old, old sound that was as familiar as my own pulse and as native to me — but in the mood I was in, the drums were a part of my thoughts and seemed to come from the inner rather than the outer world.

That way it seemed to me at first; but then I stiffened; my skin prickled all over, as if a wave of icy air were flowing over me, and my heart beat faster and faster. *There were the drums*—still far off, but real, and nowhere in the whole world but in the foreign brigades were drums beaten that way, not as the Yankees beat their drums, not as the British beat their drums, but in a cross between the skirling of the pipes and the haunting Slavic rhythms of the Polish men, singing a song of defiant, wild and angry sorrow, telling people who hear to beware of men whose lot cannot be worsened but only bettered, men who go into battle with nothing to lose; and coming as it does from the skinny hands of little children, there is a pathos added that once heard is not forgotten.

And now I was hearing it, and I began to run. Across the fields I ran, my heart pounding, bursting through a hedge, leaping a brook, panting and sobbing — but then losing all of my courage as I neared the road, and finally crawling into a patch of blueberry bushes, where I could see without being seen.

And there I lay, while the drums beat louder and louder, until finally they came into sight; and then when I saw them, I wept. First came Laurens and Stewart, leading the file and mounted finely, but it was not for them I wept, but for the little column of less than four hundred men, which was all that remained of the brigades. First there were the drummer lads, eight of them, little Tommy Searles and Jonathan Harbecht and Peter O'Conner and the rest, just as small, just as shrunken, just as pinch-faced as ever; and behind them marched Chester Rosenbank with four fifers, and then came the regiments — the two regiments that remained. But there they were and I saw them: Billy Bowzar and Jack Maloney and the Jew Levy and the Great Nayger man, Bora Kabanka, and Danny Connell — alone he was, and I

wondered what had become of his fair maid—and Lawrence Scottsboro, older than ever, his back bent as he trudged along, and Angus
MacGrath, towering over the others—yes, there they were, but many
others were gone, and I wept as the little company marched past
toward York village.

A long time I lay there, part of the time thinking, part of the time
with no thought but the sudden peace I knew. And then I rose and
walked back to York village, with my purpose clear in my mind.

PART ELEVEN

Which is the last part of my narration, and
which tells how the foreign brigades gathered
again at York village in Pennsylvania
and what befell them there.

So I come to the last part of my tale of the foreign brigades of
Pennsylvania and of their rising against the officer gentry; yet a little
more must be told before I can let my memories be and let the dead
sleep as they should sleep. Since it is of myself that I write, I must take
some time for my own thoughts and my own broodings, which is what
I know—and little enough do I know of my comrades. That they were
not mean and lowly, I do know, and this I will assert again and again;
for they had a store of courage and nobility that was nowhere found in
my own soul. This I assert, before I write what became of them and of
me.

Myself, I went back to York village after I had thought about the
matter sufficiently and knew what I was going to do; I did not know
whether it was right or wrong nor did I greatly care at the time, but I
knew that I had to do it, because a man is no good when he is broken
into many fragments, a piece here and a piece there, but only when he
is whole. And I knew that it would make me whole again in the only
way of wholeness I cared for.

So I walked back to York village after a time, and I walked down the
street to Lemuel Simpkins's cow pasture, where the Pennsylvania Line
had encamped. By now, it was late afternoon, and already the tents
were raised, the pickets posted, and the men were engaged in clearing
the grounds, laying out the parade and gathering wood for their night
fires. They had stacked their muskets in the European manner, by
fours with one bayonet fixed—which is peculiar to our brigades—and
from the look of it you would have thought that there had been an

550

encampment there for many a day past. They had put out sentries, raised up a flagpole, and were beginning to build brushwood shelters, so it was evident that this was no quick bivouac but an encampment of some duration; and everything they did was carried out in the easy, competent manner of men who knew their work well enough.

Simpkins's cow pasture rolls down and away from the road and the encampment was set a good quarter of a mile back, with the command tent on a little knoll. Already, half of the townsfolk and just about all of the children had gathered along the road to watch, and already the children had begun their game of hide-and-seek with the sentries. Oh, it was a familiar enough picture: the children and the excited people, and the seemingly bored sentries in their torn and dirty overalls, and the little knot of officers importantly discussing the situation with the town clerk and the town council, and the girls preening themselves and the drummer boys standing back and hooting at them, and the horses clustered near the command tent and the soldiers off duty sprawling gratefully on the grass, and one wretched little captain showing his authority by giving parade drill to a platoon — all of it familiar and terrible and wonderful at the same time.

For a while, I stood off, looking to see whether Molly Bracken was in the crowd; but she was not there, so I went past them and circled around, to come into the camp from the farther side. I walked up to a sentry, and it was Arnold Gary, and he took a long look and said:

By all that is holy and critical, is that Jamie Stuart himself and in the flesh?

It is, I agreed.

Then he threw down his musket and put his arms around me and rocked me back and forth, and I hugged the smell of him, the sour, rancid smell of the dirty overalls on a man who has marched all day long, the feel of him, of a man of mine own kind who was a brother to me; and he said:

I knew it, and I told them, You mark me, when we come into York village, there will be Jamie Stuart, fat as a plucked chicken.

And what are you doing here with the brigades — or what is left of them, God help me — so far south and away from everything? Is the war over?

This stinking war, said Arnold Gary, is one that will never be over; for if it was, what in hell's name would our lousy officers do with themselves? and for the sins of my blessed mother — who never teached me the writing or the reading — here I am still, and will be forever most likely. And as for being here in York, well this is a rendezvous, the way they say, to see if we can make a Line out of ourselves, so that we can march off south for a campaign upon which they have set their hearts, there being damned little to squeeze out of the Jerseys any more, while the Pennsylvania country is as fat and tasty as a pig's ass. Ye can see that I envy you, Jamie Stuart, standing there in them fine shoes and fine breeches with never a care in the world, while my own reward from the damn uprising is special treatment with the cane.

How is it then?

It is lousy, Jamie Stuart, if you must know the whole truth.

How do you mean?

I mean that they are exacting payment in their own sweet way. For the exact letter of the rising, it is true that they have kept their word and exacted no punishment, but if you break step you get a cane on your back and twenty lashes for just whispering at parade, and for the Jew Gonzales, because he talked back to that dirty little rat Purdy, one hundred lashes, from which he died, just as Jim Holt, the Nayger, died when he talked back to Butler and they 'spontooned him in the belly. Oh, Jesus Christ, that was a thing to see, for he lay there on the ground, twisting and turning and begging us not to pull out the fat spear, but we had to, and then he rolled over and vomited out his lifeblood. And you can imagine that the fools of the Committee remained? Even Jack Maloney, coming back from Philadelphia, where he said he left you.

I know that, I said.

And you are free and clear, Jamie — what a blessing!

Depending on how you look at it, I said, for I have come here to enlist.

No!

It's true, so I'll thank you, Arnold, to let me go through to their damned command tent.

Are you crazy, Jamie? Are you clear and raving mad?

Possibly. What in hell —

He interrupted by tapping my chest and saying deliberately, Go away from here, Jamie Stuart.

And why don't you run away? I demanded. Off across the fields and away, and who would ever find you, Arnold Gary?

Where would I run to, Jamie? And what do I know except to heft a musket? But yourself —

Myself is my own conscience, so let me go past.

All right, he said. All right, Jamie Stuart.

And then he picked up his gun and went on his round, and I walked along into the encampment; and one after another the men saw me and recognized me, and many of them hugged me close, so I knew how it was to be back with them again.

Here I met Bowzar and Jack Maloney, who said, Have ye come to look down at us, Jamie Stuart?

Down or up, I answered; what in hell is the difference. And I walked past him over to the command post, where Butler and Laurens stood talking and then looked up and faced me in silence. But the men, my own old comrades, they kept their distance and stood together, watching quietly.

Well, here I am, I said, and I've come to enlist.

Laurens smiled in a way that might mean anything at all, and Butler put his hands in his pockets, spread his feet, and looked me all over and up and down.

Jamie Stuart, he said.

You have a long memory, I answered calmly enough.

Longer than you would ever imagine, Mr. Stuart, and when you address me, why you will address me as Colonel Butler, if you please.

Yes, sir.

Yes, Colonel Butler!

Yes, Colonel Butler, I repeated.

Now in that there is the making of a good soldier, Jamie Stuart, so if you go over to the tent, the Jew will make your papers for you, and then you can draw a pair of overalls from Captain Kennedy at the supply depot over yonder and report back here.

I answered, Yes, Colonel Butler.

But he paid no more attention to me, going on with his conversation with Laurens, who now carefully avoided my eyes; and I walked to the big tent and entered. There Levy sat at a camp table, with the journal of the Line, that old, weather-beaten, leather-bound book which we had treasured so carefully through our rising, open in front of him—wherein he was composing the details of the day's march; and he looked up as I came in, his thin face a little more worn, a little more lined, his hair streaked with gray, but otherwise no different, and he squinted at me because my back was to the light.

Hello? he inquired.

I walked over and showed him my face, and a slow smile came and wrinkled him all over, and he stretched out both his hands for mine.

Jamie Stuart, and God be praised for keeping you sound and healthy.

And how goes it with the Line, Leon Levy?

This and that, Jamie Stuart. Some are dead and some are gone, and now there is a great campaign brewing in the Southland, but where will men be found to fight it? The people are tired of war.

You look tired, my friend.

We get tired. But what should I say about you, Jamie Stuart? You are different. Are you happy here in this pretty place, and are you with the beautiful lass whose name is Molly? Is it a good life here?

It's a good enough life, I answered him, but I am here to enlist in the Line again.

To that he made no reply, but looked at me searchingly for a long while; and then he nodded and got the papers and prepared them.

Sign your name here, lad, he said.

I signed my name, and once again I was a soldier of the commonwealth, and then I went and drew my overalls and put them on, and then I reported back to Butler and Laurens.

So you see, I have a long memory, said Butler.

I stood at attention and said nothing.

An astonishing long memory, and your overalls are torn, Stuart.

They were issued to me this way, sir, and I have not had time to mend them.

And dirty.

Nor to wash them, sir.

I said before, specifically, Stuart, that you were to address me as Colonel Butler.

I am sorry, Colonel Butler.

Sorrow, Stuart, is not an admirable quality in a soldier. Discipline is more becoming, and it seems to me that twenty-five lashes would wipe out your sorrow and instill a decent regard for soldiery qualities. Do you agree?

He wanted me to plead or protest, and I would have died before I did either. Laurens stood beside him, silent, but watching me narrowly; and I knew that he would not interfere, nor did I desire him to.

Do you agree, Stuart? Butler pressed.

You are my commanding officer, Colonel Butler, I answered him.

We will add five lashes for insolence. A round thirty. Have you anything to say to that, Stuart?

Nothing.

You are taciturn, Stuart. Never were there a more loud-mouthed, dirty-spoken lot of unhanged cutthroats than the men of the 11th Regiment, but they have all become admirably meek and silent. I am pleased to find you no exception, Mr. Stuart.

So there was my introduction to the Line, and they did it properly, that same evening, as the sun was setting, drawing up the men to parade and laying on the thirty lashes with the drums beating and with a fine concourse of townsfolk watching from the road. As an evidence of humor and understanding, a short man and a tall man were instructed to handle the whips, so that Kabanka and Levy were forced to administer my punishment; and then the same two, when I was finished and fainting with pain, carried me gently to the hospital tent, where Andrew MacPherson rubbed bear fat into my back and Jack Maloney and Billy Bowzar tried to cheer me.

I am cheerful enough, I said evenly, and happy enough, so leave me alone.

And because they understood me and knew me, they left me alone there with my own thoughts and the strong, soothing fingers of the barber. . . .

Why did they whip you? Molly Bracken asked me, when I returned to tell her what I had done and that I would live at the manse no longer.

Because they have long memories, and they have not forgotten what happened in January, I answered her, looking at the fine, ripe whole-ness of her, looking at the sunlight which came through the window and lay upon her hair. She sat in her parlor facing me, her hands in her lap, her back straight, a strong, contained woman and like a rock to my eyes; and I, who would be twenty-three years old in a day or two, and old enough and proper enough to have a house somewhere and a wife to care for it and children to raise up, stood in the coarse canvas overalls that marked a man apart from the whole world.

And as I stood there, looking at her with fondness and wonder and a certain separateness too, a hint of the logic of my life came to me; for my youth had passed away, as it does at one moment or another for all men, and the cold consciousness of death faced me and I faced it and recognized it and greeted it equitably and fairly—there in that sweet and sunlit country parlor, with its soft olive-greens and pale blues that were so much a part of that era. Well and gently do I remember it, the country furniture that was already old with the satiny quality of our good white pine, shaped by German cabinetmakers already dead and moldering in their graves, and hand-hooked rugs, the small, high windows with their diamond-shaped panes of glass, not the glass you see today, but the glass of an earlier time that played with light and made an enchantment out of it, and the spring sunlight all over the place, on the pewter, on the broad, pegged boards of the floor, on my Molly's hair and on the Dutch maids who danced all over the wallpaper. In there, in that quiet place in the old manse, I began to understand the forces which drove me and the necessity which I recognized and obeyed. No man is anointed, but in many men the blood flows and the heart throbs only if they seek the freedom of their own kind; and then this freedom is not an abstraction but a liberation for themselves from their own chains. It is the salt with which they savor their food, and without it they would starve.

So when Molly Bracken said to me, Were you not ashamed that the whole town should stand there and see you whipped? I was able to answer, This was not something for me to be ashamed for.

Could they punish you for doing no wrong?

What is wrong for them is not wrong for me, I told her. Do you understand that?

How can I understand that, when I understand you so little? You love me and yet you hate me, and when you look at me a part of you is here and a part of you is elsewhere. What honor is there in a dirty pair of overalls — and why should it be you when the whole world is content to abide in its place?

Because I am not content.

And you will never be content, Jamie, never.

But I will, I answered her, I will, Molly, and you must pity me because I will.

Who ever pitied you, Jamie Stuart?

No one, I said, no one. But you must.

Why? Why?

Because I love you the way no one else will ever love you, and I can't have you.

It's a love that comes of talk and nothing else, Jamie Stuart, and your heart is not involved — for when a man loves a women, he marries her and takes her for himself.

I will not do that.

Because you cannot, she said bitterly.

Because this world is no damned good as it is, I cried, and the bread I eat is too salty for me to swallow! What cursed indifference there is in this place; and for five years I fought for the freedom of my country, and this is my country where my mother and my father died as bondslaves, chattels, flesh they were to buy and sell, and I will not be bought and I will not be sold, for there is something in me that is as proud as any man who ever lived and there is something in my comrades that is proud too, and in the gentry who lead us there is also a pride, so I will follow them and fight for them and take their lashes across my back—because now it is their turn and I move a step with them, but someday it will be my turn, even if I am dead and rotten in the earth, someday it will be my turn! But that you cannot understand, for in this cursed place there is no pride and only a crawling the way animals crawl—and that is the way I crawled into the kirk to plead with God to allow me to live forever!

To allow me to live forever, I said to her, and to hell with that! I will not crawl and abase myself and scrabble for myself and only myself and cheat my neighbor and find an apprentice whose hands I can live from while I starve him and cut muskets to sell a government which never pays or thanks the men who die with those muskets in their hands or apprentice myself to a church and pray while other men fight and die for freedom—no, thank you, I want none of it! I want no such life forever! But every one of my comrades who laid down his life, every one of them lives a little bit in myself, and in that way myself will live and can never die, because my blood is here and mixed into the earth of this land. And this will not be like other lands because the foreigns came here and died here, and that can never be wiped out—never! It's a better immortality than the other kind!

And is that what you believe?

It is what I believe.

Then God help you, she said, because I cannot.

She was crying now, and I turned up her face and looked into her eyes.

I was wrong, I told her, in what I said before. Never pity me.

I never pitied you, Jamie Stuart, but you will pity me.

I will not.

Promise me, she said.

That I promise you: that I will not. It will mean such a lonely waiting—a year or five years or ten years—

It will mean such a lonely waiting, she whispered.

And will you wait?

If you want me to, she said. If you want me to, I will wait—or if you want me to, I will go with you and live by the camp the way the other women do.

Then never cry no more, and you I will never pity but only love. For once I could not love, and there was no love in the boy you walked the fields with and picked flowers with and lay in the grass with and taught to read the printed word and taught to speak gently and softly the way you speak so gently and softly, my beloved heart, my darling. I am learning to love. I am learning to be strong and whole, the way a man should be, and I will be that way when I return to you.

When you return . . .

When I return, I whispered, when I return, my dear.

And then I held her tightly in my arms, and on my back I felt her hands, pressing against the open welts that the whips had left.

And that was in May, ten days before we marched out of York village to the South, and of those last days I must now tell and then make the finish—for though we little knew it then, we marched from York village to the last great battles of the war.

I must tell of Jack Maloney, who was in many ways like a brother to me, and few enough men like him there were; if I paid a price for my part in the rising, he paid it tenfold, day in and day out. There was a particular hatred for Jack Maloney, because he was a soldier in a way that few enough of the Continentals were, and it was through him, and a couple of hundred like him who had deserted the British at the very beginning of the war and came into the foreign brigades, that we became singular among the armies of the states. In his lifetime, he had forgotten more of soldiering than most of our officers ever knew, and for this they could not forgive him. His discipline, his exactitude, his bayonet which always sparked like it was made of silver, his overalls, clean and neat always, his face shaven in field or camp, his manner, his bearing like a king, his inner calm which was never shaken—all of these combined in a goal which they must conquer to prove themselves. But it was no easy thing to conquer Jack Maloney, and he took what they gave. I think only I knew what it took for him to stand up to the cane and the swordflat; and he said to me once:

Jamie, we should not have taken them back. When this is over, they will cast us away like dogs.

That's done with, I told him. That's over and done with, just as the old Line is done with.

How much can a man stand?

What he has to, he can stand.

It was about then that our recruits began to come in, a handful of raw lads from the militia, some sailors from Philadelphia, some Naygers of the Virginias and some riflemen from the back country. One by one, the brigade officers returned, each with a handful of men, until the new recruits numbered a little better than three hundred, and they were formed into two regiments and kept carefully apart from the rest of us, of the old foreigns. Day after day they were drilled, in a hurried attempt to make some semblance of soldiers out of them, and the very haste of the officers made us think that the Southern campaign would be joined soon. Often it occurred to me that this forming them into separate regiments was the best proof of the absolute incompetency of our officers, since without question they would bolt at the first volley of ball or the first load of grape; but afterwards I learned that our gentry were by no means incompetent in their plans.

Soon after this, all leaves were canceled, and I saw no more of Molly Bracken. Pickets and sentries were drawn from the militia, and the camp was closely guarded as final preparations were made for a long march. And then, a few days before we left, Anthony Wayne arrived, bringing with him four cannon, an artillery company of some sixty men and a small baggage train, which held a few hundred pounds of corn meal and a great deal of coopered powder and shot bar. The artillery company were all of them strange men, and many of them had the voice and appearance of Yankees. They encamped about half a mile from us, on the edge of York Common, and we saw nothing of them before we marched.

The day after Wayne arrived, the two regiments of the foreign brigades were drawn up for parade inspection. Having no trumpeters, we were awakened before dawn by the drums beating us to arms, and we turned out in the smoky, wet morning with full equipment and knapsacks on. No one knew what this meant, whether we were about to march or whether there was some trouble in the area or whether this was an ordinary parade. If the last were so, it was exceedingly early in the morning, without even sufficient light to allow for any kind of proper inspection.

The only officers present at the beginning were four captains and seven lieutenants, and they ran back and forth as we turned out of our brushwood shelters and our tents, shouting at us to double our time and bend our legs and laying their canes across our shoulders with lusty abandon. Captain Gresham, a burly lad who had come to us two years ago from the Light Horse Troop, went at Jack Maloney who was crouched down lacing his overall leggings, and told him to stand up like a man and get to hell into ranks.

I'm still dressing, answered Maloney, standing up.

Dress before you turn out, damn you! cried Gresham, jabbing his

559

cane into Jack Maloney's belly.

Mind the cane, protested Maloney, mildly enough. The ranks are still forming.

And mind your lip! roared Gresham. I will have none of your damned insolence! he cried, lacing out with the cane and catching little Jack Maloney on the side of the head, so that he went down like a tenpin.

As Maloney struggled to rise, Angus MacGrath thundered like a bull and charged the captain, who turned to run. But MacGrath seized him, raised him in his hands and shook him like a puppy until he dropped his cane; and, still as with a puppy, Angus cast him away, picked up his cane, and broke it into pieces. Now the other officers came running, drawing their swords, and it well might have been murder and revolt then and there, had not Maloney himself called:

Stand to ranks! Stand to ranks!

The drummer boys took his hint and beat to parade as manfully as they could, until the roll of their drums echoed like morning thunder—while we ran on the double and fell in. In less time than it takes to tell it, our regimental lines were formed, and we were each of us standing to arms and looking straight ahead. Gresham had picked himself up and the other officers were grouped around him, talking excitedly in low tomes. And still it was before sunrise, and only now was it light enough to see anything clearly. Now the drummers stopped their playing, and the officers came toward us in a group. Jack Maloney stood alongside of me, and I squeezed his arm and whispered to him:

Easy, lad, and easy does it. You're an old soldier.

God damn them, Jamie!

God damn them, I agreed. God damn them to hell and back again, but they are the officers and we are the men of the Line, and that's that. So easy does it.

Now the officers were standing in front of the ranks and about a dozen yards away, the eleven of them in a close group and still whispering to each other. The two regiments were side by side and four ranks deep, and making a right angle at the end of our parade were the drummers and fifers, with Chester Rosenbank standing in front of them, his face white and sick—for there was something terrible and brooding upon this wet field on this cold May morning, and there was something that all of us knew and yet none of us knew. And I said to myself, We are not the Line and the Line is dead and dissolved, and we are naked here. And I was afraid the way I had not been afraid in a long, long time. Then the first burst of morning sunlight—not the sun yet but just the light—cut into the gloom, and the night mists fell until we stood knee-deep in a sea white that slowly broke up and rolled away; and then all around us was the gracious Pennsylvania countryside, bathed in the pure morning light and cleansed with the pure morning air. The crows rose from the meadows and sadly bid the night farewell and a rooster somewhere sang the morning in. The mists fell away from the tents, and from the other end of the encampment we heard the drums beating to parade, beating up the militia and the recruits. All this we could see on that green and golden morning: the distant figures of the new recruits, the horses grazing in the pasture we had made, the morning birds in the air—the intolerable sweetness of a new day still unmarred.

The officers came toward us. Captain Purdy stepped forward from the group and called:

Stand to arms!

We stiffened and presented.

MacGrath!

Angus MacGrath stepped forward and waited.

Advance six paces, soldier MacGrath! snapped Purdy, and in answer to his command Angus counted off the six paces and stood waiting. Watching him, I wondered again as I had wondered so often in the past what force commanded us and moved us; for here was this miserable little man, Purdy, hurling his orders at the great Scottish dignity of Angus MacGrath, Angus MacGrath who was like a mountain of endurance and courage and forbearance, tireless and simple and wise in a manner Purdy would never know and could never know. Yet because we were steeled in the years of discipline, we responded and obeyed.

Then why, I had to ask myself, had we revolted once? What had happened then, and what was lost now?

Kneel down! said Captain Purdy.

Like a man made of stone, Angus stood there, motionless.

Kneel down! cried Purdy.

Still Angus stood like stone, and like stone stood the ranks of the regiments.

Drawing his pistol, Purdy cocked it and presented at Angus, but I saw that his hand trembled and the big pistol wavered back and forth in front of the motionless man.

I gave you a command, he said, pitching up his voice. Either obey it or take the consequences!

And then Billy Bowzar spoke up, relaxing the awful tension of myself and of others. Billy Bowzar spoke up in that dry and even way of his, his voice cutting the situation into all of its separate parts, and . . .

May I speak a word, Captain Purdy, sir? he said.

I think Purdy welcomed the interruption and welcomed the opportunity of a way out. He had gotten himself into a bad position, and I do not think he would have had the courage to shoot Angus. It is a bitter thing to kill a man in cold blood, as well I know, even if you hate the man, as Purdy hated Angus.

So he said, This is no part of your affair, Bowzar.

Yes, sir, agreed Billy Bowzar quietly. But may I say a word, sir?

Well, speak up then, snapped Purdy, still covering MacGrath.

I only want to say, sir, that it cannot possibly help either yourselves or us to go on with this matter. We stand in our ranks, and we stand under discipline now. We are good soldiers, sir—and we are ready to march off to a campaign. We are going to fight and die, together, sir, and that is what is important. I saw the incident between Maloney and Captain Gresham. It was a mutual misunderstanding, sir, and it would be better if no blame was to be attached.

I'll thank you, Bowzar, not to instruct me in matter of discipline, said Purdy. You are being damned insolent!

I am trying not to be insolent, Captain Purdy, and I have no desire to instruct you in matters of discipline. That was not my intention at all, sir. I only felt that things will go hard if we continue in this. MacGrath lost his temper, but that is understandable.

You will not instruct me in what is understandable, said Purdy. That is God-damned insolent! MacGrath was ordered to kneel down and accept punishment. When he does, this matter will be over.

I will not kneel! said Angus suddenly. I will dee and damn you!

I could see Purdy working his courage, building his courage, jacking up his courage, and then Jack Maloney stepped forward and took his place beside Angus, presenting his musket, so that if Purdy fired, he would be in a position to fire back.

Then I'll go down with him! cried Jack Maloney. Damn the lot of you, you have no hearts and no soul, and a man is a dog to the lot of you! Now who will stand with me? he threw at us over his shoulder. Who will stand with me? Is there a man left in the brigades?

The officers closed in, but the Jew Levy and Danny Connell and Lawrence Scottsboro and Stanislaus Prukish and the black man Kabanka took their places alongside the two, some quickly, some with the damned resignation of men who realize that they have come to the end of something. An officer broke away—Lieutenant Collins, it was—and ran like the very devil was after him across the fields toward the camp of the recruits. Purdy fell back, the rest of them with him, so that now a group of seven faced a group of ten, and still the regiments stood in ranks unmoving. It was not enough; whenever I recall that morning moment, I realize how precariously the scales were balanced, and it would have needed only Bowzar and myself to tip them over—so that if we had moved forward, the ranks would have moved behind us. All of it was in my mind and through my mind, and already I could see where the lieutenant who ran off was approaching the militia; and faintly, I could hear his shouting, and now I knew why Wayne had kept the artillery so carefully apart. And all of it lived and acted in my mind, and in my mind I saw the ranks surge forward behind Billy Bowzar and myself, and in my mind I saw the ten officers go down before our bayonets and our clubbed muskets; and in my mind I saw our foreigns, better than whom were no soldiers in all the world, greeting the militia with spaced volleys until the green grass was like a slaughter pen; and in my mind I saw the artillery coming, the outriders whipping the horses, the guns bouncing over hill and hummock, and in my mind I saw us retreating into the woods with the stain of blood and death all over us—we who had slain our brothers and ignited the spark that made this war a fratricide—all of this I saw in my own mind's eye in those few minutes when the two groups stood at bay. And seeing it, I knew the hopelessness of it, the uselessness of it, the deep and woeful and pathetic uselessness of it; for it was only another road into nowhere, into a hope and a dream that had no existence, and we had traveled that road once and we knew it well. And if men died now—as I knew already they must die—they would be forgotten, and the foreigns would lick their wounds and we would march off to the Southern campaign, and we would finish what we had started together with the officer gentry. And it must be finished—this I knew.

So when Jack Maloney—Jack Maloney who was like a brother to me—called out, And are there no others? And will you not come, Jamie Stuart?

I answered him, No, I will not, Jack Maloney—I will not because there is no hope here, and once I did it!

Then be a man and do it twice! cried Danny Connell.

No—I cannot and I will not!

And then the time was past, for two men on horseback were spurring down on us, whipping their mounts, Wayne in the lead and Butler close behind him; and after them, at a headlong run, came the regiments of the militia and the new recruits. The officers reined up their horses, and the militia, panting and sobbing for breath, made a ragged line at right angles to our regimental parade, covering with their muskets Jack Maloney and Angus MacGrath and the five others. Purdy and Gresham were speaking to Wayne at the same time, and as he listened to them, his face became murderous with anger. And through all this, the sun rose and bathed the morning in its golden light.

Stand back! cried Wayne, and he reined his horse back, followed by Butler and the officers, until there was a clear space between the militia and the seven of our men. Then Wayne swung out of the saddle, strode over to the militia, and cried, Take aim at those men!

There was a sigh, like a woman in pain, out of the ranks as the muskets converged on the little group of soldiers. They drew closer; they pressed against one another—and frozen, paralyzed, I and the others in the ranks remained without thought or movement, only looking at these seven men who were our comrades, Jack Maloney, and big Angus MacGrath, and the Nayger Kabanka and the Polish man, Prukish and the Jew Levy, so small that he and old Lawrence Scottsboro looked like children, if you did not see their faces, and Danny Connell who had once sang sweet songs in another land—and they pressed shoulder to shoulder as Wayne cried:

Fire!

Forty muskets roared out, and a terrible groan went up from the ranks, a groan of awful and unforgettable anguish. Six of the seven men sank down in a horrible mass of broken flesh; one, Jack Maloney, his left arm shattered and almost torn from his body, remained standing—and facing him, the militia stood behind their smoking muskets and wept, even as we in the ranks wept.

But Wayne did not weep. I do not blame Wayne; I do not condemn him; he is dead and gone these many years, and I have no hatred for him. What he had to do, he did, and someday what we have to do, we will do.

But he did not weep; cold as ice, he was, and hard as stone, and with no more than a glance at the awful carnage of those six dead and the one living and standing, the one who was Jack Maloney who was like a brother to me—with no more than a glance there, he approached us and walked across our ranks, looking from face to face until at last his eyes fixed on me, and he said so softly and bitterly that almost only I heard:

Stuart.

Weeping, I stood there, and the smoke drifted away across the morning meadows and little moans of pain came from Jack Maloney, and we who had known every conceivable kind of horror were unable to look at this particular horror any longer.

Stuart, he said, fix bayonet!

Like a man in a dream, I obeyed and fixed my bayonet, and this dream went on, for he said:

I have a long, long memory, Stuart. Advance!

I moved forward toward that pile of horror and toward Jack Maloney, and Wayne moved with me. He drew his pistol and cocked it and held it a few inches from my head, and the hundreds of men around us stared in silent disbelief, and Jack Maloney was watching me now.

He is dying from that wound, Wayne said softly, and in bitter pain. Drive your bayonet through his chest.

For a time I stood as motionless as Jack Maloney, as Wayne, as the men in the ranks. . . .

You have one minute, and then I will blow your damned brains out, Wayne said.

Then kill me now! I suddenly shouted. Do it now, and God's curse on you!

One minute, said Wayne.

And then Jack Maloney said, Do it, Jamie, do it, Jamie! Do it for my sake! Do it and put an end to my terrible pain, Jamie Stuart. Do it because you were right and I was wrong—for the love of God, do it, Jamie! Do it!

His voice rose to a wild, vibrant note of command, and I lunged and drove the bayonet through his chest. And then I was down beside him, his head in my arms, weeping and weeping, and trying to tell Jack Maloney what I knew but what there were no words for. And then there were Billy Bowzar and Andrew MacPherson, and they lifted me up and took me away and talked to me. . . .

We broke camp the next day and set out on our march southward to Yorktown, where we fought the last great battle; and with my musket slung from my shoulder and my knapsack on my back, with bullets in my belt and a pound of powder and a pound of corn meal to keep me, I marched alongside of Billy Bowzar. Thus we marched, and in the course of it, he would say:

How is it, Jamie Stuart?

I'll never sleep again, and waking, I'll never forget.

You'll forget enough, he said, and too much you don't want to forget, Jamie Stuart. Because there will be a time for remembering.

And when will that time come?

Not too soon, God willing, Jamie Stuart. Not before the time is ripe, and then, God willing, we will know the road we take. We are like a seed that ripened too soon, too quick, for we were planted within the gentry's own revolt, and we grew a crop they fear mightily and neither they nor we knew how to harvest it. That will take knowing, Jamie Stuart, that will take learning. Be patient. The voices are quiet this moment, but they will rise again. Be patient.

PART TWELVE

Wherein a little is told of the last days of
the Pennsylvania Line, and of those whose
acquaintance you have made.

IF THIS TALE I have told here were something spun out of my own
imagination, then this would be as good a place to leave it as any; but
it would seem to me to be incomplete without a few words concerning
the fate of the handful of us who remained from the old Pennsylvania
Line. For me at least, in the course of this long narration, they have
come to live again a little as they lived in those old, old times, and it is
hard to part with them sooner than the point of firm parting, when the
Line was dissolved forever.

From York village in Pennsylvania, we marched south to join in a
general movement of troops toward Yorktown in Virginia, and toward
the battle which to all effects and purposes ended the Revolution. Yet
for us there was some special destination.

We found it on the 6th of July, on the James River, where, fronted
by a morass, the core of Cornwallis's army lay waiting, better than four
thousand men, well armed and well placed. It is said that Wayne's
information was bad that day, that he had reliable word that less than
a thousand British troops confronted us; it could also be said that he
was looking for death, as he had searched for it before. In any case, he
led the less than eight hundred men who composed the Line into a
frontal bayonet attack upon the British—and the attack was led by the
two regiments left of the old foreign brigades.

So there we perished and there was the end of the Pennsylvania
Line. Only one hundred and twenty of us survived that attack, which
was the wildest, maddest and most terrible bayonet charge of the
entire war—and which incidently gave the British the blow which sent
them reeling back to Yorktown. Of that fight on the James River, however, I have no heart to tell in detail. We cut our way into a British
army more than five times our size, and then we cut our way out
again, but of all the men in the 11th Regiment only I was left, and of

567

the Line, only a handful of town and bleeding men. Somewhere in that swamp Billy Bowzar lay, and MacPherson, and the Gary brothers, Arnold and Simpkins; there too died the German schoolteacher, Chester Rosenbank, and the drummer lads Searles and O'Conner—and how many more I have no heart to detail. Why I survived, I do not know, but it may be that I wanted to particularly and would not die even when all law and rule and precedent said that I should. For with two musket balls in my belly, I lay for five feverish weeks in a makeshift and horrible hospital outside of Yorktown. Yet somehow I lived and survived, and eventually I was able to walk.

In November, I received my discharge in Philadelphia, two hundred dollars in Confederation money, and a certificate attesting to six years of service in the Pennsylvania Line of the Continental Army. . . .

All this was a long time ago. I have had many things out of life and much that I never looked forward to, and I would be telling less than the truth if I did not admit that life was sweet to me, and rich and rewarding. I married Molly Bracken and we saw our children grown and married to others, and we saw their grandchildren. As it is said, there have been generations in this land, and the old times are best forgotten; and who am I, who gained so much from so little, to speak of injustice?

Yet it is not for the cause of justice or injustice that I have set down this narration. When I mastered the law and took my place at the bar, I gained some understanding of justice; and I do not come with any suit in the cause of the men of the foreign brigades. However it may seem in the course of my tale, I for one do not believe that they perished in vain or that they suffered in vain. They were never causes first, but results first and causes secondarily; and it is the peculiar nature of mankind that with his life so short—and often so miserable—he will nevertheless always find among his numbers those who are willing to spend themselves a little sooner than need be, a little harder, in the cause of human dignity and freedom.

Nor is it strange that, with all the monuments that have been erected, there have been none to the men whose tale I told. A monument, it seems to me, signifies a finish, a point of rest; and if these men rest, they rest too uneasily to have tributes raised to them. Their story is only half told. Another chapter is being written by those angry souls who call themselves Abolitionists, and I think there will be chapters after that as well. There would be no hope in such a tale as this if it were not unfinished.